To Jannelle and
Tim
In friendship and
Love
Peter
Filton Ca Aug.1994

DESTINATION

DESTINATION

by

PETER CARUSO

PHILOSOPHICAL LIBRARY
New York

Copyright 1970, by Philosophical Library, Inc.,
15 East 40 Street, New York, New York 10016
Library of Congress Catalog Card No. 72-118307
SBN   8022-2342-7

Manufactured in the United States of America

To Louise

my wife and twin flame for her utter
selflessness, dynamic inspiration and
invaluable contribution to the completion
of this work.

This teaching is humbly dedicated to the Supreme Cause of universal peace and cosmic brotherhood through which every man, woman and child of every nation, race and creed, and of every intellectual level, economic status, moral standard and social rank, shall be bound together in the incoming Golden Age.

The Liberated Master-Teacher

CONTENTS

CHAPTER I

PROLOGUE

Somber and utterly fatigued, Marco and his disconsolate parents looked in dismay at the massive entrance of the high-walled Catholic Seminary of the Salesians. It had been a long and wearisome walk on the narrow, rocky road that was the main thoroughfare for man and cattle and the plodding donkeys hauling their over-burdened creaking carts. The sirocco had been blowing incessantly, and the hot, oppressive dust-ladened khamsin wind was causing not only acute discomfort to the wayworn travelers, but irreparable damage to the tender buds of the apricot and almond trees. As they passed, they could hear the distraught farmers bemoaning their irretrievable loss.

From the pastoral village on the picturesque and sun-baked hills of Surda in the Southeast of Sicily, they had descended on foot to the faraway valley, crossing the broad and undulating expanse of black turf carpeted with multicolored iris, roses and carnations, trellises covered with grapevines were strung everywhere. They passed through the open quarters of Strettu where blacksmiths, carpenters, painters and metal workers in copper and iron were engaged in their trade of constructing and assembling carts and rigs. The burning gale had driven the craftsmen indoors into narrow, crowded, sweltering sheds, where the unbearable heat and close proximity caused them to curse at each other in loud, foul language; while mares, mules and asses, beneath makeshift shelters, could be heard restlessly stamping their ironshod hoofs.

Marco and his parents moved on climbing slowly and silently upward through a steep and seemingly unending lane. Now, finally, the grim and formidable citadel came into sight. Francesco and Concetta embraced their son for the last time, then knocked at the spectral iron-bound door.

Why his parents had decided that Marco was to be a priest

1

no one knew. Unless there would be one less mouth to feed in their large family of six children, or possibly because a priest would give status to the family, or perhaps it was the prognostication of the wise man of the village that had prompted this momentous decision.

❆   ❆   ❆

Marco at the age of ten found the cloistral life very dull and the discipline irksome. The Right Reverend Petella, director of the seminary, was a tall, thin man with large protruding eyes and a violent temper which he did not hesitate to give vent to when the boys were disobedient. Reverend Don Mandano, his assistant, smoked strong cigars constantly which caused his rotund body to smell of stale tobacco; otherwise, he had a kindly disposition of which his superior took advantage by abusing and humiliating him indiscriminately in front of the students. In such an atmosphere of dissention Marco felt the uneasiness of the unwanted; the lessons in Latin were delivered in a shoddy manner and his home work was seldom checked. Thus at the end of June he returned to his parental home and no one ever mentioned the failure of the attempt.

❆   ❆   ❆

The wise man of Surda, Messer Nele, was most venerated and respected even above the podesta; and since he was consulted by the first magistrate on every major decision of public interest, Messer Nele had achieved a lofty pre-eminence in the minds of the villagers. And this was most unusual as it was customary in the old world for the priest to dominate the public life. Though he was no frequenter of churches his prestige was achieved by following the footsteps of the mystic teachings of Saint Francis of Assisi. Supplemented by a physical body that was tall and slender and by the hieratic radiance from his countenance, the thought of his presence somewhere in the village, held sway all evil and unkind tendencies of the people. Crime of any type down to a misdemeanor was non-existent. Messer Nele spoke softly and unhurriedly and in his presence all pressing problems presented by the village elders and the parents began to lighten. "Face problems" — he would say — "as if you were facing a beast of the jungle securely caged. Accept the truth that it cannot harm you, then surrender your hearts to God. Empty yourselves of all thoughts, then

2

listen to the whispers within. Listen, I say, for it is the command of God telling you what to do; then go to work. Your problems will surely disappear like mist before the rising sun."

As a lad of seven Marco had been the predilect of Messer Nele, to the intense gratitude of his parents. The wise man would take the boy for long walks throughout the countryside speaking to him of God. Here were an elder and mature yogi and a younger one attracting one another. Like a bodiless teacher he enveloped the little disciple in wisdom and love saying: ". . . . and wherever you might find yourself in the years ahead, when I am no longer visible to you, never forget the ever-living Flame in your heart, for that is God within you. Its love, Its protection, Its guidance, are always with you. Know positively that it can help you for you to help others, for you are destined to ferry many people from the sea of worldliness and dependence on outer ritual to the vast ocean of knowledge, bliss and absolute Self-reliance. And even if these people are reduced to only one you shall have lived fruitfully." Like a living gossamer that vibrates even in still air, Messer Nele sensitized the youth's whole being.

Marco at eighteen had just entered the university when he met and became a close friend of Bastiano, who was then a senior and about to graduate with a degree in philosophy. Here was a brilliant intellect and a mature soul in a handsome body. Though bordering the realm of geniusship, Bastiano was also lighthearted and enjoyed the camaraderie of friends and acquaintances.

The urge for self-analyzation, as a basic tool in the study and understanding of God, was thus cast into the inmost feeling of Marco by this unique friend and teacher. Consequently the seed that had been detected by Messer Nele was now fertilized and given the first irrigation. Seeing how attentive and eager his disciple was, the charismatic Bastiano did not hesitate to expound with prophetic fervor certain aspect of the lives of some of the great Initiates of the past: Rama, Krishna, Gautama the Buddha, Moses, Jesus and many others. "Through disciplined self-analyzation and meditation on the light within Their hearts" — he concluded — "They achieved and expressed the Christ Power or Cosmic Sexuality or Contact with God. By the same path any man can achieve the same goal."

❋ ❋ ❋

3

As time passed the outer pressure asserted itself causing Marco to hold in abeyance his spiritual heritage. The residue of orthodoxy continued to linger in his mind and feelings. Living in a world of stark materialism, trampled by the bestial hoofs of the centaurs of war, held by the giant and slippery cobra of political ambitions that ran rampant everywhere, and teased, lured and harassed by the nimble creatures of social disorder, Marco yielded to the defilement of the times. And when at the age of twenty-two he re-encountered Messer Nele a world of separation stood between them. Marco's inner eye was blurred, his heart hardened, the inner glamor and intoxicating fragrance of the master rejected. Instead, in faithful adherence to the political atmosphere of the times, he belittled and swept aside all wisdom, acknowledging only the visionary speculations created by his age.

At the turn of World War I schools were most inadequate in that part of Sicily. Youths were torn apart by anticlerical teaching in classrooms and saint and icon worshipping in churches. Inner confusion and agnosticism were the result. Where does the wealth of vitality of the youth go? It builds vanity, arrogance, rebelliousness and the sowing of the seed of social chaos.

Marco felt the pulse, the cry and the compulsion of such inner and outer disorder; yet he lived in it unshamefully. Though he never violated the code of man's behavior as established by the written law of the land, before the Eye of God he was a transgressor and often treaded perilously the razor edge between jail and freedom, social rejection and respectability. Nevertheless, the crimes perpetrated by the mind, though unrecognized and unpunished by the law of man, carve their frightful effects on the etheric sheet of one's life in the form of anxiety, remorse, disease and want. Lacking proper guidance, Marco became restless. He felt the urge to continue the inner search and submitted to harsher discipline, but the result was more turmoil. Wanting to be humble only heightened the tyranny of his mortal ego; but the search went on undiminished, enshrouded in deeper silence and mystic solitude. The breakthrough came after months, that seemed an eternity, in the form of a buoyant enthusiasm in his studies for mind improvement as well as greater and more precise self-discovery.

Whenever he found a philosophical truth, he stopped reading, closed the book, reclined his body with eyes shut, and there he began the mysterious process of cosmic osmosis, the process of self-diffusion into the universal consciousness. He tried to visualize the truth per se, then analyzed it in rapport to the outer world and his fellow man; then again he sought to delve into the mind of him who had uttered it, and finally he resolved that truth into the Mind of God wherefrom all truths issue. Slowly as proficiency was achieved his body began to vibrate every time he discovered a new truth; the rate of vibration increasing or decreasing in rapport to the degree of veracity of the truth involved.

* * *

During the decades of 1920-39 Europe went through a period of defiance. Whether justified or not, malicious forces, born of resentment, national pride and personal chauvinism, broke asunder in an attempt to uproot the last vestige of collective decency. The "have not" nations, exploiting internal discontent gave vent to an array of demolitory propaganda in denunciation of the Treaty of Versailles. The nations who had benefited by the Treaty continued to enjoy the privilege of the status quo, and paid no heed to the smothering conflagration that was to shatter the whole world in a manner never seen before. The ominous undercurrent had reached epidemic proportion poisoning the blood of all.

Marco felt the impact. Convinced that he was wasting precious time behind a desk in Rome, examining census reports, he decided to join the Royal Air Force and become a pilot. He entered the Academy and graduated as an officer. Though still a second lieutenant he was often entrusted with confidential missions reserved for officers of much higher rank. It was at this time that the Royal Air Force initiated the preparation for the mass flight of twenty-four planes from Rome to the World's Fair in Chicago. Marco had the assignment of compiling the applications of the pilots that would be selected for the historical event. He requested permission to be a member of the crew but was refused by his commander on the grounds that he was irreplaceable in the position at hand. This refusal awakened in him both the frustrations and the inner glimpses of the years past. Messer Nele and Bastiano who were no

5

longer on earth, came to him in their finer bodies stern and reproachful: "You shall no longer linger in such a world of dependency and fraud. Let the outer wings go! Resign! Migrate to the United States of America, the only land on earth truly blest by the gods. Cut thyself asunder from tradition, education and social rank. Enter the vast expanse of freedom and opportunity unlimited, both in the outer and more so on the inner. Arise, arise! . . ."

* * *

In America the straggler and the rejected are reintegrated to a status of dignity and self-reliance not found anywhere on earth. The last here is truly higher than the first anywhere else, not in pride, vanity and other outer traits, but in the subtle and almost imperceptible awareness that surges forth from within for the honor of being an integral living cell of a body politics that is destined to counsel the world for thousands of years to come, and raise the least, the poorest, the weakest and the most degraded of man to a political, economic and spiritual level even higher than itself. It is because of this global leadership that both America and the Americans are respected, feared and despised today.

All this and more Marco felt in America from the moment he arrived. Even the economic depression of the decade 1930-39, the hunger and signs of bewilderment on the faces of innumerable Americans could not erase or weaken this conviction. "The citizen of this land though on the brink of starvation, has dignity indeed, and a granitic faith in himself, his country and God," he said to himself. The voice from within now asserted itself for greater authority; words of admonition came forth in short sentences, now clear, now in a whisper, but always precise. Undetected by anyone Marco grew inwardly taller, outwardly more humble, and yet greater in self-reliance. What was this mysterious voice he was hearing? Whence did it come and for what purpose? In search of these answers the only method he knew was to tighten the bolts of discipline and the way of living so as to restrain more and more the wild, wandering and despotic mind which, he felt, was the main obstruction in his search. Years went by filled with unending hardships and frustrations; but with each conquest, with each inch gained on the path, he experienced a greater inner exhilaration and a sense of accomplishment much beyond all lofty fulfillments of the mind. Here he was at the Source of Life itself. Thus by degrees, as if guided by a loving, wise and secure hand, he came to the momentous hour, to the plateau where timelessness abides. Here he heard the Voice of the Rescuer:

"I AM thy Great God Presence. OM is My Name, and It is universal, unqualified, impersonal. It applies to you and to every being that lives and moves: animals on earth, fish in the water and fowl in the air; and also to every tree and rock. I AM everpresent. I AM the THEE of thee. I AM within thee and around thee, interpenetrating thy whole structure, causing thee to grow, move, think, cry and laugh; and you see ME not. What a pity! I make you do wise and foolish things, utter words of praise and blame to your fellow man; and because your mind is proud, it is unable to function on My terms; hence you are less than a parrot. However, My son, the hour of redemption has come. Hearken:

"I AM thy Mentor, thy guide, Thy-Self. I go wherever you go, and though I never leave you, I AM there before you arrive, to welcome you. For I love you so much, yes, so much that I want you to be exactly like unto ME: infinite in love, genius, power, beauty and life itself. I do not want you to die, I want you to learn how to transmute this body of yours until it becomes a mass of visible shivering light that defies time and space and the insensate onslaught of mass consciousness miserably steeped in the concept of aging, disease and death. But you must obey ME.

"You must allow ME to guide you. I will do so with love and severity, rewarding you abundantly though I may cause you, now and then, to stagger and bleed. But I AM Thy Redeemer!

"You must accept discipline, for discipline is the key that unlocks the gate of understanding and higher spiritual living. My discipline, My son, is not a mechanical drill; it is alive, vibrantly cogent, elevating and venturesome. I shall allow you to succeed in the present task and any other task, if you are sincere and willing. But you must cultivate perseverance, for, by so doing, you will not only nourish yourself on ancient virtues, but will also contact the sons and daughters of Mine who are your elder kin that in ancient of time expressed those virtues and uttered words of truth inspired by ME.

"I have ordered one of My Elohim to draw the plate of your life from the Universal Files, and place it in the section of Cosmic Endeavour. You are under grace. You have been drafted for cosmic duty in a war against the stolid, stupid and grim acquiescense that poverty, filth, disease, envy, hatred, ignorance and the business of war itself, both of the individual and the collectivity, and of nations and races, are a way of life. I want you to wage a war against the thought-forms that declare that God is dead. I want you to awaken certain scientists to their unilateral concept in their Space Program aiming at conquering other planets or stars for material or scientific purpose only. I want you to tell them and show them that rather than conquering another heavenly body, men of earth must so live and think as to be conquered by the higher *Intelligences* that populate lands of outer space, for in Their presence even the genius of an Einstein or the inventor of the wheel is as a child playing with primitive toys.

"For such a task I, the Supreme Ruler of all life, will assign you a divine Guide, an immortal Son of Mine. He will direct thee under My direction. You will know Him and address Him as Liberated Master-Teacher. He is a member of the Cosmic Assembly of the Perfect Ones of which you shall learn as you advance.

"It is needful for you to know that all names and deeds of humanity since Creation are engraved on plates of condensed living light and catalogued in the Universal Files. These plates are never touched; man himself transmits and engraves on it automatically his thoughts and deeds whatever their qualifications. Often, in Ages of Dispensation, I allow some of My children of earth to enter the Halls of Files for study and enlightenment, then as a reward I bestow upon them immortality. Periodically, with one sweep of My All-knowing Mind, I draw certain plates for consideration. This is what you call 'the hand of destiny'. The truth is instead that some streams of life had their plates filled with constructive deeds from previous embodiments, but in the present life they had been subjected to mass pressure of destructive nature beyond their capacity to overcome, which would have endangered their

8

spiritual progress, whereas My helping Hand retrieves them onto the path that rightfully belongs to them.

✿ ✿ ✿

"Paul of Tarsus was one of these streams of life on earth. Since early childhood he had been brought up in an environment of fanaticism and cruelty, of man hunting man for no apparent reason than disagreement with the current theory concerning My Nature, failing to perceive the presence of powerful sectarian interests motivated by political and economic reasons. Here one finds the priesthood — an evil institution that always antagonizes My Will — ruled by the House of Caiaphas, entrenched in luxury and life of ease, plotting to destroy My Son Jesus and the Message of Salvation that I had ordered Him to deliver to the children of Earth. These rulers had hired Paul of Tarsus to put an end to the Messianic Messages of love and brotherhood as expounded by the courageous disciples of the Christ, by arresting them and bringing them before the corrupt court of the priesthood for judgement and eventual death.

"I permitted for awhile Paul to offend and injure even some of his friends whose plates of life were enriched with the merit of forbearance, and for each damage caused to his fellow citizens I registered on his sensitized flesh a multiple pain, the dark shadow of doubt I injected into his mind, with confusion I filled his heart. Finally on the road to Damascus I blinded him. Enough of this! I told him with love and severity. For three days his proud mind was tossed in the eye of an enraged hurricane for clearance, but doubt and confusion still persisted, then I let the Voice of My Ever-living Son Jesus speak, delineating for him a program of action that was completely adverse to that which he had planned for himself. He was promised neither wealth nor worldly prestige, but misunderstanding, sacrifice and violent death." The voice ceased.

✿ ✿ ✿

Marco's mind vibrating in unison with the lofty teaching just received saw now the drama that was about to unfold. He saw the blind man, heavy in heart, led by his confreres in crime to the great city. Paul had almost rejected the fatidic episode by the time he entered the metropolis when a man

9

by the name of Ananias, standing at the entrance to his house on Straight Street, cried aloud in a voice filled with love and compelling power: "Come unto me, Brother Paul, and I shall restore thy sight and re-awaken thy soul. This is the command of our Master Jesus!"

As Paul, baffled still more by this new happening, regained his vision, he drew from the sack of provisions which he carried, the secret list of the proscribed persons, and found, to his amazement, Ananias at the head of it. Then he knew! A sweet sense of peace and inward harmony came to him; and he perceived with crystal clarity what his earthly role was to be: no longer a persecutor but a torchbearer of love and divine knowledge.

"The way for me was that of perdition and death" — he said to himself — "for I had bound my soul to deeds of destruction by serving a decaying teaching kept alive through fear and persecution. Now I shall enter the way of light and rescue myself by rescuing my fellow men. Henceforth Saul is dead, Paul is born. The misdeeds of the dead Saul shall be vindicated through a life of self-dedication to the dictates of my Master Jesus, whose Christ-light I had ignorantly rejected up to this day. My Destination and my Deliverance are in sight." Then he spoke aloud:

"Thy Kingdom, O Christ, is an everlasting Kingdom, and Thy dominion endureth throughout all generations. Command me, my Lord, my readiness is my all!"

But unlike the apostles whose minds, saturated with the living waters of inspiration, reflected the grandeur, love and simplicity of their Master, Paul, by his inability to free himself from the severity of the status of the Torah, expounded a Christian philosophy tinged with jewish austerity that touched the border of intolerance. To what degree, therefore, was Paul responsible for the persecution of those who, in the Middle Ages, dissented from the tenets of the Church? Marco's mind was unable to fathom. Using the only instrument of research at his disposal, he meditated. With a humble and trustful feeling he waited. Again the Voice within resonated:

"It was on the uncompromising rigidity of Paul's teaching that the Catholic Church justified and carried out the relentless persecution against both Jews and non-conforming Christians.

Likewise the edicts issued by Martin Luther. What one might call the *exclusiveness* of the Hebrew became the intolerance of the Church, whose dreadful instrument, the Holy Tribunal of the Inquisition, spread terror throughout Europe by its arbitrary and hellish procedure. No mother in the history of human behavior had ever devoured her own children with such a bestial vehemence as Mother Church did. Such is the result of sectarian rigidity. Paul would have forfeited his divine deliverance, had he not paid with his life under the Roman ax.

"Beware, My son! The rigid application of the law, the law that is uncompromising and unmitigated, the law that is not allowed to evolve and yield to the ever-expanding aspirations of the community, that law breeds vanity and narrow-mindedness in man's feelings. Such a law no longer vibrates with life; it dies, and a dying law ceases to inspire; the evolutive process is held in abeyance, and the existence and presence of God are negated.

"Though the Law of God is eternal and absolute in its fundamental premises, it is subjected — once it is released to the avatars — to the contingencies of time, country, race, local customs and psychological traits of man. Hence the need at this hour for all religious teachings to undergo epochal changes. Thus some of the great Truths uttered by the Christs of the past must be given newer interpretation so as to make them abreast with science and the arts. What remains unchanged is the process of inspiration and creativity. Man must meditate to be inspired and create. He who meditates and causes the living centers of his body to awaken and vibrate is dear unto Me; he is My son, though he rejects and denies all religions.

"Unlike Paul's, the severity of Moses was justified. He had to fire anew man's dignity and the concept of liberty in a massive way. The Hebrews of Egypt had known only, for many generations, servitude and fear; and these degrading traits had to be extirpated in a fierce manner, or the children of Israel would have disappeared into the melting pot of idol worshipping. An uncompromising Moses was needed to stem the flow of degradation and re-fertilize the seed of the One God. Without his action no prophets would have come and no Christ either. Try to comprehend, My son, at what level

11

of civilization man would be today without such a colossus of the Spirit, Moses."

What was the nature of the soul — Marco asked himself — that made the Hebrew lawgiver so dear to God? The answer came: Humility! Though an Egyptian prince, in an environment of extreme luxury, and with a vast culture in science and the arts, in astronomy and mathematics, diplomacy and government, and agriculture and military strategy, Moses waxed unhappy because of his inability to grasp the cause of life and man's ultimate goal. Hence the pressing inner urge to contact God, his Maker. In meditation he divested himself of name, fame, rank and cultural accomplishment, and called to God with childlike rapture. In the absolute abandonment of the self he renounced his royal rights and took shelter in the patriarchal simplicity of shepherd life. Alone and unassisted by any visible or tangible entity he continued his inner search not knowing what the answer would be, until, one day, while leading his flock to the secluded valley towards the hidden grotto at the rear of Mount Horeb, the Christ-light within, having reached the stage of disentanglement, came forth and stood by his side in the form of a Burning Bush. It burned not, nor did it smoke, and it gave no heat. It was unconsuming and all-dazzling. It was the visible condensation of the Breath of God according to the consuetude of the age. The Burning Bush grew and enveloped the humble sage until his countenance was brighter than many suns while his raiment shone with supernatural brilliancy. The fear of unpreparedness overtook him; how was he going to use such a release of power and wisdom? He fell on his knees and wept in repentance and shame:

"My Lord, light of my heart" — he cried — "if I have sinned of pride, strike me down and let it be finished. I am accursed before Thine Eye."

"Not so, not so, My son" — the thrilling voice from the Burning Bush answered. "Arise and strengthen thy limbs, for I command thee to go forth into the land of Egypt to set free the sons and daughters of Abraham from the abuses of their taskmasters, and bring them up out of that land into a good land. Such cosmic authority has been earned by thee because of many years of inner yearning on behalf of thy race. Continue to worship ME,

My son, I AM the Spirit-Light in thy heart. I AM THAT I AM is My Name, speaking from the deepest recess of thy being. Go now, for thy hour has come!"

 * * *

With every new inner experience Marco's determination to come closer to the Liberated Master-Teacher assigned to him, took on a deeper cogency. He understood that there is no individual on earth to whom is given the mandate to assume the role of redeemer; only an immortal being can guide unfailingly, only such a being man must seek through intense yearning and inward practice. This is the attitude of him who possesses indomitable faith and the strength to overcome passion, intellectual obscuration and bewilderment. Unto him death itself casts no fear. He moves on in life unhurriedly, fanning only great ideas and the noble impulses that reside in his heart, until they burst into sudden luminosity which we call inspiration.

Marco was now taught how to be a scientist of the Spirit. By gazing into the light in his heart, working inside the greatest laboratory — which is the human body — not made by human hands, he learned how to manipulate not ordinary chemicals but cosmic elements such as light-substance, life-energy, power, intelligence and will; for this was the method followed by the great teachers of the past, Moses, Gautama the Buddha and Jesus. In the laboratory of the heart these immortal Ones studied silently a science without books, test tubes or physical instruments, and listened, in turn, to other mighty invisible teachers, speak of truth, love, mercy and social behavior unmarred by hypocrisy and selfish interest. They learned how to prepare and project from within their own selves these supreme attributes through the re-arrangement of the subtle, everliving, elements found in their hearts in unlimited quantity.

By direct perception, that is, self-inquiry, the conquerors of life and death were able to delve into the cause of human suffering and limitation, and therein understand the forces of darkness that impel the mortal ego to justify unethical actions by an array of pseudo-reasons. Thus they became almighty and divinely qualified to teach mankind and point the road to salvation to those who ask and care to obey.

Through crystal clear revelations, Marco was now given a glimpse of the future, where he saw mankind en masse being raised to a higher level of consciousness: material, intellectual, spiritual. He saw the Great Ones of Life mingling with the Aryan, the Negro, the Asiatic and the Redskin, the believer and the negator of God, who were offered the opportunity to be guided towards new worlds, not by means of physical transportation but by mind transference.

Humanity has entered a Cosmic Age or Age of Dispensation or Golden Age whereby the planet Earth, through the conscious awareness of man, has to be raised to the level of perfection and luminosity of the planet Saturn, which is the depository of the highest wisdom in our solar system. This is the next step for mankind. There will be some recalcitrants, of course, but these will be dealt with swiftly and severely, for the harbingers of brighter dawns and the builders of a nobler world in every field of endeavour shall not be stopped. Space exploration needs inner exploration in order to be of any value to the man in the street. Hence the need for man to sit periodically in solitude and silence for a few minutes of introspection. There he summons the Powers of Creation for perfect guidance, and pierces the cosmic ethers beyond which the realm of infinite and boundless deathlessness abides. This realm is linked with the light in the heart; the macrocosmos and microcosmos are one.

This is the realization of the ancient Psalmist verse: *Be still and know THAT, THAT I AM GOD!* It is the essence of the Hindu teaching: *OM I AM BRAHMAN, THAT THOU ART* (*TAT TWAN ASI*), and it is the foundation of the ancient Greek philosophy: *Know thyself and thou shalt know the Universe and God.* To *know* here means to be at-one with God. Through such a knowledge man allies himself with an intelligence-force that knows no defeat — physical, mental, emotional.

* * *

Like a neophyte whose enthusiasm cannot be abated, Marco continued in his inner application. It was through this impelling desire to meditate that he was able to pierce the wall of separation between earthly life and the infinite beyond, contacting the realm of perfection that has neither suffering nor death. Currents of purple fire passed over and again through his atomic structure, similar to a series of electric shocks; and he felt and saw, through a gradual inner awakening, the fulfillment of the Eternal within his heart. Raised and exalted in Light, he was ab-

14

sorbed into the fiery sea of universal consciousness wherein he beheld the Cause of all causes, the Primal Essence of Light itself brighter than many suns, the Truth shadowless and unchangeable. Then he heard the exquisite melodies of the Music of the Spheres, followed by an enthralling voice saying:

"O disciple, do not tire thyself from such a practice for I tell thee thou art an ancient being of light ready to be transformed into a chosen instrument at the service of the Cosmic Assembly of the Perfect Ones. Intensify thy communion with the Light in thy heart. Let this be thy science, thy religion, thy artistic mood. Hold vividly in thy mind that thou art under grace; but also know that no teaching will be released unto thee, and no experience will manifest until thou art able to draw unto thyself — by the path of absolute adherence to the Law of Purity of mind and heart — thy intended companion as a visible source of inspiration. Beholding her, and with thy mind well inside thy heart, thou shalt behold pictures and letters of Light, and hear sounds, that will be translated into messages of higher living for the children of the Golden age.

"This companion of thine — the embodiment of beauty, purity and humility — dwells on the West Coast of America. Together you shall advance fast on the path, as her life plan and thine are the same. You shall be reunited with each other and fulfill the destiny of your present earthly existence. She is thy Twin Flame or that which completes man-woman's life leading to the extinction of the cycles of existence in the relative world.

"You are herewith commanded to be constantly in tune with each other and together with God and Me. For when two streams of life — man and woman — are united by the bond of twinship of the Spirit that antedates the present embodiment their harmoniousness shatters both visible obstacles and invisible impediments placed on the path of inner and outer success by the innumerable forces of negativity and hell. And when they understand each other in their inmost hearts their words are sweet like the tuberose or jasmine, and their deeds flow smoothly like liquid oil on a levigated surface. Together they abide always in heaven. You must remember that things that accord in tone, vibrate at the same rate, while things that have affinity in their inmost nature gravitate towards each other. This is obedience, yes, obedience to the law of harmony, and harmony creates receptivity. The receptive disciple is the groundwork of God and the storehouse of the universe.

"One of the outer signs of spiritual twinship is that while working together, should one feel indisposed unusual strength surges forth from within the other and the task that has to be accomplished is brought to completion effortlessly and on time. However, should one violate any article of the law of ethics severe penalty will be imposed upon both. In success or failure you stand together as one; as one you move abreast; abreast you shall face Life, Me and God, or death, Satan and Hell.

"You are commanded to show mankind that away from churches, synagogues, sanctuaries and temples of stone, in silence and solitude, by stilling the mind and meditating on the Flame in the Tabernacle of the heart as a daily prayer man can find himself and God. There is no book to be read, for there is no book which can claim to hold the absolute truth for all time and space. The Koran, the Bible, the Gita, the Vedas, the Upanishads, and so forth, contain undoubtedly living truths which are of no value until man finds the One Truth in his heart. Only then does he commence to be spiritual. By searching therein man opens the only living book there is whose mighty teaching is truly absolute and unconfinable. The time has arrived for man to cut himself asunder from the binding and degenerative spell of the so-called sacred scriptures which have been unduly deified and worshipped. Holding high such holy books, professional hypocrites, filled with ostentation and loathsome schemes, exploited, hated, persecuted and slaughtered innocents and harbingers of higher truths. O man, stop all this! Teach thyself by interrogating thy own heart. Feel the enchantment of the ever-living Pearl of Light nestled within. Bind thyself to it, for such a bondage is cosmic liberty, such liberty is the true religion that raises you to God and immortality.

"By such a process all man's intellectual faculties are enhanced and given the correct function, which is that of being the receptacle for an unending stream of inspiration in the field of science and inventiveness, creativity in arts, and wisdom in politics, diplomacy and social evolution, all leading to the eradication of want and disease, all leading to dynamic peace on earth. It means for man, as an individual, his rising above passions and the liberation of his heart from attachment to

16

finite desires and other fleeting aspirations. With the same facility with which he does all things by instinct, such as eating and walking, he will control his mind and cause it to lie prone at the feet of his will. He will cease to identify with his little mortal self which is linked to and a slave of the lower nature. He will face, fight and destroy all the pulls of the downward path, all the fierce forces that try to dampen or erase the urge of ascent, or to achieve the impossible and reach the intangible. By such a process only can man arise above all mental and spiritual deformations that have filled the world with cripples, crime, suffering and death. He and you too must look with disdain at likes and dislikes, pride, vanity, arrogance, hatred, envy, inordinate ambition, plotting and ignorance. And like you, all men must cultivate awareness of their Inner Masters, sent by God, to guide them towards a life of noble deeds for the good of the world.

* * *

"These are the highlights of the Law to be studied, absorbed and applied by the man of the Golden Age. Humanity has reached the historical era of the *One Shepherd and one Fold*, the *Shepherd* being the Higher Self of man, and the *Fold* all life in form. This implies that all men will be slowly and steadily directed to drop all sectarian liaisons, and be linked together through meditation on the Pearl of Light within their hearts.

"My blessed disciple Marco, I have herewith outlined thy task and given thee a glimpse of thy goal, which are also the task and goal of thy Twin Flame and of every man, woman and child. I have descended from My abode of Immortality by God's command, through the instrument of the Cosmic Assembly of the Perfect Ones.

"I AM the world-Teacher endowed with absolute and eternal knowledge. I shall train and guide you both with love and severity. I shall sustain you with light that never dims. In light shadowless, I shall enfold your thoughts, actions and constructive pursuits. I shall expound to you the One Supreme Teaching of which the highest creation of the human intellect is but an embryonic reflection.

"You are the representative human beings of the present age embodying the typical striving human soul who cannot accept a life of glitter and make believe. You shall have what

17

you deserve and more. I have contacted you at a time of severe spiritual crises, caused by an array of mental and emotional errors, to take you into an invisible academy where you shall be taught the Science of boundless love and cosmic reality.

"I AM thy Liberated Master-Teacher and the Liberated Master-Teacher of thy Twin Flame. The Lord Who abides in your heart and Mine, and in the heart of every living being has commanded Me to so reclaim your minds and feelings and instrument of realization, as to open permanently your Inner Eye and make you see the World of the Real, THAT which never changes, THAT which is unborn and everlasting.

"My guiding you through some of the worlds of the confineless Beyond is neither new nor arbitrary. The ancient lore speaks extensively of starry traveling; it is a truth.

"Now, Marco, draw thy Twin Flame unto thyself and together enter the Path. Your hour to act has come!"

CHAPTER II

THE SEARCH

Many a month went by and Marco, in his daily meditation, with the idealized fingers of the mind, molded with elusive clay, one feminine form after another. And having suffused it with color and clothed it according to la dernier mode, he attempted to animate it by breathing the Breath of Life upon its lips. But no matter how intense his visualization the feminine form remained inanimate; then it vanished leaving no trace behind. How precarious, he thought, is the creation of the mind unfertilized by the concept of God. Then humility, one of the Christine Beatitudes came to his mind, yes, the uninterrupted awareness that God is the thinker, the doer and the fulfiller. But how does one maintain such an awareness unmarred, in the outer world, in the presence of crime, abuse, dishonesty, poverty, social turmoil, and with nations threatening one another for no other reason than political and ideological ambitions? Having thus formulated the question, Marco surrendered his self to his Liberated Master-Teacher, and waited. Then he heard Him saying:

"I AM this boy and that yonder girl, and that creeping creature and that dying dog, and that ancient tree, and that old man leaning on his staff.

"This statement of truth applies to you, my disciple, in all its integrality. Make it your credo and never deviate from it. When you are able to fully live and express it, when you see unity in plurality and harmony in diversity, you have achieved that degree of inner purification whereby you will see beyond walls of stone and steel; then you will see your Twin Flame.

"Your heart and mind must be cleansed from the debris of humanly-stained concepts, attitudes, habits and beliefs. Your intellectual entrenchment made of pride and self-seeking must be ransacked of its foulsome accumulation, fully exposed and

19

burned to ashes. Tradition, education, heredity, environment, personality and family attachment, are swamps and deep ravines that separate man from truth, the Law and the Lord. The implement to move through such a jungle is meditation leading to self-analyzation and awareness of the world of errors in which you have lived.

"Man must seek solitude and silence periodically — nay daily — in order to analyze his thoughts and actions, and find the line of demarcation between right and wrong; then adhere to and expand the former. He must renew himself by seeking new ways of self-expression, for this leads to self-unfoldment, a broader consciousness and a better understanding of his fellow man and world events. Not by prayer alone is man made pure, holier and wiser, but by thought, deed, harassment and error as well.

"As for you, My disciple Marco, you are herewith instructed to proceed towards the purification of your mind and feelings, by employing the ancient method of Yoga; that is, rhythmic breathing and meditation, with the intent of giving a holiday to the busy mind and tranquillity to your emotional world. When you have the certitude of being well above the pull of the senses, when the upsurge of cravings of all kinds can be slain at will, then by directing a beam of love from your heart towards your Twin Flame, with no thought of form, personality or location, she will appear to you with the unmistakable clarity and cogency of the sun at the zenith. Let your mind rest quiescent on the Effulgent Light in your heart. In her presence this Light will flow into the sacred sexual center which will awaken your mind to a state of prophetic fervency. It will be the same with her."

* * *

Marco did as commanded; the magnitude of the reward was beyond his highest expectations. By applying minutely the Master's recommendations, a new world opened before him, a world of reality and inner stability, as against a world of illusion, turmoil and insecurity. With each passing day, for about six months, he felt as if pieces of living flesh were being mercilessly cut from his body, producing excruciating pain for one interminable instant, then being healed instantly with a new, smooth and transparent tissue. Thus, through obedience,

20

faith and grace, Marco grew inwardly happier, more resilient in the mind and more handsome in his body; no longer did outer attractions and ephemeral pleasures lure him. He faced obstacles of all kinds in a detached attitude, positively convinced that whatever was lacking in him in the way of intelligence, strength and power of realization would be supplied by God, his Eternal Father. His heart overflowed with vigilant and tranquil expectancy. Readiness was his all.

One morning, in the shelter of his silentium, at the hour of meditation, he saw slowly rising from the floor before him a filmy cloud of pink vapor. As he gazed at it spellbound, the vaporous substance changed in color and form, became more dense and assumed the contour of an oblong body of quivering fire, which gradually changed into a beautiful sylph-like form. There in the action of his intuitive power, Marco recognized the eternal countenance of his Twin Flame in her spiritual wholeness and beauty. Attracted by a magnetic force that knows no resistance, they held out their arms to each other, and the next instant they were in a rapturous embrace of divine love. "My beloved sweetheart" — Marco said — "I am born anew". "I have been waiting for you for aeons" — she answered — "grateful I am and ready, my precious, precious darling." Together they heard the blissful voice of their Liberated Master-Teacher:

"This is the end of the search and the end of the mortal road. Through tears, prayer and obedience to the Law, you have met, never to separate again, never in all eternity. Now the spiritual ascent begins. It will be strewn with obstacles, sometimes of a seeming mortal nature; but have no fear, remember that you are on the cosmic road to the extinction of the cycles of birth and death." A few weeks later they met outwardly.

As Marco released her from his embrace, she receded amidst the caressing melodies of the Music of the Spheres, and he saw her enveloped in highly vibrating pink flames in the shape of a cross. Delicate pink rays of scintillating light, the symbol of mercy and compassion, emanated from her fingertips, forehead and heart, and radiated spherically to the infinite horizon. Her backward-streaming hair transformed into countless plumes of purple fire, reached out to the millions of disciples on earth in need of self-purification and marked by God for a messianic task. Then a beam of intense blue light, issuing from her forehead, drew Marco gently to her. Presently they overcame the power of terrestrial gravitation and began floating in space, their gaze to the stars. As they started ascending, they heard thousands of heavenly voices singing: "Rise up, O son and daughter of God, to higher worlds of nobler life . . ."

❋ ❋ ❋

Soon they lost sight of the earth, and having reached the rim of outer space they came to a large and massive gate of wrought silver, wide open. Entering, they saw a series of terraced gardens concentrically disposed, forming a perfect pyramid. The magnificence of the vegetation and profuse variety of flowers in gorgeous hues, and the terseness of the air vibrating with a living hum, held them entranced. Clasping hands, they walked along the paths of velveted grass, hoping to encounter someone who would guide them in this paradisaic land. But as they became aware, that they could not rely on their physical sight and sense perception, they entered deep into meditation and therein heard the enthralling voice of their Guardian Angel:

"My brother and my sister: I AM the two of you in one, an aspect of your higher selves and a partial expression of God. My voice is the blend of your voices, and the words of illumination and guidance I read in your hearts. You are now disciples of the Solar Path; not of the physical sun, but of the Source wherefrom it derives its life-essence. Master Helios is the Great Controller and Ruler of this Source. Through awareness and continual adherence to the Law of Harmony you shall partake of His warming, strengthening and life-giving radiance in a direct manner, similar to the sun's.

"You are in the outer rim of the Garden of Saturn, still millions of miles away from Its spheric hub. You might call it, the panhandle, a starry location whereby all the Soul-flames who have experienced a glimpse of immortality converge for higher inspiration and deeper communion with God. Here they feel for the first time the resiliency and freedom of the bodiless without losing the consciousness of the mortal self. They also see their ancestral heritage whose analyzation gives them a more precise evaluation of their present intellectual capabilities.

Still yourselves and meditate on the Light in your hearts, and you will understand the meaning of My words."

Devoid of sense perception and feeling almost bodiless, Marco and Leonora saw themselves floating in a void filled with light. Therein they became less visible and less tangible, and presently they experienced the cosmic osmosis of Universal Consciousness, the state whereby man becomes all-pervading and all-knowing. In that inexpressible state, whose duration was shorter than the shortest time-unit, they lived in the boundless eternity, performing innumerable tasks, ranging from warrior to peace-maker, all of the manifestations of science, the arts and political rulership; they saw their past errors and violations, and the rescuing process; their present messianic labour and the noble results for those who accept them; and also those human beings who, steeped in materialistic endeavours by conscious choice, belittle and deny them. Slowly they ascended the irresistible Path and entered the World of the ever-free Avatars. Gazing around they saw millions of Spirit-beings, like themselves, going through the same experience, although by diverse avenues and degrees of accomplishment, all endeavouring after the same goal: lordship over life and death.

"My brother and My sister" — their Guardian Angel resumed — "behold! This is only an inkling of what man will gain through the practice of introspection and the process of self-surrender. A world of unending wonders lies before him who, with a stroke of his will causes his mind to plunge daily into the crucible of purification. You yourselves, in such a short period, have already earned the privilege to be guided into the *Circle of Fire* for still greater purification in the manner of the ancient disciple-initiates and selfless workers. Come!"

❄ ❄ ❄

Marco and Leonora ascended to the apex of the pyramidal garden and there they saw, suspended high above it, an immense sphere of quivering, dazzling light. Concentrating their gaze on the feet of their Guardian Angel, they rose and entered into the *Circle of Fire*, where they were invested, over and again, with piercing tongues of purple fire, that felt as if arrows of hot steel were penetrating the flesh reducing their bodies to shreds. After what seemed an eternity, the Guardian Angel extended his hands in an act of benediction and two new temples were formed around their pulsating essences; the human consciousness made of limitation and doubt disintegrated, and an outlook of confidence, courage and indefeatibility came over them. Their minds were keener, and their physical strength appeared ever-enduring. Then the Guardian Angel explained:

"These new bodies of yours, made of precipitated light-substance, are only a temporary gift. At the termination of the present experience, your previous bodies will be returned to you exactly as they were before entering the Circle of Fire. But the lesson that I AM commissioned to convey to you is that 'What I do, ye shall do and greater things shall ye do.' The facility with which I manipulate light, substance and energy, is an attribute which you also possess. You must reclaim its use not for self-gratification or for the astonishment of mundane eyes, but for the glory of God in the world of form; and the path to regain this lost heritage lies in the continuance of your inner work. It is a search out of which all other searches are but a chaff before the wind; and while on the road to such a lofty goal you will be encouraged by lesser realizations.

"The disciple of Light, destined to teach others of the true nature of God, must have a wealth of direct inner experiences; only thus does he make himself the perfect soundboard of the Unwritten Law. This soundboard is already, though partially, established in you; you possess a state of health that is unmatchable and you have a sensitized mind capable of receiving our messages. Be encouraged. Continue, continue, continue! And whether you see progress or not, be unconcerned. Every moment spent in meditation and visualization of God's Glory and Power is like ingots of gold piling up in the subterranean of your soul; you will use them at the appropriate time and in the perfect environment to the amazement of the unbelievers, the joy of your disciples and the exaltation of the Self of you. You will teach by radiation, thought transference and example, and with only a few words spoken now and then.

"Thoughts are powerful and tangible forces that impregnate and stain the atmosphere for a radius of many miles. They might cross oceans and penetrate mountains and reach the limits of outer space, depending on the propulsive strength of of the cogitating mind and the degree of awareness of the mass of mankind. While the average person — with either noble or evil intent — barely stirs his own surroundings by his feeble thinking and inconsequential deeds, the thoughts of him who has reached the lofty plane of discipleship of the Inner shake society to its very foundation. This is because, knowing to be an instrument at the service of the Cosmic Assembly of the Perfect Ones, he resolves his thoughts and actions into the Pool of Universal Consciousness, where they go through the Crucible of Absolute Truth and then are released to mankind. This explains the impact upon humanity, generation after generation, of the teaching of Master Gautama the Buddha, Master Confucius, Master Moses, Pythagoras, Socrates, Master Jesus, Master Albert Einstein and many, many others. These great ones were all equally endowed with the Christ-light which They expressed in a diversified manner, in rapport to time, space, cultural and spiritual levels of society, and their own temperament and inner heritage. They thought and worked detachedly caring not for man's opinion or well-rooted human dogmas and scientific laws. Such is Christship.

"In order to accomplish this mighty task, the disciple's physical and mental stamina must be made of a different substance, of uncompounded matter; he must be able to resolve his whole being into the state of an element: light, or fire, or love, or humility, or pure knowledge. And to whoever asks him, What are you, he must be able to say: I AM THAT.

"Such a state of utter equilibrium is not achieved through wishful thinking. Far from it. It is the result of a tremendous self-imposed discipline followed without the slightest sense of sacrifice or a whisper that implies heroism; for this is vanity and pride. This is the Divine Chastiser and the Holy Redeemer. It is not a person or an Angel with a flaming rod; it is an essence, a vibration, a mighty thought, an incontrovertible resolve that springs forth from the deepest recess of one's being. That is all! And when two or three of these unknown — unknown even to each other — resolute Christs in human form that walk the earth send messages of salvation on behalf of man to the Cosmic Assembly of the Perfect Ones, a mighty, mysterious and definite vibration of chastisement and redemption is projected to mankind, the earth and the surrounding ethers to strike heavily against ignorance, arrogance, ostentation, violence, despotism, poverty and hypocrisy. The worshippers of the golden calf, the ego worshippers, and the carnal lovers of fame, name and power, will be punished in a myriad of ways ranging from incomprehensible frustration, psychosis, bankruptcy, blindness and other organic disintegration culminating in cancer. But in every case the merciful vibration of redemption moves abreast and even ahead of chastisement for the benefit of the penitent.

"The vibration of chastisement and redemption demanded by the selfless Avatars will eventually raise your planet to the state of a fixed star; and this is because these noble Sons and Daughters of God have offered themselves as a willing sacrifice on the altar of the Law of Evolution. They too have come to the end of the search!"

* * *

As the ringing message came to a close, Marco and Leonora emerged from the Sphere of Light and, sustained by their Guardian Angel, descended to a lower realm and alighted on the apex of Mount Tet, in the ante-heaven of Mercury.

"You are" — the Guardian Angel continued — "in one of the abodes of repose for the selfless workers. I am about to denounce the popular belief that the higher heavens are inhabited only by spirits who while on earth accomplished showing deeds in the field of war, science, religion and the arts. Though such lifestreams deserve heavenly acknowledgement, We are also mindful of the humble, the unknown and even of him who never uttered a word of prayer to God during his earthly existence. Behold this vast gathering of spirits who followed the path of action devoid of reward. Who are they? Soldiers of the lower ranks who performed their duty and never thought of receiving a reward or promotion; civil service employees who worked faithfully and rejected bribes; salespeople who never misled a customer; housewives who sacrificed themselves, unacknowledged, for the welfare of the family; simple priests who were harassed and abused by their mitered taskmasters; farmers who refused to be attracted by the glitter of city life and remained steadfast to the soil; humble school teachers who devoted their lives to break the ground of illiteracy in remote and isolated areas of the world; country doctors and nurses who renounced the comfort of civilization and helped to reduce the onslaught of disease, hunger and malnutrition in

26

backward lands. Here they are, seeking repose and recovery of strength in surroundings of celestial beauty and elegance. Some, like you, are still in their physical bodies made, temporarily, finer as a reward for their selfless labor. Those who have passed through the gates of death are trained by Liberated Masters for easier assignments in heaven and on earth at the end of which they are promoted starry dwellers. Please, feel free to approach some of them for direct enlightenment."

Marco and Leonora saw Spirit-teachers emerging from vast halls of light after having delivered their daily lesson to classrooms filled with eager pupils. They were from all lands and historical ages. Hindu rishis, Chinese masters, mathematicians from Arabia, Egyptian hierophants, Greek and Roman philosophers, Anglo-Saxon thinkers, Italian mystics and poets, African disciples of inwardness and American-Indian sun worshippers. Among them they recognized Zen, Confucius, Mencius, Socrates, Democritus, the Bab, Lady Khema, Sri Ramakrishna, Lao Tsu, John Huss, Sir Francis Bacon, Mazzini, Ibn-ul-Farid, the Prophet Samuel, Moses, the Emperor Marcus Aurelius, the Emperor Justinian, Dante, Seneca, St. Francis of Assisi, Milton, George Washington, Abraham Lincoln and many others. Marco and Leonora were approached by Justinian, the genius-filer of the ancient laws:

"Welcome to our heavenly ranks, O fortunate beings of earth. To behold the Thrones of immortal life is, indeed, a grace very few deserve. We are burning flames of the All-consuming Fire from the Heart of God, raising the consciousness of these millions of Soul-flames to higher levels. We inject in them the impelling urge to meditate so as to feel more vividly the Presence of God in all their endeavours and thus lighten their burden on the Path of immortality.

"An emperor and lawgiver I was on earth, under the rulership of those who had attained immortality before me. In spite of my kingly duties, I never ceased offering the best of my time and the first of my energies to God. By so doing, my day lengthened to the requirement of my work, and my energy increased by the same ratio.

"In Byzanthium I worked in the greatest library of the world, deciphering, transcribing and elucidating codes, laws, decrees, procedures and regulations; and because the thought

27

of God and the desire to find IT was in me first and foremost, the Cosmic Assembly of the Perfect Ones had provided me with one thousand winged messengers to deliver legal opinions in harmony with the Law of God to the thousands of kings and rulers who requested them. A political blueprint of universal nature — ready at that time — had been handed to me by the Great Ones, the application of which would have given to the Western World a culture and a law of ethics not dissimilar to that of the great Sahara civilization at the apex of its glory. A United World, though diversified in the arts, literature, languages and spiritual aspirations, would have been brought into manifestation with war, poverty and disease completely obliterated. But pseudo-leaders, slaves of fear bent on selfish gain, unleashed a campaign of threats, bribery and false promises that caused the feeble and unaligned countries to reject the Statutes of Light. Thus the negators of God prevailed and the Novus Ordo of the incoming Golden Age came to a temporary halt; the dark ages followed. Nevertheless the legions of Searchers of the Inner, undiscouraged, continue to march on. With their minds anchored to God and their attention and love at the service of man they have brought into being the Institute of the United Nations; and this time they shall not fail.

"Blessed friends, I have met you for the second time. In Byzanthium you were my guests and co-workers, assisting me in research and ordaining. You are ancient souls and truly lovers of God. Persevere, for you are at the last leap to immortality."

Their next encounter was Lady-master Khema who, like John to Master Jesus, was the disciple most beloved to Master Gautama the Buddha. In a melodious voice she called Marco and Leonora the true students of the Awakened Path.

"I train the most advanced of this starry crowd in the difficult art of passionlessness and inner tranquility. Considering the selfless deeds performed by them during their earthly life my task is quite simple. Without a word being spoken, I expose their soulflames to the blissful radiance of the Love and Knowledge that issue directly from the all-pervading Presence of God.

"My ancient friends, to be firmly established in passionlessness and tranquillity, in the complex mechanism of your

28

present civilization, is a gigantic task. You are surrounded by cultured ridicule and cultivated graciousness, which are worse than the outright persecution of centuries past. Arrogance and intimidation gilded with material promises and rewards of name and fame, are two accursed methods employed by scheming leaders whose aim is to rule undisputed and grow rich in the process. We do not condemn material wealth in the society in which you live; we only remind those who want it, that to seek wealth at the expense of ethical principles is like issuing an invitation to mental aberration, emotional turmoil and physiological disintegration. I assure you, if you are bent on acquiring financial security, even above the need of your environment, by all means do not stop; but do so within the dictates of your conscience; incalculable then will be the reward. All the students of mine who return to earth with this philosophy of life well entrenched in their feelings, follow the attitude of detachment; they say to Lady Wealth: 'Follow me!' and keep on laboring as usual, in honesty and positive trust. And since Lady Wealth will surely follow passionlessness and tranquillity remain unaltered.

"While on earth, in the fulfillment of His divine mandate, your Master Jesus sought disciples, and though the environment from which to draw them was restricted and hostile, and the requirements severe, He remained detached and trustful. Whenever He saw one, He said to him: 'follow Me!' Whether the would-be disciple followed him or not, it was not his concern; He had obeyed detachedly and free from passion the dictates of his Heavenly Father. His mind was tranquil.

"Blessed guests Marco and Leonora, I say unto you: if those who misguide, bribe and threaten are at fault and, eventually victims of unspeakable suffering; those, the weaklings, who acquiesce for any reason whatsoever, are equally at fault. They may not be visited while on earth by the same punishment and suffering as their cruel masters, but they certainly will be degraded before the All-seeing Eye of the Law, and their next embodiment will be menial and marked for servitude. Man, O man, never yield to ungodliness, no matter how glittering and immediate the reward."

The heavenly Presence of Lady-Master Khema that was now receding — all youth, all beauty, all smiles swimming in the shoreless ocean of immortality – infused in Marco and Leonora an uncontainable determination to achieve the same cosmic status. A deeper and more comprehensive knowledge and understanding of God, that was what they needed. But what is Knowledge that is acquired without books? How does one direct and control his mind for such an ultimate goal? Where does the search begin? They returned to the earthly plane and waited humbly and trustfully. Their Liberated Master-Teacher responded and resumed His divine task of training:

"Knowledge is the acquisition of that Inner Power which pierces the screen of appearances and leads the mind to the cause of all manifestation. This power is bestowed to the pure of heart, or to him who, through continuous introspection, aims at the Supreme through a series of strokes of the iron will against all compromise with the lower ego. To aim at the Supreme means to so live as to rise above joy and sorrow, good and evil, and love and hatred. It means to tread the path of absolute interiorization without being away from the outer world, and to practice sanctity without being detected. It means finally to be able to perceive the cause behind the effect. Here are some helpful hints in reaching such a noble plateau:

1 – "Every time you say 'I AM' visualize the two words in capital letters and silently add 'OM'. This will remind you that it is God thinking, directing, acting and making decisions for you. The deeper your adherence to this visualization, the easier it is to overcome outer impasses, thus, the more perfect your accomplishments. Repeat in a whisper OM I AM at the beginning and closing of every task, no matter how outwardly insignificant. Train yourselves to be an instrument of the Inner Self Who never errs, Who does not know the torment of uncertainty, defeat and limitation, Who is the Essence of absolute triumph over all obstacles. Know IT as such. OM is ITS Name, OM is your all in all!

2 – "If you have practiced as told, you should feel – in a short while – a greater inner strength, and an increased physical and mental buoyancy. Humility and divine pride will begin to mingle and the blend thereof will impart a halo of Self-reliance around your head. No longer do you succumb to outer pressure. You are the anvil and you are the hammer, and each blow from without is made void or turned to a positive result. Thus you

30

hold at bay the reaping of unkind karma, and the damage caused to your material interests by past errors is promptly corrected through right attitude. And what is right attitude? That the self of you is decreasing and the GodSelf within is increasing and expanding Its radius of action in your mind and world. And because of this enormous fortune being released unto you, you will be able to rest quiescent and unperturbed in the presence of approaching dangers, firmly convinced that the reaction of your mind and the use of your strength are directed by God. You shall not fail!

3 — "You have reached the day whereby your inner possessions being on the increase, you require a greater Self-mastery for their protection. Hence the necessity of greater mental concentration on the quivering Light in your heart. You shall be able to contact the Superconscious almost immediately, every time you desire to do so, and therein perceive clearly the technique involved for your spiritual growth. And what is this technique? Seeing that Light rising from your heart into your head and being transformed into executive power, ready to express itself in the outer world.

4 — "By this time the awareness of God is so clear in your mind that the application of God's Law — Knowledge — takes place almost effortlessly. You are no longer at the mercy of moods, no matter how fierce and pressing, because moods are merchandise of the lower nature, and that nature has already been conquered. At this stage your power of remembrance has grown tremendously and your intuitive faculty expanded in proportion. Hold firmly in your mind the condition of instrumentality.

5 — "Now you have reached the threshold of Christship, you have aroused the anger of the powers of darkness — Satan, Mara, or Eblis — whose aim is to lure you and eventually cause your utter perdition. Their power of manipulation of matter and energy is almost as great as that of an Archangel. They make you think that your thoughts and deeds are an emanation from your mortal mind. They subtly stain your words with pride; they try to irritate you and make you feel envious at the sight of someone who is also advanced in the Light; they inject a tinge of fanaticism in your behavior; they lead you to the practice of queer and exteriorized rituals; they take

the smile away from your countenance and tell you that that is holiness; they call you vain if you continue being fastidious in your appearance, clothes and body cleanliness; they whisper in your ear words of superiority complex in the presence of any person you meet; they give you a false eloquence and a haughty attitude in the midst of people engaged in controversy. They finally cause you to do the most damnable things by gilding them with righteousness and perfection.

"I see this reminds you of Master Jesus in the desert of the ashes, Gethsemane, the olive grove and on the Calvary. And you may add in the presence of Annas and Caiaphas, King Herod, the Roman Governor Pontius Pilate, and both the rich and 'wise', and the mocking scum of society: the heartless, schemers, thieves, murderers; in short, the entire visible world from end to end clamored for His cosmic destruction. Yet He triumphed! Like Him you shall triumph, and also all those who will follow this teaching. You will be helped greatly if you maintain a strong and healthy body based on calisthenics, rhythmic breathing and simple and moderate eating.

6 — "At this stage you will have achieved Self-mastery. Human, vain, longings no longer impair the beauty and crystal-line transparency of your inner world. You are a torch unto yourselves, illumining the path of life without a single flicker. A panorama of starry magnificence, staged by the Self Whom you have obeyed, unfolds before your eyes and HIS. Such is everything you see, every person you meet. Think boundlessly, feel the joy unmarred by the senses. Approach people, conditions and events as you would approach God; this will sublimate your intelligence and raise you above and beyond the exploits of a true genius.

"Strive now for a glimpse of the Godhead, greater and deeper than so far experienced, and know there is nothing greater than THAT. Cultivate humility to the utmost; maintain your spiritual equilibrium intact before either loss or unexpected gain. Learn to perceive what is right and what is wrong on the instant, not through reasoning, but through deeper purity and self-exaltation in humility. Do not shrink from what appears to be a dangerous mission; know that it is the Self leading the Self to meet and welcome the Self. The Self is the All, the Self and you are one; therefore nothing

32

exists outside of you. Having overcome dualism, you are no longer beset by the belief of diversity.

7. — "Now you have — you are — Self-Knowledge. Why, how? Because you have gone through a process of dispersonalization and self-sublimation. You have dissolved the little self of you in the ocean of Universal Consciousness. You have risen above all that is human, limited, ignorant, depressing, herd-like, untrue, carnal, slothful, distortful and contrary to divine living. You have reached the state whereby you act only by the dictates of the Spirit within; you are so highly sensitized, as to know exactly when to talk and when to cease talking, what to do and what to avoid, what is safe and what is beset with unnecessary danger; you let your free and Self-expressing Spirit flood your mind with what is required to make you as wise as a prophet.

"Through the fiery desire to discipline yourselves and attain purity, you have caused your Souls to be enshrined in the Light of your Father-God OM, the Source of All. Hence the Search on the mortal plane is over. You have universalized yourselves; you have attained the Knowledge that knows and is God. This is the Fountainhead of immortality. Move on! There are trials and suffering of karmic nature along the narrow, crooked and impervious ascent; but they are transitory and, seen in retrospect, laughable and trivial. Aim at the summit and know that no earthly power can ever take it away from you!"

* * *

With their minds still attuned for inquiry and inner experiences, Marco and Leonora meditated and waited. Soon they heard the voice of an ancient Being from the Realm of Silence: "My friends of bygone ages: Greetings! I AM Flora, the engineer of vegetation and the Chief Aide of the Maha Chohan.

"When discipline and diversification were given to the earth and nature was commanded to produce in an orderly manner, I was appointed by the Elohim of Creation, Assistant Master-Elohim of all that grows by means of roots and stems. Self-discipline and the desire to know had given me divine attributes; cosmic intelligence and creative abilities stood at the threshold of my consciousness, ready to obey me and enrich my life for eternal years.

"When we impose the Breath of Life on an inanimate speck of matter, how do we go about it? We apply the process of purification. To isolate the elements from a compound means to free each element from the dross of unwanted matter. Now the element, liberated and pure, stands alone facing God. Seeking usefulness it goes into meditation in the same manner as man does. Both offer themselves to God for service.

"Whereas it is not my province to analyze man's behavior, his urge to criticise, argue and resist, in the living element one finds a ready response and unconditional obedience; and since intelligence — divine intelligence in fact — is not lacking, the living element is as responsive to innumerable tasks as an angelic being at the service of a Liberated Master. Knowing that what is demanded of it is of the nature of God, it goes to work with total transport, fulfilling all the tasks that appear on the blueprint of that specific commission. Can you visualize what would be the result of Nature's equilibrium if the mind of the element would imitate the mind of man?

"The average person may have a glimpse of the endless transformation, combination, association and potentiality of the living element by the manner in which animals yield to training. And in each case it is a question of intelligence and obedience. All animals from an insect to a sardine to an elephant can be taught to perform a certain task, even to read and write. And as man feels happy, enlightened and inwardly proud at the end of a well-done difficult job, likewise an animal. But only the pure in heart, the disciple of the Inner, is able to see and acknowledge the sensitivity, self-respect, love, pride and sense of responsibility, both as an individual and as a family group, of the so-called brute animals, and how much they yearn and love to be taken under their master's rulership for training. An animal at repose or in action in its own habitat is truly a chapter in the Book of Life.

"The scientist of matter who is also a scientist of the Soul is well aware of this and more. He knows as well as you that the power and possibilities of the atom are still in the infancy, for the atom is a child of the element holding in its heart God Itself in Its absolute wholeness; and what God can do the atom can do also; but it must be approached and interrogated with a pure heart. Otherwise the most cherished exploits of

34

this age of yours, the landing on the Sun and the traveling in the Milky Way will be of no consequence whatsoever. Mankind will continue to be sick and frustrated; nations and races will war against one another through ignorance; and floods, earthquakes, epidemics and fire will not cease their onslaught against man and his kin for generations to come. And believe me, O messengers from Earth, in the years ahead you will witness famine and poverty on the increase. This is not because of the inadequacy of the soil or the population explosion, but because of the hedonistically negative outlook of races and nations steeped in envy and the hypocritical pretense of spirituality displayed by the new breed living in filth and bent on stimulants and narcotics.

"The statesman, the diplomat, the philosopher, the artist and the scientist will not advance on the path of peace, progress, beauty and comfort, until they search within, that is, become aware and listen to the Voice of their Presence in their hearts. And this must be done quickly, for the time is short. It pleases me and it gives me honor to reveal to you the divine plan of the Cosmic Assembly of the Perfect Ones. They said: 'The planet Earth must be transmuted from the present status of shadow and ephemerality to light and cosmic stability. At once! A period of ten thousand years has been set apart for the realization of such a plan. Considering the colossal amount of work to be done this seeming long span of time is very short indeed. Hence the need to heed to our humble suggestions. It is the cosmic responsibility of every man, woman and child to commence the Inner Search immediately.'"

The Master Elohim then approached Leonora and touching her throat caused a brilliant luminosity to issue forth.

"This beam of light" — he continued — "is proof of your past association with me, my child Leonora. At the beginning of the present Cycle of Life, you had a taste of the bliss of purity which made you a great artist in the field of still life, color and the manifestation of beauty. You worked under my supervision, sketching leaves, petals and stems. And wherever there is a shade of pink today in the things that grow, they possess the influence of your ancient soul and hand. You suggested to arm roses with thorns as a defensive weapon, for you perceived a future age of involution in life, when there would

35

be people who would poison life at a touch or glance. Your love for pink as a tone of healing and harmony began to manifest at that time; and it is still with you, showing that on the path of perfection nothing is lost.

"And now, my blessed friends and disciples. I say farewell! Your inner search has barely begun. Please continue, for the reward is beyond measure!"

With a teaching filled with such compelling truths reverberating in the very depths of their beings, and with an enduring sentiment of gratitude in their hearts, Marco and Leonora descended to the human plane of life but not for long. The urge of the Beyond had become as vital as breathing. One morning, a fortnight after the instructions given by Master Flora, amidst the echo of an ineffable song of love, their bodies began to dissolve causing their Spirit forms to float upward, higher and ever higher, until they lost sight of the earth and came to a starry parkway flanked with lofty cypress trees. With their feet barely touching the ground they sauntered along a promenade that ran parallel to a riverbank; the slow-moving waters reflected a tenuous silver-blue luminance from the cloud-flecked azure of the sky above; the surrounding landscape was an elysium of richly-colored flowers of every variety and hue and the air was saturated with the fragrance of honeysuckle and Persian jasmine.

They were clothed with the garments of the Great White Brotherhood at the inception of the second millennium of the Christine era, the gold cross of the Crusaders, united to the half moon of the Moslem, worn as a breastplate, was held by a gold chain around their necks. Leonora had the insignia of mercy — a sword immersed in a pink flame — on her cape, while Marco had a military insignia on his. Strolling now leisurely northward against the current of the meandering river, they came to a large circular lake surrounded by luxuriant tropical vegetation. At the north end they saw a massive vertical wall of pink granite, whose summit rose to an almost unbelieveable height; against it the overhanging waterfall swirled in a misty drop and splashed noiselessly into the lake. As they sat on the pure white sand and directed their thoughts inwardly they were again contacted by the Ancient Cosmic Being Flora.

"The interstellar Powers are by your side, sustaining you and guiding you whereto new experiences will enrich your minds and make you worthier teachers. You are showing yourselves in your last embodiment, at the time of the First Crusade, as emissaries of the Great White Brotherhood whose focus of radiation and action was in the Swiss Alps. Your name, Leonora, was Santana, which signifies lover of the wise ones, and yours, Marco, was Kuntela, a fighter for divine justice.

"An amazing peculiarity of this body of spiritual brethren, so well entrenched in the heart of the Christian world, was that very few were the Christians who had enough qualifications to be admitted therein, while many were the Islamites against whom the plotting clergy and some of the ruthless European potentates had set their minds to destroy. The Crusades were concocted by these leaders of satanic instinct, not for spiritual reasons but for political and territorial aggrandizement. There were no Moslem infidels who were threatening the Christian World, but the corruption and greediness of the Church aided by a few scheming secular rulers who were thirsty for name, fame and more wealth. There was no need of crusading to save the Holy Sepulcher, because there was no such thing, since the burial place of the body of our Brother Jesus had been dissolved at the time of His ascension. The various Crusades were, therefore, contrary to the Spirit of the Christine teaching, and disapproved by the Master of Galilee.

"Your mission was entirely impersonal, taking neither side, working only for the sake of preventing the onslaught and bringing peace. Santana's task was to alleviate the untold suffering of the migrating women and children of both sides, whose dire poverty and ignorance had caused them to leave their homeland in search of wealth and comfort which were never found. Disease, epidemics, famine and death, were so rampant that the so-called army nurses were organized for the first time under her inspiration. Kuntela's diplomatic activity caused him to go to and fro the contending headquarters, where he observed not regular army units, but lawless packs of tramps and fanatical paupers that aimed at killing, plundering and seizing somebody else's property, in the name of Jesus Christ or Mohammed the Son of Allah. It was a mass debauchery of unprecedented magnitude. Kuntela's work established a cosmic record in the field of international relations.

37

"Dear ones, this episode was re-enacted for an inner reason. It was meant to show how easily false leaders can prey upon and mislead the unwary, and what powerful instruments they use to make wrong things appear right. The entities of darkness and destruction had both the Church leaders and the laical rulers in the grip of fear gilded with spirituality, which turned into fanaticism and gross misunderstanding. Such were the Crusades!

"Only through the process of inner search does man acquire the needed power to defeat the entities of selfishness; but such power is not given outright, it must be earned by each man through application. Often one seems to be engaged in a constructive endeavour, the consensus of opinion of the society is in his favor, all the signs of the age and civilization accord with what he is doing, he thinks he is moving in sanctity and glory, and yet he walks in quicksand, ready to be engulfed in utter oblivion. The faithful of Christendom were told by the Church hierarchs that by joining the expedition to the Holy Land they would be granted eternal life in heaven. A French monk, Pierre the Hermit, traveled from town to town, using his power of eloquence, to convince the man in the street to *arms against the infidels*.

"How vain it is to trust human intelligence, how truly alone is man in the world of man, with no place to turn for worthwhile help. Only the Inner Helper is the wise guide, only to HIM must man go for protection and illumination.

"The first step towards correct behavior and accumulation of noble karma is in the wise use of the power of speech. To be able to talk is a gift from on High; it must not be polluted with vain utterances, slander or gossip. Speech being the preview of action, it is the former that must be controlled if sorrow and suffering are to be avoided.

"The second step is never to speak or act on first impulse. Be slow in planning or making decisions, cultivate poise, arise above haste and dislike. And should you err, do not grieve, but make a mental note by speaking aloud the nature of your error, then proceed on, it never to be made again.

"Face joyfully and humbly those whom you have offended or caused loss or suffering, and ask their forgiveness. It is the greatest act of self-purification and discipline; it makes you eligible to face God and be cosmically forgiven.

38

"Be always guided by the dictates of your conscience, by the Law of your inner self; listen to It in the secret of your Silentium, listen to the sound of its mighty voice. Thus you grow gradually, until you are elevated to the Office of the High Priest of the Unseen Church of the Most High. Then you shall begin to live a life untrammelled by the despotic claims of the physical body, mental deviation, human concepts, outer pressure and sectarian dogma."

* * *

As Master Flora withdrew from their Inner Sight, new glimpses of a higher world were released to Marco and Leonora.

They came to a starry land inhabited by happy beings singing the song of Meditation and Deliverance. It was a song without words melodiously hummed. They were in groups of one hundred moving abreast through levitation and disappearing in the distance. As one group went forward, another arrived so that there were always twelve groups present. Marco and Leonora noticed that the group nearest them waiting to go forward had in their Spirit-forms signs of badly battered bodies, while those who had returned were perfect specimens of handsomeness and beauty. Desirous to know the reason for such a radical change, they directed their attention to their Liberated Master-Teacher.

"You are above the etheric belt surrounding the planet Earth" — He explained — "witnessing the action of the Law of Mercy upon human beings recently arrived from the plane of physical life. They had longed intensely for God and Deliverance, but were unable to attain the supreme goal because of wars, earthquakes, epidemics, drowning, floods, fire and other accidents. The Liberated Masters in charge of the application of the Law of Mercy, direct them into the Pool of Transmutation for reconditioning, as it were, and then send them to remote stars for the equivalent of seven embodiments. There they study the science, the philosophy, the art and the literature of the soul, after which they gather around the etheric belt of the planet earth, as emissaries of the Cosmic Assembly of the Perfect Ones, to assist striving mankind who are in the same plight as they were. After one hundred years they are elevated to the status of Christship without further embodiment.

"Do you see how important it is to make positive and early

39

visualization for the life of the beyond while still young? O man, do not let thyself be caught unprepared!"

Marco and Leonora stood in the midst of a group who had just returned from the Pool of Transmutation and felt the lifting radiance of their countenances. One of them spoke:

"Worthy disciples of the Solar Path: We are the proud farmers of the Garden of the Soul hovering over the earth, broadcasting the living seed of adherence to the Law of God. O that more of the earthly dwellers might feel our presence in the midst of their mortal chores. We disseminate patiently and silently the basic elements of divine ethics unobstructed by tradition, theology, ritual and mystery that are obsolete and a drag on the blessings of the Science of the Soul. The worst of these drags are religion and pseudo-patriotism, the major sources of hatred and persecution and generators of all other violations that make man unworthy of the heavenly bounty.

"If humanity would direct their intelligence and energy only to constructive endeavours ,there would be no shattered bodies, decrepitude, disease, crime and poverty. For what are the vast majority of business enterprises, such as tobacco used for smoking, alcohol for drinking, narcotics, gambling casinos, hot war and cold war, books on pornography, espionage and counterespionage and all the innumerable remorae attached to them, but a waste of wealth, energy and life, causing millenniums of delay on the path of joy and noble fulfillments on earth. Under the aegis of freedom, Civil Rights, national security, social progress and artistic expression, the wealth, the energy and the intelligence of the citizens of a nation are always in a state of mobilization for something or for some cause: now to defend, now to dissolve, now to keep the status quo and now to stimulate and advance. And in the interim the true forces of social progress and cosmic evolution are held in abeyance.

"When we do descend to earth to cast the seed of nobler living, we do so in a global manner. We touch every continent, every hamlet, every cave where man abides. We whisper into his ear LOVE GOD, LOVE GOD, LOVE GOD, over and again until his Soul is held in a trance of divine joy; then we speak of inner liberty as against regimentation of any kind, political, religious, philosophical, artistic and commercial. 'Thou art' — we say — 'indestructible Spirit, next a cosmic being at the service of God,

40

then a man of perfect thought and action, and finally a citizen.'
Those who respond make us vibrate all over our structures. What
an inexpressible sentiment of gratitude to God they give us. It
is truly a paean of gladness reverberating from end to end in
the World of God. Indeed that man has entered the path of the
Ultimate Search.

"And do you know where the harvest is more bounteous? It
is in the so-called communist countries. In the retreat of their
hearts both the people behind the Iron Curtain and the Bamboo
Curtain are preparing a bloodless counterrevolution that will
contribute to the ushering in of the Golden Age with freedom
for all in the true sense, license for none. Then you will see some
of the unethical enterprises disappearing for lack of customers
who no longer have use for their products of filth and degradation, while others will be streamlined and made to adhere to the
law of scientific truth. The government and its agencies will
be reduced to mere statistical departments filing events, and
nothing else; the people, tacitly, will guide the people; and those
who are slated for leadership will be examined not on the basis
of intellectual accruement or wealth or *good deeds*, but for intensity of inner vision. You must realize that although endowments
and largesses contribute to the realization of noble programs, it
is only the radiance of him who has had inner experiences that
raises the consciousness of the masses to a higher level in a permanent way.

"To the people of America and the Free Nations we say: Watch,
study, the nameless masses of Russia, China, Poland, Rumania
and so forth; they are your friends more so than the people of
Italy, Greece or even England. Be kind and understanding with
them, as much as you are severe and uncompromising with their
leaders. You will learn more about cosmic liberty from the slave
in chains than from the freethinker in your midst."

＊　＊　＊

As the gifted farmers of Light disappeared, a magnificent
Splendor-being of great inner achievement, embodying both the
masculine and feminine traits, appeared before Marco and
Leonora.

"Ancient friends of Light" — He greeted them — "I am here to
fulfill your unexpressed desire to know more about the process
of the transmutation of matter into spirit without so-called phy-

41

sical death. I shall also reveal My identity to you at the appointed moment. Have patience.

"As a human being I was a wise king and a humble instrument of those who had attained Splendorship before Me, oł those who through a happy blending of nobility of intellect and purity of heart had scaled the ladder of immortality. These beings are called 'Splendors', and I am one of them. They form the Cosmic Court of Justice, investigating, rendering opinions and making decisions on cases of universal import whose application would be valid for a thousand years. The Kumara Brothers, the Maha Chohan and Lord Maitreya are fully accredited members, Moses and Master Jesus are member-counselors, I am a junior member. This divine office was conferred upon Me by the Cosmic Assembly of the Perfect Ones.

"During my earthly life I followed the inner policy of absolute obedience to the command of My Godself. All my plans, judgements and decisions were conditioned to the approval of this Supreme Spirit. Every time I attempted, ignorantly, to think or plan anything outside the circle of awareness of God as the Supreme Thinker and Planner, I was a total failure, I lived in shame and turmoil and my earthly dominions shook under my feet. Thus, through painful humiliation, paralyzing defeats and stifling sorrow, I was initiated into the secret of the Law of the Self, whose comprehension and application earned for Me, by an act of grace, the All-seeing Eye, and rescued me for eternal years. From that day on I became wise and great before man's eye and mind. My prayer, my rhythmic breathing, my attunement with God had always priority in the midst of my kingly duties and responsibilities. And though now a dweller of this Realm of Splendorship, surrounded by ineffable perfection and wielding absolute power over all creation, yet tears of joy and gratitude to God gush forth from my eyes every time I think of my earthly life, and how miraculously I was delivered from utter perdition.

"Now I shall re-enact for your illumination by command of the Cosmic Assembly of the Perfect Ones, the process of transmutation which took place many centuries ago."

The splendrous form of the king disappeared, and in its place a pillar of Light coalesced, inside of which the structure of the spinal chord of the human body, made of condensed light, was seen. Swarming about it were billions of iridescent points of light highly vibrating, gathered here and there forming colonies of color in various hues. A commanding voice was heard coming forth from the pillar: "OM I AM OM!"

The fiery column disappeared and the points of light began to move in a disciplined manner. One group was transformed into the brain structure so highly vibrating that it appeared as if in absolute repose, and as brilliant as the heart of the physical sun. Around it the ideal head of man took shape. The second group took position on the site of the heart. Its color was pale-pink, vibrating in an upward motion and sending a continuous flow of specks of light into the head. The third colony that made the lungs assumed a subdued violet shade, shooting radially life-giving energy to every cell of the body. The lymphatic system and the blood vessels were electric blue, emanating filaments of light. The nervous system appeared as innumerable conduits of liquid light whose color was pure quartz crystal. The eyes were two spheres of deep blue light projected from the heart center and connected with the brain, and were constantly nurtured by the two sources. The bone structure was a combination of white light and intense magnetic force, whose power of attraction (centripetal) and repulsion (centrifugal) presided over and imposed discipline upon all organic functions. The muscular system came into being by the coordinated activity of all the other organs and centers of energy and life. It possessed and displayed all the characteristics and functions of thinking, feeling, seeing, olfactory and tactile of the whole system; but unlike the human body on earth, it had no degenerative tendencies, such as fatigue, aging and deterioration, because the impulses emanating from the brain structure were pure, impersonal and passion free. All the organs of sensation and perception, being linked to a pure mind, and this in turn nourished by the pulsations from the heart, conveyed true pictures of man, society, events and the visible nature itself. The body thus formed had no organs of elimination, and it did not require food. The same commanding voice explained:

"Tell the mortal mind to accept, by an act of will, the human body as a condensation of light; tell the despotic senses to take a long leave of absence, then compel that mind to shake off its haughty attitude of superiority and lie prone at the base of the invisible Pillar of Living Light that protects the complex human integer, and you shall have a body of condensed light, perfect, undecaying, self-existing and eternally beautiful. And now behold further!"

A brilliant sphere of light, thrice the size of the head, coalesced from nowhere and stood three feet above the body of light. The Voice proclaimed:

"This is My gift to the meditative disciple. Observe!"

A beam of pink light issued from the Sphere and struck at the center of the heart, producing a powerful magnetic eye, the All-seeing Eye of God. The Voice went on:

"When purity of heart is achieved and noble intents dwell therein at the exclusion of all else, man sees, perceives and understands all things beyond time, space and causality."

Another beam of light, almost colorless but equally intense, entered the center of the head and changed into a lobe, nearly as bright as its source. There it elongated and, maintaining its original size, projected forth another lobe of lesser brilliancy. The Voice continued:

"When through passionate yearning for God, these two living lobes — called the Pineal and Pituitary glands — become one again, man will be raised to the status of Master of Creation; he will shatter the wheel of birth and death, and will display both the masculine and feminine traits. This is called the *Cosmic Marriage of Heaven and Earth*."

A beam of purple light reached the solar plexus.

"Man has no strength of his own. By acknowledging his absolute and undeflected dependence on God, he becomes as strong as a mountain, as powerful as an ocean, and as invincible as an Archangel."

To the throat went a beam of golden light slightly hued in blue.

"Golden-blue symbolizes wisdom. When man makes his credo of adhering to the law of the highest ethics in all his dealings with his fellow man, he will speak only words of truth and wisdom, all his desires will come to fruition and all his actions will be free from Karma."

Moving downward a beam of purple-white light struck at the sexual organs.

"Sexual mergence is an act inspired by God whereby all the Powers of Creation assemble and unite to repeat in an endless

44

flow the miracle of life and Self-renewal. Let it be understood and accepted solely as such. Man and woman who thus unite procreate children by virtue of the Holy Ghost; they will grow mighty and wise, living Christs on earth!"

The Voice now concluded:

"This Body of Light is My Gift to man. To him it belongs, now and forever, by virtue and authority of My unchangeable Word and Promise. It shall last as long as the Great Central Sun shall last, and as long as the Universe shall feel and give testimony of My ever-enduring Presence!"

* * *

"My blessed friends of the Splendors, you have seen and what you have seen shall bring attestation of the Power and Love of God to men for immortal years. May all men of earth be branded with the Mystic Fire of divine yearning. Know that I shall never cease calling to God for more blessings and light for the children of Earth, and so shall you also. As you enter into the feeling of calling expand your visualization and call for more, for non-calling is stagnation, self-obliteration."

Marco and Leonora began to feel a heaviness and a density; their Splendor-friend instantly intensified His luminosity and held them from falling into the flesh prison. "Your minds are questioning, you wish to know who I was while on earth, and since your desire is not stained with mortal curiosity, I shall answer."

Enfolded in a celestial aura of blazing light, the Great Being stood before them, no longer in Its masculine-feminine aspect, but in his idealized human form, which was garbed in a luxuriant blue robe of an ancient Egyptian Hierophant.

"I am he" — he said — "who in the concept of the great scholars of Earth put morality into maxims. How much truth there is in such a definition of me, it is not my purpose to investigate. What I do know is this: My earthly life, though filled with high purpose and kingly duties, was an incessant flow of love to God. I studied because God is knowledge. I applied His Law because I knew that by so doing I could not fail to be as just and wise as the least of His servants of whom He would have been proud. I loved my subjects and also the peoples of the surrounding lands, because I had learned to see in them the delegated image of God. For many centuries I was the object of discussion and controversy of shortsighted mortals concerning my cosmic status. I was bit-

45

terly criticised because while in the midst of my royal duties I would withdraw from the throne of judgement to seek solitude, out of which I drew the required wisdom that helped me to decide a case in conformity with the divine law. Blessed friends of the Splendors, I searched all my life.

"It was difficult for me to convince my contemporaries and associates of the value and power of silence and meditation. Those who tried had disheartening experiences for, rather than being enlivened and illumined, they saw the powers of darkness and the entities of hell. They could not be convinced that what they saw came from within; that it meant they needed inner purification and the practice of self-analyzation, and that slowly and by degrees these entities would disappear, and beings of heavenly nature and messengers from on High would appear instead. The Realm of Light is barred to him who wallows in the stagnant pool of carnal cravings and selfish aspirations. Man cannot see his own vices and shortcomings until he enters the circulus of solitude. It is there that his mortal mind is made alive, vibrant and receptive to the blessings of God; it is there that man is universalized and turned into an effective instrument for lasting peace on earth, Christlike brotherhood and good will to his fellow beings. And now, my friends, behold!"

The dazzling light of scintillating colors which surrounded him was almost blinding, as they heard him say:

"I AM Solomon, the Son of David, the disciple-initiate of the Egyptian School of Light, King of Israel, a Master Splendor at the service of God and of the Cosmic Assembly of the Perfect Ones, and a dweller of the Realm of Immortality!"

* * *

As the ancient king withdrew from sight a sudden wave of transcendent faith filled the hearts of Marco and Leonora. They stood for awhile as if in a transfixion of divine purpose, cogitating, planning and inbreathing to the utmost all the courage, the exaltation and the exemplary radiance of the Immortal Ones. They saw the arduous ascent, the obstacles, the pitfalls and the subtle forces of hell that belittle, discourage, injure and even maim the most assertive on the path of the inner. But they could no longer be stopped, the search must go on. In the depths of meditation they heard the voice of Truth:

"Continue to train yourselves in tranquillity; guard your con-

46

duct and hold your tongue in check. Strive for higher states of thinking, where sensual pleasure cannot go. And should a corrupt thought creep in, be unafraid, cause your mind to create a noble thought immediately, then enliven it with the Breath of God through a strong and undeflected visualization.

"With all the inner wealth now at your disposal, and though in the world and sometimes of the world, you shall stand high above the world, untouched by the corruption of the common lot, unexalted and undecried by man's praise or blame.

"Disciples of the Inner, be alert!"

CHAPTER III

THE MASTER IDEALISTS

The drama and the comedy; the grand opera and the operetta. The human race, on the path of evolution and mental expansion, created arbitrarily these literary forms for amusement, warning, reward and edification of the mind. Drama begins lightly and almost carefree; it goes through a series of misdeeds made by the unscrupulous villain against righteous characters and ends in death. The operetta opens with an incidental occurrence, unfolds in hardships and misunderstanding and epilogizes in gladness which culminates in a happy ending.

Man is convinced that these literary compositions are suggested by the behavior of nature: the mating of animals and the pollination of trees, the life of the jungle whereby the strongest and most cunning of the beasts prey on the weaker ones, the sequence of the seasons, floods, earthquakes and hurricanes; and also the visiting scourges upon mankind, such as fires, disease, famine, pestilence, assaults, wars and massacres. These are the seeds — man says — from which the entire tree of life on earth germinates, buds, flowers and bears fruit.

Looking from a higher and impersonal point of view, that is, from the plane of truth unmarred by time, space and human contingency, this fatalistic attitude is driveling nonsense. We may affirm a priori that these scourges are not imposed upon man by any outer force or entity; they are man made and as such avoidable and this includes hurricanes and earthquakes. Master Jesus proved this by his innumerable miracles, the making of the wine and bread and fish, the quelling of the unruly waters, the overcoming of death for others and himself, and his persecution and ascension. By imbibing and mastering both the forces of creation and the subtlest vibration of the human mind, He overcame vice, sorrow, stupidity, selfishness, disease, famine, poverty, cupidity and death itself. He created a void within his human nature

49

which was immediately filled with a total glory, an absolute dominance over the three worlds and over the lesser and nagging incidents of every day living. This was his supreme victory. He had hoped man would take an example from him and change his pattern of thinking, his definition of life and his concept of God. Instead what did he do? As an individual and en masse he refilled the void with negativity; to work became a curse, a hindrance to the realization of the kingdom of heaven, while to idle and stare at nothing he defined as contemplation and treading the path to paradise.

Through fanaticism he destroyed the activism of the pagan world; no more laughter; no longer the human intellect, the only conscious link between God and man, would be thrown into the arena of philosophical speculation or directed to create works of art in painting, sculpture or architecture; no longer for almost fifteen centuries; then the men of the Renaissance by an act of uncompromising rebellion restored the pre-Christian paganism of Greece and Rome to its well-intended Christine nobility and glory. However, the everduring activism of Master Jesus' teaching must be given today a still more dynamic emphasis, not only as a directional instrument towards peace among men, but also as a basis and vital concept for positive advantage in the conquest of space.

* * *

That the teaching of Master Jesus embodies the universality of life, there is no doubt. He is the philosopher par excellence: "Love thy enemy"; the mathematician: the multiplication of bread and fish; the chemist: the changing of water into wine; the physician: restoring sight and limbs; the god: the giving of life; the psychologist: "Before the cock crows thow shalt deny Me thrice"; the architect: "My mansion is not made by human hands"; the statesman: "Mv Kingdom is not of this world". Then by adhering without the slightest deviation to the immutable Law of God, and by the way He faced the sordid and grim reality of every day living, as understood by the people of his time, He demonstrated the nature of the true idealist: fearlessness, forgiveness, generosity, indifference to praise and blame, devotion to duty, self-reliance, humility and love of the unlovable. Idealism is freedom: freedom from ignorance, malice, fear and sloth; freedom from pseudo-truths, freedom from idols made of clay, wood, gold or flesh. The idealist rejects tradition, customs, history, ritual, ages and places. He stands alone, majestic and egoless in happy communion with God and Its Creation. All this was Master Jesus, the Christ and the man, while on earth.

Who else could have been better molded to accept in the depths of their feelings such a philosophy, and display it with precision, but those who had received inner guidance? Yet Marco and Leonora failed at the first test. Proud of the sublime privilege, they forgot humility, they forgot alertness; the ego took over and false optimism crept in. Their feeling of self-righteousness ran so high that at the slightest obstacle they felt as if they had been made victims of an unjust treatment; resentment became dominant. On the human plane of living, man will never be able to destroy the ego; he can only hold it in abeyance through a continuous awareness of its existence. Hence the warning: "Be alert!"

The usurper came and they did not recognize it. For weeks they had lived in an atmosphere of elated exhilaration donned with the cloak of a tottering permanence. They had merged — so they thought — into the Christ Consciousness. No longer did they have the need to search or meditate or to visualize the cleansing action of the purple Fire as experienced in the Circle of Fire. Thus they fell into a world of shifting moods and little faith, filled with obscure forces and clashing powers; now they were surrounded by the unreliable entities of make believe and selfish gain. They thought of God only as the fulfiller of material and sensuous desires, the source of every thing that was pleasant and convenient, and failed to acknowledge Its immanence even in the midst of the discords of the world. They had been led to forget that man's supreme effort must be continually directed towards the realization of the Spirit of Christ in every incident of life, above and beyond all petty satisfactions. Out of superficiality and self-praise they had set their trap with their own hands, narrower than a cocoon, for a series of unwanted and unnecessary experiences.

* * *

In a subterranean abyss, deep within the earth, they found themselves immersed waist-deep in a dense, clammy pitch. Almost suffocated by the nauseating stench issuing from the slimy muck, they struggled desperately to free themselves. Gradually as their

51

eyes became accustomed to the Stygian darkness, they were able to discern a faint and sickly light emanating from thousands of human trunks that shone like ebony, and found that they were chained to a long interminable line of degraded beings, naked men and women of every age and race. Echoing incessantly throughout the vast cavern they could hear loud piercing shrieks that were terrifying. Peering fearfully through the gloom, they could dimly see the massive jutting rocks about them, and as yet quite a distance away, crawling backward towards them on top those close-shaven heads, a monstrous beast with the head of a condor and the body of a skulking tiger, moving on its hundred legs like a caterpillar. Its twisted neck enabled the bill to suck the blood that its stinging scorpion-like tail drew forth from the heads of those tortured writhing forms. The unceasing screech of the rapacious beast — a mixture of human, tiger and condor — seeking more blood, filled the hearts of Marco and Leonora and the rest of the victims with the consuming fear of utter annihilation. Suddenly, they felt a compelling demoniac power lift them free from that putrid viscid fluid and thrust them forward over the surface towards the oncoming beast. In the grip of inexorable terror, they concentrated their minds, their hearts and their wills on God as the only anchorage of salvation. OM I AM ALL LIGHT, they said at first feebly and almost unbelievingly; then slowly and steadily added volume and power of conviction, until they heard the mighty words resounding in their consciousness, vibrating with positive feeling, overcoming fear and doubt, and heightening their faith. OM meant: *Adoration unto Thee, O Father! We acknowledge Thy All-pervading Presence. We claim the action of the Law of Mercy for all of us. We are Thy children. Let us feel and behold the power of Thy Love interpenetrating all life, the wisdom of Thy Mind that knows neither entanglement nor confusion, and the strength of Thy Universal Body that knows no obstacles.*

They were about twenty yards from the ravenous beast, when they heard distinctly the resonance of their call to God echoing seven times, each time amplified twice as much as the previous one. As the last echo died away, thunder and searing flashes of flame tore through the darkness, splitting and shattering the cavernous inferno. Convinced of being under the test of faith, determination and courage, Marco and Leonora moved on now unafraid. The hideous creature was almost upon them, after having beaten violently the last ten beings in front of them. Its bloody tail, whirling with an ever-increasing speed, had penetrated deeper into the skulls, causing human voices to scream in agonizing pain and tears of blood to stream from many eyes. It was their turn now. As the castigating tail ceased its whirling and was about to strike them, sharp swords of scorching purple fire sprang forth from their heads and cut and consumed that dreadful instrument of torture.

Raised from their immersion, they were thrown, by an inner force, onto dry ground, at the base of two gigantic, transparent pillars which penetrated through the vault into the open, sustaining over their capitals a blazing vessel of white light. As they were about to leave the cavern, a commanding voice was heard:

"Fallen gods, long, unpredictable and heavy is the chain reaction of a negligent thought, even of an egotistical attitude of mind of short duration. And it is more so for those who are in training to become executives of the inner and spiritual leaders amongst men. You had been warned not to indulge in worldliness and easy-going, nor to tread the path of false optimism under the guidance of your treacherous ego. But you paid no heed. By so doing you caused other life streams to be unduly caught in the spires of your sloth. It is the duty of a leader who has sinned to rescue not only himself, but also those who were compelled to assist him in his unholy enterprises. You have won your personal battle against the fierce entities of perdition; you are ready to resume the ascent, but observe what you leave behind. Fed by the evil and ignorance of man this grotesque and predatory creature of the nether world of suffering and exploitation is endowed with the power to re-assemble its body and resume its dreadful activity in seven days. These human beings en masse have lost their courage and strength, and, brutalized by the merciless punishment, their desire to be rescued. It is your duty to help!"

"What shall we do"? Marco and Leonora pleaded.

"Expand the power of your call to God so as to include them. Call for seven days with unrelenting trust, irrespective of success and in total surrender to God. Pour the love of your hearts, qualified with Christ purity, to the beast Carnassa for another seven days, and you shall cause it to lose its identity and become a speck of light to bring illumination for one instant to all those

53

it has injured and punished in this abyss of spiritual degradation. Give of yourselves to others bountifully, learn to give, practice giving, enjoy the act of giving."

Marco and Leonora worked with undiminished enthusiasm and positive faith, and as each individual was catapulted onto dry ground and joined them in assistance, all signs of suffering were instantly effaced from his being. Carnassa became a pinpoint of light and vanished.

* * *

But their trial was not over; at the dawn of the fifteenth day, they found themselves alone in the desolate courtyard of an ancient castle, surrounded by a battle-worn and time-worn rampart, whose decayed and crumbling masonry discharged blinding and unbreathable dust upon them. Completely exhausted, following a day exposed to an unshaded sun and stifling heat, they passed a sleepless night immersed in shadowy darkness; their hearts heavily pressed by a forbidding silence. The vessel of Light, high above, shooting forth beams of pulsating ethereal fire, formed a gigantic fiery canopy over the countryside. Then, in the depths of the night, they heard the sweet melody of faith calling to God from within their hearts: "OM, we seek Thee, O Lord; make us see with faith-enlightened eyes!" Instantly two flaming torches appeared within the walled enclosure, and a stern voice was heard, speaking with loving reproach:

"Disciples of Light, what are you doing here? This is a prison for those who do not know any better, for those who are content with meagerness, contemptible of themselves and ignorant of God's bounty. Slay this self-pity and despondency for they drive you to madness and death. Arise inwardly! Behold the Vessel of Light awaiting your arrival for a transstellar voyage into the cosmic spaces where intellectual exhilaration feeds man's genius to boundless creativity. Arise, I say, and conquer all these nagging obstacles made of petty residue nestled in your feelings. Let dynamic faith guide you to the secret door, at the base of the pillars, wherefrom you shall ascend to the Vessel of Light. Intensify the action of meditation through the concentrated power that is lodged in your hearts, until you shed, burn and scatter into the plane of nonexistence the last layer of body consciousness. Reject all recurrence of fear and grief, anger, envy and doubt, and all the plotting entities that try to delay your victory.

You are ready! Drop all attachments, honor and shame, peace and turmoil, want and wealth, and crush the stern conflict of the opposing forces that play havoc in the consciousness of the unwary. Be established in God, cleave unto HIM, breathe His Breath, be HIM.

"I have come to you again at a moment when another fall looms before you, because of your partial adherence to the truth. Hold vividly in your minds the privilege of being disciples of Light, which implies a continual checking of thoughts and feelings, and a gradual rising above deviations and compromises. Be inwardly severe with yourselves, rather with your negative and sinful tendencies. You must remember that in claiming the action of the law of mercy for any violation makes you a beggar, always patching your old and worn out garment, never being able to see and wear the seamless robe of the Christ. Take refuge in meditation for a more rigorous introspection and plan for an Empire of Light, not for the comfort of a cave or the coziness of a bungalow. Again, arise, and ascend whereto a wealth of starry experiences awaits to unfold before your inner Eye."

With such encouragement, vivified by the vibrating radiance of the celestial voice, one would expect our marooned disciples to set themselves free from the narrowness of the crumbling courtyard by an act of supreme will. Instead they sought again physical means of deliverance. They inspected the walls and at one corner saw a series of rocks protruding from the perpendicular masonry; the secret door at the base of the two pillars of light, the only medium of self-rescuing, was completely forgotten. Marco took his companion by the hand and together started on their upward climb. As he placed his foot on the lowest jutting stone, the ground cleaved beneath their feet as if by a forceful blow, and they plunged headlong into a deep sepulchral pit, landing on a stone floor that was cold and damp.

Lying there, dismally desolate and incapable of thinking, they took refuge in the action and power of the universal Logos: OM. Slowly and steadily they rose inwardly; waves of light and energy filled their minds; newer thoughts and a keener sense of perception came over them. Then, out of the oppressive darkness, the flickering light of a candle became visible, showing them a wall of highly polished marble, and in front of it a series of statues of human bodies with animal heads: snakes, birds of prey, cats, bulls and tigers. Uttering the word OM, they followed the dim candlelight, and as they walked past each naked statue, the beastly head fell and was substituted by a luminous eye with a soft marvelous radiance. This outer manifestation annealed their faith and caused the light in their hearts to illumine the environment. They followed a narrow and circuitous passageway and came into the open. The Voice was heard saying:

"How difficult it is for man to understand how straight and pleasant is the path of deliverance. Because of his exteriorized tendencies and false appraisal he chooses devious, uneven and mysterious avenues, in order to create an aura of heroism and self-importance for himself. This has been exactly your behavior. In an unguarded moment you let yourselves be dragged by the limited human reasoning and rejected the inner guidance which would have rescued you from so much unnecessary delay, wandering, bewilderment and frustration. There, in the courtyard, a few paces from where you were standing, was the secret door wide open, leading to the blazing vessel above. Meditate, disciples, meditate! Consume the heap of confusion in which you wallow; seek further purification, humble yourselves at the Lotus Feet of the Creative Spirit abiding in the Silent Void of your hearts; face whatever there is to face in an attitude of utter surrender, otherwise called repentance; use the Purple Fire and see it passing over and again through your minds, and soon you shall be out of this unhappy impasse."

❀   ❀   ❀

For seven days Marco and Leonora journeyed, crossing valleys and rivers, penetrating forests and climbing mountains, searching and inspecting, hoping and yearning with each passing day to come to the end of their trial. At dusk on the seventh day, surfeited and grieved, they sank into a slumber and then into a profound sleep for many hours. In the inaction of the mind, the Purple Fire cleared the way and the willing spirit surged forth revealing to them all their blunders. As they awakened, fully restored in physical stamina and with a resurgence of faith, they became again conscious of divine guidance. Held in the mystic embrace of an enchanted aura, happy, radiant and forgiven they submitted their minds to undeviated discipline and thus returned back to the secret door by a more pleasant path.

accompanied by the upsurging light of the roseate dawn. Presently they came to a landscape of rare beauty; hedged by tall bamboo, a carpet of hooded violets encircling a miniature azure lake heavily mantled with exquisite pink and white lotus blossoms, lay before them. A profound peace permeated the atmosphere inundating their hearts in a sea of ineffable joy; and as they walked slowly and expectantly towards the bamboo hedge, a rishi robed in white appeared and welcomed them with open arms:

"I have been commanded to meet you here and assist you in whatever you desire. Please speak!"

"We need light" — Marco responded humbly. "Too long have we wallowed in a world of shame, mendacity and hell. . . . Never again do we want to see ugliness and deceit!"

"Blessed ones" — he answered — "meditate, and I shall meditate with you!"

Protected by the conquering radiance of this selfless friend, Marco and Leonora saw again the fearful deserted courtyard, the dismal darkness of the murky pit, the ugly heads of the beasts and their cold, confusing and threatening surroundings, nonexisting outwardly, but deeply rooted in their consciousness through the false appraisal of God's ways; and having intensified their attunement they immediately became aware of their state of grace. The action of the Purple Fire swept through them destroying the composite structure of their mortal minds. They opened their eyes and lo, they were only a few yards from the two mighty pillars which, like their hearts, were now merging into one of larger dimensions and greater brilliance. There was the secret door and the spiral staircase leading to the Vessel of light. A concentrated luminance, more resplendent than an Archangel's, was seen approaching the entrance, where it coalesced into the familiar form of their Liberated Master-Teacher.

* * *

"This day" — he said — "marks the commencement of a new and higher way of living and thinking for you. You have learned, through perplexing experiences, how unreliable is the assemblage called mind, senses and school education in the pursuit of the Intangible, the ever feverish essence that forms the substratum of the visible world. A finer tool is required, nestled deep in the head, enlivened by the heart, and called Buddhi or Christlight or Pure Intuition. This tool, smaller than an electron, smaller than a proton, yet as potent as the forces of creation put together, is able to saturate the human body and impart intelligence and prophetic power to every cell therein from head to foot. It moves mysteriously with the speed of timelessness making every organ, every muscle an independent entity capable of withstanding fatigue and degeneration, and of defying death itself. To cultivate awareness of Its presence and to let It work for you spells mastery over life forever.

"It is the scope of this teaching to give you occasional glimpses of the presence of this Tool, whose fractional use will point the way to a life of inner prestige and higher responsibility, and it will catapult you, if you so wish, into the outer spaces without our guidance. It will cause you to see not the mere materiality of stars and planets but the very life, habits and culture of the intelligences dwelling thereon.

"As you start ascending the spiral staircase, know this: it is twelve o'clock noon, the sun is at the zenith, all sentient beings cast a very small shadow. This means that in dealing with life, you must always work with absolute clarity of mind and purpose; speak tersely, intelligently and kindly, and never let the Truth suffer. Abhor pretension, white lying, acting enigmatically, and all forms of sophistication employed by the cultured snob.

"It is needful for you to analyze yourselves with more severity concerning the understanding and application of the gift of spiritual liberty. You have to improve on this a great deal. Do not be swayed by the opinion of the multitude that glorifies you today and crucifies you tomorrow, and finds arguments to justify the two opposing attitudes. Let dynamic humility rule; then you will throw onto the same heap both human wisdom and human foolishness, and all shades of reputation disgorged by the esophagus of slaves and sycophants. It is all trash. Whatever you gain on the inner places you outside the grasp of human intelligence, and if you are not attentive and strong you might be hurled into such a vortex of contradictory forces as to endanger your very existence and cut short of fulfillment the message that we want to convey to society. Think simply; idealize all experiences; follow the inti-

58

mations and promptings given to you by the Buddhi, and all that is noble and constructive shall come to pass.

"This was the attitude of the primitive man. Unable to read or write, or carry out research based on previous findings, the only way to explain lightning, earthquakes, thunder or eclipse, joy or fear, the only way to domesticate the animals or create the wheel, was to interrogate his own viscera, the seat of the Buddhi. This is inspiration which led to orderly thinking, the development of the mnemonic faculty, intelligence and genius, all linked to and dependent on the Eternal Buddhi. By using these lesser tools, by refining them and making them more sensitive through meditation and prayer, study and noble deeds, one arrives at the Source, at the Matrix, of Life itself. As you see God, science, the arts, philosophy, thought, study, noble endeavour, evolution and man himself are indissolubly united, forming a perfect Whole, which should never go out of order except for one of its components, man. It is up to man to transfer this idealized Whole into the plane of realization. Hence this teaching.

"Rama, Zoroaster, Krishna, Gautama the Buddha, Moses, Pythagoras, Socrates and Master Jesus (to mention only some of the greatest) realized this state of being in their own selves; now it must invade the plane of collectivity. They gave to mankind a pattern of life that is desirable, practical and durable. It is, to use your capitalistic jargon, an excellent investment bearing undreamed of dividends in the form of better health, unfluctuating peace, inward joy and unbounded satisfaction, and at the same time sharpening the intellectual urge to invade vaster and uncharted lands in the field of knowledge. Up to the moment of their inturning these luminaries were ordinary people; biologically like the least of mankind, mentally average, spiritually willing. Rama was a soldierpriest, Zoroaster a scribe and traveler, Krishna a shepherd, Gautama and Moses princes of earthly dominions, Pythagoras a teacher of science, Socrates an educator, and Master Jesus a carpenter; and whatever they conceived and achieved came out of their minds impelled by determination and discipline. They showed the same One Truth, wisely manipulated, colored and adapted for the people of their own time and place.

* * *

"Five thousand years ago a Vedic poet sang: 'The All-pervading Spirit is my Father. He is my Creator and my Master. All that exists above and beneath is a member of my celestial family. The gentle Earth is my Mother; Her Matrix is hidden in the fathomless bosom of God. There She is renewed in light, as a bride, as a daughter of love!'

"Zoroaster asked Ormudz, the Creator: 'What is the best thing Thou hast ever made?'

"Ormudz answered: "It is the Handsome Yima, the Christ My Son, the Leader of the daring, the Guardian of all the worlds, the First Born in the Celestial Family. My Creation is His in My Name. With a sword of golden fire He marches on towards Me drawing all men in close ranks to the conquest of the unconquerable. My scepter is His, for He obeys Me always. He makes Me work through His viscera. The Solar Path is His path".

"The Upanishads say: 'Aham Brahmasmi, I AM Brahman the One. Tat Twan Asi, That Thou Art. I am the Whole, the Invincible Absolute. I AM the Whole, the visible phenomenon. All is in Me, I AM in all. There is no separation between Me and all that exists. Loving all man loves Me. My son, come unto Me by the Solar Path inside thy heart. I AM the Lord thy God, the Spirit-Fire in thy heart. By surrendering the wholeness of thee unto Me, perfection shall be thine. Listen to Me in thy heart or in thy toe or on the tip of thy nose; it does not matter, I AM there equally real, equally whole. Follow My Solar Path and I shall set you free from birth and death'.

"The book of Life of ancient Egypt, erroneously called The Book of the dead, contains the Exhortations to the Initiates:

" 'I AM the Light of Osiris interpenetrating and dominating all life. And I reside in thy heart, My son, insinuating and projecting My Essence throughout and beyond. Through study and introspection, thou shalt behold the Imperishable Seed out of which all life comes into manifestation. I AM the Guide, the Ruler and the Goal of the Solar Path. Short is the road that leads to Me; it is as short as thy physical structure, but by knowing its whereabouts you will be taken into the mansion of the Eternal Becoming. I direct into thy consciousness luminous beams of wisdom, which I crystallize with a stylus of

60

fire. I AM come to rescue thee from the sepulchral chasm of degeneration in which My children of Egypt have fallen. I AM the Everliving Verbum-Light of the Resurrection guiding all men to mastery and immortality. I AM thy Ideal, thy Reality' "!

* * *

"Hear now the Teaching of the Buddha. During his stay at the monastery of Javatana, a monk of the congregation asked him:

" 'Blessed Teacher, O happy One, speak to us of the bliss of emancipation which comes after meditation'.

" 'Meditation — he answered — " ' is the gathering of thoughts or concentration of the mind upon a non-physical object to be followed by the obliteration of the latter. It is the initial attempt to displace the mortal and ephemeral for the immortal and the everlasting.

" 'Whenever a disciple isolates himself from sense cravings, and corrects negative or destructive impulses, if such a practice brings to him a genuine sense of joy and subdued exhilaration, he has entered the first plane of meditation.

" 'Whenever an inner tranquillity manifests, followed by a more profound thought concentration and a keener perception of things, then he has entered the second plane of meditation.

" 'And when he is untouched by mass consciousness, indifferent to praise and blame, and contemplative, and maintains such a behavior as long as he wishes, he enters the third plane of meditation.

" 'The fourth plane of meditation is for him who has risen above joy and sorrow, tradition, culture and creed. And having fused good and evil into one objectless purpose, his meditation has been transmuted into contemplation, that is enjoyment of God for Its Own Sake.

" 'The disciple of this class is a master-initiate, a Buddha, a Christ, an Avatar. He dwells on a plane of such a perfection and contentment as to transcend the most refined intellectual exploits. Having identified himself with his Buddhi, no-thing, no one could influence him in his creative endeavours. This is indeed the idealization of life. . . .!'

* * *

"In the teaching of Moses, one feels the impact of the true fighter. He gives no quarter to the forces that distract or scatter the mind. His words have the cogent dynamism of the desert ruler who has camped therein for forty years and yet folded his tent every dawn, ready to march on to a more pleasant land.

"'Beware, O son of earth' — he warned his people — 'of the slightest infraction of the Law, for there is no leniency from on High, and no matter how justified the motive of thy violation, you must pay for it up to the last farthing and with compound interest. To cheat or thieve or lie or kill or worship an idol, it is as severe as to deny God; and the physical death is the least of the punishments. Hence the need to undergo self-discipline with an iron hand and undeviating determination.

"'But, O son of earth, if you see God in His terrible aspect, and if you feel His giant fist as hard as a rock hovering over you and ready to crush you, and if you fear Him and by so doing you live within the Law, and take care of thy family, and honor thy word to the utmost, and show tangible consideration for those in need, immense, unmeasurable is the reward, for God our Lord is not a narrow-hearted being.

"'O son of earth, if you thus fear and love our Mighty God, He will teach thee directly, He will make thee a Christ, and glorify thee above all men; you will desire nothing else for you are wealthier than all the glittering gold of the world. So, my son, I say unto you: enter the path and make thyself a willing, humble and receptive instrument of HIM. Acknowledge His Presence, His Power, His Light and His Glory concealed in the inmost recess of thy being. Seek Him by the path of introspection, not through bargaining and elaborate ritual. Serve Him with no other thought but that of service for its own sake. Let silence and meditation be thy instruments. Exteriorized worshipping is an offense to HIM, a degradation of the divinity in man, and an opposition to the divine plan for the evolution of mankind. When a man feels to be directly responsible to God for every thought and deed, he ceases to be a responsible man and becomes a responsible god; sorrow and limitation vanish; his strength and his intelligence become delegated attributes which never fail to fulfill his constructive visualizations.

'"Therefore, O son of earth, O disciple, now that through acceptance of the Law and by means of its daily application in the outer life, you have become a god, what are you in reality? You are an idealized human being, you are the classic human being of the incoming Golden Age'.

❋   ❋   ❋

"When Master Jesus uttered the words, *Our Father who art in Heaven*, He did not raise His eyes skyward, but closed them and plunged His mind down into the depths of His heart. Heaven is, therefore, a state of being filled with urgency, a striving for perfection and transcendent insight. Heaven is the conscience made crystal-clear through absolute adherence to the unwritten Law of the universe. To reach such a state Master Jesus had to meditate. To Him meditation was the keystone to His messiahship, triumph and immortality. Without it man is avulsed from God and, as a riven cloud, broken into shapeless pieces, scattered and driven into oblivion. The true disciple knows that when he is beset with problems — and Master Jesus had an unending number — the only way to solve them is to sit quietly and analyze past and present thoughts, deeds and mode of living. In other words, he consciously steps aside and lets, as it were, an invisible judge examine him benevolently and wisely, and point out to him all errors and shortcomings, and also the way to correct them. Thus he contacts *Our Father who art in Heaven.*

"*Give us this day our daily bread* . . . is a call for spiritual guidance in order to draw both material and spiritual wealth from the Cosmic Reservoir of life without infringing on the Law of God. It is an attunement with honesty, good will and above all absolute faith in God. His is both the strength and the desire to call, and the manifestation thereof.

"*. . . and forgive us our trespasses.* What are the trespasses? They are failures some due to ill-will, others to sloth, both to ignorance or inability to live close to God, the Source of Wisdom. They cannot be forgiven, that is, dispelled and destroyed, no matter how sincere the feeling of repentance, unless they are studied and analyzed, and then avoided through the noble art of daily self-inquiry. This will lead to *as we forgive them that trespass against us.* It is a negative attitude to forgive a violator of the Law by saying simply I forgive you. He must be taught or, at least, given a hint of the technique involved

63

in such a process. Only thus can a trespasser cease to be a trespasser and be forgiven permanently.

"*. . . and lead us not into temptation but deliver us from evil,* is a reminder of the existence of the forces of sloth and depravity that prey on the ignorant who indulges in material and carnal pleasure. Temptation and evil do not touch the meditative soul, for he is well entrenched in the spirit of the Law.

"*. . . for Thine is the Kingdom, the Power and the Glory for ever and ever.* When these are not mere words but a truth deeply felt in the heart and sincerely. lived outwardly, the former trespasser or violator has become a resurrected being endowed with Christ-light. It being impossible to have a kingdom of his own, or to wield power or shed glory of his own, he will rely entirely and absolutely on God. He will have earned the divine right to be appointed Prime Minister of the Kingdom of Heaven for the duration of life and of God.

❖   ❖   ❖

"Master Jesus was and is Prime Minister of the Kingdom of Heaven. In the words of Ormudz He is the Handsome Yima . . . . the Leader of the daring, the Guardian of the Worlds . . . . the First Born in the Celestial Family . . . . with a sword of golden fire . . . . He draws all men in close ranks to the conquest of the unconquerable. God's Scepter is His, for He obeys Him always. . . . What a far-echoing declaration, My beloved disciples Marco and Leonora; what a solemn promise, what a poignant and priceless truth. It shall burn and continue to burn until the last living entity on earth will be raised and given the privilege to walk abreast with the 'First Born in the Celestial Family'. May these words be sculptured with a stylus of fire on the forehead of every man, woman and child for them to read and live by.

"However, Master Jesus was a Christ before He was born; and the unending difficulties and misunderstandings He encountered were meant as an encouraging lesson to the striving humanity and a merciless whipping to the slothful people. He had outgrown earthly existence prior to his last embodiment; and being accustomed to the Realm of the Spirit, where both freedom and the power of thinking are unlimited, to take a

64

flesh body again, or to be born, was indeed more excruciating than to be crucified. To assure the perfect success of his mission, He had to be provided with a flesh vehicle not conceived in the normal manner, but one projected directly from the mind of an Elohim into a human receptacle of the same spiritual lineage as his. Such a receptacle was Mary, Jesus' Twin Flame, a being of quasi-Christ consciousness who needed only the experience of one more embodiment to achieve Deliverance.

"Thus They descended from the realms of Shadowless Light into a pit of total darkness, the planet earth, to speak of light to those who knew very little about it, and to revamp all the noble teachings of the previous Masters, Rishis, Prophets and Yogins. They were required to relinquish, for the time being, all they knew of the life of the Beyond, and go through the grind of pregnancy, birth, babyhood, youth and adultship with the harsh discipline of body, mind and feeling that they imply. Mary came as the harbinger, mother and companion; Jesus as the Messiah and son.

"Jesus was a seafarer, desert traveler, mountain climber, a river wader, a tireless seeker and a perfect listener. So as not to be accused of charlatanry by his contemporaries, He first learned a trade, carpentry. This put him automatically out of the corrupt clan of the priesthood whom he rejected and condemned for all time; then he traveled East into the heart of Tibet and Persia, and west into Greece and Egypt, where He learned all that was needed to become a master of philosophy, eloquence and physical science. He never studied occultism as understood by the modern world.

"Well-provided with diplomas, acknowledgements, recommendations, and other academic certificates, all witnessing the youth's brilliant exploits as a student, our Messiah-to-be, barely aware of what loomed ahead, directed His footsteps towards His homeland. From Egypt, by a circuitous journey, to avoid the land of the Hebrew, Jesus returned to Persia where He contacted, once more and for the last time, the mystic lovers of God, a small group indeed, in the persons of the wise men who had seen Him in the manger of Bethlehem soon after His birth, twenty-five years earlier. And wherever He went, He noticed an acute discrepancy between the truth of the Law and the behavior of the priesthood. The so-called spiritual leaders offered nothing to the average individual in the way of a moral code, inner training, ethical behavior, love and sacrifice. Stale formulae, dead ritual, forced financial support of the temples on the part of the faithful, hard labour, heavy taxation and undisputed obedience to the religious rulers; this was the lot of the man in the street. All forms of dishonesty and corruption were rampant, tolerated and unchecked, as long as they produced a sizable return for the sectarian despots and their families and sycophants. The nameless masses were seething with rebellion.

"As Jesus reached Bethany, a short distance east of Jerusalem, He sat in the shade of an olive tree and for three days meditated, totally lost to both the mortal mind and senses. Therein he lived the life of the world in its harsh reality of both the slave and the worldly master, the ignorant and the pretended wise one, the poor and the rich, the ruler and the subject, the arrogant and the obsequious, and found that they were all alike, all equally lost, and all in dire need of illumination, chastisement and guidance. Then he unrolled the various parchments, one testifying of his achieved Christship at the Esoteric School of Egypt, another of the lofty eminence he had earned in Jagannath, India, in the field of Yoga, and other diplomas, certificates and academic acknowledgements from Persia and Greece, and burned them all. His age by this time was twenty-eight.

"During the next seven days Master Jesus meditated, not only for self-renewal or as a duty towards God, but also to verify what he had seen and experienced in the previous three days. All was reconfirmed with mathematical precision. While thus absorbed in the higher octaves of perfection, he found that his decision had been approved by his unseen Master and Guide. As he came back to the mortal plane he declared loudly to the surrounding light and sound waves:

" 'I have destroyed all physical evidence of appertainment to outer schools of knowledge, to man-made institutions and professional groups. I stand nowhere, all alone, in the face of the world. Freedom is my unseen, yet very real, and noble mate. I have rejected all conventional ways of human living, thinking and behaving which compel man to violate Truth and Justice and bow cowardly before customs, selfish interests, mass pressure, political patronage and religious vexation. I shall face what there is to face, unconcerned, unafraid and boldly, in absolute dedication to the dictates of my conscience as a willing instrument at the service of the Cosmic Assembly of the Perfect Ones. I shall ascend slowly and without deviation towards the Eternal, my Heavenly Father, by cultivating awareness of Its Vibrating Presence interpenetrating my whole being, nourishing my body, illumining my mind, watching my feelings. And I shall draw unto me all who have ears to hear. Thus I intend to live.

" 'I shall teach my disciples not to live as man does; now in freedom and now in bondage, now in wisdom and now in ignorance; speaking truth, half a truth and error and not knowing where and how the line of demarcation runs. I shall raise them above the fear of death or want, for unto the fearless the kingdom of heaven opens its door to immortality. To be fearless means to let go of the illusive side of human existence, even though no inkling of the Reality has as yet manifested. This I have done; henceforth, I AM free in the Light'.

* * *

"Having thus found Himself and declared His resolute and enduring purpose, Master Jesus was shown the blueprint of the unfoldment of His program. He scrutinized carefully what was ahead of Him, the messianic work; the bickering of His disciples, their thick skulls and their willing hearts; the various miracles; the malice of the intellectuals; the oppressive exactions of the publicans; the crass stupidity of the nameless masses; the everscheming and despotic Pharisees, everywhere present like a swarm of unwanted locust; His final days on earth; the persecution fomented by the vindictive hatred of the vile Abner; the pardoned highway robber, gang leader and murderer Bar Abba; the sensitive and confused Pontius Pilate; the weakling and snobbish King Herod; the road to Calvary; the wailing and bewilderment of His disciples and friends; the crucifixion, the refusal of sedatives and the lance; the scattering of the afflicted flock, the resurrection and the re-gathering of the same flock now clustering around the Sheperd; the final touch to the invisible and ever-enduring Temple of the Anointed One; and the Ascension into Life Eternal. And having aproved every

67

detail of such a plan, Master Jesus accepted both the office of Messiah and the attribute of Christship. Then he left the shade of the olive tree, waded the Jordan and proceeded northwest towards Nazareth where his Mother and Twin Flame lived on Marmion Way, to fulfill his mission in obedience to his inner Vision.

"Concerning Jesus-Mary's relationship, there is a great deal of misunderstanding among the average Christians but more so in the learned doctrinaires and theologians of the Protestant world, whose attitude is one of malice and derision. Mary was not just an ordinary woman of no consequence whatsoever, and those of today who think so possess a strong residue of unscientific, illogical and haughty male superiority complex that was in vogue a thousand years ago. Lady Master Mary had exactly the same spiritual make-up as Jesus'. She was a Christ endowed with all the powers and attributes of her Christ-son, plus the graceful mien of appearing like an ordinary woman in the neighborhood and before her contemporaries. The masterful support she gave her Son was never revealed because the society of her time was not prepared as yet to accept a woman endowed with Christ powers; and because of such unpreparedness she would have been considered a witch, and as such her life would have been endangered.

"From the time Jesus the lad left his mother's house, at the age of twelve, until his return after seventeen years, there was never a day when Mary was ever concerned about her son. With the assistance of the Masters of Light, they were in constant communication with each other by a process of telepathy. Often they met halfway in their finer bodies, Jesus from India, Persia, Egypt or Greece, and Mary from Nazareth, by the side of a mountain cave or a flowing river. She looking as young and vibrant as He, exchanging teachings, comparing experiences and enjoying each other's companionship.

"Joseph the Father belonged to the same class of spiritual elite. He had passed away when his Son was only five, and was reborn as John the Beloved, in the same year. This explains the injunction issued by Master Jesus while on the Cross to John: 'Go to My Mother, she is thy kin.' Mary was not to be seen during the trial or on the way to Calvary, as She had been commanded by her Liberated Master-Teacher to take shelter in a cave nearby, and from there project shafts of pink light from her heart as protection and love for her Son-twin. However during the last fifteen minutes of Jesus' life on earth, she appeared at the Golgotha to help the crucified Master in closing his physical eyes and to witness the opening of the Eye of His immortal Self for everlasting time. As Mary's presence was detected, the enraged populace instigated by the emissaries of the revengeful priesthood, approached her to take her life also; but they were unable to pierce the aura of protection that surrounded her body.

"The story that Mary wept during Jesus' crucifixion is a pious invention of the scheming priesthood of later centuries in order to influence and bind the little people to their plot of exploitation; the Madonna Addolorata — the Sorrowful Virgin Mary — together with a representation of a painted or wood-carved Jesus, so sickly looking as if begging for commiseration, is another creation of earth-bound and unimaginative artists, half malicious and half ignorant. A lifestream such as Master Jesus', whose enduring greatness in thoughts and deeds defies all standard conventions in language and literature, needs not sympathy from puny mankind, nor alms or candlelight, or celebration of masses and recitation of the rosary to propitiate Him. The Western World is so saturated with His Divine Light that the only requirement to receive tangible assistance is an intense desire to be helped and positive determination not to violate the law. He expects no direct acknowledgement; let that be expressed by treating one's fellow man with decency and consideration.

∶ "That Jesus and Mary suffered, however, it is true, but Their suffering occurred before taking embodiment; and again, when Mary as a maiden was told by her Guardian Angel of the coming of her Twin Flame as a son and Christ, and Their Mission on Earth; then no more. For Mary and Jesus, being absolutely aware of the ultimate goal of Their lives, had no cause to fear the events that touched Them so — let us say — tragically. They had come from the Abodes of Immortality, and the vividness of such Reality remained with them unmarred, no matter how overpowering the abject gloominess of earthly circumstances. As you yourselves, My beloved disciples, feel when I contact you and speak to you and guide you through the celestial realms, so were Mary and Jesus: they lived in total freedom, not only beyond and above the boundary of political and geographic confines, but also beyond and above the pull of the earth and solar magnetism. There is still another aspect of their lives that you must be aware of. They were not elected Son and Daughter of God by mere chance or through an arbitrary act of their Heavenly Father Who, by the Way, is also your Father and Mine and of all living beings. Jesus and Mary were ancient, very ancient Souls going back to the inception of life itself, and as they learned the Law of Soul-evolution, they made a vow to move abreast with it from one embodiment to the next growing both inwardly and intellectually; they lived in Lemuria and Atlantis and in many starry heavens, studying with humble transport all the disciplines taught in the universities of the land, and sought specialization in the Science of Love, the most arduous of all. Soon they learned, through experimentation, that by saturating thoughts, vibrations and pulsations with the concept of God as the Primal Mover and the everpresent Alchemist, they could reconstitute to wholeness living tissue in process of degeneration in man, beast, plant and organic matter. From this field of gross substance they passed into the intangible, joy and sorrow, peace and turmoil, truth and error, and life itself, and found that the universal reagent of all was love, that is, by mating anything with the concept of God the result would be enduring life.

"Whether Jesus and Mary, hereditarily, were of the House of David, has no importance. Being universal Souls They belonged to all royal houses, ergo to the House of David. The Cosmic Assembly of the Perfect Ones made them instruments of God in the fulfillment of the New Dispensation for mankind which had been announced in the utterances of the Jewish Prophets since Abraham, and which had to take place a thousand years after the ascension of King David to the throne of all Hebrews. The time was close at hand. Master Jesus the Prince and Mary the Princess were perfect vehicles, the Chosen Ones for the fulfillment of this command designed to give new direction and a fresher impetus to the masses on the path of social evolution. And so as to give a semblance

70

of legality to his messianic task, Master Jesus frequented the universities of the four most civilized lands: Persia, Egypt, India and Greece. This made him intellectually acceptable to both the scholars and unofficial rulers of the Jewish society who were aware of his proficiency in the disciplines of the times.

"Having thus established that the dramatic events related to Master Jesus' messianic work were pre-ordained and, hence, absolutely inevitable; that He had to submit detachedly to all 'abuses and vilifications' poured upon him by both the mob and some of the religious leaders who, by virtue of both their actions and the Un-written Law, had been condemned to oblivion, all the vengeful behavior of the Christian leaders towards the Jews throughout the centuries up to the present day, stands condemned before the cosmic bar. They have sorely offended their spiritual teachers, for such is Judaism, the Father and Bestower of the loftiest and noblest norm of life to the Western World. Since Master Jesus did not come to destroy the Law of Moses but to fulfill it, namely to inject into it a dynamic and evolutive vibration, and graft it into the consciousness of the non-Jews, Christianity is truly the son-daughter of Judaism, and it shall remain so until the Newer Dispensation, which is close at hand, is announced. The wretched practice, throughout nineteen centuries of a son using his father's wealth — philosophy, law, word, ritual and books — and then spitting in his face, and kicking him around, severing one limb after another from his body, causing him to bleed over and again unto death, snatching from him the material wealth by legalized acts of arbitrary nature, and driving him with the unrelenting fierceness of the hungry beasts of the jungle, forcing him to live in bondage, filth, ridicule and moral degradation, and in every case such a noble father remaining gentle, forbearing and generous, never losing sight of the ultimate triumph of the Law of God; all this, I say, has indeed played havoc in the consciousness of the gentile: hatred, wars, persecution of Christians against Christians, brothers against brothers, pestilence, earthquakes and famine even unto this day. And it shall continue to be so until all Christian teachings are uprooted and cleansed of the stench of stagnant blood found therein.

71

Christianity, the Jewish child gone astray, must return girded with sackcloth and mourn in repentance and shame before its true ancestors of blood and spirit: the patriarchs, the prophets and lawgivers, the messiahs, the warriors and the teachers. Unto thee I say, O Christian Church: should you by an act of justice restore to the Jerusalem of the Spirit all that you have stolen from it you would crumble into dust and disappear from the face of the earth as if you had never existed. Such is thy position, for truly you have created nothing that would please God. And to you all Protestant Christians I say: You must accept Mary, the Mother of Master Jesus, as a Christ and a Messiah of the same inner achievement as Her Son's. Until you do so your teaching will be nothing else but the arid babbling of a drunkard in a dark alley, full of hot air amounting to nothing.

"To the non-sectarian believer, the only person capable to reason unbiasedly, may I suggest that in order to improve the political institutions of the Western World and understand the social aspirations and spiritual dynamism of his fellow man, he must study in depth the Hebrew philosophy; it is there that one will discover eventually that this, not Athens or Rome, is the fountainhead of the real law that sustains and guides whatever is good and evolutive in public institutions, the arts, customs, ingrained behavior and even idiosyncrasies found in the white race; that the Hebrews had ordained and codified laws and decrees many centuries earlier than Justinian's; that the democratic institutions were in action during Moses' rule; and that the philosophical debates of Socrates were nothing else but maidservants of the Jewish Synagogue. Reject however all claims of holiness and perfection in which the Bible is held by church leaders and their unaware faithful; worship not books or words.

*　*　*

"As Mary and Jesus were reunited in Nazareth, after their seeming long separation, the magnetic pull of their hearts, the love, the tenderness and the cosmic radiance emanating from their countenances fused them into one entity whose inner strength and outer force of conviction clothed every utterance with the shining mantle of absolute truth. Beyond all imagining is the power of success wielded by twin flames, how well do they master their destiny. Now the time has arrived to come into the open and teach. Mary taught on Marmion Way in a most informal and casual manner; the women came from every walk of life and listened spellbound to the divine teaching of the Golden Princess, ever young and ever charming. She spoke of freedom for all women, freedom from bondage and slavish submission to man, be it father, husband, elder brother, first born son or any master that she had to serve for her livelihood. And she taught of God and of Its very Essence, dominating thoughts, deeds, and wholeness of the body and the surrounding world; and since God is life itself it is to every woman's total advantage to conjugate mind and body with Him for health, strength and enduring beauty. She never spoke of religion in the sectarian sense, but emphasized the importance of daily meditation on the light within the heart as the only scientific method for acquiring knowledge and wisdom that leads to freedom, to God.

"Master Jesus took to the road to rescue and teach. His Message of Salvation had to be delivered in the open, unconfined by walls of stone and unrestrained by the deadly orthodoxy of the clergy with all the evil that such a class of people spreads wherever it goes. In all his extensive traveling, the Master of Galilee had seen enough of the religious strongholds wherefrom the priests dominated the masses with a despotic and merciless hand; and as for teaching a word of truth to the thirsting humanity, in this they had no interest whatsoever. Egypt, Greece, Persia and India were wallowing in materialism, ignorance, superstition and exploitation; the Hebrew rulers had forgotten their mighty heritage and sold their own people to the uncouth authority of Rome. The Church as an organization of Truth and Light had come to its end at that time.

"Another of Jesus' characteristics was his clarity of thought, his terseness of speech and his swiftness in making decisions. A master strategist and a master tactician in one he always foresaw the adroit maneuvers of his self-appointed enemies and shrewd debaters and nailed them to inaction or silence at once. No great spiritual movement was ever founded through the prodigal showering of words, glittering ritual and stale and specious argumentation; no true master ever made himself chief of a clique with a sectarian organization of any kind.

❀   ❀   ❀

73

"Blessed disciples, Marco and Leonora, behold, and bow in gratitude. You have been raised onto the top of the pillar and into the Vessel of Light without any motion of your limbs. The Christ radiance of Master Jesus absorbed your consciousness into the rarefied and vitalizing air of starry life. Now attune yourselves with the Christ-light within your hearts, and you shall provide this vessel with motive power. Let us pray:

"OM is Thy Name O Lord.

"Lost is he who does not strive, for he has ceased to live.

"Hold firmly the rudder of my mind, for into the sea of delusion sinks the craft that wanders away.

"Rescue me from passion and sense craving, for my soul is driven by the wind of confusion and despair.

"A comfortless and dreadful life looms for him who has ceased to love.

"Thrice blessed is this day, O Father, for we think of Thee, we feel Thy Presence, we move towards Thy Mansion of Light.

"In the Heaven of our Soul Thy Name resounds like the haunting echo of the call of love.

"Thou art our all in all!"

* * *

The sun was at the zenith when the Vessel of Light carrying the purified and transmuted forms of Marco and Leonora, sailed into outer space towards starry spheres of life. It proceeded at jet speed for awhile then, gradually, it slowed down and stopped by the mouth of a river whose diamond-clear waters slightly hued in violet, disappeared as they reached the immense sea of cosmic ether.

Though in a strange land and in an environment, seemingly, unsuitable for human beings, our starry travelers showed neither concern nor discomfort; for having ventured there not by prying or covetous curiosity or scientific reason, but for the sheer joy of wanting to know more of the Empire of God, both mind and body had adapted their vibration to the new surroundings. They felt at ease as if they desired to stay there forever; but their wish came to naught, as a compassionate voice from the invisible was heard:

"Beloved guests and disciples of the Immortal Ones, greetings! The scope of your visit to our abodes of evolutive perfection is to study and observe, then report to earth. Upon

74

your shoulders lies the responsibility and privilege to convey to man the wonders of starry life, free from fiction and mortal imagining. You must therefore cast off from your minds the humanly preconceived idea that we live in a state of passive and static beatitude. We work, but considering the fact that we are not beset by the degenerative traits of war, aging and death, disease, floods, drought, earthquakes, money making and the innumerable maladies created by the mortal mind of man, our work is a happy adventure whose illimitable unfoldment is vivified by the concept of immortality. Think!

"Though you will never be able to express in words what you see, you will certainly achieve a saturation in your feelings, a powerful vibration, which you will transmit to those of earth who have inclinations of positive spiritual nature. Now, you must meditate by the bank of this sacred river Sattwa whose stream holds the principle of spiritual balance. You will feel purified and strengthened as if an onrush of purple fire had passed through your minds burning all human residue."

They obeyed, and with each passing moment Marco and Leonora felt a slow and continuous sublimation of their thoughts and feelings, then the voice was heard again:

"The capacity to understand God and absorb Its Knowledge, is in direct rapport to self-understanding. Each human being knows God for what he knows of himself. Hence the infinite reservoir of Knowledge is available to all at all times. Through self-unfoldment one may increase this power of absorption at a rate equal to his intense yearning, striving and application. To be content with what one is or has, in the way of spiritual or intellectual acquisition, means to live in ignorance and limitation. The highest acquired knowledge becomes a curse, the moment its possessor ceases to search for a higher one; for God is Knowledge, Wisdom and Light in eternal becoming towards the Infinitude. A man who is utterly satisfied, intellectually and spiritually, has ceased to live, his physical death is near at hand, his whereabouts in the beyond will be the realm of the unhappy ones."

Marco and Leonora were then granted permission to resume their starry navigation. It was the noon hour of the second day. Enveloped in a celestial aura they saw each other as bodies of light immersed in light and delimited by a dark-blue line shaping a perfect human form. As they journeyed, they became first unaware of the concept of time wherefore the sun ceased to move, then they arose above the need of an outer means of transportation and, lo, the Vessel of Light disappeared. Floating with ease they proceeded towards the sunbelt through labyrinthic lanes of starry lands, and were directed to a gate of light through which they entered into the Hall of Stilled Fire for further purification and attunement. For two days, in an atmosphere filled with intense blazing light, they meditated. Resuming their starry traveling, they moved faster or slower in direct ratio to their ability to concentrate their thoughts in the heart center. When an outer or human thought crept in or a slight doubt overtook them, they experienced terrific jolts which acted as awakeners. As their feet touched the mainland of this starry heaven, they were welcomed by their Liberated Master-Teacher.

* * *

"Yes" — He said. "Man must acknowledge every impediment of his life as an awakener of his mortal self in rapport to his Eternal Master-Self. He may learn much, little or nothing, according to the degree of self-analyzation, dispersonalization and humility which he has developed during meditation. 'Remember Me and fight' is the ancient warning to surviving humanity. 'Never shut thyself off the fold of the Eternal, no matter how ungodly the outer clash in which thou art engaged. Be not perturbed by adversity, do not long for temporary reward. Be steady in wisdom; let no thing vex thee. Have Me by thy side, and thou shalt be guided to what is worthy of acceptance or rejection. In the remembrance of Me, operating through thy mind, limbs, organs of sensation and perceptive faculty, all thy daily contacts and eperiences become joyful and highly illuminating.'

"A life of action is, therefore, to be preferred to a life of seclusion. But what is action? To seek divine guidance by periodical withdrawal from outer cares and preoccupations is activity of first rank. On the other hand to remain in the arena of moneymaking and feverish planning irrespective of anything that pertains to the realm of the spirit is crytallization, decay and death. It is the action of introspection, well-balanced with the pressing requirements of earning a livelihood, that

76

makes man whole, self-sufficient, happy and a perfect link between physical life and immortality.

"A typical example of well-wedded inner and outer action — work and contemplation — is found in the life of Master Dante, the Florentine poet of the thirteenth century. He was active both in his profession and politics, and yet yearned for inner light. In his travels in the Inferno, he moved through yawning abysses, beholding all sorts of horrors, breathing the murky air, listening to the heartbreaking lamentations of the karma-bound souls, speaking with a variety of sinners, as Master Jesus had done before, guilty of incontinence, brute violence, fraud and treachery against their relatives, their country and God; meeting thieves, hypocrites, peculators, diviners, simonists flatterers, seducers and panders, and feeling the slimy contact of the hideous scurf of the refuse of life. He saw the Law of Cause and Effect in action, and through the intelligent observation of other's errors, he became wise and pure, and achieved immortality. However, his inner progress was hastened by the Presence of Virgil, his Master-guide, and Beatrice, his Twin Flame.

"So it is with both of you. I have helped you to resolve into their own cause many of your blunders, errors and short-comings. You have been many a time in the grip of fear and doubt, and many a time undecided as what to do — all because of your ignorance, pride and lack of discriminative intelligence; but you have displayed courage and determination. This inter-stellar tour is one of your rewards.

"Striving disciples, we are now ready to proceed onward. Here you see a terrain similar to that of earth: mountainous ascents, and tortuous and adventuresome paths. You might even have to face dangerous and challenging situations that could be overcome only by split second withdrawal of the mind from the seeming impediment and thrown into the heart center. Do you wish to rest for a few days?"

"No, Master" — responded Marco and Leonora. "With the light of grace by our side and the all-encompassing radiance emanating from Thy Blessed Presence, we feel as invincible as Thee. We know already what is in front of us, eight lofty, impervious mountains separated by seven deep gorges filled with fetid and nauseating slimy matter, fire, diseased

77

beings of the nether world, and fanged and famished beasts, symbolizing the seven capital sins, the residue of which still lurks in our consciousness: pride, covetousness, lust, anger, gluttony, envy and sloth. We are desirous of disburdening ourselves of them at once, for these are the source of a myriad of lesser violations, subtle and hard to detect tendencies of ungodly nature that corrode the soul, the mind, the body and the society and assure the rulership of Satan in the world of man. Now, O divine Master, the hallowed hour for our atonement as promised by God since the fall of man, has arrived, and we shall not let it pass unused. With Thee guiding us we shall rid ourselves of all negative tendencies, and endure fatigue and privation which, otherwise, would have caused death, oblivion and, worst of all, cosmic involution. Blessed Master, we are ready!"

As the arduous ascent began, the Immortal Guide mounted first, then stepped aside, as Marco and Leonora continued to climb unhurriedly and at a steady pace. Feeling the heavy drag of the bodies left behind at the base of the pillars and the aroused and enraged satanic residue that now faced the approaching moment of dissolution, the two penitents found strength in the achieved sensitivity to know with mathematical precision the state of their conscience and the rate of inner growth. Thus armed they reached the first gorge and therein plunged headlong. The pride within, feeling now to be unwanted and having found its like outside, withdrew quickly from the two living forms. Marco and Leonora emerged with the speed of sound and alighted on the apex of the second mountain. "Let us rely on the Law of Grace" — they said in one voice to each other — "whose mercy and love know no boundaries, and we shall leap from mountain to mountain shaking off all the residuum of negativity."

Above them they saw a spherical luminance of pink radiance as large as a full moon shooting refulgent rays through the highly rarified atmosphere. "You are beholding a lesser replica of Venus" — the Master explained — "released unto you as a gift for your striving though often you fall by the wayside because of doubt. It shows you how a man of faith can truly wield infinite power and summon the universe itself to do his bidding. It shows also how light and darkness are attracted

78

by the mind in a given degree according to the momentary attitude of the thinking man; for wherever man goes, he immediately establishes an aura around himself, and all his surroundings are seen throught that aura, stained with the imperfections and limitations of his mortal nature. When you arrived here, your mere presence caused this starry environment of eternal light to be changed into day and night, whereas your re-expanded consciousness, having reached the desired momentum, brought the nature of things to its allotted perfection again."

* * *

The sun from its zenithal position radiated shafts of golden-blue light against a royal blue sky studded with billions of stars and innumerable constellations of which seven all similar to Aquarius were conspicuously brighter. "You are being escorted to the hidden gate" — the Master said to Marco — "by the constellation under Whom you were born on earth. You have a spiritual heritage of idealism and inner leadership which you must develop in its fullness for yourself, for your country and for mankind. The other six similar constellations are projections from the Mother-star who has decked herself so festively in your honor, and when you leave this heavenly canopy they will be resolved back into their Mother's womb."

Climbing steadily, they now stopped on the highest peak of the fourth mountain to survey a glorious kaleidoscope of colors; apart from interminable forests shimmering like a vibrating diamond of a million facets, they saw broad meadows drenched in living green and gold, terraced gardens rich with multicolored flowers, rippling rivers and translucent lakes mantled with water lillies. The brilliancy of the atmosphere had so absorbed the luculent form of their liberated Master-Teacher, that at moments it seemed as if he were not with them. Caught in the grip of doubt they called in trepidation "Master, where art Thou?" Wherefore he reprimanded them:

"Why, why, do you harbor lack of trust and faith in your hearts? Behold! A wanderer tramps through the desert on a full moonlight night; does he ever gaze at the sky to reassure himself that the moon is still there? And how much greater and nobler than the moon is the I AM in Me Whom I serve at present for your sake. If I AM your guide and comforter by divine command, is it ever possible that I should neglect my duty? I AM as a heavenly sphere that lets the light pass unobstructed; I AM within the range of the All-seeing Eye in your hearts. Cast the physical eye aside and let the All-seeing Eye work for you. Arise above the exteriorized tendencies of the human nature; perceive Me inwardly and know, without the slightest doubt, that I AM with you always!"

Fully restored in faith and strength, Marco and Leonora descended to the winding, pathless canyon for another ascent. Facing a cleft at the base of the fifth mountain, whose walls were dripping with water and covered with a slimy moss, the Master warned them:

"This is the starting point of the acclivity, the slope is steep and often vertical, three thousand feet high. It must be surmounted. Failure or doubt equals retreat, equals irretrievable material and spiritual loss. A professional alpinist armed with ropes, pitons, alpenstocks and other devices would undoubtedly succeed. Though you have none of these, you do possess, however, the ability of levitation; and for such a constructive purpose We give you permission to use it. Meditate!"

By reducing the power of thought to a subtle, delicate and almost invisible filament, they directed all obstacles into their hearts and saw them being burned by the Sacred Fire issuing from that unconsuming Pinpoint of Light, wherefore a vessel of light formed beneath their feet and they ascended at jet speed the precipitous slope in company with their Liberated Master-Teacher. Soon they stood on the rocky summit, grateful to God for the successful inner exploit. "Yes" — the Master commented. "Every achievement in the physical world is the resultant of an inner or spiritual plan. To throw the wholeness of the thinking, acting and dynamic ego at the Lotus Feet of God, to be keenly aware of the Intangible, All-wise and Omnipotent Essence dwelling within, to feel and know that IT can do things which had heretofore seemed impossible, means to approach life with the instrument of the highest scientific endeavour; experimentation, tests and trials are no longer required. Man was created perfect at the Beginning, and though in a variety of ways he chose to become visibly imperfect, limited and helpless, he is still intrinsically perfect and God-like. This inalienable heritage he must claim unto himself with every means at his disposal; awareness, prayer, meditation, study, work, while waging war or discussing peace, while making love or giving birth to a new life-stream, while in the process of immolating oneself for the good of mankind. GOD, the invisible, formless, all-pervading, all-seeing, all-knowing, never away, here and there, inside and outside the body, the mind, the feelings; directing, controlling and supervising everything; thought, action, the digestive process, assimilation of food, and the behavior of the multi-billion cells of the human body . . . if no one can get rid of God, it is a wise decision to have IT as an ally of superior stature. It is indeed the highest wisdom in the business of life.

"Think of this God-Force as you approach the hour of sleep, for at that moment there are latent forces within, capable of raising the body, mind and feelings to a state of desired constructiveness and achievement for the next day. Visualize yourself as a hub in your field of action radiating living spokes of light into your environment, sweeping away all impediments, and registering the mark of success upon your business and all those who are associated with you, then say OM, OM, OM, until you fall asleep. You may use any other name, or attribute, or endearing expression that has the quality of humility and self-surrender, and above all trust. Trust the immutable and ever-active cosmic law of equilibrium. Poverty, disease, want, anxiety, war, hatred, cheating and exploiting of man by another man, are like ugly rocks tossed from a mountain top valleyward. For one instant they crash with a shattering uproar, ending at the bottom of the canyon, never to rise again, never; life and equilibrium go on forever, the evolutive forces advance silently, they never stop or slow down. So is the life of man: each man as an individual unit is a force that runs parallel and within the Cosmic Force. He cannot be stopped, destroyed or killed, for he was created to live forever, even beyond the ascension of the Christ. A true artist, philosopher, scientist or wise ruler bear testimony on earth of this truth, for they cogitate, meditate and visualize at pre-sleep time as a condition sine qua non for their very existence; and thus they create, discover and find new living elements whose application benefits mankind as a whole; without such a process they feel irreparably lost. This is the reason and source of their humility.

"Intuitive power can be strengthened and broadened to an

unlimited degree through the practice of channeling the mind to a desired goal before entering sleep. However, it is a healthy habit, for both mind and body, to find out the exact amount of sleep required for maximum efficiency in the outer world and the understanding of God. To the best of your ability go to bed always at the same time; beware of the habit of putting yourself to sleep too late or at irregular hours, for a prolonged wakeful state robs the mind of its power of self-regeneration and creativity, it weakens the free will and enervates the body. Beware of stimulants and sedatives; the first corrode and destroy the inner forces and lead to physical debilitation and mental derangement, the latter do exactly the same thing. By their use man becomes an addict and a weakling, a fearful creature and an easy prey to the beings that negate life, light, genius and noble endeavour. Truly he is cut asunder from God."

*　*　*

Marco and Leonora, enfolded in the radiance of their Master and held spellbound by His noble teaching, were unaware of being levitated to the entrance of the Hidden Path. Seven steps appeared before them, and beyond they saw a broad thoroughfare of mystic enchantment. They climbed the steps eagerly, but as they reached the seventh, a massive and impenetrable wall loomed before them. Their Master had disappeared.

For many a day they stood there baffled, confused and in the grip of fear. Though not in the physical body, the bodily sensations were acutely felt: the belligerent and unforgiving stomach presented its sharp pang of hunger demanding appeasement. Their throats were parched but there was no water to quench their thirst. They felt the ominous cold of survivors washed ashore in the middle of the night, in the depths of winter, after a shipwreck. The acuminate tentacles of desolation and loneliness began to carve their bodies and consciousness with deep incisions. Then light appeared. And it appeared because they did not seek the cause of their predicament outwardly but within themselves; they were to blame for past violations caused by the love of the self, by inability or unwillingness to achieve a modicum of humility; in short caused by ignorance.

And having seen the Light of Understanding, three words in letters of fire became visible:

SINCERITY FORGIVENESS LOVE

Sincerity; what is sincerity? And the Voice within spoke, loud and clear: a dynamic striving for freedom from simulation, disguise, hypocrisy and false pretense; a desire to achieve purity, truthfulness and transparency of the Soul-flame. When in the midst of a social gathering, rather than saying half-truths, or white lies, plead ignorance; do not appear to be a saint or a nonconformist, or a spineless idiot. Since nothing is serious in such company talk of the news of the day.

Forgiveness is the process of the transmutation of resentment and hatred. Begin at once, do not wait two or three years from now, or even a week. Do it now and feel the exhilaration and the majestic dominance of the soul lifting your mind closer to perfection and making your body as light as a feather floating in the rarified air of beauty and peace.

And Love. . . . Though no philosopher or theologian is able to define this lofty attribute of God, let this be not a source of concern. Try to live in the spirit of sincerity and forgiveness; try to absorb and radiate these two cosmic attributes and the definition of Love will unfold like a lotus flower, like a maiden in the full bloom of youth, like the appearance of the Twin Flame unto him who has searched for many embodiments. Then you will see Love to be the energizer of matter, spirit and thought; the unifying essence of all living beings, and the substratum of life itself. It redeems, glorifies and immortalizes because Love and God are one!

As peace and inner equilibrium began to dawn upon Marco and Leonora, gradually the surrounding harshness changed into one of pristine starry beauty; the seeming impregnable wall dissolved leaving in its stead an intricately wrought gate of silver. At the threshold, with a single stroke of a two-pointed stylus held by an invisible hand, the two visitors were cosmically branded with the sign of the cross on their foreheads.

"Enter and welcome!" — a wondrous voice was heard saying. "May the path of the free be yours forever. Now that the vista of starry existence stretches before your inner eye, it is needful for you to know that it can only be remembered through a life of purity and utter dedication to ethical enterprises. You will not live in monastic seclusion, nor in isolated fanaticism and superiority complex. You will wallow in mud and stenchy vibration created and projected by dishonesty and cheating; and they shall not touch you, for the awareness of starry life will never dim as long as you live, that is, forever. Though imperfect and often enmeshed in a variety of limitations, you have been chosen out of the manifold, at this crucial hour in the history of humanity, because you display the needed traits of lean speech and humility, aversion to flattery and the glorification of the personality.

"Prior to World War I, the mass of mankind lived in fear and stagnation. From World War I to the vanishing days of the Great Depression fear and resignation dominated the hearts of men. From World War II to this day, within and without the boundary of the Great Society, and amidst a seeming economic affluence, fear is on the increase. Rioting and lawlessness are the result of fear within the hearts of the minority groups; the passivity of the official government in coping with the violators of law and order stems from stagnation and inability to perceive and apply the natural forces associated with law and order. You have a government of weaklings, which is similar to the attitude of wealthy parents towards their ill-bred brood. And this is fear!

"The so-called 'flower children', 'drug indulgers', 'hippies', and so forth, had to be by logical sequence the continuators and aggravators of this universal behavior of irresponsible parents and citizens. Fear dominates and drives them. Unable to face the complexities of the New Age, untrained in self-discipline and unwilling to share the hardships encountered in the gradual unfoldment of the process of evolution, they withdraw into the tribal shell of non-conformism, condemning the society en masse, while preaching a gospel of self-sufficiency and Christian purity. They deny their parents although they accept their money. To study, to work for a livelihood, to obey and apply the rules of body hygiene, to nourish their bodies with food that is properly balanced in its vital constituents, and to be well groomed in adherence to the conservative fashion of the day imply conformism, self-discipline and a sense of responsibility. And these they refuse to accept. They cite Master Jesus' rebelliousness against the corruption and dullness of the priesthood and the crafty selfishness of the money-changers, but forget how clean the Master of Galilee was both in His garment and body, that he allowed

84

his feet to be washed by others, that though oppressive he obeyed the Law of Caesar and adhered faithfully to tradition and local lore. He was a fulfiller, not a destroyer or antagonizer.

"The 'flower children' want to see and speak with God, but rather than applying the ancient method of rhythmic breathing, meditation and the other disciplines prescribed by the science of Yoga, they want to reach the lofty aim in a hurry; so they resort to stimulants and 'kicks', unaware that such a method not only destroys whatever they have left of the divine inheritance of inner freedom, but it also maims beyond recovery the internal organs of the body and limbs and organs of sensation. It is restlessness arising from the fear of inability to succeed in life.

"And there are the Negroes, and the 'Civil Rights' advocates, and the 'Freedom Fighters'. They all seek to improve their economic status by violence; they hate the white race but they want to mingle with it; they feel proud and honored to work and move abreast with it, contact it socially, and marry members of such a despised ethnic group. They fear their insecurity and are unable to perceive that the source of such fear is their inadequacy; intellectual and spiritual inadequacy. We say unto them: Children, O children of God, abandon your rioting and plunge into studying. Study unto exhaustion and cogitate and plan plans of love and noble endeavours. Move abreast with your God within and in a joyous mood, and fear not; recognition will fall at your feet in a begging attitude. Fear not what some of the white race has done to you, but what you have done recently to history, to the future generations and to God. Plunge into study and undo the unkind karma of rioting, pillaging, exaggerated accusations and disservice to the land that holds and nurses you and the political institutions that protect and defend you before the law. We watch you, beloved ones, and we guide you and protect you with the same intense love that we release unto those that strive for perfection and geniusship by the noble path of study, self-discipline and tolerance for those who know not what they do. To strike you must sometimes; but this We shall whisper to each one of you individually at the hour of meditation. Take no initiative in this matter or you will suffer excruciating pain of remorse in this embodiment and in embodiments to come. Beware of deceptive, selfish and unqualified leaders who preach violence as a way of achieving your cherished goal. Be steady

85

in God, in love and in the law, and you will win by the sheer weight of your virtue and intellectual wealth.

"To the peoples of the world we say: rather than leaning on this or that, on the church or the government, for moral support or economic well being, perceive, please do perceive the seed of omnipotence that lies in your hearts. Nurse and irrigate this seed, and it will lift you on its sturdy branches to unsuspected heights of happiness and prosperity. Retrace your steps by the path of humble and sincere self-interrogation. This is the Age of Maturity which needs to be fertilized and expanded through introspection. Science, the arts, political leadership and all the endeavours in the field of Space and interstellar knowledge cannot grow and evolve unless they are supported by a pensive humanity.

"The Light of Salvation, which is equally vital to both the ignorant and the wise one, does not accept spiritual cripples; for crippled indeed is the man who relies on the priest for a rule of conduct, and the sophisticated atheist who worships only his mortal intellect. Every man who truly prizes his spiritual liberty as a groundwork for mind expansion and cosmic immortality, must enter the Chamber of Light in his heart, there to learn things of science, philosophy and God, not found in books, schools, churches and temples of stone. It is by cultivating absolute dependence on God in a direct and straightforward manner that man becomes really free. It is the freedom of the Avatars, the Christs, the Buddhas and the Prophets now accessible to all.

* * *

"Blessed son and daughter, here you must pray with childlike enthusiasm and yet with the perspicaciousness of a genius. It is by displaying humility before God that the mind expands to encompass ever larger spheres of life. This magnificent starry land, composed of a myriad of fixed stars and starlets, is self-luminous, which means that everything is shadowless; and because physical darkness is nonexistent, you have the edenic state of living where man's craftiness, limitation and ills cannot enter. The starry dwellers, being always bathed in light, are never baffled, or ill or despondent, never forced to reduce or relinquish their power of absolute inner liberty of thought and action to anyone in exchange of material benefits or other worldly gains; yet they study, experiment and produce with the same ingenuity and passion of the most advanced idealist of the planet earth. We call them Master-idealists, positive dreamers and fore-runners of the wonderful things that are in process of unfoldment on Earth. They seek inspiration not by admiring a lofty mountain or the marvels of nature but rather by opening the silver conduit that connects the root of the nose and the sex organs. Thus they achieve mind expansion without the use of deleterious drugs. True inspiration, which is always evolutive and a producer of strength and joy, is a neutral vibration or friction of the pro-protons of the human body. Like storm troopers, with incredible swiftness, they rush to the creative center of the mind to bring about the coalescing of the new idea; then desire takes over and a quality or direction is imposed upon it.

"These Master-idealists rely on the so-called earthsoil for sub-stance to work with, either directly or through the inspirational labor of the earth-bound intelligences. One must remember that even the greatest genius in human form is ninety-nine percent the product of the soil and one percent the living stream from the Realm of Perfection. The opposite is true for the Master-idealists; hence their almost limitless freedom of creativity and spontaneous joy, their lack of anxiety and their assurance of ultimate success. In short, their thoughts, plans and actions are the resultant of a mysterious process which renders them free from all trace of ego of which even the saint in human form is still tinged.

"While the subsequent starry worlds are foci of life inhabited by beings who have risen in various degrees above the concept of matter and form, and, consequently, are capable of assembling and scattering worlds and systems thereof in a timeless flash, through the manipulation of light and energy, the Master-ideal-ists are the acme of human beings as conceived by God prior to man's fall from the edenic consciousness. Poverty, disease, old age, decrepitude and death touch them not. They see beyond the physical range of sight, and hear sounds from the other side of a mountain, the depths of the ocean and the etheric belt; they do not experiment with the elements of nature in order to find new truths; instead they interrogate directly water, fire, air, flowers, rocks and trees, and light and energy. These they call *teachers*. These teachers disclose newer laws, newer marvels that are destined to link the future generations of man with God.

"Here also dwells a class of intelligences of lesser inner achievement than the Master-idealists. They are the idealists of Earth who were and are systematically opposed in their noble endeavours by the narrow-mindedness of obtuse and prudish self-styled leaders in the field of knowledge. Though still on earth their higher selves are projected here for refuge and comfort, and for additional training on how to break the ego and stubborness of the enemies of progress and evolution as planned by God. However, some of the frustrations of the idealist are of his own making. Often and consciously he treads on forbidden territory whereto God, the Source of inspiration and the Conceiver, and the One whose ultimate aim is beauty and immortality, is forgotten; the transitory idea is worshipped instead, and as a result the inspiration lags and the realization dies or lives a sickly and short existence.

"Here, the deviating idealist is brought face to face with his pitfalls, errors and delusions. Then he suffers death, the last of his earthly delusions, his body is cremated and the ashes scattered to the wind. But the lesson that he has learned, the promise to God to adhere to the Law in spite of all pressure, and the sum total of his achievements, remain here solidly condensed, vibrating and endowed with a superior intelligence. All this, a living monolith, is the fallen idealist who has been rescued forever by the Master-idealists. He will take embodiment again on earth, with the silver cord in full action from early childhood; doubt and inner travail as to Who is the Master and Conceiver, and who is the instrument and the doer, shall no longer beset him. He will fulfill his earthly mission according to the Law of his lifestream and achieve immortality, which means that he will be promoted to higher levels of life.

❖   ❖   ❖

"The Master-idealists are made of condensed light born of altruism and love. They are sinless and without name and individuality, and as such they protect, train and guide the idealists of earth. They come from the Realm of the Formless and achieve tangibility through the parenthood of Twin Flames or Twin Spirits; two streams of life visibly separated but inwardly united as one.

"What is the exact meaning of Twin Flames? You know of twin brothers or sisters, and twin brother and sister, on earth; and how physically and somatically alike they are, and to a certain degree how alike they are mentally. But the Twin Flames are of a different sort of likeness. Each is the counterpart and complement of the other, and together they seek oneness. The strong, powerful and untamed yearning of the youth-man and the youth-woman to be together and alone, to embrace and kiss each other, and to unite their bodies and souls indissolubly, is only the faintest aspect of this twinship. The story goes back to the *beginning* of life itself.

"As your solar system came into being and was made ready to receive and support lifestreams, one half of the allotted number of Christ-men were released to earth, the other half was held in the infinite Compound of Light for a further and, as yet undelineated mission. This world of yours was teeming with vibrating individualities whose intelligence was of the class of the genius. They thought, planned and executed things of beauty in every field of endeavour. And being in possession of both the masculine and feminine traits, they lived the edenic state of life passionately and dynamically, their creative genius never lagging, and the handsomeness of their body-forms defying time beyond time itself. Life on earth was of the class of the starry realms, that is, a perpetual and evolutive activity as conceived by Christ-men. Then the time arrived for the second half of the intelligences to don more tangible forms and enter the manifested life. Before leaving God told them: *Survey, learn, expand.* They surveyed but did not learn properly and expanded limitedly. For many millenniums they roamed the spaces aimlessly; swarms of incandescendent sparkles floating everywhere; then they began to take scope for a global program of life. Unauthorized by God they took initiatives, and through error and experimentation, experimentation and error, they created time and the concept of space and distance, and finally they separated the effect from the Cause, which means that they created a world of their own, a life of duality based on chance. And having weakened their link with God they questioned the veracity of their own reports concerning the survey, and when a statement of truth was demanded of them, it was an arbitrary utterance based on the contingency of the moment, unsupported by proof or direct perception.

"More millenniums went by, desire for self-assertion crept in, and the delegated power from God was seized and placed under the direct control of the intellect. As a result the vivifying throb

89

of life was reduced to a faint pulsation, just enough to exist, and even to prosper and create in the finite environment of a consciousness avulsed from God. The luminosity of the sparkle was now marred by a progressive opacity, while intelligence and power were buried beneath the dross of shadow, which required strength and discipline to bring them into use. Hence the partial and defective comprehension of life and phenomena. Keenly aware of the limitation, the sparkle-Christ-men, no longer capable of making direct contact with God, devised ways and means to obtain help. Each felt to be the possessor of another entity residing within, endowed with the same degree of intelligence and will as it had. To it the sparkle said: 'Come forth', and out of its *loin* another entity came forth; now they were two, man and woman, twin flames. However the cosmic heritage of oneness in God had been broken.

"Now the Law of Mercy came into being, the first amendment to Eternal Law. God consecrated this new status of twinship with the sign of the Tau Cross forming the forehead and the nose, while the eyes at the corners, substituting the All-seeing Eye, which had disappeared, formed the sustaining beams of light reflecting the Primal Light from the Mind of God. This is the face that was called the 'image and likeness' of God.

"The first group of Christ-men who preceeded the "fallen' could not be left in an environment that had become unsuitable for Self-expression; for confusion, frustration and desperation were now the lot of man. God recalled the first group of Christ-men and assigned them as masters and rulers of other worlds and systems thereof to continue their mission untouched by negligence and the shadow of desire. They were called Master-Elohim, Master-Seraphim, Master-Cherubim, Archangels and Lords of Life founders of cosmic hierarchies and fiduciaries of God's Estate for all time. The Twin Flames who in one span of earthly life, through meditation and self-imposed discipline, had made amends for their original violation, were allowed to ascend to be appointed Master-idealists with the assignment of bearing Flames that would grace the world in the field of the arts, pure mathematics, eclectic philosophy and other manifestations of beauty unstained by the stigma of selfish desire. The rest formed the humanity to which you belong. The twin flames fell into more baffling frustrations, and beset by an ever-mounting fear that is the fruit of ignorance, their love for each other weakened, and in a frantic move they separated, lost sight of each other and became total strangers.

"This is one of the major causes of the world's instability: man-woman misunderstanding, misfitness in marriage, divorce and broken homes. And because of this, humanity wanders aimlessly in a world of self-created chaos, made of hatred, envy, vengeance, disappointment, lawlessness of every kind, shabbiness and filth, self-torturing thoughts, fear, imperfection of the body, aging and crippling diseases and death itself. Every living person is only half of his true self. This state of half-ness is the cause of the vast, disordered and unsightly array of limitation in which humanity wallows as if choking in a putrid, nauseating and slimy pond. Give each man, each woman, his or her perfect other half, and you will have destroyed, to the very root, these limitations. Man must retrace that lost half of himself.

"You are hereby authorized by the Law of Collective Karma that seeks to rescue the entire population of the world and the Earth itself to announce that there is a perfect mate for each man. This he must seek and find. It is vital not only for the limitless unfoldment of his mind, soul and economic structure of his own household, but also for the country in which he lives and the society at large. The Cosmic Forces of this age have him in their trajectory; his effort requires only the minimum if his intention is positive, serious, sacred and undeviating. Inner guidance, as tangible as the existence of the sun, will not be lacking. The same command is also directed to the woman. Her search is greatly facilitated by the same Cosmic Forces that have heightened her power of intuition to a level never reached since the 'fall' of man. But again her intention must be positive, serious, holy and undeviating. God wants homes not of husbands and wives but of Twin Flames. Is this clear?

*　*　*

"The increase of population on earth has caused an augmentation of Master-idealists in this starry realm to protect and guide the idealists of earth. And since the process of procreation here implies conscious and direct communication with God some of the Twin Flame-couples have regained their status of oneness which they had at the 'beginning', and transferred to higher realms of cosmic existence. Those who remained behind, be-

91

cause of the requirement for more Master-idealists, are given the same opportunity for atonement and promotion. This will lead to the hastening of the application of the Law of Grace whereby the twin flames of Earth who have found each other and lived in adherence to the Law of Cosmic Harmony, might be raised to this plane of life to become parents of Master-idealists.

"The Twin Flame-couples of this Starry Heaven procreate according to the Law of direct absorption of Light and Energy from the Cosmic Reservoir of Life. The vehicle of the incoming Master-idealist is created by the contact of the foreheads of the parents-to-be, after an inner preparation of prayer, meditation and visualization. For three days prior to the birth of the child, the parents retire to their silentium for the preparatory work leading to the highest mystery of life. In perfect unison of purpose, they visualize a being whose ideals correspond to their own, not in manifestation but in essence. It takes forty-eight hours to complete the visualization; the next twenty-four hours are dedicated to absolute contemplation of God.

At the appointed hour they are summoned by a winged being from the realm of Silence, who announces that by the Grace of the Law of Love they have been chosen as instruments for the manifestation of a son or daughter Master-idealist. Leaving their seclusion, amidst a feeling of unspeakable happiness, surrounded by shadowless light and humming a sweet song of love — the Ode to Birth — they walk hand in hand into the drawing room, where guests are awaiting them. The parents-to-be kiss each other in joyous, trustful expectation and then slowly cause their foreheads to touch. The contact releases a brilliant sphere of light, which immediately disappears towards the Realm of the Formless Spirits, there to rest above an unlit sparkle. 'Thou art the Chosen One, O Divine Speck of Cosmic Substance. Thy mission has begun, by the Grace of God, Our Father, through the channel of noble parents. Be grateful. Arise and follow me!' Within thirty seconds the new Master-idealist in the form of a charming youth, age thirteen, appears fully clothed, bows before his or her parents, and kisses their hands in gratitude and love. He then takes the oath of obedience to them and to God, while the Music of the Spheres swells to a tune of magic splendor.

"Thus birth occurs. The earthly parents dream of having a

child. Spasmodically, nesciently, now believing and now doubting, they make preparation, seldom aware of an angelic being
hovering over them, trying to awaken them to the sanctity of
the sexual act and the necessity of focusing their minds for
an ideal and perfect child. The result is often disappointing;
the new lifestream could be a total stranger, a rebellious or a
problem child, rarely the flawless prince charming, for which
they had hoped. On the other hand, the new Master-idealist,
possesses, as a minimum, the gifts of mind and soul to guide a
nation into an age of peace and intellectual and artistic renaissance never experienced before. The starry parents, though fully
aware of the indisputable success of their child, do not hesitate
to impose upon him an iron discipline, much more severe than
that of a military academy, while the earthly parents continue
their blunder through a series of leniencies called love, which
in reality, is sloth, stupidity and irresponsibility. In heaven it is
the son who says: 'Thy word, O Mother, is a law unto me,
to obey always. Thy severity is love divine.' On earth it is the
mother who says: 'what is it you want me to do, son, to make
you happy.' This is indeed a child lost, lost to himself, to society
and God. Both the world and the Octaves of Light have been
cheated. Follow, O Earth, the starry system of child rearing,
and you will have no second-class citizens, no misfits; only leaders leading leaders.

"In the process of learning, the future Master-idealist is led
step by step on the path of introspection. His progress is determined by the degree of application which he makes in plunging
his mind into the deepest recesses of his being and holding it
there at will and with ease. As his proficiency increases, he
gradually acquires greater facility in mastering any discipline,
from philosophy to the creative arts, higher mathematics, and
the Science of Immortality itself. By such a course he is made
aware of being the hub of the pageant of life, whose Intelligence-
force issues from within and is projected radially to the boundless infinitude. Now he truly knows himself — this being the supreme goal of life; he has seen God, his eternal and unseen
Father and Maker, stern, chastising, loving and rewarding. To
him he will stay linked for eternity, for joy, for life itself, for
without Him, he ceases to be.

"This is the Foundation of Universal Knowledge which embraces love, brotherhood, and the highest intellectual exploits in every branch of endeavour.

"The Master-idealist reaches manhood at the age of twenty. From there on he maintains the handsomeness, resiliency and vitality of a being who never passes away. His intelligence enters the creative stage. He is released from obedience to his parents and stands on equal footing with them, yet always in a starry relationship of love and respect. All his thoughts and deeds, being perfect, are karma-free; and should he take an earthly embodiment, as a holocaust to God for the love of man, all he would do will be, likewise, unbinding.

"Do not think that the millions of Intelligences dwelling here are of the same stratum of spiritual consciousness. Far from it. Spiritual inequality or inner variance is the eternal theme of the Law, necessary for cosmic evolution. As men have constructive ambitions on Earth at various degrees of intensity, similarly, the Intelligences here have cosmic ambitions at various degrees of intensity also. However, to be a great composer, painter or architect is not an aim, but a steppingstone. To attain Christship and live everlastingly in the Realm of the Spirit is their ultimate aspiration. Each Master-idealist is a universe unto himself existing as an independent unit yet operating harmoniously in the infinite scheme of life.

"Blessed disciples and starry travelers" — the angelic voice continued — "there is no resistance, no obstacles, no restriction of any kind, both physical or otherwise that is not conquered by the impact of a wave of love that surges forth from the heart and mind of him that wants to re-conquer his lost self, his Twin Flame. And once they find each other and live together, they hold in their grasp the universe and God. You know all this as it has happened to you; however, you shall now witness the re-enactment of the most salient points in the life of a Twin-Flame-couple who were re-united by the path of inner search in a past age. Behold!"

In the early dawn of the fourth day, Marco and Leonora still in a trance of divine expectancy, were attracted by a sudden luminosity in the shape of a sphere spiraling downward from a celestial source. Stopping a few feet from them it changed into a winged being of flawless symmetry and handsomeness, while the air became impregnated with the sweet fragrance of unknown flowers. In a masculine voice It said:

"Blessed are they who live under grace, for in the awareness of God they analyze, control and direct their thoughts and feelings into the right channels; they guard their souls from the pollution of transitory ambitions and sense cravings.

"Blessed is he whose companion of life is of the nature of spiritual twinship for he stands master over impediments and evil. Dynamic bliss and peace are his.

"Blessed are they who are able to see the Law in action, for truly they behold the glory of the Self in Its Supreme Immanence.

"Blessed are they who have consecrated their lives to God by the path of the highest ethics in human transactions, for they are the Light of the Christ in action!"

As He finished speaking, He extended his wings of light and then folded them vertically to the contour of a heart. At its center an eye of molten gold formed which, as it came closer to Marco and Leonora, increased in size and brilliance. Looking into the pupil they saw as if on a living screen a procession of starry heavens and solar systems marching on a track of love towards the Heart of Light. They saw the panorama of Life in its pristine beauty and perfection; the world of today, its commerce, its schools, its government, its scientific endeavours, its arts and its agriculture, unmarred by frustrations, discord, grief, disease and pollution. The Eye then moved backward to its primary position, became elongated and separated into two identical eyes, each as large, dazzling and beautiful as the original one.

A beam of pink light issued from one eye and blue from the other, and where the two beams met a heart of shimmering violet light came into being, the symbol of Love Divine. Then as they looked away from each other, the ground quaked, planets and solar systems were blown into shapeless clouds of black matter; the horrors of chaos of the early geological ages presented themselves tangibly before their consciousness; in one instant, which seemed an eternity, they experienced the sum total of all the ugliness of human existence since man's fall from the oneness with God into separation and duality: wars, atrocities against people, animals and nature, famine, despotism, plotting, betrayal of sacred oaths, luridness, disease, cannibalism and other deeds of debauchery. The Twin Eyes then turned their gaze towards one another, and again the Heart of Light and the Panorama of Life in their pristine beauty came to sight. By drawing more light from the Universal Reservoir of Creation the two Eyes slowly assumed human forms of flawless beauty and symmetry, masculine and feminine. Clasping hands they introduced themselves as Elos Perseva and Beata Lux. Elos spoke:

*   *   *

"Salutations unto you our ancient kin and friends. May the joyous radiance of the Golden Age be with you. You have seen that when Twin Souls face one another, they face the light that knows no setting, for they see God and the Law in a way that leaves no room for misunderstanding.

"The Golden Age is the age of twinship in action on Earth, the exact replica of the way of living of this starry heaven. It shall come into being; it has already begun to coalesce. Only seven thousand years ago, to speak your language, the Great Ones of Love commenced to polarize the hearts of all living beings towards the searching for their twin mates, whose spiritual oneness constitutes the rock upon which the Golden Age stands. On that oneness humanity shall build the Tower of Christship which no human power can ever dent. It will be the age of true love encompassing every aspect of life and maximum expression of intellectual power. In that age the gap between heaven and earth will be obliterated. Matter and spirit, mind and body, science and philosophy, poetry and politics, shall cease to function as separate entities and lend themselves in meek obedience, to the glorification of Life.

"This is the theme of the present cycle of life. Seven thousand years ago, the Elohim of Love found the realization of twinship on Earth to be the most powerful springboard to catapult mankind into a state of durable and constructive international brotherhood that is free from political scheming and emotional involvement.

"It is herewith established that man's earthly existence, when reunited with his Twin Soul as a faithful companion of life, shall commence with a minimum intensity of Inner Light comparable to the highest intellectual and spiritual exploits of today. He will move upward on a path of the highest dictates of the Law of Ethics without encountering the slightest impediment. The resiliency of his mind, the youthful look of his body and the never-dying urge to transcend forms and appearances will be sufficient to impel him into action under the guidance of his Buddhi.

"The searching seed of the Twin Soul was sown not only in the hearts of men, but in every being that possesses conscious life. In the boundless spaces every star is searching for its twin, the zodiac is in a state of transition, new constellations are in process of formation, new planets are issuing from the wombs of planet-mothers that have been sexually touched by their twin spheres of living fire; new solar systems are born. No longer does a living being want to live alone. In perfect companionship, the inter-exchange of thought, energy and substance produces forms that are beautiful and enduring. Negative enterprises are declining towards obliteration. Tobacco for smoking, liquors for intoxication, dope for 'trips' into the 'superconscious', increase in crime, war-mongering, espionage and all the evil of frustration and loneliness are fighting the last battle of the irrevocably and prophetically doomed. No longer does man want to waste wealth, energy and intelligence by giving himself supinely to the sinister force that takes delight in driving the unwary to hell. The vision of a cosmic future of unending growth is nearer to all. Death is in a state of coma. Life is preparing the bonfire of rejoicing for tangible dominion amongst men.

"Blessed friends, your presence here is the result of your achieved twinship, of a life lived in thrilling harmony with each other and an interchange of living thoughts and energy. You have accepted discipline, inner and outer discipline, with a glad heart; and though you have made it a way of life, yet you do not show it off. Surely the world at large does not care about the wealth and wonders of your souls, but we do care; we love and exalt those who are capable of freeing themselves from emotional friction and mental reservation for this leads to the shattering and scattering of all sectarian isms that clip the wings of the soul of man. Only by tacit and unexpressed rebelliousness, only by decapitating the head of the loud Moloch of the little self, and the merciless crushing of the rising heads of the Medusa of transitory desires, can man make

97

himself rich, wise and delivered forever. And what is the secret of all this? Meditation, yes, the subtle art of meditation that causes the body, mind, soul, mankind, the universe and God to become one.

"It is a difficult assignment" — Elos went on — "but begin one must. My first step in this blissful art of communing with God was to search for my Twin Flame. To have her by my side, and together scale the Mount of Wisdom and Immortality became the theme of my life. With a glad heart and iron discipline I studied and mastered all branches of learning and tests imposed upon me, and thus I penetrated not only the essence of my ideal, but it made me also a great scientist and inventor. Meditation, though unpalatable at the beginning, gave me, eventually, a mysterious feeling of inner strength. My feet and legs began to vibrate. All this transposed into the human body has unending implications. Meditation awakens the genital organs and the pulsations therefrom strengthen the heart and enliven the mind; despondency gives way to contentment, and fear to well grounded courage; noble resolutions are made, and an intense desire to practice generosity takes over. All the lofty traits of the ideal human being come forth, and health reaches almost the stage of indestructibility.

"Encouraged by such a process the meditative disciple moves on to more profound and loftier experiences. The body is strong and supple; and the mind now far-seeing and superlatively retentive clamors for direct illumination. It no longer begs, it demands for now it knows its rights before the Tribunal of Creation. Christhood is the goal, that is, dominion over life and death in the name of God. To pray is no longer required; whatever one wants is his for the taking; the universe is his footstool. But he will continue to meditate. I continued to meditate. A giant of the Spirit must be humble; and he must hold in check the attempts of the personality to assert itself; the oath of obedience to God must be renewed at every step of the way; the conviction that both, all visible possessions and the intangible flow of life that one enjoys come from God, must be kept cogently alive. To say Thank you O Father, is never enough, the Rod of Grace must be felt upon one's brow. Love, the most abused of God's attributes, vilified, persecuted and crucified, must be proved through worthy deeds performed without ostentation but quietly and in silence.

"A man in love has pride. It is immaterial whether it is love for a woman or for God. I was in love with both, though as yet I had seen neither; hence my pride was of a superlative nature. I wanted to feel well, to look well, to behave well. I was proud of all my accomplishments including humility. A disciple of the inner, the meditative student, must possess this inward pride for he is a messenger, a messiah, the ambassador of the King of Kings with the specific mandate to lift nations and races from all human miseries. I lived in such a feeling of divine pride expectantly, humbly and trustfully. My Twin Flame will surely come by divine command, by the Law of Grace. I had passed all the tests. Then one day at the hour of meditation I fell on my knees and uttered loudly the words of self-surrender: 'Father, Thy will be done!' This tore asunder the veil of separation between my darling companion and myself, and I beheld my blessed Beata as beautiful as an Archangel, her countenance as dazzling as many suns. Out of love imperishable she had descended from higher octaves of life forfeiting temporarily the Throne of Light that she had earned through the same process of meditation as mine, the same longing and the same faith. As I took her tenderly into my embrace of love, our minds and hearts were fused into one. Thus we became each other's custodian for everlasting years. Thus ended one cycle of life — limited, functional and changeable — and commenced a higher one, a life of never-ending spiritual growth and absolute joy."

*   *   *

Elos' narrative had raised the minds of Marco and Leonora to a state of joyful exaltation; here they were facing two beings whose attainment was incomparably greater than those of the greatest chief of state, artist or scientist; masters over matter and mind, light, energy and vibration. Now, Beata, perceiving the embarrassment of the two youths approached them and caressed their faces with the loving touch of divine reassurance.

"Be happy" — she said. "Lift up your heads, for you are standing on equal footing with us; and as brothers and sisters we are standing on equal footing with God. How can man know God unless he lives with Him in a joyous and relaxed manner, studying His behavior, pondering on His Word, analyzing His command, and most of all absorbing and living in the Spirit of His Law. On Earth when a slave serves an enlightened master faithfully and intelligently, the day will come when the master takes him first into his confidence, and then bestows gifts upon him, until he actually delegates power for specific missions whereby the slave discusses deals, makes decisions and signs contracts in the name of and for his master. And whatever he does, it has the seal of approval. Likewise with God. The more one advances on the inner path, the more intense the desire to relinquish the gift of free will and become a slave of God, to abide within His Shadowless Mansion and serve Him faithfully, consistently and intelligently. You feel at ease as a slave because you know with mathematical precision how far you stand in His Presence. And this is knowledge of humility, the propulsive force that thrusts you forward. God, on the other hand, does not look at you as a slave, but as a son, a prodigal son much beloved indeed. And He projects at you the magnetic beam of the Law of Grace, while at the same time pretending indifference; for He surely wants you to feel that you have reached Him by your own effort, trial, disappointment and suffering. Then you feel proud of your accomplishment; He wants you to; for it is through divine pride and divine humility intelligently blended that the disciple on the path holds firmly the position of command delegated to him by God, the Father, the Ruler of the Universe.

"The citizen of the Western World must reduce his overrajasic tendency, this perpetual rushing, this endless craving to project his mind outwardly for visible accomplishments. It is a sign of immaturity, of insufficiency, of fear and insecurity. Unable to know himself, and no matter how worldly wise and intellectually brilliant, he trembles in agony at the thought of the inscrutable tomorrow, even, of the next day. Hence he is easily mesmerized by unscrupulous entities: smoking, dope, intoxicating beverages, gambling and, worst of all, insurance companies of all types. That he would learn, O Father, we entreat You, to meditate. This is the only proven method that opens the Inner Eye and makes him see with absolute clarity what lies within and beyond.

"I am one of the Directors of the Guardians of Life for the

planet Earth. They are the recorders and analyzers of every thought and deed projected by man. We are the custodians of the Akashic Records, listing on tablets of imperishable material all the transgressions, blunders, stupidities and noble exploits of every lifestream that walks the Earth. How childishly unsuspecting are human beings, especially those whose life revolves around matter and dollars and cents. Wait until they are released from the body of the flesh and presented, by the Guardians of Life, with a bill of particulars copied from the Akashic Records; then they will realize how negative they were, in spite of their acquired wealth and fame; and also how selfish in spite of their seeming altruism displayed while on Earth. Negative because they contributed nothing to the life of the spirit, and selfish because they abused the Guardians of Life who had to file their thoughts and deeds born of ignorance.

"In the starry halls, wherein the Akashic Records are filed the Guardians of Life study every thought, every little vagary projected from man's mind; every slight change of mood or feeling goes on record. Nothing escapes. The sensitive tape of each man's life runs on a twenty-four hour basis, recording new impressions that only a Liberated Master is able to read.

"Now, a large percentage of these Guardians have acquired enough merits for promotion to higher offices, yet they cannot leave their heavenly archives; first, because of the ever-increasing population of Earth, and second, because of the Law of Evolution whose demand for greater perfection from mankind is never fulfilled; hence, their presence is needed to guide men and expand their good work.

"In order to fill the rank and file of the Guardians of Life that in obedience to the Cosmic Law of Reward must be released for higher responsibilities, the Cosmic Assembly of the Perfect Ones has enacted the following Decree of Dispensation to mankind: 'Whoever makes up his mind to serve the Light as herewith taught in the measure of one, will receive assistance in the measure of ten'. A very simple decree as words are concerned, but the inner and outer transformation that it will bring about for every man, woman and child, individually, and the far-reaching effects for peace, prosperity and advancement for the entire humanity are beyond all imagining. And those of the first who reach the goal will be promoted Guardians of Life.

* * *

"To speak to you personally, blessed friends of ours, the Akashic Records of your past lives indicate your intense desire for freedom and truth with no clinging to sectarian institutions and their tawdry superstitions. You have always disliked, and with reason, all colorful and elaborate religious rituals for you remember very vividly how they can be traced back through an unending chain of events to the cruel and bloody barbarism of the priesthood of Babylon, Assyria, primitive Egypt, Africa and the nomad tribes of Western Europe. Since time immemorial you have been students of the Religion of the Spirit and the acceptance of this philosophy of life has given rise within your hearts to the passionate love of nature, whether untouched by the human hand or simply rearranged for the unfoldment of the soul. And having expelled base cravings, through a series of strokes of the iron will applied during the last four embodiments, you have prepared yourselves slowly and consistently for the present starry experiences. The Liberated Masters, who are distributed along the Path like pharos along the waterways, welcome you. And as you depart from the abode of One on the ascending trek you take with you something precious, intangible and enduring: the conviction that you are traveling with those who are your betters, the noble and wise companions who have helped you to set and keep your house in order. Negative teachings preach the annulment of all desires; you have combined them into one and imparted on it a dynamic and evolutive force: love for beauty of form and sound and harmony of colors, and that all mankind be lifted to the same heights of appreciation, away from ugliness forever.

"You must tell your students to cultivate abhorrence for idleness, wishful thinking, good intentions and slovenly application; tell them to keep a keen critical eye upon their thoughts and deeds, to keep a constant watch against a lapse into self-praise, and that the satisfaction for work well-done is simply a stepping-stone for nobler deeds.

"All this and more are an integral part of your lives which will never suffer loss or enfeeblement. And this is so because in passing over the threshold of the spirit you have always been careful to make precise demands on life and accepted divine guidance. For many embodiments you have lived in the same

102

sweet connubium which is similar to ours; and it shall last until inner mergence becomes a reality. You have always taken embodiment together, and duly met although born in different lands. You have always been sweethearts and never permitted to marry, because you would have so inly grown as to conquer all karma and attain Deliverance centuries past. But you were needed at this time to bring forth the present work. This was indeed your greatest sacrifice to the Universal Consciousness. The Angel of Life held your hearts united in the embrace of pure love, while your physical selves were kept apart as a reminder of the task that was ahead of you. Now you are reunited, cosmically and legally, never to be separated again for eternal years. We leave you alone now in this starry environment, to wander as you please, to attune your minds to other streams of life, and to listen and learn while yearning for the eloquence of silence. We shall see you again three days hence, when the sun of your solar system is at the zenith, in our dwelling on Venus Way. Come and be prepared for a lovely surprise."

*　*　*

In the depths of meditation Marco and Leonora heard melodious voices incomprehensible to the mind but soothing and sweet to the thirsting soul. Then they directed their attention to the relationship between the physical ear and the mind of nature, and a voice was heard above the others, clear and understandable:

"Bold travelers, do not stand still. Arise and stroll the land. See God's estate in a blaze of light, while down under the Earth sleeps and the tide ebbs. Let the Spirit of God enter the mortal mind, therein to stay, to protect, to guide and to illumine. In the stillness of the mind man binds himself to the World Imperishable, is lifted into space and made deathless. Aye, you are as wise and strong as the forces that impel the celestial bodies to rotate and evolve. You cannot fail.

"Come now, ascend onto the summit of this towering indestructible mountain of condensed fire, by relying solely on your inner strength and breathe therefrom the rarefied air. Behold the starry cities and their citizens producing masterpieces of beauty free from the crave of gains and the feelings of personal glory, but only with the humble pride of perceiving God's Presence closer and ever closer."

103

From the apex of that lofty elevation, they saw a complex panorama of breath-taking splendor: vast garden-cities intersected by broad promenading thoroughfares and interspersed with living fountains and landscapes of indescribable beauty, edifices constructed of translucent and nondecaying material, the air dust free and crystal clear. They saw thoughtful and happy inhabitants in their prime of youth, none looked older than twenty-five, none younger than thirteen, according to our earthly standards. They were dressed in the fashions of every race and land, and of every age up to the present time and beyond. Who were they? Some had come directly from the Realms of the Spirit, they had bodies composed of condensed light, masculine and feminine forms, in couples, radiating the joy of life unmarred by human blight; others were the idealists who once had lived on Earth, dreaming dreams of higher living through the medium of literature, music, the arts, philosophy, science, and their allied disciplines, and realizing only a fraction thereof because of man's mental and emotional crudity. Here they move in an environment of their own creation, unobstructed by anyone and endowed with unlimited power of self-expression.

The matchless and sublime grandeur of the vista aroused Leonora's already elevated mind to a still higher level of perception whereby she retraced herself and Marco in one of the past embodiments that they had had here together in this Starry Heaven.

"I feel a warm and sweet familiarity in all that surrounds us here" — she said, and her heart began to swell with a joyous and humble repentance. "It feels like the homecoming of the prodigal child after a tempestuous wandering in strange and unfriendly lands. I could walk anywhere without losing my way." Then a heavenly radiance shone forth from her counttenance. "Let us enter the Silent Void and ask God to guide us."

They rose vertically with the speed of thought and stood in midair wherefrom they saw an S-shaped valley covered with glistening villas, each nestled within a luxuriant garden vivid with flowers as yet unknown to mankind. They saw parks of enchanting beauty and splendor, yielding a semitropical vegetation. There were winding ribbons of superb parkways paved with faultless lawns, public squares surrounded by buildings of palatial artistry, and airdromes suspended in midair for interplanetary communication and transportation. Looking westward they saw Astrapel, whose name in immense letters of light, was floating in the sky above the city in changing patterns that had the semblance of plane and solid geometry. Powerful telescopic instruments were placed everywhere on transparent pinnacles atop templelike structures for interstellar observation. They saw Spirit-forms of thousands of the youth from the planet Earth being taught astronomy by Liberated Master-Scientists, the discipline that appears to be the most important branch of scientific training for the future generations of earth.

"Astrapel is a city of mathematicians and astronomers" — Leonora explained — "and though it seems as if the master-masons had completed it only yesterday, it is actually more ancient than the pre-Neolithic culture, more ancient than the apparition of the first blade of grass in the land that would have been called ten thousand years later Babylon or Susa. From this City departed those who were released to Earth to become the Creators of the wheel and the numbers, the carriers of seeds, spores and bulbs for the process of forestation of the wasteland that was beginning to emerge from the ice age, the teachers of agriculture, the first drovers of domestic animals that were destined to play such a vital role on the evolutionary path of the helpless, inane and frantic human race. Master mathematicians were dispatched beneath the sea with specks of light that were to become fish, vegetation and vital organic minerals; and Master astronomers were also released to give to man the rudiments for interplanetary and interstellar training."

Southwest of Astrapel the City of Luxopolis came to sight. It was an assemblage of exotic Oriental temples, mostly Chinese, gorgeous and awe-inspiring. Leonora again explained this to be the temple-city of Quan Yin, the Lady master of Mercy of the brave Asiatic people, and She is the presiding cosmic leader preparing a bloodless revolution for the spiritual, intellectual and economic re-awakening of the yellow race. On its outskirts facing West Leonora saw a lovely pink villa. "There" — she said — "I abided in the far gone antiquity, during one of my starry embodiments, while being trained in the art of being an idealist. There too you came to visit me during the same span of time, for you also had an embodiment in this starry heaven but for other reasons than mine."

105

East of Astrapel lay a large body of water, similar to the Eastern Mediterranean. Inland, about a mile from the shoreline was a magnificent atheneum, whose columnated faculty buildings displayed the most refined architectural designs of classic China, Persia, Egypt and Greece. They were constructed of marble, onyx and alabaster and were rendered imperishable by the treatment of cosmic rays. At such a noble display of works of art, their wealth and mystical radiance, Marco's mind was also awakened to the knowledge of the events that followed:

* * *

They were looking at the University of Usarco, one of the highest centers of culture and knowledge of this lofty realm of divine living, and the Alma Mater of the various foci of learning that came into being throughout the historical ages on Earth: the school of Oratory in Athens, the Museum of Alexandria in Egypt, the Atheneum of Rome, the universities of Salerno, Padua, Paris, Belfast, Edinburgh, Cordoba, Boston and so forth, and the Florentine academies Della Crusca and Dei Lincei. There is not one college of higher learning on Earth that is not linked to or does not receive inner guidance from this Mother School of Usarco. But much is yet expected to come, and be accepted by these universities for expansion on the path of perfection.

Each of the various buildings was dedicated to a specific branch of learning which was indicated by its architectural design. The cylindrical structure surmounted by the semispherical dome, was the Hall of astronomy, the science of the infinite, upon which the true idealist reflects for inspiration. It is conclusive, therefore, that pure science and idealism are closely linked to one another. In fact, ninety percent of the Liberated Masters were scientists.

The next building was a perfect cube, the symbol of divine stability, encased in pillars of wrought gold and dedicated to the study of philosophy, the Science of the Soul, through which love, compassion, humility and brotherhood, are scientifically explained and understood, and scientifically applied. At the end of each academic year, the four pillars which symbolize the four aspects of man — body, mind, feeling and soul — emanate light for the equivalent of seven days, in the colors of pink, violet, golden-blue and white announcing to the starry dwellers and to the world of man that the wholeness of universal life has been raised one step higher on the path of cosmic evolution.

The Hall of Agriculture and applied sciences was pyramidal in shape, multifaced and multicolored. It meant that their findings were constantly and selflessly given to mankind and all the researchists who practice introspection. They saw an amphitheater where drama, music and public speaking were taught; and nearby was an immense gymnasium, used only for the cultivation of pure aesthetics of body form, free from the concept of competition.

The campus was intersected by lovely paths and smooth silky lawn, edged with incense-mingling flowers and shrubbery which required neither irrigation nor cultivation; they simply obeyed the visualization of the landscaping architect who directed the arrangement and growth from his office through electronic devices. Irrigation and pollination were effected by periodical showers of negative ions which acted simultaneously on both the roots and buds.

Marco and Leonora were now walking within the perimeter of the campus of the University. Had they made an effort to be seen by someone for guidance, they would have accelerated the rate of vibration of their body-forms. But they preferred not to be seen; they wanted to see and relive the Akashic Record of the age of their association with the activity of this great university.

They paused for meditation! It was Marco who, while still in samadhi, broke the silence: "What is this? O tingling ecstacy, so joyful and yet so anguishing, so mysterious and so revealing. The base of my spine is on fire, and a fiery tongue of gold is moving and enveloping my sexual center. A thrilling vibration is spreading throughout my body, my spine is all aglow, my solar plexus is pulsating faster, a warm and gentle wave is investing my throat from within and from without. And now the top of my head throbs faster and faster. The body-temple is on fire, and yours too, my sweetheart; I feel a rapturous bliss. What is the meaning of all this? And a Voice answered:

"Your body-temples have been invested by the fire of purification. The Christ-light of knowledge and revelation cannot operate in a consciousness clogged by the dross of limitation and mortal thoughts. Meditation sweeps out the unwanted accumulation of unbelief and belittling, the mind becomes buoyant and the perceptive faculty keen. The intangible and yet all-powerful atomic forces of the human organism are drawn centripetally to the Speck of Light that governs life in form. At this stage man becomes all-knowing. And now behold!"

As with a motion-picture projector the Akashic Records began to unroll on a living screen. It showed Marco whose name was Kuntela Usarco, frequenting this university which was called 'Stel'; he majored with honor in pure mathematics and cosmic physics. Following the day of graduation he was appointed as a member of the faculty staff; later deanship was conferred upon him. It was at this time that he developed a method of teaching which aimed at self-discovery while listening to the professor or studying the lesson from a book. The students applying this method were able to achieve the highest grades in every subject. Because of his utter devotion to counseling, guiding, teaching and directing both the faculty staff and the student body, Marco caused all the residue of petty compromises and mental deviations to be dissolved both within himself and everyone else, and thus he was catapulted to the apex of a flawless idealism. Idealism leads to selflessness. To the selfless one all honors are bestowed. The name of the university was changed from Stel to Usarco in a plenary assemblage of the starry citizens. On the day of the official inauguration the amphitheater of the University was filled with spectators eager to witness the ceremony. Presiding over the momentous event was the ancient Cosmic Being Agricola, Master of the earthsoil. He spoke thus:

"It is a divine usage, both in heaven and on earth, to honor worthy streams of life; not for their sake for, as a rule, they are masters of humility, but for those who, being on the upward path, need to witness such public recognitions so that they may replenish themselves with unfaltering courage and godlike ambition.

"The Usarco Age of this focus of higher learning is about to begin. For the outgoing dean Master Tucanus this is also a day whereby a more scintillating crown will be set upon his head. The Cosmic Assembly of the Perfect Ones have promoted him Master Contemplator and active ruler of a system of stars. Kuntela Usarco will succeed him by virtue of many a deed, performed in a spirit of humility and altruism that dwells on the plateau of the highest wisdom and discrimination. The Usarco pattern of teaching shall take root, and the undecaying fruit of this invisible tree shall be given freely to both earthly and starry institutes that are prepared to receive it. And whoever welcomes it and applies it will experience a levitating power in the field of dynamic idealism that will crush to dust and scatter all the plotting forces of negativity." As the spectators stood silently radiating their overwhelming approval, Usarco was called upon to speak:

"The Usarco Age means that my work will increase by leaps and bounds. To work is a dynamic gift, a privilege of the gods. What a distinguished and enduring honor has been bestowed upon me. It feels like a boon, a propelling force that will catapult me, sooner than expected, to absolute liberty. And with a joy that knows no bounds I shall bend my will in service to life and man.

"It is a mathematical law that energy wisely spent shall, eventually, return to its source multiplied ad infinitum. Hence I will think, plan, act and meditate free from anxiety, well-aware of God as my sole thinker, planner, doer and enjoyer of all my accomplishments. Unto HIM I surrender this self of me, with a trustful heart, mind alert, and limbs supple and ready. This is the noble path."

Following this eventful ceremony the living screen showed an acceleration of activity. New edifices were raised, services streamlined, requirements for admission made more severe, and a rigorous discriminate selection was practiced towards those who aspired to professorship. The dignity of teaching was duly consecrated as a memento to the pseudo-teachers of earth who prostitute their intellect for volatile and spurious fame and pecuniary reward. The professors' desire for greater knowledge received a fresher impetus because they made constant and effective appeals to the Liberated Masters for inspiration, teaching and guidance.

* * *

Now the screen brought the above episode to its close and turned to the enchanting pink villa. At the sight of the lovely garden and the seven marble steps leading to the entrance a warm feeling pervaded the body-forms of Marco and Leonora. With a stroke of the will held in the iron grip of uncompromising determination, and aided by the boon of Grace they passed through the screen and entered into the living reality of the episode. Entering the house they saw again the various rooms in delicate shades of pink, with the exception of the study, which had been especially decorated in green and gold, the colors so much loved by Usarco. They touched everything with a cogent urge and yet in a dreamlike and romantic attitude. The furniture, tapestry and draperies had the cleanliness and freshness of being new; for here nothing soils or ages. An unwanted object may be made to disappear and merge into the universal substance by the power of thought of its creator and rightful owner. They remembered the days of starry happiness they had enjoyed together in these divine surroundings, away from faculty cares and responsibilities. Entering the study they picked up a book lying on the table and opening it read:

"How often does man realize that all his accomplishments are the resultant of a borrowed energy and substance? Very seldom. How often, in performing his duties, does man acknowledge the Presence of an Intangible Essence directing his mind, senses and limbs? Again, very seldom. Does he know that he cannot even carry himself or hold a tiny straw on the palm of his hand? No, he absolutely does not! Then is not this man's worst pitfall and mark of ignorance, the cause of his suffering and limitation? Yes, it is! And what is man's greatest asset? It is the knowledge that no power of any kind is his own. It is the Ever-present Spirit of God who works in the world of form through man's mind, senses and muscles. The acceptance of this truth leads man to immortality!

"One of the differences between a Liberated Master and a human being is that the former never faces a situation without calling ahead of time the intervention of His Immortal Essence, while the poor mortal, stupefied by his ego, has to stumble several times, (often too late) before he cries for mercy."

They closed the book and fell on their knees in humility and gratitude. And being fully aware that all things are possible in God, they transmuted themselves into Luxana and Usarco, two beings of love: young, perfect and sinless. They embraced and kissed each other in a rapture of cosmic joy. At times they felt to dissolve into each other's pulsating essence, losing body, ego, perceptive faculty, personality and individuality; each free in the other, both in God, and feeling the inexplicable exhilaration of such a stupendous and indescribable mergence. Then they heard their Guardian Angel whispering admonitions and responsibilities, warning them — now sweetly and now sternly — that the law of mercy does not apply to the student on the Path that transgresses the principles of ethics. Only the uneducated deserves mercy and compassion, for they do not know the power of thought vibration and radiation.

*　*　*

Luxana and Usarco now levitated their forms to the University grounds, and passing through the outer gate they meditated as in the cosmic past. Enchained to each other like two living links, index finger and thumb of one hand touching the corresponding toe, and index finger and thumb of the other touching the toe of his companion, the right arm of one entwining the left arm of the other, thus locking the universal energy within the body, and then setting it in motion; the motion that propels man to noble deeds. Raised above the concept of time and space, Usarco re-enacted and lived in a timeless flash his ancient activities and duties performed in a day as university dean. He felt the far-reaching powers that were at work within his being, smoothing difficulties and solving problems as they began to be sensed. The keen awareness of the All-knowing Mind in which he continually bathed himself, gave him the wisdom to make precise and immediate decisions, and thus influence, without compulsion, every member of the staff in making the required move for perfect results. He had cultivated through unending years of patience the seed of inner leadership, and now that he was gleaning the effects, he wanted to give it unlimited sway.

As he sat in the Hall of the Elite listening to the Liberated Masters delivering lessons reserved for the teaching staff, he was invested with their powerful radiation which he transmuted into instantaneous knowledge and conveyed it with originality and freshness to those about him. Often he heard the voice within his heart speaking: "My son, be my harbinger. Go! Know that I think for thee, for thee I create, through thee I evolve My Law. Thee I pervade through and through."

*　*　*

111

In this Civitas Dei, a veritable center of culture in its broadest aspect, the university dean, in collaboration with both the faculty and the administrative staff, and with the contribution of the leaders from the student body, has a threefold responsibility: cultural, spiritual and governmental. Politics and clergy being nonexistent, the institute of marriage, as understood on earth, is unknown. Each celestial intelligence may search for its twin flame, or it may not; and having found each other, they live together in obedience to the unwritten law that governs this matter. Disobedience means self-annihilation, but no one disobeys. Their union is filed in the archives of the university for the sake of statistical data only. Likewise for the births, as well as cultural, artistic and scientific achievements. Special records are kept for those who are elevated to higher realms and those who are sent to Earth for special missions. There are no compulsory laws, hence no judiciary institutes, nor jails or police; there are no taxes or currency, and no institutions of political rulers as understood on Earth. There is however a Body of Intelligences devoted to the study and analyzation of Cosmic Jurisprudence. It is presided over by a Liberated Master who has been trained by the Legal Intelligences associated with the Cosmic Assembly of the Perfect Ones. A different Master presides over each session. Whatever they agree upon that reflects a higher and closer understanding of God, is entered in the Akashic Records and, by a process of cosmic symbiosis, reaches throughout all creation and made to filter into the minds of the people of Earth.

This City-State of God has no hospitals and consequently no medical doctors who have to dedicate their lives, not to constructive and evolutive work per se, but to patching up decrepid and crumbling human organisms. There is however a body of Researchists who carry out — ideally — experiments on the human body for the benefit of the receptive scientists of earth. Often a Master researchist descends to earth to direct the mind and hands of a surgeon engaged in a delicate operation. With success achieved He withdraws. Similary with the invention of new surgical instruments and discovery of new drugs.

Those who feel inly qualified to run for the few public offices — Park Commissioner, Art Exhibition Commissioner, Director of the Board of Sciences, President of the Philosophical Society, and their respective aides — are elected by the method of universal suffrage in its absolute sense. A bulletin showing, in a very terse manner, the degree of culture, attitude, and the type of public service each applicant is qualified to render is printed and released by the Board of Public Affairs attached to the University. The report is then sent to every starry citizen. That is all! No one sponsors anybody. There are no committees, no speeches, no music, no dinners, no bribing and no cajoling. The citizen, irrespective of age, consults the Akashic Records which are presented to him, devoid of comments and lean in literary style. Then he casts his vote uninfluenced by anyone. Such is the pattern of public life in this ideal land.

This system of screening and consultation, carried out in the most impersonal manner, was conducive to producing a government that was well-geared and precise in all its functions and duties; and contributed to the creating of intellectual giants. Actually it is the citizen who, assisted by impartial boards, possesses the key to sound government. When the citizen, through meditation, becomes keenly discriminative, he does not need to be told what to do, nor is he apt to be influenced by political schemers. He is so public spirited that his interest in collective rulership is as great as that of ruling efficiently his own household.

* * *

Walking on public thoroughfares, where sidewalks and buildings looked as clean and new as if the city had just been built, Marco and Leonora saw the equivalent of stores and shops as conceived by the man of Earth. Here they were enormous art galleries, filled with original masterpieces of painting and sculpture, furniture, glassware, china and silverware, tapestry, fabrics, books, musical instruments, laboratory equipment, and so forth, all tastefully displayed and unattended by sales-people. The starry inhabitants may select whatever they require according to their desire, comfort and artistic sensitivity, in exchange for what they may have to offer from their own workshops. Values are estimated with obvious generosity in favor of the collectivity. No imposition from outside is seen or felt. Objects that are no longer needed in a house or office are returned to one of these galleries and re-displayed. And since nothing ages nothing is marred or appears to have been used. Merchandise may be removed from public display but only by the producing craftsman

113

who will then re-manipulate the material for new works of art. New wares arrive continually from the various studios and laboratories of artists, writers, scientists and technicians, who work only for the sake of self-expression. They never engage themselves in producing a replica of any masterpiece, for this is considered spiritual stagnation; nor do they feel attached to their works. Whatever they create is immediately dispatched to the galleries and forgotten. Their creative power is so advanced that as a work of art reaches completion, a new and greater idea unfolds and takes shape instantly. There are metallurgical plants where electronic devices are used for metalworking.

All objects, large or small, from a letter on, are delivered through underground conduits, electronically operated, or through the system of tele-transportation. Sewerage systems, street cleaning or garbage collection are unknown. All actions are free from the pain which is associated with work done for profit or reward. Here one serves and pleases God in being engaged in constructive endeavours for the joy and welfare of his fellow man. This is the work, the profit and the reward.

❊   ❊   ❊

Luxana and Usarco now re-transmuted into the twentieth century disciples Marco and Leonora traveling through the Starry Heaven of the Idealists; body-forms and perceptive faculties gathering deeper and deeper conviction of the indestructible reality of life, of the care of God for all Its children, and of the astounding nobility of man and his limitless potentialities for mental and spiritual growth on the staggering and trackless avenues of infinitude.

They heard the call of Elos and Beata, sweet, delicate and compelling. They levitated themselves to Venus Way and entered the lovely mansion, where they were warmly welcomed by their host and hostess. Mingling with the celestial guests they were recognized by many from other stars and planets, and congratulated for being the cause of the re-enactment of the sublime episode — the Ascension of Elos — which took place thousands of year ago.

The drawing room in which the guests were assembled, was extremely large and palatial. The walls and ceiling were covered with square tiles of dull apple green veined with the darker

114

shade of olive leaf. Each tile emanated its own light which could be softened or brightened according to the host's desire or requirement. Strips of leatherlike material were set between the tiles with the words OM SUM I AM embossed on them in gold. The floor was carpeted wall-to-wall with a thick fabric that had the texture of raw silk, in the color of olive leaf asymetrically streaked with rose pink. One end of the room was elegantly furnished as a study, while the rest was arranged for entertaining. Dainty baskets of flowers that never wilted and in a myriad of colors were placed everywhere. A musical instrument, the size and shape of a grand piano, occupied one corner of the room. It was electronically operated and could produce a single instrument, or several thousand of the same type, or a large orchestra, by simply obeying the inspiration, impulses, moods and desires of the player. There was also a television apparatus, the size of an ordinary book for interstellar receiving and transmitting.

The decor of the dining room was pink. Walls, floor and ceiling were covered with a one-tone fabric of different textures. Furniture, linen, draperies, china and silverware were all in various shades of pink. The house had no kitchen, for cooking was unnecessary. All food made of luminous substance and devoid of fibrous matter, was precipitated directly from the universal reservoir of life.

The master bedroom was decorated in soft shades of violet. Because the inhabitants here have no need of rest, beds are unknown. They use relaxation chairs designed to hold the spinal column erect and the legs in a horizontal position. Such a posture is conducive to meditation, inspiration and creative work.

Here the bathroom becomes a chamber dedicated to the ritual of spiritual purification. It is only a ritual and a formality for these noble beings, although it had, for Marco and Leonora, a powerfully exhilarating effect. As one enters, the interior is transformed into a mass of incandescent purple fire blending with water sprays which gush forth from innumerable orifices located in the walls, ceiling and floor. This shower of fire and water, which leaves one unwet, is followed by a shower of white light, symbolizing the reintegrated purity, buoyancy of eternal youth and mental attunement with the Universal Consciousness. In the human body such a ritual opens wide the ideal conduit between the genital organs and the pituitary gland causing intermittent illumination which in turn produces impulses of physical love of the most exalted nature of nobility and sacredness. And if this impulse is well restrained by a capable and disciplined mind, it imparts handsomeness to the human body, it smooths wrinkles from the face and gives luster to the eyes, it brings forth and heightens constructive traits: love of life, forgiveness, generosity and intense yearning for service to man, society and God; it leads to mind expansion of the most exalted order to merge finally into creativity and prophetic wisdom.

An open patio surrounded the house, and the lawn on every side was bordered by a living hedge of young cypress trees. Miniature fountains, shrubbery and a profusion of brilliantly hued flowers were interspersed throughout the grounds. At the rear of the mansion, hidden by slender fir trees, was the Silentium or chamber of silence and meditation. It was sound-proof and endowed with the power of making invisible all who entered. It was used only on occasions of universal emergency affecting steps to be taken by the Cosmic Assembly of the Perfect Ones in dealing with the destiny of a star, a planet or the Earth and its inhabitants. Like an ideal democratic institution the Perfect Ones need the support of the starry population and their concentrated energy assembled during meditation. The name THE KUMARAS was carved on the door of the silentium as a dedication to the ten great sage-brothers who, in the antiquity of individualized life, instituted the act of meditation as the most important method to achieve Deliverance.

* * *

As Marco and Leonora returned to the drawing room, they found Elos and Beata utterly absorbed in divine contemplation and surrounded by a wall of pulsating light which could not be pierced by either sound or thought projection. A vibration of bliss imbued the atmosphere. Faces of peerless beauty were seen appearing and disappearing, beings with the All-seeing Eye on their foreheads, others robed in garments of fire, and winged beings of matchless handsomeness in toga candida. A seraphic symphony of silence was being played softly by an unseen orchestra.

They observed the ceiling slowly beginning to vanish as if by the increase of its luminosity, and the walls also commenced to fade away. The room now emptied of all furnishings was raised by an invisible force, and the floor changed into an immense platform which was now seen as if suspended in midair. Surrounded by chairs, a wide oblong table with a highly polished surface of golden onyx veined with antique green and white, in the motif of flames, appeared from the unseen. A crystal brazier, emanating unconsuming and smokeless purple-white fire, formed at the center of the table. The starry sky, altered to a darker shade of green jade and studded with rose-quartz luminaries, was their celestial canopy. The symphony of Triumph, superseding the symphony of Silence, swelled to heights of majesty and sublimity. Heavenly guests began to appear, and as each one arrived, the radiance of the surroundings became brighter and ever brighter. Soon all was enveloped in a world of highly shivering dazzling light as if in the heart of the sun.

As everyone took his assigned seat, a winged being in a garment of soft violet hue, symbol of protection, appeared behind each chair. Beata and Elos occupied the two seats at the center of the table, the winged beings at their back wore robes of white and were armed with flaming swords of white fire. These were the same Angelic Beings that had stood behind Master Jesus on the Hill of Bethany, at the hour of His Ascension. Marco and Leonora sat opposite Elos and Beata; the Lord Maha Chohan graced one end of the table and Agricola the other. Flora sat next to Leonora, and the Liberated Master-Teacher by the side of Marco. Master Jesus was contiguous to Beata and Mary His Twin Flame by the side of Elos. They saw Melchizedek, Moses, Krishna, Homer, Dante and Beatrice, Gautama the Buddha and Yashodara, Solomon, the Emperor Justinian, Socrates, Virgil, Milton, Mahatma Gandhi, Ramakrishna and Sarada Devi, the Venetian Master, Leonardo da Vinci and Mona Lisa, Galileo Galilei, Joan D'Arc and Louis de Conte, Martin Luther, John Huss, Pythagoras and Teano, George Washington, Abraham Lincoln, and in their finer bodies General Douglas McArthur, Herbert Hoover, Dwight Eisenhower, and many other Liberated Masters and Splendor-beings, all in the attire of the land and epoch of their last embodiment. There were present seventy great masters endowed with eternal life.

All was enshrouded in silence; each prince of light and celestial guest now projected a luminous beam from his forehead towards Elos who began to slowly rise until He stood high above, his feet on the converging point of the seventy luminances. They all uttered the Sacred Word OM, invoking God to overshadow and sustain them in the completion of this sublime event. Beata now began to ascend by virtue of her own power and came close to Her beloved companion.

Each beam of light was of a different hue and degree of intensity due to the fact that each Master has dominion over a specific action of the Cosmic Law. Justinian, Solomon and Agricola emanated blue and gold, the Maha Chohan gold and green, Master Jesus white, gold and brilliant blue, and Mary of Nazareth pink. Leonora and Marco made also their modest contribution by virtue of the Law of Grace aided by the greatly accelerated vibration of the surroundings. Leonora's was pink and Marco's gold and green.

Amidst this stupendous spectacle of power and glory, multicolored sparkles, flashing intermittently from the environing meadows and hillside, began to be seen; they were the starry dwellers. For many miles in every direction this eager crowd of Master-spectators gathered to witness the greatest and holiest episode in man's life — the Ascension — which has to be repeated in the future ages as many times as there are human beings, until the Earth itself, made also pure and holy by man's thoughts and conduct, is transferred to a higher orbit. From above, legions of the Angelic Host and Shining Ones were seen gliding downward towards the stage of this cosmic drama of life.

Now one after another the heavenly guests commenced to withdraw their flaming beams, letting Elos stand on his own light. Followed by Beata, He continued ascending steadily and majestically, and presently his cosmic color — blue and gold, symbolizing perseverance and wisdom — appeared. Ceasing his ascent, He gazed downward in the attitude of surveying his life in this starry land, instructing the two guests from the planet Earth to behold in a detached manner all strivings and accomplishments. As He stretched forth his arms to bless the vast assemblage beneath, they all answered in one mighty utterance: OM I AM LIGHT EVERLASTING! He then intoned:

"To the rim of Thy Dazzling Vessel of Life Immortal I cling, O Father-God OM.

"Through obedience, perseverance and service, I have found refuge in Thy Heart of Light. I AM about to enter, O Lord, into the vast ocean of Universal Oneness. Absorb me into Thyself, O Father, and hold me therein for eternal years.

"I salute Thee, My All-wise Teacher and Dispenser of life and bliss. Thou art my Law, my Essence, My Presence and my All in All!"

Slowly Elos and Beata resumed their rise into higher empyreal realms, leaving behind streams of light and fire in their individual colors. As the Music of the Spheres played the Symphony of Life Eternal, seven Master-contemplators were seen descending, escorted by three hundred forty-three Splendor-beings clothed in scintillating garments. They formed a spiraling cone ablaze with the colors of the solar spectrum, and having encompassed the ascending couple all disappeared.

* * *

Agricola, who had been Elos' Master-Teacher, informed the assembled guests that the newly liberated couple would return anon for an act of grace towards the guests from the planet Earth. In the interim Marco and Leonora were privileged to be near their Liberated Master-Teacher who radiated the eternal youth, wisdom and handsomeness of the immortal ones. "I am pleased with your attainment thus far" —He said — "but it must be protected through continual awareness. It is a possession more precious than the most costly jewel, more deserving to cultivate and expand than the highest human ideals, for it leads to the Source of Wisdom." Other Masters congratulated them also; then they met the Maha Clohan. He took Leonora aside and spoke to her softly of things of inner nature, of things intimate and transcendental. To Marco He related in a spirit of admonition one of his blunders typical of youth, a solo flight executed over the Swiss Alps.

"As a flying cadet" — the Master explained — "you disobeyed your instructor's orders by rising 5000 feet above your assignment of 17,000 and overstayed your allotted thirty minutes. In spite of these violations you incurred no military punishment. In addition you had committed several other flying errors, which were not noticed because We clouded the atmosphere above the Cameri's airdrome, hiding your plane from the ground observatory. Your errors were grave enough to take you out of the physical body, thus Our intervention became imperative, for you had to be protected for the mission that was ahead of you.

"If the youth of the world knew how often We shield them from their innumerable blunders, caused by their ignorance, restlessness, stupidity and vanity, they would fall on their knees in submission to their parents, teachers, elders and to God. And I dare say that without this Invisible Hand of protection, seventy-five per cent of the young people would not reach adulthood. Your daring attitude in physical flights, stressing the aerodynamic characteristics of the plane beyond its capacity, was a sign of inner restlessness, heavily tinged with ignorance. You were a wandering disciple of the spirit in frantic search of the path, and flying was your only escape.

"We have bestowed upon you both the honor of discipleship in Our Retreat of the Swiss Alps, of which I am in charge. Henceforth you are brother and sister of the Green Toga, whose field of action is Central Europe and the Western Mediterranean. You are worthy of this endowment."

Then Master Agricola conversed with Marco and Leonora, and in the course of the conversation, they learned of all the grace and the heavenly gifts that were released to ancient Rome at the dawn of her birth: courage, initiative, a superior intelligence and the knowledge of a true democratic government in opposition and as a corrective example to the political disorder that stemmed from the chauvinistic supremacy of the individual in which the Greek world was wallowing. The Romans began well, and their first act of universalism is to be found in the concept of citizenship to be extended to the non-Romans. This was to be the root of the Empire of Light and the Commonwealth of all nations. This is the only constructive idea that they transmitted to the future generations. And it is still an idea waiting for unfoldment and fulfillment. The Romans then fell into the grip of superstition, greed and fear. "Because of such a mortal deviation" — Master Agricola explained — "the Romans turned out to be the most despicable warmongers of the ancient world. They invaded many lands and for no justifiable reason, subjugated their inhabitants, seized their wealth and drove their citizens into abject slavery. No other country, earlier or later, practiced slavery in such a savage manner; it was viler than the slavery of the sub-civilized Babylonians, more repulsive than the practice of vivisection upon human beings in the museum of Alexandria of Egypt. The institution of the gladiatorial games, where educated captives and criminals alike were forced into combat of wholesale murder for the delight of both plebeians and patricians, of rulers, literati,

120

preachers of morality and the seething masses, show to what state of degeneracy the Romans had fallen. By comparison Homo Neanderthalensis was a god. The Romans made a profession of denying promises, scraping treaties, and insulting and manhandling other heads of state. Fear and a feeling of superiority complex breed arrogance, arrogance leads to criminal irresponsibility, to murder. Prior to the rising of Julius Caesar many a city was plundered and the people slaughtered of which Carthage is to be remembered above all others. In vain our disciple Scipio Nasica — who happened to be you Marco — after pointing out over and again before the corrupt Roman Senate, the importance of a prosperous Carthage to the welfare of the Western World, cried aloud 'Carthage must stand'; but the suicidal forces of degradation prevailed and Cato's curse 'Delenda est Carthago' — Carthage must be destroyed — became a fact. Had the great city and her noble citizens been allowed to live and prosper, or forced to inactivity by the tools of competitive fair trade over the land and over the sea, they would have avoided the tyranny of the Empire and the ineptitude of the emperors, the obscurantism of the Middle Ages, the abuses and corruption of the Papacy, the persecution of the innocent and free thinkers, the incongruous and un-'Holy Crusades', the disease, famine and squalid poverty of the masses, and all the legalized thievery and mob coercion that have festered within the human society for unending centuries. The United States of Europe, the least on the path of a nobler world, would have been a fact ages ago.

"Julius Caesar, an initiate of the Etruscan School of Light, exalted and vilified by false historians and political meddlers, was the first Roman ruler who wanted to revamp in an organic manner the political doctrine of the Republic on the basis of the Pythagorean teaching. He was the re-embodiment of King Asoka who two centuries earlier had ruled India in light and justice while the Romans were taking delight in the gory spectacles of the arena. We had entrusted him to create an office for diplomatic intercourse whereby the native representatives of the conquered provinces would have been allowed to approach him in a spirit of mutual equality and absolute freedom, for political, cultural and economic discussions. Following this initial achievement Caesar would have suggested the formation of a universal body for permanent peace on earth. But his closest collaborators,

121

impervious to light, crude, greedy and fearful of losing prestige and wealth could not accept his recommendations; hence the many fratricidal wars, the persistent and vindictive antagonism of both friends and relatives, the waste of wealth and the debilitation of the state. To avoid anarchy, ruling by decree became imperative; plotting and assassination were the result.

"As an initiate Julius Caesar could not avail himself of a police escort; he had to walk to the office as an ordinary citizen; he knew with uncanny precision what the state of the Republic was, its virtues and its vices, and how to properly handle both for constructive expansion; and he knew also how the growing discontent of the political vampires towards him was changing into hatred for a sanguinary deed. When he saw the conspirators approaching him for the kill, he faced them unafraid but reproachfully. The Republic already prostrated to inaction but still breathing and endowed with the power of self-regeneration, felt now the deadly thrust of the parricidal dagger. Julius Caesar forgave all, covered his head with the green toga and passed away immediately, untouched by physical pain.

"With Caesar's departure, the Etruscan School of Light — heir to the Egyptian spiritual greatness — was transferred to the Swiss Alps with the same laws, codes, statutes and rules. The dynamic urge of the evolutive instinct of every sane man became static first, then went into hibernation. From that time to the present day, the land of the Romans has been unworthy to sustain a focus of light. It has never had a generation going through life without having seen, at least once, the clash of war weapons. It has persecuted, killed and burned at the stake many a messenger from on High, harbingers of liberty and peace. It became the battleground of Europe and the world. Great Masters in every branch of learning have taken embodiment there, to awaken the masses to a role of leadership for international brotherhood, but they have been unheeded. Even today, in many respects and in the field of politics and international trade, the heirs of the Roman world fall behind the average of the rest of Europe; hence the internal convulsion and economic lag."

The tolling of far away bells was heard; seven ponderous strokes clear and commanding. Then silence, followed by the echo knelling seven times rhythmically. The star-strewn sky

122

was invaded by beams of light that pierced the atmosphere with dazzling brilliancy. Oblivious to both the surroundings and the circumstances which had elevated them to the present level of consciousness, Marco and Leonora felt a thrilling vibration pass through their spirit-forms; they retired into the chamber of the soul and said: "We are ready!" A voice of authority and loving reproach spoke:

"Usarco, Usarco, hasten thy way! Retrace yourself to your princely ancestry in behavior and wisdom. From the apex of spiritual aristocracy you have descended valleyward to a plane of life slightly higher than mediocrity. It is enough. Slay all residue of earthly inhibitions, slay such unbecoming modesty. Yield, yield, yield, to the magnetic pull of thy star of triumph, and let thy starry radiance unfold and conquer in a starry manner.

"Behold these surroundings; they are your Empire of Light. It is the pattern of what is expected of you on earth. The many millions of streams of life herewith assembled are the counterpart of a similar amount of anxious and noble souls on earth awaiting their divinely appointed leader. Who are these seventy Masters and princes of Light? They constitute your executive force at the service of God for the triumph of man over the nagging and unrelenting powers of negativity, limitation and disease. For though fluid wealth and physical comfort are on the increase the gap between those who have and those who have-not has widened immensely. Bewilderment, inner turmoil, crime, civil disobedience, rioting, debauchery, pollution of the mind and body, international hatred and other forms of suicidal attitudes have also increased, parabolically. Why? This you will discuss with your Staff for them to convey the answer to both the rebellious and the receptive ones. You have learned, O disciple-teacher, how flimsy actually is the line of separation between the law-abiding ones and those who deny the law, the saint and the sinner, and life and death. They all stand on a precarious and pseudo state of equilibrium. A slight thrust and they will fall into each other's arms and together praise God in a spirit of cosmic brotherhood. This *thrust* you shall provide.

"The hour is close at hand; men want to know. Those who have experienced mind expansion through the seeming easy

123

path of drugs, return disappointed but undefeated in their urge for inner revelation. They know that there is a Way. And the key to this Way is the acceptance of the existence of the Liberated Masters, their overshadowing presence behind every man engaged in constructive endeavours, their irrefutable tangibility amongst the striving humanity. All truths uttered by men are inspired by these selfless Beings standing near them. No man in the flesh can ever pronounce worthwhile statements out of his own personality, because no man is ever capable of freeing himself entirely from likes and dislikes, ego pressure and mental reservations. Even in the most ideal conditions and surroundings, even when the Buddhi truly guides, there is need of a Liberated Master to give consistency and driving power to man's thought and plan. But only he who seeks within, he who aims at self-discovery, can ever hope to feel the guiding hand of his own Liberated Master-Teacher, and to perceive, with mathematical precision, the nature of the ego with its lurking vices and cheaply boasted virtues. This leads to the statement of truth that no man can ever lift a tiny straw out of his own power.

"With such a conviction set granitically in the mind of man intuitive power begins to dawn. And what is intuitive power? It is a process of cosmic osmosis whereby the interstices of the perceptive faculty vacuumized by the introspective labor are filled with the knowledge of the Beyond unto a progressive and higher saturation. Now the aura around the head of man — a mechanism not made by human hands, unfailing and ever perfect — held inactive since the fall, reassumes, at is were, its astounding mission of receiving, recording and transmitting. It creates its own power, and adjusts itself to all wave lengths throughout the infinite spaces. Its field of operation, whereby man becomes conscious of his immortality and cosmic greatness, is contained in the ideal triangle or Holy Tabernacle, formed by joining the center of the head, the center of the heart and the root of the nose.

"With this mechanism well in hand no one will ever cheat or lie, or have fear, or do anything that will cause disturbance to the cosmic equilibrium; nor does he ever allow others to disturb him in any way. The resurrected man feels now the exhilaration of this undreamed of achievement and proceeds with greater alacrity to higher conquests and deeper seeking, accepting humbly whatever seeming punishment or impediments that he encounters. The student-painter of the Renaissance suffered unending humiliation at the hands of his master, simply to learn the technique of color and perspective; the creative genius had to be developed through the discipline of finding and applying the vibrating essence of the Ideal Triangle.

"The unusual analytical power displayed by the great mathematicians, their transcendent ability to draw new principles and new laws, which have remained unchallenged throughout the ages, came to them through the Knowledge of the Self and the assistance of the Liberated Masters. Their extraordinary intellectual gifts were a release and a dispensation from on High. On the triangular screen of the Holy Tabernacle they saw the wheel and the peg, the lever and the circle, the tridimentional nature of space, the parallax, the equation, the logarithm and the trigonometrical calculation. They were great beings of faith and iron discipline who, having perceived the inanity of their highest intellectual reasoning and the impossibility of trusting the human mind, felt the need to interrogate the Supreme Source of Knowledge.

"Usarco, Usarco, arise and behold!"

* * *

The radiant atmosphere of the surrounding countryside darkened as if a lingering sunset would take place. The sky behind the fringe of slender fir trees on the mountainside appeared tinted with prismatic colors of fire, now pale and soft, now vibrant and intense. As it grew darker, they saw first a myriad of brilliant stars and then a moonlike luminosity produced by concentric bands of light. Amidst this silent tournament of light, Elos and Beata reappeared and, followed by their celestial guests, walked on a winding path between majestic oak trees towards a large and tranquil pond fed by the falling waters of a mountain brook. The air was impregnated with a delicate fragrance of jasmine.

As they reached the lacustrine gem, Marco and Leonora felt that another precious jewel was about to be added to their treasure of inner experiences. Elos and Beata walked on the starlit waters towards the center of the pond, while the guests disposed themselves along its flowering banks, and the starry

125

crowd stood suspended in midair, forming a vast amphitheater. All sounds ceased; the misty liquid swirl from the falls solidified into an immense drapery of glistening filigree. It was an opportune moment for Marco and Leonora to summon the Akashic Records. In a dimensionless time unit, with the tape running at jet speed, they saw themselves on the screen of life, entering the womb of the mother many times, many times born in a variety of races, countries, families and environments; going through childhood, now in harassment and want and now in comfort and love. Working, studying, probing and striving, many times ending in utter failure, and many times in what would seem enduring success; belittled often and often honored.

To an uncritical mind endowed with an untrained eye with a narrow visual arc, man's existence might appear as a prosaic, shattering, aimless and perpetual recurrence of Sisyphean labor; a nerve-racking, maddening and useless meniality, ending nowhere. But this is not true, man was born as a god at the *beginning,* and through disobedience and misuse of light and energy descended to the state of quasi-animality. And through mercy and divine dispensation he was allowed to return home by a series of slow and progressive tests imbibed with love and directed by the Immortal Brothers called Liberated Master-Teachers. Marco and Leonora had already passed a long series of these tests. They saw themselves being honored by many a Conqueror of life and death serving Them with distinction beyond the mere call of duty. Rama, Krishna, Zoroaster, Gautama the Buddhi, and Master Jesus, had them as faithful and dynamic disciples. They saw themselves as master-teachers and directors of many foci of light in every continent and in every historical age, and also in the long-forgotten civilizations of Lemuria and Atlantis.

In the ancient of time, long before the dawn of Babylon, thousands of years before the apparition of the so-called "ape-man", there were lands on earth highly civilized, where the law of ethics was carved in the hearts of men rather than written in codes. The most advanced scientific exploits of today were known then and more, and often brought into manifestation through the practice of introspection and the awakening of the sexual center whereby the pulsating energy rose through the conduit leading to the pineal gland. This was the source of inspiration, illumination and creativity. Marco and Leonora saw themselves visiting foci of light in Central Africa meeting great initiates and dark-skinned emissaries of the Great White Brotherhood. The people were versed in philosophy, science and fine arts, the finest of which was the pursuance of the science of peace which opens the gate for the knowledge of God. They saw no temples of stone and no priests but human bodies which had the appearance of living temples filled with the ever-enduring spirit of Perfection and Beauty.

* * *

As the screen of life ceased to run they found themselves at the edge of the pond facing Elos and Beata. Heavenly guests who had just arrived disposed themselves on the rocks by the stilled cascade, their winged feet barely touching the ground. Elos spoke:

"I have taken the liberty of re-enacting, as it were, this panorama of terrestrial beauty and charm for the benefit of our guests from the planet Earth. It is mankind that we want to raise to a higher status of life, not ourselves. May they be able to re-enact there, by virtue of the same power and intelligence, panoramas of starry beauty for the edification of man.

"We that dwell in the Realm of everlasting perfection, though in process of ever greater unfoldment, shall never cease to labour to draw men away from their earthly limitations and life of duality.

"The day of blessedness is fast approaching when the minds of men shall no longer rely on the physical sight and the mortal mind for observation and knowledge, when man's energy and intelligence shall no longer be directed to produce merchandise for self-poisoning: fear, doubt, envy, poverty, crime, disease, senility and death; when men shall set ablaze the inmost shrine of their hearts to express beauty, truth and love in a continual flow; when the vibrating and pulsating energy within will be felt beyond all doubt. Blessed indeed are they who are able to expand such inner wealth, for here resides true love.

"How indolent is mankind; even the most dynamic of human beings, possessing the subtlest, most creative intelligence, is indolent when compared with the least of us. And the fact that he dies in the average at an early age, shows how little he knows of man's infinite potentialities. Simply a minute knowledge of the mechanics of the present teaching, properly applied, will raise the life span of Earth to a minimum of two-hundred years without the slightest mar of physical indisposition. May dynamic and wise shame fill the hearts of all sentient beings.

"Disciples of Light Marco and Leonora, you are herewith required to hold vividly in your consciousness both the present experiences and the wondrous teaching that you are about to encounter during this starry pilgrimage. Practice God in the manner of the ancient sun worshippers. Expose your bodies to the rays of the morning sun and feel the living warmth rising, rising, rising, into your heads whereto most of the creative power is stored. Keep yourselves in a state of subdued exaltation. Learn to see and feel this creative power in every person you meet; it deepens in you the awareness of God. Be patient listeners, it leads to wisdom through discrimination. And when a discriminating mind rules a healthy body one sets afire the sacred centers within; it is like unlocking the gates of Heaven. And radiate daily thoughts of reverence and love to your ancient Master Jesus whose heavenly gaze was fixed on you, almost two thousand years ago, at the fateful hour of His Ascension from the sacred hill of Bethany. You stood thereon, amongst the adoring crowd watching the Victorious Master ascending heavenward, exactly as you are watching now!"

* * *

A prolonged meditation greeted Elos' message. Then Beata extended her arms in a sign of invitation to Mary of Nazareth and Leonora to join her at the center of the pond. Forthwith she spoke:

"O Lord-Father-God, I salute Thee in my heart. In Thy Formless Nature, Thee I salute.

"When I think of Thee, O Handsome Father, it is like being approached by the ideal lover; a balmy vibration of contentment, assurance and usefulness pervades my whole being; energy surges forth from the lesser Centers and rushes irresistibly into my head spelling illumination, brotherhood, love, peace and the will to conquer the unconquerable THEE.

"When such a sentiment, such an attitude is transmuted into

a cogent, burning, almost disturbing impulse, one feels catapulted onto the highest octaves of creativity and intellectual
exploits; and where there was selfishness or an irrepressible
desire to commit a crime, a wave of generosity unto self-im-
molation comes over the illumined being. It is time for mankind
to understand and feel that there is nothing in God that is
static, weak, half-measure or contemplative; there is no sanctity
in God, no humiliation, no attrition and no repentance as understood by the suicidal tenets of organized religions. HE does
not want man to depend on HIM in the outward orthodox
manner. Pleading and mea culpa and silly invocations for obtain-
ing forgiveness are out of the range of His Law of Mercy.
And do not pester HIM for miracles. Face yourself and in so
doing see that your visual range does not go beyond the tip
of your nose; list all blunders, failures and crimes; call them
aloud, one by one, take a deep breath — the living BREATH
OF GOD — and start immediately the painful, healthy and
noble labour of self-rescuing. Be a man, a being of stamina and
pride forging ahead with unrelenting thrust born of study, meditation, love and sincere desire to serve your fellow man and God.

"In order to move on such a path with a minimum speed for
worthwhile progress one must possess a healthy body but not
necessarily athletic. This body must function properly without
the use of laxatives, drugs, medicines, stimulants, antibiotics and
other habit-forming concoctions. Spirituality and body resiliency
are coexistent. Foods must be simple without being drab or
monotonous; variety unlimited; surroundings as elegant as one
can afford. Craving for rich food goes deeper than simple gluttony, it is a glandular disarrangement of nutritional nature re-
quiring medical attention; such disarrangement is often caused
by the imbibing of hard liquors, an unvaried diet and smoking
of tobacco. Overeating, overfasting, overworking and overplay-
ing are a torture to the body and debilitating to the mind.
Avoid them. Likewise, to be constantly doing favors for friends
and relatives, and thus forego physical and mental relaxation
so necessary for self-appraisal and knowledge of God, is an
act of insubordination against the Law of Life and a sign
of servitude towards the whims of inconsiderate human creatures.
This too must be avoided.

"The Law of the middle Path is a golden law indeed. However its correct appraisal and wise application requires careful study and keen analyzation. It is philosophy, science and esthetics blended into one, a field for a mature mind to encompass profitably after years of serious probing. But begin one must."

* * *

Now Beata spoke directly to Leonora:

"My gracious sister; in bygone ages during one of your celestial embodiments you were my sister, a younger one and another sparkle produced by the touch of the same foreheads. As you see, the affinity between heaven and earth is incontrovertibly tangible. Come closer, my darling, and let the limpid transparency of your heart be the recipient of greater light from the inmost recess of my being. And now allow me to dispel a doubt that is casting a shadow in your mind.

"To dwell in a human body and partake of all the pleasantry that earthly life affords, while the soul staggers under the pressure of its limitations is not sinful. Organized religions such as Brahmanism and, though partially, Christianity depict earthly life as contemptible and worthless, undesirable at its best, and earmarked for an early end. Not so, not so, my beloved kin. Life on earth is a test and a challenge, the result of a violation to be redeemed. It is therefore a privilege to be on earth, for it means that the opportunity was given to the soul to restore the cosmic equilibrium that it had broken in a previous life. Human embodiment is a dispensation from on High, an admission to an unseen university where one majors in the Science of the Self. Blessed is he who knows this much, for he will surely take full advantage, wherefore, deliverance is achieved. Unhappy is he who rejects the opportunity and continues indulging in a life of sloth, or mere pursuance of material comfort, or further degradation.

"Supremely blest are you, my fair and adorable sister, for you know all this and more. Do continue to apply yourself as of now, and you shall behold and conquer the mount of deliverance.

"Behold" — she said speaking to both Marco and Leonora — "the sun of cognition hovers over you both. In humility and pride you let its rays enter your world for precise and unfailing guidance. Pause and rejoice! Wave after wave of cosmic love is investing your hearts drowning all unlike itself. Be trustful! Surrender at the Lotus Feet of your Godhead all you possess, your highest aspirations and ideals, your very lives, and worship IT as Spirit and Truth. Resume your ascent and waste no time. Remember at least one of the infinite aspects of God: unborn and unending evolutive vibration. And this means work and study wisely wedded to rest and recreation. Smile at life always and cultivate elegance to the utmost.

"There is an imperceptible, concealed nook inside the heart of every man, not to be seen with the mortal eye, yet it is very real. Therein all the powers of the universe dwell, as direct ambassador-emissaries of the All-pervading Spirit-God. May all men consult them at every step of the way, by the path of meditation. It is healthful, rewarding, elevating. Teach this to all who come to you; there is nothing else! Our love shall follow you both forever."

* * *

Silence ensued. Then the Logos OM was heard, again and again, musical, vibrating, commanding and all-pervading. It came from beneath and above, from every rock, tree, bush and flower, and from the surrounding valleys, rivers, lakes, forests and mountain tops. The starry luminosity slowly reappeared, while the unseen orchestra of the Spheres could be heard playing the symphony of the Triumph of Life. Beata, Mary of Nazareth and Leonora clasped hands and disposed themselves in a circle with Elos standing at the center. Powerful shafts of dazzling light, projected at them by the celestial spectators, caused them to resemble a brilliant sphere of unconsuming, quivering fire. Slowly They began to ascend, and as They passed over the towering vertices of the snow-clad mountains, they were surrounded by legions of winged Beings clothed in shimmering robes of white, each holding high a torch of blinding light. The Masters of light and starry guests followed silently and majestically, until the boundless sky was filled as far as one could see. They remained motionless for awhile, then slowly resumed their ascent, each proceeding to his own abode elsewhere in space, for the everlasting and noble mission of work, study, pause and rejoicing, for the glory of God.

CHAPTER IV

THE MASTER STATESMEN

While Leonora was on her escort trip to the celestial realms of higher understanding, Marco was urged by the voice of his Inner Self to draw around himself the circle of fire and water, as a protection against the sinister forces of distraction. "Heighten thy enthusiasm, straighten thy spine, move on with the humble pride of a true master!" He was then beckoned forward through more profound attunement to make preparation for newer experiences, where the Soul is given greater freedom and human relations are raised whereto the law of ethics is not stifled by human expediencies, or viciously lowered to the standards of the jungle, or recast to fit the aberration of short-sighted politicians in the name of national security.

He entered meditation with the utterance of the First Word of creation, the Logos OM — the living, impersonal, formless Christ — and heard its innumerable reverberations on the evolutive planes of life. As his Spirit began to soar, he experienced flashes of total communion with his Eternal Self. Then the voice became more insistent: "Hold thyself on the path with a firm hand, my son. You are now in the public eye, a true ambassador of the Empyrean. Not by begging and bargaining shall you win, not by promising and enticing, but by fusing into one love and wisdom."

❋   ❋   ❋

On the ascending path towards the cosmic heights, Marco's Spirit-form was escorted by seven masters robed in glistening garments of white and gold; their headcaps in the fashion of the ancient Hebrew Seers were adorned with oriental emeralds and amethysts. Their faces were so enveloped in brightness that they resembled the brilliancy of seven suns. Suspended

133

in space and seated on stools of condensed air they gazed earthward over the continent of the Americas from pole to pole, and saw the new cities of the Golden Age hovering above the present ones, ready to descend. They saw the new inhabitants, marvelous examples of living beings, demigod artists, scientists, philosophers and public leaders, utterly dedicated to projects of universal scope — a life simplified at its base and yet complex and far-reaching in awakening the unending desires of the heart and in firing the sparks of genius in the minds of all men and lower creatures alike. Because they were free from taxation, cancer, polio, alcoholism, narcotic addiction, use of tobacco, communism, democracy, religious sects and priesthood, international espionage, fear of want, hidden urge of colonialism, national boundaries, boycotting, juvenile delinquency, vandalism and all sorts of crimes and hazards — and because they were unencumbered by Social Security, Medicare, Unemployment Insurance, labor-management controversies, Life Insurance, Blue Cross, blood banks, antibiotics, Red Cross, March of Dimes, preschool vaccination, passports, and all the vast array of rules and regulations required at present to keep a childish and heedless humanity from driving itselft to utter self-annililation, such a race of intellectual and spiritual giants was devoting its energy and intelligence to further scanning life in the upper spheres and on earth, inside the rocks and in the depths of the oceans; new discoveries were no longer choked by the unilateral concept of curing this or that disease, or exploited for material gains, or harnessed for destructive purposes. Instead it heralded a series of festivities of philosophical and artistic nature which resulted in greater and deeper self-understanding and more precise knowledge of God.

As each Golden City descended to its appointed site, slumless, uncongested, vibrant, well-ordered and resplendent, as if planned and executed by architect-idealists, with no cemeteries, smoking chimneys, smog or traces of pollution, it produced a widespread conflagration which destroyed all people with stubborn carnal instincts and base materialistic inclinations, all the institutes of gambling and their advocates, all the tools of subversion, vice and crime, all the parents branded with laxity and irresponsibility towards their children, all the vampires of the youth, the spies and the demagogues.

With the merciful displacement of such useless and unwanted human dross, there was an immediate intellectual and ethical expansion in the rest of the citizenry which predisposed them to the permeation of the culture and moral conduct of the space dwellers. The two groups thus merging formed the first nucleus of the society of the Golden Age.

As the cities of the Golden Age began to dim and disappear, Marco stood in awe before the Seven Seers. One of them came forward and with his thumb touched Marco's forehead three times. "Who am I" — he asked. "I do not know, Sir!" Marco responded. "Give ear, my son: 'come, and let us return unto the Lord: for He hath torn, and He will heal us; He hath smitten, and He will bind us. After two days will he revive us: in the third day He will raise us up, and we shall live in His sight.' "

"I know" — Marco said — "Thou art Hosea", and he kissed his hand.

And another Seer came forward and spoke: "now it came to pass in the thirtieth year, in the fourth month, in the fifth day of the month, as I was among the captives by the river of Chebar, that the heavens were opened, and I saw a vision of God." Marco recognized him as Ezekiel and kissed his hand.

And Jeremiah came: "Order ye the buckler and shield, and draw near to battle. Harness the horses, and get up, ye horsemen, and stand forth with your helmets; furbish the spears, and put on the brigantines."

And Isaiah spoke: "Then shalt thou call, and the Lord shall answer, here I AM . . . And the Lord shall guide thee continually, and satisfy thy soul in drought: and thou shalt be like a watered garden, and like a spring of water, whose waters fail not."

The fifth Seer was Daniel who related how unprepared he was when called to give interpretation to the King's dream. But as the words: ". . .there is a God in the Heaven of the heart that revealeth secrets" . . . were uttered, anxiety disappeared and the correct interpretation that saved his life came forth.

"And you shall know that I AM, and that I AM the Lord your God within your hearts and none else, and you shall walk erect, proudly. And it shall come to pass afterward that I will pour out my Spirit upon all flesh, and you shall be cleansed and purified, and being so you shall prophesy." And this was the prophet Joel.

Now the last and the youngest of the noble escort, Malachi, shook hands with Marco in the manner of today, then spoke:

"As foreseen we have shown you what will be the day 'that shall burn as an oven' and the unwanted dross, the filth and the scum 'shall be stubble'. A New Elijah shall come to men, and He shall pour living water on the Christ-seed of every living being, and whereto that seed germinates, the bearer shall be lifted high at the dawn of the Golden Age; and whereto the water flows like unto stony ground. . . ."

Marco again kissed the hands of the Seven Prophets and thanked them. Hosea embraced and kissed Marco and said:

"Tell all men how alive, real and vibrant we are!"

❖ ❖ ❖

Graciously the seven Masters took leave of Marco. Unable to hold himself in that state of consciousness by his own yet undeveloped inner power, Marco descended, rather erratically through a series of severe jolts, to the human plane. Still in a trance of wonderment and gratitude he found himself in a great redwood forest walking on a narrow, yet enticing path that seemed to lead nowhere. Thick macerating foliage was underfoot, and as he moved on, he stopped occasionally to admire lush groups of fern growing parasitically at the base of ancient redwood trees. Eternity was with him and around him; he felt the dynamic vibration of ineffable peace that had not been interrupted since the inception of life in form. He wandered up and down hill, pausing now and then to enjoy the beautiful landscape with its luxuriant carpet of crimson-petaled flowers and embowering trees. He saw a bottomless pond of clear still waters hidden by gigantic ferns, and further back the overhanging woodland of giant oak trees. There was no sign of human hands having deviated the pattern of vegetation, therefore all was unmarred by man's concept of profit, all was a theme for cogitation on God's love, power and glory.

Entering deeper into the dense forest, he found pleasure in the placid humming of lower life, the inordinate murmur of a rippling brook, and the silent work of the beings of the shade. He moved surrounded by life which cast no opinion at this intrusion, yet he felt greatly assisted by its indifference. Sitting on a rock he renewed himself in meditation and before long was contacted by his Liberated Master-friends. He saw first the dazzling radiance of his Liberated Master-Teacher who touched his forehead and said: "Never relent the practice of inner discipline and awareness of God. Stay on the path and know that all tests are conquered. And what is the path? Constant interiorization. When an outer task is completed, it is man's duty to re-link himself at once with the Light in his heart in humble gratitude to the Self for all that was accomplished and in preparation for what lies ahead."

Master Jesus appeared and said: "Some of the many aspects of love are kindness, tolerance, understanding, an encouraging word, a pat on the shoulder, a disposition to listen and to agree, and even a simple smile. . . . Add them up one finds himself on the summit of the hill of Bethany, ready to leave the earth a victorious Lord and Master."

Master Flora came and His words changed into luminous roses. Soon Marco saw a scroll of roses in front of him alive with Light and Wisdom. "Defend and love Nature. It is thy only source of beauty and inspiration. It sustains thee, it strengthens thy limbs and recharges thy mind on the path of truth. Let thy mode of living be simple, yet lacking nothing. Achieve beauty and elegance not through costly clothes, mechanical comfort and imposing surroundings, but by renewing thyself and thy home with the fruit of the severe work of introspection, and the difficult task of directing thy mind to God for pure thoughts and inspiration. And do not expect to succeed entirely, for absolute beauty and ultimate perfection are not of the world of man."

His next visitor and Teacher was Justinian. With a stylus of condensed light he carved on a sheet of gold: "Justice is the law applied, Order is the law accepted, Peace is the law lived, Love is the law made manifest."

Then he heard the voice of Agricola:

"Silence is the realm where creative work is nurtured. Observe the earthsoil! It neither speaks nor advertises, yet it creates incessantly and sells all it produces. O man, ponder on this with the instrument of discrimination, and behold thy delusion crumbling, thy creative ability heightened and thy link with God made stronger."

Solomon came in kingly garb surrounded by his royal court. He sat on the Throne of Life and said:

"Only the humble is wise and the wise is king. On the evolutive trend of society all human laws are subject to abro-gation and derogation. Let this be done with the tools of philosophy, not through rioting or threats. Only the weakling and the uneducated rebel, and to yield to their intimidations is a sign of political inadequacy within the leaders."

The youthful forms of Elos and Beata appeared and in one voice they spoke:

"OM I AM with you forever! When man identifies himself with the I AM, the Ever-living Self, he ceases to doubt or have fear; he rises above limitation and bewilderment; his consciousness expands and becomes almost all-pervading; he *knows* that it is the most intimate, omnipotent, indestructible Essence within that fires his mind for wise and noble decisions whose impact on the outer world spells absolute success. However, when he says 'I am sick, I am destitute, I am afraid', what does he do? He brings to a focal point for a negative and destructive impact upon himself, all the stupidity, all the ignorance and all the limitations of the mortal world. Sickness, poverty, failure and so forth are merchandise of hell thrown at mankind by sinister forces that are not forces at all but a mongrelish and pretentious melange of nothing ready to disappear at the sight of a raised finger.

"The thoughtful individual, the man of the world, is never assailed by the powers of failure, even though he might fail now and then. And when this occurs, he enters the world of cogitation, there to re-capture new forces and more modern weapons, to reshape his seeming failure into a better equipped battleground. Unknowingly he has surrendered both intelligence and will to God. A slight acknowledgement and the victory is assured."

❂   ❂   ❂

As the Cosmic Visitors disappeared, the Inner Helper beckoned Marco on. He took him by the hand and led him along a riverbank towards the source. The atmosphere was becoming more vibrant by the presence of unseen beings who were converging there for reasons as yet unknown. Seven giant eucalyptus trees came to sight; their transparent trunks issuing from the bed of the river were placed in tandem at a distance of about fifty feet from one another; rainbows of light radiated from their crowns. Floating on the water, at the base of each tree, were water lilies in rich profusion, and in the midst of them seated in the lotus posture was a Shining One holding in his hands a gold tablet and a stylus that emanated sparks of fire.

Marco's Inner Helper re-entered the temple of the heart as a sign that visible assistance was not required for the time being. Actually it was a test to establish the degree of his Self-reliance in faith and mental power. Now he felt the presence of the unseen beings more powerfully and of being carefully scrutinized by them. He realized that they were writing about him, and for an instant he faltered; then summoning all his inner forces to a focal point as he had done in past years when he had to face his professors during an examination, he walked confidently beyond the seventh tree. There he saw a scene of awesome magnificence. Seated on a throne of light at the center of the river, a few feet above the surface of the water, was a youth of about sixteen enveloped in a mass of gold and blue liquid fire, which poured down upon him from above. His head however, being self-resplendent, was not touched by the investing flames. At the sight of Marco, rays of light issued from his forehead and throat and were projected radially towards the far-off horizon. Behind him were twenty-four Splendor-beings forming a semicircle. The eight at the center were robed in white, the eight at the left were in blue, and the eight at the right in yellow, all equally dazzling. From the top of their heads beams of light in the colors of their vestments were cast upward, and as they converged the column was formed, of gold and blue fire, that decended towards the head of the Youth.

Impelled by an inner urge that could not be restrained, Marco levitated his form over the water and came face to face with the Master on the Throne. The seven Shining Ones delivered their tablets to Him, and as each one passed his scrutiny, it disappeared.

"Marco, disciple of light"— the Master said in a voice permeated with a commanding and loving sublimity — "I welcome thee. You have been inly guided from the moment you fell onto the narrow winding path that seemed to you to lead nowhere. I assure you that there is no 'nowhere' for the disciple of the inner, for every earthly nook up to constellations and solar systems are permeated to full saturation with the Presence of God, guiding, sustaining, chastising, rewarding, protecting and illumining whoever is on Its path. Therefore, he who cheats or steals or kills, where does he go to hide? The more he violates the law the more he exposes himself to both the physical and the unseen Eye of Justice.

"Here, in front of Me, carved on a screen of light, are the reports compiled by the seven faithful Devas, proving our assertion. Though unseen they have scrutinized your thoughts, feelings and aspirations, and this is what they say:

"1 — 'He is striving for a more accurate balance between dynamic humility and constructive pride. His mind yields to the knowledge that comes to him by direct perception; but not enough to truths conveyed to him through human channels.

"2 — 'His yearning for the vision of God is on the increase.

"3 — 'He is well-advanced towards the effacement of the ego.

"4 — 'He accepts beyond all trace of doubt the concept of deathlessness and continuity of life. He sees every human being as a lesser Christ on the path of maturity.

"5 — 'He sees salvation through introspection leading to noble endeavours.

"6 — 'He labours for Self-finding, Self-fulfillment and Self-realization unaided by any outer media whatsoever.

"7 — 'His body is physically ready to undergo strain and stress in the service of society, the Liberated Masters and the Light.'

* * *

140

"Marco, Marco, we praise thee indeed. You have the secret of ultimate success: standing alone on the rock of life, unconcerned, unafraid and dynamically aloof; yet keenly aware of danger as if treading on a razor edge. This is the philosophy of him who truly has placed his country at the right side of God; giving to it love, ideas and ideals, service, honor and prestige, and asking nothing in return. There is no dignity, no true and lasting opulence and no greatness both on earth and heaven, and above all no deliverance from want and ignorance for a man or a firm or an ethnic group that goes a-begging for favors, recognition, contracts, power, money, justice and unilateral legislation. All things received without the counterbalance of study, discipline, hard work and individual sacrifice, are a curse to man, his country and society. A beggar remains a beggar as long as he continues to beg no matter how pressing the outer factors.

"At the inception of the industrial revolution there commenced an undreamed of growth of fluid wealth which had been planned in the higher octaves to flow and permeate both the working class and the employer. Instead a new type of parvenu arose — men in whose genes there were traces of envy and hatred for the wealthy and despotic barons of centuries past. As a helpless servant he had been born previously slaving under the bloody lash of a cruel master. He wanted to crush him and spoke to himself in a whisper of a revolt that would benefit the suffering downtrodden. The mental pattern of such a plan was registered in the Akashic Records with a variation. Now he was reborn with the intelligence, the will and the tools that would make his noble dream come true without any uprising. Instead he reverted to imitating and worsening the merciless and inhumane method of the despised feudatory sub-ruler. He became rich by the application of the law of the jungle in a more cunning way, indeed, in a series of unmentionable ways. He gave himself to vain pursuits, crudeness and snobbishness; showing off with the precise aim of humiliating and tyrannizing employees, sycophants and 'seeming' friends to the best of his deviated and degenerated instinct. He did nothing for his inner growth; and whatever he left behind that seems constructive and noble, such a thing has a heavy crust of vanity.

"With the advent of the Russian Revolution the employer began to stagger under a series of responsibilities and harassments of his own making. It is the eternal law of physics that for every action there is a reaction equal and opposite, which when applied to human behavior — both individually and collectively — is called Karma. However We do not justify the exhorbitant and often untimely demands of the Labor Unions on behalf of their members. We beg them to surrender to Us the sword of Damocles forged without our permission and out of revenge. With love and firmness We warn them of the ever-living, ever-acting Law of Karma. We trust their intelligence and We know how much they think of and love their country. Both members and leaders should pause, now and then, nay daily, and meditate, and ask God and the Liberated Masters for guidance, not selfishly but for the good of their land. Such practice must be intensified as the hour approaches for the renewal of the labor contracts. Otherwise, We commend the Labor Movement as a whole, and the management also whose acumen and ingenuity have contributed in making the land of America a vital focus of light and prosperity that surpasses the rest of the world combined.

"The Golden Age is not to be understood as an age of ease, passive contentment and laissez-faire. Far from it. Its realization demands of each man and of each nation a preparatory age of fire and steel and a merciless siege against the obscurantistic tower of the ego and its ponderous barnacles of chauvinism, pride, assertiveness and despotic disposition. Each individual and each nation, without the slightest tinge of backsliding, must carry on his shoulders the constructive aspirations, with all the implications involved, of the rest of mankind. His whole nature must burn day and night with a permanent fever for self-improvement, his imagination vivified and exalted by seeing God in every face, man or beast; his will, the active force within, turned into a whirling and cutting whip, must hold the turbulent and petulant mind well-concentrated on the realization of lofty ideals; his faith in the Self must be boundless, and his desire to help his fellow man must be kept alive through enthusiasm. Humanity will not make a worthwhile inroad to peace unless there are people of this caliber, willing to rise above the deadly drag of mediocrity, worldliness, stupidity, cheating and crime, all merchandise of the ego. The Golden Age is a society of masters who will be required, at their lowest exploits, to nail to immobility death itself."

As he ceased speaking, the unknown Master and his cosmic escort turned into blazing flames and disappeared. The placid river and the majestic panorama vanished; Marco's path changed abruptly.

* * *

He came to the rim of a crater — immense, deep and frightening. Gusts of radiant heat surging forth from its depths struck him with their fiery blast. Isolated, surrounded by precipices and desolation, unable to retrace his path, he closed his eyes and composed himself in meditation. Like a combatant pressed on every side by unrelenting foes, their faces a stony mask of death, he arrayed himself to die unconcernedly for his God. This is self-surrender.

The volcano began to erupt. Shapeless masses of ignited matter, in various degrees of brilliancy, were launched skyward and then rained down upon the marshy soil, causing thick vapours of unbearable stench to rise from the earth. As the eruption continued to grow in violence, noise and destructiveness, gigantic columns of liquid fire and incandescent basaltic splinters were hurled forth to great altitudes and transformed into black, menacing clouds, which completely obscured the atmosphere. A lashing rainstorm accompanied by a piercing wind loosed its fury as if a divine chastiser wanted to punish the rebellious earthly elements for their defiant attitude against the cosmic order. Marco perceived the two contending forces challenging each other, and therein saw the ideal man, severe and godlike, standing with upraised hands trying to appease the two warring powers. Perceiving his inability to cope with the situation, shame overtook him.

Presently the starry memento began to resound in his consciousness: "Usarco, Usarco, cut thyself asunder from unbecoming modesty, and assert thy divine birthright of wise leadership and justice. Gather knowledge and strength from the Self of thee and issue the decree that gives thee executive power over life. Arise, Usarco, arise!"

It was enough! He stood supreme master over the self, its limitation and negativism. He entered the Hall of Justice, sat

143

on the kingly throne of the Universal and commanded the two contending forces to cease warring and stand before the bar of justice, to hear the Law and abide to its dictates. He saw the Universal Self embodying the Law, the Judge, the Counselor, the Public Accuser, the plaintiff and the defendant.

The scene changed as per command. Two youths appeared before him, equally handsome, equally intelligent and equally eager to learn and to obey. The first one spoke:

"Master-justice, I am a rebel and intend to remain so as long as the forces of the status quo persist in their haughty stubbornness of infallibility and presumptuous wisdom. Too long, your Honor, we have tolerated such a trash, such a pomposity, such rotting corpses. And believe me, your Honor, I am not boastful and much less a rebel; and it would please me very much to lay down this assumed garb; but I cannot.

"I am a dweller of earth and thereon one lives and moves in a maze of confusion, misunderstanding, ignorance and malice. That which is legal and permissible today becomes a violation tomorrow. A man's deed is defined heroic by some and treacherous by others. Envy runs rampant in the professional world, among the artists, priests and politicians. The business world is a cheat. Under the glitter of a photographic lens accompanied by a gesture, a glance, a meaningless phraseology, and the lure of sex, every dispensable item is made to assume inestimable value in the life of the consumer. Brand names are a protecting shield for legalized cheating, often in the quality of the goods, always in the price.

"Gambling houses, insurance companies and banks, behold, your Honor, there is nothing that they do not promise one at the end of a transaction. Masters of cheap psychology, cleverly expounded and relentlessly applied, they are destroying the dignity, the sense of values and the spark of life itself in every human being. In the name of God and for the sake of the evolutive process of society, your Honor should issue a mandatory injunction which would assess precisely the wreckage caused to the soul of man and correct the damage with compulsive and clearcut decrees. Gambling should be outlawed, not by forcible methods, but by a sudden uprising of noble consciences and an educational campaign that would instruct the masses of the emotional damage brought about by the

144

anxiety between the placing of the bet and the results thereof. To this one must add the support and comfort given to the vicious elements of the underworld whose ill-gotten wealth is used to foster more corruption and breed more crimes, which then must be counteracted with a larger police force at the expense of the taxpayer.

"And finally we have the government, the master-cheater. How can I, your Honor, list here the unending blunders, the deeds of hypocrisy and the outright violations against life, liberty and the pursuit of happiness committed by the guardians of law, justice and order. States are the result of acts of thievery and murder. A few individuals organize themselves as a gang with the determination of seizing and ruling the country, the same way as another gang would rob a bank, and through vague promises and audacious deeds they attract the malcontent, the idle, the school dropouts and some lifestreams with evil karma. With such an initial strength, based mostly on bold speech and manner, they cow the worker, the producer, the law-abiding citizen and some of the undeserving leaders, and by the enticement of wealth and prestige beyond their lot, as well as threats of steel and fire, they reduce them to impotency and make them tools of their sinister plot. Should such a gang succeed in seizing the land, these elements will constitute the founders, the heroes, the hallowed leaders deemed to fill the Hall of Fame for school children to honor and remember, and for future leaders to emulate and quote their sayings with reverent hypocrisy. And now that such a gang of thieves and murderers is well established in power, its components form the hierarchy of worthiness with lofty titles of respect and acknowledgement and unending privileges: Sir, Illustrious, Honorable, Earl, Excellency, Eminence, and, until a few years ago, even your Royal Highness and Imperial Majesty, while at the same time they draw schemes for heavier taxation, and snatch the youth from the pursuit of education, family ties and ethical livelihood, and train them in the art of war and murder.

"What are crime and evil? The offsprings of selfishness, the result of mishandled justice and unwillingness to conquer igno-rance. The courts of law and their administrators groan heavily under the hypnotic spell of "legal precedents' manufactured by the thieves and murderers before mentioned, worn out traditions of ages past when life was harsh and people cruel and merciless; and there is political pressure to consider, and the pressure of the business world whose trusts and cartels aim at paralyzing individual initiative in art, science, social reforms and the interpretation of God itself. And we must not forget the Civil Rights movement whose impudent policy of threats and demagoguery, which amounts to nothing, has dispatched our laws to a dusty attic and scared the wits out of a spineless Congress and an equally spineless Department of Justice. The lawmaker is a child of his highly refined intellect, a proud twister of the reflected light of the Buddhi. Hence all his laws are limited and a breeder of innumerable loopholes. Those who take refuge in the Roman Law as a source of justification for their decisions, are indeed a poor lot, for the Romans did nothing that was selfless and just even in rapport to the age in which they dominated the world. Remember the murder of Carthage and Corinth guilty only of trading according to the law of competition and in obedience to the rule of demand and offer; remember the massacre of the gladiators, guilty only of seeking that minimum of liberty conceded to a diligent slave; and let us not forget the wholesale slaughter of the early Christians bent primarily on the realization of the kingdom of love on Earth.

"The lawmakers, the leaders in politics, religion, business and education, and every individual entrusted with duty and responsibility towards his family or his community, must learn how to consult the files of the Self, whose laws and codes are interpreted with the key of interiorization. Until they do this, I shall remain rebellious."

❋   ❋   ❋

And the second youth spoke, his voice tinged with sadness. "Master-justice, salutations unto thee.

"The day is near at hand when this brother of mine and myself shall walk side by side in twinship of mind and soul. The two aspects of man's nature — good, the real, and evil, the unreal — which we so distinctly represent, will be inwardly reconciled, and perfect outward equilibrium will ensue. Then each man is elevated to a lawmaker unto himself and a law-abiding citizen of the highest order. Such a highly-prized goal is achieved through daily practice of self-interrogation. Let no one try to learn the nature of *good* or the behavior that is lawful through books. It cannot be found on printed paper, nor in the word of mouth, for these are subjected to a series of factors as numerous as there are human beings, and tend to change with the swiftness of two consecutive thoughts. Remember St. Paul: 'Slave, go to thy master!' and the Gettysburg Address: '. . . .nation, conceived in liberty and dedicated to the proposition that all men are created equal . . .' and how much these two statements and many similar ones have been discussed pro and con by philosophers, statesmen, church leaders and simple folks. Results? None so far, even in this age of space exploration. Only the conscience can answer truthfully. Only a conscience lying prone at the Lotus Feet of the Conscience is able to issue truths that defy time and space, and dominate human relations in a spirit of love for eternal years.

"Such a modus vivendi, being within the grasp of an average human mind, such as mine, can be brought to realization at once. I believe so, your Honor; and with such a feeling of positive and dynamic optimism I am able to delve deeper than my rebel brother into the still waters of the collective conscience of men and see therein the seed of goodness in process of germination. It gives me joy to have detected the presence of many active, noble and determined lifestreams in every field of endeavour, including the government and the armed forces, both in our land and elsewhere in the world. I have even noticed a sense of fatigue, a desire to withdraw, in many a war-minded soldier as well as manufacturers of war implements. Are we bolting the doors against all armed conflicts and throwing the keys into the ocean? Are we in an age of transition whereby the various academies of the armed forces and their magnificent buildings and surrounding countryside will be transformed into Academies of Health and Body Beautiful, Philosophers, Statesmen and Initiates, Space Science and Cosmic Forces, Interracial and Inter-continental Love and Respect, and Truth and Immortality? If so, we are indeed close to the dawning of the Golden Age. As of this moment on, it is the peremptory duty of every student of law and order, every lover of light and beauty, and every perceiver of the undying Essence dwelling in one's heart to heighten and expand any trace, any

147

evidence, no matter how faint, that might give an indication of the existence of a desire for inner striving in any person they meet.

"It is not my purpose here to disclaim the veracity of my rebellious brother's accusations against society and the existing laws. They are truths and they need to be corrected at once. Neither of us has a practical suggestion as to their rectification. We have come to thee for enlightenment. Please, pronounce the Law of Conduct."

* * *

"Sons of Light" — Marco responded — "I beg of you, hear me.

"Like unto a mountain must a wise leader be. The mountain gives abundantly to the valley below. The forest, the meadow, the lake and the creatures therein, by their presence and their appearance bear witness of the wisdom and generosity of the mountain above. The wise leader, the philosopher and the man of genius, must direct their attention to the masses below, observe them closely, converse with them, eat of their food, and acquaint themselves of their mores and aspirations, and, as you yourselves have wisely suggested, enhance any constructive desire, and return it to them garbed in wisdom and holiness. This will generate enthusiasm and joy in their hearts, which will resolve into a noble pride, a fiery determination to advance on the broad avenue of universal good.

"Man being real is innately good, evil being unreal can only touch the reality like a passing wave. When the man in the street is convinced that an outer incentive or a noble deed can cause his soul to vibrate faster and his heart to rejoice, he begins to see that morality and truth are exclusively within. Saints, gods and guardians of law and order are no longer needed. Now he stands alone before the Law, conscious and proud of his achieved height and mastery. At the slightest violation he will not go into hiding, for the entire world is seen as an open court of law and the Self within as judge and jury, public prosecutor and defending counsellor, accused and accuser; the Self within punishing justly and qualifying the sentence with the light of redemption. That man has ceased to violate the Law of God forever.

"As a test for such a high goal, litigants, facing a court of law, should confront one another, alone and in silence. They

148

should be left there until, passions and disagreements subsiding, they feel and see their common spiritual lineage which goes back to the inception of life itself; the judicial contest has come to an end untried.

"How unending and varied are the gifts of God to man. He is truly the Mount of Wisdom and Love feeding the shallow and sluggish rivulets below that are the minds and hearts of men, that they may grow and prosper, and bring tangible testimony of the Law of Cosmic Harmonies in the ever expanding human society that, though now and then bewildered and in despair, thirsts for peace and deliverance from evil.

"These suggestions are not directed to collective groups, political parties, ethical societies, religious organizations, and educational institutes. Not even to the government. They are directed exclusively to man, each man singly taken as the basic unit of life, without whom life itself and God cease to be. To thee and to thee alone I speak, O Man. Take hold of thyself and cling to the Self within with all thy strength, with all thy mind, and with all thy heart. Do not impose upon the simple; do not be insolent to the mean; do not join those bent on plundering the few, nor those that would make prey of the weak. As a father and husband check thy responsibility daily, as a son be obedient and grateful, and in each case loving always. At your place of business be gracious and loyal to thy superiors, gracious and understanding to thy help. In assisting others go out of thy way to the best of your strength and discrimination. This, again, is love. Know that upon your shoulders lies the self-appointed task of making love universal. God depends on thee, on thy love, for the cessation of all wars, for the mutual cohesion of families, and for the opening of the heart of man to man. And remember also that thou art heaven and earth. As heaven you are incorporeal and creative light endowed with the power of regulating and determining anything that happens with absolute perfection; and as earth it is your duty to apply the dictates of heaven. And when every trace of antagonism has ceased, you have grasped the law of the world in its entirety; you have triumphed over limitation and death itself; you are a Christ.

"Sons of Light, this I feel is the Rule of Conduct!"

＊ ＊ ＊

At the exact moment Marco was initiating his return from the Higher Octaves, Leonora was initiating hers also from the Realm of the Splendors, farther away in the immensity of space. Their meeting was one of great joy and love, while waves of ethereal music, coming from an unseen source held them elevated and attuned with the world of perfection. Friends and acquaintances who found themselves within the circuit of their auras were invested by an unusual and inexplicable feeling which took on diverse forms according to the temperament of the recipient; the loquacious spoke with greater wisdom, the mischievous became pensive, the sad, happy, and the idle, suddenly ashamed, made noble resolutions. Indeed the gifts of God are not talked of nor demonstrated by an organized process of the mind or will; they are transfused by behavior and silence.

Many an uneventful month went by; Marco and Leonora working at their assigned tasks in the outer world, grateful always to their Liberated Master-Teacher who had guided them to such a lofty state of consciousness. Then one day they were thrilled by His now familiar voice:

"I am here" — He said. "Transcending distance and time schedules, I AM always by the side of all my disciples scattered in all lands. And I guide each one according to the law of his own being, which never coincides with that of another, yet they all move abreast towards the same goal. Now another series of experiences is in the process of unfoldment for you. In your daily meditation you must arise above the element of time. You must gravitate towards the effacement of all opinions in the presence of events that appear damnable even to a hard-boiled sinner.

"Should you see a person lowering and pulling a basket from a well with the intention of drawing water, you must not interfere until you are asked to do so. You must neither harbour nor show the slightest feeling, nor formulate any judgement concerning the soundness of mind of the person involved. Should a tottering drunkard cross your path, minding his own business, do not play the moralist, even in thought; above all do not feel proud of yourselves for so doing. And if life is endangered give assistance in utter detachment and never play the hero. See God in every incident that you encounter; accept it for the moment as an expression of HIM. However when alone in meditation, ask HIM in your hearts, in the name of cosmic discrimination, to put each event of the day in its own niche.

"Have your daily lives free from unbalanced moments and doubts, free from unfinished business. You are ready to do so. Action and repose, thoughts and plans, intelligence and feeling, must proceed harmoniously. Have no thought of reward or fruition; learn to wait. Ability to wait is the highest wisdom. Apply your mind and strength constructively at all times.

"Every man is endowed with the ability to reshape his own world from one of misery, limitation and dissatisfaction, to one of joy, abundance and inner certitude. He must commence by bidding farewell temporarily to his mode of living and outer associations, and re-enter the Chamber of the Soul in utter faith and with a feeling of expectancy that leaves no room for hesitancy. Sitting alone in a corner of a clean well-ordered room, he opens a book of ancient wisdom, and therein, at random, reads a saying, and perhaps another and another, until he feels a strange current pass through his body, a lifting vibration of wonderment and pleasure. It is enough. He puts the book aside and closing his eyes begins the marvelous work of cogitation and visualization. How far he may go on the path of genuine happiness and inward exaltation, no one, not even a Liberated Master, is able to foresee. He could be so inly blest as to be touched immediately by the hand of his Immortal Teacher.

"This experience, even in its mildest degree, will never, never, be forgotten, and it will constitute the foundation upon which a new world, a world of charm, happiness and inward satisfaction is built."

* * *

Marco and Leonora had learned that to obey the suggestions and recommendations of their Liberated Master-Teacher with enthusiastic transport brought always spiritual rewards of higher and ever higher nature. There is one point here that needs to be emphasized: the Masters of Light never command, never compel or impose; and having absolute respect for the free will of their disciples, they never intrude in any manner into the inmost shrine of the heart; gently, lovingly, patiently and unobstrusively they come and wait for his readiness to receive instruction; and having given the instruction, if there is no explanatory question being asked, they bow and withdraw.

151

During the following weeks our disciples meditated and prayed for greater light and inner strength. The more they saw and learned, the deeper their sense of spiritual inadequacy. The Master's voice was again heard:

"Blessed is he who lives under grace, for he has reached the turning point of his life. And you have, My students, for you have sought and found the Shrine of Oneness. This means that you shall no longer dwell on the concept of age, or of aging or disease. With the spark of genius in your hearts brought into action you shall live in the spirit of the Eternal Now which is the mode of living of the Golden Age. You shall rise above the manifold and see every living being as an organ of God, capable of expressing at every moment all the attributes of the Self. You shall direct your attention frequently and with dynamic and positive intent, to all those who are engaged in bringing peace to the world, mainly to the noble but harassed body of the United Nations. Tell the members of that body that their task is primarily a spiritual one, then humane, social, economic and political. It means that they must learn to meditate first as individuals, then as members of the Cosmic Body of God. By so doing, I assure you, the practice of meditation will spread like wild-fire throughout the world; the obscure and demoniac tendencies lurking in the hearts of men will begin to be eradicated.

"The economic blessings of the society in which you live have thrown an unusually large segment of the population into a pathological extrovertness that is almost suicidal. People have debilitated the power of thinking, their creative faculty has been reduced to a shambling parrotry. Observe music and the arts; nobody creates, except children up to the age of ten. After this age they fall into the web of pleasure seeking and wild indulgence like their parents'. Out of mercy We, the Guardians of Life, save some from further degeneracy in order to hold human society from engulfing itself into deeper abjection. Like the ancient initiates and teachers we do proclaim the vital importance of meditation as a means of raising humanity from the jungle of bewilderment and involution. Give up the church, synagogue, temple, pilgrimage and all exteriorized rituals as an instrument of salvation; they are nonsense; they are tools of schemers and profiteers bent on keeping man's mind on the

152

same level of a child's. Observe and study nature and the sky and constellations, how they express themselves, silently and without a sound of gossip. And then observe and study thyself, O man; see the citadels of light of thy body flashing back and forth to each other messages of wisdom and life beyond death. A simple partial understanding of this process is sufficient to give you all that is required to make you a god.

"When excess extrovertness prevails, the society is diseased, the masses lack discrimination and the leaders are corrupt. As a certain level of degeneracy is reached, the Guardians of Life release a divine Chastiser, an Awakener, a Christ who, on assuming the human form, causes a revamping of the unwritten laws of ethics; all men pass through the test of the Purple Fire, some to emerge from it, others to be consumed and quasi-annihilated. Those who survive constitutive the Living Verbum of the New Cycle of Civilization. Such was the Messianic Age of Master Jesus.

Sometimes the reaction to mass indolence and political ineptitude comes from an individual who all his life has been in the midst of them, as in the case of Socrates in Athens. His teachings proclaiming virtue and truth did not have immediate result, nor did they act as a mass awakener, yet they influenced the philosophy of the successive four centuries, and will continue to do so for many centuries to come.

"The sublimity of Socrates during the trial and at the hour of death shows one of the greatest spiritual triumphs since the commencement of the human race. 'Be virtuous and truthful, and yearn for an unseen Master by the path of introspection' — He said — 'and the Knowledge of the Self is yours. There is no man who can live constructively without a Master. There is always a Master who sustains the spiritual climbing of a disciple of the Inner. I had my own, always close to me, guiding me, correcting my thoughts, words and deeds. Because of his nearness and fatherly love, I won my trial before the Court of the Eleven, exactly as He had forseen it, leading to the discarding of the flesh and the Triumph of the Spirit. My daily meditation brought me rewards of everlasting nature.' Thus Socrates attained immortality and became a Liberated Master. This same teaching and guidance are given to you now, My disciples, and are intended to awaken the world.

* * *

153

"In order to hasten the process of spiritual reconstruction, I hereby announce the existence of the Inner Schools of Light which, though unseen by the physical eye, are, nevertheless, as tangible and real as the physical sun itself, for the benefit of those who have reached the 'turning point' in their lives. Classrooms are hovering over every hamlet, every house and even over open fields. Individuals with sound thoughts, lovers of discipline and responsibility, and with a slight yearning for truth are eligible for admission. Those who display diligence and humility are first strengthened in the body and mind, and then taught how to shun traditions, earthly culture, family links, blood relationship and all the fads of the world of appearance. We teach them how to walk straight and unafraid before God, and how to cultivate the noble pride of true humanhood, without which Godhood and Immortality remain a pious dream. These are the trail blazers, teachers, harbingers, prophets, initiates and messiahs — individuals endowed with enough courage and wisdom as to shake the human society out of its moral degradation and material want. And as it is unnecessary to possess academic diplomas to gain entrance to one of these schools, the humble laborer, the farmer, the street cleaner, the scientist and the seeming wise diplomat may claim admittance and stand on equal footing with each other in a spirit of cosmic interest and universal brotherhood.

"The first inkling of this inner training is perceived by a partial but continuous alleviation of physical toil, mental bewilderment, and the recurrence of doubt and passion. The laborer, the soldier, the judge, the civic leader and the businessman will find themselves facing newer, easier and higher avenues of self-expression. They will face tasks with unusual self-assurance, and solve impasses as if by magic. In the awareness of this mysterious power and its origin, their hearts will swell with uncontainable joy; they will fall on their knees and weep in utter gratitude to God. Thus he who has gone astray returns to his Father's House for an eternal stay. This is the first and least of the rewards bestowed upon the contrite prodigal son. As for you, my disciples, behold the new experience that is unfolding before your eyes."

Marco and Leonora rose to a higher realm of consciousness and found themselves walking in the manner of Spirit-forms that need no solid ground beneath their feet towards a towering, pine encircled mountain. On its declivitous slopes above the timberline, near the summit they saw a magnificent celestial Being enveloped in pulsating light. A series of flashing letters issued from his forehead:

"Be guided by the Cosmic Law of Justice, ye that are destined to show the path, deflect not. Live and think as one." As they came closer to the Great Being, they bowed their heads and prepared to receive instruction. Free from the limiting action of the sense-organs, they were able to translate the vibrating pulsations of the Master's mind, into thoughts.

Gazing around they found themselves at the center of a clearing in the heart of an impenetrable forest of silver spruce. Twenty-four of the trees encircling them began to lose their normal appearance and changed into gigantic pillars of light shooting luminous beams from their capitals. The ground became levigated as if made of polished purple marble. Surrounded by golden flames and standing on an altar, the Angelic Being now appeared before them, the letters of light continued to emanate from his forehead:

"Son and daughter of Light, behold, listen and learn. . . "

Two rays of light came forth from his throat. With one he drew a flaming cup from the heart of Leonora, with the other a blazing torch from the forehead of Marco. He held the cup and the torch in front of him.

"Son and daughter, I am happy of you! This is the true ritual of the Sacred Fire. Man and Woman that so behave constitute the perfect and integral unity of life. He the temple, the high priest and the custodian of the Sacred Fire; she the Flaming Vessel of Beauty and Love, the Priestess-companion and the custodian of the substance around which life gravitates and is delivered to God whole and unmarred by the concept of death. Together they build a temple of imperishable material. Only that which is created by man and woman divinely united is fully protected by the Law of Life under the ministration of the Liberated Masters, because it contains all the elements of divine architecture, the elements of continuity and harmonious evolution. Such couples move in an aura of certitude in all their endeavours, their daily lives are filled with achievements beyond all imagining; never being tired or despondent, always happy and buoyant, always wiser than the day before.

"In a home where life vibrates in such a high degree, there is a leavening power capable of encompassing the whole creation, urging every human being to imitate, emulate and attain. From the seed of a family so divinely knit, springs forth the public leader who knows how to serve the community for an ideal social order. The devotion and obedience of a child to his parents whom a Liberated Master guides, clear the way for the child to be contacted also by his own appointed Master, thus widening the field of action for a universal brotherhood. The masses of the world are eager to follow such leaders, irrespective of race, creed and nationality, and show them their attachment and love.

"If the policy of the American people to flood the earth with money in their Foreign Aid Program, could have been coupled with pensive political representatives of the meditative class, students of inwardness and discrimination, and aware of their role of instrumentality at the service of the Immortal Ones, the global reconstruction could have been a fact. We know it is in the heart of every American to show the world how sincere he is in his display of generosity, but he is unprepared to prove his feeling in a cosmic-scientific way. Hence, the worldwide misunderstanding and fear. Humanity is no longer satisfied with *panem et circenses* in the form of a dole. Both within and without the geographical borders men want to be guided to the spiritual source of life, wherefrom all blessings come forth clothed in shadowless light, the true garb of enduring substance.

"O My country, O My country, where is thy universal destiny of trail blazer and peacemaker? Tell me, where is it? As husband and father of the world, thy behavior is similar to that of a typical American man towards his wife and children who yearn for his companionship and guidance: 'here, wife, take this check and buy yourself whatever you wish. Here kids buy yourselves some toys and candies. And now scram, I am busy.' Yes, busy with irresponsibility and extrovertness. The elected leaders are busy with winning popularity contests and high-handed methods of coercion towards critics; the appointed leaders play the sycophant, the bureaucracy follows suit. O visible leaders of My Country, awake, arise and obey the Invisible Leaders. Then truly you shall save the world for the glory of God."

❉   ❉   ❉

The letters of light died away, and the Angelic Being and the mystic setting vanished. Exquisite strains of music floated about

156

Marco and Leonora causing their spirit-forms to tingle and throb with blissful expectation. They sat on a massive rock chanting the Holy Name of God in tune with the heavenly rhythm. A procession of Spirit-splendors passed by on their way to empyreal realms for higher duties; some were ancient, while others were of the present age. They were informed by the voice of wisdom in their hearts that they were beholding legislators, rulers and leaders of men who had performed their earthly tasks in harmony with the Law of God. They had dived deep into the fathomless depths of their hearts, and the inexhaustible knowledge and wisdom they had found therein they had given away without any concept of reward. He who maintains this attitude purifies the mysterious centers of his body and becomes flawless and almighty. How little is required of man to be lifted high in the Presence of God.

The last of the Spirit-splendors had passed by when Marco found himself again in the midst of a new test. The Akashic Records of one of his past embodiments flashed before him and he saw projected against the shoulder of a mountain the spirit-form of that embodiment in gigantic size. A ray of light struck the head and the reflected beam absorbed Marco into the actual event of many centuries past. He was a patriarch-ruler of an ancient tribe in Chaldea. Robed in white linen and encircled by a wall of white fire, he was ascending onto the summit of a holy mountain to hear the voice of wisdom direct him in the solution of problems that were vital to his people. It was night, but the bare and awesome plateau that stretched before him was flooded with stilled light. He was about to fall on his knees in adoration to God, when he saw a woman of exquisite beauty approaching him. Her long wavy hair, which was golden, fell softly over her shoulders and upon her head was the crown of a ruler. In a submissive attitude, her blue eyes filled with sadness, she came closer and said imploringly:

"Teacher of antiquity, I beseech thee for the Light of Liberty that casts no shadow. What is the way, the way without return? My name is Lea, and it was Lea in my last embodiment, and I was your daughter; do you remember?"

"My daughter, my darling daughter . . ." Marco answered. "But you were a queen and an initiate. . . ."

"Yes, Father I was. And I had disciples, and some of them

157

surpassed me in wisdom and inner light. And this was my downfall, because I envied them. Thence I lost my way. For many centuries I have dwelt in the realm of transition with little or no inner progress, hoping against hope to shatter the wheel of birth and death and achieve deliverance. Filled with confusion and doubt I have wandered aimlessly in surroundings that keep on shrinking and getting darker and darker; I have visited sanctuaries and holy foci of stone, and met many learned priests, but nowhere have I found the fruit of truth. Teach me again, O Father, that I might go beyond death."

Marco perceived her earnestness, yet being unable to formulate an answer without first consulting the Voice of Wisdom, told her to still herself and, in a one-pointed visualization, utter silently and without moving her lips the Name of God OM; then to wait for his return. He walked away and came to a solitary place. Here he meditated for enlightenment to render immediate assistance; but no answer came. On his way back to Lea, he realized that his meditation had been stained with the clause of *immediacy* which had blocked the flow of knowledge. He sat again in absolute abandonment of mind and body. Now the Voice of Wisdom spoke:

"You have disappointed the Self of you. Ponder and retain that this failure will not be repeated; learn to live in the awareness of eternity where nothing happens too soon, nothing too late, where all events fall into place at the appointed instant. Life was created and functions in obedience to a precise rhythm that no force can ever disarray. Death for those who deserve it never takes one by surprise. Disappointment is the fruit of ignorance. Now go, and face your disciple, I shall speak to her through you.

"My daughter of ancient and of today and forever. For such thou art, noble, wise and enduring. And being so, how can you be so despondent or confused or grieved. Search within, search . . .; and now let peace manifest . . .; see and feel the conduit of light between your sexual organs and the root of your nose; see the liquid fire ascending and descending. Now, my child, be still and wait for revelations. . . ." And the Voice of Wisdom spoke no more.

Lea understood and directed her mind to meditation. From the depths of the self there surged forth one after another the fiery and lurid dross of mortal habits, feelings, passions, belittling, social rank, opinions, desires and even outer education.

They fought fiercely against her, resenting their displacement. She fell and rose, and advanced courageously against the viscid tentacles of the common lot of human existence, against the derision and smearing of false friends, and against hypocrisy and gossip. In the stillness of her mind she saw the fearful scramble of the merciless vampires of life preying on the ignorance of human beings who take delight in the illusion of outer goals, material possessions, tinseled trappings, name and fame. All this she saw and overcame.

In the process of her inner unfoldment Lea felt her body tingling, vibrating, pulsating at a rate never experienced before. For the first time she perceived the difference between a human soul in its pristine state, and one with the superimposed qualities attracted during the earthly life. Her sadness had now disappeared and her form was almost transparent. Without any motion of her feet, she moved backward, her garment shining like a mass of liquid gold, while her countenance was as lightning. Now the royal crown, the last vestige of human attachment, fell to the ground and was shattered into dust, while a dazzling luminous star appeared on her forehead giving her a god-like majesty and glory. The star began to increase in size and brilliancy, until Lea's whole form was absorbed into it. Free from all earthly pulls, she commenced to ascend into the upper atmosphere to be welcomed by a multitude of celestial Splendors. Then Marco heard the Voice of the Self, speaking words of encouragement:

"Disciple of Light, We thank thee, for through thy assistance another being has been released from the world of form and limitation, into the fold of Life Eternal. Distress and confusion shall no longer beset her. Thanks to thy sagacity and selfless help, another Christ has risen.

"Yes" — the voice of the Liberated Master-Teacher echoed. "Another Christ has risen! It is the refrain of the Cosmic Harmonies. How tremendous is the power of a noble thought, a gracious word, an affectionate gesture. Behold our Master Jesus; He sat at meat in the hovel of crime while publicans and sinners came and sat down with him and his disciples. And every one who gazed at him and felt his magnetic pull, took embodiment soon after death and became a citizen par excellence, raising many degrees higher the moral standard of his community. How contagious and uplifting is the radiance of a Master, and what impelling force it has upon human beings with receptive hearts is difficult for man to evaluate, because the structure of your society and the extrovertness of the human mind do not lend themselves to the things of the Spirit. Rather than giving publicity to the compactness of families and to men and institutions engaged in tasks of education and alleviation of physical pain with no aim of profit, the press glamorizes divorces, crimes and other deeds of destruction. How can one ever measure the contribution of the photographic equipment alone to the plague of rioting, strikes, hippiehood, assassinations and defiance of the police force, where the deviated and uncouth youth shows himself as if playing the role of hero and liberator. It was not so during the last Golden Age where scientific achievements were more advanced than today. Conditions were reversed; mind interiorization was predominant, newspapers were bulletins of information, lean and straight to the point, and television programs devoted to the arts, science and philosophic debates. Families or members thereof that were spending an evening at home sat around the hearth, the children relating the experiences of the day, the parents united in love indissoluble, commenting, guiding and instructing for a nobler behavior on the morrow. The late hours were devoted to meditation and the practice of setting afire the sacred centers of the body with the intent of purifying the blood stream, charging the muscles with newer strength and reactivating the mind to the peak of alertness. This is in the last analysis the process of oxygenation achieved in obedience to the Law of Universal Harmony. This is the philosophy of life in action of which medical science is one of its branches. As positive disposition, otherwise called faith, and medicine cure ailments, likewise keen visualization and knowledge of the unending potentialities of the body cause the Sacred Fire not only to maintain the human vehicle healthy and resilient, but also to enhance the creative possibilities of the mind. This is the never-ending, never-failing action of the Sacred Fire, and it goes even beyond into the regeneration of diseased or decaying tissue to absolute wholeness."

* * *

If these were the requirements for the realization of the Golden Age, Marco and Leonora felt that they were living in it now. All

160

the elements of physical well-being, mental vigilance and emotional equilibrium were solidly in their grasp; constructive desires came to fruition effortlessly, and the world at large, though always stormy and threatening, yielded always the right of way every time they faced people and events. Problems, pressing and baffling appeared daily at their threshold, rudely clamoring for attention. But Leonora with the flaming torch of positive thinking met them on their own ground, barring the way against further inroad. Looking in retrospect at a frightening situation, days and weeks later, she would remark: "Thank God, the Master directed me. I could not have solved the problem alone. . . ."

Their Liberated Master-Teacher did indeed direct them and prepare the way for new inner experiences with the intent of leading the soul, mind and body closer to unreachable perfection.

* * *

Seeking new inner contacts for the sake of greater knowledge, Marco and Leonora walked towards the southern slope of a densely timbered mountain, where the trees hold discussions of vital importance for the welfare of man. Sitting at the base of one of these noble giants, they heard it saying: "Why do men die in the infancy of life as compared to the average lifespan of one of us?" "The reason is very complex to them but utterly simple to us," a nearby tree answered, and continued: "They investigate our lives, mores, and appearance with the instrument of the intellect which, in its pride, fails to reflect true wisdom. They come to us with an array of mechanical tools, test tubes and chemical reagents, chopping us to pieces. . . Oh, if they only came to sit in our midst and listen to our talks and partake of the food which we manufacture for them and find out how we go about producing life from the dungeon of death. . ." And another tree spoke: "Poets and artists visit us often; the former are caught in the vise of rhythm and literary restrictions, while the latter take delight in our garb, and thus both miss in understanding the true essence of our being. . . ."

Gazing into the westering sun, Marco and Leonora saw the youthful Master-judge of the river approaching. "Please" — He said — "do not try to learn who I am; besides my nonidentity is meant to convey to you the sublime philosophy of service detached from the concept of reward or recognition.

161

"I have come impelled by the law that governs your lives, which in turn is dictated by your progress on the inner. You deserve the service of love that I am about to render for, though it may cause you to bleed and stagger, it is love nevertheless.

"You are required to prove to the Cosmic Assembly of the Perfect Ones, that you are able and willing to tread on every path, make a hall of learning out of every street corner, and raise every concrete block on the waterfront to the status of a pedestal of light. You must be capable of feeling the grief, disillusionment, suffering and temptation of your brother-man in order to learn exactly how to rescue him by the use of his own dim and fitful light and feeble faith, and without outer assistance. You must learn how to guide him towards salvation by showing him that all the powers of creation are concentrated in his heart. Man is willing to undergo discipline if he is convinced of this truth.

"Mankind is at the threshold of a messianic activity. Hearken! All human distinctions — race, color, creed, social rank and economic status — are obliterated from your consciousness. Foe and friend, saint and sinner, and encomium and censure are leveled before your perceptive faculty. You must accept and know that they are unreal and, as such, nonexistent, hence wherever you see imperfection, sloth, darkness and disease, you must transmute them by the impact of your own radiation, into perfection, fervor, light and health. In short, you must be guided at every step of the way by the Effulgent Being dwelling in your hearts.

"Disciples of Light, the Cosmic Assembly of the Perfect Ones requests that you so live as to blot out all earthly pulls, desires and worldly aspirations. All the teaching given to you so far, must be accepted solely as a stimulus to delve deeper into the realm of the Fourth Dimension for further self-renouncing and Self-asserting, self-losing and Self-finding, self-dying and Self-living. You must arise above false modesty and the feeling of inadequacy, concerning the task that is ahead of you, for they are in truth, a form of withdrawal from life. Are you able to comply with these requirements?"

* * *

The unknown Master disappeared before Marco and Leonora could formulate an answer. They felt now that they were about to face a severe trial of an unknown nature. Their surroundings changed drastically; the atmosphere had become dark and hos-

162

tile; the soil, water, vegetation and rocks had all turned to a deep brownish blue; an insidious vibration crept over their body-forms; all was devoid of sound, the sense of smell and touch vanished; all seemed dead. They wallowed in a vacuum of loneliness and mental disruption and were affected by an incapacitation to either rejoice or suffer.

Thus they stood and waited as if in a rudderless vessel floating dangerously in the vast and tempestuous sea of nonbeing; and as the first inkling of perception returned they saw and smelled uncleanliness, disorder and fetor masking their Spirit-forms. They were lashed mercilessly in the body, mind and soul; the pains, aches and misery of the physical nature returned augmented incredibly in all their brutishness; the assertive ego was now subjected to the most abhorrent humiliation, and the soul groaned under an unendurable pressure that held it back from Self-expression. Their hearts and minds quailed and would have been glad to turn back to the dreary stockade of common human existence. Streaks of livid, reverberating lightning, now and then, pierced the dark surroundings, revealing the squalidness of the soggy, crumbling soil of the tundra extending for many miles around.

The stillness and solitude, although oppressive and undesirable, were interrupted occasionally by inimical sounds accompanied by physical outbreaks of a worse nature. Electrical discharges, thunderstorms, icy winds and a fearful sussultorial motion of the ground warred madly against each other, causing the marshy land to solidify for a moment, break the next, melt and solidify again.

Was all this the expression of some punitive karma, an unknown residue of error from past embodiments? Marco and Leonora felt indicted by an inexorable and invisible judge for crimes committed in the past, and pleaded guilty. They were in no one's world but their own; they were responsible for its unattractiveness, primitiveness, discomfort and lack of light. On these premises they slew all feeling of self-pity and desire to lean on outer assistance for the rescue of their Karma.

And now the work of reconstruction began. It was heterogeneously complex and global, much similar to the act of creation. First the soil was restored to its pristine wholeness of stability and productivity, but it reverted back into instability and barrenness. Perhaps streams and canals were needed, but upon their completion the water refused to flow and became stagnant; seedlings broke the ground but grew no further, the grass was gaunt and the bushes wilted. No flowers or fruit were to be seen anywhere. The creatures of the wild were plentiful but stunted and listless; the air was heavy and stale, the sky overcast with dark foreboding clouds. Marco and Leonora were striving for color, form, symmetry and asymmetry, beauty and life, all as a vibrant and harmonious whole. In vain! They analyzed every detail of their plans but could find no flaw and no missing element as far as the acme of intelligence could conceive. Sad and baffled, and unable to find a way out of such a perplexing impasse, they fell on their knees and cried for mercy. Entering into the realms of slumber the Merciful, wherefrom they passed into the Chamber of Revelation, they waited absorbed and transfixed not knowing what to expect; then letters of light appeared forming the words *Self* and *self,* and the next instant they were catapulted back into the midst of their creation.

SELF and self, God and Christ, Father and son. The rescuers had toiled humbly and bravely, and everything had been molded to perfection; but like a walking doll it was lifeless and mute. Why? Because they had forgotten to insert, to transfuse into it the concept of God. And though it is true that God is everywhere, still IT must pass through the crucible of the self, the soul and mind of man, in order to be perceived outwardly and brand life with LIFE. Now they meditated and asked for instructions from their Liberated Master-Teacher.

"Yes" — he said — "one cannot see or perceive in an enduring manner the beauty, majesty and wisdom of the outer until he feels the Presence of God flowing through his blood, sinews and muscles. And the more he heightens the intensity of this process through the medium of the mind, the greater the degree of appreciation and understanding; and it could be so raised as to reach the state of creativity. This is one of the facets of the miracle worker. Master Jesus could not have healed the sick or caused the dead to rise, or multiplied the fishes if he had not felt such a trememdous flow of ENERGY in his body, energy that he qualified and directed according to the requirement of the hour."

Exploiting the radiance of their Master for maximum results, the negative pulls of their striving dissipated and Nature again sounded her paean of life; their Spirit-forms reacquired the freedom of the Fourth Dimension. Rivers of advancing light flooded the cerulean sky and crisscrossed the atmosphere in exuberant colors. Gorgeous gardens and orchards in full bloom, cascading waterfalls and lakes of sheer beauty, and mountains with grandly timbered slopes, their peaks helmeted in snow, spread endlessly before them. In the distance they saw a series of rocky elevations and in the midst of them they recognized Mount Meru, and on its eastern slope the picturesque and fertile valley of the Himavat. Impressed by the unusual wealth of tropical vegetation, they directed an inquiry to the Master-guardian of the mountains Lord Tabor.

"This is not the Mount Meru of earth" — He explained — "but its spiritual counterpart in the belt of perfection that encircles the planet earth. Your Mount Meru is a replica of this, with all the limitations and imperfections imposed upon it by the human mind. It is needful for you to learn that all rocky elevations of at least three-thousand feet above one of their adjacent valleys are Foci of Light, meeting places for Liberated Masters and spiritual adepts in charge of the destinies of the surrounding villages and cities, their people and vegetation. Mountains are, therefore, living organisms constantly radiating health, strength and wisdom to those who approach them in a spirit of receptivity. However, if a mountain is neglected by man, its beauty marred, its vegetation mistreated or destroyed, in short, if it is not loved, it withdraws its living radiance and begins to disintegrate and will eventually vanish. The surrounding cities and their population suffer disruption of political, economic and spiritual nature; and even if the mountain does not show physical degeneration, nevertheless it no longer radiates health, peace, strength and wisdom.

"When organized religions were still unknown mankind worshipped nature, mountains and the sun, a truly healthier and much wiser approach to God than genuflecting before a helpless statue of a St. Anthony or the like. With the adoption of anthropomorphism and other absurd, diabolical and even lurid rituals, man artificialized himself; his physical stamina collapsed, his mental alertness weakened and his spiritual outlook shrunk to a pitiful state; mountains lost their lifting glow almost entirely, only a tenuous trace remained, a gift of mercy to man from the Guardians of Life.

"It is my pleasure and my honor" — the Lord Tabor continued — "to guide you into the heart of Mount Meru where you shall receive the seamless garment and the sandals of the ancient wandering disciples of Light. Herein all the activities of its earthly counterpart are analyzed, corrected, recorded and returned to earth for man to accept or reject, as he sees fit. Be attentive and free from anxiety and curiosity."

Through a circuitous path Marco and Leonora were led inside the great mountain, where they entered a magnificent and idealized civic center. It was the combined counterpart of the finest architectural creations of the arts and music centers of the United States of America, extending in every direction and embracing the residential sections of the Master-technicians employed here. Along the broad parkways there were members of the Great White Brotherhood acting as guides to the many thousands of diplomat-visitors and tourists of the inner from every land. Although there was no sky or sun to be seen, no one had the impression of being indoors; the air was cool and fragrant, and a series of contiguous luminous arches, high above the buildings, provided an ideal lighting system.

Entering one of the halls of justice they saw a group of Liberated Masters seated in session listening to individual soul-flames, representing the business world and seeking approval of their plans. They heard the presiding Master-Judge say that whoever has a constructive plan to bring into realization, shall receive full support from the Great Hosts of Light; those whose plans are defective in some form, are greatly assisted, through the illumination of their minds, in perfecting them; and finally those who are engaged in destructive enterprises and unethical schemes, are no longer left to themselves, either to succeed or fail. The energy poured into those activities shall be seized by messengers of this Court of Law and held bound within its creator's aura, and eventually be forced to return to its own source with an amplified effect of destructiveness. The Master-Judge said also that every attempt to disturb the forces of peace, or to corrupt or mislead certain strata of human society, or to weaken the youth through dope, the press, radio

166

and television, are doomed to failure, and the qualified energy released there shall revert to the creators to spell suffering, mental derangement, blindness, cancer and death. The presiding Master-Judge was also heard remarking, regretfully, on the absence of political leaders. "It is a pity" — he said — "that neither government executives nor elected rulers come to us, and yet they are the pulse of peace of a distraught society. Even schemers and meddlers come to us in the attempt to have their programs enshrouded in the mantle of morality, no matter how flimsy this mantle. This shows that unethical individuals feel, now and then, the touch of God and the shame of their behavior, while most politicians rely solely on the questionable strength of their proud intellect, preferring the ephemeral success that might keep them in office to the enduring praise of history and God."

Marco and Leonora were unable to comprehend this inner process whereby man's spiritual counterpart uses an outer agent, as it were, and in the present case a court of Justice invisible to the physical eye, to influence and make the mind accept a more perfect plan. Master Tabor intervened and gave the following explanation:

"In every form of cogitation intended for outer realization, there is a subtle flow of energy or vibration that issues from the root of the nose and travels internally to every atom of the body. The atoms acknowledge receipt of the message and return it to the center of the feeling world — the heart — for further analyzation, eventual change and approval. Now the plan, being complete and ready, is transmitted to the mind for execution.

"The mind of man is a recording device clogged with a massive amount of material of photographic, sound, olfactory, taste and tactile nature; a limited portion of which is well filed, the rest stacked in a heap of incredible confusion, worse than the warehouse of a peddler of rags and junk. When a new plan arrives, the mind frowns or, worse still, rejects it. It takes ton after ton of energy and pressure from the converging strength of the atomic structure to convince the mind of its duty to accept and execute the plan; but before it begins to yield it has to dig into the pile of unfiled material to find out whether there is any connection between the new assignment and whatever it has done previously; this inward research coupled with the slothful tendency of the mind is time consuming; hence the need of an outer-inner agency, the Advisory Board of a mountain retreat. The heart collects the details of the plan and projects them to the nearest focus of light where the Board adds its own positive vibration. Thus charged the plan acquires executive force that leaves no room for delay in fulfillment; the mind bows and goes to work.

"You have learned of the existence of the foci of light inside mountains, and have had a cursory idea of their method of operation. The United States of America has an abundance of such centers of Wisdom and Tribunals of the Inner. It is a mark of far-seeing statemanship for any political leader to consult them. If these could only equal business and banking executives who plead for assistance day and night."

* * *

The gracious Lord Tabor suggested to our disciples to remain a little longer in their exalted state and visit the spiritual counterpart of the river Ganges whose holiness in not marred by human fanaticism and misconception. "Have no preference as to the place you want to visit" — He counselled — "for you might be misdirected by the subtle traces of likes and dislikes that is accompanying you. You will learn much and in the process you have a debt to pay."

They alighted somewhere on a hidden spot of its eastern bank. The water was crystal clear, running lazily with a sweet and melodious hum, the river-bed was covered with rocks that glimmered like precious stones in all sizes and colors. They saw many foci of Light along the shores and the Masters therein were specialists in therapeutics, eugenics and the science of health. Spirit-forms seeking health for their bodies from all over the terrestrial globe were assembled here in immense spherical halls filled with sparkling pink light. In one of the healing centers, a Master stood high on a platform delivering a lecture without words; he was completely nude, his form truly superlative in symmetry and handsomeness. As he turned around showing his spine, a jet of warm golden-pink water issued from an orifice in the ceiling and sprayed his back from neck to coccyx, then as he again faced the classroom his body slowly became transparent, its internal organs visible to all. A spark came forth from the root of his nose, traveled over the head, down along the spinal column and into the coccygeal center, causing a brilliant conflagration. The body became a flaming pillar of unquenchable fire, which lasted only a few seconds; then all returned to normalcy. The unknown Master bowed and disappeared.

Marco and Leonora moved inland, traversing gardens, orchards and woodlands of celestial beauty, crossed a grove of banyan trees, and came to a broad meadow where a magnificent white elephant stood motionless. As soon as it saw Leonora, it ran swiftly towards her and knelt at her feet, seemingly, in a pleading attitude. She extended her hand and touched the elephant's forehead, issuing a silent call to God for its blessing and liberation. Presently the animal rose, stood still for an instant, then burst into a dazzling flame and disappeared. Like superior men, superior animals aspire to immortality through the medium of a son of God, and Leonora in this instance gave proof of such an achievement.

Continuing across the open meadow, they passed through a hedge of tall cypress trees, and entered an arcade of light; the ground beneath their feet was alive with innumerable little purple flames rotating like whirlpools. With circumspection and awe, they walked a short distance, when looking back they saw a curtain of unshadowed light advancing while in front another similar wall of light was moving towards them. Soon they were submerged in an ocean of dazzling splendor. They sat on the ground in a meditative posture feeling that their Spirit-forms were about to undergo a further transmutation. Impelled by the pulsating effulgence in which they were immersed, they crossed over the boundaries of the last and subtlest trace of the ego, surveyed for the last time the imperceptible borderline between the highest intellectual exploit and the domain of the Buddhi, and having become as light and weightless as the free atom, lost themselves in the Realm of Unchangeable Truth. In it they enjoyed the ineffable taste of universal citizenship, the trait that makes man beloved by every other man and trusted by every soul. They were thus cogitating on the stupendous experience when they heard the Voice of Wisdom speaking:

169

"O beings ethereal, O pure intelligences, arise above and beyond the consciousness of contemplation, where things are greater than the greatest, where time, space and causality no longer hinder, where the pair of opposites cannot dwell, and where birth and death loosen their grip and vanish. Follow your divine Guide, THAT which is unseen and untouchable, but only felt and awful real. Make way for IT, for IT is thy Genius. Through IT you shall be linked to the Eternal Self and know the unknowable. Follow no one else.

"Beings refined and primeval, enter the Master Hall of your wise Self wherein the Unseen Teacher shall make thee know that when life dies in purity of heart death dies along with it, never to resurrect again. With such an end life grows richer and the world is raised higher; and as you return to Earth hold yourselves enshrouded in such a beautiful mantle of perfection.

"Arise above the pain of birth, the pain of unwise and heedless youth, the pain of personality, the pain of sorrow and happiness, and the pain of want and wealth. Walk in light, be humble, love all that lives, shun offense, speak kindly, be ready to help, and rise daily one step higher in the love of truth.

"Beings ethereal, tell all to enter the Way, the Way of meditation. And now behold!"

* * *

Enfolded in an aura of mystic joy and divine exaltation, Marco and Leonora bowed to one another, and in so doing their foreheads touched and gave rise to a sparkle which changed immediately into a youth of thirteen, embodying both the masculine and feminine traits. Clothed in light it stood before its parents and said:

"Blessed parents, I thank you. I AM the pure Christ-Light, because I AM untouched by worldliness: hence, I AM the Light of the world, the Fire of Man's mind, the undying Soul-flame in his heart. I think, plan and work in absolute obedience to the Law that governs the Universal Consciousness; hence no karma can ever bind Me, no illusion can ever make Me fall. I AM free and immortal!"

Then translating Itself backward, It gathered more light

about Its dazzling form, and transmuted it into twelve beautiful beings of white fire, who immediately encircled their creator. The Son-Daughter smiled at Its parents and began to ascend, followed by Its adoring ones, the creation of Its pure mind. The arcade of Light vanished.

* * *

Proceeding further in their starry wandering, they came to a circular pond of opalescent pink water set like a living gem in a filigree of forestal verdure. Pink and blue lotus blossoms floated thereon, while the broad shoreline was rampant with wild fllowers of every shade and fragrance. On the opposite side of the pond, they saw two contiguous sheltering palm trees, under which a great rishi sat in contemplation. Walking over the water they came close to Him and knelt at His feet. As he returned from samadhi, He quickly bade them rise, and touched their foreheads. "You are back in the estate of Mount Meru, and I welcome you with much love, travelers of the beyond." He extended his hands with the palms upturned and, lo, three exquisite crystal goblets appeared. "Please drink" — he said. — "It is liquid light. In the morning it tastes like your favorite breakfast, at noon like your favorite lunch, and in the evening in any way you want it to taste, always at the peak of perfection. My name is Vasikta and I am, and have been for the last thousand years, the guardian of this retreat, although my apparent age may seem to you to be about twenty-five."

"My Raja Sahib" — Leonora interrupted — "what is the secret of such a complex radiance that you project. You are handsome and wise, and you seem to have strength unconquerable and an enduring will to be and to do. Not only time have you subjugated; all else and unqualified life too hold you in their protective embrace of dynamic and resurgent love."

"My noble Sahibah" — Vasikta explained — "what I do is what you have seen and learned in this starry wandering of yours. Try to remember: the body is the living temple, the dwelling place of the Holy of Holies. You are at the service of this Holy of Holies, otherwise called I AM. This service you promised to render in a solemn oath at the time you entered into the womb of thy mother. The maintenance of this temple is therefore your sole and absolute responsibility.

171

Mind, free will and yearning are the instruments; these in turn create the material for the upkeep: meditation, pure thoughts, athletics, Sacred Fire, work, study and awareness. The pharisaic society in which you live speaks of love. You do not have to love or say to anyone 'I love you'; simply take care of the Temple as taught, love becomes all-inclusive and all-conquering.

"Now, my darling, as a housekeeper you do not own the Temple, you only service it. If you are careless and slothful, if you waste time and energy in silly and destructive endeavours, such as gossip, unethical business ventures, outer uncleanliness, smoking, immoderate drinking or eating, intake of drugs and dope, cheating, misleading, envy, war, and other vain pursuits where honor, security and life itself of your fellow man are involved, you, naturally, neglect your primeval duty towards your Master, the I AM; you allow the instruments to rust, the material to rot, you fail to fulfill the articles of the treaty, so solemnly accepted when embodiment was granted to you. By such behavior you have become useless and discardable — you die — and no amount of earthly praise will save you from utter oblivion.

"But if you serve HIM faithfully, if you fulfill the requirements of the Law and adhere to the terms of the Contract . . . behold, you are given — as a minimum — a body-form like mine, in itself a source of wonder and joy and satisfaction unspeakable, and it is all yours forever; an intelligence that transcends the human genius in its loftiest exploits; an absolute mastery over your own destiny, you 'die' if you wish, or live for eternity unstained by the degrading process of birth, and un-humiliated by the inevitable stage of childhood, where the helpless human soul is mercilessly subjected to the deadly blows of parental limitation, constructive laws of behavior that are today and changed or gone tomorrow, and all types of meaningless tabus imposed by the sophisticated and despotic society. You are raised in the estimation of your Lord and Master; then HE adopts you, takes you into HIS BOSOM and bestows upon you the supreme gift of Christhood, meaning that HE makes you Heir to HIS Throne of Power, Majesty and Glory forever and ever.

"Please" — he now spoke directly to the two listeners — "cease doubting. You are gathering around your body-forms matter from the earth, which makes you heavy and unfit to stay here for further instruction." He touched their foreheads. "The fact that, unaided by any outer assistance, you have come here, impelled by an inner force; the fact that you, of your own volition, are able to draw such knowledge from the mouth of a Seer, who, humanly speaking, has no interest in you, save the impersonal urge to serve the Light, is proof of your hearts' passionate and unquenchable desire to delve into the unknown and learn things that are outside the circulus of the highest human reasoning. You are coming to the stage whereby the Logos will rule your lives, you to serve IT and apply ITS dictates. Only a short while yet and you will live in the spirit of Master Jesus' utterance: 'It is finished; into Thy hands, O Father, I commend my Spirit.' You have come here as a prelude for the dawning of such a marvelous occurrence. And it shall come to pass.

❋ ❋ ❋

"You have also come here to meet a humble member of the Vanguard of the Cosmic Assembly of the Perfect Ones. From the profound recesses of the starry forests and mountain retreats, we are the eyes of the Law in action fixed on the world. Men do not see us, but we see them and follow their thoughts very closely; we guide them towards the dormant Logos, so that they might acknowledge and express it. And those who are receptive to guidance we attract unto us for higher training in Self-leadership. For exactly this reason you have come to us; but you have an additional task, that is, to absorb the Law so that you might express it in its genuine purity, in its universalized spirit transcending the social garb and individual idiosyncrasies of every race and nation of the globe. Remember always that the essence of truth is the simplicity that does not give rise to abusive argumentation. Hence, you will refrain from bringing into play the ancient symbolism of the Circle, the number Twelve of the Hebrews and the Seven of Pythagoras, the Triangle, the Serpent, the Narrow Passage, the Chamber of Mirth, the Bird of Prey, the Blooming Lily, the Labyrinth of Death and similar inconsistencies with the Space or Universalized Age in which you live. Exteriorized rituals are clannish and sectarian, and the source of much hatred

173

and spilling of blood. Remember: all sects and religions are a categorical denial of the true Spirit of God.

"All that is inherent to man's welfare and evolutive process, the scientific approach to better health, the laws of dietetics, housing, harmonious sexual intercourse, education, sports, music and the arts, sound government, work and repose, buying and selling, transportation, farming, mining, industry and banking, international trade and tariff, collaboration and diplomacy, must be acknowledged as branches of the Primal Science, the Science of the Spirit, embodying all mankind and the animals and the gods too.

"It is the teacher's duty to spread this New Verbum to the man in the street who truly constitutes the substratum of the New Age. We want a society of Aristrocrats of the Spirit rather than of money or intellect. You must strive to reproduce on earth the hierarchy of the starry realms; the Angel-laborers, the Archangel-foreman, the Prince-poet, the Power-writer, the Cherub-scientist, the Elohim-prime minister, all . serving the Empyrean-ruler, God. By living and working in such a spirit no one will assume an attitude of superiority, no one will dwell in the debasing feeling of being useless or quasi-so. After all it is God and the Liberated Masters who set afire the minds of certain living entities called men and release unto them specific plans for global evolution; not for a race only, or a nation, or a social group. It is important to know that the shorter work week, the higher wages, the cleaner and better factories and the longer yearly vacation, were ordered by God and not by the puny egos of certain labor leaders. And this imposes a higher responsibility upon the laborer, that is, striving inwardly so as to become an Angel-laborer.

"The masses must be made aware of the technique involved in the realization of all the things that have the mark of excellence, and how the Liberated Masters work through men in the field of science, politics, labor and the arts. To cultivate such an awareness means to cultivate God, to come closer to IT and to claim the birthright of the First Born.

"Social involution is the result of spiritual aridity and intellectual debilitation. Ancient Rome collapsed into oblivion because of such an interplay of evils. The gladiatorial games made them obdurate, and the persecution of the early Christians reduced their mental discrimination to that of an untutored child's. The British Empire was in the same state of collapse at the time of the American Revolution. Spiritual aridity and mental debilitation made it blind to the — as yet — unexploded inner power (mental strength) and humility (spiritual wealth) of the people of Colonial America. Though America lacked everything: manpower, weapons, culture, the subtle reasoning, the legal cavillousness, the political training, and the liquid wealth of her mother country, she had everything: the guidance and protection of the Liberated Masters. The British Empire on the other hand had everything, but it was haughty and obdurate to the gifts that are eternal: the Spirit that always wins, and the humility that never loses.

"The American Revolution is registered in the Akashic Records as the revival of the battle between the lonely Arjuna and King Duryodhana and his tens of thousands of picked soldiers fully armed and equipped. It was a bloody battle in the two instances but the lonely one driven by his invisible charioteer won because he fought not for conquest but for the right to live. The American patriots were men of insight and humble disciples of the Inner who, in the secret of their hearts, had contacted the Logos and the Liberated Masters, and, unconcerned of their fortunes and lives, had offered themselves without hesitation to the noblest cause on earth: Liberty!

* * *

"Do not be misled by those who speak of freedom vehemently, of the freedom fighters, of the Civil Rights advocates as an organization, of the fellow travelers who find heaven everywhere and the corruption of hell only in your midst, of the new breed who want to live their lives unhindered by the existing laws, and of all those who oppose the status quo forcefully, substituting — at its best — nothing — and, at its worst, — social disruption and self-annihilation. Freedom does not require a banner, or parades, or threatening marches, or boycotting, or abusing those who are in charge of law and order, or casting vituperations at the Chief Executive. Freedom is not a doctrine subjected to discussion or human appraisal like a political party; and it is not an institution with statutes and by-laws where one can join as a member and then go out with the intent of pioneering his tenet for the purpose of attracting new adherents. Freedom is not an academic degree bestowed by an outer agency. No one can set anyone free by saying 'Freedom I grant unto thee' without generating laughter of commiseration from the Masters of Life.

"Like the genital organs — vibrant, functioning and product-ive — identifying male or female as such; like the physical eyes acknowledged as the organs of sight, and like light being the offspring of fire and heat, freedom is the essence of life. It pre-exists to man's birth. The minute sperm-cell inside the womb must travel in freedom in order to manifest life, and this is so in all forms of life; hence, even animals are born essentially free.

"By such an inalterable principle freedom is a gift from the Self to the self; it is an inalienable endowment. It is generated from within, comes to the surface of the skin, saturates the aura, radiates outwardly in a spherical form, travels to the utmost boundary of creation, and returns back undiminished and unincreased. It is like a wave produced by a rock thrown into a pond of still water; they are integral parts of each other. And wherever man decides to go, freedom travels with him and ahead of him, and it is there to welcome him: freedom welcoming freedom. It cannot be given away, nor can it be taken away from one. It cannot be lost, but it can be neglected, or left behind unused. In this case seek not outwardly, blame no one but yourself.

"Freedom, therefore, is self-determined, self-realized, self-fulfilled and intended to benefit subjectively. If one does not know that he has it, or is not intellectually aware of having it, and makes no effort to bring it forth, he will never find it outwardly, no matter how much he yells, or curses, or threatens or kills. In fact every word or act that might harm his fellow man while in the process of seeking freedom, results in greater bondage, deeper moral degradation and lesser awareness of the spiritual endowment of freedom.

"The people of France under the rule of Louis XVI felt that in order to set themselves free from the tyranny of the Bourbons they had to start a series of uprisings. On July 14, 1789, a mob of Parisian freedom fighters attacked the Bastille with the intent of freeing the 'hundreds' of political prisoners.

There were none except seven common criminals; but the freedom fighters had to march on in search of freedom, and being disappointed at every step of the way, rage and lawlessness engulfed them; and having divided themselves into gangs they roamed the city perpetrating acts of thieving, raping, destruction of property and massacre, but they did not find freedom. Then they thought that the royal family should be executed. It was done, still no freedom. The new regime, also in search of freedom inaugurated a series of trials that led to the guillotine thousands of innocent people; but no freedom was achieved. When Napoleon Buonaparte appeared on the political horizon he was looked upon as the champion of freedom. Both the mob and the advocates of liberty acclaimed him as the saviour of France and of Europe and of mankind. They hastened to serve him in a series of wars that were meant to be wars of freedom. Tens of thousands of young men perished ignominiously in campaigns that raised Napoleon to the temporary status of tyrant and a worse negator of freedom than the regime of Louis XVI. O man, seek not freedom outwardly.

* * *

"An organized society, based on true and lasting evolution, consists of a series of public institutions of restraining nature; restraining instincts and tendencies of egoistic quality of both the individual man and groups thereof. Society requires discipline to function properly, to evolve and to develop God's attributes in man unhindered by negative forces. These public institutions are called to oversee, investigate and sometimes check private organizations engaged in money-making ventures. Sometimes public institutions investigate each other, and at other times for the sake of balance of power in domestic politics bodies of spirited citizens arise to investigate everybody. Such a society is indeed healthy and free and on the broad avenue of greatness.

"There are however two institutions which no one ever thinks of restraining or even investigating. The Supreme Court of the land, because of its recent deliberation and policy making in the field of the administration of justice, has shown that it should be overhauled and its members subjected to

177

disciplinary action of some sort, nor should they be permitted to stay in office for life.

"The second of these institutions is the church, the organized religions. God and religion do not blend. God stands for freedom, for unrestrained expansion of mind and soul under the guidance of the Buddhi. Religion or re-ligio means taboo, to restrain, hold back, bind fast, to compel conformity. Why should it be so? Like cigarette selling whose strength rests on commercials made of a sequence of meaningless words against an unrelated background; similarly the priestcraft, in order to prosper and achieve importance, must play with words — morality, sanctity, obedience, hell, paradise, love of church — of ambiguous meaning, against a background of rituals — gorgeous robes, gestures, Mass, confession, rosary, candles, statues — whose scrupulous performance degrades man to a state of infantile helplessness. Because the church lives in a temple of cardboard with an inside and outside veneer of granite, ready to be blown into oblivion at the slightest pressure of constructive criticism, it resents both innovation from within and from without. The only institution that can loosen the grip of sectarianism and break through the tyranny of debasing saint worshipping, is the unorganized and ever-expanding body of freethinkers, sun worshippers, lovers of nature, students of meditation and disciples of light.

"Those who fear to take such a step should analyze the behavior and teaching of Master Jesus Who was freedom incarnate, Who meditated in the desert of the ashes, prayed beneath an olive tree or by a stream, and Who never indulged in crystallized rituals of any kind.

"At the dawn of the Golden Age you shall have a spiritual-laical society, free from priests and professional guardians of the Holy of Holies, free from saints and gods and tabus: every man a creator in his specific field of endeavour. You are the harbingers of such a society, working as you are without a distinctive robe, lean in words, rich in love, patience, true humility and desire to serve. Do not run away from the world. Instead plunge into it when you must, and do not be content with a mediocre job. Enjoy all that life offers you: health, comfort, elegance, intelligent merriment, friendship and scientific progress. Cultivate sensitivity as to what is desirable and

178

unbinding and what is impelled by a carnal urge. Constructive desires are devoid of driving power, unconcerned of the time element for their fruition; they are qualified energy placed at the Lotus Feet of God and then charged by the Masters of Creation with the power of realization in the amount deserved by their creator and more.

"A worldly desire, fulfilled through the driving power of the ego, is a curse, a source of fear and anxiety, and a contributing factor to the furtherance of unethical plans. What it does to one's own karma is gruesomely appalling; while the desire brought into realization through the power of God, constitutes a memento of the ever-promptness and ever-present companionship of the Immortal Self to man.

* * *

"My noble ones" — Vasikta concluded — "the truths which I have conveyed to you were given to me by a great Teacher whom I AM privileged to serve. And because in this test you have shown worthiness you have made yourselves eligible to meet Him. Come!" Like an elder brother he took them by the hand and together they rose to the summit of Mount Meru. At the entrance of a sheltered grove they found themselves facing the youthful Master-Judge of the river. Vasikta addressed Him:

"My Master-Teacher and wise Initiator Lord Maitreya: I have guided back to thee these worthy disciples of Light. Uncluttered by the theological tenets that have dragged the Christian world into a sanguinary arena since the ascension of Master Jesus, and unstained by the concept of 'I' and 'mine', I release them unto Thee".

As Vasikta mentioned his name, the exalted Master began to assume the outer aspect as known to the ancient initiates, chelas, Avatars, adepts and Liberated Masters. The two disciples were no longer standing before a youth of sixteen; He was a mature being of thirty, with a face of stainless beauty, enveloped in a radiance of strength, love and wisdom. His hair was shoulder-length, gently waved and the color of molten gold with a slight shade of copper alloy. His beard was short, and his eyes of deep violet were charged with a tremendous magnetic force. His white seamless robe, lined with a glisten-

179

ing blue fabric, was edged with a cord of dark gold, while his breastplate was a twelve-petaled lotus of platinum and precious stones, with a blue diamond at the center.

The Lord Maitreya is one of the most distinguished members of the Hierarchy of Life. Unto him is entrusted the task of molding humanity into one vast organic unit which shall, in the near future, generate the perfect collective man of the Golden Age. Soon, his master voice shall be heard by those engaged in international affairs and diplomacy for the realization of enduring peace on earth. Soon he will be heard by the members of the United Nations when convened in plenary session. They shall acknowledge him as their wise counsellor and guide.

All the spiritual awakeners of the world from time immemorial are closely linked to the great Lord Maitreya. Rama, Krishna, Gautama the Buddha, Zoroaster, Confucius, Zen, Lao Tsu, Mencius, Moses, Samuel, Pythagoras, Jesus, Muhammad, Dante, Joan d'Arc, and others of the same lofty rank, acknowledged him as their inspirer. In the present age his radiance hovers over all writers, poets, philosophers, scientists and public leaders who are endeavouring to bring peace and enlightenment to earth. As the Great Initiator was about to speak a concentrated light of blinding intensity blazed forth from the top of his head.

*　*　*

"The Great Ones of Life" — he commenced — "those whom I humbly serve, the Cosmic Assembly of the Perfect Ones, have ordered me to cast another seed through which They expect an unusual harvest in the field of international collaboration and universal brotherhood. They want to draw men away from self-created materialism by injecting a vibration of universality into every little chore of the day. They want every man to speak to himself in a whisper or even aloud 'how can I improve this, how can I do better, how can I relieve my fellow man from pain, distress and want . . .'. This They want to accomplish, not through forceful methods, or sacrifice or renunciation, but through self-discernment. Let man live as he wishes, undisturbed, uncriticized and unreproached. Let him fail and stumble and fall, again and again, and dispose of himself as he sees fit, as long as he does not interfere with his fellow man's freedom and pursuit. But add a little note of diversion to such a tiresome extrovertness, that is, a few minutes a day of pause and silence, in order to review and even approve his own conduct. Is not man a master of his own inner world? And is not such a world fundamentally constructive?

"In a week or so his world will begin to undergo a process of remolding, for powerfully intoxicating, remarkably contagious, are the experiences of the inner. What a sensation, what a wealth of teaching, what a noble religion, are hidden in Man's heart. Hypocrisy and churchgoing gone forever.

"Does man want to shake off political despotism, economic pressure, a mean executive or the nagging of his companion? Meditation is the first step to be taken. Only for five minutes and he rises unafraid and dominating over the seeming obstruction and the lurid tormentor. If such is the first fruit of meditation, how can one measure the flood of inner and outer wealth, the physical buoyancy and mental alertness, and the unending stream of victories and satisfactions that fall at the feet of him who practices inner contact daily. This is like meeting the Holy of Holies, not in fear and contrition but as a junior partner in a business of never ending growth. Thus, out of a simple incident of life, out of a slight deviation from an attitude of superficiality, to one of mild severity and quietude, man ascends the Mount of Success and Immortality.

*　*　*

"How do you suppose all the teaching of the ancient Masters, who never wrote anything, was put down in writing? Exactly through this same process of self-interrogation. You know — in your present age — of sounds, images and colors, being impressed on plastic and celluloid; you know of mechanical instruments transmitting and receiving the same elements; you are fully aware that the atmosphere is teeming with life much beyond what is shown you through highly sensitized photographic apparatus and other recording devices; and you believe in these beyond all trace of doubt; but do you know that the whole human body — skin, limbs, organs of sensation and perception, and even every single hair — is the greatest and only perfect recording instrument in existence? It is so absolutely perfect that it cannot be improved. All that takes place on earth, beneath the earth, above the earth and in the beyond, is neatly and faithfully registered on the human body ready to come forth through the speaking voice without an extraneous speaker, tuner or amplifier.

"Now, let us apply this same process of recording to one of the teachings of the Avatars of the past: Master Jesus. Two hundred years after His ascension, all that pertained to His mission and even His existence had almost faded away; all was confused and misty. Then the spiritual revival began. Meditative scholars and seers decided to delve into the Master's utterances. Helped by the scanty information found here and there, and assisted by some of Us, they tuned their minds with the Akashic Records. In A.D. 325 at the time of the First Ecumenical Council of Nicaea they announced some of the aspects of the Master's teaching. Other similar councils followed, each enriching humanity with newer and higher aspects of the Truth. Had this truth been given the correct interpretation as expounded by the living Receivers, the world today would be living in the Golden Age.

This for the white race and the Negro of Africa. In the East where spiritual discipline had elevated the mind even higher than the status of an earthly genius, there was no necessity of calling councils. One man was sufficient to delve into the etheric record of past teachers and draw forth, with uncanny precision, all that had been said and taught. After all what is an inventor but a man of insight, rarely relying on what had been done previously, but mostly on mental concentration, intuition and faith. And isn't this meditation?

* * *

"Let us now speak of inter-continental and inter-racial collaboration, for the Euro, the Afro and the Asian are like three families crowding an average room and separated from one another by a flimsy partition of bamboo. Such are the living streams of your solar system when compared with the universe. Collaboration, therefore is vital for survival. In so small a room the most important piece of furniture is a sturdy dining table; and while the women prepare dinner, the men around the table talk and scream and let their fists fly wildly; but as the steaming viands appear, each housewife is entitled to

182

be complimented by the husbands not of her race for her culinary masterpiece. Here at least is an opening for agreement; many others will appear.

"The people of the East need help; not any more however than the white race or the brown Arabs or the deeper brown Africans; each lacks something that the others can offer. And it is not a question of giving, but rather a process of perceiving and analyzation, while each allows the others to enter his own sanctuary. We advocate a mass migration on a temporary footing, from the East to the West, to the South and vice versa. Allow the Asians to absorb the marvels of technology created by the West and study the uncompromising love of nature of the Africans, and the yellow race will rise to a level of world pre-eminence that will astound even the Octaves of Life. Allow the white race en masse to learn the art of stilling the mind for a spiritual purpose; convey to it the true meaning of tolerance and gentleness, some of the Confucian etiquette, the tranquil behavior of the unacquisitive soul, the strength of the self-reliant spirit, and the love for all life; open unto it the inner sanctuary of true Islamism where the sacredness of the spoken word abides, and you shall have a race fit for the Golden Age. And do not be dismayed, O white man, if you seeem to lack so much. Try to absorb at least one of the requirements listed; I assure you, the others will fall in as if by a miracle, impelled by the law that governs the force of cosmic gravitation. We intend to stop the Asians from dying of malnutrition and lack of proper sanitation; and also the European man from dying of anxiety, overeating, smoking, and drinking, and the abuse of drugs and stimulants. We intend to fill the gap of misunderstanding created by the villainous and egotistical attitude that each possesses a superior religion.

❋ ❋ ❋

"You, My disciples, must tell man, nations and society, that such a plan can be brought into realization as easily as changing one's shirt. All this confused and unbalanced arrangement of the human outlook — the sorrow, frustration, disease, hatred, and war is like a veneer, a layer of dust on a marble slab that any child can wipe out with a single blow. Two groups of diplomats face one another discussing ways and means to settle

183

a dispute; then one of the members utters an unkind word; immediately war becomes inevitable. How childish! Why don't they pause instead for a few minutes or a day, and then resume negotiations? Are not lives more precious than personal resentment or even this seeming national pride? And how rash for the chief of a state, who should be the quintessence of intellectual equilibrium devoid of personal feelings, to go about casting derogatory remarks against another nation or its chief of state. It is in fact a contemptible behavior, whether justified or not (for it is absolutely unjustified before the Presence of the Inner) to indulge even in unkind thoughts against anybody.

"Here is indeed, O noble princes of Light, the source of all evils — personal, national and of the entire earthly globe: the individual man. The ills of society are the sum total of unwholesome thoughts and deeds created by such an unreflecting man, and piled up in obedience to the economic law of dumping. An overproduction of goods creates an economic and financial crisis with dangerous international repercussion; an overproduction of degenerative thoughts and actions creates something far worse: a spiritual crisis and a mental debilitation not easy to erase. Even the Guardians of Life with their unlimited power cannot erase the dreadful toll demanded by the inflexible Law of Karma; they can only soothe the anguished soul during the actual process of the irreparable destruction of the physical body. The average individual, caught in the slimy web of mass consciousness, begins to decay at the age of puberty. He may retard the degenerative process if he has been reared in a family of responsible parents, father and mother united by the bond of spiritual twinship, inly educated, even though they may be outwardly illiterate. Or he may learn how to exploit properly the sexual power, directing the urge to the enrichment of the mind and strength and symmetry of the body, rather than to an ill-advised coitus. In this case he may be able to nail to immobility the continuation of decay. A man or a woman with rich and vibrant sexual glands may not only live forever, but excel also in many fields of endeavour, including the triumph of the Spirit.

"This is the nature of the man and woman of the Golden Age. But why wait? Start today, at once, and be the harbinger. Cast into the fire of the Gehenna the negative side of thyself,

O man, and live in the infinitude of immortality while still in the physical body; you could speed up in a few years thy cosmic evolution equivalent to a millennium. Practice interiorization by visualizing a subtle vibration rising from the sexual center and reaching, in wave after wave, the center of the head. You do not have to be an expert in anatomy to do this, whereas you might bring into the plane of actuation wonders in science, art, philosophy, politics and longevity; you could sweep away in one stroke all the negative drags on life, and turn the hours of your daily labour into an avalanche of spiritual invigoration, mental resilency and physical well-being.

"This is indeed the science of the Spirit and the Spirit of science, the groundwork upon which stands the springboard that shall catapult man onto the plane of Christhood and cause him to live in the marvelous environment that this supernal expression embodies. It is the task of every true spiritual leader to hammer into the consciousness of every man, woman and child the need of inward seach, as the only avenue that leads to the annihilation of the global obstructions of the human society; for mankind has definitely entered the cosmic cycle of meditation.

"Peace on earth does not materialize through the verbal, or even mental acceptance of the symbol of the physical sacrifice of a Christ, nor through blasting sermons, nor through the good intentions and hard work of the members of the United Nations. It is the responsibility of every individual, in every walk of life, to so think, live and behave as if desiring to be no less than a living Christ. Even if the bodies of a legion of Avatars were to be sacrificed on the cross, or slaughtered on a battlefield, humanity would not be raised one step higher in brotherhood and peace. This is because without intense introspection there is no contact with God, there is no Direct Perception of the things that are real and eternal, and there is no way of evaluating the forces of good and evil. The incorrect interpretation of the death of Master Jesus has truly debased the Christian world. Without meditation man rots and dies many a death.

"Where meditative citizens are absent or insufficient, the nation falls into a depressing ennui, a perfect ground for the growth of despots, an ideal medium for the hatching of crooks and unfaithful public servants; the youth rebels, sneers at what is left of social order and rules of ethics, and plots against his parents; pornography takes root and women give birth to Judases who will, eventually, sell their country to any enclaving foreign nation for a medal or a praise. For seven generations such a nation will cease to grow, and when it begins to grow again much blood will be spilled."

* * *

The Lord Maitreya ceased to speak and as He gazed around a radiance of joy registered on His face. The grounds had expanded considerably, and standing thereon were one thousand couples, disciples of Light from all races, creeds and nations of the world. The Master did not speak English but a language that was the root-language of every spoken tongue on earth, and no one had any difficulty in translating his words into his own native idiom. He continued:

"Since you all know what is required of man for tangible spiritual progress, will you be kind enough to adhere to simplicity when teaching, and see that no one starts with inordinate enthusiasm. Excess eagerness leads to disappointment and defeat. Advise your students to practice only a few minutes a day, and then gain momentum by and by. Hold each one on the Middle Path in everything: meditation, work, play, nutrition and love making; be mindful of him always like a tender-hearted mother, like a chastising father.

"Do you remember what happened to all of you at the beginning? How the beings of the suspended world preyed upon you with nagging and belittling? So it will be with your future students. All men have a more or less hidden weakness, often unacknowledged, that one day is kept in abeyance, and the next day goes haywire. Now this infirmity (alcoholism, smoking, sex gratification, and all the vast array of social and moral violations) is actually under the rulership of the disembodied entities of the suspended world. As long as one does not try to expel them through a definite method of self-discipline, nothing happens; but the moment one enters the path of the Inner and displays the needed will power to slay, once and for all, such an elusive tendency, then those sinister forces try to lure, threaten, drive to desperation and persecute him in the attempt to hold him bound to their will. They project thoughts of doubt and malice, they call him a fanatic and a weaver of self-destruction; they depict his future with the dark colors of misery, loneliness, frustration and all the obnoxious traits of the socially-rejected person. Meditation, however, makes the student aware of the existence of these suspended beings, and provides him with the proper weapon of battle and victory.

"This explains certain decadent and morbid propensities in some youths and adults alike of the society in which you live. It is the work of these unhappy and cruel discarnate entities that crowd the atmospheric belt around the world; and the human beings who fall under their sway are lay figures made of clay and devoid of common sense. Sexual abuses, alcoholism, drug addition, vandalism, setting forests on fire, abduction and all sorts of crime, are of their making. They organize themselves into gangs, exactly as those of the underworld, and take hold of certain public leaders whose minds are diseased for power and supremacy. They work patiently, and with the use of usurped intelligence and energy, they inflate the ego of these pseudo-leaders, and through false reasoning they change the definition of love, truth, liberty and even established scientific axioms. They make them appear as forward thinkers, political reformers, lovers of humanity and messengers from on High. Then other weaklings of lesser intellectual ability join them; human elements filled with turmoil and disappointment, who now perceive a chance to climb the ladder of eminence.

"People such as these draw programs of great daring, filled with words that glitter and deceive, disregarding history, justice and established laws. Soon they attract the unguided youth, the youth of the slums, the youth that grows in an unhappy environment in the midst of ignorance, bickering and alcoholic parents, and intoxicated with the glittering uniform and attention from the mob, set out to dominate the world. This is the origin of dictatorship and of organized crime of every form.

"These hovering creatures of vice and immorality do not dare to approach the meditative man, for his aura is so powerfully charged with cosmic energy that as they touch its borderline, they are transmuted into vapor and despatched to the realm of disidentification. Therefore it is to the supreme interest of every student to make earnest application in both meditation and

187

inner work so as to overcome the harassment of this miserable heap of hellions. Continuous self-supervision must be practiced, then the noble road of Christship comes to sight, broad and shadowless.

"The Golden Age, the age of greater intellectual enlightenment and vaster spiritual conquests, the age of sunward flights, cannot come into full realization until the air is cleansed from the mephitic exhalations of these negative entities. We need, therefore, this prelude of inner awakening, this cosmic uprising from every one of you and from every constructive individual who honors, respects and loves his family, his country and God. Let no one stay neutral, but all enter the battlefield of bloodless fight within the meditative heart, and gather with full hands the blessings of the Novus Ordo Seculorum. This is our loving request, and the request of the Cosmic Assembly of the Perfect Ones to all men of good will."

✿ ✿ ✿

The Lord Maitreya again interrupted his talk, as if wanting to give his audience the opportunity to dwell for awhile on his teaching, and make it an integral part of their consciousness. Changing his voice to a more intimate tone, he resumed:

"Disciples of Light and candidates to Christhood, you are such a magnificent group, well determined and fully equipped to scale the Mount of Wisdom and attain the Ultimate Reality. Dive deeper into the heart of your Inner Helper, the Saviour of the World, the Cosmic Christ. Never cease to obey his every command.

"Know that upon you, disciples of inwardness from many lands, rests the arduous task of outlawing wars, of ennobling every living being by grafting on him the seed of meditation; of teaching him, gently, how to contact the Inner Helper by the simple shift of the center of spiritual gravitation, and by attuning his mind to the voice of the Logos within. Do not expect to be perfect or always successful in all your endeavours. Work and, while working, laugh at obstruction, discouragement, doubt and failure.

"Do not lose sight of your mission: you are the pioneers of the Science of the Soul; the hidden living spring, highly vibrating force of the members of the United Nations. Support them wholeheartedly. Each one of you is a focus of rectitude, a broadcaster of international good will, a fiery denunciator of incorrigible public misleaders, and a master of love and mercy.

"You will tell the world how fraught with karma of unnarratable future suffering is illiteracy, uncleanliness, malnutrition, and backbreaking toil for a mere physical sustenance. Tell both your scientists and political rulers how much more rewarding space exploration would be without these shameful blots that still plague the man in the street. Verily, with a healthier and happier humanity down under, spaceships would fly farther and bring more intelligible information to man. Unto you all, disciples of the Inner, We entrust the task of making men artisans of the Spirit and lovers of beauty in every form.

"Industry, business, banking, the Trade Unions, publishers, sports organizations, schools and lodges, should join forces in drawing plans for a revival of noble exploits in every field of endeavour, in order to disseminate constructive ideas for the youth to pick up and contemplate. Do not build youth centers without corresponding adult centers. Correct behavior in children is instilled through example rather than words. Therefore all planning for better youth must embody a cogent desire for self-chastising in the adults. Let the father stop smoking, drinking and cheating, and the son will follow him effortlessly. Allow the youth to mingle periodically with the elders, and if they are engaged in a discussion of important matters, the youth, impelled by curiosity and respect, will sit down quietly and listen. This is the proper way to create a correct mental outlook which is the foundation of spiritual growth.

"A youth raised in an environment where words and behavior do not contradict each other, where truth and action are harmoniously wedded, must, by necessity, by the law of action and reaction, continue to display such noble traits in his adult life. Now imagine a group of such lifestreams leading a great nation, or being members of the United Nations, speaking softly, unrhetorically, casually, and yet displaying a power of conviction that allows neither doubt nor contradiction. Let truth and sincerity prevail, and the age of debates, legalistic stunts and fear of war is over.

"This could very well be the basic constituent of the idealized collective body, the Avatar-body, otherwise called mankind. Such a body existed in past civilizations; then, meditation weakening, it fell into disrepair; the jackals of evil pierced it with their venomous claws, wounded and mutilated it to such an extent that healing would have been impossible without the intervention of the Liberated Masters. Now these Liberated Masters and Cosmic Workers are on earth by the tens of thousands, each projecting innumerable replicas of himself so as to touch and help every living being anywhere. Blessed are those who are initiated in the art of meditation for they shall see their Master as tangibly as you see me now.

"Who do you suppose cast the seed of dis-nationalization into the hearts and minds of the workers of the United Nations? It was a gift of the Liberated Masters to deserving and receptive lifestreams who now constitute the founders and first citizens of the commonwealth of nations. Soon many national boundaries will fall into disuse and be replaced by magnificent parks and parkways for the enjoyment of the vacationing masses, mingling with one another, each absorbing the finer traits of the others, and making continual efforts to behave in a manner that is pleasant and attractive — a stimulating and happy process of living cosmically. It will be found then that to exist within the shell of the sect, the social clan or political party, means to force the Soul-flame — which was born for starry flights — into a Procrustean bed. The man of the Golden Age will think and act with a universalized consciousness, and will be endowed with power and knowledge capable of guiding stars and solar systems towards greater harmonies and more profound truths.

* * *

"Beloved disciples, see that you map your daily activity and behavior with due wisdom. Make a habit of visualizing ahead of time the various incidents that you might encounter. This will prevent the subtle forces of evil from causing you to fall by the wayside. Do not envy your competitor and do not covet his customers, rather rejoice and bless both. I speak for those of you who will teach outside of the boundaries of America. In the old world merchants of small towns waste time and energy in destructive projections at each other. Speak to them of the law of karma.

"Do not leave your abode anytime unless genuine happiness radiates from your countenances. Tell your disciples how friendly life is with no enemies to be seen anywhere, but only one to be felt and disposed of by an act of the will, that is, the puny ego, the chronic complainer, the vampire of life and the tireless troublemaker. As long as this little 'I' is allowed to exist, man cannot collaborate with society and life constructively.

"Do not apply unwisely the law of detachment, for it breeds hypocrisy. Adhere to all constructive enterprises, work with love and diligence, and see the result as a gift of God. Enjoy it in this spirit, then move on to higher achievements.

"Do not live in a neighborhood of poverty and slums; aim for physical comfort, spaciousness, cleanliness, pleasant surroundings and a touch of elegance, whenever possible. Be mindful of your personal hygiene.

"Do not be impatient, nor issue negative or unkind statements. Should any of your calls to God remain unanswered, stay on the path and wait with alert and positive feeling. You are under test, and your trust is a siege against the citadel of obscurantism. In the end light must triumph because Light is God.

"Courage is a sign of perfect discipleship. It is a perfect blend of mind and physical strength. He who indifferently yet with a firm step walks to the stake or to the cross for the sake of an ideal is as wise as a Christ and as strong as an Archangel. He weakens his foes for many a life and strengthens the hearts of the receptive multitude for many a century, while he himself attains immortality.

"The age of the haughty employer and the narrow-minded rulers, and cowed and submissive subjects is a thing of the past. There is a spiritual, intangible and yet real oneness between the two which has to be taken into consideration at every step of the way. To neglect it means to produce a severe damage to both the society and the cosmic order. A harmonious collaboration and a genuine feeling of friendship are demanded of both. When the Roman emperors identified themselves with the gods, they did not express an untruth, but an incomplete truth, for their subjects were also gods.

"A community of people, therefore, is the most comprehensive expression of the cosmic hierachy. It is God who displays Himself, in various degrees, through the human body. He interpenetrating all things. He works, strives, loves, creates, loses and wins. He breaks human resistance; He castigates and rewards, and by so doing raises the human society closer to perfection. It is God who is born with the birth of every being: Negro, White, Hebrew, Latin, Asian, etc. How much truer and more consistent with His Law is, therefore, the concept of the Commonwealth of all Nations as against those who still proclaim the doctrine of chauvinism and isolationism.

* * *

"Truths such as these, or any truth by that matter, must not be accepted blindly, or in faith, or because of the authority wherefrom they emanate. And this is a severe warning to all of you. Do not disobey, do not weaken, or you will forfeit any future contact with us for the duration of your present embodiment. Faith unsupported by direct perception is worse than political sycophantism; it is utter degeneration of mind, body and soul. The doctrine of the infallibility of the Church has spread over the conscience of the masses a thick layer of infernal fetor, which for many centuries held man in an abyss of eerie darkness and devoured his soul almost beyond recovery. There is still a subtle residue of this condition in some of you.

"Innumerable are the ways that lead to direct perception, and some are very harsh indeed. When disease befalls suddenly on an unethical businessman, the first thing he experiences is the loss of all cravings: drinking, smoking, inordinate sexual intercourse, the urge of money-making, ambition and other material desires. In the quietude of his hospital bed, he muses on the organization that he owns and directs, and realizes for the first time that his employees are not beings to be exploited but faithful helpers and intelligent collaborators. Slowly, step by step, an actual heaviness is lifted from his chest; his grasping tendency dies out, a deep desire for self-analyzation, to study and know himself, changes into a force that is impossible to put aside.

"This is initiation, a resurrection, the Renaissance of the Soul; a process whereby the mind is redirected to its allotted task of obeying the Buddhi rather than acting on impulse based on flimsy appearances. The rude awakener is no one else but the loving and chastising Self. Now the new initiate can truly say with the words of the ancient teachers: 'Blessed be this day, O Lord, for Thou hast guided me onto the Path of no return, awakened in me the desire to seek Thee, given me proof of Thy awful Presence, and made me ready to accept Thy Law and follow Thy Command. Release me, O Lord, into the world of the manifold, and make me worthy of Thy trust in every incident of my daily life unto the end of my days.'

"This affirmation of faith based on proof elevates automatically our returning prodigal son to the status of citizenship of the Commonwealth of all Nations. His mission is well delineated; no more feverish striving for results that are personal and avulsed from the good of his fellow man; no more rushing into a task without pausing first to visualize God for inspiration and guidance; no more vain aspirations or inordinate passions. The realization of universal brotherhood is his all in all!"

* * *

The Lord Maitreya entered samadhi, deep communion with God. His resplendent form grew dim until only a soft golden-blue light was seen. New Spirit-forms were arriving, aspiring citizens of the Universal Society blending with the sea of youthful heads that stretched before them on the hallowed grounds. All was encompassed by innumerable flags of light with staffs of fire, representing every nation of earth. Presently the Lord Maitreya made himself visible, this time surrounded by a large group of Splendor-beings, who remained at his side; amongst them was a Master of towering stature and greater brilliancy who stood at his back. The radiance of their combined auras extended in every direction beyond the circular horizon, and held the vast audience in the spell of life beyond death. The Master resumed his talk:

"These immortal Splendor-beings, whose identity shall be revealed to you gradually in the near future, as you grow inwardly, are honoring us with their Presence at this gathering of interplanetary brotherhood. It is the first of the series forecasting annual meetings whose precise aim will be the consecration into the Spirit of Universal Brotherhood of Twin flame-couples as well as individuals who want to become active citizens of the Commonwealth of all nations.

"Blessed citizens of the world of God, and you also aspiring candidates, listen and learn: Your annual dues have to be paid in light; light that is produced from within and projected outwardly, silently, in the form of noble thoughts and deeds and without interruption. Such a behavior, as you very well know, will be registered in the Akashic Records. The Guardians of Life in charge will examine them and issue report parchments that are helpful for self-analyzation. Some of you will advance faster than others, and more than a few will bring testimony of experiences similar to that of Master Jesus at the time of his physical death: loss of the physical body without the so-called physical death, ecstatic moods, boundless joy and infinite peace. They will have sensations which cannot be described in words, nor can they be affirmed or denied. They are of the realms of the Soul, all-transmuting, all-elevating and all-encompassing.

* * *

"Because of your combined radiance of positive love and good will, a City of Science shall be built somewhere on earth; We know where! It will be an international pool of all the scientists of the world — East and West, United States and Russia. They will meet periodically, and like sons of man they will argue and threaten; and like sons of God they will open their hearts and minds in a commonwealth of endeavours and close their conference in a symposium of divine brotherhood.

"In dealing with the people at large, the Cosmic Assembly of the Perfect Ones has armed legions of Liberated Masters with weapons of blue fire. As the fire invests each individual lifestream it may result in annihilation, awakening or liberation, according to the residue of past karma, present thoughts and deeds, and the nature of a planned resolve in process of unfoldment. Men and families will be set free from hardships, while those who persist in violating the law will be shifted aimlessly for many aeons amidst mental disruption and spiritual distress worse than the most barbaric torture. Then, out of mercy, they will be permitted to take embodiment and start again on their ascending path from where they left off. By that time another planet will be ready for them, a medium of primitiveness and physical discomfort, for the planet earth will have been so elevated in spiritual consciousness that it will have no room for those who had gone astray. It shall be raised to the status of a self-luminous star by the concerted thoughts and deeds of the men of the Golden Age.

"In the field of education the weapons of blue fire will bring to an end the conflict between natural sciences, the arts, philosophy, political science and economics. Religion will drop off entirely;

194

the Spirit of Immanence will take over weaving into one harmonious unity all branches of learning.

"Coming back to you, my precious disciples and starry guests, I want you to know that the weapon of blue fire has passed through your physical bodies on earth and through your mental and emotional world, and no one was rejected. You have passed the test of Service. And while the cosmic orchestra plays the Symphony of Triumph, you shall be initiated into the Order of the Knights of Cosmic Service. The Light of Service pure and unqualified will saturate your minds, bodies and feelings. Henceforth all your thoughts and deeds, study and meditation, eating and sleeping, walking and athletics, buying and selling, teaching and listening, work and vacationing, shall be a resounding board of cosmic activity; no drag, no discordance, absolutely in tune with the celestial harmonies.

"Teach your disciples the Spirit of the Law; let them coin the words to express themselves before God, or to convey a truth. Stay away from stale formulae, slay uniformity, they clip the wings of creativeness, they are degrading. Issue a new and different prayer with the dawning of each new day and in the face of each new happening. Bind no one. Freedom must be absolute. Do not organize groups; refrain from preaching. Teach upon request, and aim for inner membership of the Invisible Church, both Militant and Triumphant.

"Consecrate yourselves in light as often as you wash your hands. Let it be the Baptism of the Soul in the fountainhead of bliss. Let the higher forces descend upon you and your fellow man, to sustain and protect you against temptations and distractions. Avoid idleness, it is a waste of God's time. Observe the world that surrounds you, from the insect that crawls at your feet to the starry procession above, it is life advancing unfalteringly towards nobler goals. Do not stay behind or you will come to naught. Continual watchfulness and self-analyzation are imperative. Feed the Sacred Fire with a well concentrated mind, and fan it to shadowless brilliancy with the Holy Breath. These are your soil, your seed and your tools. You are richer than you think.

"Watch the youth; they are the recipients of higher blessings in process of manifestation, but they must be prepared. They must undergo discipline intelligently blended with love. Leniency no, intelligent severity yes, and continually. And what is intelligent severity? Exemplary behavior on the part of the parents. Loud talking, foul language, interparental bickering, gossip, criticism, smoking, inordinate drinking and disorderly house, are the negation of 'intelligent severity.' Such behavior dulls first the mind of the child, confusion and emotional disarrangement follow. The spark of intuition which would have yielded new ideas is buried beneath a thick layer of damp ashes. Neither corporal punishment, nor erudite dissertations on what is right or wrong will ever re-channel him into the path of noble living and constructive deeds as planned by the Guardians of life. If he has a kind karma inherited from a previous embodiment, an Inner Helper may appear to rescue him in adult life. In the meantime he gives himself to petty crimes against his ownself and others, then more serious crimes and all sorts of violations, causing costly damages to society. Lifestreams who had planned to dedicate their intelligence and energy to constructive endeavours of cosmic nature are thwarted from their aspirations and assigned to this half-wrecked child to keep him in a vegetative state, more or less, and in repair at best.

"Such is the inestimable damage caused to the Cosmic Order by such ignorant and unloving parents. Worse than many deaths is the punishment imposed upon them for their crime.

"Intelligent severity is the subtle art of education that benefits both the teacher and the pupil. It is a process of adaptation without yielding, a faculty of foreseeing the child's reaction to outer impressions generated by either thoughtful or thoughtless people and elaborated upon in a spirit of realism that leads to truth and a desire to delve deeper into the cause behind the effect. This intelligent severity, therefore, is a task of the teacher towards himself rather than the child. It is the radiance of the effort that strikes the pupil, holds him compact and happy on the path of correct behavior, which is transmuted into respect and awe for the adult educator.

✦ ✦ ✦

"Noble disciples of Light, Knights of Cosmic Service, wise educators: You are about to descend to earth; meditate and listen."

The vast audience, now tens of thousands strong, silently stood in unison like one man.

"Nameless is the Lord; yet He is in every word of every spoken language. He is Silence, He is a Hum, He is a Song, He is in the wind and the trees and in the depths of the waters. He is in the Symphony of the Spheres. He has form and He is formless. The tiny pebble contains Him and the systems of worlds too; and He contains them all and more. Nothing else is but HE!

"He is the Thinker behind the thought, the Doer behind the action, the Silent Speaker and the only Listener. He is the wise and the fool, the Power behind the Breath, He is the Seen and the Unseen, He is the all in all. Nothing else is but He.

"O mind of man, O prodigal being, cogitate on HIM. He is thy Maker, thy Ruler, thy Guide, thy Inspirer, thy Educator. He is the Essence of thy success. Cogitate on HIM! And now behold. . . ."

High above, the atmosphere was filled with colossal letters of light in prismatic colors, floating aimlessly; then they disposed themselves to form the words: OM, I AM, Allah, Light, God, Dio, Genius, Father, Spirit, Life, Fire . . . and an infinite number of other words, each representing a name given to the Supreme Maker by every man of earth. As the letters of light began to disappear, thousands of Liberated Masters were seen wearing seamless robes of gleaming white. They mingled with the audience while Marco and Leonora enjoyed the company of their Liberated Master-Teacher. Now a voice from an unseen source spoke:

"Disciples of earth, Spirits of Liberty, Pioneers of the Golden Age. You have herewith re-established the foundation upon which you shall rebuild the Temple of the Soul whose duration defies the corruptible forces of the mortal world. While still here, enjoying such a wondrous state of consciousness, with our immortal radiance protecting your Spirit-forms, be it known to you all that any wish that you desire to make will be fulfilled at once. The nature of such a wish will guide and direct you to the task that is best suited to your temperament. Thus, by a path that is all your own you shall reach the Source of Immortality.

"It behooves you to be keenly aware that your responsibility to life has grown by leaps and bounds. You shall not make inner progress worth a farthing unless you live nobly, think nobly, approach nobly all that lives and radiate nobility in a continual flow and as a matter of course. And should you, somehow, be

197

forced to deviate from such a conduct, do not be frantic, fear not, retrace your steps, make amends and move on. Since perfection is not of the world of man, there is a constant need of re-initiating oneself before the all-encompassing Presence of the Self. By such a process you do away with churches, metaphysical societies, pilgrimages and other exteriorized rituals — whose inner value is very meager indeed — while perceiving more intensely the merciful work of the Law of Grace.

"You are at the threshold of the Christ Consciousness wherein the Second Birth or the Birth of the Spirit takes place. The growth into Christ adulthood is not a matter of course, as in physical growth, but a conscious process of inward expansion, intellectual refinement and sublimation of thoughts and deeds. You have cast aside the estate of the flesh, as large as a shell, for that of the Spirit, as small as infinitude itself. Your responsibility to your fellow man and to life has increased in proportion.

"Now the silken cord of Deliverance is in your hands. It is barely a thread, but it shall become thick, strong and secure through adherence to the Law of Love and Divine Service in the world of man. Know that every time you fall or deviate, every time you think of it in social belittling, persecution and even torture, it grows in strength like the mounting sun of dawn. Human existence, at its best, is ninety-nine per cent death; with the gift of initiation it becomes ninety-nine per cent alive; therefore, your effort consists only in that one per cent. The Law of Grace is active and directing. In your daily life, or in whatever service you render to your community, remember this: no longer do you serve a personality or a man-made institution. If they appear to be so, if they harass you beyond endurance, we shall take you away and place you in a position of prestige and soul-expansion. No longer do you strive to keep your head above water, such as struggling for physical comfort, physical health and paying taxes and bills; no longer shall you create unkind karma that saps your life now and degrades you in your next embodiment. You have risen above such nagging obstructions forever.

"This is the goal, the true dynamics of life, the urge of all men; and you are far ahead on the path. Tell the political leaders, the intellectuals and the man in the street that the Commonwealth of Life for all the children of Earth is already in action in the Realms of the Perfect Ones. It is up to humanity to claim it or reject it.

"This is the Supreme Way, the Way of no return, the Way that leads all children to their Destination: Immortality. As you are about to descend into your physical minds and bodies rejoice greatly for the consciousness of the bodiless shall remain as alive and vibrant as it is at this moment, while our Presence shall overshadow and sustain you to the end of your earthly days. You shall live in the boundless Infinitude of the Spirit.

"O disciples, O teachers, O Knights of Divine Service: once more, as of yore, because of your readiness, the Logos has taken flesh, the Truth incarnate lives again. Man's march on the path of eternal becoming is on."

* * *

The vast audience descended to Earth. On the summit of Mount Meru Marco and Leonora stood in awe beside the Great Lord Maitreya, the Master-coordinator of all the noble aspirations of mankind, the Supreme Watcher and Protector of the unfoldment of the Golden Age. Surrounded by His heavenly escort, they were invested with an aura of cosmic peace and beatitude. The starry meadow below was a sea of liquid fire burning and melting to a cosmic oneness the glorious banners of light left behind by the noble pioneers of the Commonwealth of all nations of Earth.

CHAPTER V

THE MASTER SCIENTISTS

It took Marco and Leonora many a dawn to descend from the towering peak of Mount Meru, after musing for days on the wondrous teaching of the great Lord Maitreya. And why should they descend? "Earthly life" — Marco remarked — "even at its highest level of consciousness, has nothing to offer to assuage our hearts for the great privation. We are idealists. . . ."

"No!" — the severe and commanding voice of their Guardian Angel interrupted. "You are not idealists. You are dreamers of foolish and idle dreams, caught in a web of irreality and negative thoughts leading to stagnation of mind and degeneration of body, denial of comfort, disavowal of progress, and decrial of the constructive contribution of the working man to the welfare of society. Should you continue in this attitude of indolence, you will soon cease to exist as active and productive citizens, and enter the world of the juggler, of those whose existence is based on begging, gambling, sloth, hypocrisy, cheating and childish make believe. You must work, or forfeit the gift of cosmic liberty. You must bring into realization the mandate entrusted to you by the Master Instructors. You are a living link betwen heaven and earth."

Shaken and humiliated they again touched the earth soil; from afar, coming towards them they could hear the bold music and the enthralling voices of the Gandharvas singing and playing stirring martial music which soon aroused them. Physical strength, more positive thinking, and the will to do and to dare, flooded their beings. The task ahead having been carefully delineated, the tools and material forthcoming, they now prepared to meditate for enlightenment and consolidation of their plan. As evening approached they became aware that the voices had ceased to sing and they detected ominous overtones in the music, which then became discordant and threatening as if produced by the hellions of the suspended world. Marco and Leonora were now convinced that because of their unwarranted attitude of superficiality another test of inner nature had to be faced and conquered. They gathered courage and, without hesitation, boldly started to climb the steep dorsals of a rocky elevation that had appeared before them.

As they neared the summit, they heard the rumble of thunder announcing an approaching storm over the mountain range. A shrieking, driving wind was uprooting trees and rocks and hurling them forcefully down craggy mountains into yawning crevasses with an echoing crash of indescribable fierceness. In the stormy darkness, a dim, flickering light appeared above them; following it, they came to a high narrow ridge overlooking an immense and fearful vorago filled with semiliquid matter in continual ebullition expelling mephitic vapors. Tremendous igneous rocks were thrust upward into space from where they plummeted back into the voraginous pit, causing the fetid substance to splash high above the jagged ledge in the grey tinged colors of yellow, blue, orange, green, violet, indigo and red. A fiery voice of authority was heard:

"These symbolize the end product of the mortal traits of man: envy, jealousy, rage, hatred, ignorance, avarice and pride. As they are released from man's mind and feelings, they gather at the center of the earth to be returned, at the appointed hour, to their creators by the force of the inexorable law of cause and effect. Man, individually and as a member of the collective body, called society, nation and race, must redeem them through personal and direct effort, or else. Good intentions or prayer avail him very little. Self-analyzation that leads to enlightenment, that leads to sacrifice and actual renunciation, that leads to abandonment or even complete loss of material wealth, is the only scientific way. One may encounter, while on the path, the Angel of Grace or the Christ of Love, but it is supreme wisdom and a sign of fortitude not to expect them. If this procedure seems harsh, remember this: it is man who made it so. To Us, to Those who have conquered life and death, it is just, wise and perfect, it is love made manifest. Though traces of these pernicious traits still linger in your consciousness, you shall no longer fall under their dominance, because you know the science and possess the scientific knowledge that leads to their dissolution. We shall continue to chastise you in the absolute awareness that this is what you want, that this is the most efficacious method of protection against the vicious assaults of physical, intellectual and moral filth that still plague the world.

"Disciple-initiates, be alert, be determined, be self-reliant, never take the Master, the Light and God for granted. As the cosmic forces never for one instant cease to sustain life, likewise you must proceed, through awareness, to meet these forces on their own ground, and mold them to your own needs and aspirations. If you have not meditated, or if your meditation does not have the fervor of the perennial dedicated one, what are your needs? Not much higher than those of the beast of the jungle. And your aspirations? A more or less vegetative life. With daily meditation and periodical self-interrogation and keen analyzation of your thoughts and motives you enter at once into a physical environment as vast as infinitude itself, an intellectual world of creativity, and a moral realm of angelic nobility."

As the elemental rebelliousness gradually subsided and the stillness of the night was fully restored, a beautiful spiral of luminous filaments, as fine as gossamer, rose from the center of the volcano and illumined the sky above intermittently. With each emanation of light a myriad of white sparkles rained down upon the earth. The same voice, in a gentle tone, spoke again:

"Sooner or later the Light of Peace and Understanding shall emanate from the fiery turmoil of man's spiritual destitution. In the world of the manifold light and ignorance are strangely related to one another, but never are they mixed or united. And when the latter rules the former stands in waiting, but when light rules ignorance ceases to be.

"There is a focus of light and virtue in every hovel of crime and vice; it is an advanced garrison at the service of God, waiting for an inkling of remorse; then it strikes with amazing swiftness and scientific precision, to punish and forgive, to illumine, sustain and elevate. How deeply aware of God is a sinner in the midst of his sinning, in the interspace of two consecutive violating thoughts. His doubt, anxiety and fear, concerning the outcome of his evil deed, are generated by an inner rebellion, an unconscious awakening of the law of ethics within, demanding and commanding him to cease violating God's Statutes of correct behavior.

"When humanity persistently disobeys the Law of Life, that is, when the Light and Energy with which man is endowed are misused, God, out of mercy and love for the world at large, raises Its hand from within man's heart, to accelerate the swelling of corruption and bring all defilement to a quick termination. And as soon as man becomes aware of his violation, God, again, out of supreme wisdom, opens immediately the path of spiritual ascendancy. This is, in essence, the mechanics of truth and error, punishment and forgiveness. It is all within. It is light and energy springing forth from the heart, pure and unadulterated, misqualified and polluted by an ignorant mind, forced to commit all sorts of violations which revert to sorrow and suffering for the user, and then it is reclaimed again by another wave of light and energy issuing from the same source.

"The same Light and Energy are also stored, in tremendous concentration, in the Etheric Belt and at the center of the earth. This shows man to be an integral part of the Cosmic Order, and how indissolubly linked he is with every form of organic life and inorganic matter. All destructive thoughts and deeds, after the indescribable havoc produced in man's mind, feelings and world, go downward into the center of the earth, where they are charged with the quality of redemption or evolutive vibration, and returned systematically to man in the form of wars, cataclysms, epidemics, poverty and other scourges. Then as they are acknowledged and expiated, they go upward to the Etheric Belt to be taken by the Liberated Masters and charged with the quality of durability in the form of new scientific inventions and philosophical teachings whose application gives to man greater physical comfort and closer understanding of the Law of God. And this is evolution.

"The cognition of this activity is a supporting pillar to him who is beset with grief and doubt as a result of his many violations. At the first appearance of a disturbing force, rather than running here and there in search of human help, he should face himself squarely and submit meekly for punishment, whatever it may be. This simple and courageous decision elevates him to the lofty status of a Son of God. His heart and mind emptied of all opinions, excuses and self-justification, become a Holy Grail waiting to be filled with the Grace of Understanding and Wisdom that knows no human failure. From now on this man so transformed will meditate daily for guidance and help in the transmutation of all conditions interfering with the normal flow of divine blessings into his world. A Liberated Master-Teacher will not be wanting.

"Thus step by step man conquers himself until he stands supreme master and ruler over the self. One by one, all the imperfections and shortcomings hidden in the subconscious are destroyed; he rises above fear, doubt, loneliness and the damnable concept of insufficiency; he feels strengthened and unerringly guided in every thought, at every action, and with joy unbounded he transfers this wealth of blessings to whoever is receptive, at no cost whatsoever and with no questions asked. Physical health and economic well being grow side by side with spiritual expansion. In the shadowless Light of the Self, no traveling is required to hear the Buddha, the Christ, the Avatar; no temple to frequent, no ritual to follow, no prayer or rosary to recite. By sitting in meditation, man's future life is woven on a canvas of light. The theme of his visualization impresses the canvas, while the displaced light enters his mind for further material and spiritual conquests."

*　*　*

Many a month went by as Marco and Leonora worked on self-refining. There was no sacrifice involved, only the acquisition of a deeper and ever deeper awareness of God in all their daily activities. In the meantime they were building the needed momentum whereby they could be contacted by their Liberated Master-Teacher for more intimate teaching, teaching of universal nature, for revelations of the things of life not written in books. Night and morning, day after day, they meditated in absolute trust, visualizing the Master's effulgent Presence illumining their study in the depths of the night. He came exactly as pictured, his voice youthfully bewitching:

"Worthy disciples, it is God Who causes me to hear you, Who moves me towards you, Who enlightens me concerning your spiritual welfare. It is God Who does all. When we welcome and see God's Presence in all our endeavours, antagonism and misunderstanding cease, all things are seen in unity. Spirit and matter, science and philosophy, capital and labor, are not each other's enemy. Only ignorance is the enemy of all; and ignorance stems not from lack of school education, but from inability or unwillingness to meditate. Teach man to meditate, and within seventy-two hours you shall have a new society. Teach the white and the Negro to meditate and in seventy-two hours you shall have the dispute over the Civil Rights movement solved as if by magic, each party claiming an overwhelming victory, each party disappearing into the other. And do not be discouraged, O my disciples, for this seeming lack of interest in meditation displayed by the people at large. We, in the Octaves of Life, are working, and the fruit is not far off. Have patience. Accept the truth that the universal awakening is at your doorstep, that the East and the West, the Free World and the World behind the Iron Curtain, are about to initiate discussions of enduring collaboration in politics, science and economics, all based on spiritual oneness; and as in the meadow of Mount Meru, every member of the Cosmic Congress will be overshadowed by his own Liberated Master-Teacher. And because the practice of meditation amongst the masses of Soviet Russia is more widespread than in the Free World, greater is the pressure there for the founding of this Cosmic Congress.

"Because the democratic society is not any less plagued with political, social and moral diseases than the regimented society of the communistic countries, and because freedom is often abused, and too much of it in any organized society leads to license and disruption of law and order, we shall bring to light an ancient teaching which was successfully tested in the laboratory of public life. It did not last because it was meant to be a test case only, molded by a genius who took embodiment more than two thousand years too soon. I refer to the teaching and experimentation in political science of Master Pythagoras of Samos. You also took embodiment during the same time, and as students frequented with him the same esoteric school of Memphis in the land of Egypt. Marco's name was Arcus, and Leonora's was Lunide. In the unfoldment of the experiences that follow you will be convinced once more that in the light of modern science, Pythagoras' teaching and what you have learned in the present embodiment are exactly alike, that is, the realization of a Christ-like society based on meditation.

"The school that Pythagoras founded in the 6th century B.C., in the city of Crotona, Magna Graecia, though basically scientifico-spiritual, was essentially non-sectarian. The concept of the Immanent God was predominant in every phase of the curriculum. Silence and stillness of the mind were the method whereby such Immanence could be scientifically grasped. He achieved such marvelous results in every field of endeavour that none of his contemporaries had a feeling of indifference towards him. He was loved and respected by those who had a happy karma, and feared and hated by those whose program in life was to steal and cheat, mislead and exploit, their fellow man.

"During your early youth, each of you individually in the sanctuary of family life, were trained in the ancient philosphy of Hermes Trismegistos, or Three Times Blest, Father and Founder of the Egyptian civilization. Hermes' teaching was the exact replica of the Vedic Philosophy taught by independent gurus in the caves of Tibet, along the banks of the rivers, in the forests of India, Burma and Siam, and on the island of Ceylon. Every teacher helped himself unstintingly from the Upanishads which were older than any existent philosophy of life, and adapted them to his own moods, environment, traditions and aspirations. When Moses came, he expressed the concept of God in the clear sentence: *I AM THAT I AM is My Name and I reside in the heart of every man. Know ME thus!* Apollo revealed it to the Greek World as *KNOW THY-SELF and thou shalt know the universe and God.* And Master Jesus transmitted it to the Western Man in the still misconstrued words *I AM the Way, the Truth and the Life . . . I and My Father are one . . . I AM with you always . . .*, meaning not the personality of Jesus, but the Christ-light which he had drawn forth through meditation.

"I must emphasize the words *independent gurus,* to show that there were no religious sects. These teachers were not appointed by a king or a high priest, but having attained Direct Perception by the path of inwardness, they were divinely appointed and qualified to teach whoever had the desire to learn. They did not frequent seminaries or theological schools, but simply sought within, exactly as you do, exactly as you did, not only in Egypt but also in the embodiments of India and Persia. This explains your proficiency in meditation, and the help you will be able to render to your fellow man.

"What caused the practice of meditation to fail? It was a multiple and complex assault from many sides waged by the obscure forces of priestcraft, politicians, criminals, gamblers, cheaters and exploiters. None of these wants man to meditate. What use has the meditative disciple for pills and drugs, of life insurance and books on pornography, of blood banks and guns, of costly funerals and police protection, and of name and fame? Absolutely none. The modern priesthood does in a very mild way approve the doctrine of meditation, but woe unto him who dares to substitute meditation for the Mass, the recitation of the Ave Maria, the communion or the Sunday Sermon. Meditate, O man, and you will strike at the roots of all war, espionage, hospitals, shylocks, tobacco stands, dope traffickers, gambling casinos, and similar practices and institutions including Monte Carlo and the whole state of Nevada. What a society it will be, simpler, truly elegant, and geared for absolute evolution.

"Some of the ancient teachers, such as Pythagoras, Socrates and Jesus, in order to leave behind a tangible focus of their truths as entrusted to them by the Cosmic Assembly of the Perfect Ones, had to allow their bodies to be torn apart by the mob of human society. No longer! The Supreme Rulers of Life have decreed that the accredited Teachers, Christs and Buddhas, in human form shall broadcast the Verbum of Meditation to every nation and in every language fully protected from belittling, calumny and physical violence attempted against them by anyone, be it a tyrant or a priest. A wall of light impenetrable to physical weapons or mental projection will surround each teacher of meditation. Mankind has already much evil Karma to redeem: the persecution of the early Christians, the treacherous butchering of the Albingenses instigated by the 'saintly' Dominican Friars, the wanton slaughtering performed by the crusaders in the name of 'Christ the King', the massacres of the Night of St. Bartholomew, the hundreds of thousands of sons and daughters of the Christ that perished under the bloody hands of the Holy Inquisition, directed by the bestial priestcraft that called themselves 'the Protectors of the Faith', the Hitler regime that killed millions of innocent Jews, and many other similar tragic events. And there is the damnable projection, that still goes on, of derisive thoughts of a Catholic against a Protestant, or a Jew, or a Buddhist, and vice versa; it is a massive build-up of destructive forces powerful enough to blast the terrestial globe into a shapeless mass.

"No longer, we say! The Hand of Heaven has turned to a compassionate severity, exactly, to a merciful mercilessness. Should the patriotic historians of nations, and the custodians of the Halls of Fame with their display of relics and mementos, see the Akashic Records of their 'saints', 'heroes' and 'great' leaders, they would be bitterly disappointed. Many of these were reborn crippled, blind, epileptic, physically malformed, diseased, sexually impotent, prone to cancer and other organic degeneration, and with an I. Q. not any higher than a total idiot. Think of Napoleon, for instance, so exalted and worshipped by his contemporaries; and even today considered still as a star of first magnitude in the firmament of France. Since his death in 1821 he has been reborn six times and died as a monstrously deformed being before reaching the age of twenty, his glandular system in a pitiful state of disarrangement, and his perceptive faculty barely clear, now and then, for him to see in perspective the unending crimes that he committed to satisfy his assertive ego. It will take him another five-hundred years before his I. Q. begins to rise again.

"In the present century you have had various lifestreams with similar karma: Stalin, Hitler, Mussolini, Roosevelt, and their sycophants; rulers of Imperial Russia, Germany, Austria and Japan; British and other European political leaders involved in the maladministration of their colonial empires; and, with only a few exceptions, all the popes and the heads of the Roman Curia. Some of the latter are even slated for sainthood. The truth is instead that everyone of them is, at this moment, in the midst of you, with a more or less defective physical body and impaired mind, in his millennial task of redeeming all the suffering that he has caused to society. Life can wait. The wheel of birth, death and sorrow shall never cease turning for him who does not meditate.

"This is the result of man's extrovertness; a series of false appraisals at every step of the way, suggested by his incapacity or unwillingness to seek interiorly. It is a scenario of confusion that seems orderly, of evil that appears constructive and noble, of permanence without principle, and of reality devoid of the central nucleus of living truth."

* * *

As the Master withdrew, the somber shadow of the night returned. Marco and Leonora felt waves of light pass over and again through their minds in a cleansing and purifying activity; all specks of worldly thinking were temporarily washed away and a feeling of eternity encompassed them. They took refuge in the Unwritten Law and humbled themselves at the Lotus Feet of the Creative Spirit. "Speak to us" — they entreated — "guide us, teach us. We are thirsty and hungry for truth and wisdom and for everything that springs forth from Thy mind . . ." An invisible hand touched their foreheads, and they felt resurrected and renewed. Then the voice of their Master was heard again:

"Let a feeling of wonderment and joy pervade you through and through, for you are at the threshold of a new experience that touches you both directly and intimately. But first behold what you leave behind, and beneath your feet: a dark star, the earth, which neither generates life, nor is it able to sustain it; yet once it was a fixed star of first magnitude, a starry mate of the Sun. Behold the vast majority of human beings, heavily chained with disease, poverty, fear, idiosyncrasies and every type of crime born of ignorance; adhering strangely to habits and traditions that are childish and incongruous. See how they race, in a frantic mood, towards self-annihilation, concerned primarily with the gratification of the senses, seriously convinced that this is the supreme aspiration in life. See how they rush madly for the limelight, towards name and notoriety, wealth and a dignified funeral, causing the earth to stagger beneath an unwanted burden.

"Behold other human beings standing still and confused at the crossroads of life, incapable of making a decision. What fodder they are for the scum of death, the discarnate entities of crime and depravity who, riding on ugsome beasts

210

of their own making, prey mercilessly on such a forage of weaklings, driving them to premature death, or turning them into plotters for more heinous crimes of social and moral order — alcoholism, sexual abuse, dope, theft, murder, gambling, bribery, threat, kidnapping, usury, misleading advertisements, political and religious despotism, espionage, lynching, treason, slander and war — and making them their own comrades for further suffering and spiritual involution.

"Observe now that group of youths, so handsome and happy, and exuding the absolute conviction of success in life. They are lawyers, scientists, artists, medical doctors, Ph.D's, and so forth — just graduated from the university — and about to enter the productive world with a purpose. Alas! Only a few will adhere to the law of ethics that holds them on the path of spiritual ascendancy; the rest are ready and willing to forfeit their minds, energy and life itself to the pursuit of activities that are the very negation of common sense and basic existence as intended by God, as if their intelligence were still in the stage of the subhuman. With a superficiality that denies the fundamental instinct of survival, they give themselves to espionage, or to the manufacturing of bubble gum, or to printing pornographic books, or to selling dope to the youths, or to broadcasting to their own people, in a truculent and bellicose attitude, carefully garbed in a scholarly aura, outright lies against a foreign nation with the intent of creating a casus belli; or to defending members of the murderous Cosa Nostra, or to the exaltation on the Radio and Television of the virtues of such and such a cigarette, or to make a shamble of another human being's character who happened to disagree with their political tenets. And I could continue here indefinitely. And at the end of the day each of these wasted and unrepenting intelligences goes home, happy and satisfied for a *good day's work* measured, naturally, in terms of money and outer success. Now he turns his corrupt and deadly wits upon his children, elaborating on his noble behavior, honesty, fair play, justice and so forth. No wonder the earth is so dark in spite of the light shed upon it by the blazing sun.

"Now, O awakened disciples, deepen your meditation and behold! See here and there tiny specks of light, coming and going like fireflies. It is another multitude of men striving for light, now failing and now falling, yet determined to ascend and triumph. These we do help; these you must help, and the rule of conduct is: *Seek within. Know thyself. Hold thy mind from wandering outwardly. Confine your thoughts within thy heart. Shut out all external objects. Rid thyself of all negative qualities.* And sooner than expected the Angel-helper will come to guide each one towards the dissolution of all obstruction and limitation.

*   *   *

"I want herewith to issue a statement of truth for the benefit of the worrying demographists who are concerned with the complex problem of overpopulation. The Cosmic Assembly of the Perfect Ones is about to take steps to bring the demographic growth to a standstill. Not because of lack of food or water or space. It is instead a hastening process of cosmic cleansing. A lesser amount of lifestreams with unkind karma will be permitted to take embodiment on earth: a greater number of lifestreams now living on earth, who persist in disobeying the Unwritten Law and refuse to heed the recommendations suggested by our accredited teachers, will be dispatched to far away islets of the Milky Way, there to dissipate their ill-qualified energy against themselves.

"Blessed disciples, I AM pleased with your inner progress and high level of thought upon which you stand at this hour. You have stood bravely before the onslaught. Be vigilant, inly vigilant, and watch the enemy within for, by comparison, the enemy without is a bosom friend. Know that the higher you go, the easier it is to fall. It is through alertness and practice of what you already know that you protect your spiritual acquisition against scattering and depreciation.

"Make every outward movement the expression of an inner visualization of perfection and beauty. Hold undiminished for the whole day the happy resiliency released to you at the morning meditation; link the evening meditation with that of the morning in an unbroken stream of lofty thoughts. See the people that you meet not as ordinary individuals but worshippers like you and greater than you. This is working for God consciously and continually; this is living eternally.

"Know that the moment you project an unkind thought to your fellow man, you shatter the living temple in which you dwell and expose yourselves to greater danger than that which you have projected. One may have his house fire insured through the purchase of a policy, but no one can ever protect your Soul-flame; only inner vigilance can give this protection. Therefore stay away from inward and outward idleness.

"The fact that I AM ready to answer your calls does not imply that you should lean on your Master, for this will lead to self-defeat. My appearance to you is, partially, the result of your meditation and noble living. Should these be lacking or insufficient, I would be compelled by the Cosmic Law to sever my connection with you. The lotus bud blooms beneath the water, well-hidden from physical sight; then it comes to the surface and displays itself to the appreciative onlooker. Be as a lotus bud: strive incessantly with no thought in mind but to rise and rise and rise from beneath all that is human, limited and mortal. And now behold the Akashic Records projecting on the screen of life some of the highlights of one of your past embodiments."

❉ ❉ ❉

The Pythagorean Era — sixth century B.C. — appeared on the canvas of time. There was the island of Samos, floating leisurely on the sparkling blue waters of the Aegean Sea, of the Sporades group, off Asia Minor, northwest of Miletus and southeast of Chios.

It was late spring: aboard a sailboat fully equipped for seafaring in the Mediterranean were three handsome youths, Pythagoras, Arcus and Lunide, manning the beautiful craft. All were similarly garbed in pleated knee-length lightweight woolen skirts with bloused shirtwaists of a dull silk fabric. A wide dark silken sash was wound about their waists. Sandals and full-length socks completed their attire. Lunide was tall and slender, with dark-brown eyes, of a wondrous beauty, golden olive skin, and copper-brown hair that shone with a high natural luster. Pythagoras and Arcus were taller than Lunide but of the same complexion. They had the mien and poise of two well-nurtured youths of well-to-do Grecian families.

213

Pythagoras' father was a goldsmith of repute, while Arcus' was a lace merchant whose trade extended as far as Carthage, Rome, Etruria and Fretum Herculeum.

At this time Samos — Pythagoras and Arcus' birthplace — was a focus of culture: art, philosophy, literature and rhetoric were prospering; sculpture and fine pottery were at their peak. Its maritime power was competing successfully with Carthage, Egypt and Tyre. Although linked to Greece for language and religion, Samos was a political entity per se; and because of its wealth derived from agriculture, trade guilds and exports, the citizens were always able to bargain for their liberty with their powerful enemies: Persia and Greece.

Lunide was the only child of Lucerna, governess in the princely household of Sonchis, the Chief Hierophant of the famed esoteric school of Memphis, Egypt. Lucerna was a disciple-initiate of this school, and because of her great inner light, she was highly trusted by her master.

Desirous to know how it was possible for Lunide to be the daughter of a member of Sonchis' household where the vow of celibacy was mandatory, unbreakable and absolute for everyone, Marco and Leonora saw the screen changing to give them a pictorial history of Lunide's birth. Erect and pensive, his head shaven, and clothed in imposing state vestments of white and gold, the Chief Hierophant, followed by thirty-six hierarchs walked towards Lucerna's apartment at noonday. He took the baby Lunide, less than two days old, and carried her through unending corridors and columnated halls to the majestic basilica of Osiris. There, amidst music and clouds of incense, he placed her on the altar and offered her, with the ritual of royal consecration, to the Verbum-Light of the Resurrection, in homage to a being of celestial descent.

A similar ceremony was being performed in Samos at exactly the same time. A masculine child, Arcus, three days old, is taken by his mother Devna to the Temple of Hera to be consecrated before the Holy of Holies and dedicated to the Light of Apollo.

The Akashic Records showed Devna and Lucerna as bosom friends of the same age, in the prime of womanhood, making a pilgrimage to the Temple-garden of Delphi, at the foot of

Mount Parnassus, in the city of Athens. While meditating, they heard the Delphian Oracle speak:

"Virgin flames rejoice! Hear the happy tidings. Erelong you two shall separate. Devna shall be the vessel for a Soul-flame who seeks embodiment for greater Light, and when such a He-light manifests, his companion of life will also take embodiment, through Lucerna, after the manner of the gods. A mysterious stream of fire shall descend into Lucerna's womb for a feminine lifestream, the embodiment of charm and compassion. And all shall be well." The two maidens understood very little of the words of the Oracle, but they were unafraid. And thus it came to pass as foretold.

Lunide and Arcus met for the first time in Memphis, at the age of seven, when Arcus' parents were visiting Lucerna. The two children were inseparable playmates for several weeks, roaming together in the sequestered garden of Sonchis' pontifical palace. Lucerna had planned to introduce the little boy to the Chief Hierophant in the hope that he would be consecrated to the Light of Osiris in conformity with the Egyptian religion. A few days later the two children were taken by their mothers to the basilica, with Arcus attired in the vesture of the land of the Pharaoh. Walking slowly towards the altar, where the ritual of the Perennial Fire of Consecration was unfolding before thousands of faithful worshippers, they kneeled on the first of the seven steps leading to the holy shrine. As Sonchis, arrayed in his magnificent vestments, turned to bless the awed congregation, he saw the two mothers and their children looking up at him in mute supplication. Reading their thoughts, the high prelate extended his hands to Lunide and Arcus as a sign of invitation, then placed Lunide's hand in Arcus' and amidst exalted music and singing led the two little neophytes towards the Sacred Fire where he caused their foreheads to touch. The children stood transfixed, their countenances glowing with the reverberation of the fiery-flaming tongues emanating from the immense brazier. As the music ceased, Sonchis opened the ceremony of consecration with a brief invocation.

"OM, Perennial Light of Osiris, Thou sole Dweller in the heart of every man. We call unto Thee. Speak through us the Word of Truth, the Logos, THAT which shall guide the lives of these two children, Lunide and Arcus!" He remained silent for a moment, then spoke again: "I thank Thee, O Father OM!" Now he addressed directly the consecrated ones:

"As in the past, so it is today and in the ages that are to come. You have passed from a starry abode to an abode of starry possibilities on earth; and you shall draw many a man to higher planes of life. It is herewith decreed that you shall never separate, for in your oneness of mind and purpose lies your usefulness to society and God. Let meditation on the Verbum-Light of the Resurrection be the instrument of attainment, and the source of material prosperity. Live in accordance with the Unwritten Law, and let the Truth flow through unhindered. May your parents so live as to justify the grace that is theirs. And may the grace of the Inner Sight descend upon you and upon those who accept and practice meditation. Go now, grow in love and purity so that you may serve God accordingly."

* * *

Lunide visited Arcus' parents seven years later when she was fourteen and approaching womanhood in all the glory of unmarred beauty and charm. Side by side with her splendid physique, she possessed a subdued and evanescent light which gave her the ability to make herself invisible whenever she desired. Her skin was almost transparent and her walk had the grace and elegance of the royal personages of her land. Arcus was not in Samos at this time; he had been sent to Miletus to the famed school of Thales to study under Anaximander, whose knowledge of physics and matter, and the theory that the latter was endowed with boundless possibilities of transformation, had attracted scores of students from all over the Eastern Mediterranean basin. None of the great teachers of Greece of this time taught or spoke of God. The Hellenic culture of that age produced only shrewd politicians and despots; most of the students planned their careers in terms of monetary gain, crushing mercilessly ideals and ethics, and showing no interest in human values. All was foul and fast decaying. It was no wonder that the Egyptians despised everything that was from Greece: people, goods, culture, religion, political institutions and the arts.

The screen of life now runs fast, without pictures or sound; there are only blank spaces with occasional vertical bars in jet black, interrupting the whiteness of the canvas. Seven went by, then new episodes appeared.

Lunide at the age of twenty-one returned to Samos to find Arcus fully graduated from Miletus. The age, the education and the diploma had made him the classical by-product of the Greek civilization of that time. Inwardly he was pensive, severe and humble; outwardly superficial, boastful and proud. But Lunide's presence changed all this. Under her probing and loving eye, he began to unfold his true nature, to express the anguish of his heart, and his yearning for truth and real knowledge. She recited poetry and sang verses of profound symbolism, and as she chanted or spoke, Arcus saw chariots of light moving in midair propelled by unseen powers. White-robed beings of celestial handsomeness, their heads immersed in light, passed and repassed before his vision. He heard arcane instruments playing intoxicating melodies, and the Egyptian idiom spoken with indescribable mastery and grace. One syllable meant the vast and roaring ocean, another the infinite universe, and then OM, the first of all sounds, the shortest and most melodious, the all-pervading Spirit that creates, transforms and destroys, THAT without which all is chaos and void, THAT whose gaze or touch exalts and immortalizes. As Arcus' consciousness unfolded, powerful currents of light caused strange waves of energy and intelligence to rise up through his spine into his head, sweeping out all the debris of a decadent outlook, and all residue of fear, duality and delusion. He began to live in bliss.

One afternoon the two youths walked barefoot to the temple of Hera and therein knelt for awhile in meditation before the main altar. As they were about to leave, they saw the high priest Mordecai in his gorgeous liturgical attire of the highest religious ritual, heading a procession of lesser priests and musicians, moving devoutly and with synchronized gait, towards the Holy of Holies. The long train of his white linen robe, richly wrought with embroidery of purple and gold, was carried by seven laical brethren. The priests sang and swung their censers causing thick clouds of hallowed incense to float above their heads. As they reached the seventh step leading to the innermost sanctuary, they knelt before the Sacred Fire of the Holy Grail, then prostrated themselves in a wordless offering of their thoughts, actions and aspirations to God.

As the sacrificial ceremony ended, Mordecai invited Lunide and Arcus to kneel on the first of the steps leading to the altar. Then extending his hands above their heads, he pronounced the solemn prayer of divine solicitation:

"I invoke Thee, O Light of Orpheus, Father-God OM. In the vastness of Thy Creation, the Twin Flames mindful of Thee, search for one another. It is through thy grace that they succeed. Only they who thus descend to earth never forget their source, the Fatherland of the Spirit. In the remembrance of THAT, they think and work in harmony with Thy Law, and with every passing moment they come closer to Thy Mansion of Eternal Light.

"This is the article of the Covenant between Thee and these two youths, Arcus and Lunide. Through the knowledge of the Golden Verbum of the Resurrection, they will easily find the path of return.

"O Great Spirit of Orpheus, Formless One, Cosmic Liberator, make these youths a temple unto themselves, filled with Thy Light. Before their achievements in the Light I bow. I thank Thee, I thank Thee, I thank Thee."

❀ ❀ ❀

Ten days have elapsed; the screen of life shows Devna and Arcus entertaining Lunide in the lovely garden of their villa. The Egyptian maiden, happy and carefree, sips from a Phoenician amphora a beverage of fruit and honey. Suddenly her joyous mood changes to one of sobering reflection. Begging forgiveness, she sits on a low reclining chair and, with her eyes closed, loses herself in profound reverie, as if absorbed in thought transference. They hear her saying:

"I see my mother lying on her couch, in physical anguish, but inly happy. She holds me close to her, and I feel the warm gaze of her beautiful eyes. Now she speaks to me: 'My child, I am about to go, for I did not take embodiment to be a governess, but to prepare the way for thy coming. This has been accomplished according to the Law that governs thy destiny. Now, hearken, my child, unto what I am about to say, for I repeat what I have told you in years past. Let my

218

teaching, which is the teaching of your invisible Father, stay with you until the day of your triumph over birth and death. Thou art a child of heaven: heaven is thy beginning, thy medium and thy goal. Thus far I have been thy visible teacher; henceforth a greater Teacher shall be thy guide. Obey Him. The Path of Light is, in truth, the Path of Love. Make Love thy credo. The more you love, the higher I shall be raised; the closer you will be to Cosmic Triumph. Love is what links man to God; Light is the reward, and Light is all-inclusive. He who loves, his earthly existence is enshrouded in heavenly bliss, every thought of his generates a healing tune, and every action is bathed in beauty.

"'Now I am ready to ascend, my child: be not dismayed, radiate joy instead, for this is what I need at this hour. My love unto Arcus and his parents, unto you and all life.'

"I see my mother growing pale. Through a telepathic call she has summoned Sonchis. 'Thou hast been released from earthly links for eternal years!'—he is saying. 'A life as broad as infinitude awaits thee. Thou hast triumphed by the Path of Love!' He touches her forehead. The dazzling luminance of Hermes, surrounded by a legion of Splendors, has descended and now stands waiting high in midair. My mother's Spirit, in the shape of a lotus flower, leaves her body and begins to ascend. She is welcomed by Hermes, her Twin Flame, who holds her forever in his embrace of immutable love and happiness. Now they direct their gaze to earth where her physical body lies, and through intense visualization transmute it into light and resolve it into the realm of Primal Energy."

* * *

Another episode which occurred a few days later appeared on the Screen. It was early morning in late spring. Lunide and Arcus, their hearts in love, took a stroll on a lovely country path flanked with agnus casti heavily ladened with fragrant white blossoms. They were discussing Arcus' education received in Miletus; its superficiality and lack of constructive purpose. In a tone of bitterness Arcus said:

"The ancient philosophers and wise teachers who made our land great and noble by following the doctrine of the Master Initiate Orpheus, have been substituted by petty despots surrounded by spineless sycophants and a brutal military machine. I am of the opinion that the inner teachings should come out of the esoteric schools and be made available to the common people. Only in this way can ethics and constructive leadership be reinstated. If the Hellenic world is out of the fold of enlightenment, it is because the basic teaching of *Know Thyself* is forgotten, no longer applied. Behold: in Rome the wise laws of the king-Initiate Numa Pompilius are illumining the minds of many a legislator and tribune, political corruption is denounced vehemently. In India Buddhas and Avatars are gathering spiritual laurels everywhere, while Egypt stands high in the doctrine of the Verbum-light of the Resurrection. What is happening to us? Why do I feel so helpless notwithstanding my diploma?" He ceased speaking as if wanting to force an answer from Lunide, but she remained silent and thoughtful; then Arcus concluded:

"I have such a powerful yearning to be taught how to deepen my meditation, to improve my inner growth . . ."

They walked slowly; the sun was at the zenith, and the air was warm. A farmer came by pulling an ass loaded with covered baskets containing live poultry and provisions of fresh fruit and cheese. Arcus purchased some food and the two youths ate their lunch sitting by a brook under a sycamore tree. During the afternoon they wandered a little, gazing at shepherds and sheep and country folk in their untroubled happiness and pastoral simplicity. At sunset they returned to the stream for meditation; a sense of tranquillity gradually came to Arcus.

As they emerged from the introspective discipline, they saw, a few paces away, a well-dressed and strikingly handsome youth of about their age. He radiated all the traits of a perfect son of man: poise, respect and innate intelligence. As he spoke however, one could feel the forces of a complex spiritual crisis warring within.

"Greetings, my friends" — he said, bowing almost reverently before Lunide. "My name is Pythagoras of Samos; my father is a goldsmith, away now and working in the new palace of our tyrant-ruler. Partenide is the name of my wise mother. Twenty-one years ago, when I was only three days old, I was blessed by the noble Mordecai, and at the age of seven my parents took me to the Temple of Delphi to be consecrated to the Light of Apollo. After the ritual, and in the midst of a clamoring crowd of worshippers, a flash of blinding light issued from the main altar and struck me, wherefore a divine voice spoke: 'This child is marked by destiny; he shall be a wise teacher to all men of every land and for many ages. Let him go to the land of the Pharaohs and there learn what is needed to fulfill his destiny, for while there he will be crowned Master-Initiate.'

"Because of my parents' wealth and love, I have traveled extensively and have been taught by famous teachers, but with meagre results. All I see in Samos is a veneer. Our Tyrant Polycrates rules with a heavy and bloody hand. God is mocked and the people have lost their liberty. I am restless and unhappy, and often driven to the brink of self-annihilation, but now my day has come. I must prepare myself for the task that is ahead of me. Last night in a vivid dream the Voice of Destiny spoke to me again, and it directed me to seek after a maiden from Egypt who is visiting Samos at this time — a wise disciple of the Verbum-Light of the Resurrection — who shall intercede for me with the Chief Hierophant of the School of Light in Memphis. Certitude and doubt, fear and joy are battling against each other within me. In the awakened state I wept in gratitude and begged my guiding voice to direct me whereto that maiden was to be found. 'Walk' was the word that I heard. Walk I shall, hoping. . . . Please forgive me. Perhaps you will say a prayer in my behalf, and wish me success."

"Blessed be your unseen Guide" — Arcus said. "Be still and behold, my brother!" A light shone around the head of Lunide, and Pythagoras saw and understood. He bowed again before her and kissed her hand in gratitude in the manner of a disciple to a holy man.

❋ ❋ ❋

"We shall go to Memphis" — Lunide said. "Seven days hence we shall be on our way. I must warn you, gentlemen, to keep our plans in the utmost secrecy, for in the things of the Inner secrecy is the key to success. The disturbing and envious entities that surround you both are too powerful to be underestimated. Your mother (speaking to Pythagoras) is, at this moment, being inly instructed by the Voice that guided you here, to let you go without a tear or the slightest sign of grief, although she will never see you again. Throw away all your diplomas, forget your book knowledge. In Memphis truth and knowledge will come to you by Direct Perception. Study and cultivate self-confidence; your Inner Helper will guide you towards your cherished goal. You may know the definition of matter, but you will never know its living essence until you are able to penetrate and transmute it, not by laboratory experimentation, but by the power of your mind, made pure, omnipotent and all-wise by means of self-analysis. Pythagoras, my brother, I welcome thee!"

Devna and Partenide met and welcomed each other with the kiss on the forehead, in the manner of the feminine inner sisterhood. Together they provided the three youths with a graceful sail, elegantly equipped.

During the voyage Lunide continued to instruct her two companions: "Cultivate enthusiasm . . ., accept discipline without the slightest feeling of resistance . . ., obey, and offer yourselves for service . . ., observe the Law of Silence at all times. In Greece you were taught how to draw the gods to the highest level of the human intellect, and often lower. In Egypt man ascends towards Godship through the Science of the Verbum-light of the Resurrection. Man's mind is limited in all of its exploits when left to its own resources; it becomes all-pervading when forced to listen to its greater Master residing in the heart. You will be taught how to live by what you learn, because what you learn is living science, not dead formulae or man-made laws. I love the discipline of the School because, in spite of its severity, it is still within the circulus of acceptance of the average student with firm resolve.

"If Hellenism teaches one how to be a brilliant speaker, Egypt teaches instead the eloquence of silence; for when one is self-possessed, the utterance of a simple statement is the result of a long and severe analysis; hence it must be a truth. Forensic eloquence or political oratory or dramatic recitation die out as soon as the speaker ceases to speak, all is forgotten within an hour, while a truth pierces both the heart and mind, in spite of the simplicity of its literary style; it produces such a conviction and acceptance that it causes a radical change in the life of many a listener.

"As you shall see, the land of Egypt is a starry heaven unto itself. Those who are planning our destruction and trying to menace our free institutions will never succeed in grasping the secret of our teaching. A few years after your graduation, you shall witness the invasion of our land by the hordes of Cambyses. There will be massacres and pillaging in the lower valley of the Nile. Barbarian dialecticians will search and search, but to no avail; the mouth of God is sealed tight, and without Him all seeking comes to naught. King Cambyses' dream of a vast political empire will crumble like a dry leaf. What mankind should aim at is the empire of the Spirit in the midst of diversity of culture, language and traditions. When this will be a fact, I do not know, but it shall be so. This is the Science of God, the consciousness of liberty and true brotherhood. There will be political entities, but not physical nationalities. The teaching of the sacred lore of Memphis is about to be transferred to an unknown land surrounded by two vast seas. The Light of the great foci of wisdom of India, China, Persia and Arabia, will join the New Memphis in this unknown land.

"Since I know there is no failure in either of you, I shall tell you some of the wonders you will find in our halls of Light unknown in the outer world. We have tubes of glass filled with vapour that emanates light at the touch of a button placed on the wall. The Hierophant-teachers do not even touch the button; they concentrate their minds on the heart center and the light goes on. The electrum that in Greece is looked upon as a mere toy, has been found to produce healing vibration in preventive medicine and also vibration of cold and warmth whose application maintains the interior of our buildings at a pleasant temperature irrespective of the heat or cold on the outside. The same electrum has been exploited to enhance sound and bring closer to one's physical sight far away objects; it is applied to register rain, wind and drought, and to estimate with mathematical precision the quantity and quality of crops months ahead of time and without the inspection of the fields. Through what you might call counting devices, placed strategically throughout the land, we know how many heads of cattle there are and the state of their health, and foresee any impending disease. You have heard about condensation of heat from the sun, sound waves, friction, pressure and vacuum;

in Memphis you will be taught the cause and law that governs these physical manifestations. To manipulate the five elements — earth, water, air, fire and ether — could constitute the culmination of all your aspirations, but this is as a rubbish when compared with the scientific understanding of the process that governs the physical resurrection of the human body from death. Sonchis declares that even this is less than a trifle; we must learn how to be reborn in the Spirit. This is the Science of sciences, the Science of God.

*　*　*

"You, Pythagoras, may ask, in fact I read the question in your mind: 'how is it that Egypt came to be the possessor of such unlimited knowledge?' Please, be attentive:

"Ammon-Ra was the first god-king of the land of Egypt. He was the embodiment of the great Hindu ruler Rama, the founder of the Sun worshipping philosophy in opposition to the widespread lunar idolatry, or the worshipping of matter as an end, such as rocks, trees, rain, animals and all the forces of darkness. Ammon-Ra means: OM RAMA N or *I AM Rama in my conditioned nature,* corresponding to: I AM the Buddha, or I AM the Christ. 'N' is a symbol denoting a mathematical sequence of unknown value, for such is the value of life on earth outside the Spirit of OM which is the name of God and the embodiment of all the attributes of God. Therefore, Ammon-Ra was God individualized. He assumed this name as a self-reminder, in his daily work, of his immortal descendence.

"Let us dissect now the word Rama: Ra is the name of the sun, the bestower of light and energy to our planetary system: MA means love, fertility, work and manifestation. These should be the qualities and attributes of a king and, for that matter, of any ruler. Failing in this, he becomes a deceiver and usurper.

"Now this sun-seed is present in the heart of every man, making him a potential being, capable of displaying all the sun's qualities and attributes, through a series of spiritual rebirths into nobler realms of life. The sun-worshipping ritual is not confined to kneeling on a rock and stretching one's arms towards the sun, and repeating mantras, or asking for boons. It has a deeper meaning. It implies continual awareness of

God at every step of the way, in thinking, planning, working and playing.

"In Egypt the Word of Light or the Name of God is Osiris. In dissecting this word, we find that all religions, in their pristine, unpolluted state, have the same origin. O SIR IS means OM THAT BEING, or I AM the Unqualified Consciousness, the Buddha, the Christ. Osiris is the equivalent of the Sanskrit expression OM TAT SAT (I AM THAT). The Word OM, therefore, is the oldest name of God. The tremendous power which It has derives from the fact that It was sounded into the physical ear of the first man directly from the great Elohim of Creation. Its utterance illumines the mind, protects the body and makes us do the right thing at the right time. It is because of the Word OM, uttered often by the members of the Great White Brotherhood, that the foci of spiritual learning are hidden from the barbarians who seek their destruction. With OM on one's lips martyrdom becomes a wedding march towards the Universal Bridegroom: God!"

* * *

The Screen of Life now showed the three voyagers approaching Memphis, in their beautiful white sail. They were deep inside the Nile, south of Sakkarah, in late September. Although enshrouded in pensiveness by Lunide's revelations, Pythagoras and Arcus were attracted by the magnificence of the quay. Almost a mile long, it was made of solid blocks of granite in various colors; and as they drew nearer they could see it was teaming with activity: the loading and unloading of vessels by half-naked Ethiopian slaves; port authority officials inspecting all goods in transit; well-trained dogs, bearing the royal badge on their foreheads, were sniffing at men and parcels for contraband. They saw Phoenician, Greek, Carthaginian and Etruscan merchants checking their freight and loading their asses, mule-drawn wagons and camels, bargaining loudly with brokers and prospective buyers. There were idlers, sistrum players, fakirs, charlatans, thieves, Chinese peddlers and fortune tellers, all intensely occupied with their trades. Indigent freedmen were roaming everywhere, re-offering themselves for sale.

An Egyptian police officer, brandishing a brutal whip high above his head, was seen approaching a disorderly and noisy group of vagrants, and as he came closer he lashed them indiscriminately. In the scramble to escape the itinerants trampled on each other; arms and legs were bruised, eyes blackened and heads contused. At this moment the healer-physicians arrived with their boxes of surgical tools, bandages and unguents. They were easily recognized in their professional attire — white skirt, shaven heads with a blue headband to which was attached the badge of their guild, a metallic disc on which was engraved a snake coiled around an arrow. The doctor now faced a would be patient offering a gradation of services at different prices ranging from simple bandaging to washing of the body, sterilization of the wounds with alcohol, perfumed unguents and a written guarantee of complete healing. Bargaining ensued, often with an exchange of insults, the fee was lowered and the treatment began.

The two youths marveled at the grandeur of the quayside: white temples with gilded domes silhouetted against the blue sky; columnated palaces, mausoleums of glistening marble and variegated granite, magnificent fountains, pillars and obelisks of every size and color, monuments of gigantic sphinxes, luxuriant flower gardens, public parks with artificial lakes swarming with tropical fish, and cascading waters which splashed against metallic blades producing simple melodies. Within the perimeter of the city, the thoroughfares were broad parkways, the vehicular sector appeared to be more than fifty feet wide. It was a two-way paved road for horses and carriages, four feet lower than the promenading level, and at intervals it was surmounted by high arched overpasses; however, at the intersections it was completely sunken beneath the street level. There were parkways where vehicular traffic was not permitted, these being reserved for military and religious parades. On either side of the vehicular sector were broad promenades bordered with palm trees, flowering bougainvillae, fern, evergreens, philodendrons, periwinkles, climbing grapevines and other tropical shrubbery, forming interminable arcades of shade and fragance.

Arcus and Pythagoras were seen strolling along the Boulevard of Mars, crossing the Avenue of the Winged Virgins, two of the most imposing thoroughfares of Memphis. These were elegant parkways lined with gorgeous temples and stately palaces, glittering obelisks elevated upon pedestals of porphyry,

226

pyramids of finely carved masonry, miniature orchards, exotic gardens, and rows of inscrutable sphinxes reposing majestically on broad dromoi. Lunide had already taken leave of her seafaring companions, explaining that a messenger from the School of Light would contact them. Mingling with the crowds on the promenade, they saw many richly dressed people: wealthy citizens, officers of the Army and Navy, political executives, architects of the royal crown and hierarchs of the church, princes and princesses of royal blood, in splendid attire, each followed by a retinue of secretaries, bodyguards and messengers. Veteran soldiers were seen walking proudly with martial stride.

Continuing along the same boulevard, Arcus and Pythagoras came to the Temple of the Dead, an imposing basilica of white marble surrounded by a portico of brazen columns and walls paneled in limestone. From the palace adjacent to the temple, the high priest, followed by a procession of lesser prelates carrying lighted candles, and robed for a religious ceremony, walked to the main altar for an offering of propitiation to Osiris. The officiating ecclesiarch wore a tiara studded with jewels and emblazoned with a winged disc, symbolizing the sun; at the tip were two identical ostrich feathers, the symbol of Truth and Order. Suspended from the tiara, adorning his forehead, was the uraeus; over the robe of white linen which flowed loosely to his feet, was a waist-length cape of crimson embroidered with gold volutes, flowers and animals. His breastplate was of platinum studded with diamonds, rubies and other precious stones. A leopard skin edged in gold rested on his shoulder, held by a chain of platinum around his neck. At his waist was a featherweight dagger, whose hilt shaped to a Tau cross with a globe at the center symbolized power bestowed by God.

Arriving at the altar the high priest called upon the faithful to recite the appropriate mantra with each of his ceremonial rites. As he rose from a kneeling position, he held the tip of the dagger high, and caused a spark of blazing light to flash forth. Simultaneously the two priests close to him swung their thuribles, letting clouds of incense veil the dagger. A second and a third spark emanated from the dirk, which greatly bestirred the hundreds of faithful, convincing them that God had answered the priest's call. For such a privilege the people were invited to make generous contributions to the church. Coins of gold, silver, copper and leather were thrown on the floor by the worshippers.

A virgin maiden, the daughter of the officiating priest, now entered the temple and walked, at a slow pace, towards the altar. The long train of her white silk gown was held by six younger maidens. Her hair was adorned with white and pink roses and a light blue veil shaded her face. A plaintive sound coming forth from the sistrum which she played signified that God was not pleased with the first voluntary contribution, and that another collection would be taken at the close of the musical performance. As the player reached the altar, the congregation commenced to sing; an enthralling solo was then heard from another maiden entering the temple, and soon by a third appearing at the entrance. The ceremony was concluded with the entire assemblage singing the last passage of the hymn, while the maidens and a score of priests moved about with large baskets collecting coins.

Shocked and confused by the despicable behavior of the idolatrous priests, Pythagoras and Arcus left the basilica and wandered on in this magnificent yet strange city filled with grandeur, wealth, extravagance, corruption, hypocrisy and venality. In the evening they saw groups of musicians in public squares and parks, and by the porticos of temples, playing religious music that would sensitize the souls of the uncouth populace; and surrounding them were the everpresent church clerics demanding alms of the spectators for the glory of Osiris. They saw playhouses monopolized by Ethiopian impresarios, actors and actresses, houses of prostitution and gambling casinos. Along the waterfront and in the quarries slave workers, unable to fill their daily quotas, were mercilessly beaten by Egyptian taskmasters. Elegance, refinement and comfort were at the acme in the homes of the well-to-do, ignorance, filth and disease were rampant in the hovels of the poor.

Without a definite objective the two youths moved about, passing the night wherever they happened to be at the end of the day, for guest houses were plentiful. They sauntered along the Avenue of the Sphinxes, a thoroughfare flanked with colossi of granite: heads of bulls, rams, birds of prey, and other beasts, on human bodies. At the end of the Avenue they came to a gateway of forty eight red columns of various heights, some surpassing a hundred feet. Entering they walked towards a large square occupied by gigantic statues of gods, sacred animals, and winged globes of crystal filled with shivering light. At the east end of the square they saw a fenced garden whose gates of gilded steel were heavily guarded by armed priests. All visitors were seached and their sandals removed.

Pythagoras and Arcus ventured themselves inside. The landscape was a dream of artistry and perfection; the lawn on which the visitors walked was as thick and soft as heavy carpeting, while the rest of the vegetation was in a state of faultless beauty. They walked towards what appeared to be a series of animal cages, made of burnished copper. They were, in fact, the sanctuaries of the sacred beasts of the Egyptian firmament, each attended by a score of keepers in white uniforms, who kept bowing contritely before the dumb creatures while polishing the floor of the cages. The hide of the sacred bull had a magnificent luster, and the sacred cats' fur was equally soft and glossy. There were cats out of the cages, roaming everywhere, pestering the people, but nobody dared to touch them.

A visitor, whose appearance was that of an Arab merchant, was suddenly attacked at his ankle by one of the felines. In the struggle to free himself from the vicious hold, the man kicked the cat on the head. Some of the bystanders — fanatic Egyptian animal worshippers — witnessed the scene and immediately emitted cries of deprecation and vengeance. In the attempt to escape the man was seized by the infuriated mob and his body mercilessly beaten, crushed and cut to pieces with knives, axes and clubs, and the flesh, still quivering with life, was thrown into the cages of the god-beasts. Pythagoras and Arcus, who had tried to intercede for the doomed victim, were also beaten and expelled from the desecrated grounds, called the Sacred Garden of the living gods.

With swollen eyes and bleeding noses the Samian youths walked dejectedly home, gazing at each other silently but interrogatively. The Akashic Records projected letters of light radiating not physical pain but a soul-searching anguish of a deep emotional crisis.

"Who shall ever save" — Pythagoras cried — "this accursed race from total destruction and utter oblivion? What a savage brutality lies beneath their evanescent layer of make believe graciousness and intellectual veneer; and while their cancerous flesh is covered with silken garments and adorned with garlands of flowers and precious stones, their souls emit a mephitic stench generated by the rottenness of their thoughts and feelings. Woe unto thee, race of hypocrites and criminals; woe unto thee, land of marvels resting on sand, for as the true foci of light are withdrawn from thy midst, darkness and annihilation shall be thy lot!"

To this justified and prophetic utterance of indignation, Arcus replied:

"Maybe, maybe all these seeming disappointing events and tragic occurrences are the prodomes of spiritual unfoldment that awaits us within the walls of the School of Light which we are about to enter. And suppose it is a test of faith, or a method that leads to deeper self-analysis and truer comprehension of life and society? Should we leave Egypt now, not only would we reject what Lunide has told us about the school, but also forfeit all the prophecies uttered in our behalf. Let us meditate for faith, inner strength and the all-inclusive Cosmic Light."

✿   ✿   ✿

Avulsed from the world of form and grateful to God and the Masters for the release of this experience, Marco and Leonora moved swiftly into another realm for deeper pondering and instruction. Departing from a spheric hub of purple fire and sustained by a beam of light they proceeded radially towards starry regions where the carnal ego cannot enter. Looking back at the hub, they saw an infinite number of spoke-like beams of light issuing from it, each one attempting to raise an individual towards this realm. But, alas, very few reached the goal; the majority, taken by fear and loneliness, unable to live ethically, and unwilling to let go of the bundle of earthly attachments, yelled frantically and fell back into the rot of self-regimentation, self-made constraint and the choking stockade of human thinking. Onward, they moved into the consciousness of the fourth dimension, until they lost sight of every beam but theirs, and then that too disappeared. Adhering to the Law of Sun Worshipping, they knew they could not fail. Leonora's Spirit-form was ablaze with intense white light tinged with pink. How truly real she was now without the deceiving human shell. "How lovely and beautiful" — she said "to be here, in this realm unconstrained by time and space, undivided by good and evil, and unmarred by intellectual pride."

"Yes!" — the Sun Worshipping Consciousness answered. "This is the state of One-ness and peace where even the noblest of passions cannot enter. This One-ness is achieved only through the perfect harmonization of one's triune nature — physical, intellectual and emotional. Crippled is the athlete whose aim in life is to develop muscles and body symmetry for mere competition or breadwinning. Crippled is the scientist who attributes his discoveries to the intellectual exploitation of the law of action, reaction and chance. Crippled is the merchant who plans to undersell in order to destroy his competitor. Crippled is he who makes a profession of mysticism through self-torture and unnecessary renunciation. Do not scatter thy precious inner wealth, O man. Raise the protective walls of light and abide in the vast expanse of undifferentiated universalism. If you only listened to the voice within in the solitude of thy silentium, be attentive to thy inner urge and be receptive to inspiration and guidance, what an awakening, what a power, what a triumph over limitation, sorrow and death.

"Blessed ones, at the close of your studies in Memphis you had reached the portals of this lofty realm. Such a heritage will surely set you free sooner than dreamed of. Disciples of the Verbum-Light of Osiris, the Solar Path, listen now to the Spirit-form of Master Rama, in His ever-enduring reality."

❋   ❋   ❋

"I AM Ammon-Ra, Rama, the I AM, the Brahma, the Buddha, the Christ, the Eternal One, devoid of human traits. When the lost continent of Atlantis was at the apex of its glory and the Sahara was the seat of an unrivaled civilization, I was the embodied Christ, the Son of God and the Father-ruler of the Aryan race of Europe and Asia. My name was then Rama, the Light Bearer, signifying that I followed the Voice of God in all my endeavours. My dominions extended eastward to what is known today as the Bering Sea, and thence southward to the equator. In Europe my ruling power was limited between the Barents Sea, the Mediterranean and the Atlantic Ocean.

231

"I was also the Christ-counsellor of the Hindu-Aryan-Caucasian continent, a federation of free states on the pattern of your United States of America. The continent of north and south America and the islands of the West Indies were another political federation of highly civilized peoples. South of my Asiatic dominions was the land of the Southermost or Austro, ruled by another Solar-king, a true Christ-king indeed. How ancient I AM it suffices to say that I had been a citizen of Lemuria for one thousand years prior to its disappearance beneath the waters.

"Amos, who was a brother of mine, had been the Father-ruler of the Sahara civilization for five hundred years before my elevation to rulership. He ruled for another four hundred years, and as he was about to join the ranks of the Immortal Ones, he visited me and entrusted to me a solid block of laws and decrees which had been given to him by God. With his departure the Sahara Kingdom began to decay. During my fifteen hundred years of rulership, I saw this great land, once peopled by a magnificent race of high intellectual and spiritual attainment, decline into a state of nonentity. God was first substituted by the power of the intellect, then by the idolatry of physical objects and finally forgotten entirely. The edenic climatic conditions, unsupported by the awareness of God, also began to change; the atmospheric temperature rose sharply, dessicating lakes and mountain springs, and making edible vegetation impossible to grow. This imperiled the sanitary conditions of the inhabitants causing disease and epidemics. The stronger people migrated north and south, through indescribable suffering and further spiritual degeneracy. Those who came north, eventually, reached the Mediterranean shores of North Africa and faced us. They were no longer the same original race of physical handsomeness and inner light. Their golden-brown skin had darkened considerably, It was almost black; their lips had thickened through long generations of promiscuity with the lower creatures of the jungle, which had been created by their base thoughts and visualization, and their flowing brown hair had become crinkled due to the intense heat of the desert.

"What had remained in them, and somehow even developed, was an intellectual alertness capable of astounding exploits in the field of mechanical science. They had conceived innumerable weapons of destruction, similar to what you possess today; and they used them against each other with the firm belief that they would be reborn with indestructible bodies. They crossed the Mediterranean and contacted us along a strategic line corresponding to forty degrees latitude north. And having refused to meet their demands which meant, in essence, the forfeiting of our God-given liberty, a state of unrelenting and bloody war ensued, which lasted over one-hundred-fifty years.

"During this period of massacre and destruction, we learned a great deal. First of all we copied and improved on the weapons of our self-styled enemy; then we copied and improved on their method of warfare. We had never had a war before, so this improvement was actually in being more merciless on the field of battle against our armed foe, and more merciful to the prisoners and the wounded. For us it was a test of survival for that time and for the ages to come, for the enemy it was a recoil of karma. Apparently neither side could claim victory; ravage and desolation were on both camps, and the southern part of Europe was made uninhabitable. But the conflict had a far-reaching effect on the future of mankind.

"While the war was still raging, the Cosmic Assembly of the Perfect Ones ordered a mass migration of children and young women to the luxuriant valleys of southern Tibet and southward still to the land of Ceylon. Seventy disciple-leaders of the Solar Path, from the Seventy United Federated States of Europe led the youth, together with cattle, horses, sheep and other supplies. It took twenty-five years to complete the itinerary; and apart from the fact that not one of the seven million travelers perished, none added one year to their earthly life, nor did they change their physical lineaments until their destination had been reached. Spiritual training and scientific knowledge were imparted to them during the migration.

"Because of the unadulterated teaching given to these migrating youths, a teaching that corresponded exactly to the irreproachable conduct displayed by the adult leaders, the new race had no difficulty in developing pure inspiration which lead eventually to the founding of the noblest philisophy of life as expressed by the nonsectarian Brahmanism, Buddhism and Confucianism. This philosophy, still unchallenged, shall save humanity. Such is the origin of the greatest spiritual race on earth.

"In the course of time this philosophy of life was simplified with the institution of the Sun Worshipping ritual which consisted in the utterance of the Word OM and the daily practice of meditation. It was quickly accepted by the leading minds of the civilized world, such as Persia, Arabia, Egypt, Greece and Etruria, and in each instance the people — both individually and collectively — who practiced the teaching became wise and strong, and impregnable to the forces of darkness.

"I had conquered death and earned my body of Light for several centuries, when a group of youths from the fabled and sun-baked valley of the Lower Nile arrived at Darbhanga, in Nepal, and knocked at the door of the School of the Initiates. Hermes, a youth of twenty of striking charm and inner light, as the leader of the group pleaded with his companions to be admitted into our School and undergo whatever discipline or hardship or test that would be imposed upon them. They wanted the spiritual training that leads to Christship. So ancient indeed is India's undisputed mastery in the field of the things of God that, even the present age, notwithstanding the chronic famine, political harassment and unjustified epidemics, the Indis possess, above all other races, the connate elements, the spiritual characteristic, the hallowed ground and the intangible wealth to conduct successfully schools of cosmic knowledge. You will derive comfort and courage to know that you have a Hindu heritage of blood and spirit. Your success is, therefore, assured. Hermes and his friends having fulfilled the necessary requirements, returned to Egypt and founded the Doctrine of the Solar Path which conquered Memphis, Sakkarah, Thebes, Luxor and all the cities along the liquid highway of the Nile. For five thousand years the teaching remained pure and vibrant and during that time Egypt had become the land of the living devas, whose political organization was based on the Science of Osiris, the OM TAT SAT of India, the Fire-Principle and the Verbum-Light.

"The greatness of Egypt in every field of endeavour and the high standard of living of its people, were envied by the barbarian rulers of the interland of Africa, who could not accept the simplicity of the Solar Doctrine and its astounding results.

234

Unable to win through armed conflict, they polluted the lofty teaching with the spreading of idolatrous and revolting rituals. Altars were erected along the borders where the bull, the cat and the hawk were worshipped and given daily sacrificial offerings. Hermes saw the danger, the menace to his universal mission, and called to God for help. Thus another phase of the noble teaching began. A Master Elohim contacted Hermes and advised him to relinquish his body and enter the realm of the Immortal Ones. The Great Leader departed from his awestricken disciples and ministers in a halo of light and glory without leaving one speck of his physical body unclaimed. All Egypt saw in Him the Symbol of divine power and the fulfillment of the highest human aspirations.

*　*　*

"One hundred years passed and Hermes had become a myth vaguely remembered. The same Master Elohim who had advised Him to take leave of earth, ordered me to go back. As a youth of twenty, I presented myself to the Pharaoh-hierophant, and showed him how well versed I was in the doctrine of Osiris. I related to him the striving and sacrifices endured by the youth Hermes during his initiation in Darbhanga, his progress, his purity and godlike mien. The King tested me over and again, and although he considered me the epitome of all that was needed in a spiritual leader, yet he had neither the power to accept me nor to support my mission in any way whatsoever.

"'My son' — he said — 'there is a radiance emanating from thy forehead that bespeaks of thy spiritual worthiness. My office being consultive I have no authority to recommend thee to any of the various governors of the Egyptian Federated States. However, the world is in dire need of an Avatar capable of making the Logos OM resound again in the consciousness of every citizen, as it did during the rulership of Hermes. Whoever is able to issue such a sound with the power of conviction that leaves no room for doubt or defection, that one could be elected as the founder of the spiritual and political dynasty of our land. Son, art thou able to display such a power?'

"'My Lord' — I replied — 'I shall tour the land in a fortnight and broadcast the seed of the happy tidings. I shall speak with the eloquence that is inherent to an Avatar, and awaken the people to the danger of the corrupt foreign teaching and gross idolatry.'

"Under the tutelage of the Cosmic Assembly of the Perfect Ones, I went to work immediately. Flooded with light from of High the masses showed an unusual eagerness to accept the resurrected Verbum of Hermes and merge into a political and racial unity. The infiltration of the foreign cults was stemmed at once. A general assembly of the twenty-four governors was called, and soon after I was elected the Ruler-Initiate and Supreme Arbiter and Defender of the physical and spiritual welfare of the people of Egypt. I assumed the name of Ammon-Ra and became the founder of a glorious dynasty that upheld the philosophy of the Solar Path and made Egypt the cradle of a civilization that was the twin sister of the more ancient Hindu-Aryan civilization of Asia. Such is the origin of the greatness of the land of the Nile.

"I met you at that time, embodied as Lotha and Sacur. Lotha was the daughter of a provincial ruler, Sacur the son of her father's bitterest political enemy; yet the two youths were close friends and frequented the same school. Through them, through you that is, their fathers accepted the teaching of the Solar Path and became my wise ministers and collaborators. After graduation Lotha was appointed teacher and confidante of my princess-daughters, while Sacur assumed command of the army in charge of the defense of the borders.

"My disciples, this celestial abode wherefrom I speak, holds the records of the constructive deeds of Egypt. Here are the cities of Memphis, Luxor, Thebes and Assuan, with their schools of initiation, the royal palaces of the Pharaohs who adhered to the noble teaching of the Solar Path, the houses of the hierophants, and the citizens themselves who practiced the teaching. Your graduation in Memphis is the last episode registered here, together with Sonchis' ascension and Pythagoras' mission and liberation. Then all that followed — with the exception of Jesus' visit to that land — the decline of Egypt, was entered in the records of the moon consciousness.

"This is called the Heaven of the Master Scientists, because it is based on the principle of inward observation as a starting point for self-unfoldment. By studying the degree of resonance produced in the mind by the utterance of the Word OM, one is able to establish the degree of inner growth, health, strength and possibility of success in the outer world. It was because of this inward observation that none of the students of the Solar Path was ever harmed by the barbarians that invaded Egypt after your departure. In fact, those who were massacred, were the people of the same level of consciousness as those who participated in the gory dismemberment of the body of the Arab merchant. Ninety-nine per cent of the Egyptian populace at that time had this type of karma. No wonder Hermes, who had foreseen the final collapse, had said: 'O Egypt, land of light and darkness, only tales will be spoken of thee by the future generations, and nothing shall remain of thy greatness but a few words carved on stone!' It is so to this day.

"Eager disciples, it is needful that you intensify your introspection, for I AM about to take you to a starry rampart from where you shall see the city of Memphis and the lodging where Pythagoras and Arcus stayed after being mauled in the garden of the animal-gods. Thence we shall follow them through all the main episodes of their lives as students of the Solar Path up to the day of graduation. Afterward, having bid you farewell, you will be directed to meet Pythagoras himself."

A few days later Ammon-Ra reappeared, touched the foreheads of Marco and Leonora and said: "The Eternal Logos OM is thy Mystic Order of Everlasting Life!" Then they rose onto the starry rampart. A messenger from the Chief Hierophant Sonchis appears on the Screen of Life, and enters the youths' lodging:

"Salutations unto you from our Fatherland and from our noble Chief" — he said. "I have come to implore your forgiveness for the ill treatment imposed upon you this afternoon. It is an omen of sorrow for our city. You were denied the reverence and honor which are due to visitors from foreign countries. It is still worse in the present case, for you are students of the Solar Path. May you be kind enough to let us know the amount of gold pieces you desire, as well as other conditions you wish to dictate, so as to allay your moral and physical suffering. I have been instructed not to bargain, but to comply unconditionally with your request, whatever it might be. . . . In the meantime you may command me to perform any menial task in your behalf."

237

Pythagoras and Arcus gazed at each other in amazement, then replied: "Please, brother, allow us a few minutes to examine ourselves, so that we may give the correct interpretation to your message." They retired into another room, and upon their return said to the messenger: "Please, convey to your Chief our humble salutations of respect, obedience and love, and tell him that the only thing we ardently desire, is for him to take us off the street and admit us as regular students into the great school."

"This was their first test" — Ammon-Ra explained — "and they won it. They had been lured in such a subtle fashion, and given a chance to argue and fight in the manner of the Greeks, but innate humility and poise prevailed."

Early the next day, a carriage arrived with four students harnessed to it, and the two youths were invited to ride in state. But perceiving another test of humility, they not only refused to board the vehicle, but harnessed themselves to it and helped to pull it to their destination, which was the Hall of the Sun.

* * *

Guided by the radiance of the Solar-King, Marco and Leonora were able to follow, from their starry observatory, all the thoughts, moods, behavior and tests of the two youths within the school. They saw them entering the rotunda, a museum of relics and outdated scientific and astronomical instruments; from there they toured the various halls and columnated corridors filled with imposing obelisks of marble or wood on which were carved the deeds and glories of the past Pharaohs. All was strange, impressive and stimulating, a foretaste of what lay ahead in the years to come. Towards evening, a group of students appeared offering to escort Arcus and Pythagoras to the dormitories. As they walked merrily along, the lights began to dim perceptibly, the escort to disappear, and the splendor to vanish.

As they reached the last corridor, narrow and bare, linking the main building to the sleeping quarters, the scene changed abruptly; the remaining students receded from sight, the lights went out and the two youths found themselves alone in total darkness. Raging with frustration, gripped with fear, they lay on the floor in a sea of contrasting thoughts and shifting moods,

238

now of disappointment and regret, and now of fury for the undeserved abuse imposed upon them by the ill-mannered students. However, in spite of these self-hindering elements, traces of calmness and mental equilibrium gradually returned. In the achieved state of inward peace and unconscious self-surrender, a ray of light issued from their foreheads and converged about ten feet in front of them, illumining the surroundings. Exalted again in spirit, they arose and gazed fixedly at it in mute expectancy. As the light increased in brilliancy, they saw within it the form of a wondrous Being.

"Blessed sons, I AM the Logos within your hearts, seeking freedom from the prison walls of the flesh. There is no hastiness in Me, for I live beyond time, in the boundless eternity. However I AM compelled by the Law of Grace to see that in the future you do not bind Me to more than My allotted embodiments. The sooner you achieve liberation the sooner I will glorify you in the Eyes of our Father-God. Should you decide to allow Me to guide you, I will so illumine your minds as to enhance your intelligence to the state of an immortal Master's. Study and strive with the intent of overcoming mortal thoughts and unkind feelings. Be not dismayed by these seeming obstacles and hardships, and do not blame anyone for their appearance. They are all yours and must be conquered through an intensified process of self-analysis.

"Blessed sons, be happy in Me and grateful, for I have directed you with your permission, to this noble focus of inner teaching. Work earnestly! Pythagoras, My son, the ascension awaits you at the close of this life span which, according to human standards, will be a long one. Lunide and Arcus shall be prepared to meet and walk with the Son of God and Master of Love on the plains of Asia, and be His ambassadors in awakening all of Europe to the doctrine of the Christ, at the commencement of the New Era. They shall gain entrance to the Cosmic Halls and be taught how to read the Akashic Records. And afterwards, in the Twentieth Century of the incoming era of the Christhood, they will return to earth for the last of their cosmic tasks; that is, the announcement of the Golden Age and the method through which it is achieved and maintained. This being their mission, it shall come to pass."

✳ ✳ ✳

The Guardian Angel then ceased to speak and vanished from their sight, but the light continued to shine until the two youths reached the cell assigned to them; then it went out. In the attempt to establish the size and appointments of the room, they crawled in opposite directions to reach the wall, and as they became separated from each other in the dark and windowless enclosure, a frantic vibration of fear began to churn within them; it caused the mind, untutored and unreliable, to build a wall of separation within the cell. The unreal solidified and each youth felt himself incarcerated as if in a stone sepulchre. Now seemingly inaudible to each other, thinking thoughts of annihilation and oblivion, each was certain that the other had been destroyed. Seven seeming interminable days and nights passed in what appeared to be darkness, loneliness and martyrdom.

The cell was, apparently, quite small, furnished with a cot, a stool, a folding table attached to the wall, a sink filled with water, a towel, and toilet facilities. The water remained always clean, in spite of its constant use, and the towel never became soiled. A loaf of stale bread, which never ceased to be whole, and a jar of water which was always full, no matter how much they ate or drank, were their only source of nourishment.

During these seven days the two youths showed undaunted courage and faith. OM was the theme of their breath; It was their rock, their lamp, their path and their law. It was the teaching of Lunide bearing fruit. Now the battle between reality and illusion began. They heard a voice saying that the vicious priests had condemned them to hard labor for life. "Let it be so, I shall not fear. OM, I AM." These words were spoken exactly alike by the two youths, and in perfect unison. The second test aimed at convincing them that they were kept in captivity in order to be burned alive as a sacrifice to the animal-gods. They answered: "Begone! OM I AM is my protector. In OM death is life, In OM life is eternal!"

The third test was a powerful one. The two captives were lured into the freedom of the outer world, holding positions of importance, surrounded by luxury, and accumulating wealth through unethical deeds. But they answered: "OM, I have spurned all human desires in exchange for the Wisdom of the Self, the sole reservoir of perfection, beauty and wealth. I shall serve only God, for all that I gain through IT is mine permanently."

After three days of stale bread and water, and threats of physical and moral nature, the two youths could no longer be deluded; but the tests continued to come, and in each case an ever decreasing amount of mental and emotional dross (the residue of false impressions and erroneous concepts of life) was burned. This time it was the test of the belly. The cell was expanded, illumined and transformed into a sumptuous apartment. From an unseen source heavenly feminine voices were heard singing, accompanied by stringed instruments playing exquisite melodies. A table appeared before them, elegantly arranged with fine china, silverware and cut crystal, ladened with Epicurean viands. Then a masculine voice spoke assuredly: "It is all over now, my brother, no more tests, you are victorious. Eat, drink and make yourself strong, for this very day you shall meet the Chief Hierophant." Pythagoras and Arcus reacted at once and in unison:

"Away with thee, diabolic tempter; bread and water are enough for me for the rest of my life. . . . Blessed Osiris, nourish and strengthen me with Thy Light instead." They walked towards the table and with a powerful kick caused the whole setting to scatter and disappear; the lights went out and the cell was restored to the size of their still restricted outlook.

"The fact that those eatables vanished from sight at the impact of a physical thrust" — Ammon-Ra explained — "shows that they were real and tangible, visualized perhaps in years past or even in past embodiments, and nestled somewhere in the subconscious. This proves that nothing is lost, nothing goes astray, and also that *visualization is creation*. In the present instance, a dynamically malefic force was added to those victuals with the intent of weakening the spirit. Their disappearance was the result not only of the kick, but also of the uncompromising self-possesion displayed by the two youths, the effacement of the personality, the subjugation of the ego, and their self-surrender to the Godhead. This again is the result of the practice of introspection. What a nobility, what a wealth, what a joy are his who is capable of relinquishing personal preferences, aspiration and even constructive habits, at the hour of an inner trial. What our two youths lacked were awareness and continuity of these inborn gifts; hence their need of frequenting this School of Light whose program is to build character and release quasi-Christs to society.

241

"From this, one infers that the Christ-seed is implanted within each individual. No one is exempt. It is man's duty to nurture it by seeking the guidance of a guru whose love and depths of understanding rescue his disciple from the negative traits of doubt, fear and ignorance, and then, gently, guides him towards Self-mastery."

Arcus and Pythagoras must now submit to the fifth test, the test of fire. An intense and stifling heat has enveloped the dingy, dismal cell. Our youths, their mouths parched, reach for water but, alas, the pitcher is empty. Perspiring profusely, almost naked and gasping for breath, they see a reddish light penetrating into the tiny, narrow room; the light changes first into the heads of many snakes whose diabolical hissing not only raises their blood pressure, but adds still more to the unbearableness of the suffocating atmosphere. Now the snakes vanish and fire appears in ugly, devouring flaming tongues. It burns through the floor and soon attacks the cot. Forgetful of the previous tests and the reason for their being imprisoned, surrounded by mean, menacing and vindictive entities, they become panic-stricken, but only momentarily. Seeing the inanity of their attempt to rescue themselves from the lurid flames, they direct their attention to God. At ITS Lotus Feet they take refuge: "O Father-God, mercy, mercy, mercy! What am I doing here . . ., what, whom, am I protecting? A worthless conglomeration of blood, muscles and bones? Away with it. Set me free from such a bondage by an act of mercy from Thine Heart of Love. I know there is no death!" In one leap, and in absolute self-abandonment, they jump into the flames, but the fire disappears and our unrelentingly tested students stand there disappointed but much stronger in mind and body.

"You can see" — Ammon-Ra commented — "that an invisible power was holding the youths' minds sway. Was this power beneficent or malefic? The answer is obvious. Had their bodies been injured? Were they starving or resentful towards anyone for these unhappy experiences? Did they blame Lunide for having invited them to Memphis? All the answers are in the negative. Therefore, the power was a power of love directed by a wise being who was manipulating currents of thought and the residue of false beliefs nestled in the youths' consciousness, causing them to come forth and be destroyed once and for all. Now behold the test of water."

242

A driving rainstorm starts to pound heavily on the roof of the cell. The water seeping through the ceiling causes the plaster to crack and fall, and wherever the water touches the floor a hole forms, out of which, fetid, boiling mud gushes; steadily it begins to spread and slowly rise. The harassed youths, reared in comfort and cleanliness, can bear neither the look nor the touch or odor of the slimy matter. Seeking protection and finding it nowhere, they stand on their stools, hoping against hope that the mud will cease rising; but the putrid substance soon touches and covers their feet. Terrified by what seems to be an approaching death by drowning in this muck, they cry in sheer despair: "God, God, please, lead me to an open field and let me fight and die in defense of a worthy cause, or burn me on a sacrificial pyre in exchange for a crime committed by another human being. O Father, Father, though in the grip of fear I am fearless!" Holding their breath they stare in front of them as if beholding a vision; a ray of light illumines their countenances: "Ah" — they exclaim — "this is an illusion. Lord, let this illusion go!"

❊ ❊ ❊

Thus the dross of illusion and misconception concerning the initiation into the esoteric school of Memphis, having been removed by the painful process of a physical and emotional nature, Phytagoras and Arcus feel reborn, resurrected. Like an ailing person from whom a malignant tumor had been extirpated, like a yogi who after a lifetime of intense discipline finally sees himself as a being of absolute dispassion and utter detachment, so with our candidates: rootless — humanly speaking — and keenly aware of their unbreakable link with the Eternal. "It was Sonchis himself" — Ammon Ra explained — "who directed this cleansing process telepathically from his study. How vitally important, therefore for the aspiring disciple to seek the guidance of a guru. Go to him, O man; surely you will be happier and more protected the moment you touch his aura. And no matter how stubborn and rebellious, or burdened with unkind karma, he will not allow you to depart empty-handed. Give thyself wholeheartedly into his holy patronage.

"Immersed in space, comfort and elegance, people conceive narrowness and meniality; surrounded by light and peace, they prefer the dark den of plotting and anxiety. Why is it so? Because

243

man never or seldom, seeks within. Lacking the broadness of thought that comes from self-inquiry, he wallows in a world of error, misjudgement and illusion; and usually he blames others, even society or the government, for his mental sloth. And when an emergency arises, confused and baffled, he curses the collectivity and often his own parents, for his inability to cope with the problem at hand. Some individuals read good books and become spiritually inflamed. While reading they make wise resolutions, plan to change their way of living, to disburden themselves of certain unbecoming habits, to radiate love and so forth. But as soon as they close the book, there again are the self-created forces exerting their tyrannical pulls. Instantly all is forgotten. Another man makes a firm resolve to get up early in the morning for fifteen minutes of meditation before going to work. He may succeed for a few days; then, seeing that nothing happens, the enthusiasm wanes. Such a man, who was born for Christhood, has decided to remain a mortal nonentity.

"He who practices interiorization, day after day, year after year, even unto the last earthly breath, in absolute trust and with no mind for results, achieves Deliverance and Dominion over life and death. The touch of God will surely come, and when it comes, its duration will be shorter than a split second but enough for the meditative one to inherit Heaven and Earth."

❖   ❖   ❖

The Akashic Records unfold swiftly on the Screen of Life. Marco and Leonora see Pythagoras and Arcus meeting Lunide and other coeds and fellow students on the campus, all happy but pensive. It is a day of inner vigilance for those who seek admission into the School of Light. Tomorrow their souls will be exposed naked and helpless before the all-seeing eye of love of Master Sonchis. As in the School of the Prophets of the classic age of the Hebrews, here too, the only requirement for admission consisted in possessing a wealth of noble tendencies accumulated in past embodiments. And unlike some of the youths of today who take for granted frequenting a university, twenty-five centuries ago it was the acme of all privileges for every one including the offspring of royal blood.

It was an auspicious day also. The sun had entered the sign of Libra, in the constellation of the zodiac of the autumnal equinox. Throughout the City of Memphis there were religious festivities. Hierophants toured the various temples to speak of God in Its spiritual aspect to the masses engulfed in animal idolatry. Lunide escorted Pythagoras and Arcus on a tour of the campus, showing them the various faculty buildings in their massive architecture typical of Egypt, disposed like an amphitheater and separated by variegated landscaping.

"This is the Hall of Perseverance" — Lunide explained — "in brown granite, where grammar, elementary music and arithmetic are taught to children irrespective of their future aspirations. Next to it is the Hall of Faith in light-yellow granite, for mathematics, physics and chemistry; the Hall of Mirth, in green granite, is for the study of agriculture, husbandry and forestry. The Hall of Justice is in blue granite; here history, geography, biology, civics, philosophy, commerce and international arbitration are taught. This edifice in purple granite is the Hall of Sound where the student learns silence as the foundation for eloquence, languages and experimental sciences. The Hall of the Sun, in green and gold granite, is devoted to astronomy, medicine and higher mathematics.

"Through the foregoing disciplines one attains the highest level of intellectual knowledge, but only from the human standpoint. The student is still unable to cope with worry, moods, cravings and inordinate desires. He is still subjected to disease of mind and body, is ignorant of human relationship and true happiness; he ages and dies. The buildings forming this wide circle are either rectangular or prismatic in shape conveying to you the concept of incompleteness and limitation.

"The edifice you are now looking at is a marvel of architecture, a divine idea projected to earth by the Elohim of Creation, and is unmarred by man's genius or mortal consciousness. It is the Hall of Light, a perfect sphere standing on these consecrated grounds of pure white sand. Composed of light-blue transparent and imperishable material, it has no windows or doors, yet people can go in and out with ease; may look on the outside from within, but cannot see inside from without. It is illumined day and night with heatless light gathered from the sun, and no physical person or object casts a shadow. Its immense auditorium is provided with invisible acoustical devices which carry the voice of the speaker to within three feet of the listener. A person approaching this

245

structure, becomes invisible to the outside onlooker as he reaches an unseen line one-hundred meters from the vertical tangent of the spherical wall. From that line on the visitor ceases to walk, he translates himself inside without moving a muscle."

"How did such a marvel come into being?" — Ammon-Ra interposed. "It is the result of cosmic planning, organization and co-operation; the sum total of love poured to God by thousands of rulers, teachers, hierophants, and common citizens of Egypt who had lived a life of self-dedication to universal brotherhood since the Age of Hermes. They had visualized a pattern of earthly existence whereby all men could surround themselves with beauty and comfort unmarred by wear and tear, and without the sweating of the brow. Such a pattern still exists in this Starry Heaven, and it is ready to descend to Earth in all of its infinite aspects of perfection.

"The Hall of Light was the bone of contention and the constant source of envy and hatred of the petty tyrants surrounding the land of Egypt. Steeped in materialism and bestial aims they thought that by invading this country they could acquire the secret of building structures similar to this, simply by uttering a magic word, or striking the soil with a rod. They had no time for meditation or inner search.

"In this Hall the student learns the transmutation of matter after the manner of the ancient Hindu Masters; and although he possesses a body, here he loses his body consciousness through total adherence to the doctrine of the Solar Path."

* * *

Now the formal ceremony of admission into the School of Light unfolds. The student body is gathered in the auditorium of the Spheric Temple. A group of novitiates to which Pythagoras and Arcus belong stands by with mixed feelings of renunciation and hope, under the supervision of a lesser hierophant. They wear coarse robes of white linen with a heavy blue cross of iron as a breastplate, a symbol of the long years of discipline and study ahead. An invisible orchestra plays the Symphony of Adieu to the world of appearances. Thirty-six sub-hierophants robed in white and blue surround the lectern, while twelve hierophants in white and gold enter from the wall above the speaker's platform, floating noiselessly and disposing themselves in a semicircle behind the speaker's chair. Now Master Sonchis descends, also floating from the domelike ceiling, wearing a jubbah of pure white silk trimmed in gold. His breastplate is a nine-pointed star of gold with an enormous pink diamond at the center. He possesses the handsome features of the classic aristocratic Egyptian youth; and though his actual age is nearing one hundred, he looks like a youth of eighteen. In him death lies prone at his feet and life serves him unconditionally.

"Blessed disciples of the Solar Path" — he commenced — "let us pray to God:

"O SIR IS, OM TAT SAT, OM, OM, OM . . ."

For about five minutes, the audience uttered the Name of God with an ever-increasing transport and devotion; and as it stopped the mighty Logos echoed for another five minutes without losing power. In the interim the hall expanded, walls and ceiling disappeared and the audience was seen standing high in midair, as if on an invisible platform. The freshmen were elated at the novel experience. A range of mountains came in sight at the far-off horizon; some were forest-crowned, others helmeted in snow, while still others were ablaze with golden-blue light. The sky was cloudless and the sun emanated shafts of light in the shape of purple swords.

"Such is the power of prayer, O Lord of Creation" — Sonchis resumed. "When Thy awful Name is uttered, O Father, without selfish motive, untold wonders appear to the sight of man. Any desire that is less than absolute mergence into Thy Universal Self is a severe blow to the Soul; it clips its wings and holds it earthbound.

"When we call to God for ITS own sake, we throw etheric waves heavenward to reach out to the Heart of Creation. The response is sure to return to enrich our worlds beyond all expectation. It is through this simple process that disciples of the Inner are rocketed to Godship while still on earth; and it is through ignorance of this same process that man is continually beset with grief, limitation, birth and death. However, man will not keep on being ignorant forever. When through meditation, or agonizing search, or intense yearning, he forces the first ray of the dawning sun to dispel the gloom of his heart, and lets the blessed light from within burst forth to scatter negative thought-forms, he has begun to learn cosmically. It is a wondrous process worth the inundation of the Nile. Try, O man, try. And if you want to accelerate results re-learn to cry. Let tears of repentance stream down your cheeks beyond restraining; they fertilize your soul for an abundant crop.

"Strive for truth, O mind; and no matter how arduous the ascent, seek strength and determination in calmness and self-control. Should a negative entity obstruct your path or frighten you, shout loudly the name of God OSIRIS, OM, I AM, and know that nothing, no one can resist the Power of the Logos. It is the Ruler of the road, of life and of death.

"Strive for inner realization and slay, once and for all, any desire for outward physical vision. Whoever conceives God as having hands and feet, and a long chain of attributes and qualities, does not belong here, he is doomed to self-oblivion. When we speak of God as the Ultimate Reality, we do not imply physical tangibility to be realized in the near or far-off future, but as an Eternal Becoming, a realization beyond the grasp of time and space. Less than this God is an entity of the mortal mind and, therefore, shifting and unreliable, whereas it transcends all measure, definition and even the loftiest intellectual exaltation.

"When we call a temple *holy*, where the worshipper feels an inner exaltation and a sense of peace, it is not so because of a deity standing therein, but because of man himself. It is man who sanctifies the temple of stone. He is the true, living temple where the Holy of Holies resides. That inner exhilaration is the high priest, the Christ-force officiating for man's awakening and blessing.

"The religion that relies on statues, ritual, chanting, relics, exteriorized worshipping and blind faith, must disappear. It is inevitable that it is so, for the man of the future, imbued with the knowledge of living science, will reject with inconfutable proof the concept of the personal God.

"The scientist of tomorrow is the true spiritual teacher. With every new discovery, he will prove both the existence and presence of God as an eternal Essence, the Cause of all manifestation, and a Goal that will never be reached. Applied science is the expression par excellence of the Eternal Becoming; a progressive scientist is ITS instrument, always ready to reject old methods of research for new ones. The upholder of a creed never questions the statements written on the crumbling parchments of the sacristy, nor does a priest ever dare to contradict a doctrine from a master-theologian of the past. Therefore the Law of Eternal Becoming, the Truth in action, is difficult for them to accept; it is indigestible food.

"The fact that our school of initiation is so eagerly sought by the youths of the civilized world, proves that the inner awakening of our society is broader than the universal animal idolatry in which the masses seem to wallow. Scantier is the number of people who accept in faith the paternalistic utterances issued by self-appointed teachers. We ourselves believe in nothing until we prove it, not collectively in the classroom, but individually, and this includes God. Every student must have his own proof. Nor do we believe what he says; his body, mind, speech, behavior, power of understanding, his way of sitting, eating, playing, walking and state of health, must unmistakably prove his inner glimpses and communion with God. We show him a way but not the Way, for each man's way is his own; it cannot be used or copied by others. Every age must produce its own teachers and revelators, conveying the One Truth with new words, and applying it with new methods. This school is a spheric hub with an infinite number of spokes, one spoke for each man, all bound to the same Law that governs the universe and Life.

"When a scientist fails to draw certain conclusions from a laboratory experiment, what does he do? He sits in a quiet corner of his study and analyzes step by step all he has done, trying to find the loophole. He turns inwardly as far as that specific experiment is concerned. He does this detachedly, without feeling, blaming no one. Thus he prepares himself for further and more enlightening investigation.

"A man engaged in buying and selling legumes studies the fluctuation of supply and demand, and investigates the nature of the coming crop. By so doing he learns when to buy and when to sell to the best of his interests. Should he fail in his forecast, the blame will be all his and no one else's. And if he acknowledges his shortsightedness, he will learn a lesson for the next transaction, otherwise he is doomed to bankruptcy. The same law applies to the realm of the spirit. It is man himself who must investigate the existence of God through the discipline of the mind and the power of the will; and the field of investigation is the self. The self is the mine, the field, the laboratory, the shop, the market and the consumer. It is the most marvelous store-house of knowledge that leads to Self-mastery and immortality. Our teachers do not teach, they guide; they stimulate questions and provide partial answers in order to arouse curiosity and self-reliance in the mind of the student; they encourage and support the timid with appropriate loving severity. Emulation is discour-aged, and if a student excels, he is directed to show gratitude to God in his heart, and a more profound analyzation of the process of self-unfoldment. Now he understands one of the simplest laws of the Science of the Self:

$$\text{Mind} + \text{inspiration} - \text{ego} = \text{Humility}$$

"The teacher's success resides not in the fact that he has years of experience with other students (for in spiritual guidance this is a pitfall), but rather in his own personal experience; he knows himself, he became a teacher through Direct Perception. Hence he knows the way of others, which he indicates — the student must tread it with his own inner equipment.

"By such a process, the student — alone and unaided, aware of the uselessness of external support, and constantly challenged by the world of appearances — is forced to face life in its own tenet with the scientific praxis of inwardness. He will win through a series of lesser revelations leading, step by step, to the Triumph of the Self. He is now at the threshold of the Christ Consciousness.

"And what about the intellect and the reasoning faculty? Fully aware that a fine, healthy and vibrant intellect is capable of smashing any obstacle that tries to befog both the Universal Truth and the Unqualified Light through false reasoning, we develop and train it with the severe study of mathematics until, unable to go any higher, it becomes a footstool for intuition and prophetic power. Our goal is receptivity to the Wisdom of the Self, that is, Direct Perception.

"Through such a process, our students acquire the power to convey the traits and attributes of the Christ not by oratory or seeming wise utterances, but through silence, reverent behavior, an orderly and noble way of living, and other inconspicuous virtues of the soul. This is the true nature of a duly majored hierophant. It is the result of a happy union of faith and science. It makes the mystic a scientist, the scientist a mystic."

✿ ✿ ✿

Now Master Sonchis spoke directly to the candidates seeking admission.

"Blessed students, children of light: I welcome you into our ranks. As I call the roll from the current parchment of admission, please walk forward and place yourselves in a semicircle before the lectern:

"Aphos of Ethiopia, Arbaces of Assyria, Arcus of Samos, Berosus of Babylon, Coctos of Thebes, Daluh of Arabia, Gileah of Judea, Gubarru of Assyria, Hicos of Memphis, Monica of Sicily, Philone of Athens, Pythagoras of Samos, Tarsus of Galicia, Uruk of Babylon, Yasma of Persia.

"Thank you and now behold. . .!"

Master Sonchis entered samadhi. Slowly his body lost contour as if merging into a vast ocean of light, until only a tiny sphere of ethereal fire remained rotating clockwise and displaying in succession the prismatic colors of the solar spectrum. The audience stood transfixed, each person radiating the supernal joy that comes from the privileges of witnessing such an event that attests of the greatness and immortality of man. Now gleaming red and white roses issued forth in great profusion from the luminous sphere and floated high above the heads of the assemblage. The celestial voice of Sonchis was heard:

"O Mother Isis, feminine aspect and Twin Flame of our Formless Spirit-Father Osiris. Gracious One, come! Thou awakener of the sacred centers of our bodies, come and dance about our new students, flowers and pride of Thy Womb. Dance in the lotus of their hearts, and seal therein all Thy world-bewitching beauty. Place Thy Mystic Rose on their foreheads." A fiery light enveloped all, and as it evanesced a fragrant white rose appeared on the brow of each candidate. "O Father Osiris" — the voice continued — "loving and chastising One: hold now, in Thy strong grasp of determination and manly behavior every one of us until the hour of Deliverance." The sphere of light vanished and Master Sonchis reappeared:

"Candidates, you are henceforth duly accepted members of the student body of this School of Initiation. Adhere to the rules of discipline with a joyous transport, and let all your activities — study, athletics, play and rest — be enwrapped in the living mantle of meditation. May the Christ light enfold you all!"

❋   ❋   ❋

251

For Marco and Leonora to see themselves so vividly and vibrant in a previous embodiment, was a divine dispensation of supreme value, both in rapport to the society in which they live today and as candidates to Christship. They wept and rejoiced. What a truly instructive lesson in realism to stand naked before the mirror of life and see oneself with a mind detached from every trace of egotistical appraisal. Their gratitude to God, to the Liberated Master-Teacher, the Cosmic Assembly of the Perfect Ones, Ammon-Ra, and to the land that now shelters and nourishes them broke all bounds. They cried aloud as if issuing a prophetic pronouncement:

"Glory unto Thee, O hallowed land of heroes and lovers of liberty. Thou art the Pole-star of our lives. It is by the grace of thy dynamic and evolutive stability that we have found our way on the trackless sea of life.

"Thou, O fearless, O Victorious One! Where else, in this turmoiling world of envy, plotting and ingratitude, could such a grace be found? Hail unto Thee, O Land of America!

"O enchanted soil of infinite blessings, O Father-Mother of the incoming nations of the Golden Age: Be thou like unto a Liberated Master who has conquered life and death forever: a relentless and daring pioneer, humble, generous, detached and alert, alert, alert!"

The Screen of Life came to a stop and Ammon-Ra declared: "With the power invested upon Me by the Cosmic Assembly of the Perfect Ones I hereby ratify your prophetic call to God with the Seal of the Fire of Realization. It shall be so!" and with his thumb touched their foreheads. As the Screen recommenced, He continued:

"Here one finds that class distinction and social inequality are unknown, though in the outer world the society is choked by taboos, castes, creeds and racial discrimination. In the classroom, the students haunted by the shadow of bondage are the happiest, the most studious, the most polite and those who never infringe upon the rules of discipline. They know there is no way out but to be a god unto oneself, facing society and life with a mind and soul made strong and all-conquering through study and self-discipline. Their graduation means the liberation of their families from slavery. At that time, there was an agreement called the Covenant of Liberty in God, between this school and the various rulers of the known countries whereby said rulers would burn the rope of vassalage, servitude and slavery of those families or members thereof who could prove that at least one of their kin had graduated from this school.

"Advocates for Civil Rights were extant at that time. They divided themselves into factions: some stirred up hatred and fomented revolution, others incited plotting and assassination, while still others resorted to demagoguery and street corner debates. None of these won an iota of the liberty they sought; on the contrary, some were punished with death, others forced to commit suicide, and many others were deprived of their citizenship and banished into exile. Only those who bent their backs on the benches of classrooms, studying until quasi-exhaustion, succeeded in achieving their most cherished goals: economic well-being, social status, intellectual wealth, spiritual wisdom and comprehension of the Godself.

* * *

"We shall now skip" — Ammon-Ra went on — "seven years of the academic life of the student body, and analyze some of the activities that were unique and contributed to the success of the school. The university student endowed with an exuberance of health and vitality, and deeply aware of what is expected of him by his teachers, family, society and his responsible self, must, perforce, find a form a relaxation that is meaningful and worthwhile. In the ancient world and in other lands outside of Egypt students indulged in moderate athletics with little or no thought of competition, and moderate sexual promiscuity. And I say *moderate* because the sexual act — the orgasm of the coitus itself — was enwrapped in the concept of a deity, a god or goddess watching over the couple, reminding them of the malediction that would befall them should moderation be overstepped. The result was by far a happy one. In the society in which you live, the university student, with a biological exuberance greater than ever, and with an intellectual and social responsibility that has grown by leaps and bounds, and forced somehow into a system of sports that relaxes neither the mind nor the body, due to the aggressive and unbridled competition with which it is qualified, your student, I say, is driven to unrestrained sexual promiscuity that is devoid of every trace of beauty and spiritual touch; thus he fails to derive the sense of relaxation which he sought. Hence the bewilderment, unhappiness and rebelliousness amongst the youth, and the mounting need of psychiatrists in the adult population.

"In the School of the Initiates in Memphis these degenerative tendencies in the biological makeup of the student had been solved successfully. The genital organs were considered the most important center of the human body where physical strength was generated. This physical strength was required to heighten handsomeness and enthusiasm which led to noble pride and kindled the desire to excel in the classroom. The school had the most elaborate gymnasia where the students exercised freely; gymnasiarchs though present did not interfere unless requested. There were steam rooms and masseurs armed with strigils whose use was not limited to scraping sweat and dirt from the body; they removed dead tissue that caused formation of wrinkles, letting new skin grow fresh and youthful. Women gymnasiarchs massaged gently the genital organs of the students while the latter saw to it that the vibration thus produced was distributed evenly throughout the atomic structure of both body and mind. When the spermatic substance, though ready to issue forth, is held in abeyance and the ecstatic pulsation raised, by the power of the will, upward into the head, man passes from magnetic charm to inspiration to sudden enlightenment and superconscious revelation. This is the healthiest, most delightful and most durable form of mind expansion. Gymnasiarchs worked likewise on the girl-students, massaging their breasts and genital organs, and the effect was similarly one of supernal exaltation of body, mind and soul. As the academic years went by the student produced this atomic arousement without any outer assistance, solely by the power of his disciplined mind.

"Because of this unique and daring system of education, based mainly on the bio-cosmical knowledge of the human body, ancient Egypt achieved an intellectual, political and artistic preeminence in the contemporary world, and became a focus of spiritual training in the domain of the philosophy of life that had already given birth to the stern monotheism of the Hebrews, and was to influence both in ritual and theology Christianity and Islamism. Even in the fields of engineering and medicine, Egypt was far ahead of anything known to the Near East and the Mediterranean basin before the Industrial Revolution.

"How similar you are, my disciples Marco and Leonora, to Arcus and Lunide. Behold! As in ancient Egypt you Arcus still arise at four in the morning or even earlier, you still practice fasting and make use of enemas. You never required medical assistance then, and you have never seen a doctor in this embodiment. The color of your eyes, hair and skin, the shape of your faces, straight noses, long necks and smiling mouths, the slenderness of your bodies, the absence of any abdominal protrusion, the long and shapely legs, all attest to your classic heritage. Your breast, Leonora, is the exact replica of Lunide's for firmness and magnetism, revealing the care and manipulation given to it at that time, and demonstrating the harmonious interrelation of the endocrinal structure of your body. The overall vitality that you display today is linked to your aristocratic birth in the house of Sonchis.

"Your yearning for truth and the desire to contact the Liberated Masters go as far back as your last embodiment in the land of Lemuria, two hundred and fifty thousand years ago, when that continent was blazing with sparkling luminance throughout the world, and sheltered a population of giants of the Spirit. It was there through your infant lips, that the Word AUM resounded for the first time in the consciousness of man. *OMLAT, OMLAT, OMLAT* . . . (AUM is Light) was your baby talk; for thousands of years, previous to your Lunide embodiment, you lived, in the realm of the Spirit, a life of undeflected application in the pursuance of inner and outer purity. Therein you learned what a tremendous responsibility, to God and Society, it is to be born. As a reward for your pioneering labor in the field of the Spirit and the pursuit of excellence that leads to immortality, the Cosmic Assembly of the Perfect Ones granted you the privilege of choosing your parents for the embodiment to come. It was the Eternal Self of you who, from the Octaves of Life, prepared your future mother to be a wise teacher, and gave her strength and courage to conceive you in what the outer world would call *out of wedlock.*

"And who could be the Bridegroom of such a mother? He had to fulfill the cosmic aspiration of the incoming You, as Lunide, who was already destined to display all the traits of a perfectionist and striver for beauty, and a seeker of wisdom,

255

worthy of the visualization of the parents. Thus you knocked at the gate of the highest wisdom, Saturn, where Hermes had taken abode since his ascension. The celestial spaces were so filled with the reverberation of your desire that when the Rebuilder of the Egyptian civilization saw you, He absorbed your Self into his heart and held you there until the fateful hour would come to release your soul into Lucerna's womb, the youthful and unwed governess of the House of Sonchis. Such is Virgin Birth, a transference of a formless and vibrating *intelligence* into the crucible of living liquid matter within a feminine body.

"As Pharaoh of Egypt, centuries prior to your Lunide embodiment and in possession of the all-seeing Eye, I saw you in one of the Egyptian schools, a meritorious student worthy to be teacher and confidante of my princess-daughters. You performed your assignment in perfect adherence to your noble aspirations, and never sought royal reward or verbal praise, as if you already knew of the incoming boon of celestial parentage. Be aware, O disciple Leonora, of this living heritage, and strive incessantly and with abiding joy to behold the Presence of your Father Hermes and Mother Lucerna who are overshadowing you with their protective Love, Wisdom and Knowledge.

* * *

"We shall now observe on the screen of Life, a group of students moving about on the campus, on a holiday, unhurried by classroom attendance. As a responsible and successful businessman, his mind filled with vision for his commercial house, his heart full of love for his family, and with no sign of anxiety or doubt, so is each individual student, solidly lodged in the concept of his mission. Much is at stake. His thoughts and inner forces are intelligently and carefully harnessed for the ultimate objective. Yet he keeps on saying: 'How can I be worthier to myself, my family, my society and God'. In the unfoldment of his work variation of details and minor deviations from the main path he does admit as a certain possibility; but the final goal that looms ahead clear and tangible has to remain inalterable. And what is the final goal? Scientist-avatar, philosopher-avatar, artist-avatar, and ruler-avatar of body politics, which means reflecting perfection and Godlike nobility at every step of the way.

"Such a precise objective leaves no room for slackness, idle talk, gossip, vain argumentation, disrespect of other's opinion, malicious behavior and unethical thoughts towards life. Discussion yes, wrangling disputation never. Students with such moral and intellectual makeup did not need supervision. In fact, they had none; freedom was absolute. Classroom attendance was not checked, yet absenteeism was almost nil; the dormitories were never inspected, yet the students kept their rooms clean and orderly, their clothes fresh and always appropiate to surroundings and circumstances. Mealtime was unscheduled, each student maintained his own in harmony with his inner and outer work, and nutritional requirements. The tendency of the youth to carouse and be boisterous was here checked and disciplined through stage acting and singing, ennobling thus body gesture and the sound of the voice. Sunset was the peak of silence. As the campanile of the campus chimed the vespers, all activity ceased. Teachers, students, office workers and visitors alike sat in meditation wherever they happened to be. For one hour everybody sought God.

"Occasionally, however, some of the students fell into the grip of self-defeating thoughts; moodiness, discontentment and pessimism engulfed them. These lead to obscuration of the mind, emotional disarrangement, crime and suicidal proneness; for he who antagonizes life disrupts the normal flow of the cosmic harmonies and treads the path of self-annihilation. Behold, my disciples, one of such students crossing the screen. He is so morose and almost lifeless; his heart is heavy, pounding clumsily, and his mind barely vibrating. It seems as if the Indwelling Presence is no longer wanted. What is happening there?

"Harassed by the crisscrossing of the negative vibrations of the world which his untrained mind was unable to detect, the holy centers of the body — the base of the spinal column, the sexual center, the solar plexus, the heart, throat, and the pituitary and pineal glands — were thrown into a state of confusion whereby they no longer collaborate with each other for an optimum biological efficiency. They still secrete their mysterious substances, but they do not travel through the atomic structure; instead they stagnate and poison the body;

257

hence the greyish color of the skin, the adumbrated aura, the lifeless gaze and the failing physical strength. You are watching a heap of organic matter in process of decomposition. Human entities such as this cause the earth to groan and stagger, and to grow darker and unfriendly even for a Christ. The united forces of good must be harnessed to correct and obliterate such a plague. And what are the united forces of good? Science, philosophy and the arts; for these indeed are the tangible tools that remold the defective and degenerating man into one that is *real*: the image and likeness of God.

"Do you know that a living human body with a happy, buoyant and noble disposition weighs upon the earth half the poundage actually shown on the scale? Do you know that a brilliant mind devoted to constructive endeavours reduces the weight of the body by at least two thirds? And do you know that a Christ incarnate is weightless? And may I tell you that one of the major causes that contributed to the sinking of Atlantis and Lemuria was the pessimistic and suicidal attitude of some of their inhabitants? Should the people of earth who negate love, order and happiness, reverse their feelings, the earth itself would immediately respond by changing into a self-luminous star of higher vibration and perennial beauty. Is it not, therefore, logical to declare that the unhappy, pessimistic and destructive individual is not the legitimate, lawful and *real* dweller of earth? He is an unwanted guest, a thief, an impostor and a cancerous entity that requires expert supervision before the entire human family is trapped in the same virulent web.

"Let us follow again our dejected student. Who can ever set him free from this comatic condition? Behold a hierophant in his secluded study; observe him radiating vibrations of love to his students. Now with his all-seeing Eye he scans the campus and sees his ailing student in need of assistance. He closes his eyes, utters the Name of God OSIRIS three times and plunges the mind into the depths of his being. The cosmic forces are now ready to do his bidding; a blinding spark of light is directed to the coccygeal zone of the student's body and sets it on fire. It is enough; the holy centers are reactivated and the biological processes resume their function.

"This hierophant, this *real* and quasi-complete man, wield-

258

ing almost Christ powers has performed an act of cosmic re-integration, that is, a miracle. And because this miracle is known to no one in the outer world but to Master Sonchis, he has fulfilled an assignment of cosmic import qualified with true humility. The student has learned a lesson that he will never forget, because, undisturbed, undistracted and seemingly unaided by any outer agency, he was able to follow, step by step, the resurgence of his inner forces; he has had an experience of Direct Perception, and as such, he is wiser and closer to God.

"And finally: These teachings and these experiences, disciples of the Solar Verbum, Marco and Leonora, are intended to sink deep into your consciousness. Please, make them an integral part of your selves: flesh, blood and mind. You have been granted a privilege and charged with a responsibility. In the not far off future, the Cosmic Assembly of the Perfect Ones will request you to apply these healing powers on behalf of some of your ailing disciples. And you must be ready. You need an intensive course in higher humility to resist and dominate the obstinate demands of the ego who never ceases pestering you for outer praise. You must be able and willing to set on fire the basic center of the human body of a discontented person, and do so in utter secrecy from a sheltered corner of your study, without even knowing where the person is, nor giving even the slightest hint that it was you who did it. Honor and praise you will receive from the Unseen Ones. Meditate, work and rejoice."

Ammon-Ra bid his disciples farewell, his commission being fulfilled. Before ascending he made this prophetic pronouncement:

"Ere the closing of your present embodiment, you shall witness and preside over a universal gathering of men, women and children, in an unheard of revival of Sun Worshipping; peoples of every land and faith, and unbelievers too, offering themselves as a foundation for the most enduring amalgama of science, philosophy and the arts; every lifestream a perennial devotee of light that casts no shadow, studying and producing for a society of gods. And out of that coordinated activity you shall announce the dawn of the Golden Age!"

With his thumbs he again touched their foreheads as if

sealing his mighty utterance on a living parchment; then issuing the mighty decree: "AUM is Light, AUM is Light, AUM is Light. I AM!" they saw Him floating in midair, his dazzling form of unconsuming fire stood majestically above the apex of Mount Moran of the Grand Teton National Park, one of the retreats of the Great Ones who guide America towards her spiritual destiny. Then he was seen no more.

*　*　*

Using the still pulsating radiance left behind by Ammon-Ra, Marco and Leonora were able to hold in action the Screen of Life for one more episode of the Egyptian School of the Initiates: Pythagoras at the commencement ceremony delivering his farewell address:

"I AM on my way to the total consummation of my mortal ego. O Star of Humility, absorb me into Thy Fiery Essence.

"I shall endeavour to apply the method of teaching of this magnificent Atheneum to my future students, that they may properly comprehend the doctrine of the Solar Path and the Law of Cause and Effect in a way that will preclude all doubt, mystification and misunderstanding.

"I shall inculcate upon their minds and hearts never to aspire to anything but the highest, and never to be satisfied with second rate knowledge. I shall teach them to cultivate awareness of God at every step of the way of their diurnal labor.

"I shall demand of my Father-Self to chastise me whenever I am in default, for I intend to tread a path filled with momentous experiences that will be remembered for thousands of years.

"May whoever follows the teaching of the Solar Path be forever released from the world of duality and delusion.

"Gratitude from my heart goes first to God directly. To God again through my choicest friends Lunide and Arcus. To God again through my noble Master Sonchis and the faculty staff. To God again and again through my blessed parents, and everyone who directly or indirectly contributed to the realization of my life's dream.

"OSIRIS I AM OM".

*　*　*

As the Screen of Life ceased to run Marco and Leonora returned to the multifarious complexities of human life. The urge of the upward reappeared with uncontainable force, but the necessity of bread-winning, orderliness of home, personal appearance, duty as citizens and social intercourse had to be met.

With a faith still tinged with a trace of ego they worked facing stubborn obstacles; mornings and evenings, however, were reserved for God, irrespective of the demands of the outer world. "Light of Osiris, Light of Osiris, Light of Osiris . . ." was their call and prayer, and the answer came in due time and in obedience to the law of cause and effect. "Son and daughter"— the Inner Master responded — "speak, what do you wish?" "Open the gate of our hearts and minds, O Father, that we may comprehend the meaning of true humility . . .", the blinding brilliance of the Self vanished.

Enveloped in darkness and tossed into a pit that seemed bottomless, Marco and Leonora found themselves floating leisurely as if gliding in space, the Word OM reverberating in their minds. A false sense of security was beginning to pervade their beings when, suddenly, they felt a terrific downward pull, as if caught within the power of terrestrial gravitation, which caused them to plummet with ever-increasing speed. Their descent was halted abruptly a few feet above the surface of a large cloaca filled with putrefying waste matter. They saw coming towards them naked human beings — their bodies disfigured with unsightly, gaping wounds and pustules — screaming frantically: "We are lost, we are lost . . . help, help!" As they came closer, Marco and Leonora who were about to issue a call to God on their behalf, noticed that the suffering creatures were all blind; the prayer of rescue died on their lips, and only meaningless syllables, lacking love and conviction, came forth. The voice of Osiris spoke again within their hearts:

"Son and daughter, this first experiment in higher humility has failed. Like a man puffed up with self-love you wanted to render assistance, but only on the condition that you would be noticed and thanked. Disappointment is an entity of ignorance, a sour pill of the heedless. Only he who is totally entrenched in ME, even while cleaning the sewers or being crucified can truly act and comprehend divine humility which My Son the Christ spoke of. For such a state of consciousness the disciple on the path needs a wealth of inner experiences.

261

Your merciful Liberated Master-Teacher shall provide them for you. Listen and obey. You will see and hear of those who win and those who fail in the game of life; of those who win though losing, and those who having won, are actually reduced to a wretched spiritual pauperism choked in the slimy tentacles of despondency, loneliness, fear and incurable disease. You shall learn about striving lifestreams, the foundation of hope, human diversification and tendency, of the indestructible and eternal life of the Soul, and how it travels and forges ahead in the infinite and ever-evolving realms of Creation. Be attentive!"

* * *

Locked in the tranquil embrace of objectless meditation, Marco and Leonora soon found themselves alighting on the borderland of the sunbelt. Aided by the gift of the Verbum-sight, they saw a staggering panorama of intersidereal splendor: the procession of the equinoxes, the motion of the zodiac, the starry heavens and an infinite number of celestial bodies, all unaffected by the concept of time and space, translating around the Heart of God, in adoration to Its Creative Mind. They saw ninety-one solar systems — a fraction of the whole — the dimmest one being one thousand times brighter than ours. Each of these systems held within its orbit seventeen star-planets, populated with magnificent lifestreams whose foreheads glowed with shadowless light in various hues and degrees of brilliancy. None of the inhabitants showed signs of age, nor did they appear unhappy or in any way inharmonious with life. Brotherhood seemed to be the resultant of strength, love and wisdom fused into one.

High above their heads, in the empyreal expanse, was the Milky Way, a broad concave lane of light studded with fixed stars of every dimension and degree of luminosity, and in their interspaces, as if roaming in no man's land, they saw innumerable dark islets covered with specks of moving matter which emanated dim and intermittent light. "Each vibrating corpuscle is the last elemental residue of what was once a complex and highly specialized human form" — their Liberated Master-Teacher explained. "He was a human being that walked the earth. Through a series of misdeeds, embodiment after embodiment, he descended to a state of living whereby he lost both his precious individuality and the gift of the awareness of God; and because he is keenly conscious of his ultimate destiny, he surges and strives incessantly on the path of evolution. Like an amoeba, billions of years are required to be a human being again, and have the privilege of uttering the name of God."

Turning their attention to our planetary system, Marco and Leonora saw seven concentric lanes of light rotating at various speeds in a clockwise motion. They were disposed conically with the vertex resting on a luminous rod that issued from a mountain peak of the physical sun, while the ever-widening lanes stood suspended higher above it in perfect symmetrical order. The narrowest section of the cone was almost dark and very slow in both its speed and rate of vibration; the upper lanes were brighter and rotated faster, and the uppermost was as brilliant as the heart of the sun. Their Divine Guide now gave an interpretation:

"These seven circular lanes are the seven stations of man's ascendancy towards cosmic mastery after the so-called physical death. They constitute a series of tests followed by promotions onto higher plateaus of consciousness. To have enough merits on earth to reach the first station or circle is the most ardous task. This explains the merciful assistance given to mankind by duly appointed teachers, incarnate Christs and Liberated Masters who are exactly the equivalent of first grade teachers in the system of earthly school education. As a child who has been promoted to second grade, never returns to the first, likewise a man lifted onto the lowest of these planes of overlife will never again return to earth but proceed forever and ever into higher states of cosmic existence. Man is indestructible! A Liberated Master himself, having fulfilled his assignment on behalf of a certain group of aspiring disciples, is promoted to higher cosmic hierarchies which are as far distant from man's intelligence as a living cell is from an Avatar. A Christ recently promoted may be given the spiritual government of a nation or a race or continent for one or two or three thousand years, after which he might be elevated to the rulership of a planetary system for another ten thousand years, as it were, and on and on. Such is the staggering infinitude of life, marching unrestrictedly in the infinitude of space. Such is the grandeur of God.

"How is it conceivable, therefore, that a disciple of the Solar Path, once ascended, returns to earth for another embodiment? It is done, now and then, as an act of supreme dispensation, as in the case of Master Jesus, but never twice with the same Liberated Lifestream. And though Master Jesus — still one of the rulers of the spiritual destinies of the white and Negro races — might project a replica of Himself to some deserving disciples, this is not a sign that he will take embodiment again. A Conqueror of life and death is an anachronism amidst the mortals.

"Now, my disciples, observe beneath and learn. Behold the narrow neck of this funnel of human existence. This is the recruiting center of the soul-flames who are about to take embodiment on earth. Those who are endowed with noble karma come from higher planes of consciousness, while others, stained with vice and sin have lingered here for decades in cold, greyish, sad and deathlike surroundings, hearing only the voice of teachers, speaking of love, law and obedience, trying to inculcate on their consciousness the wisdom of studying, positive thoughts, humility, respect and harmonious collaboration with their fellow man. They are shown all the incongruencies and idiosyncrasies in which the members of the human society below wallow, and how to avoid them. Those with a karma of violence and incipient crime against man and nature, laugh at the teachers, and sneer defiantly at the law and order down under; while the souls with meritorious karma cry for mercy and forgiveness, that they may be allowed to stay and avoid embodiment, submitting to whatever tests the Master-teachers might impose upon them. But it is of no avail; down they must go; it is the dictate of a cosmico-scientific law. Even he who is destined to be a genius, or a great ruler, or an industrialist swimming in wealth, must re-enter the thorny trap of earthly embodiment. You noticé, please, that all countenances here look alike, individuality has temporarily disappeared. This is the moon-consciousness.

"A soul who, in the interim of two embodiments, is forced to stay in this shadowy and slumlike enclosure, has no specific intellectual or spiritual traits. And though he might acquire wealth and seeming fame, it matters not; he will return here, unless he devotes a portion of his wakeful hours of the day to God directly. Noble deeds without meditation do not raise the conscience of man.

"When a soul descends to earth from the next Circle which is ruled by the Elohim Mercury, he brings to human society the gift of the arts and sciences unstained by greed. Before he descends, Mercury touches his forehead and warns him: 'Son, that you may devote thyself to scientific endeavours (or the arts), and never allow thy noble profession to be polluted by selfish aspirations. Work under the tutelage of thy Godself and return to Me as a Prince of Light. Go, My son, and know that I AM thy Godfather!' He then shows him the pitfalls and delusions of those who forget the admonition, and the spiritual degradation that follows. In the fatal plunge those who yield to temptation and prostitute science and the arts for personal benefit are barred from Mercury's Presence for thousands of years; the intervening embodiments could be as low as those of the primitive beings of the jungle.

"The Circle of Venus surmounts Mercury's. Here the Soul is given the supreme touch in the expression of divine love on earth. 'Love dispassionately, My child, and beware of the illusion of the form. Walking on a lonely path, should you hear the lamentation of a wounded being, go out of thy way and render the required service to the best of thy ability. Do not say *I must go to my mother's house first for she is sick unto death*, for this is selfish love. Every form that lives is mysteriously linked with God; it deserves thy wholehearted attention, respect and love. Wherever there is a thing that breathes, there is a flame that yearns for love. Love that, My son, irrespective of the size, color and shape of the vessel; it is energizing; it activates thy intelligence to a state of undreamed of creativity.' This admonition, whose application could bring peace to earth, is rarely practiced, most often wholly forgotten. This is the cause of individual and collective frustration, double talk and circumventing attitude of political leaders in internatíonal relations.

"Above Venus is the Circle of the Sun whose Guardian Elohim holds the triumphant torch of immortal beauty. This is the academy of the gurus and yogins whose athletics of the mind, the discipline of the body, love of God and detached attitude for the things of the world, constitute the crucible of enduring beauty in form and essence. When they are despatched to earth they spread the verbum of joy and handsomeness to a score of adoring disciples, who then express themselves in the field of the arts, dancing, music, poetry, painting, architecture, landscaping, interior decoration, fashion, beauty contests, Olympic games, and all the noble niceties that spring forth from a healthy mind and a state of affluence. If these receptive disciples would only reflect upon and analyze the root and essence of their creative urge with the instrument of meditation and humility . . .

"The Fifth Circle is ruled by Mars, the Guardian of Justice. From this heaven the justices of the supreme courts of the civilized nations are released to earth. Through the gracious will of Mars, assisted by a Board of Liberated Masters of Jurisprudence, a designated lifestream becomes president or secretary general of the United Nations or one of its consultive members. The tribunals of the world could improve markedly on their rendering of justice by cultivating awareness of the Eternal Presence of Mars hovering above their benches. It is through Him that they must report to God concerning the administration of justice. It is a grave crime to subordinate justice to the selfish whim of dictators, political parties, private interests, transitory ideologies and fashionable moral trends. And we may add another violation; yielding to arbitrary threats from racial groups.

"Surmounting the Circle of Mars is the Heaven of Jupiter, the Wielder of Supreme Power entrusted upon Him directly by the Cosmic Assembly of the Perfect Ones. Here dwell the souls of those lifestreams who are destined to exert a cosmic vigilance over a planet. They are the impersonal Buddhas, Christs and Avatars. With the speed of Light they cross a territory or a continent to cast silently the seeds of a new and higher civilization. These seeds fall into parcels called Copernicus, Newton, Galileo Galilei, Giordano Bruno, Ashoka, Socrates, Moses, Alexander Graham Bell, Marconi, Einstein, Fermi and a few others. Jupiter's radiance of wisdom is projected into the lower Circles of Life, and could greatly enhance the prodding minds of human beings, were they conscious of His Presence.

"The Seventh Circle is the last one available for partial comprehension by a genius. Only the Inner Eye liberated from the flesh prison can see It, and only the mind of a Christ can explain It. Hence, my disciples, be of good cheer. As an act of grace for your patience and sincere yearning, I tell you that this Circle is a link between your solar system and ninety others, and it is placed under the rulership of Saturn, the Prince of Light par excellence and one of the Masters of Universal Wisdom. He possesses visibly the All-seeing Eye of God, a band of light adhering to his head which widens to the shape of a disc of dazzling luminosity on His forehead. What can I tell you of Him, my disciples. When, in the line of service, I behold His wondrous Presence, it is as if I were standing face to face with the Universal Countenance of God; I fall on my knees in grateful adoration of the All-encompassing Logos, and lo, He kneels by my side and kisses my hand in humble submission saying: 'Son, mayest thou soon be master of my dominion'. Such, indeed, is His humility. He is the Householder and the Supreme Host of all that lives in the planetary assemblage of your solar system; and whoever thinks of Him with true humility realizes with absolute certainty the concept of infinitude and immortality of the soul.

"These mighty Rulers have been placed also at the service of mankind by the Cosmic Assembly of the Perfect Ones. Unlike a Liberated Master whose power of instantaneous mind-penetration is limited to only one solar system for the first thousand years of his ascension, these Great Beings are equipped with a power of perception capable of embracing one-hundred solar systems in a time flash. The researchists in the field of psychology would do well to ponder over this astounding characteristic of the human mind.

❊ ❊ ❊

"You shall now behold, my disciples, the path of return of those lifestreams who have achieved liberation either through the so-called death or through direct transmutation of matter. Be attentive and observe their behavior. To convey to you their feelings, try to visualize a child who at the age of four entered a kindergarten and remained there until the age of one-hundred

267

because of his inability to master the elements of the alphabet. Such a retarded child is man, even the man-genius, in rapport to a newly promoted Christ. His thousands upon thousands of embodiments, and his incapacity to understand the mechanics of transmutation of his own body have held him bound in the kindergarten of life. Now here they are, happy, humble, eager, and wielders of powers greater than the force of terrestrial gravitation, interplanetary attraction and solar magnetism put together. And what is their most outstanding virtue? Humility, my children, humility. It is the humility of the true wise one whose mind is constantly directed to the ever-present and ever-active Law of God.

"Their first self-imposed and gladly performed assignment is to linger in the moon-consciousness, the melting pot of creation and quarantine of life, to assist and train the unhappy souls on their downward plunge, who must meet and rescue the unkind karma of their previous embodiments. They pray to God that those who have committed themselves to new crimes will be immediately arrested at the first attempt to cause further damage to life. Then They resume their ascending path towards Mercury. Those whose earthly activity was tuned with this Circle of Life, stay here as messengers of Mercury inspiring and assisting the people of earth with Mercurian traits. The others ascend towards Venus, the Circle of Life of Divine Love. If they are Twin Flame-couples, they stay here temporarily as teachers of love to the down-going souls, and then proceed ascending towards the next Circle of Life. As Venus is the meeting place of the Twin Flames, those who are alone remain here, not only as messengers of Venus, but to rescue their twins still living on earth, or to be joined by their divine mates who may be engaged in duties of cosmic import in higher realms. The dwellers of this Circle who have earned Christhood, undergo a transmutation of form through a grace from the Circle of the Sun. Beauty and Tranquillity are bestowed upon them.

"From Venus on, only Twin Flames ascend to higher heavens. In the Circle of the Sun they learn that beauty cannot be maintained unless it is constantly polarized with love and grafted to the Heart of God, for this is purity and understanding. Twin Flames are best qualified for such an activity for they live in an aura of harmony, joy and peace, the three pillars upon which beauty stands.

"The busiest of the ascending souls are the Godchildren of Mars. Like the honor students of any university who are invited to join the teaching staff after graduation, the ascended lawmakers, justices and attorneys are given the mandate to project shafts of light into the minds of those of earth engaged in drafting evolutive legislation in behalf of the people. They inspire the members of the United Nations, NATO, SEATO, the Summit Conferences, the Halls of International Arbitration and Peace, and every other gathering of lawmakers where the welfare of the masses is codified.

"It was through the selfless labor of love of the victorious children of Mars that the Declaration of Independence of the United States of America, their Constituion, and Lincoln's Gettysburg Address, came into being; so it was also with the much abused and controversial legislation on Civil Rights. I dare say, however, that this noble document will be, erelong, taken as a guide by other nations plagued by racial discrimination. What a dark karma is in store for those who are maliciously opposing the normal unfoldment of the Civil Rights Laws; and how much darker will be the next embodiment for those who are exploiting, for vanity or selfish gains, the dispensation of equal opportunity before the Law. Beware, O man, of the subtle and inconspicuous feeling of social, economic or racial superiority. It is thy downfall for many embodiments to come.

"Since Justice and Liberty are closely interrelated, the messengers are always busy. No community of people, since the outset of the present cycle of life, has received more tangible help from the Great Ones than the Continent of the Americas, Canada included. They have been hammered with such awareness and strokes of light, that their inhabitants are the most freedom-conscious people of earth today. For this reason they should, not as a courtesy but as a duty, be sensitive to the call of liberty raised by other peoples who live under unwanted rulers. However, they should never enter into alliances or sign political treaties favoring any nation whatsoever. Foreign entanglements are extraneous to the Law that governs their lives. Their mission and duty are to radiate love to all, backed with power and preparedness, and to assist wisely those who ask for help. As the Custodians of Cosmic Liberty and the Guardians of the Commonwealth of all Nations they must be strong and alert both in the field of the Spirit and matter.

"The Twin Flames who are armed with the Torch of Eternal Beauty and the Sword of Divine Justice, continue moving higher and ever higher to make room for the incomers from lower realms. They ascend towards the Circle of Jupiter where they become Junior Executives of the Cosmic Order of Life. Being trained for interstellar duties, they seldom come in contact with the people of Earth. By gazing at each other and together at a star, the Twins have the power to raise the luminosity and rate of vibration of that star. From now on they derive their nourishment from the Consciousness of Saturn.

"Blessed searchers of knowledge and astronauts of the Spirit, you have seen the ascension of man, the celestial ladder through which the striving soul climbs to realms of existence where the earth is completely forgotten, yet true life has barely commenced. Even Christship, so exalted on earth and sung by the Angelic Host as the loftiest event in the procession of the equinoxes, is nothing else but the beginning of man's Self-discovery. Billions of years are required to carry him to the confineless threshold of the Mind of God. However he can never fall again, because suffering, ignorance and death are no longer of his world. May man live in the awareness of this truth, by any path that he might choose: meditation, love, humility, service, study, worship; by one, two or all of these paths, and join the ranks of the Liberated Ones."

❖   ❖   ❖

The fountain of Wisdom halted its flow, and all was enveloped in silence. The Master had graciously withdrawn from the presence of his adoring disciples, but they could not descend from the lofty realm of the Spirit; instead, they levitated their forms to a starry meadow of semitropical vegetation that faced the Southeastern slope of Mount Vesuvius in Italy. It was the etheric counterpart of that famed rocky elevation which periodically curses with harsh desolation a people and a country snugly entrenched in self-praise and dreams of unequaled greatness. Wandering aimlessly, Marco and Leonora came upon an extraordinary and magnificent garden hidden on the slope of this heavenly mountain. The lawn, trees, flowers and shrubbery were so arranged as to form precise geometrical figures; even

270

the jets of water from the various fountains formed in midair solid figures, such as cubes, spheres, pyramids and cylinders. As they stood spellbound in silent admiration at the strange yet picturesque spectacle, they noticed the absence of winged insects so indispensable to pollination, wherefore they directed their attention to Master Flora for an explanation.

"What are insects and bacteria?" — he responded. "They are organic units endowed with a distinct and specialized function in obedience to a higher impulse that issues from the Mind of God or, to appease the skeptics and atheists, from the Law of Nature; and like other living beings, they are subjected to the law of evolution. This means that as time goes on they will be able to perform more complex tasks and, compelled by the law of love or harmonious coexistence, some will lose their lethal traits against vegetation, domestic animals and man. By such a process they acquire merits exactly as man does, and eventually achieve a status comparable to that of an average human being who is engaged in constructive work.

"In the life of Earth, insects and bacteria are both teachers and chastisers, and also awakeners of man's power of observation. We, in the ascended state, have nothing to learn from them, and whatever they perform that is useful, it has no field or expression in our environment of perfection. The day will come when these units of life will not be required on Earth for pollination, nor will there be deleterious bacteria whose control baffles the world of man. Pollination, being a process of fertilization similar to the erotic vibration projected at each other by a man and a woman in love, can be brought about by radiating thoughts of love to the trees of an orchard. And this is what we do here. Our vegetation has no need of insects or insecticides, as you have no need of horses for transportation in the large cities of your land. And as the horse is being educated, as it were, for nobler activities — racing, stage appearance and so forth — through a process of selection and training, likewise the insect. In a few years you will be able to set the dog free from the inhumane boredom of guiding the blind; an electronic detector is in the making for the gathering of intelligence from the surroundings to be transmitted to the brain structure of him who lacks physical sight, until such a time when man evolving also on the path of ethics, will no longer be born blind or suffer blindness through misconduct. Animal life — helpless and bound — is undergoing accelerated evolution, faster than man's, until it reaches a status of respect and freedom comparable to man's attitude towards his own family."

* * *

Marco and Leonora returned to Earth and made preparation for the forthcoming encounter with Master Pythagoras and his activity as a philosopher and teacher of the youth in the City of the Chosen Ones, twenty-six centuries ago. The ideal community living that he brought into realization in the city of Crotona, in southern Italy or Magna Graecia, as it was called at that time, gave luster to that age and raised the democratic system of government to the acme of perfection. The famous center of higher learning that he founded had the same topographical layout of the School of the Initiates in Memphis, with the exception of the Spheric Hall of Light.

Pythagoras had enemies from the outset of his activity, though he was not their enemy. He was constantly harassed, envied and falsely accused by the so-called freethinkers who, under the aegis of freedom of thought and speech, fabricated the most diabolical insinuations against the great Master. Summoned time and again before the City Senate at the instigation of his detractors, whose way of life was injustice and corruption, Pythagoras came out glorified and exalted, and with his hands filled with gifts, endowments and subsidies for the expansion of his program. Consequently, the energy of destructiveness directed at him was transmuted, by a higher power, into a constructive force, which caused his teaching to cross many boundaries and conquer the political leaders of many communities. He possessed the charm and magnetism of a Christ, and wherever he spoke, his words and inner radiance held the audience spellbound.

So highly constructive was his program, that an outer brotherhood, composed of farmers, tradesmen, literati and men of arms, was formed to sustain the Institute of Higher Learning and spread its philosophy. As a result, crime, poverty and disease decreased considerably and, as if by reflection, Pythagoras' adversaries increased in number and depravity. The Master aimed at the application of a philosophy of life based on scientific investigation, namely, the dissection and exposure of moods, desires and aspirations arising in man, by the path of self-analysis and with the instrument of mathematics. By such a process, he proved, crime is eradicated without physical coercion, higher profit in business is realized by the application of the law of ethics in all transactions, and intercommunal peace and collaboration are achieved simply by the comprehension and application of the Law of Cause and Effect. A few years later, when he was summoned again before the investigating committe to give an account of his method of training the youth, he walked to the witness stand and said:

"O noble assembly of City Fathers: Greetings! What we do in our classrooms, I shall expound it to you now. Let us still ourselves and visualize the Fire in our hearts ascending towards the head, there to lie humbly at the feet of Jupiter AUM. Let us listen to Its Voice concerning the raising of funds that will build the aqueduct that you are planning, and the stamping out of the epidemic that rages in the suburbs. All this, Wise Ones, without any increase in taxation. . . ." There was stillness for awhile; then an avalanche of practical proposals were submitted through the illuminated minds of some of the members. "This" — Pythagoras declared — "is what we teach to the youth: self-inquiry and the search for God, not in outer symbols of wood or stone, nor in rituals and empty words, but from within, through an upsurge of light and energy from the heart to the head." He was dismissed, amidst a roaring ovation from the tribunes of the people, and with new monetary endowments.

The City of the Chosen Ones was a college of higher education in both sciences and humanities, a focus of initiation leading to Christhood, and a model civic community of the Golden Age. It was surrounded by a wall having four gates that faced east, west, north and south; the gates were always open, symbolizing the open heart of God wherein all men find light and comfort at all times. A statue of Hermes placed at each entrance bore the inscription: THE PROFANE KEEP OFF, meaning that whoever is not open-minded and desirous to learn cannot receive divine illumination.

At the time of admission the freshman was told and made to understand that he was embarking not on a program of memorizing, but on one of cogitation and analyzation which extended beyond classroom attendance to conversation, recreation and repose. He had to accept the truth that in all his thinking, talking, learning and dealing with his fellow students, he was continually checked by an invisible teacher who was always present, entrenched within his heart and in touch with Master Pythagoras. Because of this continuous supervision, the student had neither time nor inclination to dwell on unethical thoughts, use foul language, or be noisy and uncouth. In the gymnasium, wrestling, boxing or competitive games were forbidden because they gave rise to pride and revenge, a reprovable state of being that burned the seed of brotherhood which had, instead, to be fostered and brought to fruition.

At the end of the term, the examinee had to stand before a board of elder students, chosen for their exceptional intelligence, humility and moral integrity. Thus from the very beginning the students were trained for leadership. The members of this board, in accordance with instructions received from Master Pythagoras, were requested to bring forth, through harassment and exaggeration, certain shortcomings of the examinee in order to test his feelings and determine his character, poise and sportsmanship for future amelioration. Both mind and heart had to grow and evolve side by side, and this could not be achieved unless the student submitted to dissection by a group of junior scientists of the soul. With each new test he came closer to the perception of his Godself.

These were the revelations that came to Marco and Leonora while meditating on their ancient Friend, their attention directed without deviation to the Akashic Records. They were eager to see Him and learn from his living voice more of his classic method of training the youth, and how much might be accomplished today in the field of education by applying his teaching, intelligently revised and adapted to our modern age, yet left basically unchanged. Now the last veil of separation, growing more tenuous under the inexorable power of a disciplined mind, broke asunder.

❊   ❊   ❊

Appearing not on the Screen of Life, but directly in their home as an ancient and much loved friend, Master Pythagoras warmly embraced both Marco and Leonora while tears of joy and gratitude to God streamed from their eyes. The perseverance of the long and strenuous vigil to be transmuted into such a tangible reward, was truly the acme of felicity. "From the woodland of Samos" — He said — "to the School of the Solar Path in Memphis, to sunny California, I have watched you with love and respect, hoping and hoping that some day you would make the Herculean effort to shatter the impediment of the flesh and behold me as I have seen you in your last several embodiments all filled with noble exploits. How privileged, and yet deserving, you are to have been chosen by the Hierarchy of the Liberated Masters as a channel for a divine mission on earth. What a crowning reward for your faith and untiring effort in self-discipline. If the outer world were informed of this visible encounter between Heaven and Earth, between the mortal and the immortal, some fanatics would not hesitate to burn this house as they burned mine long ago. For the elect, earthly life is extremely arduous, while for those steeped in the philosophy of the belly, it is a generator of hatred. May you never come in contact with them; may the law of the land protect you, and may the millions of devotees shield you from physical harm.

"You have established an almost Christlike affinity with the Liberated Masters. This affinity is the resultant of two forces originating from two fountainheads and flowing down to the same stream. When a Liberated Master and a non-liberated being meet, the atomic vibration of the latter is stepped up to the rate of the former; and if the non-liberated being responds to the Master's call, it means, that there is spiritual affinity between the two, or a harmonius relationship and understanding that complement, strengthen and hasten the evolutive process of the human soul. Such a soul is under grace, signifying that he is prepared and willing to offer himself to the Liberated Masters for a task of spiritual import amongst his fellow men.

"But what guarantee do the Masters have that the chosen channel will continue in his obedience to Them? None, but one! The channel must live with his Twin Flame, and the two must enjoy the same level of consciousness. This condition you also fulfill. When Twin Flames meet, their common destiny is sealed for eternal years. They influence each other so thoroughly in thinking, planning and striving towards their ultimate goal that they seem to merge into one, without, however, forfeiting their individuality; hence they are mindful of one another as if they were eternal sweethearts. They know that a thought or deed that pollutes one, pollutes the other, resulting in the law of rebound that strikes them with twice as much force as it would an ordinary person. Their cultivation of sensitivity to outer stimuli becomes a protecting wall of light and fire against incomprehension and hasty decisions, an illumining factor for self-knowing, leading to self-improvement and correct judgement of people and events. And those whom they meet are deeply influenced for love and noble behavior.

"Twin Flames are neither impractical nor dreamers. Their status may not be detected with the physical eye, but is intensely sensed by the responsive souls who approach them. Their lives are not avulsed from the contingencies of every day existence, for they are surrounded, like every one else, by the forces of darkness and sloth that love so dearly to disrupt happiness, the pursuance of ethical goals and the concept of God in man. These lower entities, however, cannot dent the Twins' aura of protection built through years of introspection and yearning for inner realization. In short, they so live as to see perfection with discrimination, making one-thousand-one allowances for the web of confusion in which man enmeshes himself, and plan way ahead so as not to be caught in the same trap. With such a psycho-scientific attitude they are seldom harmed.

"The average person may find comfort in believing in the power of destiny, the drag of family pressure, economic depression, tradition and mass consciousness. This is because of self-pity or innate sloth or unwillingness to arise above the seeming; and because he cannot see *through* or sink his mind into the depths of his being, he is a victim of his own intellectual exploits all bent on misleading him. The Eternal Self that truly guides and elevates is by-passed. Having thus failed to meditate, our unfortunate man lives, or rather exists, by appearances and effects instead of Reality and Cause. He may be a Texan millionaire or a shipping magnate or a maecenas surrounded by the acme of comfort and luxury, nevertheless he dwells in a musty, crumbling and dark house filled with fear. To him who through years of interiorization has perceived the Imperishable World of the Spirit, it is like majoring in all the disciplines taught in all the universities of the world of man and more. This, however, must not be interpreted as suggesting that we decry the importance of attending school or studying philosophical truths as found in books. The exact opposite, indeed, is the truth. A university diploma is basic in the formation of character, but only basic. Of what avails one to possess a brilliant intellect without humility, or to know how to transplant a human heart, and yet suffer from arthritis, or some emotional lacunas concerning the coessential conviction of what is right or wrong? To overcome such impasses one needs to go beyond books or mere cogitation. He must utter the Name of God to himself, and meditate with grim determination.

"It was through this process that I was able to found the City of the Chosen Ones with the precise intent of attaining Liberation. But in order to convince the families to entrust their children to me, I needed humility, that type of humility that aims at the rejection of the glorification of the personality; my countenance had to be overshadowed by the Effulgent Light of the Self and seen outwardly by the citizens of Crotona. My project was out of the world of man, unapproachable with human power, therefore, God had to be my foundation and my director. I had gone beyond my fiftieth birthday and as yet had manifested nothing of what I had planned while at the School of the Initiates in Memphis; and I was still alone, searching for my Twin Flame, trusting that the blessed day of her coming would not be far off. In the interim, I had experienced the physical hunger, hardships, humiliation and moral dejection of him who, though an honor student, was laughed at by despots and exploiters and their sycophants.

"Now there was a culminating point in the esoteric doctrine of the School of Memphis which I shall bring to your attention, so that you may feel spiritually refreshed. It was the secret of secrets. After having received the diploma of Initiateship in the Spheric Hall of Light, all ablaze and shadowless, we were called, one by one, by Master Sonchis into his private study for the following words of farewell:

" 'My brother and disciple, you are now an initiate in its fullest significance. It means that you are at the service of God exclusively. You shall have no other master in the visible world. Unto him whom you serve you shall look at as an emanation

277

of God. And should you perceive a persistent malice in his behavior coupled to your inability to correct it, you must withdraw from his presence and seek employment elsewhere; and in the meantime look forward to the blessed day when you shall be a director thyself at the service of God. Know that you are above the dual world, signifying that you are free in the absolute meaning.

" 'Be aware, however, that freedom is not a free motion of the limbs, or abusing those who depend on you for their livelihood, or imposing your will upon others. No, indeed! Freedom is a condition of your whole being that lives and expresses itself on the plane of Christship. Extend this privilege to your fellow men.

" 'Should you return to earth, know this to be only for a divine mission similar to that of an Avatar's. Think and work in this spirit in gladness of heart, and all shall be well. Know that the most grievous failure and the most agonizing experience are nothing but shadows. Go my son, and broadcast the seed of immortality as it was given to you. Blessings!' An embrace and a kiss followed. This statement of truth was delivered to all of us, to both of you and me. It is yours, make full use of it and you shall cross the sea of life and reach the shores of immortality.

* * *

"When I reached the city of Crotona, I found a replica of Babylon at its worst. Wealth, corruption, disease, crime, illiteracy and pauperism were rampant; the social and political structure, as a whole, was crumbling to pieces. Families were ill-ordered, with husbands and wives wrangling at each other; men were busy with their trade of money making irrespective of ethics and human consideration; mothers extensively engaged in social activities and vain pursuits. Indigent children had no care because of poverty, while well-to-do children were similarly neglected because of their mother's sophisticated negligence. The priesthood was usurping political power and fattening its treasury by bribing bigoted bureaucrats. I succeeded in gathering some of the youth of the slums, and God spoke to them through me with the love and eloquence that are all His. Having gained their trust, I began training them outside in public parks and empty lots. By the end of the first year, juvenile delinquency was on its way out. Shabbiness and foul language amongst the teenagers

278

were no more. There is no better soil receptive to the things of the Spirit than the hearts and minds of young people, and in this field my pupils put to shame the hypocrisy of the priestcraft and the skepticism of both the intellectuals and political leaders.

"Thus the Pythagorean Institute came into being. Having investigated my character and my intellectual ability, the City Senate assigned to me a hill that dominated the city and its Forum, the sea and its quay. Temples, halls, dormitories and laboratories, surrounded by landscaping, were erected through gifts and endowments; the students themselves helped in the actual construction. A broad parkway flanked with cypress trees connected the City of the Chosen Ones with the seashore. At the north entrances was the temple of Apollo, reserved for the boys; at the south end the temple of Ceres for the girls, and next to each temple were the dormitories. The faculty buildings were at the center on a circular layout. The temple of Vesta, at the center of this circle, corresponded to the Spheric Hall of Light in Memphis. My sleeping quarters were an integral part of this temple.

"Thirteen months after his admission, the student took the test of friendship or civic behavior, for what avails one to achieve proficiency in rhetoric and accounting, music and athletics, if his emotions are left unbridled and his instincts in the state of a jungle. Conquer the heart of Nature, son, he was told; she is thy first and true friend. Marvel at and respect the beings of the field and forest, the sparkling lakelets and the patient flow of the brooks, the sprouting seeds and the bursting buds, the chirping birds and the swift hare, the endless aspects of the sky and the imperturbable radiance of the stars. Marvel at them, son; it reinvigorates thy body and elevates thy soul to God. Do not kick a rock and do not mar the lonely wild flower that grows by the path. Observe everything with loving curiosity, and absorb its strength and grace. And if they suffer, try to suffer with them. Weep a little.

"Then came novitiateship or test of silence, the duration of which was sixty-five months. His task was very simple and yet very difficult, that is to listen. The student was taught to listen to the voice in his heart, repeating to him what he had heard in the classroom. His daily routine was so arranged that nothing was overlooked to insure his physical comfort; a weekly medical checkup was also provided. All his activities: written tests, rhythmic breathing, meditation, classroom attendance, athletics, meals and recreation were carried out in mute behavior.

"The scope of novitiateship was to cultivate intuition by the path of introspection and self-analysis. To achieve this goal, we had to hit hard at the most predominant tendency of the youth, namely, the desire to dominate others through boastful utterances. During this period the student was assisted in the unfoldment of an inner feeling of gratitude and love, first towards his parents, then the world at large. With the concept of the physical fatherhood as an emanation from God, well established, his mind was then raised to God, as a greater Father of all fathers and men, to Whom everybody is bound, and through Whom all men are linked as brothers. Jupiter was the King of the gods and the Father of mankind; Cybele was His consort, and Demetra, their daughter, the mother of productivity and the goddess of pregnancy in women. Thus earthly parents came to be considered as humanized gods to be loved and honored by their children at all times. And having accepted such a hallowed family overshadowing earthly life, the student concluded that to have a city that is clean, well-ordered, wisely ruled, and free from crime and disease, was the least a citizen could do to honor the Heavenly Father. Any less than this was a betrayal of the land, and as such a mortal sin.

"Love for the land of birth will eventually lead to civic pride and an expanded sense of hospitality applicable to *foreign* visitors with the intent of lessening, and ultimately obliterating intercommunal rivalries. This is diplomacy.

"As the student reflected on this basic teaching, a tremendous transformation took place in his inner world. Our next step was to throw his mind into the field of intuition whereby misjudgement is reduced to a minumum while foresight is raised to the point of prophecy. 'Citizen' — we whispered into his ear — 'now that you have such a clear concept of the relationship between God, men, parents and society, tell us who you are, and with whom you intend to associate yourself, and how do you plan to strengthen this relationship that will, in the end, result in a more stable social order and deeper recognition of God. . .!' Thus he grew to ideal manhood, perceiving with an ever clearer mind, what his role in the community of men and in the presence of

God would be. At this stage the student was, indeed, a being of considerable power of insight. Morning and evening he would recite to himself the golden maxim of the ancient philosophy:

OM I AM the Eternal Law. Adhere to It with happy
transport through study, discipline and introspection.
Seek Me within, and honor Me above all things. Renew
thyself in the arena of the world. Have reverence for
all life.

"The statues of the gods and goddesses, considered up to now as symbols of qualities and attributes, were no longer accepted as a source of inspiration, and the concept of the Formless God, dwelling in the depths of his heart, as the Beginning and Goal of his earthly life, was given absolute priority.

*   *   *

"The next cycle of teaching commenced with a revamping of yoga exercises. Dimly aware that the universe without and the world within are closely interrelated, and that a disordered society cannot be redeemed as long as the ego continues to negate the harmonies of Creation, limbs and internal organs, the senses and the seats of the ductless glands, were made supple, vibrant and responsive to the magnetic forces of nature. Although the importance of the endocrine glands has been mentioned previously, I would like to point out to you the repercussion of their activity on the moral and social aspect of life on earth.

"The ductless glands are invisible centers or foci of forces whose task consists — at their lowest expression — of holding the physical body together. Without them the body would waste away and disappear like a snowball under a hot sun; but when properly exercised, they can transmute the flesh vehicle into a state of indestructibility. It was our purpose, and it is the goal of every true yogin, to harmonize and enhance their activity to the point whereby man could break asunder the degenerative process of aging and disease, and raise his mind onto the plane of Christhood. The first center is located at the base of the spine; it is a furnace filled with live coal smoldering beneath a thick layer of ashes. As in a locomotive whose driving wheels, rods, generators, steampipes, valves, levers, and so forth, rust and cease functioning if the boiler remains inactive for a long time, likewise with the human body. Revive the reddish-brown fire at the base of the spine and the first and immediate effect is to make the body impervious to disease.

"The second center is the sacral plexus or holy braid. It is the sanctuary of the sex organs; holier indeed than all the churches, temples, ashramas, synagogues and mosques of the world put together. The genital organs are held therein in a state of watchfulness. When the fire from the furnace reaches this center for the first time at the age of puberty, the entire atomic structure of the body glows like a star of first magnitude in the firmament of life. The Immortal Master within rejoices greatly in the hope that the lifestream will continue to expand the radiance that he now possesses. When through meditation the fire is made to travel consciously into this sacred cove and placed at the service of an ideal, man becomes master of the elements and friend of man and beast.

"The third center is the solar plexus, the exact replica of the physical sun. Again, when the disciple is able to draw the fire up into this center together with the vibration that emanates from the sacral plexus, he can do precisely what the physical sun does: heal all disease in others and radiate the same vivifying energy to his surrounding world.

"The fourth center is in the heart and its environing region. As a rivulet flowing towards a large river loses its characteristics in the new body of water, likewise the fire of the first center on reaching the heart changes its color into a rich crystalline red. At this stage the disciple enjoys the use of the all-seeing Eye and the power of levitation.

"The fifth center is in the thyroid gland and the region of the throat below the larynx. It communicates directly with the sacral plexus, and is the seat of the Golden Voice. The warmth around the throat experienced by a man at the sight of the woman he loves, issues actually from the genital organs, and it is a sign of physical and spiritual twinship. Through the cultivation of this center eternal youth is attained.

"The sixth center is at the root of the nose between the eyebrows. When the fire finally reaches this plane, heaven and earth merge into one, and the recipient of the grace is no longer affected by the law of karma. He is a resurrected being and stands, like the Immortal Ones, on the apex of the Mount of Wisdom, ready to enter the Seventh Center which is the Mansion of the Lord and the Abode of the Law. Though still in the flesh he is a Liberated Master.

"It was not compulsory that the student achieve control of the sixth Center, although a few, as you will learn later, did. To gain mastery of the sacral plexus was sufficient to make him a model father and husband, and a responsible citizen. However, over fifty percent of our students who had entered the age of puberty were incapable of fanning the fire of the furnace. They were listless, unhappy and unresponsive to kindness and affection, and their progress in studying and learning was alarmingly below par as compared with those who had shown sexual sensitivity. Our clinic, called Physio-cosmic Center, was equipped to cure the malaise. Our physicians and nurses treated the genital organs — penis, vulva and breasts — with competence and in a spirit of dedication and love; most of the students undergoing this treatment were reintegrated to perfect health of body and mind without the use of drugs, hormones or psychiatric therapy.

* * *

"The astronomic season was the chosen time for both commencement and the opening of the new academic year. Coinciding with the festivities of Apollo, both the student body and the teaching staff gathered to welcome the freshmen. The coeds played the sistrums and performed the Doric ballet in their pink and white costumes. The Terpsichorean art had reached such a high level of perfection and gracefulness that Greek and Roman impresarios did not hesitate to offer attractive contracts to some of our best students. It was here that the Doric fugue originated. It was also at this time that the parents, having seen the result of our training on their children, became active supporters of our Institute.

"Dear friends, do you remember the joyous excitement of our ancient days, the thrill that pervaded our hearts as we crossed the Mediterranean together towards the land of the Nile, the subdued happiness that we felt as we were promoted from one degree to the next? Now I want to describe to you the feeling and attitude of one of our students who had attained mastery over his solar plexus. It will remind you of our noble days in Memphis when the unending hours of meditation brought the precious reward of inner revelations. To control the solar plexus is higher than to possess the most cherished diploma cum laude from one of the best universities of your land. Well, the same spiritual exaltation pervaded the student here, as he was ready to enter the Inner Hall of the temple of Vesta, on his way to the threshold of Christhood. The whole universe sang for him only, the celestial orchestra played at his bidding the melodies that were dear to his heart, and his Twin Flame he saw inwardly as an angelic being of faultless beauty, approaching him with outstretched arms. It was the resurrection, the radiant day of the Solar Path. The student body feted him lavishly, as if he were to enter marriage with a maiden of the beyond.

"As he passed through the portico on his way to the Inner Hall, glimpses of the past crowded his mind and made him realize the magnitude of his progress and the unfathomable possibilities of the future. For the first time he understood truly the need of humility. As he approached the cell, without a stylus or a piece of parchment in his hands, he saw immediately the extent of his mighty task: to dispersonalize himself and reduce both the intellect and the will to a pinpoint of light, so as to cause the Logos to become active and all-commanding. This is the process of initiation, or the conquest of the most formidable fortress ever created by man: the assemblage of mind, senses, ego, cravings, family links, culture, tradition and racial traits. He was on his way to self-universalization. Will the enemy submit? No! It will fight back in a most vicious and diabolical manner until complete annihilation.

"I took the student's hand and led him towards the fiery pyre of spiritual transmutation, which was a lovely, soundproof, subterranean chamber in the temple of Vesta, simply furnished and immaculately clean. The people of the outer world had invented fiendish tales concerning the halls of initiation; the candidate was thrown into a dark pit, amidst slimy beasts and demons, in filthy surroundings and fed with abominable refuse. A more deceptive accusation was never uttered. The student-initiate was left alone with a ruthless war to wage, against his past karma, a merciless and relentless foe; and against the mind whose tyranny is worse than all the forces of darkness of the nether world. We, the teaching staff and the student body helped him from the outside through prayer and visualization of his victory."

Master Pythagoras now caused the temple of Vesta to appear on the Screen of Life. It was a magnificent structure of the purest Doric architecture. Between the columns of the circular portico surrounding the temple were marble statues of the various goddesses. "Vesta or Hestia" — the Master explained — "corresponds to Isis of Egypt, Mother Kali of the Hindus and Quan Yin of China. They are the embodiment of Love that emanates from the invisible God. The disciple on the path, the spiritual babe who needed temporary support, saw in Her the expression of the highest mercy, love, perseverance, the arts, science and philosophy and every attribute that was supernal.

"Vesta was a child of condensed fire, or a being born directly from the Buddhi of a parent who had embodied both the masculine and feminine aspects of life. Her body, therefore, was not a compound as in an ordinary mortal, but an element — Fire — in a human contour. She required neither food nor sleep, nor could she die, for death is the disintegration of a compound. However, we warned our students not to dwell on the Vesta-shell, for that would have meant self-defeat. To utter such a truth to the masses, steeped in idolatry, would have resulted in death similar to that of the Arab merchant in the garden of the animal-gods in Memphis. This was the main reason for keeping the inner teaching enshrouded in secrecy. The other statues represented the lesser goddesses, each symbolizing one of Vesta's disciplines, such as astronomy, music, poetry and so forth. They were there to remind the student never to be discouraged for the seeming slow progress on the path of the Spirit, for the least attainment through meditation is worthier than the highest earthly success. When the divine attributes are perceived within, nursed and outwardly expressed, then man truly begins to live. Until that time he is a shifting, fearful and mortal entity.

❊ ❊ ❊

"The progress of the coeds moved abreast with the rest of the student body. Their achievements contradicted the current attitude that man possesses more intelligence than a woman. The fact that there were more feminine than masculine statues in this institute, was an incentive for the girls and a constant challenge to the boys. The result was a secret, lovable and sweet competition, all rejoicing when one of either side excelled. Thus I came to the issuance of the famous pronouncement taught in Memphis concerning man-woman relationship, but primarily directed to man:

"'Man, honor thy woman and, by reflection, all women on earth and Heaven. She unfolds before thy eyes the inner significance of the created world. She symbolizes Nature, the bestower of tangible joy, grace and opulence. She assists thee to ascend by degrees towards the Universal Soul. Place her on the altar above all created things as the all-comprehensive and holy image of God.

"'Honor thy woman, O man, and behold thyself raised onto the heights of freedom, enfolded in Light and Glory.

"'Honor thy woman, my son, and love her as thy own god. And as you reach the Ultimate Goal, turn thy gaze to the world of form and there she is, the humble instrument of thy victory. Now draw her into thy cosmic heart and together ascend to the Octaves of Life Everlasting.

"'Man, be thou perfect, and know that her imperfection is the reflection of thy negligence!'

"This ode of love and wisdom, put to music, was sung and played on holidays in the parks of the City of Crotona; then it became the anthem of the City-state, and as a result the society changed its face. Both the wife of the toiler and the woman-slave of the well-to-do were raised to the noble status reserved until then for the wives of the religious and political hierarchs. Husbands stopped frequenting gambling dens and unethical establishments. No longer were the children running to and fro homes and shops to gather news of the delaying fathers. Bickering between men and wives gave way to harmony and reciprocal respect. I was the beloved of the feminine world, the friend of the law abiding citizen who saw in me an impersonal reminder of noble conduct, and a piercing thorn in the flesh of those engaged in dubious enterprises. As my host of admirers and defenders grew, likewise, my pack of foes.

* * *

"At the last stage of our teaching, the disciples were few, often none. We were not organized to produce avatars, but citizens of first rank. When, however, a student reached the lofty status, I, his teacher, kissed his hand and made myself ready to obey; like your Master Jesus with his disciples, I could have

286

washed his feet. We enriched the various city-states with public servants and political leaders of sterling integrity, officers of the armed forces bent on peace and negotiation rather than war, business men of high ethical principles, brilliant attorneys in search of justice by the way of truth rather than forensic eloquence, celebrated architects, and other noble lifestreams with their hearts set on constructive endeavours. Of those who achieved initiateship, I mention only three: Milone, Archippus and Lysis, all master of teleiosis and Christ Light. The eye of the soul, closed for thousands of years opened to the full blaze of universal wisdom and immortality.

"Every day, at the noon hour, the advanced student came out of his solitary confinement into my study for a three-hour lesson on higher mathematics, an uninterrupted pounding and discussion on algebra, trigonometry and calculus in rapport to life. My aim was to tire his physical mind and draw it away from all sorts of vagaries; after the lesson he would seek the solitude of his cell for deeper introspection leading to teleiosis.

"The magnificent physique displayed by the disciples who had reached initiateship explained the evolution of matter. When matter is enlivened by the propulsive power of the soul, all tangible substances undergo a process of sublimation. If the mind, the intelligence and the will, by their perfect accord, can draw the body away from decay and make it imperishable, likewise, the concerned action of men can cause the planet earth to be shifted from an orbit of lower vibration to that of a higher one, a path of life unmarred by crime, war, poverty, earthquakes, floods and disease. The earth has a soul exactly as man's. The Solar Soul is the father of the Soul of Earth. By the law of the gene, father and son possess the same chromosomes; why then does not the earth radiate the same luminance as its father's. It does, but it is hidden beneath the heavy crust of man's ignorance, vice, malice, fear, anger, brutishness, fraud, treachery, thievery, forgery and hatred. Burn these downward pulls, and the earth will shine of its own God-given splendor, and will no longer need the sun's radiance to produce and live divinely.

"Initiateship is the crowning aim of life on earth for every man. He who has attained it, has the Way, he is the Way, the Christ incarnate. However, this much I want to convey to you, and it is a serious warning to the world. Life on earth is the lowest

287

in the hierarchy of universal existence where the right to mention the Name of God is exercised. Should man forfeit this privilege, the sublunar world will be his next step where intelligence and will are unusable. He would have cognition of the value and power of these faculties, but would lack the knowledge of their use and the external environment upon which to apply them. This state of being, although one step higher than the disidentified existence of the Milky Way, is, nevertheless more excruciating because the individual is conscious of his intellectual and spiritual stagnation. Consequently, for an initiate or even a disciple whose status is not any higher than the control of the second center, his life on earth is a veritable immolation. It is like a bird of the snowcaps caged in a dark cave. Should he incline towards the standardized morals of the society, he is likely to forget his spiritual heritage; and should he hold fast to his cosmic aristocracy, they call him queer, they revile him, persecute and crucify him. Such were Socrates, Jesus, Joan D'Arc, the Bab, Hallaj, and many others.

"Let us consider now the average individual, the so-called law-abiding citizen. He does good, and by his deeds he acquires merits on a limited scale, a short and joyous starry existence in the higher Octaves; then he returns to earth for another test. But unless he develops the holy foci of his body whereby he learns the difference between the relative *good* and the absolute *good*, unless he cleanses his thoughts and deeds from egotistic stains, he will remain the eternal traveller between the earth and the moon, the moon and the earth, corresponding to a frog which never goes beyond a few square yards of muddy water. A selfless deed is that which if fulfilled with the clear and precise awareness of God as the doer and man the instrument of manifestation. To reach such an understanding man must become sensitive to the action or to the participation of the Soul in his daily life. He must learn with accuracy the use of the power of free will, and how to surrender his dynamic thinking to God in exchange for discrimination. The quasi-totality of the good people, unaware of this relationship, bind themselves with childish superficiality to seeming innocent practices of political and religious nature, that cause them the loss of either freedom of thought or their cosmic individuality, or both, and yet they continue to swear that they are still free according to the Law of God.

"Then there are individuals whose use of free will is limited to the kind of food they want to eat, the type of tobacco they want to smoke, at which bar they want to spend their evenings, and the amount of money they decide to throw away on gambling. *Upon the shoulders of these bound people lie and prosper all the forces of ignorance, involution and human exploitation.*

"There is another group of lifestreams whose intelligence and environment, though not any higher than the previous one, yet they feel that they should improve themselves; and they succeed in various degrees, according to the amount of dynamic thinking (free will) they surrender to God in exchange for discrimination.

"You have still another group of individuals whose cruel misdeeds from previous embodiments have led them, in the present life, to be arrested and put in prison for many years. In their long hours of solitary confinement, in the grip of shame and fear, and weeping inwardly, they are forced to self-analyzation in rapport to life, events, aspirations, scope of human existence, and the action and reaction of man's behavior. They read in books and on parchments the description of noble and selfless deeds performed by wise men, and come to the conclusion that it would be wise to try to follow them to the best of their ability. Blessed be the hand of the police that caught them. And thus, instead of applying their free will to further cheating and scheming, they begin to experiment with the opposite. And having found the experiment restful and rewarding, they go on and on, and eventually come in sight of a new panorama of life where they decide to stay.

"When a man's free will is directed solely to the satisfaction of carnal and egotistical desires, the physical body is his hub, name and spurious fame his goal. He lives by instinct or wellnigh. He may be a laborer or a prize-winning athlete, or a stagnating scientist who, for the sake of wealth or fleeting prestige, has renounced the ethics of his profession, it is all the same, they are slightly above the instinct of the beast of the jungle.

"The man whose free will is applied as a propulsive force to hold at bay passions and cravings, to impel the mind to delve into philosophical truths or to investigate the realm of pure science, that man constitutes the salt of the earth, the torch of the world. He is the upholder of the Law of Evolution and the true harbinger of international peace on Earth. And if he continues on the path, he will reach a state whereby he no longer wastes his free will to hold at bay passions and cravings, they simply drop entirely from his world, never to appear again, like a fried kernel whose power of germination was killed forever. This man is at the threshold of Christship and qualified to sit at the round table with masters of the class of Krishna, Rama, Hermes, Zoroaster, Master Jesus and all the Liberated Masters.

"As you see the heedless and indiscriminate individual is a dead weight in the cosmic order of life, and when not actually violating the law of man, he is a parasite of both the visible and invisible society; and the least he should do on the path of self-recovery, is to attune his life with the accepted good of the community in which he lives, though this *good* might seem far from perfect. Simply obey that, O man, and let those who know more plan the improvements; your negative behavior makes you unworthy to investigate and legislate.

"At the hour of death the Soul-flame — through God's wondrous mercy — makes Herculean effort to draw the mind and ego to an inner conference with the proviso of analyzing the various blunders and misdeeds of the earthly life. With marvelous clarity all violations are projected on a screen of light similar to the one that has shown to you the present experiences. According to the degree of acceptance of such a vision as a tangible happening, the dying individual can so obliterate his ignorance as to prepare himself for a higher existence in his next embodiment. By the same degree of acceptance, people whom he had wronged during his life, could be reintegrated, through strange and undreamed of channels, in their material and moral losses, thus curtailing the unkind karma that looms ahead. If the vision is rejected, the divine lesson is also rejected. The loss is immense, the individual's next embodiment will be heavier and darker.

* * *

"On the borderline of the etheric belt that surrounds the earth, parallel to the Moon-consciousness, there are tangible classrooms where proud hearts and stubborn minds are mercifully trained by Liberated Masters in the Law of humility and selfless deeds. They are taught how to heed and expand the finer impulses that now and then issue from the depths of man's heart. They are shown what a poor investment it is to be entangled in the slimy matter of pride and capriciousness, and also given a glimpse of how to go about finding their perfect companions whose presence dispels their antagonism towards the Law of Life.

"Happy and constructive will be the forthcoming embodiment for him who has profited by this merciful training. Let all men make positive visualization of this help as they approach the sunset of life, and see themselves rising above meniality and coarseness, conquering drudgery and economic limitation, and feeling the warmth of the Breath of Life that has no end. Thus they shall begin to perceive, in a way that leaves no room for doubt, that there is no death, that nothing is destroyed, and that all existing matter, impelled by the law of evolution, must, per force, move towards perfection, towards God.

"At the hour of return to the new human body, the enlightened mind and heart — intellect and feeling — merge into one entity called Psyche, a brilliant, vaporous essence of heavenly fragrance. Its luminous companions left behind bid It farewell and make It utter aloud the pledge of love, humility and obedience to God. It solemnly promises to engage Itself in constructive endeavours, to serve the Light in a world of shadow and sloth, to express the truth in the midst of illusion and make believe, and to expand the Christ-light within through daily meditation. Thus It leaves Its spiritual realm of perfection, passing through the moon-consciousness for the last lesson on love and self-surrender. Then down It goes into a pool of blood, flesh and darkness for nine months, to emerge thereafter as a human being endowed with the privilege of reflecting the Light of the Immortal Self.

"A human body so equipped must truly be the most perfect living organism ever devised by God. In fact, it is. There is nothing that can compare with this globule of living matter whose potentialities extend beyond the boundary of infinitude. It can shatter and reassemble a world in a timeless flash. It has a City of Light — the head — whose resplendence far exceeds the brightness of many suns. It has a Creative Intelligence — the pineal gland — before which both matter and spirit bow and serve. It has a Court of Justice — the throat — whose legal wisdom could rule all creation for everlasting years without a single friction. It has a Temple — the heart — whose love and mercy can bind life in the embrace of eternal peace and happiness. It has a Reservoir of Power and Energy — the solar plexus — which is capable to heal disease, destroy sorrow and hold suspended in space the infinite number of planets, stars, suns and celestial bodies. It has a Laboratory — the genital organs — endowed with the unchallenged authority of recruiting Soul-flames from the Unseen, and clothing them with the imperishable armor of the Legions of God. It has also other minor centers which are highly sensitized to the call of absolute beauty and truth.

"This is Man, and this is how I presented him to my adoring disciples. And those, the very elect, who had reached the Chamber of the Self, found him exactly thus."

* * *

Master Pythagoras beckoned Marco and Leonora to stroll with him along the beautiful cypressed parkway towards the seashore; his powerful aura held them secure in the awareness of life eternal. Although pensive, he radiated boundless happiness. He was tall, well-built and with a martial bearing; his skin was olive-tinted and a seraphic light shone forth from the depths of his magnetic brown eyes. His chestnut-brown hair was brushed back in the fashion of the twentieth century, leaving well-exposed a broad forehead which enhanced his youthful appearance. He was robed as an ancient Egyptian Hierophant.

From the sandy shore they looked back hoping to see the City of the Chosen Ones from afar, but saw instead the classic city of Athens at the height of its glory on the luxuriant plains of Attica. Northward, against a crystalline sky, was a series of hilltops dense with blooming orchards and tropical vegetation and overspread with gorgeous villas. They recognized the summits of Hymettus, Pentelikon, Parnes and Aegaleus. At the southeast was the harbour of Piraeus, bathed in the opaline waters of the Aegeaen Sea and filled with graceful yachts of every description. At the center of the plains of Attica was the Acropolis adorned with architectural masterpieces. They saw the winding parkway or Sacred Way leading to the Propylaea, and further on the massive bronze statue of Athena Pallas. At the eastside stood the Parthenon or Temple of the

Virgin Goddess. Here and there at street corners and by fountains beneath wide-spreading shade trees, were spirit-forms of ancient sages in their white linen robes, surrounded by eager and attentive youths.

"You have seen" — Master Pythagoras explained — "the Akashic Records of two cities that were once foci of light. This is the heaven where all the cities of the world that have spread truth and light, are filed, exactly as documents, letters, charts and other important papers are filed in a well-organized office. We could cause Athens to disappear and another city to appear, but this has no importance. What is important is this: All thoughts and deeds of man are duly filed both for single individuals and collective bodies. The balance sheet between constructive and destructive deeds tells of man's position in the scheme of life. These records are as near to the mind of man as the tip of his nose. They are, in fact, in the imperishable Fourth Dimension, that is, the Pinpoint of Fiery Flame in the heart, where the infinitely great and the infinitely small meet and become one, the Intangible and Indestructible. This again affords two lessons for man to learn:

"When your mind, seemingly out of nowhere, gives birth to an evil thought, a thought that might threaten to stain your soul, fear not. Let it come as it will, only see that it remains within the boundary of your head by sealing the throat center. Apply Dante's maxim: 'be unconcerned, but look and pass'. Detach your feelings from it and declare to yourself loudly that it does not belong to you; it is an unwanted guest. Presently that evil thought will lose pressure and disappear. As you grow inwardly such repulsive villains become rarer until they cease to disturb you entirely. When this occurs you have reached the stage whereby you can create constructive thoughts endowed with a force of immediate realization. One might, if he so wishes, plan with uncanny accuracy in what country, city, race and family he wants to be born in his next embodiment, what profession he would embrace, and how long he desires to stay on earth. And he will retain the clear knowledge of his previous embodiment. By disciplining his mind now, he has made himself a genius in his next existence. The Cosmic Assembly of the Perfect Ones and the Liberated Masters encourage this activity. It is the most rewarding of all hobbies man can indulge in. It costs nothing and sets one free from the diabolical escapism of drinking, gambling, gossip and mind expansion by the way of hard drugs whose degenerative effect is too frightful to put into words. This process of cogitation is also an escape, but into reality, the reality that liberates the mind from the shackles of frustration, stupidity, ignorance and limitation.

"We humbly suggest the philosopher, the scientist and the artist to experiment with this process of thought-projection into future embodiments. With the intellectual discipline that they already possess, it would not take long for new horizons to unfold before them. They would also have mathematical proof that all philosophical truths, scientific discoveries and artistic creations in the field of form, sound and color, emanate from the same source — God — and that they are all fundamentally alike. For indeed one and undifferentiated is the Thought of God, and being so that ONE can never be at war with itself. This ONENESS being thus crystallized in the living concept of the Eternal Becoming, deviation and dualism are illusory and ephemeral, and always a source of unending tragedy. This tragedy, however, can be erased through one instant of sincere and determined visualization of that cosmic ONENESS. CHIT or Universal Knowledge follows.

"We are eagerly waiting for man to ask for direction on how to plunge and swim in this Reservoir of Intelligence. We want to give him new and more tangible proof of his immortality and godlike potentialities. We will tell the artist how to draw forms, sounds and shades from that ONENESS and, through daily introspection, enliven and clothe them in flawless beauty; the philosopher how to herald truths that withstand the onslaught of time, space and causality; the scientist how tangible objects can be transported not through electronic computers and atomic energy, but by the power of mind alone prodded by the utterance of a syllable; and the medical profession not how to transplant a heart, but how to graft life itself.

"It is imperative for the Western World, at this hour, to praise, encourage and sustain students who are desirous of dedicating themselves to the pursuance of pure disciplines —

philosophy, mathematics and the arts. And in what country can such a program be established successfully but in the United States of America? It is unfair for parents to stifle a child with unkind remarks, simply because he has no tendency to go out and earn a little money on odd jobs; and it is unwise to feel proud when another child shows signs of *practical* initiative at the expense of healthier visions and a more worthwhile and far-reaching vocation. Insight is the salt of evolution.

* * *

"Our girls were not released from the Institute as the boys were, namely, after graduation. They had to study another year to gain initiation as wives and mothers. The most intimate details of married life were unfolded to them, in an atmosphere of sacredness and beauty, by teachers who had reached the threshold of Christship. Many of the students took post-graduate courses in this field. Sexual relation — they were taught — is not a pastime, but the highest of earthly duties. To be able to function sexually is a gift of inestimable value; it is like a diamond with a thousand facets, each reflecting a commission from God whose execution moves heaven and earth and all the celestial bodies therein. An attitude of respect and reverence is imperative. Love making, either for providing a garment for an incoming lifestream into the world, or in fulfillment of a biological urge, requires inner attunement before the consummation, a word of gratitude to God after. Rules and regulations, as precise as science itself, were taught concerning mental outlook, feeling and physiological hygiene for approach, orgasm, coition and pregnancy; physical and mental fatigue had to be avoided, the proper diet was suggested, intoxicating drinks and magic potions were tabu. It is the fine art of married life and the science of motherhood.

"Celibacy was discouraged as not conducive to spiritual growth. A man and a woman — husband and wife — living at the threshold of Christhood, may bear children without relinquishing one iota of their lofty status. Only they possess the physiological excellence, the mental equilibrium and the emotional stability in such an abundance as to give birth to children capable of lifting the world onto higher octaves of consciousness. In the realms of Perfection there are legions of Soul-flames with angelic traits, ready to descend to earth, but they cannot because there are not enough mothers to fulfill their requirements. This is the tragic result brought about by a code of pseudo-morality created by a sectarian doctrine steeped in negativity.

"An important factor that could truly foster the realization of a nobler society of men, would be a further reduction of the working hours for both employees and employers, and housewives also, provided that the longer hours of leisure are devoted to constructive hobbies: reading, music, dancing, singing and outdoor sports. A brotherhood between economics, science and philosophy could bring this suggestion into immediate realization. The soil is ready. There is today a fiery yearning among the masses to study, to know and to improve their minds, and to sensitize that elusive sense of appreciation. Cosmic forces are flooding the world like a transcendent manna, but the people are unable to assimilate them because they lack the required time for self-attunement. And because of such fundamental negligence and unpreparedness, a breeding source of fear and anxiety, women of great spiritual merit, born to bear sons of light, are thrown into the market place to earn a mere living, barely enough for bread, clothes and shelter, and thus forego the more important function that justifies their physical existence.

"In the City of the Chosen Ones, we trained the girls how to sublimate love for a perfect marriage, and how to draw and hold the mate for an exemplary life. The thorns of rudeness of man's superiority complex were softened through the noble art of intelligent adaptation. By making him her ideal, she became, by reflection, his ideal, and as a result the happy medium was easily realized. The two ideals thus fused formed the compendium of the whole universe. The ideal wife is spiritually greater than man, because she is self-forgetting. In his embrace she becomes an intangible attribute; in his arms she can submerge her soul in his soul and lose her identity. Another step and she will be in the embrace of God. This is sublimity or mergence with the Inner Reality. A wife so endowed can surely raise a man with mediocre intelligence to a plane of creativity; and no man of genius could really achieve eminence without that elusive force of fiery vanity that smolders like an undeclared holy war in the heart of his beloved. This is the ideal woman who impels man to do and to dare.

"Couples such as these are increasing steadily in your world; there will be an avalanche of them in the incoming twenty-first century. Great men and women are in the making who shall appear greater than Arturo Toscanini and his Carla, Rama and Stea, Krishna and Radha, Pindaro and Corinna, Plato and Diodina, Jesus and Mary, Gautama and Yashodara, Dante and Beatrice, Leonardo da Vinci and Mona Lisa, whose happy blending shall cause undreamed of manifestations in every field of intellectual and spiritual endeavour, for peace, brotherhood and the Glory of God. And they will beget children whose handsomeness, nobility of heart and mental power will usher society into the Golden Age."

* * *

Master Pythagoras extended his hands to Marco and Leonora and together they translated themselves towards the abode that he occupied in the City of the Chosen Ones during his earthly mission. He felt their unexpressed desire to meet his twin companion, known in history as Teano, and had planned to have them meet her. As they entered his commodious study decorated in soft elusive shades of green and violet, they became aware of a tenuous fragrance of jasmine, which became more intense as they approached a brazier at the center of the room. He bid them gaze at it and at the same time visualize the action of the Sacred Fire in their hearts. Slowly a golden-pink flame spiraled upward and gently assumed the contour of a beautiful feminine form of about twenty-two. Leonora recognized her immediately as one of her ancient friends. She was Teano, Pythagoras' Twin Flame. He took her in his arms and kissed her tenderly. Then she turned to Marco and Leonora:

"My greetings and my love to our starry travelers and guests, and to you Leonora — my ancient Lunide — my heartfelt gratitude for the love, training and encouragement, which you poured to me so lavishly while serving you in Egypt. Do you recall? I was a Shining One from the Realm of the Spirit, a babe of Light, hungering for greater Light into which you initiated me, and in exchange I kept your living quarters immaculately clean. You were so stern and generous and an efficient teacher also; and as you released me I was raised into the Heaven of Venus from where I saw my Twin Companion in Crotona, working on a mighty project: the founding of the Institute of Higher Learning. He was then thirty-nine years old. Using the energy and light of your training, I took embodiment as a virgin maiden, and as I came of age I entered Pythagoras' school as a student. Now come, please!"

The Akashic Records changed swiftly and another episode came to view. Holding Leonora's hand, Teano left the temple of Vesta and moved eastward followed by Master Pythagoras and Marco. They came to a mountain retreat, a palatial abode hidden within a rocky elevation. Traversing majestic halls and columnated corridors of breathtaking splendor, they came to an immense rotunda surmounted by a semispherical dome made of laminated gold and studded with precious stones, forming the twelve signs of the zodiac. At the center of the floor stood a colossal chalice, seven feet high and seven feet in diameter at the brim and base, which had been hewn from a single golden-blue diamond. Scintillating flames of smokeless fire rose from its depths.

"We are inside the etheric counterpart of Mt. Gargarus in Asia Minor" — Teano explained. "In this cavern lived Master Saturn up to twelve thousand years ago. Before he was promoted to his present starry office by the Elohim of Creation, He beautified and expanded this abode to its present shape and size by the manipulation of Light, Energy and Substance. He lay on the floor with his head where the chalice stands and called to God for the boon of Elohimship: 'Let there be a visible expression of the conjunction of the masculine and feminine traits as a symbol of God's power in a human form'. And as the desire was fulfilled within his own self, he then issued the command:

"'Let the Quenchless Fire of God coalesce and rise visibly from a Grail of Imperishable Substance', and the chalice and the fire came into being. 'And let there be a Guardian of this Sacred Fire, a human form, uncompouded and imperishable, to teach men the Eternal Law of Oneness. And let her name be Hestia, the Daughter of the Flaming Vessel, the Hearth of the Western World and the Fireside of humanity'.

"Thus Hestia or Vesta was born. She came forth from the Fire as a youth of twenty, clothed in a robe of gold. As I descended from the Heaven of Venus and took embodiment as Teano, She contacted me while in my teens and unfolded to me the principle of spiritual twinship. When I reached the age of thirteen She directed me to the Pythagorean Institute for further training, but mathematics were not exactly my vocation. Every time Pythagoras entered the classroom, his radiance was so overwhelming that I could not concentrate, I could only feel my intense love for Him. Thinking of him, in the solitude of my cell, all depressive moods gave way to elation and spiritual exaltation, and the formulae and equations which I could not comprehend by persistent study, I understood through my heart with the instrument of love. Once I asked him whether it was possible to cultivate awareness of God by the path of love alone, without the martyrdom of algebra. 'Not as an emotion' — he answered — 'but as an active force that begins and ends in the concept of God, love is the greatest awakener of intuition which leads to foresight and thence to the knowledge of the universe.'

"I held fast to my love-instrument as the only means of inner progress. By the age of seventeen I had the inner proof that Pythagoras was my twin flame, and for two years I battled with myself and prayed to God to open the way, yes, the way to our eternal reunion. I meditated with ever greater fervor. Finally the auspicious day arrived. On my nineteenth birthday, at the hour of sunset, I felt an invisible guide take my hand and direct me to my Master's cell in the temple of Vesta. There I found him meditating, completely lost to the world, in the embrace of the Superconscious. I stood close to him and waited; and as he returned to the earthly plane, he opened his eyes and, lo, we stood facing one another. Without giving him the opportunity to utter a word, and with that feminine determination that never accepts *no* for an answer, I declared my love for him and related all my inner experiences of the past six years. He made no attempt to interrupt me, which I considered an encouraging omen. The sweetness of my voice and the sincerity of my heart enveloped him, not for bondage, but for liberty; not for personal desire, but for collaboration, devotion and love. We gazed at each other transfixed and happy, then in one voice, as if inspired, we said: *We are Twin Flames!* He held me in his manly

299

embrace of love and kissed me again and again. I was lost, lost in him for cosmic freedom, for eternal years.

"Our marriage sealed the realization of his master-program. Some of his disciples were somewhat shocked by the event; he was almost sixty while I was nineteen. However this shock was of very short duration, for the reward of living divinely soon became visible. Public estimation towards us grew by leaps and bounds, and more so when our first child was born. Those who had accused my husband of making secret preparations to sell the City of the Chosen Ones outright and flee with the money, lost face and disappeared. Every thought, every plan, every action and achievement of ours, proved unmistakably that it was love that justified our marriage, not the latter that sanctified our love for one another. The aura of blessedness that surrounded us at that time, surrounds you both today; therefore, fear no obstacles but move forward, happy and trustful, towards liberation."

They returned to the temple of the Goddess of the Sacred Fire, and as they entered they saw a replica of the Flaming Grail that they had seen in the rotunda of Mt. Gargarus. They sat in meditation in the lotus posture of the Oriental yogi, and directed their attention to Vesta. After an elapse of a few minutes they heard the musical tones of her golden voice:

"Disciples of the Solar Path, Marco and Leonora, I greet you! You are in sight of the final goal whereby you shall stand above all earthly hope, master of the self and dispenser of comfort to those who approach you. A wealth of precious gems of liquid light are already in your hands, earned through discipline, study and faith. However, you may not release them until you have the needed discrimination as dictated by the Law of Cosmic Wisdom; more intense study and self-analyzation, with the aim of purging away the last residue of mortal dross, are required. The condition of the world demands from you total victory over the self. Then the golden glow of heaven that will make you invincible in the art of peace and brotherhood shall be yours. You have exhausted your worldly duties and attachments; and having no desire to please personalities, or gain name and fame, you are henceforth commanded to serve God in a direct and uncompromising manner. Such a task befits you perfectly, for your courage and spiritual awareness are of the loftiest nature.

300

"Blessed Lunide, it is needful for you to know that another factor which contributed to the realization of your dream of virgin birth, was the selfless help that you gave Me from the Spheres of the Spirit, in the establishment of the first Temple of Fire of the Vestal Virgins in the ancient world. All the energy that you poured to Me, I presented to Hermes to be credited to your spiritual account. And to you, Arcus, I say: There is no need at this time to give a detailed list of your achievements in past embodiments. It suffices to say that they are all constructive and elevating, and that We, the Immortal Ones, trust you and support you in what lies ahead for both of you. Now Teano, the charmer of the gods, shall make you richer with a new jewel by relating to you the experience of their earthly life; how they were able to transmute the cruelest suffering, persecution and injustice into an apotheosis of light and love."

❀   ❀   ❀

As the melodious voice ceased, they beheld a dazzling Spirit-form of incomparable beauty, which soon revealed itself as that of the great Goddess Vesta, the Daughter of Saturn. For an instant they saw the neat contour of Her exquisite physique, then gradually it became diffused and soft, softer and more diffused. Concentric discs of light emanated from Her heart center which increased in size and brilliancy until they resembled the radiance of the sun. She remained visible for a few moments, and then disappeared leaving behind an intoxicating fragrance of jasmine. Marco and Leonora fell on their knees in a feeling of intense gratitude, while Teano and Pythagoras, though accustomed to living amidst starry realities and glories, stood transfixed by the supernal experience.

"You have been tested in humility" — Teano said — "and have won. How else can you explain this divine grace of beholding the Immortal Goddess of the Sacred Fire. Humility truly transforms man's heart into a holy grail into which God pours Its Light, Love and Power. With such a wealth in his hands, both heaven and earth fall at his feet for unconditional obedience and service. During my earthly life I was repeatedly tempted in this field. Some of our students in their youthful exuberance praised unduly both my intelligence and my somatic traits, and in the domain of man-woman and husband-wife relationship they posed questions of such intimate character that only a Liberated Master could have answered satisfactorily. When they came to me, the interview was always planned a week in advance; this gave me time to humble myself at the Feet of the All-knowing Spirit.

"Is celibacy desirable? They would ask. Not until every effort has been made to find one's twin flame; and this is undoubtedly the most worthwhile search in life from the biological standpoint and for cosmic fulfillment. If one prays to God with intense yearning, He will surely reveal how to go about finding one's perfect companion without resorting to that complex and sophisticated machinery called social parties, whose results are often very frustrating. Be not frantic, have no doubt, attune your mind and heart with the Pearl of Light within, and know positively that God does not want stray children roaming the world aimlessly. And do not put shackles on the search, such as wealth, social rank and so forth, for if you do this you are cheating the law and will be punished accordingly. The life of a celibate is arduous indeed, no matter how seductively glamorized by the unwary.

"Marriage elevates man to the status of a king, woman a queen. His dominion, being spiritual, has no boundary. Forced to project his soul outwardly and concerned of the unforeseen impression that he might leave behind, he is forced to a continual and exhaustive self-analyzation; and this is a course in higher learning. Yearning for self-respect, he must cultivate reverence for his wife while applying loving severity to his children, and this leads straight to love and reverence for the deity that protects his household, thence to the Impersonal Spirit. Being under constant supervision by the members of his family, every little chore must be carried out with an eye for perfection, not only as an example for his growing children, but also because his own pride is at stake. And this pride is the key to noble deeds that are the foundation of meritorious karma that leads to the immobilization and dissolution of the wheel of birth and death.

❊ ❊ ❊

"As time elapsed I became the faithful interpreter and

302

divulgator of my husband's teaching. I no longer studied or frequented his classes, but learned through meditation and love. And this any woman can do. Our love for each other was based on the freedom of our souls which, in turn, yearned for mergence and oneness. This is the secret of Self-surrender. I had so developed my intuitive power that I became receptive to my husband's creative ideas like the Holy Grail into which the Wisdom of God is poured unobstructedly. We were each other's ideal, heaven and star.

"My family grew as expected. We had two sons, Arimestos and Teulage, and a daughter, Damos. Teulage became later the founder and master of the Pythagorean School of Light in Empedocles; Damos was appointed her father's messenger, and after his ascension, she inherited his manuscipts. Arimestos was executive director of the City of the Chosen Ones. Our three children found eventually their twin flames.

"The Pythagorean doctrine spread throughout the Mediterranean basin and northward of Italy — Rome and Etruria; institutes of Light thrived everywhere, and where the Pythagorean Constitution had been adopted political corruption, crime, poverty and disease disappeared. The Constitution provided for the establishment of a legislative body whose members were chosen from the constituents of the Lower House of Representatives elected by popular suffrage. A council composed of Pythagorean adepts, who had reached the threshold of initiateship, constituted the Supreme Consultive Body in all matters concerning the welfare of the people. All grievances were presented to this body whose wise recommendations were inspired by the scientific principles of the Doctrine of the Solar Path.

"In his later years Pythagoras became a wandering master, visiting the city-states where his Constitution had been adopted. He also accepted invitations from rulers of other communities who were desirous of being initiated into the Doctrine of the Solar Path; and wherever he went, as he entered the assembly hall of the city-state where he had been invited to speak, there were crowds gathered waiting eagerly to hear him speak on the Master-constitution. He would stand facing the audience for, perhaps, ten minutes without uttering a word. During that time he prayed to God in his heart: 'Let the awakening take place, O Lord of Light, that they may know what I know, and see the Truth with Thine Eye. Let the throat center expand and the wisdom from the head center descend to be expressed with the eloquence of an Elohim.' The halo around his head then became visible to all, and as they stood there under the mighty spell of his power of spiritual penetration, they perceived the truth and saw the answers to their questions in living letters of light above Pythagoras' head.

"Although the Pythagorean Constitution did not provide for taxation, the public treasury was never empty; monetary endowments kept pouring in; the estates bequeathed to the state were either transformed into public parks, or allotted to deserving citizens, or used for schools, or temples without officiating priests. In the field of trade and commerce, both the employer and the employee rose above personal interest, the former by raising wages, the latter by improving the quality and volume of his production.

* * *

"As Orpheus earlier and Apollonius of Tyana later, likewise with Pythagoras: the earth was no longer worthy to bear him. His adherence to the law of love, his selfless dedication to the good of his fellow man, and his forgiving attitude towards those who had declared themselves as his enemies, had raised him to the plane of an embodied Christ. Those who had to be exposed — for the good of society and in obedience to the Law of Cause and Effect — in their treacherous plans, felt that as long as Pythagoras was alive and had prestige, they were unable to bribe, plot and thieve against the community. The Institute of Higher Learning and its surrounding campus must be ransacked, burned and reduced to ashes together with their founder and staff. This was their plot. Pythagoras, whose age at this time was ninety-five, had the foresight of a living Buddha. He knew what was in store for all of us, and acted accordingly.

"In the nearby city-state of Sibaris, where the Pythagorean Constitution was in effect, people with evil karma, plotters, gamblers and outlaws, were infuriated and filled with frustration, not only because they felt that they had lost their wits, but also because they could not intimidate or subject to extortion the businessmen who had no fear of them whatsoever. Even armed robberies were fruitless. Every law-abiding citizen was prospering, disease had disappeared, and notwithstanding the fact that the police force had been reduced to a mere shadow of its former strength, still no crime could be perpetrated successfully.

"After continuous and futile attempts the members of the underworld came to the conclusion that this state of affairs — this ethical way of living — was ungodly, unnatural, demoniac and a foray of an impelling universal disaster. The cause: the Pythagorean Constitution. The New Society, being still young, the majority of the people were unable to perceive the Eternal Cause, the Law of the Self, behind all manifestation; and unsupported by knowledge and faith, these people were easily swayed by the demagogues. 'Away with the Constitution, away with the Supreme Consultive Body, away with the emissaries of the black oligarchy of Egypt. Destroy them all; death unto the evil before it is too late.' Thus they cast the stone.

"The Constitution was overthrown. Pythagoras' disciples were threatened with physical violence and forced to flee. A week later the rebels, armed for the kill, appeared in Crotona and besieged our beloved City of the Chosen Ones. We were handed an ultimatum requesting us to surrender into their hands some of the Sibarites who were in our midst. When a note of refusal was forwarded to them, a state of war ensued. Following the Egyptian method, Milone was appointed supreme commander of the army of Crotona, and in a few hours the invaders were forced to withdraw.

"But the fear of universal disaster descended also upon the population of Crotona for the same reason that it had attacked the Sibarites. Fomented by the defeated candidates for public offices, and led by Cilone— a former student expelled from our school for unworthiness — the Crotonians were now ready for an open revolt. In public harangues Cilone accused Pythagoras of being a demigod and the emanation of a foreign occult organization whose aim was to destroy the democratic institutions and enslave the people. 'He tells us' — he said at a mass meeting — 'that we are a flock of sheep and he is the holy shepherd. Watch well these initiates; with their refined manners and wise talk they draw money out of your pockets by a diabolical power . . . Observe them carefully, how well organized they are, how they love one another . . . Examine their standard of living . . . Aristocrats, yes, that is what they are . . . Away with them, death unto them all. Long live liberty and democracy!'

"Some of the bystanders proposed to summon Pythagoras before the People's assembly in self-defense; but Cilone could not permit that, his democracy was one-sided. He accused those whose who made the suggestion of being the Master's emissaries. The mob wanted to stone them to death, but Cilone had no intention of harming anyone but Pythagoras, his personal enemy. Thus he held the attention of the crowd on what he wanted to say: 'As we, the people, have no place in the Pythagorean Constitution, and as the right to decide and to judge has been taken away from us, likewise we shall deny them the right of self-defense. Death unto Pythagoras and the Pythagoreans.'

"The time to spill blood had arrived. They came in search of us as wild and fierce as starving bloodhounds. Soon we were under a state of siege, completely cut off from the outer world; but through the power of the Inner Eye, which can see where the physical eye cannot, Pythagoras informed us of our enemy's every move. We were assembled with fifty disciple-initiates in the temple of Vesta. As the revolutionaries arrived, they spread straw soaked in naphtha around the building; then it was set afire. The interior of the temple was a mass of incandescent luminance from the light that emanated from our foreheads and throats; a stilled peace and unspeakable joy abided in the hearts of all. One by one, forty disciples were released from their physical bodies into life eternal in less than thirty minutes, and as their forms dissolved and disappeared, a fragrant mist of roses, jasmine and daphne impregnated the circular nave.

"Archippus and Lysis were ordered to gather some of Pythagoras' manuscripts and deposit them in the Masters' Retreat of the Swiss Alps, while Damos was entrusted with other philosophical documents, some to be taken to the School of Light in Memphis, others to be delivered to her brother Teulage in Sicily where she went to live. With the power of levitation and invisibility they crossed the fire and soon were on their way. Arimestos stood outside, in the midst of the assault, unrecognized, pouring love to the insurgents. With the grace of remembrace that was released unto him, he went to Athens where he taught and wrote on the Pythagorean philosophy of the Solar Path.

"The golden cupola of the Temple of Vesta, now split silently as if by cosmic command; Pythagoras and I walked to the chalice of the Sacred Fire and sat on the brim, close to one another, my hand in his, our feet and legs inside the flaming vessel. We looked as young as we do now. Smiling at each other, we commenced to utter the Logos: OM, OM, OM. . . . in perfect cadence with the throbbing rhythm of our hearts made one. The sky lowered towards the temple as the Holy Grail with us inside slowly moved upward. As we reached the apex of the dome, the celestial canopy opened and two-hundred-fifty Twin flame-couples, descending from the Heaven of the Contemplators, clothed in glistening white togas and wielding the three-edged sword of purple, pink and gold fire, surrounded and welcomed us.

"Gazing earthward for the last time, we saw Cilone and his unwary followers stricken dumb upon the ground, each trying to hide himself beneath his evil companions, like earthworms burrowing under the mud. And while surveying that miserable heap of flesh rotting in the slimy substance of hatred, passion and ignorance, Cilone gripped by harrowing fear and despondency, thrust himself into the burning straw. Still uttering the Name of God, we kept on ascending, surrounded now by a legion of heavenly Gandharvas performing the Symphony of Triumph. The stupendous vision of our ascension was witnessed by our faithful disciples in Crotona, our children and a score of other students scattered over the Mediterranean basin.

"The relentless persecution against the Pythagoreans continued; the people reverted to where they belonged, in the pit of the Moon-consciousness. Disease, ignorance and political bondage were their lot, and they accepted it as a normal way of living. The great Lysis appeared once more in Crotona, secretly, to cast the seed of the Pythagorean Brotherhood, then directed his footsteps eastward and settled in Athens; here he achieved an enduring reputation as philosopher and teacher. Epaminondas, one of the greatest Greek strategists, was his pupil.

❋ ❋ ❋

"How much and how far did Pythagoras' teaching of the Solar Path influence the ancient world? The spiritual renaissance which began to unfold in Greece after our departure, was based on the Pythagorean doctrine. Through love of truth and virtue Socrates, Plato, Xenophon, et al., raised the intellectual and individual dignity of the masses against the skepticism of the sophists and the bigotry of the rulers. Rome was strengthened in her democratic institutions while the tribunes of the people gathered new impetus which helped to consolidate the Republic. For the first time in the history of the Western World an organic plan for economic assistance to the poor was devised and put to work. The esoteric societies of Etruria opened clinics throughout Tuscany for free medical care to the needy, while the well-to-do citizens abandoned their leisure and founded the merciful White Cross; they toured the city every day to help alleviate suffering. Scientific research began to unfold; painters, sculptors, musicians, poets and philosophers were able to inject a new touch of inner beauty and harmony into their works. Greece was awakened from her lethargy and became again the moral and cultural center of the Mediterranean. Ancient rivalries between individuals, families and city-states were mitigated and interstate arbitration came to be more effective. All this was the result of an inner awakening in man brought about by the partial acceptance and application of the Pythagorean method of a scientific approach to life.

"But soon Greece had to pass through the valley of despond as a test of her people's renewed character and spiritual stamina. My Twin Flame had foreseen the Asiatic invasion which came about twenty years after our departure from the earth. All that was great in the field of the spirit — liberty, science and ethics — had to be protected against the barbarians from the near and far East. During the battle of Marathon, both the Athenian phalanxes and the battalions of the peltasts, newly created by Epaminondas, were overshadowed by white clad beings moving in the air, pointing out the strategic sectors that had to be held in order to protect and save the republic and its vast spiritual heritage. As the Greek army, lean in number but courageous in heart, was unable to withstand the onslaught of the invaders, the Shining Ones led by Pythagoras' Spirit descended into the ranks and fought with it. Again, it was Pythagoras' ever-hovering Presence, through the Oracle of Delphi, that directed Themistocles during the naval battle of Salamis, causing the destruction of King Xerses' fleet and thus forcing him to renounce the plan for the subjugation of Greece. At the Thermopylae, where Leonidas was defeated, Pythagoras directed the evacuation of Athens. 'Abandon the city' — his voice warned — 'take nothing with you. Leave the doors of your houses open and do not extinguish the Sacred Fire. You shall return triumphant three days hence. Go! Let a piece of board, a rock or a bush be your shelter. Let me greet the enemy alone.' As the inhabitants fled their homes to take refuge in the caves of Mt. Parnassus, the Persian invaders entered the city baffled and mystified by the vacant enviroments. They were shaken by the echoeing of their heavy boots tramping on the empty pavements and terrified by the presence of the Shining Ones standing silently and unarmed at the threshold of the temples. Dark clouds began to gather and press downward, the weather turned cold, and the feeling of an approaching storm penetrated the bodies of the marching troops; the ominous atmosphere fanned the fright already mounting.

"In the distance the roar of an avalanche was heard, and earth and rocks were seen hurtling down the side of one of the hills surrounding the city, crushing many of the soldiers. The hoarse yelling of vengeance that rose from the unslaked throats of the troops was drowned in violent claps of thunder, while bolts of lightning streaked across the sky, followed by a chilling torrential rain. Tongues of unextinguishable fire sprang forth from everywhere: buildings, temples, fountains and pavements. It started from the perimeter of the enemy outposts and closed in towards the center of the city where the invaders were concentrated. Isolated and unable to communicate with their commanding officers, the soldiers gripped by a paroxysm of mortal fear, sought a way of escape. Turning towards the harbour, which had become a furnace of uncontrollable flaming fury, the frantic troops now in the throes of the lowest aspect of the law of survival, trampled on each other and made a carnage of themselves. It was the action of the law of karma, for nothing was destroyed but the sons of the lunar consciousness. The land of liberty had been saved.

"From the temple of Minerva came the clarion call of redemption directed to the youth. Pythagoras' Spirit again spoke: 'O Eternal Youth, the Solar God has defended thy City, alas, for the last time. Henceforth, you must take over the custodianship of the intangible wealth which has been poured to you from on High. No steel safe or mountain cave, no navy or brave military strategists can ever protect the spiritual patrimony of a race. You must protect it by the path of meditation and action harmoniously blended into one. Seek admission into the Schools of Light and arm yourselves for a bloodless combat against ignorance, fear, envy and mental sloth. Meditate on the Effulgent Light in your hearts; for there is the Infallible Oracle, there is the enduring Source of true Knowledge and Liberty.'

*　*　*

"Dear Marco and Leonora" — Teano concluded — "we belong to the youth of the world. We do not pamper them, on the contrary our training is based on wholesome severity in a wise amalgam of love. A youth so trained cannot be anything but scientifically just, scientifically noble and scientifically wise. Such a scientist could never deviate from the Solar Path. We will never lose him.

"We live in the Starry Heaven of the Master Scientists, the Cosmic Workshop of the most eclectic intellects of earth who, through the medium of introspection, bring forth new scientific discoveries leading to nobler standards of living. Pythagoras is the Foreman, as it were, of this philosophico-scientific research center, working under the direct supervision of the Cosmic Assembly of the Perfect Ones. Assisted by a score of Liberated Master scientists, he impresses the consciousness of receptive youths and points out new avenues of research for ethical scientists of earth as a share of the divine dispensation which humanity enjoys in the present age.

"As for me, I hover over the wives of men of responsibility trying to suggest to them how to love their mates and fire their intelligence for greater and nobler exploits. And this includes the sensitizing of their hearts for holier family life. Those who are united by the bond of twinship, I enhance in their hearts the awareness of this sacred gift in order to bring them closer to Deliverance. Man, woman, husband, wife, scientist, philoso-

310

pher, artist, businessman, politician, humble farmer or ruthless criminal, are, in the last analysis all children of love. Love rescues, ennobles and liberates. Let us use it!"

✳　✳　✳

Teano drew close to Pythagoras, her eternal companion, and leaned her head against him in an attitude of utter abandonment. She was as petite, beautiful and childlike as she was wise and immortal. He inclined his head towards her and together they stood there smiling, happy and divinely radiant. Then gazing intently at each other, their luminous auras merged and became brighter and ever brighter, until gradually they fused into a mass of quivering gold and pink flames whose expanding radiance enveloped Marco and Leonora completely. For one speck of eternity they lived in the consciousness of the bodiless, egoless and immortality.

CHAPTER VI

THE MASTER TEACHERS

Each year, beginning with the first day of December and for seven consecutive weeks, Jesus, the beloved Master of the Christian World, pours an avalanche of love to the earth. All life is raised by his mighty radiance. Joy, generosity and lightheartedness are felt more intensely by every sentient being. Whatever man's visualization of the Great Lord of Life, so it is: peace to the heart in turmoil, hope to the despairing, companionship to the lonesome, wealth to the merchant, health to the ailing, toys to the child, food to the starveling, renewed faith in the immortality of the soul for the selfless individual, and wisdom to the disciple on the path. This was the theme of yearning for Marco and Leonora. They longed for deeper and ever deeper inner experiences.

For many weeks, lost to the world, they meditated on the Master of Galilee with the absolute conviction that He would not deny them the ineffable grace of beholding His all-triumphant Presence. They saw Him ascending the sacred slope of the hill of Bethany, on the fortieth day after the Resurrection, clothed in a purple-blue robe and followed by the proud and imploring gaze of his faithful disciples, Mary of Nazareth, his Mother and Twin Flame, the enamored and sobbing maidens Mary and Martha, and a multitude of ardent believers. It was a beautiful sunny day, but the Master-sun that was the Incarnate Christ outshone the physical sun as the latter outshines the moon. Soon He reached the crest, turned and surveyed the throng as a true conqueror who had fought and won, with the invisible weapons of love and self-discipline, against all the negative and abhorrent traits of the mortal man. All was held in the dynamic aura of silence that is preparatory for a momentous event that is about to unfold. Marco and Leonora translated themselves towards the adoring crowd; and as they came nearer, saw them disappearing until they found themselves alone facing the Master on the summit of the hill. They bowed before his luminous Presence and said: "We are ready!" "Follow Me, my beloved disciples . . ."

They moved eastward, held suspended in the air by virtue of His omnipotence. Crossing a series of mountain ranges and many a river, they alighted on the eastern bank of the Ganges in Allahabad.

"The radiance of this holy river graces your countenances" — the Master began —; "and your auras bespeak and confirm your readiness for the teaching that is about to be released. Behold the flowing waters stilled by the command of your Master Presence. Behold this sylvan loveliness, trees, bushes and flowers, how they hum, bend and swing, as if to welcome you. Indeed, they know you, and are expressing their joy in seeing you once again. Many centuries ago, this was a land of great light, and an oasis of divine justice. Many a Christ lived here, teaching tolerance and gentleness, and enriching the soul of man with the ever-resurgent spirit of self-reliance that does away with the insane acquisitiveness of name, fame and material wealth which are the source of arrogance, cruelty, spoliation and war. This is the birthplace of the mature mind that is destined to unify and pacify the world; at this visible fountainhead of wisdom you shall renew yourselves for the worthy task that is ahead of you.

"Three thousand years prior to my apparition in the land of the Hebrews, you were dwellers of these sacred groves. Saru and Lis were your names; and this lovely temple, now filed in the Akashic Records, saw you as its priest and priestess. Here, under the supervision of a great Master, who had attained liberation during the sinking of the continent of Lemuria, you practiced and taught the art of silence. Facing one another, you drew the light of understanding by looking into each other's eyes, causing the Sacred Fire to spring forth from a brazier in front of you, which you fed with four shivering rays that emanated from your foreheads and hearts. Thus you communicated with each other the subtlest shades of thought and feeling. What a matchless set of twin flames you were. Pilgrims and rulers came from every land to study your behavior as a means of self-discovery and thereby learn a lesson which would benefit them in rapport to their fellow men and their subjects. Those who were mute acquired the power of speech and manly eloquence, while

314

those who had indulged in demagoguery and misleading rhetoric lost the precious gift of the speaking voice, until they would submit to the process of self-purification, and declare their positive resolution to abide by the law of ethics in public transactions. Many noble maharajahs rather than punishing some of their unruly ministers, sent them to you for training.

"Your method of teaching was based on the philosophical truth of 'know thyself', not by merely saying so, but by actual demonstration. Since the human body is a live recording mechanism upon which all the happenings of creation register with absolute precision, you had within yourselves the power to read, in the aura of any person who came, or was sent, to you for assistance in overcoming his trespasses, all his faults and misdeeds. Facing one another, in full view of your patient, you delved into each other's soul and brought forth with matchless clarity, all his past and present thoughts, feelings and behavior, which you presented to him not through the spoken word, but in letters of light. The impact of being so discovered and exposed caused such a radical self-appraisal as to change his life from one of compromise and half-truth to one of self-dedication to the welfare of his fellow man. But mainly he learned the noble art of meditation through which he contacted his Father in Heaven for daily protection, guidance and worthy deeds.

"One of the factors that today is causing so much disorder and misunderstanding between races, minority groups and nations is exactly the inability of both the common man and the political leader to pause, cogitate and seek silence. The jobless, the Negro and the indigent, living in congested and defiled slums, gaze around their dwellings, and without a second thought they blame the society for their wretchedness. The envy, bitter hatred and violence that they pour into their surroundings seem to relieve the inner tenseness. Karmically speaking they aggravate the situation. Some day, in the near or far future or in embodiments to come, the unwritten Law will compel them to reclaim at greater suffering this destructively qualified energy. Had they been taught the art of silence and self-analyzation perhaps they would have found that they were a school dropout or that they were reaping the effects of some brutal violations against life committed in previous embodiments. Man's predicaments are self-created, he himself is to blame. This however does not justify

315

the egotistical attitude of both the political leaders and business executives. Should they fail to exert themselves in alleviating suffering, their next embodiment will find them in an economic and social status of wretchedness comparable to that of their now maladjusted brothers.

"The mental and spiritual aridity that prevails amongst the political leaders of the world, and of their advisers and experts, has to be sought also in their inability or unwillingness to pause and cogitate. Meditation? Silence? It is all a waste of time. The mob clamors for panem and circenses; the unfit leader, a victim himself of a democratic precept that no longer works, calls frantically the speech writer and demands that a speech on the current event be written *by tomorrow*. This implies much search in dead books and dusty archives, none within, and without inturning there is no creativity and no way of solving the dangerous social turmoil of this world of yours. The same self-defeating attitude prevails amongst a vast majority of religious leaders, parents and university students. From the inner standpoint you are so miserably poor, so lethargically lazy. With so much material at your disposal and free for the taking, your spiritual garment is extremely shabby. Why so? Because mankind as a whole, and the *savants* in economic sciences in particular, have a deep-rooted consciousness of global poverty. And because of this refusal to let the mind soar into cosmic space, the burden of lifting the earth out of this vegetative state and onto the plane of the golden era, falls on a very few disciples whose wings are continually clipped by the sneer of those who should know better.

* * *

"My noble discipline-initiates, observe: the crystal gate that once admitted you into the Temple of Silence shall now lead you into the Seventh Heaven of Splendorship under the rulership of Saturn, the Supreme Advisor in the field of wisdom. As you cross the threshold both the structure and the surroundings will execute a one hundred eighty degree turn which causes you to face westward, in the direction of the continents where the white race predominates. The Christian world is in such a sad state. The papacy still clinging to an arbitrary and unauthorized spiritual supremacy whose theocratic claims of infallibility are nothing but a cover up for its doctrinary stagnation and justification of abuses. The Protestant Church is equally guilty of narrowmind-edness and sectarian intolerance. Whoever authorized these packs of wicked beasts to ridicule, persecute and murder my people on the ground that they had crucified me? Who ever gave them permission to institute 'holy' tribunals for the prosecution and burning at the stake of innocent people guilty only of rejecting their childish teaching and barbaric rituals. I would rather see the white man a disciple of the *pagan* Socrates, Seneca or Epitec-tus than to call himself a Christian as defined by the self-appointed vicars and ministers of my Gospel. The Cosmic Assembly of the Perfect Ones has studied this shamble of a religion, a potpourri of Machiavellian chicanery, demagoguery and tinseled ritual, a crime against the very sacred life of man, philosophical nonsense and, now and then, true sparks of spiritual sublimity, and has come to the conclusion that the three major denominations of official Christendom — Catholic, Protestant and the Orthodox Church — are beyond rescue and repair. Heavens, solar systems and constellations are working towards the gradual obliteration of this hopeless confusion that permeates the consciousness of the Western Man concerning God, Christhood and the immortal-ity of the Soul. Primarily, we intend to destroy this idolatrous attachment to Me as a person, which has filled the Western World with helpless hypocrites and sycophants, and bring forth the consciousness of the solar path whereby man stands straight as an Archangel, master of his own world, and fully aware, day and night, of the immortal Self that never leaves him. This Im-mortal Self, being the Source of his pride, peace, wisdom and glory, is his living Model into Whom man wants to be absorbed and become a living Christ. And to give you an intimation, my disciples, be it known that those who love Nature and the Stars more than churches and saints, are closer to this ideal man.

"Please, O my disciples, cease thinking that I am disturbed for this state of affairs in the world, for I am not. Remember, I AM a Liberated Christ, a conqueror of passion and mortal traits. The Christ and I are one. As Jesus I do not exist, and as a Christ I AM with you always."

Master Jesus paused for awhile, his eyes closed, his head slight-ly inclined, his countenance ablaze with heavenly light. As he returned to the plane of Marco and Leonora's exalted conscious-ness, he extended his hands and, lo, twenty-four chelas appeared,

317

clothed in white and yellow robes, intoning the Ode of Obedience to the Light. As they approached the crystal gate, the magnificent portal swung open: Master Jesus, with Marco and Leonora at his side, followed by the chelas, four abreast, crossed over the threshold, traversed the forecourt and entered the temple. They passed through the Sanctuary of Silence, which was symbolized by a blazing heart of white fire, and soon were in full view of a sequestered garden whose luxuriant vegetation far surpassed anything ever seen on earth. Passing through a circular hedge of ferns, they entered the Court of the Fountains, a large enclosure interspersed with flowering trees and gorgeous fountains of every size and architectural design, from which jetting streams of water in rainbow hues gushed forth playing a symphony of motion and shades. Each fountain had been hewn from a solid block of precious stone. There were massive yellow diamonds, garnets, amethysts, onyxes, topazes, rubies, emeralds and others, each representing and symbolizing one of the constellations of the zodiac. Master Jesus and his escort disappeared, leaving Marco and Leonora in this oasis of celestial artistry.

Seated in the lotus posture, on the scented grass, by the fountain of aquarius, they entered meditation, absorbing deeply the heavenly vibration from which they acquired prophetic power. Their spirit-forms then moving with the speed of thought alighted on the summit of a rocky elevation, from where they beheld an incomparable panorama of grandeur, towering mountains of sublime ruggedness with snowy peaks thrusting shafts of blinding luminance against the blue sky, thundering, foaming cascades of sound and energy, peaceful valleys with tranquil mirrored lakes, winding rivers, parklike glades of multicolored wild flowers, and gardenland covered with palatial abodes inhabited by celestial beings who possessed the knowledge of the Science of the Soul. The starry panorama then slowly moved westward, crossing both Europe and the Atlantic Ocean, and descended upon the continent of North America. As it touched the earth, it produced a devastating conflagration destroying an unwanted accumulation of decaying corpses of men and beasts and rotting mephitic matter, then it settled there peacefully; the celestial land and its Elysian mansions and their starry dwellers forming the dawn of the Novus Ordo Seculorum of the New America, the cradle of the New Verbum of the Golden Age.

Coming down from the Eastern sky, and moving towards North America, Marco and Leonora now saw another scene that seemed prophetically awesome: an immense escalator with thirty-three broad platforms in various colors of the solar spectrum. On each platform stood a Master-Elohim, clothed in a mantle of dazzling blue and white, surrounded by seven Splendor-beings from the Heaven of Saturn, in robes of yellow and blue; their aspect the perfect expression of love, wisdom and power, yet divinely formidable. High above the thirty-three groups, his form ablaze with light and fire of blinding splendor, stood a Director-Elohim issuing wordless commands. By projecting powerful shafts of light from his forehead, he directed each group of wise ones to take over the rulership of one of the thirty-three centers of higher learning in America spread along the Atlantic and Pacific seaboards and the Gulf of Mexico. The latter, first in the cosmic mission, will be gateways of love and brotherly amity looking southward. The splendor-beings of these eleven foci of cosmic learning will issue daily, with compelling sincerity and like a chorus of dedicated muezzins from a minaret, the clarion call of invitation to the noble people of the southern land: "Come unto us, come unto us, O children of Liberty, and partake of our spiritual bounty. Let us brand each one of you with the mark of Splendorship that you may raise your kin, your waters, forests and mountains to starry perfection. You are equal to the best, second to none." From the Pacific Coast to the western shore of the Indian Ocean, the clarion call shall be one of humility and awe: "O wise ones, Sons and Daughters of Heaven, come unto us, we beg of you. Bring to us the secrets of your greatness, that the Western Man may learn how to rule and be ruled by philosophy and the humanities. Teach him how to apply compassion and fellow-feeling at every step of the way of his daily life, that you may return to your sanctified homes enriched with positive and dynamic gratitude, from which you shall be raised onto heights of comfort where the spirit of the totality of all souls begins to unfold."

"The eleven groups of Splendor-beings, from their campuses, strategically located along the Atlantic seaboard will speak like a legion of Archangels to the slumbering people of Europe, Africa and the Near East: 'Awaken, O beloved elder ones of ours and learn from your children who have made good. Come to us open-minded and bold. We shall make you one without words or compulsion. From the moment you touch our shores and breathe the rarefied air of our political institutions, you will scrape and burn your parochial habits, your anachronistic social distinctions and national provincialism, born of fear, jealousy and ignorance. We respect you. Why do you ridicule us? Are we not your sons and daughters? Open your minds instead and learn proudly from your children. Learn how weakening it is when you call yourselves Germans, French, Italians or Ethiopians, and how strong and truly protected you feel when instead you call yourselves Euro or Afro. Do it now, be the pioneers by erasing this inglorious trait of your past. You shall earn undying gratitude from your future generations and a spiritual dispensation from the Cosmic Assembly of the Perfect Ones.'

"Disciples of the All-seeing Eye" — the Director-Elohim announced — "when these calls are issued, the people of other continents will separate into two groups: those that belittle and refuse, and those that respect and accept the invitation. The former, though in the minority, will be the noisier; they are the enemy of civilization, progress and God. However, victory is ours. We are the ones who have chosen the land of North America for this task; we also chose it as the seat of the United Nations. The thirty-three foci of cosmic learning will train the true political leaders of the world, to be spiritually equipped to rule their countries for practical programs of universal good."

✿ ✿ ✿

As the Director-Elohim completed his revelation, Marco and Leonora returned to the Court of the Fountains, where Master Jesus awaited them.

"What you have seen" — He explained — "shows how deeply concerned we are of this un-natural and un-Christian division of the races and nations of the world. Our first aim is to liberate the consciousness of man from religious sectarianism which, frankly, is the root of all evil. We want no priests, and in order to achieve this goal, we must emphasize the immanence of God in the life of every single individual. The more one feels the nearness and tangibility of his Immortal Self, the weaker is his link with the professional preacher, the truer his appraisal of his own shortcomings, the more severe his restraint in criticizing his fellow man, the prompter his desire to listen and cooperate for the common good. As I have declared previously, my Message was not meant to be monopolized by any clique wearing a special uniform, nor was it intended to give rise to theological disputations, and, above all, I never authorized anyone to ridicule, persecute and murder those who disagree with my teaching. The fact that I spoke from street corners without music, singing, incense and chalice, demonstrates that I did not intend to create a new religion, but to cast a living seed for a nobler manhood based on the philosophical truth of the ancient Greek philosophers: 'Know thyself, O man!' This truth is still valid today and forever. Man must be made aware of the responsibility towards himself directly and without outer interference, degrading self-pity or binding oaths to any oligarchic or theocratic conventicle. One does not need to study psychology, or the mystery of the virgin birth, or the meaning of the Trinity, to comprehend the importance of uniting mind and feeling; nor does one need a priest to understand God. One's conscience is more accurate in determining what is right or wrong.

"Behold the luminous stars of the Soul, some barely tolerated by a church wallowing in corruption and theological farrago: St. Francis of Assisi, Galileo Galilei, Giordano Bruno, and others. None of these actually cared about me personally; they wanted truth, simplicity and freedom of mind, things that were precisely denied in 'my name' by a corrupt syndicate of cardinals steeped in ignorance, vanity and bestiality. How wonderful the sensation of the First Visitation when, unaided and absolutely alone, the heart begins to vibrate while the mind responds in sheer wonderment and holy fear: 'O God, O God, how limitless Thy Mercy and Thy Love', the pigmy changes into a giant, the ailing person is healed instantly, the dark shadows from the criminal's mind lifted for ever, and the student of meditation stepping up to the threshold of creativity: man finally inheriting the kingdom of Heaven. How does he protect and invest such unexpected wealth. Daily meditation is the answer, the basis of self-discipline, the living soil for the growth of the Soul to Godhood. Be thou, O man, the depository and the investor of this wealth. Entrust it to no one. Behold the fast accruing interest: thy body stronger, thy mind more vigorous, thy heart freer, thy home made cleaner, thy outlook in life broadened to encompass infinitude itself.

"Well established on his seat, in a posture that best accords him physical comfort, the newly self-discovered man embarks on one of the most astounding experiences of life: the search of the Self, the mysterious Being whose power and grace are the true reservoir of peace and wisdom. Imagine solving baffling problems all by one-self without outer help, hardships reduced in intensity, seeming unjustified and frustrating delays looked at detachedly and with equanimity. And having to wait, to wait patiently, he now faces God in humble defiance, as it were, declaring his determination to resist fear and threat, no matter how pressing. This is spirituality indeed, and the most fascinating of earthly adventures. It is ten thousand times more stirring than any other human enterprise, including space exploration. Think a little, O man: in a sheltered place of your house, with your mind alert and in full possession of your perceptive faculties, hearing a voice within speak, pointing the way to a certain goal; or beholding pictures moving with sparkling clarity, or being touched by an invisible hand and taken into celestial realms such as this. What other human exaltation, except the merging of the bodies and souls of twin flames, could compare with such experience. Where else could one find happiness and mental equilibrium? In what manner could one enrich his soul and advance towards omnipotence, omniscience and immortality?

"Yet sadly for the human society as a whole, only a small percentage of human beings attempts this initial, though difficult, deviation to venture into the exciting world of the inner. You may say that it is karma, and I respond that the willing mind has the capacity to re-direct man's karmic baggage from one of dominance to one of obedience, that is, subjugation of the burden of demerits to a well planned goal of mental and spiritual elevation. The ultimate result, I assure you, will exceed one's fondest expectation. When one considers that the mind, aided by positive determination that comes from the knowledge of the Self, can do and undo anything at will, smoking of tobacco or gambling or drug addiction or other similar acquired habits, can be dismissed promptly and without a second thought.

"Like a runner in training for the Olympic Games, practicing faithfully and methodically, day after day, accumulating endurance and experience — which may be called merits — and looking forward to the culminating moment of victory, so it is with the student of meditation. He is the athlete of the spirit, labouring on the transmutation of matter, aiming at the conquest of death and the triumph of life. The ascent is not easy. Doubt, despondency, skepticism and a sense of guilt will pester his mind; surrounded by the forces of evil and the lure of sensuality, many a time he is tempted to give up. 'What is the use' — he would say — 'behold, O my Soul, men exalt the deeds of those skilled in murder; they belittle the humble who has done no sin; they justify the strong who does wicked things; they persecute the man of God who seeks the kingdom of Heaven. Did you not see recently, O my Soul, a famous American magazine with nationwide circulation calling the wife of a chief gambler *her most serene highness*, and taking films of their mansion, with reporters standing in awe before her'? Yes, O Junior Christ, I agree with you. And things worse than this happen in the field of politics. The Presidency of the United States today is the goal not of the wisest and most capable but of the richest and most inept. No wonder you are going through an age of blunders in both foreign affairs and domestic policy. The masses have ceased to think and their power of discrimination is at a very low ebb, but to follow them and be ensnared by their glitter, makes thee, O my disciple, guiltier than they. You must stay on the path, for you are more precious to us, to life and to the welfare of the world than the Presidency and the State Department put together. Your meditation and your inner search that seem so remote from politics are actually influencing and molding minds, thoughts and decisions of both the Senate and the House of Representatives of the United States of America. In mastering yourself, you are mastering your nation and the world.

"You saw a little while ago the Splendor-beings descending upon North America. You felt the penetrating power of their Buddhi, charging every atom of your bodies with the intuitive intelligence which they possess. Believe me, thousands upon thousands of other spiritually receptive students throughout the world, felt their presence and heard their call. When this information will be released to earth you will receive thousands of inquiries from these noble lifestreams who will want to compare notes. Mark this day well! Who are these splendor-beings? Simple folk they were long ago on earth, devoted to decency and justice, unsung heroes, artisans, and laborers of the field, whose every stroke of hammer and dig of hoe were qualified with the thought of God. They thought intensely of righteousness, unaware that some day they would be masters of it. Some of them were rebellious to despotism and fearless before the rack or scaffold. And those who heard their call, heard the call of their forefathers. I am not — using your terminology — any greater than they. They are all Christs who never entered a church, never attended a theological discussion, never genuflected before a bishop, never took communion. Not one ever earned a monument while on earth; no one ever wrote a fascinating biography of any of them, and their bodily remains are nowhere to be found. What are their feelings, how do you define them with earthly words?

"Tentatively, they may be compared with the behavior of a true philosopher, educator, scientist or artist, whose sheer joy in discovering a new truth, a new element or force, or a new living form in nature, escapes all monetary measurement. You can compare them with the fearlessness of a Socrates, or the selfless innocence of a Joan d'Arc, or the seraphic aloofness of St. Francis of Assisi. One thing, however, they have in common: Humility, of which they knew nothing. While on earth, they never dwelt on heavenly reward; they simply attended to their tasks and ennobled them with the thought of God. The intellectually brilliant may define this behavior as passive resignation, we prefer to call it spiritual insight.

"I see your minds brimming with questions and, thinking of my power of omniscience, you refrain from asking. What is the status of those who possess a college diploma, who, for the sake of livelihood prostitute their conscience and minds by yielding to employers who are bent on misleading the masses through the avenues of radio, television, advertisement and the press; of those who devote their lives and energy in dealing with gamblers, drug peddling, prostitution and organized crime, their lawyers and accountants; of those involved in espionage and counterespionage, manufacturing implements of war and lobbying for the continuation of the existing armed conflicts in order to accumulate wealth and gain political power? What shall I answer to you, my disciples. Sad indeed are their future embodiments. The sum total of the evil deeds of each violator coalesces and seals his mind and feeling world, which is then

324

kept intact as if under refrigeration one thousand degrees below zero. When he takes embodiment again he is directed to the locker room to pick up his unholy baggage. With such a heavy load he staggers back to earth and passes his next existence as a blind, a cripple, or as an idiot. He may be affected with cancer, or severe arthritis and sometimes with a new disease that baffles medical science. He goes through physical life in a state of unnarratable suffering, his mind in a vegetative condition. He will be a burden to society, that same society of men that had refused to curb his misdeeds in the previous embodiment. If through the mercy of some friend or teacher, he is given a glimpse of his past violations, his heavy load of destructive karma is made lighter but only a little. Then he dies, as it were, but another embodiment is close at hand, plagued with different handicaps. Thus slowly, very slowly indeed, through hundreds and perhaps thousands of embodiments until he reclaims all the damage caused to society, life and God. Then he begins to ascend; however, in rapport with those who had devoted their lives in accumulating merits he is like a man of the Stone Age before an Einstein.

"I may sound scandalous to many a reader if I, a Christ, justify the art of compromise, provided that it is carried out on a temporary basis. A magazine or newspaper writer, for instance, who all of a sudden finds himself involved in an unethical situation and is forced to write articles that conflict with his conscience, and is unable, for economical reasons, to resign from his job, it is pardonable for him to compromise his outer vesture without staining his inner life. He will continue in his task in a spirit of detachment while at the same time directing his attention to finding a new occupation. He must be like a deep ocean that remains untouched and unpolluted by the continual flow of sewage from the earth. He has to watch his feelings at every step of the way, intensify his inner application and speak to God aloud: 'Hold me, O Father, hold me untouched by this miasmic pressure that tries to engulf me. Set me free'.

* * *

"Life on earth is like walking on a razor edge or, rather, like the attempt to make a pin float on the surface of still water; it must be dropped on gently and in a perfect horizontal position. No man who has gone through life in adherence with the law of ethics, has done so all by himself. A Liberated Master has been by his side always, urging him either to action, study or meditation, never allowing him a moment of leisure. There is nothing more devastating in life than human leisure, the dolce far niente of the well-to-do and playboy; and there is nothing more reinvigorating than the self-submission to discipline and the constant checking of unbridled desires and the wandering of a wild mind. Purposely God did not give to man a perfect world; He gave to him a Nature that is wild, incomplete and in need of transformation. Man must carry out this transformation by the path of self-analyzation, study and work; and no man, no matter how active, can ever fulfill his assignment, in the evolutive process of nature, in one life-span. Hence the need for every man, woman and child to work, that is, to express themselves outwardly. Methodic application of the hands and mind to transform or mold matter and energy is a form of self-discipline, collective order and evolution, whereas to indulge in idleness rots the mind and body, degrades the soul and leads to collective chaos. The visible man, being essentially a product of the ever-active nature, must work along with it, not against it. Nature compels him to do so. But if he refuses, nature throws him into a state of personal and collective disorder, and when such disorder accumulates beyond certain limits the body politics, nations and continents are flung into confusion by wars, floods, drought, fire and other cataclysms. Then whatever was accomplished by previous generations in the field of comfort and beauty, is lost, and man is forced to work for mere physical survival. Like a crew of engineers and workers entrusted with the maintaining of a bridge always at the peak of efficiency, so is man with himself, his family and God.

"When wars come and cannot be avoided, they must be waged manfully and unrevengefully, seeing in it the dissolution of age long ill-will, injustice and mental limitation born of leisure, that is, misdirection and misuse of man's thought and energy. The conflict itself is a cleanser and an inner awakener leading to a better understanding of both one's self and the seeming foe. You will ask: how about yourself, Master; were you indulging in unwanted submission or trying to awaken a tired society that was wallowing in self-defeating inertia? And if you had Christ powers why did you endure such a horrible persecution and the seeming inevitable crucifixion? And what were you trying to demonstrate?

"Yes, I was sent into a tired, confused and soul-less society by the Cosmic Assembly of the Perfect Ones. Both the Roman world and my own people were in a state of coma and in dire need of an awakener. Trained by my earthly teachers of India, Persia and Egypt, and protected by the Great Ones who were guiding me, I succeeded in drawing unto myself the accumulation of age long hatred, abuses and spiritual stagnation born of haughtiness and lack of introspection. And those who had eyes to see and minds to understand saw and transmitted to future generations the undreamed of potentialities of the human soul: its victory over death and its everlasting dominion in the infinitude of life. I did not save anybody; man saves himself not by believing in me but by accepting and applying day in and day out my message of truth. Away therefore with the tale fabricated by the Church that man must believe in me to be saved. As for the *abuses* of which you speak and the suffering of the crucifixion, I assure you that I know nothing about it; it is a display of gross ignorance by the world at large which knows nothing of the infinite knowledge and strength lodged in the heart. I walked to the cross unconcerned of my earthly surroundings, with a body as handsome as any of your finest athletes of today, totally absorbed in the Self of Me, my Father in Heaven, happy and radiant for my well accomplished mission. I, therefore, reject all the so-called 'works of art' in painting, sculpture or drama that show me as a frail, bleeding, sickly looking and helpless fellow.

❁   ❁   ❁

"Physical suffering is a state of being purely subjective, and it cannot be described in words. In fact it is so elusively subjective that its mental reactions are innumerable, varying according to an unending series of situations, such as age, gender, time, place, education, fashionable thoughts, economic condition, state of health, and many others. Therefore, whereas one may suffer excruciating pain at the prick of an ordinary pin, another may walk on a bed of nails, or through fire, or have his body trespassed by a sword, and still remain untouched by the slightest physical discomfort. This is a state of self-control upon which the Knowledge of the Self begins to unfold. The physical body, as a temporary garment of the soul, must serve the Higher Man who is above suffering; it is this Higher Man, this Indwelling Spirit, who molds the flesh vehicle according to the requirement of the hour.

"The true disciple of the Inner does not waste time training his body to walk on a bed of nails, for such a feat has absolutely no bearing on his spiritual growth. Instead, he trains himself, through meditation, to gaze at every human being as if he were fleshless; and whether in the act of meditating or committing a crime, he sees himself in him as an expression of the ever-dominating Presence of God; hence he is not at war with anybody, for everybody being an integral part of himself, he cannot be harmed or suffer thereby. On my way to the field of the skulls where crucifixion was awaiting me, I saw the face of God in every person that I encountered, and there I saw myself as a runner who had outdistanced all the other contestants and was in sight of the Ultimate Goal. How could I have suffered when every detail of the setting was bespeaking *triumph, triumph, triumph.* Instead gratitude and love were in my heart for the assistance that I was receiving from those who were otherwise called cheaters, thieves and killers. 'Killers of God', the Christian mob, instigated by the Church leaders, has called the Jews. What a nonsense. If any killing at all was committed it was death itself that fell by the weapon of Self-Knowledge that I possessed.

* * *

"The Soul-flame, the Indwelling Spirit of Man, is God's sole begotten son, the releaser of Self-knowledge. It is THAT which knows everything of the past, present and time to come. It must be contacted through conscious meditation, that is, meditation on thought, motive and deed. It requires no setting aside of time, but simply determined reflection and analyzation of what one is thinking or doing at the moment. The personal experience connected with this process is a subtle sensation of warmth in the heart that spreads like a sudden fire throughout

328

the atomic structure of the body. It is a feeling of gladness to be alive, a sense of delightful wonderment typical of first love, a mixture of adoration, passionate yearning, devotion to duty, generosity, adventure, desire to be silent and alone, forgiveness and noble resolution. It is an inner synthesis, a perfect equilibrium of mind and body, thought and deed, feeling and perception. No pulling apart, no waste of energy. Once savoured, man has ceased to exist by the law of survival, for a vast estate opens before him, and nature herself bows as a humble and dedicated maidservant. Naturally such a state is slightly more difficult to achieve than to grow intellectually or economically, but the results escape all comparison, because they are everlasting. The rich have nothing to offer to the poor but material sustenance, while he who has sought and attained Self-knowledge needs only to utter a statement to enrich the whole humanity and raise their spiritual level for many a millennium. Why does mankind feel so powerfully the impact of a truth? Because the sage who pronounces it never speaks to the personality, but to the Soul of man, that is, to his own Self.

"The man of Self-knowledge is a scientist of the Everliving Soul. He deals with intangible substance that never changes nor undergoes the vehement attacks of time and space; hence the results of its manipulation are precise, unchangeable and uncontradictable. This inner inquiry leads automatically to the astounding revelation that man and God are identical. In such awareness one never loses sight of another supreme truth that all life, outer and inner, emanates from God. With such knowledge, accepted and lived by, the recipient is entitled to guide his fellow man on the ascending path of eternal freedom.

"On the path of Christhood is he who through the discipline of meditation has set himself free from outer ritual, and idolatrous begging and imploration. Shun, my son, shun the Olympus of man-made gods and saints, and accept discipline with a glad heart and determined mind. Do so now, at once, and be a god unto thyself. Time is short.

❊   ❊   ❊

"Though Love is my cognomen, it is the least understood by the people of Christendom. In the name of Love horrible

329

crimes against life and God have been committed since my apparition on Earth. The basic cause for this behavior is to be sought in the uncalled for eagerness of Christians to love me while actually I never asked to be loved. My commandment was 'love one another . . . love your fellow man . . . love your enemy . . .' No man ever accumulates merits by glorifying me to the sky, but he can certainly earn Christhood through love on Earth and respect and protection of life in every form. I have no use of man's proffer of personal love, but I may assist him in attaining the Kingdom of God if he obeys me to the letter: 'Love one another' and 'Love your enemy'.

"Through this misapplication of my teaching a Church hierarch condemns a heretic to death, and as soon as the sentence is executed, out of love, he enters the Church to give thanks to the Lord (Me?) for the extirpation of another withered branch from the Tree of Life. Is not this Church leader himself a branch of the Tree of Life also withered and ready for the fire?

"In the name of Love a conscientious objector refuses to fight on the grounds that war is un-Christian and the negation of love. However, he would not hesitate to kill or maim anyone who tries to interfere with his own personal life and possessions. Two Christian nations face one another in battle array, and in the name of Love, Justice, and what not, the respective bishops implore my intervention to help one against the other. There are also certain Christian fanatics who refuse to bathe on the grounds that soap and water may cause the death of the insects that crawl on their bodies. Many strange and queer things are done, and many mortal sins are committed in the name of Love. What a pity! St. Bernadino of Siena, for instance, while denouncing corruption and preaching love for Mother Church, condoned and approved the beating of unruly wives by their husbands, and was a most rabid persecutor of heretics. He is a saint, or is he? And most of the saints of the Christian firmament are of the same class or worse.

"True love is that which arouses tenderness at the sight or sound of a suffering living creature, of a human being irrespective of race, color or creed, or of a deviated individual. It must impel one to leave behind everything and run over to the assistance of a fellow man in need. It must be self-fulfilling,

330

like unto a star of light hovering over one's head, penetrating deeply into the heart, casting no shadow."

*　*　*

Master Jesus paused. His form shone with resplendence and glory, his feet sparkled with light, an aura of pink luminance encircled his head, and his eyes bespoke all the attributes of the perfect lover of the Indwelling Self. He enfolded Marco and Leonora in the radiance of his Christhood, and the next instant they were translated onto the same rocky rampart from where they had witnessed the coming of the Splendor-beings into the land of North America. Now another vision of prophetic import began to unfold.

From the far-off horizon, moving towards them, hundreds abreast, was a seeming interminable column of Cosmic-Governors in blue togas, each holding high a caduceus of flaming blue fire. Mighty and severe in their bearing, they were so numerous they could have girded the earth. Halting a short distance from where Master Jesus and his guests were standing, they bowed before Him and stood awaiting his command. Shafts of pink light emanated from the forehead of the Living Christ which enveloped the Cosmic-Governors forming an engirdling ring of pink-blue enkindling light around the earth. This being the *Seal of Approval* the Cosmic-Governors descended to earth and mingled with men, women and children of every walk of life, in silent observation. Some of the people avoided them in fear, some were indifferent or bewildered, others rushed towards them to be touched on the forehead with the caduceus of light. These were mostly children under the age of seven. Suddenly, as if impelled by a mighty command, all activities on earth ceased; all structures — houses, apartments, office buildings, factories and so forth — lost their walls and ceilings, and the inhabitants of the cities and country stood still and hushed, visible to all. The workers of the open fields dropped their implements and waited. The workers of the mines, tunnels and underground transportation were raised to the surface as if driven by a levitating force over which they had no control. All people traveling stopped their vehicles — carts, automobiles, trains, ships and aircraft — all were held immobilized, as if caught in cages of glass. The earth was afire and the sky

331

ablaze with unconsuming flame. The Cosmic-Governors approached every man, woman and child, and touched the forehead of each one with the Scepter of Light. From the contact a luminous sparkle flashed forth which remained suspended above the head of the individual. The Cosmic-Governors examined the sparkle: if it showed crystal-clear transparency, the individual was given a parchment of laminated gold, with the Law of Ethics written upon it, and the nature of his task for the incoming Golden Age. His service was to be that of a scientist, philosopher, artist, statesman, educator, or spiritual leader; if the sparkle beshowed opacity, lesser offices were assigned, according to the degree of transparency, while the parchment of the Law of Ethics was made of silver, copper or other baser metals.

The individuals who gave no sparkle at all were catapulted forward and backward, downward and upward, and in every direction, criss-crossing the atmosphere with the velocity of lightning, and were directed towards cosmic halls of learning, under rigid discipline.

As the whole humanity was examined and tested, and the unworthy ones removed, the Cosmic-Governors began to ascend, leaving behind blueprints of beauty for the earth: starry-like cities to be populated with human beings engaged in constructive activities according to the principle of absolute progress; homes to be occupied by couples in their prime of youth and remaining so as long as they adhered to the Law of Ethics specifically drafted for each of them. Men and women duly married to their twin flames or other perfect mates. Teenagers raised in an atmospherse of love and master severity.

The Cosmic-Governors again presented themselves before Master Jesus in the same formation. "These noble rulers and chastisers" — he explained to Marco and Leonora — "are the harbingers of the Golden Age, an age whose realization demands the application of disciplinary methods. They are due to descend to earth unexpectedly and, like crashing thunderbolts, hit heavily on the accumulated dross of idiosyncrasies and pseudo-definition of whatever seems — and is not — good and lawful. Material wealth, derived through shady or difficult-to-detect activities will be exposed to the sight of the world, bringing disillusionment and shame to both the possessors and their families and friends. Just, stern and impersonal will be the work of these Cosmic Redeemers. There will be neither leniency nor delay. Each man will be judged not only with absolute exactness, but also in a way that precludes the repetition of the same violation. With the completion of this unhappy but necessary task, you will see the commencement of the teaching of the Science of the Soul in the colleges and universities of the world."

The Cosmic-Governors bowed before Master Jesus and withdrew silently, and while standing in midair they let the caducei of light descend to earth, one for every man, woman and child, as a living memento of the visitation from on High. Returning to the Court of the Fountains, Master Jesus smiled at Marco and Leonora as a host who is about to surprise his guests of honor. "Would you like to meet the hostess of my starry mansion?" — He asked. "Yes, indeed!" they answered eagerly. "Then behold . . ." The Spirit-form of Mary of Nazareth, Jesus' Mother and Twin Flame, coalesced before them.

* * *

"Do not be so pensive" — she said — "about that which was just revealed to you. Suffering of the flesh is a cleansing of the Soul. Not that the Soul needs actually cleansing; it is the dross that accumulates around It that needs to be removed; and this dross is like a leech that has grown large, fat and brazen throughout many embodiments in contravention not only of the cosmic laws, but also of the basic practices of everyday decency. We do not pull the leech; the Law of Life does not permit us to force ourselves into another lifestream's world. We simply awaken him to the existence of the intruder in his conscience; he has to pull it off all by himself, unaided by anyone. Often he does not succeed, the pain is too excruciating, and rather than make the supreme effort, he lets the leech go undisturbed and plunges his whole inner world into more lurid deals, bigger showoffs, noisier social parties, filthier debaucheries and other serious and mortal crimes. When this stage is reached, the Law of Life takes over by an Act of Dispensation made of steel and fire, floods, earthquakes, epidemics, famine, economic depressions and other cataclysmic events that hit directly those whose leech was left undisturbed.

333

And let it be known, Marco and Leonora: the innocent, the law abiding, the strivers for good and the disciples of the inner are not touched. Those Cosmic-Governors, though merciless, humanly speaking, that is, lacking the degenerative sympathy of the weakling, are indeed Cosmic Redeemers and Masters of Love. And for those who are not able to comprehend the significance of LOVE, let it be known that the true Wielders of LOVE are highly specialized surgeons of the Spirit.

"People, and more so the grown-ups, dream of a gentle, lenient and yielding Comforter to nurse their whims and satisfy their petty desires, no matter how childish, morbid or brutal. How many deviated persons go to church to ask the intervention of a saint in the destruction of their 'enemies', or of those whom they dislike or envy. Only the very elect visualize and ask for a Comforter with an iron hand ready to crush them at the slightest infraction. Of this class was my Comforter and Harbinger during my early age while frequenting the School of the Essenes. He made me a giant of the Spirit. At the age of sixteen, after ten years of training with relentless severity, I was able to wield cosmic powers: the lilies bloomed in my hands. I was impressed and frightened, and, in utter surrender, I begged my Comforter to train me in humility and purity. 'You have them, my child' — he told me. 'Should these powers fail you, it will be a sign of arrogance'. 'And what shall I do to keep them forever, and even expand them?' — I again requested. 'Listen, my child, and learn:

" 'This body of yours does not belong to you. It was given to you by God in trust. Keep it strong and resilient at all times through rhythmic breathing, physical exercises, proper diet and an elevated frame of mind. Cultivate the sacred Centers of the body through meditation. Know that they possess the secret of eternal youth and beauty. Know that they are the Source of the Infinite Wisdom and knowledge of God. Offer thy body to Me, thy Invisible and Holy Comforter, and I, with my Universal Organ of Love, shall awaken thy holy centers so as to achieve absolute synchronization with the Cosmic Harmonies of Creation. Be always aware, day and night, of my uninterrupted closeness, nay amalgamation, with you.'

"At the age of seventy and up to the hour of my Deliverance, I continued to enjoy the physical freshness of the days when the lilies bloomed in my hands, plus the almost infinite knowledge and wisdom of my ascended Christ-son and Twin Flame.

* * *

"In the matter of proper nutrition, it is important to emphasize how people grow more heedless with age. As they grow older they develop a craving for richer foods at the expense of wholesomeness. Being quasi-immobilized physically by lack of exercise and a complex of small and nagging ailments, aware of their malfait bodies, mentally affrighted and negligent as a result of sexual abuses and disarray of the endocrine glands, incapable of competing with the youth in sports and other physical prowess, they find an escape in concocted foods and other tidbits that stimulate an already corrupt palate.

"Austerity in eating, that is, simple, natural and well-balanced meals, elegantly spread on the table, served on fine china, tasteful glassware and silverware, is indeed an important factor for spiritual unfoldment. Fatty foods, spices, processed starches and commercial sweets, soft drinks and alcoholic beverages, smoking, drugs and stimulants, lay inside the body, ugly sediments of toxic material whose ill effects, from simple tiredness to lugubrious cancer, plague humanity; but what is thrown mostly into irreparable disorder is the relationship body-mind-soul. So indisputable and precise is this correlation, that when the internal organs of the body are unhindered by excess toxic residue, and richly bathed in oxygen through rhythmic breathing, the mind yields quicker to the wisdom of the soul, and the creative power is raised to undreamed of levels of productivity; here the lower self ceases to antagonize the action of the Buddhi, the Knowledge of the Self becomes all-revealing, and peace that passeth all understanding manifests.

"Total or partial ignorance of these truths is the cause of an unhealthy body and confused mind, and the binding of the Soul to the wheel of birth and rebirth by the growth of unkind karma through social and ethical violations. Everything in that body undergoes degeneration: sight, taste, smell, touch, hearing, voice and thought. Without an efficient control and functioning of the senses, mind concentration fails, meditation

335

fails, wisdom fails, ethics fail, everything goes topsy-turvy. This is the road to hell — self-created — the road of bondage, limitation, drowsiness, affliction, wickedness, deturpation and disease, all leading to cosmic death.

"Where do you think covetousness, hatred and infatuation arise from? Fear, yes, fear that stems from an unhealthy mind dwelling in a diseased body. So man becomes covetous, resentful and a needless grabber; he cuts himself asunder from the evolutive characteristics of noble living, whereas when he knows the state of his being, when he is capable of cementing together the various organs — limbs, senses, ductless glands and mind — then his courage and spirit of generosity break all bounds, and man moves without pause towards lofty realizations, towards the One Realization of Ultimate Freedom.

* * *

"I would like to speak to the very elite of the intellectual world who, though deeply convinced of the existence of God, from both the philosophical and scientific aspect, nevertheless they display an attitude of sophisticated indifference when they move in the official circles of their profession. Why is it so? It is a mental residue of nineteenth century rationalism when reason and logic were based on what the physical eye could see, or combination of what chemical substances could produce, or machines could perform; it was the glorification of effect and the negation of the Cause. Busy as man was at that time with the exploitation of nature on behalf of the Industrial Revolution, the concept of God had weakened considerably, while the moral collapse had grown parabolically, reaching the acme of brutality with World II. But today the spirit of man, thirstier as never before for the things of God, wants to scale the mount of true wisdom, and quickly; and it cries for guidance. Where is such a guidance to be found? Not in the priest, not in the political agitator, not in those who babble opinions on ethics, or obedience to the law based on the political status quo, or on a *noble* past which never existed. Only the fully accredited philosopher, jurist, educator, mathematician, geologist and astronomer, can assist man in his spiritual ascendancy. We demand of them, whenever and wherever they gather for professional discussions, to open their meetings with a prayer to God and a request that a Liberated Master makes himself visible to preside over them. What an epoch-making day it would be for the whole human society, when one of these intellectual aristocrats will rise up from his seat to utter such a prayer.

"The man of today wants to be taught how to live undeviatedly and continually as an offspring of the Mind of God. He craves for intelligence and energy, not dogma. He wants to solve problems and overcome inner clashes through the Mathematics of the Cosmos, not through timid imploration or supine acceptance of saintly utterances on patience and resignation. He wants to be taught and shown, consistently and scientifically, that he is at the center of creation, and that all his thoughts and deeds influence life for which he intends to assume full responsibility; he sees himself as a god capable of ruling the phenomenal world not by the bluffing of his ego but by the application of the Law of Self-mastery.

"And this is the task of science and philosophy, planning and working in unison like twin flames, forming the intellectual and spiritual vesture of the true preacher, and achieved through study, meditation and autoanalysis. The society in which you live is torn asunder by two extremes: the ultra-conservative which makes no history, and the *flower children* and Civil Rights advocates with radical tendencies who deny the evolutive process of thought and conscience, and are bent on destroying the existing social order in exchange of chaos. Some of these, perceiving the inanity of their plan, will eventually join the middle path which remains the living hub of positive progress. The people of the middle path are the architects of the Golden Age. Whatever they perceive while studying or meditating, they experiment within themselves, in silence, and without disturbing the world at large. Like new wine in old casks declared worthy of aging, their teachings are for future generations to enjoy.

"The difference between the ultra-conservative and the man of the middle path is that while the latter experiments with the world of the inner and enriches his own life with new wonders which may influence indirectly the social order, the former, like a sheep, submits unresistingly to worn out dogmas and the exploitation of political demagogues and business schemers. Like the inventor of the wheel, the domesticator of the wild horse, and the builder of the first flying machine, Gautama the Buddha, Zoroaster, Master Jesus, Copernicus, Edison and Einstein, were not in any way extremists or revolutionaries, but members of the middle path. They neither insulted nor disturbed anyone; they had only an intense yearning for self-expression; the revolutionary effects, as it were, of their findings, which began to unfold after their passing away, and which are still in the process of expansion, did not aim at the spilling of blood, like certain malcontent Civil Rights leaders, but at the demolition of worn-out institutions and anacronistic ways of living.

"Speaking of myself, and applying your terminology, my earthly mission was of the same nature of your Civil Rights movement. As a representative of the Liberated Masters, I had to preside over meetings where there were women, many of whom had, in various degrees, radical tendencies. I neither antagonized, nor went along with them, but patiently and wisely instructed them on the necessity of intelligent adaptation and compromise. 'Study nature' — I said — 'and behold the fir tree. It grows everywhere, by the seashore of the tropics and on the snowy slopes of high mountains. Through the process of compromise and adaptation it has conquered the earthsoil.' The lot of the average woman two thousand years ago seemed hopeless and beyond all trace of recovery, all the glimpses of the former Golden Age had died out in her heart. Although trembling and somehow insecure, I did not hesitate to cast the seed of freedom and respect in such a way that not a branch of the precious tree should ever wither. This I accomplished by communing every night with a most intense yearning with my Godhead and my Liberated Master-Teacher.

"Blessed friends, though often you feel to be moving amidst skepticism and spiritual bleakness, you will be pleased to know that the seekers of Light in this age of yours and in rapport to the population, are more numerous than during my time. This increase is due to scientific research and new discoveries, not to organized religion. During my time we had only Nature to marvel at, and in her name praise God. A very few of the elect knew about the harmonious relationship between the microcosmos, the body, and the macrocosmos, the universe.

338

Today, wherever you look, you feel the reality of God as exacting as the touch of a rock: labor-saving devices, rapid intercontinental transportation and communication, exploration beneath the sea, inside the earth and in space, the intelligent behavior of animals and vegetation, the living vibration of metals and precious stones, the vast knowledge concerning the wisdom of the human body, and so forth, and in the presence of any of these truths, no one could refrain from exclaiming: 'Praised be the Lord of Life!'

"More and more is science approached with the instrument of the Intangible, the Soul with the sharp bistoury of science. When the two converge, heaven and earth will meet also, and the whole world will benefit as a result. One of the main obstacles to such a realization is the bickering of theologians and mediocre philosophers, and the concept of certain economists who still hold to the erroneous doctrine that society must be made of rich and poor. The Great Society, the society of plenty in physical comfort, health, hygiene, intelligence, spiritual accomplishment, peace and brotherhood, is feasible and within the grasp of every man, woman and child. It must be accepted in the feelings first. The wealthy in spirit see life amidst death, cleanliness in filth, and virtue in depravity. My Christ-son spent many a day in the desert of the ashes, and by visualizing the impermanence of the human body, he strengthened himself for his triumph over birth and death. Today science is giving hints that even the human body might not be, after all, as impermanent as it seems. Rejoice! When, by the path of meditation, man unites himself with God, and makes a solemn promise to obey and love, everything is possible because nothing is impossible to God. Love, peace, brotherhood, wealth, science, philosophy, immortality are thoughts of God nestled in man's heart, while man himself is the supreme and visible compendium of God's power and intelligence.

"Listen, O man, listen to the Voice of Wisdom. It is there inside your throat wanting eagerly to be heard. It wants to shower thee with love and divine care. It wants to shield thee from unnecessary grieving and bewilderment. Listen to the Voice of Wisdom at every step of the way in your daily thoughts and deeds. Offer thy mind, body and will unto thy Father in the Heaven of thy heart, and you shall be graced with the tangible Presence of a Liberated Master-Teacher!"

* * *

Mary of Nazareth moved towards her Christ-son, and together they stood close to one another not as mother and son, but as Twin flame-sweethearts of the starry realms. They told Marco and Leonora to continue in their striving for spiritual illumination and commence to draw a program of inner teaching on behalf of the millions of students all over the world who seek divine guidance. "You must now return to earth"— Master Jesus concluded — "and formulate with scientific accuracy what you want me to explain to you when we meet again before the expiration of the seven weeks of intensified Christine radiation to mankind." The magnetic attraction that had held the two disciples close to the Masters began to weaken; then they were released back to earth.

Encouraged by the divine promise and assisted by the wealth of spiritual experiences enjoyed thus far, Marco and Leonora found it easy to attune themselves with the Pearl of Light in their hearts. And remembering what Mary of Nazareth had said concerning the Voice of Wisdom inside the throat "wanting eagerly to be heard", they directed their attention to their throat centers and waited. After a few days the Voice spoke:

"Labour, O man, Labour! Labour with passionate faith and undaunted will, and behold all woes retreat and vanish. Like a slow rising flood, the waters seeping everywhere, advance, O man, and leave nothing behind unconquered, for this is Knowledge. Through it you shall be relieved from thy bundle of toil, thy mind catapulted onto plateaus of superhuman power. Cogitate, obey, labour!"

Marco and Leonora meditated individually on Master Jesus' request, and on comparing notes, found the resultant to be the same: the Sermon on the Mount. Immediately they were released from their bodies and their Spirit-forms soared back to the Court of the Fountains where they found Master Jesus and Lady-Master Mary graciously awaiting them:

"I AM happy" — the Lord of Love commenced — "that you ask me to comment on my Sermon which, frankly speaking, needs to be remolded in the light of truth for the twentieth century man. In fact I want to elucidate upon it so as to serve the society of the twenty-first century. Let us call it Rules of Conduct for the Universal Man. The teaching is not original; it is a compedium of the more ancient utterances given to mankind by those who are now greater than I — Rama, Zoroaster, Gautama the Buddha, Moses, Confucius, and many other cosmic Masters and Brothers. When I said 'I did not come to destroy but to fulfill', I did not have in mind the prophecies of the Bible alone, but also all that had been taught to mankind since its spiritual re-ascendancy after its fall from the previous Golden Age. It embodies Judaism, Buddhism, Hinduism, Persia, Egypt and the constructive paganism. After all my cognomen — Christ — links me to the vast family of the Liberated Ones; those are my true and permanent brothers of the spirit, the relationship of blood being only incidental. More than being a descendant of David, I AM a descendant of Rama the Christ, Gautama the Christ, Moses the Christ, etc. Once a man is resurrected, whether a Christian or a Moslem, Negro or Eskimo, he becomes automatically our kin."

Master Jesus approached the two disciples and touched their foreheads. He pressed his left thumb on Leonora's forehead, his right on Marco's. Instantly a brilliant sphere of golden-blue light enveloped Marco, while Leonora was sealed within an orb of shivering pink fire; their outer garments changed into the Arab-Hebrew vesture of two thousand years ago, golden-green for Marco, white and pink for Leonora.

"Fear not my disciples" — Master Jesus resumed — "I have returned you to the embodiment of the ancient days, during the three years of my messianic work in Judea; at that time you were brother and sister. I have not done this arbitrarily. I read in your auras that you wanted to know whether you had ever been associated with me in previous lives. You have! The contents of my Sermon had been given to you by one of my disciples soon after we returned from the Mount: and though visitors from a foreign land, you remained in my country and followed me wherever I traveled, witnessing the drama of my person up to the culminating stage of the ascension. This knowledge will give you the needed awareness for the precise comprehension of that which follows:

❈   ❈   ❈

341

1 — *Blessed are the poor in spirit*: *for theirs is the kingdom of heaven.*

"Through the power of my direct radiation, supplemented with repeated hammering and warning my apostles understood clearly the esoteric and exoteric significance of all my teachings. In this instance, however, and due to the vital importance of the truths that I was going to proclaim, I instructed my Twelve to go on a three day meditation and inner purification prior to the utterance of my first article of this block of inner laws. Conviction had to take place by absorption in the feelings aided by a stern and uncompromising self-analysis. Severe indeed was the discipline of the spirit that I imposed upon them.

"To be poor in spirit means to possess a mind uncrammed by complicated intellectual exploits, undistracted by the splashy events of the outer world, and capable of reflecting intensely upon a truth imparted by a worthy teacher. It means also to possess the inner strength to sweep out at will and effortlessly all extraneous and mortal thought-forms nestled within. With the issuance of my first beatitude, I released my blessed apostles from all outer breadwinning tasks; for a week they disappeared — each alone — into the surrounding countryside to study and analyze the spirit of my statement, while I supplied their families with the needed food and material comfort. It took nine weeks before the full text of the Sermon reached completion.

"Not the poor, therefore, in your pecuniary significance, is worthy of the kingdom of heaven, but the deserving, the virtuous, the sincere and the spiritually determined, for such must be the attitude of those who intend to scale the Mount of Wisdom. It is a realized status of inner simplicity which means freedom from cravings, fear, insecurity, limitation, doubt and attachment to material possessions. It means again to be always ready and willing to re-examine habits and ideas inculcated by tradition, and let them go, if necessary, without the slightest feeling of loss or regret. Wealth, ethically acquired, is for selfless use, not to be hoarded or squandered.

"We, the Immortal Ones, do not condone poverty in any form, whether material, intellectual or spiritual. Penury is the result of some violation of the Law of Life which clearly compels man to make every moment of his life count. If you are economically indigent, do not boast about it, trying to convince others that

342

you are blest because you are poor, untemptable by the sort of evil under which many of the rich groan miserably. You are wasting your time and degrading your soul further. Study instead, improve your mind and work with the concept well-fixed in your consciousness that you are a member of the Cosmic Family whose riches are boundless. Study and work, wisely associated with repose, recreation, meditation and the proper care of the physical body, must be the tune of one's life. He who so applies himself overcomes all aspects of poverty, including economic want; he comes closer and ever closer to the realization of the kingdom of heaven.

2 — *Blessed are they that mourn; for they shall be comforted.*

"Mourning is weeping, and weeping is a process of inner cleansing and spiritual illumination whereby the Soul sees with irrefutable clarity the Abode of the Self, the gate wide open, ready to welcome the returning prodigal son. A true teacher must possess the inner force to induce weeping, periodically, in his neophyte-students. You Marco have this power! Like a duly accredited guru, let an élan of love and tenderness follow a deserved reproach; the student will cry and see in depth that you have made him a junior-initiate. Now he is comforted forever.

"In the life of the outer world, mourning is the result of a definite and seeming irreparable loss, be it a relative or friend, an estate, a limb, a set of ideas or a way of living. But to be comforted the bereaved must acknowledge the impermanence of earthly existence, and the action of a higher power trying to awaken him from the slumber of illusion into a more profound understanding of the Law of Life. Often a person in spite of repeated warnings, in the form of slight disappointments or minor losses, is unwilling to let go of unbecoming habits, ideas and unethical enterprises. His pride and stubbornness — the depraved traits of the mortal ego — make him more tenacious in the pursuance of nugatory aims; hence the violent and painful rupture; a flimsy world that had appeared so solidly built gone to ruin. Displaced from the main current of life the mourner retreats to a secluded spot, and there, alone, with tears streaming down his face, he weeps convulsively. Lumps of dead matter, thoughtforms and the residue of past errors are thrown off from his mind and feeling. He actually sees and smells the slimy drippings falling from his eyes, forehead and neck, and wipes them off in disgust. He now plunges his mind interiorly. What a blessing! Whereas in his previous state he would have scoffed at the pre-monition of oncoming disasters, such as disruption of family life, poor health, failing business, and waste of time and energy on worthless objectives, now in closer touch with the Self — his Father in Heaven — his mental equilibrium highly enhanced, he perceives and analyzes his past blunders and makes positive resolutions for a nobler future. This is indeed a courageous fare-well to a defective norm of life. This is Self-purification. Our mourner is approaching the silver gate of Self-understanding that leads to the Hall of Truth, in full view of the blazing kingdom of spiritual freedom. O, that he would tarry a little longer in such a blissful suspense, until the waning ego is out of sight, and the Holy Comforter appears and stands by his side forever.

3 — *Blessed are the meek: for they shall inherit the earth.*

"When I enrolled at the esoteric school of Heliopolis in Egypt, the chief hierophant, having examined my credentials from the school of Jagannath, informed me that I did not need any addi-tional teaching, for I knew all that was required for a successful leader. I answered that I wanted to go beyond mere leading. I wanted to learn how to serve and rescue the lowly and the sinful, how to feel their sorrow and temptation. I wanted to attain Christship. 'If this is your goal' — he said — 'you must pass the test of humility, that is, you must go through the trial of sincerity, justice, faith, philanthropy, heroism and love divine, and then pass through the chamber of the dead'.

"Such is humility, O my disciples, O thou universal man. I sub-mitted. Had I been satisfied with the Hierophant's alluring and encouraging remarks, my path towards supreme Self-mastery would have been barred. I had to reach the most profound depths of dispersonalization, dispassion and mind control. Like the flow-ing waters of a river saturating the surrounding soil, I had to expand my consciousness to encompass the world of man; his most hidden self I had to absorb into my world.

"And this is humility, blessed ones, that which makes one master of the world, not a beggar of man. A king went into a forest to visit a sage of great renown. He bowed before the hermit,

344

but the latter gave no heed. Then he presented him with gifts, but the sage refused them. 'Thank you' – he said – 'there is nothing that I need. The fruit of the forest feeds me, the water of the brook quenches my thirst, and the bark of the trees covers my body'. After much supplication, the king prevailed upon the man of God to visit him at his royal palace. Entering the throne room, the sage found the king kneeling before the statue of a god to solicit favours: 'Give me more children, give me more cows, give me more slaves . . .' At such a spectacle of mental deficiency and spiritual bondage, the sage went away. Whereupon the king ran after him pleading: 'Master why do you leave me?' 'Go away', the sage responded, 'I have no use of beggars!'

"This is the humility that conquers fear and rejects human power, kingly station and the lure of gold. This is the behavior of the meek who acknowledges only one Master – God – his mind attentive to the call of the Inner: 'Yes, Father' – he would say – 'I AM here, I AM ready', with his eyes downcast, his body trembling and his voice choked with emotion. For, who dares to raise his gaze, or make a move or utter an idle word, when the Effulgent and Eternal Presence of the Godhead is felt or seen. Humility is a wise surrender.

"And why and how does the meek inherit the earth? Because having surrendered the whole of himself to a power that knows no limitation, and having been guided by that power with an unfailing hand, and having seen how willing are Life and Nature to submit to a pure and selfless soul, the meek has reached the enviable stage of universal ownership; all the visible things of the invisible cosmos – physical comfort, men and living beings – rush to him for protection and use; they love such a master in whose pure and outgiving hands they feel glorified and immortalized. Master indeed is the meek; master of Light, Force and Matter.

4 – *Blessed are they who do hunger and thirst after righteousness; for they shall be filled.*

"Righteousness is a state of inner purity, a conscious awareness of being – to one's best ability and understanding – just, fair and correct in all his endeavours. There is no man on earth, no matter how degraded and, seemingly, beyond moral recovery, that does not *hunger and thirst* for purity of heart which is the foundation of clear thinking and a healthy body, while these in turn are the main pillars of personal and collective peace. Now we want to rescue such a lonely and distraught human being who, though deprived of the basic essentials of common decency, still possesses the undying urge to enter, unaided and all by himself, the path of righteousness, so as to feel proud and self-reliant from the very inception.

"Walking into a forest, he sits on a rock or under a tree and directs his attention to the creatures of the wild, or the sway of the foliage by the wind, or the murmur of a brook. Gently he lets himself become absorbed into his surroundings until he becomes an integral part of the whole. He analyzes carefully all that he sees and feels inly touched, that is, the atomic structure of his body vibrates at a rate higher than usual. This is the beginning of a spiritual awakening. Pressed now by an array of interrogatives he asks himself constantly WHY? why all this, what does it mean! Sitting on a bench in a public park, he observes people of all ages and in various attire strolling to-and-fro, each in his own individual gait, each absorbed in his own thoughts of merriment or sadness or indifference. WHY? In the marketplace he sees other lifestreams, no two alike, engaged in buying and selling, engaged in a myriad of activities. WHY? WHY? WHY?

"It is *hunger and thirst* to know the answer, and this compels him to study, to probe and to interrogate himself. He has seen mysterious forces clashing against one another, harmony and cheating, disruption and constructiveness, and has compared them with the residue of his past conduct, felt ashamed and, by an act of courage and supreme determination, rejected them entirely. Our lonely and distraught man is no longer so; he has entered the path of righteousness, and he intends to tread it, cost what it may.

"From now on, this new citizen, this disciple of righteousness, shall not live a life of disruptive passivity, nor be inharmonious with the world at large. He shall be an integral part of the striving and struggling of his fellow man. He will be careful not to formulate thoughts or issue statements that may shatter either his world or others'. He will check his own intention and motive behind actions with the severity of an uncompromising chastiser. Having tasted the living water of such spiritual aristocracy, he does not intend to pollute his inner mansion with the mephitic

346

exalations of the least unkind thought. So well entrenched in the truth or in that which never changes, such a man cannot be anything but a disciple of righteousness, a dweller of the realm of Self-knowledge. He is *filled* to overflowing with whatever is required to appraise properly and broadcast harmony and good will. He adjusts himself promptly to outer situations without yielding a farthing of his immense inner wealth; the staggering vista of his ultimate goal will never be clouded.

"Because the make-up and spiritual chemistry vary — often strikingly — with each individual, the rate of inner growth and the perception of the truth vary also. The paths of heaven are as many as there are human beings. Achievements and conduct in past embodiments are responsible for such variance. As for the final victory there is no doubt; the celestial bounty belongs to all.

"Multitudes of men and women live, in this age of yours, in a spirit of positive expectancy of things and events which they are unable to define with proper accuracy. Like true adventurers, explorers and inventors they dream, however, of the obliteration of wars, disease, crime and poverty; they dream also of gardens of Eden, eternal youth, works of art, universal brotherhood, blending of races, luxurious homes, elegance, cleanliness and smiling faces everywhere. Is not this the exact equivalence of the Second Coming of the Christ? The greater the number of people who do *hunger and thirst after* righteousness, the closer the vision, the visit and the touch of the Christ. Strive, O man, strive!

5 — *Blessed are the merciful for they shall obtain mercy.*

"Mercy is an active grace, a beatitude, endowed with a tremendous power of penetration. It conquers at a touch, rescues both the giver and the receiver, cleanses their hearts and minds, strengthens their bodies, and delivers the recipients from further error and sin.

" 'Mercy and truth preserve the king and his throne is upholden by mercy.' This is one of Solomon's thoughts of wisdom, and it means that a ruler devoted to dispassionate justice wisely blended with mercy is in no danger of being deposed, because the masses who want to be governed see in him a severe and watchful father who punishes and rewards in the name of God. By his example, the subject is compelled to reflect on the relation-

347

ship between good and evil, and derive a lesson of higher ethics for himself, his family and the society at large. This process truly ennobles and enlightens the world of man.

"With the practice of introspection, the disciple of mercy unveils the true nature of his being almost effortlessly; spiritual insight comes to him, and whatever he sees interiorly he will use it in molding his life for greater achievements. 'Be ye merciful, even as your Father which is in heaven is merciful'. This pronouncement of truth conveys the concept of tolerance first, which must lead to compassion, forgiveness and love. By forgiving those who have caused you harm, by being compassionate for their lack of discrimination, and by expressing an inner urge to help them, in a loving and detached attitude, you actually execute a process of self-purification from pride and anger, and impart to the offender a positive lesson which causes him to reshape his life from one of superficiality and irresponsibility to one of deep concern and constructive scope. You have expanded his horizon beyond the enslaving thought of color, creed and racial differentiation. And is not this true brotherhood?

"When an act of mercy is withheld, notwithstanding the persistent prompting to release it, the individual involved entangles himself in a series of cosmic violations; he condemns without sufficient evidence, reasons with a carnal and vindictive mind, and issues opinions that tend to pollute society and God, as well as himself from head to foot. The man whom he should have forgiven and restored to the status of a free being, remains in bondage. The releaser of mercy, having missed the supreme opportunity, degrades his soul for further suffering. Because society maintains a feeling of condemnation and discrimination towards a criminal who has duly paid for his crime with a prison term, such a criminal is driven to new and perhaps worse transgressions of which society itself is co-responsible.

"Why does this happen? Is mankind revengeful? No! It is because people have never studied properly the moral teachings of the Masters of the past, teachings which are reduced to a few sentences. 'Man, know thyself, thy moods, thy desires, thy cravings, thy aspirations. Meditate, analyze thyself'; and having always depended on organized religions, rather than self-interrogation, for inner guidance, they have remained ignorant of the dynamics of the Law of Cause and Effect. Ignorance has a two-fold effect on the mind and body: it stains and corrodes, hence it causes physical disease, poverty and intellectual limitation, and it leads to confusion as to what is right and wise, and what is wrong and foolish. What poor investors, what reckless squanderers are the people of earth. It takes much less energy to forgive than to condemn, to love than to hate, to cultivate peace than to wage war, to direct one's call to God directly inside the heart than to a far away saint. It is more exciting, more adventurous and truly elevating to feel an overpowering, thrilling vibration moving through the spinal column than to watch a television program made of cheating, maiming and killing. How depressing the latter, what an overwhelming torrential bliss induces the former.

"He who cares to study and reflect on my humble utterances, all by himself and without any priestly commentary, will come to know that all living beings, himself included, are made of the same substance, only differently qualified, and this qualification is self-imposed. Try, try, O man, to visualize the wondrous feeling of being an integral part of My Nature, of possessing the same spirit — which you actually possess — that I possess, and of being endowed with the same power of Self-mastery, wisdom and glory. Do, I beg of thee, try. Try to see My Living Flame in every person you meet, and work with him as if you were working with Me. Commence at once to unfold thyself by applying these celestial attributes to the people near you, thy kin, thy neighbor, thy servant and thy enemy. Train thyself to behold living sparkles walking the earth, instead of human beings, and enjoy the kingdom of heaven thereof.

"The deeds of a man of mercy are like explosions of light emanating from a mind that, having become pure and stainless, has accepted the Presence of a Higher Guide whose earthly counterpart is the Christ-light residing in his heart. Both the dispenser of mercy and the recipient will walk side by side in oneness of purpose, praising God and thanking each other for the opportunity of seeing the Law of Mercy in action.

6 — *Blessed are the pure in heart: for they shall see God.*

"Is there a definite sign that labels a man as having an impure heart? Yes, there is! It is his failure, his inability, to contact and feel the Living Pearl of Light in his heart. This Pearl of Light is the only Reality that explains and justifies man's earthly existence. The moment the Presence of that Living Pearl is accepted and truly felt, that moment man has ceased to violate the Law of God. This means that he has become a disciple of the Inner, a being of cause alone; and having merged in the universe, and having the universe merged in him, he has risen above ignorance, duality and death. This man has a pure heart.

"What are the obstructions on the path of purity? Clinging to earthly life for the sake of sense pleasure, having a feeling of indiscriminate attachment for the passing phenomena of everyday existence, doing work contrary to the law of ethics or for mere selfish motives, to do good with an eye on praise or outer acknowledgement, to be unconcerned about the downtrodden, to live aloof from constructive politics, to antagonize — even passively — international collaboration, to betray one's land of birth, to be engaged in espionage, to wallow in the mire of personal desire, vanity, greed, passion and envy, to boast a superiority complex, to display false modesty, to utter white lies or statements of slander, to judge or criticize, to gossip, to play the sycophant or overpraise the good conduct of others, to be inordinately loquacious, to be untidy in the body, clothes or home, to overeat, overplay, overwork or oversleep.

"How does one throw off these fetters born of ignorance? By conquering ignorance itself. How? Through the art of meditation, the cultivation of discrimination and the discipline of yoga. One by one the shackles of the transitory world will break asunder and disappear, and man — unburdened — will develop a keen alertness of mind and litheness of body, and will see the light which he thought never was. Then slowly and gradually the face of God begins to loom on the horizon of the heart. It is there that one *sees* God first, everywhere next. It is through becoming and sensing that one sees; and in order to be-come man must obliterate the stagnant impedimenta of the ego.

"Purity of heart is not a gift reserved only for the nuns, monks, hermits or celibate-mystics; hence it has nothing to do with avoidance of sexual intercourse. Parents bearing children are as eligible to purity of heart as saints and rishis. If sexual activity were a hindrance to purity then its effect would also be irremediably impure, and there would be no man qualified for Christhood.

Every Soul-flame in the realm of the formless must pass through the portals of the flesh to be useful to God. Therefore, to be born may not be a punishment, but it certainly is an act of obedience to a law that no one can escape. What is imperative is this: Once in the flesh man must seek God through introspection, and unaided by robed professionals. And whenever sexual intercourse is desired, it must be prepared and performed as an offering to God, visualizing ITS Presence standing close by during and after the consummation, and dedicating unto IT the incoming Christ-citizen.

"The husband and wife with pure hearts live in the proximity of blessedness, and through their children, as an offering unto God, they sublimate their souls and contribute to the purification of the heart of the world. The starry heavens must be populated with beings from below issuing from divinely mated men and women. Therefore, if it is difficult for children born from such parents to rise high in the Light, how much more difficult it must be for a Soul-flame whose law of life compels him to take embodiment irrespective of the worthiness of the parents. Hence, judge not, help and be compassionate at all times.

"To those who are pressed on every side by the sinister forces, and find it arduous to progress inwardly, to the minority groups who find themselves hemmed in by the discriminatory behavior of those who know not the law of cause and effect, and to the sons and daughters of man who seem to be always facing unyielding limitations of economic nature, I say: Do not despair, try to practice meditation, no matter how hectic or bleak your surroundings. Plunge your mind into your heart methodically, even if for one minute, and try to feel the lifting hand of the Christ-light within. All of you, my beloved ones, are under dispensation, and for every thought of self-surrender to your GodSelf, be it known that you come closer and ever closer to your earthly victory and cosmic triumph. Look your self-styled enemy straight in the eyes, with compassion and love. Plan for immortality, not for earthly limelight.

"Purity of heart — Christ purity — is a realizable must for every human being. All men are endowed in equal measure with the powers and attributes of God. It is man's duty to awaken them and fan them to blinding brilliancy through the art of meditation, the cultivation of discrimination and the discipline of yoga.

351

This is the method followed by the ancient teachers, gurus and rishis, and by Me, since the dawn of life on earth. Thus is God felt, seen and known. Once in the radiance of ITS wondrous Presence one will never err or fall again, for in that radiance the mind is made pure, all-wise and almighty forever. Practice, practice, practice; it is the surest way to see God.

7 – Blessed are the peacemakers: for they shall be called the children of God.

"A king entered a forest and found a sage seated beneath a tree. Utterly absorbed in God, tranquil in mind, it seemed that the holy man had stilled time, space and life itself. Deeply impressed, yet with an eye on vanity and pride, the ruler invited the hermit to his palace; but perceiving the selfish motive hidden in the king's heart, the sage declined the invitation.

" 'No, thank you, sir' – he said. 'I love the forest, and you are not prepared at this time to receive instruction.' The king who was accustomed to absolute obedience from his subjects, threatened him with his life. Whereupon the yogi gazed at him with compassion and love saying:

" 'My son, listen and learn: Thy threats have no power over me. I AM so well established in divine harmony, and so totally at peace with thee, and with matter and energy, that the steel of thy sword cannot pierce me, thy pyre cannot burn me, thy water cannot drown me and, truly my son, deep in thy heart you have no other desire but to love me. I AM at peace with all the forces of creation, and what are you but the sum total of these forces ready to serve only God and Life. You and I, O my king, are one in Essence and Existence, one in Knowledge and one in Bliss, under the tutelage of the same Father-God. Peace be with thee, my brother!' The king bowed in respect and left the forest.

"This is the way the peacemaker labours: humble, unconcerned, direct, detached, dispassionate, fearless. He is a living, intelligent and vibrating integer of the cosmos moving abreast with stars, constellations and solar systems in obedience to the law of absolute evolution, that is, unbroken and enduring Perfection.

"The peacemaker lives in the Eternal Now with the keen

352

awareness of him who walks on a razor edge; the past is dead and the future is a thought. Only this very instant is alive and active, like a diamond needle, impressing a mute and indifferent disc with the Harmonies of the Spheres, and the peacemaker sees to it that these harmonies are in no way marred or muffled by the faintest trace of human interference. To do this he must be able to dominate life from above, like an undefeated conqueror, like a god. Suspicion, vexation, anxiety, doubt, rebuke, injury, sorrow and temptation are not of his world. To radiate love and good will, to foster the arts of peace, and to bind hearts with hearts for the kingdom of heaven on earth, are of his world.

"The peacemaker is untouched by the acclaim of the outer world; hence he remains undisturbed by pillory, persecution, condemnation and even threat of death. He is like a beacon, much beloved by the captain of a freighter who wants to deliver his precious cargo on time, and much hated by the smuggler; but in either case the beacon remains unconcerned, devoted only to the task assigned to it by the science of navigation. How does a peacemaker reach such a noble state of living and dynamic stillness fit only for the gods? In meditation he saw the various forces of the ego warring against each other. He called them to a conference and therein he saw what a miserable lot they were: spineless, noisy and full of bluff. Shame overtook him, and divine pride followed; and since life admires the daring, an iron fist was released unto him, and with a mighty blow he crushed and scattered the contemptible heap of troublemakers. And having achieved enduring peace within, he was promoted a Christ, a child of God.

8 — *Blessed are they which are persecuted for righteousness'*
   sake: for theirs is the kingdom of heaven.

"This beatitude brings before man's mind the existence of the so well known forces of good and evil, creation and destruction, evolution and involution. Where the forces of involution are rampant, the life of the upholder of law and order is beset with difficulty and often endangered. A messenger of righteousness is easily detected. He is like a city set on a hill; he is like a lighted candle in a room at night, and when the prowler enters, the first thing he does is to knock the light off, so that he may ransack

as he pleases. Because of man's fall from the edenic consciousness, this bewildering conflict of forces must be expected, hence
the need to be alert each moment of the day. Were he to watch
a television program with an episode of violence, whether taken
from *real* life or not, he must create within himself an upsurge
of compassion for the villainous dramatis personae: actor, writer,
director, producer and sponsor. These are in themselves tools of
involution that insinuate the very marrow of life; they persecute
true evolution. Under the aegis of name, fame and monetary return, cleverly blended with the term *educational*, they declare
that their aim is to show that crime does not pay. What a pity,
what hypocrisy! The truth is instead that as long as these arid
and spiritually depleted intellectuals exist, unable to search nature for totally constructive inspirations, the upholder of good
is inwardly persecuted, and the energy that he would have spent
spreading the gospel of righteousness, must be used for self-
defense. Thus is evolution hindered, and the realization of the
kingdom of heaven delayed.

"During my earthly life, a messenger of light who had been
entrusted with a messianic task, had to have an exceptionally
healthy body and a mental stamina of great magnitude for, often,
at the end of his day's labour, he was unable to find shelter or
purchase a meal. The local priest who, the previous day, had
felt humiliated by the disciple's wisdom, had seen to it that none
of his flock would give physical assistance to the wandering
teacher. For the sake of truth, he had to be a master in the art
of disputation.

"Proceeding further with my teaching, I said unto my disciples:
*Swear not at all, neither by heaven for it is God's Throne, nor
by earth, for it is His footstool; neither by the power of the invisible Temple, for it is an emanation of the Will of God. Neither
shalt thou swear by thy head, because thou canst not make one
hair black or white. But let your communication be: yea, yea,
nay, nay: for whatsoever is more than this comes to evil.*

"Swearing is an act of self-binding, either to the will of a man
or to a doctrine. It makes man a slave. Because of this ingrained
and universally spread tendency of swearing, I want to be very
emphatic regarding the spiritual danger involved in taking oaths
and pledges. A man who, in a moment of uncalled for enthusiasm, underwrites and solemnly promises to adhere to certain

354

laws and rules of conduct issued by a political party, a religious order or an ethical society, may bind his life for many embodiments to come, and thus enslave his conscience that was created to be the carrier of, and to express only, the eternal truth. There is not one thing upon the earth to which man may claim ownership: not a hair of his head belongs to him. By what authorization does he then swear for this or that? Be free, O man, free in the cosmic significance. Seek the comfort, the protection and the Truth by the path of thy heart; for this is the only tested method that makes thee wise and fearless. However, should one find oneself in a situation where an answer is imperative, then the art of lip compromise is the best way out. Say that you want to study and analyze the facts. Take time. And should you decide to accept their program or adhere to their tenets, swear not at all, but make clear that you intend to follow the day by day prompting of your conscience; respect and admiration for your stand is the reward.

> 9 — *Blessed are ye when men shall revile you and persecute you, and shall say all manner of evil against you falsely for my sake. Rejoice and be exceedingly glad: for greater is your reward in heaven: for so persecuted they the prophets which were before you.*

"As you see this article of the rules of conduct was solely directed to my disciples, the Twelve, not to the people at large. And because they were worthy and inly prepared to teach, I compared them to the prophets of the past. And prophets they were indeed, the largest number ever produced at one time by any school of that age. The words *my sake* were not meant to refer to me personally but to the Divine Office as a Christ. I should have said *for the sake of the Truth which is invested upon me as a Christ.* Truths had been given to other Christs before me, and were and will be given to others after me. Truths had been given to Gautama Siddhartha the Christ, Moses the Christ, Maravira the Christ, Zarathustra of Persia, Lao-Tze and Confucius, Jeremiah and the Second Isaiah, Pythagoras and other pre-Socratic philosophers in Greece, who were persecuted and reviled in one way or another with their disciples. All these were immortal Christs of my class, and in their teachings there is no hint that they wanted to be elevated to the rank of deities; yet people light candles and kneel before some of them, including myself. And this is one of the major obstacles on the path of the kingdom of heaven. O that the Western World would have accepted me as a philosopher-Christ, and expounded my teaching in classrooms and theaters instead of churches.

"There is no reward in heaven for beggars, pilgrims, implorers of saints and Sunday churchgoers, for heaven is a state of inner poise. It is the satisfaction of possessing an expanded spiritual horizon, and of knowing precisely how to evaluate outer events that lead to the understanding of the cause behind the effect. It is a continual striving for self-overcoming and Self-mergence, and a dispassionate attitude towards good and evil. It is forgiving and forgetting through an inward identification of both friend and foe. It is to feel the dismay and bewilderment of the sufferer above and beyond the confines of color, race and creed. The reward in heaven is the universalization of the soul, and more.

*　*　*

"We have said again and again: *blessed, blessed, blessed* . . . What does this word signify? A sad face perhaps, or a horrified attitude towards an unavoidable war, or a display of disdain at the sight of a prostitute, or a recoil from action, or a tour of the churches of the town, making the sign of the cross upon oneself and reciting *mea culpa, mea culpa, mea culpa . . .?* No, indeed! *Blessed* means worthy , fortunate, candidate to gracehood. A man needs only one glimpse of the Reality to find or be contacted by a Liberated Master or by Me. Then accept guidance and obey thereof. He will achieve this state of grace with or without the knowledge of my Sermon on the Mount, with or without a college education, whether rich or pauper, white or Negro, in a palace or in a slum. Hungry or well-fed, working for a king or in the sewers, clothed in silk or in rags, it matters not; the path of the inner is within everybody's reach, and it costs nothing.

"With this initial contact, a treasure house opens wide its doors, revealing an immense wealth for ready use: a wealth of courage, ideas, intelligence, physical endurance, desire to do and to dare. A delightful and bewitching smile that infects

356

everybody sets on the countenance of our resurrected man. He is on the go as if propelled by a mysterious force, and wherever he goes, he leaves behind a radiance of mirth, orderliness and good will; and if he has to deliver punishment he charges it with love and a vibration of redemption. The awareness of being an instrument of God makes him as keen in circumspection and discrimination as a prophet, as happy and carefree as a healthy and well-tended child. No thought of the morrow will ever becloud or unduly brighten his mind, for he stands on the rock of evenness wherefrom he dominates life. And if you think of him as a visionary, avulsed from everyday occurrences, you are misjudging. Well-rooted in him is the sense of truth and its deviations in the outer life, and this means that he possesses a more profound sensitivity in the evaluation of practical things. He sees with unfettered mind the savage conflict between evolution and involution, good and evil, the force that elevates and the nagging drag of ignorance, and into the fray he plunges, with undeviated determination to bring harmony and restore peace between the warring powers. And he does all this with true dispassion, hating none, grieving not for those who must perish, redeeming the sinner, mindful of justice, and unafraid for himself and his life. Truly he shall not fail.

"This is the credo of the master-man in the making, the yielding in spirit, the merciful, the humble, the peacemaker, the pure in heart, and the upholder of righteousness. It is the philosophy of life of the resurrected man who has adorned his brow with the resplendent jewel of divine awareness in thought and action, at rest and repose, while asleep and while awake. Indeed, he is a Christ, and the infinity of life stretches before him!"

* * *

With the closing of the commentary on the Rules of Conduct for the Universal Man, Master Jesus and Lady Master Mary, smiling at each other with the mystical intensity of the true lovers of God, merged into one and disappeared. Out of mercy they had lowered their vibration and made themselves visible to two humble and believing disciples who had yearned with abiding and passionate faith for this jewelled occasion. With the departure of the Masters, Marco and Leonora fell on their

357

knees in rapture and gratitude. Unsupported by the radiance of the immortal Ones, they slowly descended to earth; it seemed rather as if the earth itself had been raised whereto the celestial Court of the Fountains had stood, drawn by the dynamic faith of the two wandering lifestreams. For seven days they lived in a state of pristine harmony and confineless majesty of starry visions, practicing thought transference that would lead also to the fusion of their bodies into one. Invested by brilliant shafts of unconsuming fire in the colors of gold, green and pink, they were tossed in space and shaken violently over and again. As this cleansing process terminated, they were given the taste of mergence in immortality, but only for a flash of time. At the beginning of the eighth day, they again heard the Master's voice of love, instruction and warning:

"You are treading the razor edge flanked, in equal number and strength, with the forces of righteousness and the powers that want to violate the noble law of divine living. It is the latter's most important task to prey upon people of your spiritual attainment. They love to disrupt, although temporarily, the flow of harmony and peace directed by the Liberated Masters to the disciples of Light in the world. They love to misguide, deceive and cause sudden confusion in the rank and file of the striving students on the path of Deliverance."

Due to a feeling of false self-assurance, they failed to heed Master Jesus' warning. Thus, unconsciously, they weakened their spiritual link with Him and a few days later, at the hour of meditation, instead of Master Jesus, they faced unwelcome and unwanted visitors. Leonora saw a tall, handsome male, well-groomed and with magnetic brown eyes. Marco saw a comely female in gipsy attire, with flaming black eyes and long flowing ebony hair. They were disarmingly suave and prudent, and quite persuasive for the unwary.

"Friends" — they said — "why do you subject yourselves to so many hardships. There is no need of discipline to memorize a few wise statements to impress the crowd or even the so-called intellectuals. Just look around, friends, look around. Here an accomplished financier delivers a ponderous lecture on the wisdom of inflation as a cure for deep-rooted economic ills; there an illustrious political leader crusades on national austerity and higher taxes as a means of fiscal solvency and balance of trade, and both find audiences ready to applaud. The most important factor that elevates a candidate for public office to the desired goal is not knowledge, wisdom and ethical background, but the amount of money spent during the campaign. 'After all' — say the thoughtless crowd and the slothful intellectual — 'anyone who spends millions of dollars to be elected, deserves the job, irrespective of all else'. Your politicians of today are not any higher on the ladder of moral behavior than the peddler of last century who sold sugared water as a cure-all. And look at your drug manufacturers, food processors, makers of household devices, and all dealers thereof . . . If there were not a few conscientious inspectors and a handful of public-spirited citizens to check on their multitudinous forms of greed and cheating, your nation would be in a state of jungle. And observe the three major television networks. Every morning, after a prayer of words delivered by the local minister, priest or rabbi, channels throughout the land open their activity by declaring solemnly to adhere to the Code of Ethics of the National Association of Broadcasters, and then allow cigarettes to be advertised, a food item depleted of almost all nutritional value proclaimed to be good for you in a dozen ways, soft drinks glamourized to the sky for the purpose of binding the youth. Everything must be presented as superlatively excellent, and advertisement sees to it that the ten per cent of truth is raised to ninety. As a result, in this society of yours global exaggeration is a modus vivendi.

"Friends, we take pity on you. Don't be eccentrics, fools and dreamers; follow the mob and be like everybody else, that is, clay in our hands. Thinking of the overlife? What a nonsense. Leave that business to the priests. He is the master-mind of Madison Avenue. A Mass, a Paternoster, a sprinkling of holy water, a Jesus Christ meek and obedient to his call, and unkind karma is no more.

"In the field of the spirit the vast majority of mankind ceases to grow beyond the age of seven. Cultured people and successful industrialists go to church every Sunday to swallow worthless stuff about salvation, the crucifixion of Jesus Christ, and God. When turmoil and fear hold sway, nobody thinks of self-analyzation and meditation; a trip abroad or a pilgrimage to a famous sanctuary, duly approved by the church authority,

359

are deemed sufficient to assuage the thirsting soul. Interiorization? It is a waste of time. Men are not children of God; they
are restless apes, thoughtless, superficial and dangerous. I work
with the mediocre churchman and make him greedy, the shrewd
politician and make him a liar, the warmonger and make him
bloodthirsty, the misleaders in the field of science and the arts,
industry and commerce, and make them money hungry, and
those who consciously withhold the truth from the people
for pecuniary reasons; all these I direct and sway as I please.
This is my empire, my friends, a very tangible one for the
earthbound people. Come with me, leave behind the things
of the spirit, join the common lot and gather the results thereof
in name, fame and material wealth. I assure you, you will do
well. . . ."

Thus spoke the tempters and belittlers; then they merged
into one, half male and the other half female. They were ugly
and repellent now, and stood watching, tense and worried, yet
hoping that Marco and Leonora would yield. But as their
minds were again re-anchored to the incorruptible heritage of
the Spirit every thought of positive adherence to the way of
light caused the tempter to be jolted by terrific shocks, the size
of its body began to shrink until it was reduced to the size
of a pitiful and scrawny pigmy, finally it disappeared. The
tested disciples now took inventory of their spiritual wealth
and found how much better equipped they were to withstand
the allurement of the world. They thought of the great teachers
of the past, the spiritual seekers, who were ridiculed, censured
and persecuted unto death by the so-called custodians of
religious orthodoxy and moral code. Their antagonistic behavior
and seeming defeat became, eventually, their vindication, and
paved the way for higher truths that would lead to the One
Supreme Master-Truth. Thus, recharged with greater determination, they turned inward for deeper search. The tempter
returned boldly and defyingly, pressing at their heels and
obstructing the way. And what is the way? A more critical
analyzation of thoughts, desires and planning, a more severe
study in evaluating the far-off consequences of today's thoughts
and deeds. That is all! No prayer and no supplication to any
hypothetical deity. The Living Presence of the Master of Nazareth then appeared:

"Peace unto thee" — he said to the tempter whose countenance had turned ashen with terror. "Peace, love and illumination unto thee, unhappy child of the nether world. That you might be receptive to Truth and Virtue, and thus bring to a close this unwanted mission of yours. I know thee well Satan of ancient, thy suavity and persistence could do you honor if they were qualified with noble intent. Now begone and do penance thereof, for thy merchandise shall find no market here. These two disciples have a quasi-Christ consciousness, and many a man will they rescue from thy dominion. Of this we do assure you. And when mind, intellect and heart will unite for a one-pointed thought, plan and goal, then anything contrary to love, truth, peace and beauty shall scatter, be dispersed and disappear. And this includes you. As for now, my blessed brother of deviated consciousness, know that no one but a Liberated Master has any power to test a disciple of Light!"

* * *

Now that by an act of grace the tempter was no more, Marco and Leonora turned their gaze towards the blazing luminance of Master Jesus. Their Spirit-forms left the earth and passing through the stratosphere, proceeded northwestward until they reached the etheric counterpart of the Stikine Mountains, a lofty range of the Rockies, north of British Columbia. They alighted on the shore of a forest-bosomed lake whose shimmering waters issued from a cave of liquid light in the depths of a snow-crowned mountain. The gentle sloping terrain towards the lake was covered with unusual and charming habitations in the architectural styles of every land and civilization of earth. Some of the dwellings were enveloped in a tropical atmosphere with the corresponding vegetation surrounding them, while others beshowed the severe and rigid environment of high mountain life. Master Jesus acting as a guide explained:

"This earth of yours is intended to be inhabited from pole to pole, and from the beds of oceans, lakes and rivers to snowy peaks, without marring in the slightest the asymmetric beauty of nature. From barren sands, hard rock and stony plateaus food will be produced in abundance for every human being, bird and animal. Cemeteries must disappear; and those who antagonize the divine Will or turn their energy to destructive aims, will be crushed by the immediate recoil of their own thoughts.

"Behold, my disciples: faces of every race and garments of every nation and age, are assembled here in this starry land that dominates the continents of the Americas, the cradle of liberty for the people of earth. I say the cradle, not the vast and wide field. Thus liberty is in the making, notwithstanding the seeming signs to the contrary, and it shall come to fruition on time, exactly as it appears on the cosmic blueprint. The Cosmic Assembly of the Perfect Ones has begun to recruit Liberated Masters possessing certain traits that would blend with India, China, Japan, the New Australia, North, Central and South America, Russia, Europe, Near East — the Hebrews and Arabs — Africa, the Eskimos and the American Indians, and send them here with the precise mandate to make concerted action to influence the hearts and minds of the people of Earth towards a beginning of understanding that will lead to tolerance and liberty. They will work alongside of the other Masters, Splendor-beings and Cosmic-Governors mentioned previously. Special attention will be devoted to minority groups, the economically indigent, the politically oppressed, and those who feel to have been wronged in the field of Civil Rights. Each Master will teach and counsel people of the land of his last embodiment, his own people, as it were, so as to create a quicker response through pride and emulation. A term of fifty years has been given to them to complete their task; and those who accept and live up to their message will first be appointed assistants and eventually raised to the status of their Masters'!"

By the attentiveness with which Marco and Leonora listened, Master Jesus was convinced to have found two disciples whose behavior was similar to the chelas of ancient, humble, egoless, eager to learn and obey, and ready to serve. This is a turbulent age, they thought, an age of exaggerated assertiveness, and unwanted and undisciplined individualism. Somebody has to yield, yes, yield even unto death in order to break the social tension and show the way. There is a dire need of reassessment of the political structure of the nations of Earth, both in the democratic countries and the communistic ones. But how fast and to what extent without shedding blood and the risk of involution? Men are required by the cosmic plan of the incoming Golden Age to think and act in a way that is positive and constructive at all times and without the slightest deviation. And this thinking and doing must be blended with love. Thoughts and actions nursed with love are the great solvent of social inharmony. They remembered Paul of Tarsus who, by direct instructions from Master Jesus, had taught the masses, with sternness and love, the need of self-discipline as a basic preparation for the acceptance of the New Verbum that had superseded the old teaching without antagonizing the existing social order. They were convinced now, more than ever, that salvation is not a prerogative of churches and sects, that heroism is not associated with physical courage, or stolid indifference at the sight of the rack, and that true patriotism consists in defending the rights of man, irrespective of race, color and creed.

The task of Marco and Leonora in this field was now becoming more precise; instructions and explanations to be given with the clarity that is based in equal measure on knowledge and love. Knowledge implies inner discipline, study and observation. Love is the cultivation of selflessness the binding of their hearts to the hearts of their fellow men and together, to God. Master Jesus who was standing by invisibly now spoke:

"Yes, selflessness! This is the opposite of personality, the number one villain on the path of spiritual ascendancy. Its aim is to kill all God's attributes nestled in the heart of man. It blinds and causes one to change from a giver to a grabber, from a master to a slave, and from an immortal being to a mortal nonentity. Yet, in spite of its powerful dominance, this personality will flee miserably at the first attempt of man's turning towards self-mastery. As the personality dies, the divine traits, which had been forced to inaction, rise again to dominate life for unlimited self-expression in every field of endeavour. *This is individuality!*

"Individuality is a divine reward, a means whereby man is distinguished from the rest of the world, nay from the rest of the living entities of the universe. It is therefore a trait of the free soul who has rejected regimentation of every form and shade. It is a unique, constructive and impersonal way of approaching man, society, politics and religion; a way that gives rise to admiration, envy and even hatred in the hearts of those who from generation to generation and from embodiment to embodiment have bent their will and conscience to exploiters and enslavers. The man of individuality is unafraid, open-minded and straightforward, seeking no approbation for his deeds, and showing indifference to either praise or pillory coming forth from anyone, rich or poor, weak or mighty, intellectually brilliant or fool. He is however inly disturbed when, for the sake of truth, he is forced to attack tradition, tenets, rules of conduct, and all that appears sacred to the common lot. And this inward distress is generated by the obtuseness of his contemporaries who are unable or unwilling to see the new light of truth. This is the source of sorrow of a true teacher. Moses, Gautama the Buddha, Pythagoras, Meng-ste, Matheno, Zarathustra, Confucius, Socrates and Myself were, in this respect, men of sorrow.

"The man of individuality has a way of defining things that is scandalous to the unthinking crowd and its leaders. In the average person, for instance, the concept of 'neighbor' is very restricted; so restricted, in fact, that it very seldom goes beyond the postal zone. To the seeming eccentric and anomalous human being— the man of individuality, the one who treads the steep road of the high search — a neighbor may be the one next door or the one who lives at the antipodes. He loves both with equal feeling and helps either one in a spirit of utter dispassion, no matter what the color of their skin, their creed or political affiliation. He is also a person who looks benevolently at a man who lives in the straight jacket of prejudice, superstition and hatred, fully convinced that sooner or later the Light of Knowledge will burst forth from the mind of that bound soul to shatter all man-made impediments.

"Individuality, therefore, has nothing to do with showing off, intellectual stunts, outward anomalies, gestures, pseudo-originality and similar clatter. It implies detachment from the sacred lore of orthodoxy, indifference for the social musts, self-analyzation in order to find fresher and livelier ways for self-expression, silence amidst inordinate babbling, a spirit of independence devoid of antagonism, humility where pride and vanity rise high, initiative where dead routine is long estab-

364

lished, and, above all, awareness of being an instrument of a higher power. This is individuality and selflessness made one.

"The disciple who has thus achieved such an enviable state of consciousness, no longer follows a fixed method of meditation; he creates his own, fitting it to his own temperament. He approaches God and the Liberated Masters in a way that, although in compliance with the Eternal Law, it, nevertheless, contradicts all the methods followed by the teachers and disciples of the past. He discards the orthodox way of praying and constructs his own according to requirements, time and circumstances.

"I suggest to thee, my disciple-reader, to commence at once to cultivate your own individuality. Cease to be a sheep of this or that sectarian fold; be a shepherd instead. Here is the staff, the power of the will made invincible through study and discipline; go and gather into one fold the sheep-body, the sheep-mind, the sheep-senses, cravings, idiosyncrasies, lassitude and menial aspirations that at present run wild and uncontrolled. Expand your conscience, stretch your spiritual outlook, give new food to your intellect. Discipline yourself more severely by arising above all shades of compromise. Sever for awhile all affiliations with your church, synagogue, political party or libertarian conventicle. Enter solitude and silence. Analyze, dissect, invade new territories; then re-gather and re-build. Love new adventures, and know that in the field of the Spirit they are infinite in number, exciting and challenging beyond all imagining. Be a celestial athlete qualified for the Cosmic Olympics.

* * *

"The first thing that you will learn on the path of tolerance and love, is the fact that true Buddhism, Hinduism, Zoroastrianism and Islamism are comparable with true Christianity, and that there is no necessity for the Western World to preach my teaching to the Eastern minds. Likewise, to speak of Buddhism in the West as a militant doctrine is also unwise. Why? Because as Master Gautama the Buddha is one of the spiritual leaders of the East exclusively, I AM, also exclusively, one of the spiritual leaders of the West. I did not take embodiment in Judea by accident; I was commanded to do so by the Cosmic Assembly of the Perfect Ones. The purity of the Oriental

365

Teachings, because of the worldly-minded and corrupt priesthood, had so degenerated that it could not be disseminated in the West. The people of the Western World having reached spiritual maturity, could not be entrusted to an already debased philosophy of life; hence, My appearance. However, no European or Christian can truly understand, live and apply my teaching without a thorough knowledge of Buddhism, the Vedanta and the Upanishads. Inly Gautama Siddhartha, Krishna and Myself, belong to the same cosmic hierarchy, although Krishna, as you shall learn later, is slated for higher duties.

"Three great Lady-masters, working under my supervision, are in charge of the application of the Law of Love on Earth: Mother Kali for the Hindus, Quan Yin for the Buddhists, and Mary of Nazareth for the rest of the world.

"Now hear and learn: every time a European, or either a non-Hindu or a non-Budhist — no matter what his creed or the color of his skin — attunes himself with either Quan Yin or Mother Kali, the energy of that attunement is automatically transferred to Mary of Nazareth. She takes that energy and uses it in behalf of the one making the call. Similarly, all energy directed to Lady-master Mary by either a member of the Buddhist or Hindu World is transferred to Quan Yin or Mother Kali. This shows the inutility of all missionary work tending to gain adherents in other lands where one of the three major religions is predominant. It shows also the cosmic oneness of Europe, Africa and the Americas. How childish is, therefore, the attitude of certain Christian leaders who extol the virtues of one master at the expense of another. We do not approve the militant activity of Christian churches in the Buddhist or Hindu World, except where economic or sanitary assistance is involved, considering that the Western World is so well-advanced in this field.

"There is another important reason for our rejection of this militant policy of the Christian Church, and it is this: the Cosmic Assembly of the Perfect Ones does not want humanity to be dominated by one religion, for it tends, sooner or later, to those unspeakable abuses of theocratic rule already registered in the history of mankind. Today you have five major spiritual philosophies, namely, Hinduism, Buddhism, Judaism,

Christianity and Islamism; but in the future there shall be as many philosophies as there are human beings, each garbed to the need of the cosmically free individual whose clear vision reflects in its entirety the Law of Divine Harmony. On that day all organized religions shall cease to exist, for humanity will have reached spiritual adultship, each man his own shepherd, his own Master, his own Christ.

"Through the comparative study of the various religions, the now freer individual comes to the conclusion that each man is a potential sun, with its own magnetic field of action. As no two solar systems or even two stars, are the same in radiance and rate of vibration, likewise no two men can equally share the same religious doctrine and, at the same time, render justice to the law of their being. The disciple will learn also that if the billions of cells of the human organism would behave as man behaves — as a member of the society — there would be no human body at all. The cell, through the impersonal use of its God-given intelligence, is able to renew itself, while man, having submitted to the mortal mind and abandoned the Buddhi, can only create physical and social decay, sorrow, and many a death for himself.

"How did this happen? It happened the moment man allowed another man to rule his conscience. *It happened when man ceased to meditate,* to contact directly the source of life, and relied instead on what another man told him concerning his soul, his self. At that moment both his spiritual and physical decay began, fear penetrated into his heart, and the seed of enmity for his fellow man was cast therein. What a chain reaction of degenerative events. The power of will shifted from the eternal to the ephemeral, man became intoxicated, entranced and held spellbound by an array of menial desires. Then his intelligence, no longer functioning under the inspiration of the Buddhi, caused the eternal values to be reversed: ignorance, poverty, disease, hatred, war, class distinction, vengeance and death itself were accepted as normal constituents of life against which there was no power. Now to bow before a man in priestly robes was considered noble and in tune with the Divine Law. Thus man forfeited his birthright of indisputable supremacy over nature and life, and accepted the role of slave and the lot of death. The Ancient Acquaintance, the Supreme

Companion and Advisor, the Fountainhead of Intelligence and Wisdom, the Very Self residing in the heart of every man, became a total stranger, almost unknown, nonexistent. Yet it is an absolute necessity that this Supreme Being be retraced by the path of meditation. There is no other way.

"When the Ancient Friend and Father is felt and found again, man resumes his true and eternal role for which he was created: to achieve Christship or near-identification with God. This is the inner work of the prodigal son on his returning path towards the Father's House.

"Blessed disciple-reader, these instructions are meant to penetrate deep into your heart. I love you! If you want to conquer sorrow, defilement and ignorance, follow them. Feel the radiance which I have placed around thee as a protection against doubting. Make thyself acquainted with that strange *something* within thy heart, for that is the call issuing from thy Father's House, the call of forgiveness and love, the messenger of peace and wisdom, the carrier of supply and comfort. Accept this avalanche of blessings by the path of meditation. Still thy mind and, while doing so, visualize a pillar of fire inside thy spinal chord moving towards the head. See the fire being transformed into liquid light, interpenetrating thy atomic structure, giving thee strength, mental alertness and true awareness of thy inner forces. I love thee."

As Master Jesus brought his instruction to a close, his Body of Light began to dim and gradually disappeared. Marco and Leonora stood there, still and grateful. Then a thousand-faceted diamond appeared at the base of their spinal columns where the *Lotus of the Kundalini* resides. As in a true yogin and by the power of an undeflected visualization, the diamond rose through the hollow conduit of the spinal column towards the head. It projected warm beams of light in the colors of violet, indigo, green, yellow, blue, orange and red, and, like a king mindful of his subjects, visited its domain — the various organs and centers of activity of the human body, whose proper function forestalls inharmony and decay. And wherever it went, it left behind precious gifts. Without diminishing in size and degree of brilliancy, it gave of itself to the genital organs. "You have been obedient to the Law of Life and Eternal Youth, my children" — it said. "Here is more light!"

Then it touched the solar plexus: "Here is more light for you, my son. Use it to strengthen the wall of protection against further incursion of the enemy: doubt, fear and negativity." Into the Hall of Love in the heart, it then entered, and was greeted by the Master seated therein as the ancient Torch-bearer of the world whose resplendence shall raise the earth — body — from the status of a dark planet — transient and mortal — to that of a star of first magnitude, that is, immortality. The living diamond then ascended towards the throat and bequeathed unto it a greater power of eloquence to be used exclusively for the defense of Truth. It then ascended towards the head . . . How did Marco and Leonora feel at this point? They cannot say; we cannot say. The experience cannot be framed in words. Let every man find it out for himself.

Holding their attention on the Living Diamond within, they now levitated themselves towards a towering mountain, on the etheric counterpart of the continent of Lemuria. On its densely timbered slope, they came to a very ancient temple-abode. Twenty-one giant fir trees flanked a sacred path leading to the rock-hewn temple. Guarding the entrance gate of intricately wrought white metal, were two angelic beings with gossamer wings of azure fire; as Marco and Leonora approached, they bowed and let them pass.

Entering the main hall of the cylindrically shaped temple, they found it to be mammoth, having a diameter of over three thousand feet. It was called the Circular Hall of a Thousand pillars of Fire. The dome - ceiling was massive and majestic, and it had, seemingly, no visible support, for it was suspended about ten feet above the annular wall, letting beams of sunlight enter continuously without casting a shadow. The floor of highly polished fossil mahogany, showed an irregular grain filled with highly vibrating emerald-green light. Carved in the circular granite wall of olive-green, were one thousand spacious alcoves paneled in laminated gold, and within each alcove was a suspended sphere of fire, three feet in diameter. Two spheres of fire, each forty-nine feet in diameter, floated in midair at the center of the hall, one above the other. A tiny sphere of fire, with a pink radiance, about seven inches in diameter, was seen moving from alcove to alcove, touching the spheres therein, producing a soft bell-like sonorous vibration. Desiring an explanation, Marco and Leonora directed their attention to the Akasha and, lo, the voice of Master Jesus was heard:

"This masterpiece of indestructible architecture came into being long, long ago at the apex of the Lemurian civilization. It was a temple of silence and meditation for the advanced disciples of earth — philosophers, scientists, statesmen — who wanted to contact in full the Creative Intelligence while still in the physical body, and convey the experience to their own people.

"Each sphere of fire represents a disciple who achieved liberation. The first disciple, whose sphere is the most brilliant, occupied, during his meditation, the alcove opposite the entrance gate. At the time of his ascension, he brought into visible form the two spheres of fire suspended at the center of the hall, symbolizing the eternal and unbreakable link between man and God. The fact that these two spheres are suspended from nowhere signifies that when man truly relies on God, he need not worry about human support or approbation. It tells also how illimitable could be man's achievements when he dedicates himself wholeheartedly to constructive endeavours devoid of pecuniary aims.

"The first Lemurian disciple dwelt here, in his physical structure one thousand years, in constant renunciation and austerity, yet with his mind on the world as a genuine expression of God. He drew artistic, mathematical and philosophical truths from the vast reservoir of creation and, in a spirit of love and altruism, conveyed them on beams of light, to his receptive disciples in the outer world, who were engaged in fostering the law of evolution in every field of endeavour. He was, as you see, very active in spite of his apparent renunciation and withdrawal from the world. Completely absorbed in the thought of immortality, and immersed, as he was, in such altruistic pursuances, he gradually ceased to breathe and rose above all the contingencies of the physical life (food, biochemical changes, etc.) and, consequently, maintained eternal youth.

"This episode conveys to you another truth, namely, that beings of My spiritual stature had walked the earth before Me; I was cognizant of their existence and deeds before I took embodiment.

"The cylindrical shape of the temple symbolizes human

perfection attainable on earth, but impossible to hold, unless it is overshadowed by the dimensionless thought of God, represented by the semispherical dome and the foundation beneath the floor of the same contour. Only one thousand perseverant and stronghearted disciples were able to pass the test in that long span of time, until the day of the sinking of the continent. This temple is a veritable jewel of light, fruit of the highest intellectual knowledge wedded to humility. It was not carved with physical tools, but by the projected thoughts and visualization of the many adepts, in harmony with the original ideas of the first disciple.

"Now observe the little sphere of pink fire, bouncing from alcove to alcove and striking a musical note with each touch of the spheres. That is you, Leonora. At that time — 250,000 years ago — your name was Sile; you were an eager seeker of light, soliciting the company of those who were well-advanced on the path of the Inner. For twenty-five thousand years, you took embodiment in this land, close to this temple, reached the age of seven and departed; then returned after one hundred years or so, for another seven years of earthly life, and often you found a few of the meditative disciples whom you had left a hundred years earlier. Thus, being taught by these blessed ones, you grew inwardly. It was here that you learned the many different patterns of arousing the inner light in order to contact God. The disciples themselves continued to change their methods of application also, and even their prayers to God, whose answers were never the same, although related to the same subject. God never speaks the same word twice, nor does He give a standard method of communication with Him. Freedom of Self-expression is absolute."

From the ancient Temple of Meditation, Marco and Leonora levitated themselves again to the Court of the Fountains. Silently they called to Master Jesus, and sought His Christ Radiance in their hearts. As the element of time disappeared from their consciousness the Master appeared, and resumed his instructions:

"A spiritual leader is a teacher who has added love and humility to his academic degree. When these three elements are wedded in the same person, spiritual leadership becomes more organic and effective, and, I might say, more reliable.

With the severe discipline of the classroom, the compulsory requirements of moral conduct, the daily routine which does not permit a let down, and the grinding of the mind under ther heavy blows of mathematics and the study of ancient dead tongues, the emotional world of the student is brought to a standstill. Then by adding the practice of meditation, the mind is subjugated and the despotism of the senses obliterated in a manner that is acceptable, pleasant and healthful. The individual then does not have to contend with repressed emotions, because the entire process is based on and accomplished through science. This is what makes spiritual leadership organic, effective and trustworthy. It is the typical Pythagorean method of attaining Self-mastery.

"Now what happens to a person of such moral and intellectual stature? Simply this: he unfolds automatically into the Fourth Dimension — the threshold of Direct Perception — and therein he is contacted by a Liberated Master for an assignment of universal import in the field of the arts, science and international ethics. It is thus that a true artist, a true scientist or a true philosopher becomes a spiritual leader, more so than a person who embraces religion as a career.

"The priest is the guardian of the moral code. To him ethics are a trade, a profession, and as such resented at times. Away from the church, his priestly robe is an obstacle to self-expression which forces him into a world of fantasy and make believe, even hypocrisy. How often does such a priest curse the role that he plays; born in freedom, he is now most hopelessly regimented. By contrast, the artist, philosopher or scientist accepts and applies the rule of ethics with the absolute freedom that comes from an inner urge. To him meditation is not an article of monastic discipline, but the expression of a superior will, an overpowering desire to surrender himself to God for greater knowledge and spiritual refinement. These are the tools that impel the mind to enter uncharted fields in the realm of science, philosophical truth and the arts.

"When a priest devotes himself to his trade with the proviso of glorifying the Church, he writes books on theology which are, at their best, a jumble of half truths and sheer nonsense whose practical results, however, are to cow the simple-minded faithful into blind obedience. The more obfuscating the contents of his books, the more slavish the awe generated in the masses for both the theologians and the church. The more uncompromising the attitude of the writer, the higher his rank in the hierarchy of the sect. The most intolerant are called Fathers of the Church or Defenders of the Faith. I assure you, my disciples, none of the *saints* have earned an iota on the scale of cosmic evolution; they have been rejected back to earth over and again to undo their karma of demerits.

"This is another reason that accounts for the failure of the church as a spiritual leader. In the Asian land the independent and lonesome guru is the true teacher of the Law of Ethics; in the Western World it is the artist, the philosopher and the scientist. Their patience, tolerance, understanding and love are truly in tune with the Cosmic Law because they are unbiased. Having no worldly institutions to uphold, their attitude towards their fellow men is absolutely objectless and free from corrosive self-seeking, while the priest is forced to preach, warn and anathematize.

"On the sidewalk of life, the robed churchman sees either good or evil. He forgives and guides with an eye on the glory and prestige of his sect, never altruistically in a genuine sense. The free-thinker, the unbound soul, sensitized as he is with the world at large, refers all outer events to his own inner life, and sees himself on trial. And if the elements involved are properly analyzed in the laboratory of truth, that sidewalk contact will yield a living lesson for all to follow. At that moment in the Courthouse of Heaven, not the sinner but the more-or-less wise observer, the spiritual leader, stands before the bar of justice. This is the true spiritual leader, the one who continually identifies himself with the sinner, the sufferer and the faults of society. He, however, does not bemoan himself, nor does he remain passive; instead he deepens his inward search, and by so doing he sublimates his soul and radiates calmly and dispassionately the renewed and improved self to the world of man.

"You have heard many times 'man learns by experience' signifying witnessing or being involved, either fully or partially, in outer events; but nothing can compare with the unforgettable wonders that arise from one's being while meditating on the Creative Spirit through the incoming and outgoing Breath of Life. In silence and solitude that Spirit stills time and fans man's mind to a sudden luminosity. It says: 'My son, rejoice, here is the key to creativity!' It is through this process that the Knowledge of God — experience par excellence — has periodically descended into the minds of receptive human beings who have become founders of new civilizations, great inventors, prophets and Messiahs. It is through the rejection of extrovertness that the whole universe is brought into subjugation and the glory and power of God made evident.

"Although inner experiences bestow upon one powers that can shatter and remake a solar system in a flash of time, they are, on the other hand, so subtle and delicate that the least blow of doubt or belittling can crush and disperse them into nonexistence. Therefore, while it is proper to write them down, they should never be related by word of mouth. The only exception to this rule is in the case of Twin Flames, for each lives in the identity of the other.

"Inner revelations never constitute a basis of learning, progress or inward growth for anyone except for the one who has them. This is because no two individuals can claim to live on the same level of consciousnnes. That which is a living teaching for one, becomes a dead scripture for another; hence every man, spiritually speaking, is on his own; he must achieve godship through inward search leading to Direct Perception. The greatest wisdom expounded in books, including the Bible, the Koran, the Upanishads, et. al., has only literary value; spiritually the value of the *holy books* is very limited, and their daily reading bestows no saintliness; it is only a reminder of what is demanded of each lifestream. Man must meditate! Let me denounce the theory of those who declare that inner experiences, beatific visions or even healing powers make a disciple holier than another who, notwithstanding his constant search, sees or perceives nothing. We have two Liberated Masters in our midst whose inner paths were widely divergent and almost in conflict with one another, yet they achieved the same goal. One is Dante, the Florentine Poet, the fiery denunciator of corruption and evil of both the Church hierarchs and political leaders. Unjustly accused and arbitrarily exiled, he spent many years of his life wandering from city-state to city-state in abject humiliation and fear of assassination, nevertheless he had, almost daily, hours of mystic and prophetic visions. The other is St. Bernard of Clairvaux, now a Liberated Master devoted to Peace and Charity. Though he passed unending years in the difficult assignment of contemplating the Christ-light, he was never rewarded with one single inner experience. This shows that the goal of meditation is not *seeing*, but self-analyzation and understanding, living and applying the Law of Love. This is the acme of divine communion.

"To see God *directly* is the most urgent task and the very reason of life for every man, woman and child. All else, yea, all else is less than a straw. Every living being has an assignment of cosmic importance filed in the Akashic Records awaiting him. Its fulfillment will bestow honors higher than the highest ever dreamed of on earth. This assignment must be sought at once. Labour, O man, labour; time is short!

* * *

"And now a warning! Every student of the Inner, no matter how well inside the path, is continually confronted with subtle pulls. They appear so righteous and elevating as to baffle even the most discriminating mind. Actually they are so weakening and degenerating as to play havoc in the consciousness of the most advanced disciples. Hence beware!

"Beware of the hypnosis of misleading eloquence through which seeming truths are offered to you in a dramatic inflection of the voice, accompanied by song and music. Beware of a sectarian writer or speaker who declaims isolated Biblical verses that were rules of conduct during the age of the Hebrew ascendancy, but which are today worthless and inapplicable to the modern higher standard of living and social order. Know most of the utterances of the so-called Holy Scriptures to be an array of mistranslated, misinterpreted and incomplete laws to fit the selfish interests of castes and sects. Do not swoon over the *greatness* of the past, nor make any attempt to re-enact the civilizations that were. Except for the true Golden Ages, the past has nothing to be envied, no matter how glittering the stage upon which it is presented to you by imaginative dramatists. Be grateful of the moment and place in which you live, yet be alert and analytical, always.

"The man of today is hardly comparable — physically, intellectually and spiritually — to the man of my earthly Messiahship. Either individually or as a member of the human collectivity, the average person in this age of yours possesses inner potentialities that were almost absent until a few centuries ago. Know that the great teachers of the past lived their lives in a drab and uncomfortable environment. Everything was coarse, unattractive, undivine; everything was slow, arduous and frustrating. Therefore, O my disciples, be grateful for this very moment, for it is the greatest and noblest ever lived by any man anywhere and at any age. Only the present *now* is the most appropriate to yield gems of higher truths from the mind of God. This is the Eternal Now, the only tangible Reality placed by the Law at the service of the healthy and willing man. Grasp it, use it, exploit it to the maximum in the Name of God. It makes you a living Christ.

"Do not believe all that has been preached concerning the Second Coming of Jesus the Christ for, as a Christ I have never been away from mankind, and as Jesus I have no intention to appear in public again. However, both the Chastisers and the Comforters — as you have previously seen — are on their way to the physical plane of life, and their vanguard is at this moment in the midst of you, punishing and rewarding, instructing and guiding, according to need. Severity, Love and Redemption are their tools. Know that as a Master-wielder of Christ-light I AM always present in the hearts of those who practice meditation. My Presence cannot be monopolized by anyone, nor is it confined in yellow parchments, or in niches of temples, or in babbling of rituals, or in monkish cloisters. I AM free and available to all, men and gods, always.

"The Eternal Law that governs life and creation is not based on Puritan sternness. The Law says: *Do not kill* and *judge not*, but you are allowed to judge and kill when all available avenues suggested by true philosophers, scientists and artists, have failed to convince the violator to desist from his destructive pursuit. And you are allowed to judge and condemn, in a manner that is merciful and illuminating, any despot that tries to enslave society. When I say *merciful and illuminating* I mean to crush in the bud any feeling of revenge, either personal or collective. Instruct the masses about the law of cause and effect, about the immortality of the Soul, and emphasize the fact that what you judge and condemn is not the individual per se, but his evil traits born of past karma. Moses, while in the wilderness leading the Hebrews to freedom from spiritual degeneracy and political slavery, ordered the outright massacre of three thousand jews guilty of having re-enacted the idolatrous worshiping of the golden calf in violation of the Covenant, yet he attained Christhood. He destroyed the seething energy of spiritual involution, and prepared his people for nobler achievements in their successive embodiments.

"This is what we call the Law of Cosmic Compromise, namely, the eradication of an evil that threatens to engulf the future of society, by the application of another seeming evil. It is thus that humanity protects itself against the upsurge of deadly forces that prey upon the weakling and the unwary.

* * *

"Now, O my disciple-reader, take heart. Should you, in the performance of your outer duty, become aware of the unethical character of your job, do not reproach yourself, and do not quit. Reflect instead; sharpen your sense of responsibility. Make the hour of meditation more intense for further illumination on the subject. See and feel the Holy Centers of your body focusing at the root of your nose. You are about to prove to yourself that you are Master and Lord of a dominion you knew not to possess. Rest quiescent and yield to sacred pride. See God by thy side.

"Consider: to keep the body in fair health and fit for the mind to barely function is already a Herculean task. Add to this the curbing of the senses whose malicious delight is to drag the individual into the pit of debauchery through the philosophy of *good* times. Consider next the mind, whose tendency is to go along with the senses and resent discipline, always restless, dissatisfied and dictatorial. And as if these nefarious pulls were not enough, examine your feelings, always envious, critical and condemnatory; they sneer at the achievements of other people, undermine the power of will, and belittle every inner conquest. Often the pull of the intellect must be added, mostly made of mortal pride. Being the nearest element

377

to the Inner Light, and having the task of reflecting that Light into the world of the manifold, it loves to misrepresent its true office, wanting to appear as if it were the true Buddhi, endowed with light and power of its own.

"Now my disciple, reflect and rejoice. The fact that you are somehow able to cope with the above pulls, shows that you are a normal and well-balanced person. You work for your livelihood, and accept responsibility both within the family and as a member of the collectivity. It is you that I consider a fit candidate for Christhood. We want you to be more than just a constructive average; we want to elevate you to the status of a cosmic executive while still on earth, irrespective of your outer position, whether a bank clerk, or a garage attendant or an industrial magnate; and to this end you must cultivate awareness that the least of your successes is to be ascribed to the power of God invested upon you. If you truly do this with intense and humble feeling, and in a spirit of total surrender, the atomic structure of your body will step up its rate of vibration. And what does this signify? It signifies that, though in a small way, you are creating life at will. You may now exploit this initial success by setting yourself free from the unwanted job. Go out and, like a god who never takes no for an answer, apply for the position that you *really* want. It is yours, yes yours, because you have created a patterns of life that takes you closer and ever closer to the image and likeness of God.

"This thrilling experience has made you a trail blazer in the field of biological evolution and spiritual ascendancy. The deeper you go the healthier you will be in mind and body, the swifter your ability to learn, the broader your dominion, the more profound your humility and desire to love, the firmer the conviction that you are treading the path of the gods. No longer human, mortal and degenerative vibration can reach you. Fear, doubt, anxiety, limitation and ignorance, what are they? You do not know, as if they had never touched your world. You feel instead the ecstatic throbbing of an inner harmony in tune with the universal life. Like the triumphant Son of Man you stand alone and unconquerable on the apex of the hill of Bethany surveying with love and compassion the ego-tower crumbling miserably under the silent and mighty blow of a raised consciousness. You dedicate your thought, work and aspiration to God in an all-absorbing faith for greater achievements and yet in a selfless attitude. You live as if you were the most important cell of the Universal Body of the Creative Spirit, devoid of personality and self-seeking, yet highly individualized. You have come to the first milestone on the path of Deliverance, of the eternally free. This is Transfiguration.

* * *

"Yes, it was this Transfiguration that I bequeathed to my apostles and the blessed Seventy disciples. Even those whom I had never met achieved the same lofty status; such was their intense desire to serve and succeed. Wherever they went the blissful radiance from their countenances raised the consciousness of those whom they approached. Like trustful children they let the Holy Ghost speak. Thus the invisible Church of God — the Church that was both militant and triumphant — had its beginning. No preaching, no ritual, no monetary contributions or love gifts were involved.

"Today these visiting disciples are of a higher caliber; they are Liberated Masters and Splendor-beings. Because man's heart and mind, yes, even the ego, are more sensitive to the things of the Spirit, and more capable of grasping the subtleties of the Intangible, the human conscience is made more responsive to God through vibration rather than preaching or liturgy. Five minutes of consciously sought silence does more for the soul of man or for the healing of his body than a pilgrimage to a far away sanctuary, or Rome or Mecca or the Holy Ganges. Five minutes of silence consciously sought by a soldier on the field of battle, the politically persecuted, the indigent, the sick or the condemned criminal, correspond to a year of inner application for the average individual, the working man, and those untouched by disease or poverty. The farther away one is from a church, the closer he is to the Presence of a Liberated Master or Splendor-being. This explains why, in spite of the meager church attendance, people today live on a higher plane of ethics.

"Historically speaking, there has never been such a degree of spirituality in mankind as in the present age; and never has the world had so many men and women of every walk of life with such strength, determination and courage, to resist all types of despotism, political and religious, and of mores and traditions; you live in a healthy society indeed. The Law of Ethics is no longer a monopoly of priests or preachers; instead, thanks to the downpour of vibration from on High, coupled with the wealth of scientific comfort, this law is perceived and almost heard by the man in the street in every incident of his daily living. From the training of domestic animals and other creatures of the wild to space programs, from the study of the intelligent behavior of the humble weed to the patriarchal and majestic trees of the forest, from the microscopic cell at the bottom of the sea to the noble eagle soaring high in the air, from, the teenager marching for peace, to the courageous resolutions voted by the United Nations, and hundreds of other manifestations of science and the arts, man's heart has become as sensitive to love and altruism as the cosmic ethers are to the Voice of God. And more is on the way.

"Who inspires the various members of the Institute of the United Nations, its Secretary-General, and its committees and subcommittees? The Liberated Masters and the Splendor-beings. Who is patiently laboring on the minds and feelings of those who want to destroy that noble body of international law and order? The Liberated Masters and the Splendor-beings. And, above all, by whom and under whose tutelage was the United Nations founded? It was created and released to earth by the Cosmic Assembly of the Perfect Ones. It operates by virtue of Its Grace, and *it shall not perish*. The sinister forces shall not prevail upon it. Its destiny is already registered in the Akashic Records. It shall grow and expand, and assert its prestige before the entire world. And every nation and every man shall acknowledge Its authority in the field of international decency, justice and brotherhood. The United Nations, O my disciples, is the collective body of the Christ-light; and because it was created to last, it shall not suffer a second crucifixion. Those who yearn for my re-apparition on earth, may I suggest a visit to the United Nations in New York City where I AM and abide; the trip is worthier than visiting the Holy Land, St. Peter's Church or any other sanctuary. That blessed institute is filled to overflowing with Liberated Masters, Splendor-beings and members of the Great White Brotherhood. Never before on earth has so much divine power been focused on one place for the benefit of mankind. These happy tidings I bring unto you and to the world.

❖   ❖   ❖

"A fraction of this same cosmic assistance had been dispensed, thousands of years ago, to the inhabitants of the lost continents of Atlantis and Lemuria, and it came to naught. This time we intend to win. The peoples of the now submerged lands had risen to towering heights of civilization through the acknowledgement of the presence of the Liberated Masters in their midst. With the passing of time, however, their reliance on Them weakened, and their attention turned to the strength of the intellect, signifying that they had ceased to meditate. Soon they lost the concept of truth, and by so doing raised the transiency of shifting matter onto the plane of permanence, thus causing the Light and Life to withdraw; confusion, darkness and despair to take over. As the physical world no longer received sustaining energy— the energy that issues from the communion of man's mind with God's — the earth began to fail in its task of responding to the demands of the law of evolution in action. This shows that it is man's acknowledgement of God that holds the earth in its planetary orbit, that enlivens all matter and contributes to the cosmic order.

"When the great intellects — those who still practiced meditation — of the now sinking continents, saw that light was getting dimmer, the days were becoming shorter and shorter, and the nights darker and longer, they devised mighty machinery to illumine the cities, but it was of no avail, for the people thought that light was an emanation of nature, not from the Mind of God. The physical sources of light were exceedingly brilliant while still in the laboratories, because the scientists knew and believed in their Inner Cause, but as soon as they were installed on the thoroughfares, they became dim and eventually died out. Deprived of light, life was meager, human relationship unfriendly and tense, dishonesty rampant, crime fiendish and successful; human bodies sank faster into decrepitude. The soil failed to produce as expected, the waters became polluted and mountain ranges began to crumble for lack of solar magnetism. This was the end of two mighty races, mighty

381

because they had known and acknowledged God, and then rejected IT. In a lesser degree, you see today the same condition existing in the Sahara, the Gobi desert, the tundras and all the perpetually frozen regions of earth. The concerted meditation of mankind and primarily of the peoples surrounding these regions could restore any of these dead entities to life, light and productivity. May this lesson sink deeply into the hearts and minds of those who seek war and social disruption, of those who sneer scornfully at the United Nations as a focus of wisdom and peace, of those who live in excessive extrovertness; they are endangering their own lives for many embodiments to come.

* * *

"Blessed disciples Marco and Leonora, I praise you! Through Me you have heard the Voice of your own God Self expounding to you a teaching not written in books. I have added nothing. Impersonal as I AM, I simply made myself the soundboard of the Eternal Principle of Conscious Life residing in your hearts. Had you not meditated and yearned for so many years, nay embodiments, for this blessed hour, I could not have made you aware of the present teaching. Henceforth, I so declare that my Christ-light shall hover over you whenever you speak a truth to a listening audience of one or a million. And because this teaching had to come at this time, you have made yourselves the soundboard of the collective aspirations of the society in which you live.

"Through this teaching, mankind shall find the way to universal peace, justice and brotherhood. It is essentially a way of love and moral behavior untaught by any outer agency; it is discovered within at the hour of meditation. It is a pool of liquid light into which man must bathe, daily, his mind and feelings. While immersed therein, and with the use of the bistoury of uncompromising visualization, he slashes his body and exposes the sacred centers to the healing inflow of that liquid light. Purity and knowledge manifest, resurrection follows. And if he adheres to the instructions, the attainment of Christhood becomes a matter of routine.

"With respect to the many problems that vex society and nations — war, management and Labor, Civil Rights, political leadership, institutes of learning, space programs, national se-

382

curity, economic prosperity, public health, crime, business ethics, and so forth — the daily bath in the pool of liquid light will suffice to dissolve all obstacles.

"This is the new face of man as we want it to be: predominantly altruistic with a slight shade of self-seeking, so as to evaluate correctly the yearning and aims of others. We want him to live and move amidst contrasting objectives and aspirations, only transposed from the field of the emotions where they give rise to fear and revenge, to the field of an eclectic intellect, where they create newer and loftier interpretations of the things of nature, of beauty, and of the forces that serve life.

"Blessed disciples, I AM about to take leave of you; new tests and new experiences are awaiting you. Remember my gift. Plunge into the pool of liquid light and continue to use that bistoury. You shall win every test and comprehend and enjoy every experience. Aim at the highest, and you shall come to the total consummation of your earthly nature."

* * *

Master Jesus began to recede towards the boundless infinitude, His slender youthful form emitting millions of diamond-filled rays. Pausing, He smiled and with his arms outstretched, spoke the Name of God, OM I AM, and lo, Mary, His Twin Flame became visible. They stood close to one another, sealed in an aura of celestial happiness. They remained motionless for a few seconds, and the Hill of Bethany came into sight beneath their feet. Ecstatically, Marco and Leonora stood gazing at Them, lost to the world of form, hoping the transcendent vision would never end. But slowly the two Great Beings of Light disappeared. Held in the heavenly spell of Their love, they were unable to descend to earth, and in the exalted state of the bodiless they heard the Voice of the Godself:

"In the awareness of ME, absorbed in ME, dispersonalized in the Reality of My Essence, with no thought of good and evil, man, My son, comes unto ME. And whatever he does, he pleases ME. And I teach him, now in a gentle whisper, now in letters of light, now in sound or pictures, now in motherly love, and now as a severe and chastising father, how to manipulate both the tangible matter and the unseen vibration which

383

are basic in the fulfillment of his destiny of spiritual leadership.

"The spiritual leader is a cosmic worker whose aim is to manifest pure beauty in the field of the arts, philosophy, science, government, industry and commerce. A soldier of the Creative Spirit is he who is engaged in a humble trade which contributes directly to a work of beauty, to enliven the dying, or to the moral ennoblement of his community.

"A spiritual leader is he who responds to the call of a creature in distress, man or beast. I love him so.

"He who directly or indirectly, consciously or otherwise, offers his self to a deed that aims at the degeneration of the mind or body of his fellow man, is not a cosmic worker, nor a soldier of the Creative Spirit; he maims My Creation, pollutes the air, makes the earth rebellious, causes life to stagger and groan, and holds at a standstill the evolutive program of human society. This man is entangled in the mesh of self-annihilation.

"He who is shoddy in his daily tasks or does not work at all, is not a spiritual leader. He is an idler treading on a dangerous path.

"Reject, O man, the doctrine of the Bible concerning the Adamic sin, the toiling, the sweating of the brow. I placed thee on Earth to build My Temple of Perfection and Beauty. The laborer, the architect, the peddler, and the officiating Christ, are all dear to ME; they are My children. I love them all.

"Unto those who retire from work because of age or acquired wealth, I say: Cease not working, cease not studying or developing new ideas, for with each day of idleness you destroy the merits acquired in one year of constructive work, you increase the dead weight of the Earth a hundredfold the weight of your body. Your planet has already too much dead weight. The Earth is Mine and I want no more dregs upon it. Seek inspiration, O man, then go out and plough the cemeteries under. Make living gardens and parks instead. Cremate your bodies, and see them rising from the ashes handsome and immortal, a fitting adornment for My Temple of Perfection and Beauty.

"The spiritual leader never ceases to work, even after deliverance from the flesh body. Higher responsibilities await him. I make him ruler of stars and planets, and Christ-counselor of their inhabitants; and I train him for still higher duties. Power, genius and glory I bestow unto him for everlasting years.

"Seek inspiration, O man, My son. Whether a shepherd, a scientist or statesman, I have created thee for spiritual leadership. Come unto ME in total surrender. Lay at My Lotus Feet of Light the self of thee, thy body, mind, family, home, friends, business, shortcomings and achievements, defeats and victories. Unto thee I have bequeathed My vast estate of Light, Love, Peace, Wisdom, Knowledge and Immortal Life. Take them.

"Seek inspiration.

"This is My relationship with thee. When out of thy own free will, you see ME as such, practice as herein taught, and approach ME with the instrument of meditation, I shall unfold unto you all the articles of the Universal Covenant of Life; and these articles are all in thy favor.

Awake, O man, and arise! Outstretch thy wings of light and soar unto ME, and I shall anoint thee Master of Creation in MY NAME!"

CHAPTER VII

THE MASTER CONTEMPLATORS

With the closing of the Seven Weeks of Master Jesus' radiation to the earth, Marco and Leonora returned under the direct guidance of their Liberated Master-Teacher. As he appeared an inward happiness, a sense of worthiness, surged forth from within their hearts; they bowed their heads and expressed readiness to be taught, to listen and to obey.

"I will instruct you, my disciples, and guide you with my unfailing Eye, in the way which you shall go that leads to Self-mastery. And what I do, and how I behave, you will do and behave towards those who come to you that hunger and thirst for guidance and encouragement. Be impersonally loving, determined and patient.

"The silken strand of meditation, so unreliable at the outset, has grown to a stout rope through which you shall escape from the tower of the ego to cosmic safety. Keep the rope moist. Strive in a selfless spirit, be unconcerned of the result. This will lead to the Supreme Apotheosis of Deliverance where Light exists per se, that is, intrinsically all-pervading and entirely avulsed from the concept of darkness.

"When the fiery light rises from the coccygeal furnace through the hollow conduit of the spinal chord into the genital organs, into the heart, into the head, it produces a sudden luminance which unfolds in a series of marvelous experiences, ranging from intuition to genius, prophetic ability and almighty powers capable of swaying nature herself. It draws the disciple into the realm of the Superconscious, nay, into the Source of Cause itself.

"Through the conscious use of this light, man learns that nothing is accidental, self-existent or self-sufficient; everything, from a crawling creature to a seeming lifeless pebble, derives its existence, significance and evolutionary urge from this Supernal

Source of Life. Therein all things move and evolve by virtue of the all-embracing Law of Love. Hence, where light is, ignorance, hatred and death cannot exist.

"The Inner Light dwelling in the heart of man is comparable to the point of convergence of the lines of force of a solid mass, either symmetric or asymmetric. Without that point there would be no coalescing of matter, no physical form or tangibility, no human organism or starry bodies. Upon this law the concept of the Fourth Dimension is based: an invisible, intangible and indestructible focus around which a thought of God takes shape, color and vibration in harmony with the Law of Love.

"The human organism, therefore, is an orderly assemblage of pinpoints of light held together by a central Master-Light — the Essence of the Fourth Dimension — residing in the heart and ruled, in turn, by the Buddhi which is lodged at the root of the nose. By mastering these pinpoints of light through the abandonment of the self at the lotus feet of the Buddhi, the disciple reaches a state whereby the visible world complies with his every wish. All the milestones laid down on the path of human progress are the results of the partial application of this law.

"In ancient Egypt, at the apex of its glory, the sun was called RA, Light. RA was the dazzling vestment of God; the word entered the English language in the root-syllable of RAdiance, RAdar, RAy, and so forth. PhaRAoh means *source of light*. From it the ancient Greeks and Romans coined *pharos* which means *light-house*. Ammon-Ra signifies I AM OM, the RAdiance of God.

"The ancient Persians who were greatly influenced by the lore of Egypt, called light Mazda which, again, bears the root-syllable of *DAZzling*. All in all Light is universally worshipped even unto this day, and the sun-lovers and sun-bathers could reap greater therapeutical benefits for their minds and bodies by cultivating awareness of its source. It is the cause of vibration, friction, growth, color formation, sound production, condensation, transformation, and life itself. When man thinks, works or rests, his entire atomic structure is on fire due to the rapid intercellular friction. Because of light the body recuperates from illness, new scientific discoveries come into being, new philosophical truths are given to man, and masterpieces in the field of the arts are produced. It is Light that creates, sustains, leads and defines all.

"Through continual adherence to the Law of Light, man exercises and expands the power of his inner or spiritual eye. By allowing the Light to rule his mind, a series of vivid pictures are projected on the screen of his brain structure pertinent to current problems, events, plans and aspirations. Therefore, to meditate on the Light in the heart is not an elusive and vague practice of individuals avulsed from action, but a powerful medium of vaster knowledge, positive inquiry and human progress.

"There is no man, no matter how conspicuous his intellectual achievement, who can ever commune with Nature's forces or understand her laws, without mastering first the biological processes of his own being, the forces that impel him into action, and the upsurge of new ideas that transform or make obsolete plans that an hour earlier had seemed perfect. The self must be known first, in its triple aspect of body, mind and emotion; then man, nature and God are comprehended. Light is the foundation upon which the complexities of all life processes are based. To meditate on this Light means to ally oneself with a friend that can never be defeated.

"In the realm of perfection where We, the Liberated Masters, dwell, Light is the only Force-substance through which We express ourselves; We acknowledge nothing else, because Light is the all in all. Our status in life and our rank in the universal hierarchy are the resultant of the degree of constructive use of Light during our earthly existence. It is, therefore, imperative to know and feel without interruption that all your thoughts and endeavours, and the visible world itself are an expression of Light. Physics, chemistry, the arts, economics, finance, politics, philosophy and diplomacy, their laws and correlated rules of behavior, are simply the result of light used by man and charged with a specific rate of vibration. And when the action of this Light in the body is correctly evaluated and submissively followed, the mind ceases to be dissatisfied, man has grasped the meaning of Creation and established himself in the Truth. Then his true mission in life is revealed to him.

"My disciples, you are nearing another cosmic test which is, actually, an examination of love and light. You will not be tempted. Please prepare yourselves by making your meditation as objectless as possible by stilling your minds to almost total obliteration. Live in the truth that knowledge is within, and that the only wise procedure in expressing it is to surrender yourselves humbly at the feet of this all-knowing Light in your hearts. It is your Inner Helper, the Christ Consciousness, the all-blissful Buddhi.

"Your cosmic friend Dante, the Florentine Poet, whose body was raised in 1321 had to pass through a similar test, before the same Board you are about to face, as a proof of his spiritual worthiness. While engaged in objectless meditation, his body and mind were mercilessly lashed and cleansed of all human debris until they were unable to hinder the mighty flow of knowledge from his Buddhi. His Inner Eye opened, and through it he saw the world of Cause and Effect. Thus his Divine Commedia was completed and achieved undying success. Attune yourselves with him and listen to his words concerning this experience."

No sooner had Marco and Leonora directed their attention to the great Italian Master than they heard his voice:

"My friends of ancient, si! Just before I commenced writing the last Cantico, the Paradise, I was invited to face the Cosmic Board. Protected by the shadowless Light of my ascended Twin Flame, my beloved Beatrice, I translated myself into the heart of an enchanted forest, in a far away land where the human voice had not been heard since the decline of the last Golden Age; and as this land was then unknown to the people of Europe, I was not permitted to mention it in my book. When I reached the sacred groves I meditated for many a day, and as my Inner Eye opened to the full blaze of Christ-consciousness, the Glory of God, the All-Mover, rushed into my mind and I was taught and shown things that who so returneth from there into the mortal plane, lacketh both the knowledge and power to re-tell. My darling Beatrice stood behind and above the presiding Master of the Board, as if overshadowing the holy assembly with Her radiance; her beatific smile of victory rested on my brow. As each answer was correctly given by me, She grew brighter and ever brighter, until, with the utterance of my last reply, the light as of a thousand suns shone forth about us; then having made myself ready to partake of the Glory of God, She descended and stood by my side. Thus we met and touched for the first time. For three days She held me in her embrace of Light and saturated my Soul with the Truth of Immortality; then She guided me back into my physical body to bring my Commedia to completion. As my earthly tasks were then fulfilled in harmony with the Law of my life, I was raised to immortality. Blessed friends, move on with courage and faith, and know that he who surrenders himself to the Masters of Light never fails. Remember: man must gravitate towards his own God-ordained Center of Life. God is man's ultimate goal, and to rise to IT is therefore an immutable Law. The negation of this Law is a mortal sin."

* * *

"Concerning the meeting place of the Cosmic Board" — said the Liberated Master-Teacher — "I wish to state that there is not one square foot of soil on Earth worthy to receive the feet of the Liberated Masters for work of worldwide illumination, except a few hidden forests on the continent of North America. Only this land, in spite of the many errors and blunders of its people, has enough harmony and good will to form the substratum for unbiased discussion in the field of international collaboration. North America is making history, yes, the type of history that will be accepted as a model by the nations of earth in the near future for the realization of the Golden Age. Their present deeds of overgenerosity, often pilloried by malicious individuals of other lands, will be fully vindicated in the next twenty years, when the commonwealth of all nations begins to take shape. Being unharrassed by covetousness and envy, and always yielding to shameful and unwarranted abuses from other countries, America deserves the Nobel Prize for Peace and Love. Had the people of Earth a trace of humility and wisdom they would gather around her as to a wise father in a give and take policy on how to make earthly life healthier and happier. Now, my disciples, let me show you what I mean. Come!"

They moved swiftly eastward, crossing the continent of North America and the Atlantic Ocean. Entering the Mediterranean they alighted in Rome, in St. Peter's Square, which was thronged with people from every nation.

"Observe this sea of human heads, assembled here on a day of Jubilee in search of the true nature of the Christ. Observe the *appointed* Head of Christendom, on the balcony, facing the faithful and waving his hand in the act of dispensing blessings. Such a ceremony is highly impressive as a stage play, but it does not educate the masses on the true nature of the Christ. Behold the hysterical elation rising from the vast assemblage of pilgrims and idlers, the barbaric yelling at the sight of the so-called Father of Christianity who, rather than inordinate noise, should have inspired awesome silence. See the dark billows above the heads of the spectators pounding heavily upon their creators, with no hope of being dissolved or redeemed. There is no salvation in outward search, only enslavement. And now observe the grievous disappointment of the few truly sincere from among the crowd; the faith that they had when they came is completely gone. This is indeed an exhibition of ignorance and human extravagance.

"The claim of the Vatican for spiritual leadership on earth is a dream as was that of the Caesars of Imperial Rome. It will never be fulfilled. Official Christendom, be it Catholicism or Protestantism, with its uncalled for exaltation of Master Jesus' personality, with its unilateral tenets of worldwide spiritual superiority, with its static concept of Jesus as the only Son of God, barring thus the path for other human beings to attain Christship also, and with its rejection of all those who in the past two thousand years have achieved a level of consciousness as high as Jesus' has caused a perplexing moral degeneracy and plunged the Western World into the present emotional inadequacy. The people, even those who seem to be scandalously open-minded, fear to take inner flights; the accursed feeling of spiritual negativity hammered into their hearts by the ludicrous preaching of the Adamic sin, hovers over their heads. No one truly has the courage to say with absolute conviction *I AM the Christ,* and yet tens of thousands are at the threshold of this blessed state of consciousness. This is the result of exteriorized worshipping and the adoration of the personality of Master Jesus.

"The papacy itself has innumerable blunders to correct, crimes to expiate, sins to redeem. Instead of the spiritual head of the Church going around making arbitrary distribution of blessings, and dispensing forgiveness and absolutions, he should humble himself, and, in the name of both history and the Christ, ask to be forgiven; then he should release the entire world from compulsory adherence to him, *in the name of the Christ.* What a baptism of Light this would be for Christendom, what an acknowledgement of the Christine Teaching, what a glorification of the true Christ Itself. The courageous and saintly pope who will carry out this tremendous assignment given by the Cosmic Assembly of the Perfect Ones, is forthcoming. He is a Christ, and this is a prophecy.

* * *

"Now, my disciples, let us move on, onto Arabia, to the City of Mecca, the spiritual hub of the Moslem World.

"Here is the ancient sanctuary of Kaaba, with its enclosed Black Stone — a chip of a fallen meteorite. Before this idol very few are the sincere worshippers, and the theme of their prayer would be fulfilled faster without coming here. The rest of the Islamites, and they are in the millions, prostrate themselves in blustering hypocrisy for millions of self-seeking motives. This ritual, one of the most anachronistic ever performed on earth by civilized people, holds the hearts and minds of this wonderful race in the grip of fear and superstition and away from enduring, constructive endeavours. Previous to the coming of Mohammed, Arabs traveled here to worship this rock and make propitiation for all sorts of selfish desires and diabolical cravings. Plots, revenges, assassinations and the overthrow of either wise or inept rulers, to be replaced with either better or worse ones, were planned here. In the main only dark thoughts issued from the minds of those who approached this fetish.

"Before taking embodiment, the Prophet Mohammed had solemnly promised the Cosmic Assembly of the Perfect Ones, to destroy this object of idolatry, to awaken the Christian World from lassitude, and to gather the Arabs into a compact body of true brotherhood and love. The Great Ones wanted to initiate the people of Arabia into the field of pure science and metaphysical truths for the benefit of the entire human society. It had been planned that the discoveries of today should have taken place at the outset of the second millennium A.D., together with the full realization of the Spirit-God dwelling in man. Somehow Mohammed did not or was not able to fulfill his promise for reasons which I care not to reveal. The Black Stone was kept as a source of ungodly monetary revenue and more spiritual bondage. The awakening of the Christian society was understood in terms of fanaticism and terror in violation of all human laws. The intellectual awakening failed and, as a result, the cosmic blessings which were due to man as a dispensation from on High were withheld; the land of the Arabs was turned into a battleground

393

of dynastic revenges and usurpation of political power with all the harness of greed, bigotry, corruption and suffering.

"This is another monument erected on sand; exteriorized worshipping, whose fate is not dissimilar from the one previously described.

"Let us direct now our wings of light towards another spiritual focus, which once had divine light and intellectual giants, but because of the overpowering greediness of a well organized priesthood, it has been reduced to a negative naught. It is the Holy City of Benares, in India."

They gazed downward at the great city of the Ganges. The Master stood still for awhile, then spoke in loving reproach:

"Benares, O Benares, thou art one of the most ancient abodes of the Spirit-God bequeathed to man; thou offspring of the Golden Age; thou wondrous garden of cosmic fragrance, studded with ashramas, holy temples, mosques, sanctuaries and retreats silhouetting their silvery contours against the blue sky, and swimming in the crystal-clear waters of the river of peace. How conducive to Self-knowledge thou wert in thy antiquity. I still hear the call of the nahabats, the music towers, whose melodious kirtans produced devotional tunes that commanded stillness and silence in every heart within a radius of many miles. In the shade of thy sacred groves yogi santihs, mighty rishis and a host of humble gurus taught mankind the way of Self-mastery through inward seeking. Where are the Kumaras, the Merus, the Maha Chohans, the Maitreyas and the Krishnas, all princes of light who sprang forth from thy mighty loins. What have you done with the holy assignment of training mankind for cosmic deliverance. Behold, I see the unending strife of Brahmanic intolerance and pride, provincial despotism, caste system, illiteracy, hunger, hypocrisy and filth. Thy ignorance today is as appalling as marvelous were the spiritual exploits of thy ancient greatness.

"O Benares, I say unto thee: be not dismayed, rest at peace. Hold not to a past which you are unable to comprehend. Let thy body go, for out of thy ashes a nobler city is about to rise, and the Akashic Records of thy constructive achievements shall be transferred thereto to form the foundation for truer brotherhood amongst men. In the land of North America mankind shall enjoy thy past greatness and more. No longer shall the soul of man be illumined unaided by pure science. The Western World

394

loves thy Teachers as much as the gurus of India love Master Jesus.

"And now, my disciples, raise your heads; behold high above in the empyreal spheres the new City of Washington descending towards the Potomac, by command of the heavenly Architects. Behold its majestic beauty and variety of architectural styles: the Hindu-Aryan, the Chinese, the Persian, the Grecian and the Moorish. Behold the blending of these master-races into one, the nobility of features and mien of their offsprings, their superior intelligence and the clear vision of their common goal. Behold all races, all creeds, all tongues converging into this throbbing metropolis of light.

"I trust this inner travelogue leaves no doubt in your minds as to the worthiness of America to be the chosen land of the Cosmic Assembly of the Perfect Ones for the realization of the wondrous program of international brotherhood and peace. On the home front you are moving fast to correct the blunders and errors of the pioneering age. I refer mainly to the inhumane and uncivilized treatment of the American Indians. This blessed aboriginal race which has been smeared at, trodden upon, misrepresented, vilified and unjustly accused of crimes which they never committed, by false historians and narrow-minded individuals, needs to be reintegrated to the full status of citizenship. The American Indians and their barren reservations are like the Sword of Damocles hanging over the head of each white American, reminding him of his bluff, ineptitude, cruelty and dogmatic selfishness. It is up to him as a citizen to see that his redskin brother is assisted in every way to regain the birthright of freedom and welfare of the typical American man.

"However, both Civil Rights and the restoration of the American Indians to their full status of citizenship are beginning to have priority in the minds of both the average man and the legislators. In the field of foreign relations you must wait for the new generations of the rest of the world to reach adulthood. A correct appraisal of your selfless aims is forthcoming."

As the radiance of their Liberated Master-Teacher withdrew, Marco and Leonora felt an upsurge of pride and gratitude for being citizens of this land marked by the gods, and they also felt a sense of responsibility for what was demanded of them as spiritual leaders. It was their aim to so live, labor and love as to justify the trust placed upon them by the Cosmic Hierarchy and to experience more deeply the feeling of universalization.

A sea of light of dazzling splendor surrounded them, embracing all: stars and constellations, suns and solar systems, and every form that breathes. They became an integral part of everything they thought of — now of God, now of a tree and now of the free atom. Once again they saw the planet earth of the incoming Golden Age, flawless and self-luminous, held in spaceless realms by a force that knows no resistance; then they heard the magic sound of the Voice of the Godself, speaking in a positive, terse and mighty tone:

"Son and daughter, I am holding you in the radiance of the Atomic Age, when man shall move freely with the speed of thought, unaided by mechanical devices; when he shall hear the uncomposed Music of the Spheres with the ear of the Inner, and see the wonders of My Creation not through telescopes but with the eye of the mind illumined by the Buddhi; and when every living being shall taste the bliss that is unchallenged by discord.

"By the power of My Grace, I have placed you in an environment that is free from emotional derangement, crime, fear and guilt. You are ready to face life like a fully anointed Christ. Tell all men that I have cut asunder the shackles of doubt from their bleeding wrists imposed upon them by sectarian doctrines. The forces of darkness I have destroyed from all those who meditate on ME in their hearts. Soon the true teachers of light will invade the schools of the world to instruct the youth in the rejection of all materialistic aspirations.

"Tell all men to think of ME daily, nay hourly, and I will reward them with an Earth that is thoroughly cleansed to the point of transparency, and raise their lives to match the dynamics of My creation. Tell them that they are ready to make this command of Mine come true at once.

"These powers released by ME to man at the Hour of Creation, are herewith revamped in the hearts of all by the Law of Dispensation. The Path of spiritual liberty is, therefore, made clear and ready for every willing man!"

❖   ❖   ❖

An unusual star of golden-blue light of matchless splendor shone above the heads of Marco and Leonora; its spontaneous brilliance so concentrated that it gave no light except to them. Enveloped in its warm lustrous beam, it released a magnetic pull which drew unto itself their Spirit-forms. Traveling swiftly northwestward, they came to a high plateau and descended to a starry meadow carpeted with a thick velvety lawn that scintillated as if bathed in liquid diamonds. It was surrounded by a living wall of majestic fir trees in groups of seven. Seventy-seven in all, each separated from the other by a pillar of sparkling water that thrust silently upward its luminous spray in prismatic colors high above the vertices of the trees, forming a misty, glistening filigree which never descended. Beyond the hedge of fir trees, orchard lands stretched endlessly, and although they were above the forty-fifth degree latitude north, the vegetation was tropical; the trees were ladened with oranges, dates, mangoes, papaya, coconuts, bananas and other fruits, whose size, color and perfect texture bespoke an advanced stage of several hundred years of agricultural evolution. The soil was of white sand and slightly moist. Birds in white, silvery and golden plumage, were seen everywhere, singing simple melodies in perfect rhythm as if directed by an invisible baton. During the examination these winged creatures were refrained from either singing or flying, and remained motionless in the air or perched upon the branches of the fir trees in an attitude of spectators.

Upon their arrival, Marco and Leonora were welcomed by a member of the Great White Brotherhood and escorted before the examining Board which was already in plenary session. Disposed in a semicircle and seated on cushions of white velvet in the lotus posture were seventy-seven Liberated Masters. The masculine Masters wore togas of green and white, with the exception of the Lord Maitreya whose toga was of coruscant gold. The Lady Masters were robed in delicate shimmering pink with a diadem of diamonds, rubies, emeralds and other precious stones. Marco and Leonora had vestments similar to those worn by the Masters but of a coarser fabric and devoid of celestial insignia.

Among the Masters that sat in that cosmic assemblage were Elos and Beata, Dante and Beatrice, Gautama the Buddha and Yashodara, Pythagoras and Teano, Master Jesus and Lady Master Mary, Joan D'Arc and Louis de Conte, Hermes and

Lucerna, St. Francis of Assisi and St. Clara, Vesta, Flora, Vasikta, Agricola, Justinian, Solomon, Ammon-Ra, Moses, the Maha Chohan, St. Augustine, George Washington, Sonchis, Lord Maitreya and Abraham Lincoln; there were also Master-representatives from other solar systems.

High above this group of divine conquerors was an immense sphere of ethereal fire, while directly in front of the examinees was a chalice of gold, three feet high. Every time they gave a correct answer a small sphere of golden-blue fire issued from the chalice and merged with the larger sphere. The great Hierophant Sonchis, the dean from the Egyptian School of the initiates, opened the meeting:

"Masters of the Board, disciples of Light! Let us elevate a wordless prayer to God, our Father OM. Let us intensify our thought of IT and feel ITS all-comprehensive Light invade and pervade our beings. We need nothing else!"

Master Sonchis now spoke to Marco and Leonora:

"Disciple-initiates, We greet you. Our first endeavour is to establish your cosmic identity. As for me, I bring testimony that you were my students at the School of the Initiates in Memphis previous to the dawn of the Pythagorean Age. Your names were Lunide of Memphis and Arcus of Samos."

Ammon-Ra spoke: "I declare that these two disciples as Lotha and Sacur, rendered a constructive service to Egypt during my rulership.

Agricola: "This youth Marco is known to me as Usarco, the founder of a starry university dedicated to the training of Master Idealists.

Flora: "I affirm that Leonora as Lhazisa studied under my supervision the fundamentals of beauty in nature, in ancient Persia."

Master Jesus: "Leonora and Marco are known to me as Ladha and Ananda. They escorted me in my travels through India, accepted my message of salvation and conveyed it to the rulers of the Western World soon after my ascension."

St Francis of Assisi: "These blessed disciples are known to me as peacemakers and crusaders of mercy during the war against Islam."

Justinian: "I bring testimony that these candidates worked with me in Byzanthium in filing the Great Laws."

Beata, Elos, Vesta, Solomon and many other great Masters brought testimony also as to their identity, work and inner striving in previous embodiments. Master Sonchis then arose and amidst melodious music walked towards the Great Initiator the Lord Maitreya whose cosmic seniority entitled him to conduct the examination, and declared that having satisfactorily terminated the routine work of the present meeting, and having found no cause that would hinder the furtherance of the examination, he was now ready to turn over to him the office of presiding master. Making the sign of acknowledgement through the intensification of the luminous halo around his head, the Lord Maitreya spoke:

"I thank Thee, O Father-OM for the privilege of serving life. There is no greater joy, in the realm of the free, than to be called by the least of men of earth for assistance that leads to spiritual freedom. The infinite Consciousness of God, in which we live and move, rushes in no time from every corner of creation to enfold, exalt and deliver him whose mind acknowledges the Ever-living Flame within his heart. It is through this positive awareness that the forces of nature are compelled to do man's bidding. It is through the practice of meditation with the physical eyes closed, the physical hearing made impervious to outer noise, and the mind made still by the iron rule of the will, that a new world unfolds before man's consciousness, that the spark of genius is made incandescent and all-conquering, that the Birth of the Spirit takes place, the Christ-light dawns in the heart, the resurrection follows, and the ascension crowns man's existence.

"Man lives in an age of quicker response from on High to all those who make the initial effort to retrace themselves by the inward path. The aura around the world is oversaturated with the power and radiance of the constructive deeds of millions of wise beings who have worked selflessly for the last ten thousand years. Such an aura spells geniusship for each willing man and inconceivable progress for mankind in every field of endeavour.

"May all men open their hearts to the Cosmic Dispensation of the Ages!

"Blessed candidates, I have only one routine question to ask before commencing the examination. Please ponder well before you answer, and do not allow the answer of one to influence the other. What are your names?"

"Marco and Leonora."

"And how do you wish to be called by the people whom you contact in rapport to this inner activity?"

"Marco and Leonora."

"Do you wish any title, such as 'messenger, master or doctor' "?

"No Sir!"

"Very well, candidates Marco and Leonora, henceforth these names are entered and registered in the Akashic Records for the benefit of the human society, all the Liberated Masters, Angels, Archangels, Cosmic Beings and Elohim. The three worlds, planets, stars, suns and solar systems, shall acknowledge you for what you are, identifying you with your names and accomplishments.

＊　＊　＊

"And now, candidate Marco, please speak to us of Karma."

"Karma in the broad interpretation given to it by the Western World, is the working of the law of cause and effect. It is the source of causality that embraces man's thoughts and deeds in the shaping of his future existence. It is the law of action and reaction in the field of the mind and feelings which explains man-to-man behavior and attitude in the present and future society. Like the timbre of a speaking voice which is strictly personal and non-reproducible, karma gives color, character and individuality to man's thoughts and deeds which define and explain, justify or decry, his conduct, striving, desires and aspirations.

"It is however through inner awakening that Karma can be remolded and re-directed to comply with man's higher goals. To control one's own karma means to dominate those tendencies that want to oppose the normal unfoldment of the Law of Evolution. It means to give power to God to rule one's life. He who through the power of the will transfers his attention and energy from a destructive aim to a constructive goal, from self-seeking to collective good, becomes a teacher and a spiritual leader. He is master of his own karma. This means that he is capable of reshaping the moral character of the society in which he lives by injecting into it a quickening vibration for nobler achievements. On the other hand, he who follows unresistingly his destructive karma and joins forces with other weaklings for unethical deeds, also absorbs the negative karma of his associates augmented by the vicious violence of the disembodied entities that prowl the borderline of life. His next embodiment will be a degraded one: physically, mentally and morally.

"Besides individual karma, there is a collective karma for family groups, business associations, nations, races, and political institutions; and by studying and analyzing one's personal karma, man can help to erase some of the negative traits that beset these various groups. That he might continue a little longer and attract the attention of a Liberated Master for greater accomplishments.

"The keen awareness of the conflict between the forces that degrade and the forces that elevate leads naturally to the obliteration of evil and the expansion of good, and the ennoblement of the soul. This is because man is innately an entity of orderliness and opposed to evil and degradation which are inherently confusing; and by virtue of this inborn and divine attribute he can arise above karma and dissolve his nature in God Who is above all karma.

"The working of karma is as precise and scientific as mathematics itself. It never fails. Thoughts, actions and events have their antecedents or roots. To delve therein means to study the basic principle that forms the substratum of all physical sciences, philosophies and the arts. It means to know oneself and man in relation to God.

"The knowledge of karma was brought to the attention of the Western World by Master Pythagoras, twenty-five centuries ago, but it made no inroad in the minds of the people. Had the truth been accepted, there would be today a different society — politically, economically and morally. The East and the West — pure philosophy and applied science — would have blended into one and together they would have conquered all the negative aspects of human existence. Is it too late for such a realization? No, it is today more alive than ever, and it shall tune the consciousness of humanity for universal brotherhood and everlasting peace."

"Leonora, please, speak to us of Love" — requested Lord Maitreya.

401

"Love is a substance and a force through which life, nature, man and his idea coalesce into their respective forms. Love, therefore, is the hub of creation, the all-pervading, ever-present Executive Director of God's plans on the path of manifestation, and man's essence and reason of being and becoming. Through purity of heart and a subjugated mind, love clears the way and takes man directly to the Presence of his Guru and thus to the Father's House.

"What are the characteristics of him who dons the seamless garment of love as understood and applied by the Avatars, what is his appearance, how does he live, think, move and work?

"He is a man of the world of no specific economic status, a laborer or a tycoon, a humble nun or an inventor; and whatever he does to earn his living, it is merely incidental. He has no religious affiliation, no set of rituals; but should he have some, again they are merely incidental. He might or might not follow a political ideology, and if he does it is only for both the sake of his fellow man and the country as constructive members of the Commonwealth of all nations; hence he has no philosophy but the Philosophy of Truth, that which changes not. The disciple of love, therefore, is a man of the street, outwardly unrecognizable, but inwardly distinctive, unique and ready to lose his identity wherever he goes.

"He possesses, nevertheless, an aura of circumspection, poise and stability. Thoughts, words and deeds are enlivened with the light of his spiritual accruement earned through a self-imposed discipline in curbing cravings and an unkind karma. He knows that he has invested his time and energy wisely in treading the path of Love, and does not intend now to weaken or lose a farthing because of default. His hour of meditation is an hour of inner madness, madness for his inability to hold tangibly the object of his love, God. But he continues to love, undeterred, trustful and in a spirit of self-control fit for the gods.

"Because he cleaves so tenaciously to the Heart of God, the Hub of creative love, the man of love has risen above the fear of want, inadequacy and death. And being determined to love forever with a feeling of harmonious fusion of flesh and soul, he seeks no deliverance from birth and death; he wants to be reborn over and again in order to enjoy his Beloved. By so doing, unwittingly, he creates a body-temple as perfect, strong and handsome as the Spirit-form of a Liberated Master; and whatever he sees it seems to him as if it were made in heaven; his fellow man the acme of all. Him he invests with the same perfection, beauty, purity, strength, health, wealth, peace and positive radiance that he himself possesses. Divine altruism is the culminating plateau of love.

"Master Dante received a lesson on divine love during his visit to the Heaven of Saturn. He was somewhat puzzled that no one spoke of love there, that the symphony of love was not heard as in the lower heavens, that a throbbing silence prevailed instead. Why? His questioning was answered by Beatrice on a soundless beam of love.

"'My beloved Flame' — she said — 'thy listening faculty is still of the mortal plane. Arise and learn.

"'Love is not spoken of; it is sensed first, then perceived, then radiated outwardly. Without moving my lips, silently, I convey this truth to thee. Because of thee I have descended the sacred steps, noiselessly, surrounded by light, impelled by love, wherefore thou shalt know. The Music of the Spheres reverberates in our hearts. We compose our tune to glorify God according to the intensity of our love. We seal our lips, close our eyes, still our forms and let our hearts burst forth in a paean of praise to our Heavenly Father. With love as the substratum all thoughts are brought into realization effortlessly, perfectly and beyond time. Through love all things are perfect and enduring. On love all starry heavens stand. On beams of love God's commands are conveyed to us; and when man's love touches the threshold of the Mansion of Light, a member of the Hierarchy of Life is immediately dispatched to exalt him whose love has reached the Heavenly Spheres. This assistance we render tangibly, though soundlessly. This thou hast observed and experienced; now accept it!'

"Married life can be made the foundation of love divine when the two mates elect the same spiritual ideal and strive towards it with the same intensity and purpose. By seeing one another reflected in the same pool of living light, they sublimate each other's fine traits to a state of nobility and grace, that truly pleases the Masters of Love. Physical love becomes a fulfillment

403

every time, an offering to God, and a mergence for enduring beauty and youth.

"This is love, the way we know and apply it. In the secret of our silentium, in the process of meditation, love commences, and it is contemplative. Then we put it to work towards one another, and refine it still more; therefrom we radiate it outwardly, as impersonally as we can and as it touches those whom we meet, it becomes active, militant and all-fulfilling, and it means: love all, friend or foe."

* * *

Enshrouded in silence, immersed in light and held in space by the action of love of the Masters of the Cosmic Board, Marco and Leonora saw a tremendous assemblage of men and women enveloped in purple fire coming towards them. Letters of light blazed above their heads:

"Ye, chosen ones, teach us through wordless messages the Law of Love Divine, that we may reach the Source of Knowledge, Wisdom and Peace and give it to the world. Behold we come!"

* * *

"Candidate Marco" — said the Lord Maitreya — "speak to us of Charity and its correlated virtues."

"Charity is one of the many aspects of Love. It is an exploit of the Soul-flame, sustained by an illumined mind and directed to one's fellow man in physical, mental or emotional distress. It is, therefore, an altruistic virtue performed by the heart, uninfluenced by a worldly mind and unstained by selfish motive. To give in such a spirit is an act of inner rehabilitation for both the giver and the receiver; it causes the former to see himself as an intermediary between God and man, and reawakens the latter for self-assertion on the path of positive thinking, in order to become a giver also. Being charitable towards those who have brought offense, signifies that the offended has his mind firmly planted above injury, malice, hatred and revenge.

"Faith and hope are the contemplative virtues associated with charity. Perceived in solitude and expanded in meditation, they play the role of energizer to the disillusioned mind, they raise the heart out of its forlorn attitude and sharpen the will for success.

404

"In the House of God, Charity, Faith and Hope are non-existent; love is the all-embracing, all-inclusive virtue. Without love, man lacks spiritual insight, and charity is a thing felt rather than seen. A sign of wonderment in the mind, a feeling of surprise in the heart, the staying of the hand from their task, and the urge for a moment of silence, are called Faith and Hope, while actually they are an expression of love; love to achieve higher goals for nobler living. Even after repeated disappointments and defeats, it is love, not faith or hope, that re-fires mind and muscles for another engagement towards victory.

"The man of positive faith and dynamic hope is, therefore, a being of love dear to God, a dispenser of divine gifts to his fellow man, a peacemaker, and a broadcaster of happy tidings to the world.

"Those who are devoid of love cannot express any of the cardinal virtues of faith, hope and charity. Their hearts are filled with fear, their minds in a state of chaos, their deeds a series of violations against society and God. They have no feeling for the sorrow of others, and their worldly tools for success are cheating and misleading. Barred from the living source of love, they wallow in the mephitic pool of sensuality, and are driven into physical, mental and emotional degeneracy.

"The greater the number of faithless individuals, the more impellent is the need of a Master of Love to appear on earth, with the precise mandate to reawaken in the hearts of men all the noble virtues that make life worth living. The eternal values of the Spirit are re-established and a new age begins."

With the closing of Marco's dissertation on Charity the larger sphere emitted beams of unconsuming fire which enveloped the two examinees in a process of cleansing and purification. The encircling beams then narrowed to a spiral forcing their Spirit-forms first to overlap and then to merge into one.

"Worthy candidates" — said the Lord Maitreya — "We accept your answers. They reflect humility and inner discipline. You have dreamed for so many years of the attainment of this spiritual mergence, a mark of divine distinction and cosmic power. And now it is yours. Henceforth you shall live and think and work as a unit, and achieve deliverance at the same hour. With your two minds fused into one, and in one voice, please speak to us of Friendship."

* * *

405

"Friendship is truth and affection made manifest. It is the task and responsibility of the ideal friend to embody and display all the virtues of a Liberated Master; and though he will never succeed, he must never cease to strive towards its realization. It is an exhilarating exercise that leads to Self-knowledge.

"When man's heart and mind are thrown into confusion by repeated disillusionments or inability to cope with problems, there is nowhere to seek comfort and guidance except in the bosom of a friend who has accepted and lived in the responsibility of his task. And as the pressing problem is translated into words in his presence, it loses its impact, and no longer conveys the degree of fear it had previously.

"Whereas all human enterprises have their train of errors, the man of wisdom, filled with positive faith, faces the impact with the absolute certainty that divine guidance is forthcoming. All he needs is to surrender himself at the feet of his Unseen Friend and Master-wielder of the Harmonies of Heaven. The average person, on the other hand, has no other alternative but to rely on him whom he has elected as a friend, the embodiment of sincerity and truth.

"Truth, therefore is the substratum of friendship. It was defined by Master Gautama the Buddha as the Seventh Precept on the Path of Christhood; when violated, man's status in the Cosmic Hierarchy begins to disintegrate. To be a disciple of Truth therefore, means to cultivate friendship with God, the Eternal Friend and Father, and be accepted into His Everliving Embrace for unerring guidance and loving comfort."

* * *

"We have perceived" — the Lord Maitreya remarked — "the majesty of your Godself speaking for both of you. It is wonderful! Now, please continue in the same manner and speak to us of Prayer."

"Prayer is a surrender and a communion. It is the most intimate approach of the Soul of man to God for the acknowledgement of a grace already received, and for the offering of the self for a task of collective good to perform. Man does not pray in order to extol his virtues or confess his vices, exchange of reward or punishment; he prays to listen and submit, then conform his life to the rules of conduct that were revealed to him.

"At work or at rest, the disciple of Light prays, and by enfolding every achievement in humility and gratitude, and by disclaiming authorship for whatever he does, he renders unto God what is God's, and receives in return gifts of great value in the form of more abundant health and wisdom, and also newer and higher responsibilities.

"He who prays for selfish reasons degrades his soul, for he worships a lesser god, a man-made deity which is beset with all the traits of man's limited outlook; the response cannot be but meager, while the prayer that reflects the spiritual and material welfare of the world, returns to the sender charged with the good will of the whole humanity.

"The highest form of prayer is silence and objectless meditation. Apart from the fact that loud appeals issue from men in fear, they also disturb the currents of thought and deviate the directness of man-to-God communion. The stilling of the mind and the no-thinking that follows an intense visualization, produce a void in man's consciousness which is immediately filled with divine light.

"When a man cogitates on a truth, or loses himself in reverie or smiles detachedly at the abuses received many years past, what does he actually do? He listens unconsciously to the Voice within. Let him link this process directly to the Flame in his heart, and he has issued a perfect prayer to God.

"Not for bread alone man lives, but for ideas, guidance and inspiration. This is the prayer of the man of science, the eclectic thinker and the true artist. And when they feel the warmth vibrating at a higher rate at the root of the nose, they know their prayer has been answered.

"In conclusion, O Most Serene and Loving Guardians of Creation, we think Prayer to be an arousement of the Sacred Fire from the base of the spinal column to the head leading to the union of earth and heaven. It is an urge which leads to the absolute certainty that God is the sole Author of all that is true, noble, holy and beautiful, and man the sole recipient of ITS unlimited estate."

* * *

The examination having terminated, the students were now subjected to the silent scrutiny of the seventy-seven Masters, as to behavior, poise, sincerity, alertness, humility, love and detachment from name, fame and ego-pursuit. Marco and Leonora also analyzed themselves as to worthiness and inner strength; the the Voice of the Self spoke in their hearts: "Persist, persist, persist. Enfold yourselves in the Christ-Light from dawn to dusk, and face the ascent with undaunted determination. Climb whereto no one can climb, and I shall raise you thereon and higher, beyond the inconceivable!" Now the Lord Maitreya spoke:

"Candidates Marco and Leonora, and thou, O reader, listen and learn. The statement that God is the only Indweller and Overdweller everywhere, is mechanically uttered by all, accepted by a few, expressed by fewer. But with you it has become a passionate reality. Strong in you is the spirit of the mighty Ones who commenced from mere scantlings, as sinful beings, and scaled the Mount of Wisdom unaided by any visible teacher and unassisted by man-made doctrines. The heroic age of an uncompromising attitude in the field of the Spirit is not over, and it will never be over, because God needs this type of courage from every man to reach IT. Those whose striving is padded with litanies, novenas, chanting and rituals, are simply delaying their progress. Those who try to acquire merits in the Eye of God by cheating first and being generous afterward, hoping, as it were, to enter heaven by the side door, are wasting their time. The Way of God is one only for all men and for all time, namely, inner search and direct perception; the real value of action is subjected to this work of self-discovery. Aside from all this, all else is child's play.

"Those who are mostly responsible for the delay of the full influx of the blessings of the Golden Age, are the religious leaders, the so-called official dispensers of grace and anathema. They guide the unwary, the slothful, the unthinking people on a path made crooked with idolatry, fear and planned negativity. *Thou wert born in sin.* What an appalling statement, and what a nonsense. Thus they encroach upon man's conscience with the shadows of demigods, dogmatism, display of relics, holy books and a superiority complex, in order to weaken his power of initiative, degenerate his soul and turn him to wickedness.

"The teaching of the official church in any nation of the world, generates a feeling of uneasiness in the average individual who does not frequent the church periodically, confess periodically, and take communion periodically. As a result such a faithful one

408

is forced to assume a defeated look and an air of compunction every time he goes in and out of the church; for it is there that the harsh heavenly Judge stands terribly dissatisfied with man's conduct, ready to let loose his rage and wreck the world. This is the moronic and untenable interpretation of God handed down from a narrow and unscientific past. Such an interpretation has no place in today's scientific advancement.

"Nor are the ethical societies any better. They talk of moral laws and right living for the sake of intellectual gymnastics, rather than spiritual elevation, and they waste time and energy in unending argumentations. Here again one finds leaders of the same caliber of the sectarian priestcraft whose links can be traced to the black magic of decadent ancient Egypt.

"These spiritual vampires must go; they are holding back the realization of the Golden Age. They must be uprooted, not through a conflict of steel and blood, but through the withdrawal of support and adherence by all the true lovers of liberty. The concept of the One God — Formless, All-pervading and Beneficent Spirit — must stand clear and high in the consciousness of every man. Neither through begging or purchasing, nor through propitiation or bowing before a priestly robe, or intellectual stunts, or cultural exploits, can God be found. No, we say! Throw away these crutches, O man, and contact God within thy heart by the power and action of silence and mental concentration. See nothing else but the majesty of thy Soul. Learn, once and for all, that neither the Liberated Masters, nor incarnate Christs or Buddhas, nor acknowledged saints or madonnas, can ever bestow salvation. They — We — only point the way, repeat the law over and again, then wait patiently. Man must ascend towards us all by himself, unaided by outer forces, as if he were in a dark dungeon on a lonely planet in the vast universe.

"It never dawned in the mind of Master Jesus that his sacrifice should have meant wholesale salvation to a crowd of churchgoers, wishful thinkers, externalized worshippers and idolaters of well-polished moral sentences. The law of uninterrupted daily practice of introspection is absolute, not only for man but for us as well. Should we miss for one single moment our conscious link with God, should we issue a statement unaware of HIM, we would plunge right back into the human plane or worse.

409

And from the human plane, it is the continuous awareness of God that raises man's consciousness to our cosmic status. There is more truth and spirituality in one inner glimpse than in a pilgrimage to a famous sanctuary.

✿ ✿ ✿

"Children of God, sons of man, offsprings of karma, listen and learn: when the earth was still engulfed in darkness, I was swimming in Light, for I had found God, and known HIM and worshipped HIM as Spirit and Truth. I knew of no master to whom I could go for help. There were no physical temples, stoneworks of human skill, nor custodians of knowledge and mysteries to whom I could direct my footsteps. None! Running here and there was of no use, for the earth was almost empty. The few inhabitants were either illumined or nonillumined. The nonillumined knew nothing of the Law, and the others kept on saying: 'Be still, O man, and know that I AM OM within thy heart. Be still and search for ME there. . . .' And having no other pulls, I let myself be drawn by the magnetic force of the sacred words I AM OM, I AM OM, I AM OM . . . This was my lifelong prayer; simple words, the true logos, accompanied by undeflected visualization and power of will that broke all bounds.

"By such a process I uprooted my family tree of earthly pride and carnal instincts, and linked myself to the Tree of Life whose roots are planted in the heart of God. I learned about the Divine Oneness of which every living being is an integral part. The sun and stars offered me shelter of undecaying beauty; light and silence, humming God's glories, were my friends and companions. Darkness was beneath my feet and around me, interrupted by the illumined Souls who walked the Earth, forded rivers, crossed oceans, penetrated forests and climbed mountain peaks, repeating the sentence I AM OM, I AM OM, I AM OM . . . in obedience to God's command and without any pressure or missionary intent. Then the Logos ordered me to go here and there and yonder places to speak of God whenever I felt the inner urge. I spoke often in solitary steads, or by the edge of dangerous mountain ridges, or at the foot of a crashing waterfall. I never saw a human being, and at that time it appeared to me that I never attracted an

410

unillumined soul. Yet I kept on charging the atmosphere of Earth with the simple, ringing and mighty words *I AM OM*. I lived in the flesh two thousand years, and it took that long span of time before I commenced to hear the sound of my words, echoing throughout the world and penetrating into the consciousness of man. People by the millions accepted my message and practiced the Law that I had spread for twenty centuries. Unmindful of results, desireless and unattached, I was not aware of the time and energy spent for a cause of such universal import. This is missionary work with no intent of proselitism.

"This was the law of my being, and it had improved but little until after the coming of Master Jesus. It was almost as difficult for the Teacher of Nazareth. But today it is not so; because of the Law of Dispensation, it is as easy as driving a car on a freeway. Though every man has the same powers and possibilities of a Lord Maitreya, no longer are such tests imposed, nevertheless those who attain total cosmic freedom are few. There is a greater collective spiritual advancement on Earth today, but a lagging in the number of single individuals who knock at the gates of the ultimate goal.

"Mankind must awaken. Spiritual expansion does not move abreast with scientific progress. Blind leaders, tools of reactionary theocratic teaching, lacking imagination and will to learn, have defined the behavior of the atom, mechanical inventions, the expansion of chemistry, electronics, and the achievements in the space program, as an emanation of the over-squeezed intellect, the triumph of the mortal mind. After all none of the holy books mentions such a thing as mechanical flight, and any attempt in this direction is a defiance — a *sin* — against the *immutable* teachings of the Sacred Scriptures. In politics, the much praised concept of democracy has lost all vitality and turned into an abhorrent fetish. Conceived to serve man, it now dominates tyrannically a crowd of short-sighted and spineless intellectuals who stand in awe before its Molochial presence. The concept of freedom must be understood as not violating the basic rights of others, nor of making arbitrary demands of existing institutions for sudden concession of reforms by a show of force led by professional demagogues; for this is indeed lawlessness bordering on civil war. Freedom

411

embodies the concept of respect, reasoning, and give and take.

"In the field of economics, while science declares that there could be jobs and prosperity, food and comfort for every healthy individual, economists and financiers respond with oracular pronouncements, based on the past, of inevitable recession following periods of prosperity. They toy arbitrarily with real wealth, balance of trade and other aspects of production, consumption and exchange, for the purpose of demonstrating that poverty is an inalterable fact of life. Unable to attune themselves with the cosmic or super-scientific laws of Celestial Harmonies, they fall into a maze of contradictions and to save their pride they expand definitions of old economic *laws* with the intent of confusing the public and enhancing their prestige. In this they succeed, for the masses already steeped in negativism born of a fatalistic tradition of fear and submission, yield like sheep to whatever these *savants say*. This will not be for long, however.

"Because of this intellectual and spiritual inadequacy, radical political movements come into being. How is it that no one learns from past history until it is too late? Students riot because of the appalling doctrinal confusion which they have to accept as basic truth from their professors. The Negros organize uprisings because they see the government ready and willing to spend billions of dollars for wars — whether justified or not — and then declare that the national economy does not warrant the same expenditure to educate the underprivileged or to do away with slums and endemic poverty. The youth of every country rebel because they see their elders preaching one set of laws and practicing another.

"There is another problem that calls for immediate attention if the present generation is to be saved for a more constructive adulthood. Society en masse must be taught how degenerative is the practice of gambling, for the mind, body and soul. It weakens the will to the state of a prone beast of burden, it destroys all trace of initiative, even of mere existence, by making man dependent on the illusion of a chance to be wealthy overnight. It causes bitterness, fear, graspingness and outright crime. May all the gambling dens of the world be reduced to ashes.

"These centers of vice, ignorance and crime, shall be erased

412

from the face of the Earth; the sooner the better. Since we cannot rely on the legislative institutes of the land, we appeal to parents and the thinking masses. We are eagerly awaiting a spontaneous outburst of inner light from the mind of every intelligent person. That light we shall take and expand it a millionfold for the benefit of mankind.

"Blessed candidates, these teachings and all that they imply, the unspoken words and their radiation, are given unto you both and to all men, out of love of our hearts, as a source of strength and renewed faith in the Ultimate Goal. You have revamped and given cogency to the ever-living concept of the ascension of man and the immortality of the soul, as very few have done since the Ascension of Master Jesus. However, the message that follows is for you only, as future messengers at the direct service of the Cosmic Assembly of the Perfect Ones.

"You are herewith commanded to forget yourselves as human entities. This is accomplished through absolute severance with the past, even the immediate future, even from the good deeds performed a little while ago. Keep the six cup-centers of the body unobstructed, empty and constantly directed towards the Source of Light, Energy and Substance. Burn and shatter all residue of tradition, attachment and family traits, and link yourselves indissolubly to the One Unqualified Cause. Thus you shall change from beings of limited consciousness to beings of becoming, fully aware of the Eternal Now, gazing at the Infinitude of life.

"Of the things of God, which come to you by direct perception, speak to no one who is not qualified to receive them, who lacks faith and humility, who takes delight in extrovertness and rhetoric. Refrain from teaching where cleanliness and orderliness are in default, where the listeners are rude and rough-mannered, where clatter and irresponsibility prevail. Where personal instructions are needed, speak not, but write messages.

"Reveal unto those who are worthy to receive it the overpowering reality of the life of the beyond, that they may commence to lose all fear of death. Tell them that their connection with God has never been severed, but only forgotten. Help them in the restoration of this connection by the path you consider best in each specific case; for whoever does as taught by the appointed messenger shall surely reach the goal.

413

"This God gave to us in ancient times, as a result of our obedience and determination. This we give to every man who likewise obeys and practices.

"On the Path of Truth you have had moments – nay days, months and years – of hesitation, which you have overcome through the discipline of meditation. Hesitation is a part of man's process of becoming; to doubt and reflect means to search and find, and reach the goal.

"The deep meaning of our teaching can only be grasped by those who seek inwardly; it does not convey conviction from without; it leads to the realization of the ancient Truth: *Man, know thyself and thou shalt know the universe and God.* This sentence is carved in letters of living light on a monument made of everlasting material: the heart of man. It was true yesterday, it is true and feasible today and forever. It is the supreme anchorage of the Real Man, the being of becoming, the Son of God, the Christ.

"Blessed candidates, the more you enter the bottomless depths of your hearts, the closer you are to Us, the more securely anchored you are to peace and knowledge, to the riverbank of immortality. You have passed your examination!"

* * *

The words *Son of God* echoed again and again throughout the remote countryside. The celestial meadow rose slowly until it stood higher than the towering mountain ranges that had surrounded it. Marco and Leonora now stood alone, master-surveyors of a panorama of indescribable splendor: far distant mountain peaks crowned with light, the limpid blue sky adorned with whirling discs of light as large as the physical sun, spiraling higher and ever higher throwing ribbons of fire in prismatic colors into the atmosphere. The Music of the Spheres was heard surging forth from everywhere – sublime, mysterious and poignant. The Masters of the Board now reappeared, and disposed themselves along the perimeter of the garden by the fir trees, and gradually receded from sight.

Marco and Leonora entered the superconscious, and as they returned to the awareness of their starry environment found themselves beneath a shower of cascading rose petals whose fragrance reminded them of the Mystic Rose of Isis of ancient

414

Egypt. Gradually the petals formed an enormous rose of matchless beauty, which then changed into the familiar form of Master Sonchis. Embracing his former students, He drew the signet of initiation of the ancient school of Memphis on their foreheads and invited them to follow Him. He led them towards a beautiful tropical grove, in which was a secluded circular portico with pillars of tall ferns; the ground was covered with silky lawn in patterns of concentric colors. At the center stood a giant fern whose thickly foliated branches produced a twilight shade within this living rotunda, but as the Master entered, the light emanating from his countenance filled the enclosure with a shadowless brilliancy.

"This is my Tree of Silence" — he said. "It gave me shelter during my meditation in my last embodiment. I raised it to immortality after my ascension. Every Liberated Master has a tree which tells the story of his striving and triumph; within its shade now I contemplate. Master Gautama the Buddha had the bodhi tree and Master Jesus the olive tree. Here one perceives the principle of obedience and the principle of purity whose combined action unfolds the virtue of humility — a firm foundation for a spiritual program."

Leonora silently expressed the desire to meet the Master's Twin Flame. Sonchis felt the impulse and said: "Be still and direct your attention southward." They saw a pinpoint of light approaching, which increased in size and brilliance as it drew nearer. Presently the body-form of a beautiful maiden, clad in a mantilla of white velvet, became visible. She looked about seventeen with brown eyes, chestnut brown hair and olive tinted skin.

"Your invitation" — she said — "was instrumental in expediting the work in which I was engaged in the Southern Hemisphere of the continent of the Americas. The message of Meditation which you are about to convey to mankind shall touch deeply the hearts and minds of the inhabitants of Central and South America." Sonchis introduced her as Antilia, his Twin Flame, whose liberation was completed three thousand years earlier than his.

"For thirty centuries" — she resumed — "through impulses of love I helped my darling Twin in the realization of his cosmic birthday, which is the culminating episode of every man's earthly life. During that long span of time I also worked to raise the consciousness of My people, for, as you can see by My features, I am an American-Indian. I humbly suggest to the lawmakers of Washington to do something and quickly so as to alleviate the suffering and also to abrogate all restrictions imposed on my people, and reintegrate them to the full rights of equality and opportunity of the rest of the citizens. Should your country heed not my suggestions, there will be uprisings in the years ahead far worse than those you are experiencing presently with the Negro population.

"Because of My utter devotion to the cause of My people, the islands of the Antilles were given My name; the Cosmic Assembly of the Perfect Ones made Me also the ruler of the Southern Constellation Antlia.

"I am happy to perceive in your auras all the elements of perfect spiritual twinship, a condition of unending peace and joy while on earth. Be grateful to God that you have found each other; it has been instrumental in placing you under the tutelage of the Liberated Masters. However, see that you do no relent your inner application. Guard and protect with keen alertness your spiritual estate; know that as is the apple tree among the trees of an orchard, so it is with you amongst men and other disciples of light: the strongest, the humblest, the most envied and the most beloved."

❋   ❋   ❋

As Master Sonchis and Antilia withdrew, Marco and Leonora levitated themselves towards a pool of crystal-clear waters that flowed from a natural rock-bottomed basin, partially hidden by a wide expanse of living verdure. They saw approaching, floating in the air towards the pool, two angelic beings, and as they came nearer they recognized them as their Liberated Master-Teacher and his Twin Flame. She held in her hands a tray of gold on which were four chalices of blue crystal, while He held an amphora of crystal and gold filled with water from the pool. A chalice was given to each one and they were invited to drink.

"This symposium" — the Master said — "is in honor of your graduation, and the sacred water of the River Orio that you have imbibed constitutes the baptism of living light to the holy

416

centers of your bodies. It means that you are linked forever, consciously, with the Christ-light. We congratulate you. Now, please, return to earth."

Three days later at dawn, they were summoned by their Liberated Master-Teacher by the now familiar sound of tingling bells. In less than an instant they found themselves walking with Him along the left bank of the mystic River Orio. The silvery-violet crystalline waters flowed silently and peacefully, the purple rays of the seven suns above showered them with highly invigorating light, a heavenly enchantment enveloped their Spirit-forms. They followed the river along its sandy bank, for a short distance, when it ended abruptly falling a thousand feet in foaming, splashing turbulence, into an immense irregularly contoured basin, filled with rocks and dead tree stumps. The tranparency of the water had disappeared, and the spuming liquid mass was now turbid and slimy, giving forth an unpleasant exhalation. Thinking of the placid pool that they had just left behind, the contrast was startling. Down below they saw a scene of opposing elements and warring forces, of unending chaos and hatred, but as they directed their attention towards the source of the river, the turbulence ceased and the water was seen flowing smoothly and disappearing beneath the rocks, pure and crystal-clear. Perceiving their confusion, the Master explained:

"Return your gaze to that gorge of turmoil, and listen and learn: You are looking at Lake Tasimac in the sphere of the moon-consciousness; it is not one thousand feet below from where you are standing, but rather an interstellar distance separates us from it. As the profound yearning for divine guidance cherished by the disciple of light brings events of the fourth dimension within sense perception, likewise, it draws interstellar happenings within physical sight. This lake is the symbol of inconstancy, ambition and earthly love, man's self-thrusting towards self-annihilation; it symbolizes also the pressure of the outer world upon man's behavior. Because the ideal absolute is unrealizable on earth, man's noble urge to adhere to the law of ethics and the principle of tolerance, is stifled by inescapable events which force him to deviate from his path. Compelled to move from one compromise to another, it seems — like the water — as if he wallows in filth, as if his inner world

417

of peace and perfect immutability is irremediably broken down by the jaggedness of materiality and the turmoil of the world. Not so, not so! If he fastens his visualization on truth and justice — like the water down below that returns to its pristine clarity — his soul remains unstained, and advances smoothly towards the vast ocean of life, into final mergence with God.

"I perceive another question whirling in your minds. Why do these beautiful and calm waters of the River Orio — born of silence and harmony, and charged with Christ-light — have to end their existence in such a manner?

"Still yourselves and reflect: *there is no ending.* Every planet or starry body is endowed with a certain amount of water or similar liquid. You cannot destroy a drop of it, no matter how you use it. In the present instance the water, bound by its own nature, makes no attempt to overrule its own God-given attributes and prerogatives. It falls from above, passes the filter of the rocks, comes out as a stream, precipitates as a cascade, forms lakes and rivers, and reaches the ocean; and whatever burden it carries is immediately released therein. From the surface of lakes, rivers, oceans, sewers and lumber lagoons, the same water, although temporarily altered, evaporates in its pristine nature to refall to earth in the wholeness of its God-bestowed power and vibration. That is all! All the elements of the soil and of the air are likewise bound by their own intelligence; aware of their Maker they submit to transformation through unending actions and reactions without losing in the slightest their individuality, that is, their immutable nature.

"The nature of man is infinitely greater than that of water, trees or soil, for it is God-identified Nature. Man possesses the gift of mastery over the elements, including the atomic structure of his body, by the control of his thoughts and the rising of his feelings. If he would only learn how to apply an infinitesimal fraction of this power in dealing with his fellow man and nature, he could obliterate, at least, four of the negative drags of earthly life: war, poverty, crime and disease.

❊ ❊ ❊

"Having now comprehended the inner behavior of the water, we shall pass to another set of revelations.

"This starry land has not only all the physical characteristics

418

and attributes of a fixed star, it is also illumined by a circular concave band of brilliant bodies, overlapping one another, the light of each nine times as intense as the physical sun. As this heaven rotates around its axis, even as the earth does, it passes from the angular amplitude of one sun to another without any marked change in the degree of luminosity. This constant flooding of light, from within and from without, enables the starry inhabitants to visit many places simultaneously, yet without leaving their original abodes. Far and near objects are seen, felt, heard and touched with the same degree of perception.

"The heavenly bodies are at the disposal of man. They are, in fact, the proving ground for his creative ability, and the catapult that assists him in projecting the mind towards the illimitable. Man travels as he thinks or dreams. And if it is so with an imprisoned soul, how much truer it is when he has discarded the flesh structure and reached the celestial residence. Now the Soul travels from star to star as one would take a trip on Earth from one country to another. Like earthly tourists, the Soul has preferences based on pleasant experiences that go back even millions of years, to the inception of life. A person who declares his or her attachment for the Star Venus or the Polar Star, for example, does not talk idly, nor does he make poetry; it is an atavistic pronunciamento of profound psychological importance whose further investigation will lead to a better self-appraisal in rapport to immortality. In this starry visiting, which could be compared to a post-graduate course in the Science of the Self, the Soul finds, among other things, proof of his knowledge within, and learns the nature of his past blunders and pitfalls that held him bound to matter through an unending chain of embodiments. However if he wants to remember them for the sake of achieving a higher spiritual status in the next embodiment, he must begin to think about it while still on Earth. Through actual living tests, he is shown all his errors, antagonistic attitude and deliberate refusal to accept inner guidance. All knowledge is the fruit of experience, even in the realm of the Spirit.

"During the process of searching for a messenger or a prophet, the Liberated Master in charge delves first into the hearts of men, irrespective of faces, social rank, economic status or intellectual level; and having found the individual, he then makes an accurate study of his Akashic Records followed by a deeper examination of the starry files of the would-be messenger. And though the chosen channel may later disappoint the Master, nevertheless, this is the procedure. So unpredictable is man that even a Christ can err in defining him. Seldom the messenger marked for a divine mission remains humble and obedient, hence the saying: *Many are the chosen, few the elect.* Unable to evaluate the responsibility involved, he takes unauthorized initiatives and walks proudly amongst men, issuing personal statements and presenting them as divine, in order to impress an audience or acquire fame and wealth. A few others — perhaps one or two in every millennium — by underevaluating their inner strength, feel inadequate for the task and beg their Master to be spared. Moses was one of these.

"He who is finally accepted — the elect — is placed under intense training, yoga discipline. He is taught and shown how to separate the real from the seeming, and how all created things that serve man revolve around the same nucleus and incline towards the same focus. The saint and the sinner, the rich and the pauper, the law-abiding citizen and the lawbreaker, the believer and the agnostic, and the genius and the fool, will be seen walking abreast towards the same destination; some directly by the manly and arduous route of inward seeking and steadfast determination; others through tergiversation, cheating and aeons of ignominious suffering. He will be instructed on how to find elements of wisdom in all he sees; beauty and ugliness, good and evil, birth and death, virtue and vice, love and hatred; and out of them draw worthy lessons to live by. He will be guided with a loving hand into the retreat of the heart, and taught how to bring about the dissolution of all past, present and future karma.

"Notwithstanding our love, patience and wisdom, some of these chosen ones will fail to pass the test. These we do not reject and send back to earth; instead we take them under our wings and enroll them in one of the starry colleges for Self-reclamation whereby they graduate as Brothers of the Inner, Divine Helpers, Scientists of the Soul, or even Master-Teachers. Following a temporary forfeiture of their free will, they are taught how to take apart their mortal bundle of limitations accumulated through the ages, how to separate and dissect the billions of elements found therein, and then re-constitute them by the application of mathematical laws, to fit the specific task for which they show proficiency. Please abide in stillness, and I shall cause you to levitate yourselves to one of these colleges."

They alighted on a magnificent campus teeming with activity. The students, whose composure radiated handsomeness and majesty of behavior, wore patrician robes of the classic ages of India, China, Persia, and ancient Egypt, Greece and Rome; some were of the Inca civilization. As soon as Marco and Leonora arrived, they were welcomed by a group of students, who in one voice said: "We greet the Divine in you, Masters; in celestial blessings you have come to our shores." "We are visitors in search of knowledge. My name is Marco, and this is Leonora, mv Twin Flame" — Marco responded.

A young lady of exceptional beauty and charm, with the appearance of an American Indian stepped forward and said: "And my name is Luminia, a humble teacher of this noble group of students. There is no need to tell you that we are the backward children of heaven. Born we were on earth for spiritual leadership, but we all failed because of simple neg-ligence, not out of malice. When our Masters told us that we would have the choice of returning to earth to try again, or accept the boon of this scholarship, we surrendered ourselves to their wisdom and wept in gratitude. Having tasted the bliss of the incorporeal, we could not have enjoyed the coarseness of the physical body; hence our noble and wise choice.

"My act of negligence on earth stemmed from an unwill-ingness to resist a forced marriage. In my last embodiment I was the daughter of an Inca Chief who was a worshipper of the Sun-god, while my mother was an American Indian. One day, almost a hundred years previous to the coming of Columbus, my parents suggested that I should marry a man whom I did not love. I could have said *no*, but I did not, and accepted my lot passively. I spent my free hours in meditation and prayer and became the disciple of a Lady Master the Goddess of Liberty who wanted to initiate me for spiritual leadership amongst my people. But while in training I could not take my mind off the plight into which I had fallen; hence my negligence. When I entered this school, after my passing away from the

Earth, I applied myself so earnestly that my Goddess-Teacher entrusted me with the task of invisibly guiding Columbus towards the shores of the West Indies. And having succeeded I was appointed tutor of this group of students whom I accompany from classroom to classroom and from one laboratory to another where Splendor-beings teach the Science of the Self. We are now ready to return to Earth as giants of both the Spirit and the Intellect. Our preference is the continent of the Americas, but it shall not be so. I am scheduled to descend to China, and some of my students will accompany me as Apostles of Light, all working under the direction of Lady Master Quan Yin and the Goddess of Liberty.

"We thank you for your visit, O privileged travelers. May you succeed in making a precise record of this celestial experience for the benefit of mankind. It is in itself a message of positive hope for the super sensitive human beings who feel overly distressed when, in spite of severe watchfulness, they commit a slight violation of the unwritten law. Take courage, O obedient sons and daughters of man, and surrender yourselves at the Feet of the Self, both in repentance and joyfully. You have been rescued."

Marco and Leonora returned to the banks of the River Orio to report to their Liberated Master-Teacher.

"Because of this visit of yours" — He announced — "the Cosmic Assembly of the Perfect Ones has decreed to fill to capacity all the schools of reclamation with those who took part in World War II, the Korean War and the present war in Vietnam, and passed away while fighting. We shall cause the killer and the killed to meet and sit side by side in the same classroom, listening to the same teaching of love and brotherhood. Some will never take embodiment again, while the others will be sent to the country or people against whom they fought; and by this intermingling of souls, we shall hasten the realization of the enduring peace of the Golden Age. You have rendered a service of cosmic import to the World and God.

*　*　*

"There is a celestial gift, nay a boon, that man enjoys and whose proper use spells godhood for the fortunate one. It is free will. It has been proclaimed and sung throughout your historical centuries, from the ancient Hebrew masters, Greek and Roman

422

philosophers, the Fathers of the Church, Dante, Spinoza, Kant, Schopenhauer, Mazzini and many other inspired lifestreams, as the living pulsation of God reaching the mind of man in a straight and undeviating current. It is true, and it embodies the unrestricted pursuance of man's own inspiration, and also the clear knowledge that these aspirations can be fulfilled without interfering with the constructive dreams and desires of one's fellow man. When properly applied, free will turns man into a god, while through misuse it creates chaos for both himself and society. Every time man says *Yea* or *Nay,* either for an important decision or for a trifle, he works cosmically and assumes a tremendous responsibility. Merit and demerit, freedom and bondage are thus brought into being.

"Free will properly channeled constitutes a powerful instrument for self-purification, through the discipline it imposes upon the mind for keen analyzation of actions. It makes man independent, respected and beloved. There is neither evolutive process nor durability in an organized collectivity where laws and decrees are not *freely* accepted by the masses; that is, where the citizens do not, of their own *free will,* issue, codify and declare to obey their own laws and the institutes and organs of their application. Nor does a ruler stay long in power if he uses his free will for selfish purposes, mismanagement or persecution; for having forgotten the divine origin of this gift he is no longer able to rule wisely. His self-created doom is near at hand.

"Often men of responsibility — men singled out by the Masters for an epoch-making role — are tested in a strange manner. Beings of great merit are dispatched into the human fold as simple, unpretentious and meek individuals who, unaware of their intelligence and power, yet with a remote and compelling urge to do and to dare, rise high in the estimation of great rulers. As a powerful and wise leader and a humble disciple of light meet, they fire one another in such a way, that they both become aware of being on trial; this trial being of inner nature. And they are correct in their appraisal, except that sooner or later, either one or both, forget this initial point and, through a series of selfish actions, fall by the wayside and wreck a whole cycle of existence for themselves and others. The unwise use of free will has led to the obfuscation of the mind and rising of passions.

"In the thirteenth century a ruler of Provence, in southeastern

France, a disciple of light by the name of Raymond Berengar IV, had been entrusted with the mission of fostering the arts of peace amongst the various rulers of Europe. Raymond, who had enjoyed a long stretch of heavenly bliss previous to his birth, was an ardent lover of beaux-arts, and consequently his court had become an academy of liberal faculties for poets, music composers, painters, dramatists and philosophers from all over the continent. He declared that a covenant for universal peace was feasible through permanent exhibitions of works of art, the exchange of artists and philosophers from court to court, and the translation of literary works and philosophical treatises into every known language. Raymond's four charming and marriageable daughters — Margaret, Eleanor, Sancha and Beatrice — were a powerful incentive for the realization of his program. Guests of royal blood were always present.

"One day a wandering tramp by the name of Romeo D'Arles, knocked at the massive gate of Raymond's palace and, unconcerned of his ragged clothes, firmly requested the captain of the guards to announce him to the king. The officer not only refused to comply with the bold request, but made it known that he would not hesitate to use physical force to prevent the unkempt visitor from entering; wherefore Romeo, disregarding all threats, passed through the iron bars as easily as if riding in state. On his way to the throne room, he encountered the prime minister who became enraged at the sight of the disreputable intruder; but as he tried to stop him, he found that he had lost the power of speech and the ability to move his limbs. Romeo reached the audience chamber where the king was engaged in diplomatic affairs; as the two personages became aware of each other, Raymond dismissed his guests and secretaries, and, having accepted the marks of obeisance from the strange visitor, granted him permission to speak.

"'Sire' — he said — 'I am come to assist you in the fulfillment of your program. I am prepared to serve. Accept me unreservedly and all shall be well!'

"'Friend' — the king answered — 'I do not know who you are, but I feel that you deserve to be trusted.'

"As prime minister, Romeo was wise and humble. He ruled with uncanny mastery and penetrating intelligence, gave commissions and hired personnel with unfailing skill. All European potentates sought his wise counsel. Poverty and crime were greatly reduced through the application of the Pythagorean laws. The army was cut in half. At the expiration of his first year of service, he had given Margaret in marriage to Louis IX, the saint, king of France; within the succeeding year Eleanor married the king of England, Henry III, and Sancha his brother Richard of Cornwall, while Beatrice became the wife of Charles D'Anjou, King Louis' brother. When Raymond protested that Beatrice's marriage did not seem comparable with the other sisters', Romeo prophesied that Charles would be the most important personage of Europe for generations to come, for he would be the founder of the English ruling house of the Plantagenets whose descendants would bring forth the Constitution and the Magna Carta.

"Now the first stage of Romeo's task was completed. He was ready to begin that of peacemaker. Continental Europe and the British Isles were entwined by blood relationship, exactly as envisaged by the Cosmic Assembly of the Perfect Ones, fear of being overrun by invasion no longer existed. The exchange of artists and philosophers was about to receive a renewed impetus when, in an unguarded moment, Raymond's heart became polluted with pride and a feeling of grandeur; he listened to envious and sycophantic courtiers insinuating against the wisdom and statesmanship of Romeo. No longer did he trust his faithful servant. As Romeo became aware of his master's attitude, he spoke his heart to the king:

" 'Sire, because of your trustful acceptance of my service, you have achieved an enviable pre-eminence amongst the royal families of Europe, and also made yourself dear to the Liberated Masters. We had laid the foundation for the United States of Europe, and were now ready to bring into being the second stage of our mission of world peace. Alas, O my King, erelong all shall fall into ruins. You have ceased to respond to my pulsations of good, love and wisdom. Thy Pure Will is gone, no longer can I communicate with you. Mercy unto thee!

" 'O child of Earth, I take leave of thee. A ragged tramp I came, likewise I shall go!'

"Romeo's fine robe changed into one of a wandering hermit. He bowed before his master and withdrew. As he reached the outer wall of the capital city, his ragged appearance was transmuted into that of a master of life, then he burst into a flame and ascended skyward. Will you please direct your attention to Romeo D'Arles that he may descend from the realm of Splendorhood and tell you of the motive of his actions."

In the depths of samadhi Marco and Leonora beheld a youth, bearing on his forehead the seal of a mighty ruler of men and gods:

"Greetings, my friends and candidates for starhood. How much was Europe — then a cauldron of hatred and envy — assuaged by the perfect marriages of the four princesses, is difficult to establish by the standard of human thinking. I was a perfect match-maker in the sense that the four couples were actually four sets of twin flames whose reunion sealed their ultimate destiny which caused them to skip over many future embodiments and realize the ultimate goal of earthly life, deliverance.

"King Raymond after my departure saw his error and, because of my prompt and complete forgiveness, aided by his sincere repentance and a few years of intense meditation and spiritual discipline, he was re-admitted into the path of spiritual ascendancy. His karma being excellent and the fact that he had been a wise ruler, lover of the arts and an instrument of peace and intercontinental collaboration in an age when thieving, oppression and mercilessness were the main tools of life for both the rulers and the masses, shows that he had been chosen by the Masters for that specific assignment. Though he failed, he earned the scholarship for the college of Self-reclamation and conquered death forever. Had I not forgiven him and burned to ashes all the vibration of his unwise behavior, his inner progress would have been barred and mine too. The act of forgiving is the most stupendous dissolver of unkind karma; it restores to a state of grace both the forgiver and the forgiven, and it summons the Masters of the heavenly realms for further illumination and guidance.

"The forgiving man offers the chalice of his heart, emptied of all, to God, to be filled with the Light of Beauty, the Light of Wisdom and the Light of Peace. It is like giving a little, a few crumbs from your table to the hungry creatures of the wild, in exchange for cosmic freedom; yes, freedom from the despotic

426

oppression of death, ugliness, ignorance and defeat. May forgiveness be the rule of conduct of every sentient being!

* * *

"Another wise ruler, lawgiver and peacemaker" — Master Romeo continued — "who left behind a seraphic radiance of forgiveness and earned for himself the Triple Flame of Beauty, Wisdom and Peace, was the king-prophet Melchizedek of Salem. After the Battle of the Kings, which brought to an end thirteen years of hostilities, the warring leaders elected the noble monarch as the supreme arbiter of their future destinies. At the peace conference, held in the Hall of Judgement in the temple of Salem, nine-hundred representatives of every tribe signed the Pact of Brotherhood on earth and heaven. Prior to the momentous decision, however, the king-prophet had invited the assembled delegates to meditate on the Flame in their hearts as the most tangible source of wisdom, forgiveness and lasting peace. For thirteen hours, each corresponding to a year of war, their minds and feelings were invested with the purple fire of purification. As diplomatic peace was achieved, Melchizedek again invited the members of the large assemblage to direct their attention unto him to witness the creative power of a mind made pure through forgiveness and selfless service.

"Composed in meditation, and through the manipulation of light, energy and substance, he transmuted the Hall of Judgement into a banquet hall, and by the same creative power he precipitated exquisite viands from the unseen. Then he addressed the assembly:

" 'Salutations and blessings unto you all. When man lies prone at the Feet of his Godhead within, he becomes a miracle-producing being in every field of endeavour. Each one of us — you and you and every man, born or to be born — is endowed with enough power and wisdom as to make him grow and prosper not at the expense of someone else's domain, but through the diversified manifestations of the Soul-OM Who is the sole Releaser of Wealth. In these thirteen hours of *Life in a Retreat*, you have acquired that power and wisdom. Go, and keep them alive and active through meditation and awareness. Express the Law in a way that is all yours — *original* — by surrendering your minds to God. Do not imitate one another, do not steal from one

427

another, even in thought, but direct the power of free will to the Self within and draw therefrom all that you need for deeds of everlasting value. Blessings and salutations!'

"This" — Master Romeo concluded — "is the power wielded by a man who walks in the light, over men's thoughts and passions. It is in meditation that God's attributes take root in man's conscience, while human events bring them forth into the plane of actuation."

* * *

Held in the spell of Romeo's revelations, Marco and Leonora traveled towards a starry valley in the Heaven of Utter Silence. From the crest of one of the surrounding hills, they saw their Master-Teacher descending towards them with outstreched arms. He was robed in the garment of light of a Master Contemplator. The brightness of his countenance increased steadily as he came closer until nothing could be seen except his sandaled feet. As he reached them, the Music of the Spheres burst forth in its full-fledged splendor of the Symphony of Triumph.

"I have provided this music for you" — he said — "to fill your hearts with such joyous vibration that nothing but heavenly peace will ever abide with you. Be enthusiastic to the point of ceaseless exaltation both in meditation and in your outer activities. This is a prescription not only in the cultivation of love for its own sake but also in maintaining a healthy body permanently. Be experts on joy and love. Inner specialization is more important than an outer one; its results have the mark of limitless durability.

"The physical sun is the typical expression of this practice of love. Before the sun came into being, every living form had its own sun in its heart which was nourished and kept ablaze through love and enthusiasm. Wherever one moved, the radiance of love and enthusiasm produced a luminance which was spread radially and brought into sight the physical panorama of things. The outer circular edge of that radiance was called *horizon*.

"Helios, the Elohim of Light, loved God with such intense transport and utter detachment that He desired only to be burned in the Fire of Love in the Heart of God. The boon was granted, and as he passed through the Portals of the Almighty, a spark issued from his forehead, whirled into space, grew in size and luminosity, and condensed into the physical sun.

428

" 'This is thy child!' — the Lord told Helios — 'Nurse It, and preside over its glory and beauty with the same love and enthusiasm that thou hast poured to life and to ME.'

"Thus Helios became the Elohim of universal Light and Love, and the first wielder of Cosmic Magnetism upon which the starry bodies depend for their harmonius behavior in the unending procession of life. Again, this is another proof of the power of man. From amongst the celestial entities that constitute the theme of astronomy, man is the loftiest, the wisest and the only being endowed with life that never ceases. Planets, stars, solar systems and systems of worlds, come, evolve, go and reappear to form new entities according to man's visualization and power, while man himself remains eternally the same, the truest image and likeness of God, the everlasting Christ, And though he encases his self within a form — now a human body, and now the aspect of an angel or a Splendor-being — this self is nothing else but the unborn and never-dying Self. It is entirely up to him to express these staggering attributes.

"To accept, live and apply this truth means to reclaim one's lordship over the whole creation and, through man-to-man love and collaboration, to guide in a conscious way all existing grouped entities in the universe to higher levels of living. Great Teachers of the past (and I confine myself to your historical past) such as Confucius, Gautama the Buddha, Pythagoras, Plato, Moses, Socrates, Jesus, Vico and others, proved such a collaboration possible and feasible. With passionate and resolute determination man must rescue himself and reclaim his Noble Heritage."

The Master paused, and for awhile was absorbed in profound cogitation. He paced back and forth as if to give shape to what he would reveal next; then he stopped and gazing into the infinity of time and space, spoke to himself in a whisper: "If man would only cease, once and forever, this damnable and soul-degenerating personality worshipping . . .; if public leaders, stars of the stage, screen and sports would discourage the masses, the youth and the simpletons to stand in awe before them . . .; if both parents and teachers would teach the children that there is no God with hands and feet to serve and worship, that there are no saints or heroes to envy or emulate . . .; that neither Master Jesus, nor any other Liberated Master could ever take *offense* at the lack of *respect* displayed by him who violates the Law of

Life . . .; that the only Eternal Reality in man's existence is the Majesty of his own Soul abiding in the Throne Room of his heart, that it is up to him to so live, think, plan and work as to honor the King always, and strive incessantly to behold Its Presence until he loses himself in It." Then He turned to His disciples and said:

"We guide humanity, and the revelations that follow must be viewed in this spirit. Man's salvation relies in obeying our instructions and worshipping the Light in his heart. There are three classes of Master Contemplators in this Heaven of Cosmic Life: Seraphim, Cherubim and Elohim. The Seraphim are Master-dispensers of Love, the Cherubim Master-dispensers of Cosmic Knowledge, the Elohim are Architect-builders, Master-mathematicians and dispensers of Cosmic Wisdom. They are all junior members of the Cosmic Assembly of the Perfect Ones.

"Now, the great Cosmic Being who was recently admitted into the aforesaid Hierarchy, and who is in charge of dispensing love to mankind and to life, is Master Jesus. He succeeds the great Hindu Master Krishna who has been assigned to higher duties in other solar systems. Master Jesus, whose ancestry goes back to Helios, is the sole ruler on Divine Love for the duration and up to the consummation of the Golden Age. All the lesser beings of the same rank — Mary of Nazareth, Mother Kali, Quan Yin and the Beings of Love from Venus — are henceforth placed under the cosmic supervision of Jesus whose entire cabinet has one-hundred-forty-four members. Since some of these members are well-known to the Western World, I refrain from mentioning their names because of the objectionable practice of men to worship personalities.

"On the plane of Cosmic Knowledge, the Chief Executive is Gautama Siddhartha the Buddha who succeeds Rama who, in turn, has become a White Quenchless Flame of Divine Contemplation, occupying the rank one step below the Kumaras. Master Gautama is assisted by his Twin Flame Yashodara, plus one-hundred-forty-four lesser Buddhas of Hindu origin. Of these I am permitted to mention Ananda, Moggalana, Sariputta, Lady Khema, Lady Visakha, Subhadda, Nagasena, Malunkyaputta, Vaccagottha, King Milinda, King Pasenadi, and Rahula (Gautama's son). These Liberated Masters — the wisest and most exalted disciples of the Buddha — were assigned, after their passing away,

430

to the Star Venus to await their Twin Flames and for additional training under the tutorship of Helios.

"It is written in the Hall of Records of this Starry Heaven that Queen Yashodara and her son-prince Rahula, though still rulers of an earthly dominion, submitted to divine training under the Archangel Raphael, with the provision of achieving the same state of consciousness as Master Siddhartha's. Having fulfilled all requirements as for purity and obedience to the Light, they were made Masters of Cosmic Knowledge and given the power to bring about the perfect synchronization of mind and soul of the Twin Flame-couples and their children for the incoming Golden Age. They attained such a state of harmonius relationship that, even while still on Earth, each was able to wield the power, knowledge and wisdom of the three combined.

"The Lord Maitreya completes the Triad of Cosmic Rulers as the Elohim of Wisdom. He stands supreme as coordinator of a perfect idea and its application in time and space. His Cosmic Cabinet consists of one-thousand-seven-hundred-twenty-eight great Lords of Life of whom Master Pythagoras is the Executive Director. Unto them is entrusted the power of interpretation and timely application of the fundamental laws relative to diplomatic intercourse, international collaboration, and the welfare and peace of the world. In the field of the Science of Space they preside over the scientists of Earth, directing their minds for successful exploits in the Space Program.

" 'The Earth' — says Lord Maitreya — 'has to be raised from the dungeon life in which she wallows today, into a life of purity, strength, mastery and wisdom. Saturn, Jupiter, the Maha Chohan, Mars, Venus, the Kumaras, Meru, Neptune, Tabor, Himalaya, Lady Vesta, Lady Minerva, Lady Juno and many other great Ones are by My side. There shall be wisdom and light for all living beings, for anyone who courageously makes the first attempt to practice meditation.'

"Now, there are four Liberated Masters who have been given the task of coordinating the three cosmic services: Love, Knowledge and Wisdom. One is Confucius who works in behalf of China, Japan, Mongolia, Korea and all the islands and territories of the Pacific Ocean, except Australia. Ramakrishna is the Master-coordinator for India, Tibet, Burma, Siam, Malay, Vietnam, Ceylon, Java, Sumatra, Afghanistan and Pakistan. The third

Master-coordinator is Moses, in charge of Africa, Arabia, Iran, all the Near East countries and territories, and east of the Urals, Siberia and the northern lands. He is assisted by Mohammed. The fourth Master-coordinator is your Liberated Master-Teacher, the revealer of the present information. I shall supervise Australia, North, Central and South America, Europe and the land of the Soviets, west of the Urals. My assistants are by the thousands and from every walk of life, and you are among the first ten. Messages and instructions will be released to you in the near future and from time to time; you will convey them to the masses who have ears to hear; and, I assure you, the receptive lifestreams are by the tens of millions. May I suggest that you attune yourselves with our Master-cherub Gautama and hear his message."

And the Buddha spoke:

"Humanity has reached the rim of cosmic liberty, and stands somehow confused at the sight of the magnificent expanse. Why? The people of earth, even those who seem to belong to the vanguard of the Spirit, hesitate to detach themselves from the old and plunge headlong into the arena of Dispensation. Needless to say, it requires an act of inner rebellion. The rope of tradition and attachment which, they thought weak and unresisting, appears instead strong and unyielding. It appears, I said, but it is not so. Meditation in depth is required. Then the rope of relics, rosary and robes, of confession, communion and celibacy, of tonsure, Masses and sermons, and of fast days and ritual, will vanish out of memory and existence. Search inwardly, O man, with enthusiasm and singleness of mind.

"Between the old and dying, and the ancient and everlasting there is a desert land of farewell, a condition of doubt, fear, emotional instability and spiritual insecurity. To be in it without a strong heart and undaunted faith means to live in utter bewilderment. To lose the old without perceiving the New and Eternal could lead to a state of inner dissolution. In this land many indulge in self-pity, moaning shamefully; a few strong-hearted ones make the jump. These are the nonconformists and the leaders whom we elect as visible teachers. Be patient, loving and merciful towards your lesser brothers. Draw them into the New Dawn of Life by showing them the Majesty of your Soul dominating your world. Place your-self on trial every night and

432

morning by facing the Tribunal of the heart, with Silence as the presiding judge, Solitude the only witness, the Power of the Will the sole prosecutor. It is enough! This is knowledge."

Then they heard Master Jesus speaking:

"To love divinely is to transcend body, mind, passion, race, creed and social rank. When man faces man, he stands before the sublime Presence of the Immutable from Whom his very life derives. Love THAT, O man, and be saved. However do not bow before anyone; remain straight and humble like a god.

"The disciple of the Inner must combat with all his mind and strength the degenerative and slavish practice of genuflection, loud repentance and dejected attitude before anybody, or any statue or picture or altar. Tell your children to be humble and free by directing their thoughts and love to the Flame in their hearts. The I AM of Which I spoke during My Messiahship was a reference to that Immutable Being overshadowing Me — the Christ — under Whom I worked, Whom I obeyed and served, Whom I loved without a single defection, Whom I still love and always shall. THAT I saw and loved in every man I met.

"The more man learns to love, the more he loves learning; then all the mysteries of the cosmos are revealed unto him; that he himself is the cosmos and the mysteries; he himself is the Holy Ghost and the Holy Comforter guiding his footsteps unerringly and speaking words of wisdom to the world at large.

"He who fails to perceive this inner wealth, he who refuses to love and to learn, is called a *prodigal son* — a wasteful, superficial and fearful individual. Cut off from the source of love and understanding, his life is compared to that of a pig in a pen. How does he set himself free from such a state? By making conscious appeals to the Christ within wherefrom the Holy Comforter arises. This is called self-analyzation. Now the ascending path begins through excruciating pain of physical nature, yet soothing to the soul and ennobling for the mind. And having reached the depths of desperation, the prodigal son feels it is the end, yes, the end of the ascending path, even the end of normal human living. As he covers his face and in bitter anguish weeps and groans as if staggering under an unbearable load, the veil of separation is torn asunder, for next to the bottom of helplessness lies the blazing light of salvation, perceived this time through forced introspection. A sense of wonderment holds his mind from wandering outwardly, and an upsurge of warmth convinces him that he is capable of loving and of being loved. This is actually a contact with a Liberated Master from my Cosmic Cabinet. The prodigal son has ceased to tarry in the valley of despond. He is rescued forever.

"The act of arising and returning to the Father's house is a promise to never cease meditating, and to acknowledge one's inner potentialities.

"It is my task and privilege to fill the earth with risen Christs out of the human material already in existence. The path of Love as herein presented will facilitate the realization of our mission.

"This is the spirit of the Golden Age, the age of universal peace, health, prosperity and spiritual exploits in every field of endeavour, achieved through the correct comprehension and application of the Law of Love."

❖   ❖   ❖

Marco and Leonora directed their thoughts to the banks of the River Orio, and the next instant they found themselves seated at the feet of their Liberated Master-Teacher listening to his teaching:

"When an ascended being speaks from his heavenly realm, he stands at the center of conscious life. His voice vibrates and radiates in every direction; it penetrates and interpenetrates the structure of the ether, air, fire, water, all opaque matter, hence of every living being. It travels radially until it reaches the boundaries of creation. Then it returns, like a wave in a pool, to its center of emanation charged with the impression produced in every form of life. Thus the Master learns about thought, action, reaction and need in the world of matter and form. He is also endowed with the power of absorption and self-diffusion, meaning that by directing his attention wherever he wishes, he can draw solid objects and living entities unto himself; or he can project his luminous presence to many places simultaneously, and make himself visible to whomsoever he desires. These same powers, although very limitedly, can be displayed by the disciple of Light, or a sensitive poet, or an eclectic philosopher, an artist or a scientist, when, by transcending mental and bodily limitations, they project themselves into the Superconscious for inspiration,

434

intuitiveness and prophetic visions that lead to higher truths and new trends in their field of action."

* * *

For many a day Marco and Leonora lived enwrapped in an aura of intense gratitude to God and the Liberated Masters who, patiently and lovingly, had guided them to the present state of Self-realization. But they felt that a superior strength and a greater determination were required to remain there and at the same time continue to advance and prosper in the harsh arena of the outer world. They appealed to their Liberated Master-Teacher for counsel and guidance:

"As long as you are keenly aware of the primeval karma that gives shade and form to your thoughts and deeds, and hold it there in the grip of your will, you shall cause the Law of Grace to work for you, guiding you safely through the circuitous trek of temptation and error. This means that you must never cease to acknowledge the existence of the forces of the downward pull every time you try to go higher. Remember: you have reached the stage whereby you can love and serve in the manner of the angels, who do wonders in the world of man without the slightest tinge of ego or desire for reward. To have the honor of serving God in serving life is the highest of all rewards, you deserve nothing else.

"By being aware of this angel-consciousness, feeling it and applying it, it causes you to live above karma, that is, above the action of the law of rebound; it is as if you were obeying the same Intelligence-Force that was given to man at the *beginning* or *first birth* into the edenic consciousness.

"This is the significance of the biblical expression: *In the beginning was the Word. . . .*, meaning THAT which announced the action of the Light which had to coalesce into individualized life lived in the consciousness of God. *. . . and the Word . . . —* Light and Life — *. . . was with God.* This signifies that in order to enjoy the companionship of God, one must adhere to the Light. *. . . and the Word was God*; this explains the oneness of life, God being the all in all. *. . . and the Light shineth in darkness . . .*, that is, in an environment where the awareness of God is very dim, hence: *. . . and darkness comprehended it not*, meaning that when a man rejects God's Presence or abuses God's Power, he ceases to comprehend God's Message of correct living; that is, he ceases to exist.

"*There was a man sent from God. . . .* — a perfect individual, fully aware of God's guidance, an angel-man — . . . *whose name was John* . . . (but it could be any man of any race or historical age, a man willing to obey, listen and work for a constructive purpose).

"As you see, whoever lives in the state of consciousness in which *John* lived, *is a man sent from God,* a lifestream enshrouded in grace, free from the action of karma and destined to absolute Self-Realization. This is the edenic state of life.

"The man of the world, you yourselves, belong to the class of the individualized streams of life whose behavior lowered or weakened the action of the *Word.* These gave origin to the human race as you see it today. Of these, some made valiant efforts to retrace the Light, others remained stationary, while still others kept on going downward until, through a series of destructive deeds, they became totally avulsed from the *Word,* lost their angelic identification and individualization, and were turned into riven specks of dimmed light and relegated into the boundaries of the Milky Way. However, by virtue of the new Cosmic Dispensation, these specks of light shall be redeemed, and through training and discipline, and according to the degree of their acceptance of God's Light, they will be allowed to take embodiment on Earth, or elsewhere, and start again on the ascending path towards final deliverance.

"Blessed ones, if it is easy to fall from Light into darkness, it is equally easy to adhere to the Light and enjoy the bliss and wisdom that it gives. It takes so little energy. When meditation ceases to be an exercise and becomes a habit, then a seamless garment — a garment that never soils or wears out — is given to you. Then you shall dwell in the Realm of the Free forever."

❊ ❊ ❊

As the Master's discourse ended, he seemed to be vanishing as if consumed by fire. He had almost reached the stage of complete obliteration, when gradually he began to assume the form of a gigantic pillar of dazzling light. From the pillar they heard his familiar voice:

"Arise above discontentment and idleness. Cultivate joy. Blend wisely action and meditation!"

A shaft of light came forth from the pillar, enveloped the two disciples and drew them unto itself. Rising vertically they soon found themselves within the vast boundaries of the sunbelt whose luminosity was not derived from the physical sun, but from a greater sun, the source of light and life upon which ninety-one solar systems depend for their cosmic existence. Again the voice spoke:

"Hearken and know, O happy disciples, that the Light which I project and appear to possess is, in truth, borrowed from the Cosmic Reservoir of Life. I own nothing, you own nothing. All belongs to God, all is Light, all is God!"

Leaving the sunbelt, they floated in space, following the disciplined motion of the celestial bodies. They made seven circuits — the shortest as long as the terrestrial equator, and the longest seven times the sun's maximum circumference — and reached another starry land.

"We are in the land of One Thousand Parks" — the voice informed them. "Each park has one thousand gardens, each as vast as the continent of North America. Observe: not a square inch of soil here is either jungle, virgin forest or impervious mountain. All is highly cultivated. There is no animal life except birds made of coalesced light in the colors of the solar spectrum. They sustain themselves on the nitrogen in the air which they inbreathe. The variety of the vegetation is so prodigious that no two gardens are similar; flowers, shrubbery and trees grow everywhere, from the soil and in the air, and without fertilization. Seeds, bulbs and spores are treated with atomic energy, and once planted they allow no other vegetation to grow within the radius of their maximum development. Master-agriculturists are constantly experimenting with new species of flowers and fruits, some of which they release to receptive agriculturists of earth. Because of their continuous radiation of love deleterious bacteria are nonexistent. When a fruit ripens or a flower reaches full bloom, unless picked, they are reabsorbed into their stems, changed into fertilizer and returned to the roots. There are lakes and rivers in great profusion free from insect life but rich in underwater vegetation. Each parkland, a universe unto itself, is the private garden of a Master-contemplator and his cosmic family consisting of worthy lifestreams of earth whom he trains for noble assignments on behalf of man."

Still following the Pillar of Light they came to another park. High above it, as if suspended in midair, they saw a most unusual orchard. Translating themselves towards it for closer observation, they found the roots of the trees were bare and exposed, no soil was to be seen. The trees themselves could be moved from place to place without danger of being damaged or reducing their productive efficiency. Luminous filaments throbbing like human hearts carried pulsating light and heat through the root ramifications, which were clean, soft, warm and transparent. At the root center of each tree was an eye, large, beautiful and highly intelligent; the branches were slightly opaque and filled with a luminous milky substance, which turned golden as it reached the buds, causing them to burst into blossoms then into fruit. Birds in rainbow hues were perched everywhere, singing delightsome melodies without opening their beaks, otherwise there was only a sweet humming of inexpressible peace. Desirous to learn more of this suspended orchard, Marco and Leonora called for the Knowledge of the Spoken Word and, lo, another Pillar of Light appeared. From it the voice of Master Flora was heard:

"This type of vegetation — profuse, magnificent and indestructible — is the result of the unification of physical science and the science of the soul, mathematics and meditation, labor and love. Approach nature and the sapling in such a spirit, and you will have opened wide the door of a treasure house of unending abundance in the world of man. Both soil and vegetation respond to love not only in the form of a tangible crop but also in spiritual truths. Of this Luther Burbank, now an ascended Master Agriculturist working with me, was one of your recent harbingers.

"Very dear to us are the peasants who till the soil, and those who indulge in gardening as a hobby. Thoughts of peace and harmony and a feeling beyond the confines of the flesh surge forth in the minds of those who stroll through a well-tended garden or along pine-strewn forest trails. And it pleases me to inform you that deliverance and elevation to the rank of Master-Agriculturists has been granted to the workers of

Earth who have reclaimed barren or marshy land, or discovered devices to avoid spoilage of food products, or improved plants and trees for higher yields, no matter how limited the result, or have given themselves to constructive husbandry, the training of horses, pets and other domestic animals, or have devised methods to save the beasts of the jungle from extinction. Infinite are the paths of Self-realization.

"Marvels such as these that you are beholding in this starry parkland, are however, as a trifle when compared with what can be accomplished on Earth through the holy alliance of men and the Liberated Masters. In the field of vegetation, for instance, man could levitate his body or obliterate unkind karma while speaking to a flower or analyzing its structure while at the same time his thoughts are fixed on God. Or he can hasten the process of Direct Perception while gazing at a leaf, or heal his own body while tending a sapling.

"May the love of nature take deeper roots in the consciousness of man for a bountiful crop of spiritual strength, peace and physical handsomeness. Let the uprooting of the weeds symbolize the cleaning of the self from cravings and unkind thoughts; the growth of trees and shrubbery, the inner awakening of the soul, and the picking of the fruit and flowers the constructive idea made manifest."

* * *

The sound waves of Master Flora's teaching reverberated everywhere in the limitless expanse of the starry surroundings; some of his thoughts coalesced for a few seconds into tangible form, then vanished. As he withdrew to join the other Flaming Pillar, an immense Torch of Fire supported by shafts of light issuing from the heads of five-thousand Splendor beings, appeared between them. A chorus of angelic voices was heard singing the Ode of Redemption; then in the clarion voice of a great Master of Creation, the Torch spoke:

"O blessed disciples of Light, O blessed humanity, O beautiful and wise Nature, O Life Eternal, greetings! Your combined call for action reached me at the gate of the temple-abode of Master Saturn, in the Empire of Wisdom and Love, where I have been a guest since my last contact with you. When man acknowledges his oneness of aspiration and purpose with his

439

fellow man, nature and life, he summons God to do his bidding. And what is the culminating desire of his earthly labour? Wisdom and Redemption! The former is a virtue, the latter a gift from God. Wisdom is the result of studying the Will of God and applying the Law thereof. In the process of analyzation and assimilation this divine Will is changed into free will or power of expressing the dictates of the Self unhindered and uncolored by selfish motive. It means that both the Cosmic Order and the Unwritten Law must remain inviolate.

"When the First Cosmic Soul or Universal Will-Buddhi came into being, It was endowed with the power to bring diversification and form out of a formless and motionless mass of light, energy and substance. From Its All-wise Mind, It projected ten individualized wills, and called them the *Kumara Family*. Unto them the First Cosmic Soul explained all that was required for a universal life highly diversified. The Kumaras listened in an attitude of deep humility, but firmly refused to take part in the work of creation because they felt inadequate; they bowed their heads before their Master-Father and retired into a forest of their own making for meditation and study, in preparation for a future mission as yet unrevealed.

"As you see free will and unconditional right of self-determination were coexistent with the birth of man. The Will of God, being above and beyond compulsion and threat, could not have been marred by the Kumaras' refusal, nor were they punished or made to lose their cosmic rank. This is the essence of true religion or Science of God applied to human behavior. Its realization is destined to bring about a perfect society — the society of the Golden Age — of men governing themselves without written laws, each member living and working beyond all restraints, pressure and compulsion of contingent nature, but simply in adherence to the Will of God.

"The First Cosmic Soul, impelled by the incoming cycle of relative existence, sought new ways to bring about God's command. From Its Mind it projected seven beings called Architect-Elohim of Creation and four lawgivers called Manus. The former brought diversification and discipline to the formless light, energy and substance, while the latter became the guardians and controllers of the Cosmic Order in process of becoming. Every man that came after Them was endowed with the same

440

seed of intelligence and power, exactly as were the Eleven Great Beings of Creation.

"This seed is still present today in the heart of every man, as an inalienable birthright, which needs to be fanned into action through the discipline expounded in this teaching. It is the only direct method that leads humanity to absolute emancipation. It is the All in All of all religious teachings.

"I tell you truly that should man make the initial effort to retrace his cosmic heritage, a tremendous stride towards peace and brotherhood would follow in no time. He should apply himself to reach the lofty goal with the enthusiasm of a healthy and happy child. For even the power and wisdom of an Elohim to know all, see all, and manipulate Light, Energy and Substance, is only an infinitesimal fraction of what man is destined to accomplish in life.

"Now let us analyze the teaching of your Bible and try to draw a path out of the seeming jungle of words and sectarian comments:

"*In the beginning . . . the Earth was without form, and void . . . And the Spirit of God moved upon the face of the waters.* The concept and acknowledgement of *earth* and *waters* make the statement *without form and void* meaningless; yet it is not so. *Without form and void* means devoid of conscious life or of individualized beings capable of uttering the Name of God. The First Cosmic Soul is the *Spirit of God* in action endowed with the power to establish the First Focus of God-consciousness on earth. Man is such a focus.

"The identification of Light with daytime signifies an action imbued with the concept of God; it means that a constructive thought does not materialize where and when the awareness of God (light, daytime) is absent. Night is not physical darkness but unawareness of God which results in fear and chaos. Every time man forgets God or engages himself in unethical actions he plunges into the *void* or a state of ignorance which is separation from God. The results are physical discomfort, mental obfuscation and emotional turmoil due to a lack of inflow of light and energy from the Reservoir of unqualified Life. And when he re-establishes contact with God, through the power of the will or a constructive deed, he opens a new cycle of life; he *begins,* as it were, to live again in a state of grace,

441

which implies physical exuberance, mental alertness and a driving power to search into the field of the unknown for nobler achievements.

"*Be fruitful, and multiply, and replenish the earth, and subdue it, and have dominion,* and so forth, signifies to engage oneself in actions that are beneficent to the community (fruitful), and being so they are accepted and emulated (multiply), whereby Nature is forced to respond (replenishing), to the demand (subduing) of the constructive individual who thus achieves dominion.

＊　＊　＊

"Now the question arises: What is the relationship between the First Cosmic Soul and the man of today; where is It, what is Its task and Its name?

"It is the sole mediator between man and God, the only Being cosmically authorized to listen to pleas, calls and prayers and transmit them to God for answers. No one else is endowed with such a privilege. It dwells in the hearts of men as coalesced Light, Energy, Substance, Wisdom, Love and Strength, ready to guide, protect, sustain and illumine the mind of man, ready to solve all problems. Its ultimate task is to *replenish the earth* with Itself — in the incoming Golden Age — through the thoughts and actions of men, and sweep aside those who refuse to heed the dictates of the conscience. Its name today is the Christ, the Buddha, the Son of God, the Real Man. To contradict Him, to oppose His full extrinsication or reject Him, spells self-annihilation for both man and society.

"How does one contact the First Cosmic Soul? Through meditation, noble thoughts and constructive endeavours. It is as simple as that. In the awareness of His hovering Presence, man's conscience is shaped, slowly and by secure upward steps, into a perfect likeness of the Divine Matrix, his heart is molded into an ideal chalice of God's love, his will transmuted into the Will Divine, while his body and senses reflect the sanctity and glory of a true Christ. This is the man of the world saturated with God's transmuting Presence. With the first glimpse of this inner unfoldment, man's concept of man will run parallel with that of a Liberated Master's towards the infinitude of life. Now the path of triumph over birth and death is wide open.

"We come finally to the last phase of the present teaching. What happened to the Kumara Family? Did they bring any contribution to the pre-ordained unfoldment of the Law of Evolution? They became the Great Ones of Utter Silence. Out of their own free will and self-discipline, they became the everliving expression of interstellar stability and divine wisdom, and achieved the same cosmic rank of the First Cosmic Soul. The Kumara Brothers, each embodying both the masculine and feminine aspect, founded new Starry Heavens, and are now engaged in creating a series of solar systems to be added to the more ancient galaxies of heavenly bodies. When a new cosmic project has to come into the plane of manifestation, they project the blueprint into the minds of the Architect-Elohim, and everything being perfect and ready, they utter the word BE, and the creative powers of the universe start rolling on."

* * *

Who was the Master hidden within the Flaming Torch? This Marco and Leonora wanted to know. Impelled by the desire of pure knowledge they meditated for awhile, then the Torch began to vanish and in its place they saw the eternal and handsome form of the Maha Chohan, the cosmic Architect of Nature.

"Yes" — He said — "I AM the Archited-Elohim and Scientist of everything that grows and is subjected to cyclical and seasonal changes both in your solar system as well as in several others. Flora is my Chief Assistant. Our department uses the intelligence, energy and love of ninety-one million Masters of Life. All progress in agriculture, forestry and husbandry is directed by us. Because there is no animal life in any other solar system or planet but on Earth, we are showering your scientists with sparks of *genius*, as it were, that will hasten the evolution of animal life to a level of usefulness even higher than that of medieval serfdom. Then these so-called dumb creatures will begin to dwindle and disappear, and by virtue of a law of dispensation they will be born on a specially built star to be trained as angel-helpers.

"Some explanations of transcendental nature are here in order concerning rocks, mountains, mineral ores, rivers, oceans, air, fire and vegetation. They are all endowed with life exactly

443

as man's, each possessing a vibrating individuality of its own, a speaking voice, a sensitive nervous system with an appropriate response to outer stimuli, each displaying love and hate, joy and pleasure, pain and fear: they all undergo fatigue and deterioration, and require rest and nursing for recuperation like human beings. One can induce fatigue in a rod as well as the unseen air. A despised or unrecognized laborer will respond in kind with hatred and shoddy work; an uncared for engine projects a vibration of unreliability, and a neglected forest will yield second grade lumber. You know well what fire and water can do through love, knowledge or ignorance. Even chemically speaking, there is no basic difference between Mount Everest, an oak tree and your physical body. Should I withdraw the light from my cosmic body, and also from a rock, a tree or any other chemical compound, all would be leveled to an undifferentiated state of chaos. This proves that Light is the *thing*, and this *thing* is the Breath of God. Therefore, if you ask me who I am, the perfect answer is: I AM Light, Maha Choran is but a tag; and should another name be given to me, my essence, power, intelligence and the very nature of my being would remain utterly untouched. If such is the truth, and if any human being, through the power of speech, can say *I AM Light*, on what ground does the theory of national or racial superiority rest. If there is an intimate relation-ship — a sort of brotherhood — between rocks, water, trees, mineral ore, animals and man, how much more certain is the brotherhood between an Aryan and a Negro, a Jew and a Christian, a believer and an atheist, a communist and a capitalist, a wise and a fool, and a rich and a pauper. What other explanation does man need before he commences to apply the Law of Love.

"A mountain is also a focus of inspiration and a storehouse of silence and inner strength. Because it draws light and energy directly from the Universal Reservoir of Creation, a mountain is capable of restoring to a state of perfect harmony the sacred centers of the human body raising thus the consciousness of man to a condition whereby he can dissolve unkind karma and come closer to Christhood. Within each rocky elevation of three thousand feet or over there is a retreat or Temple of Silence where a Liberated Master dwells as guardian of the

444

sylvan territory. It is his task to maintain the vibrating aura of his domain always charged for healing and inspiration that will attract lifestreams with constructive inclination either for orderliness and comfort or beauty per se. Rocks and vegetation are held in their pristine state for students of natural history.

"Trees are beings of stillness, guardians of the soil and masters of chemistry, whose manipulation of light and substance baffles the wisest scientists of Earth. In ancient times — before the forest created by the Kumara Brothers was made known to humanity — living beings of high spiritual attainment visualized great pillars issuing from the ground crowned with light. Sitting at the base of them, they practiced meditation. The radiance of the crown, seen from a distance, was a warning to other individuals not to approach, for here was a man communing with God. As the meditative one left, the radiance was withdrawn, but the pillar remained. The surface of the earth was so covered with these pillars that the great Sanat Kumara commanded me to bestow life upon them and make them similar to those under which he and his brothers had meditated for Two-hundred-thousand years. This I did in collaboration with Helios and Flora.

"We split the foundation of each pillar beneath the groundlevel into many branches and charged them with the power of absorbing energy from the earth's structure. Similarly, we split the crown and charged each branch with the power of absorbing light from the physical sun. Then, through capillaries built within the pillar, we caused the energy from beneath to be raised to the crown and exchanged for light which, in turn, was carried back to the roots as a fertilizer or enlivener. Thus the pillars, became living beings or trees, capable of communicating with one another.

"Flowers are one of the most precious and mysterious messengers of God. They convey thoughts of beauty, tenderness and love which no other visible manifestation is able to do. Their fragrance vibrating with the heart of creation, can soothe anguish, bring harmony and raise the soul onto the borderline of Direct Perception. When the scientist of earth, through spiritual attunement and laboratory research, is able to dissect the aura in which a flower is immersed, he will gather enough energy to cleanse and illumine an average city. Fruit is condensed light and fire ready to be transmuted into conscious life, strength and intelligence. While the flower nurtures the soul and speaks of God, the fruit, by cleansing and energizing the physical structure of man, raises him to God.

"The ocean symbolizes the perpetual motion of the cosmic powers; a never-ending, self-expressing living entity whose strength, energy and volume neither increase nor decrease. The relationship between the ocean and man rests on the premise that the former without the boundary of the seashore ceases as a storehouse of planetary stability, while man without the boundary of a stilled mind and subjugated senses cannot display the Christ attributes.

"The water of a river, thundering down from the mountain spring, symbolizes the unending traveling of man who has refused to heed God's call. Tossed fearfully from steep and rugged cliffs into dark meanders and hidden caves, and out again through tortuous and narrow gorges, the water falls into roaring and crashing foam, and remains fundamentally unchanged, while man, even after a journey of his own making, a million times more fearful than that of the water, is destined to enter the path of quiescence and truth.

"Fire, called by the ancient the Father-life of the universe, is highly concentrated in the atomic structure of every living being; and when man inbreathes and outbreathes, it is the Spirit-fire that renews itself, displaying its cosmic attributes in one of the most complex phenomena in the unfoldment of life. Through rhythmic breathing and meditation man can cause the fire of the body to burn all dross of physical and emotional nature, and bring all signs of aging to a halt and raise the mind onto the vertex of life, before the Presence of the Godhead. All-embracing and boundless are both meditation and the urge for inquiry.

"My blessed disciples, I have answered all your unsounded questions propounded by your inquiring minds and humble hearts; and because of your sincere and eager attitude, humanity as a whole shall benefit thereby."

"The Maha Chohan escorted by the two pillars of light which, in the interim, had assumed the contours of Master Flora and the Liberated Master-Teacher, moved into the background accompanied by the crown of Splendor-beings. The

446

power, charm and radiance of the Master Triad were so awesome and all-encompassing that they allowed no human thought to coalesce within a radius of interstellar space. In the sweep of their all-conquering effulgence, Marco and Leonora severed the tenuous link with their human nature, and beheld the three Great Ones embodying both the masculine and feminine aspect. Enveloped in an ecstatic feeling of inexpressible happiness and peace, they also merged into one and enjoyed for a fraction of eternity the divine status of completeness. The Masters then returned to their starry abodes, while they retraced their way back to the banks of the River Orio.

* * *

While awaiting their Liberated Master-Teacher they directed their attention to the Light within the heart in an effort to review all that they had learned concerning the First Cosmic Soul. As soon as the delineation had been made they heard the First Cosmic Soul speaking:

"What a noble conqueror is he who is able to transcend all desires, yet continuing to be active, positive and all-fulfilling. Through propulsive desirelessness, man acquires that inner strength which holds in abeyance all human allurement while producing boundlessly all that is required for comfortable living and a progressive social order. Behold Master Jesus! Though avulsed from earthly desires, nevertheless he reshaped the western world for a higher concept of life. Let it be likewise with you. Wherever you go or happen to be, control your impulse as what to do or say concerning your inner experiences. Enter the void, yet be keenly aware of Me dwelling in your hearts, causing the throat to vibrate, the lips to move; I will give you wise thoughts for you to express in words. Perceive my dazzling Spirit-Fire in action awakening the atomic structure of your body, every organ, every limb, the five senses, the perceptive faculties. See me as your thinker, your director and doer. Know this to be the mental attitude of the incarnate Christs. Make yourselves Christ-acting beings, not intermittently but continually. Cultivate readiness, be devoted to Me, attached to Me only, worship Me, serve Me; for Me you must be willing to weep and endure belittling and persecution unto death. I AM the Living Essence of Cosmic Intelligence and Geniality;

447

I AM the sole Mediator between man and God. Be Me; sage-ness is yours!"

An august assemblage of Sages and Masters attired in white togas, appeared traversing the River near by. In small groups of three or four, they were directing their footsteps towards the Heart of Light where Creative Silence abides. They saw the Great Ones of antiquity whose names are already registered in the history of mankind, welcoming these new adepts who have achieved Deliverance since the Renaissance: princes and princesses of Christ-Light who had never compromised with truth and liberty, beings who during their earthly existence had antagonized both the violence of political despots and the theocratic encroachment of the Church leaders. They were of every country and creed, including some American luminaries, noble men and women, who had fought on behalf of our land, setting it free from both the domestic provincialistic prejudice and the shackles of colonialistic bigotry imposed upon it by the European political schemers. Now they were joining the more ancient Masters and Splendor-beings in a symposium of initiation.

As the last group disappeared, Marco and Leonora perceived with amazement that the starry atmosphere had lost its blissful radiance and had become dark, fearful and threatening. A violent ground-striking electrical storm zigzagged red and gold streaks across the sky. Tempestuous winds crashed against giant fir trees, followed by a blinding rainstorm. The glare of a roaring forest fire, blazing with demoniac fury, was seen across the river. Human voices — inordinate, ugly and menacing — were heard louder and ever louder, as if advancing towards them for the kill. Amidst such elemental turmoil, however, and in spite of it, the surface of the river remained tranquil; its waters continued to flow smoothly, silently and unconcerned. Strengthened and inspired by the behavior of the River of Peace, they rose above surprise and questioning, and took shelter in the Temple of the Self, in the depths of their hearts. Then their Liberated Master-Teacher appeared smiling:

"I am happy indeed to see how well entrenched you are in the tower of cosmic stability. Behold, not a drop of rain touched you. Once the Self is contacted, either directly or through a Liberated Master, the disciple becomes inexpugnable to the vicious assaults of the entities of make believe. Why? Because to be in the Self and for the Self means to so live as to know the precise line of demarcation which divides the relative-absolute from the Unchangeable Truth. The seeming jarring experience of a little while ago, did not actually take place; and it could not, in such highly rarefied surroundings suitable only for the contemplation of God. Whatever you saw and felt, it was a test of inner nature, and you passed it. But how did it happen?

"The atmospheric pressure of the sea level of earth was placed around your Spirit-forms, making you fall, as it were, into the physical plane of living. There the low-vibrating elements were gathered and given only certain destructively qualified impulses. I said *only* because they needed the energy, the driving power of man's free will to be tangible and actually cause harm. All you saw and heard was the effect of light and sound production in a static form, similar to that created in a motion picture studio, where neither the makers, nor the listeners or beholders are impressed, yet they appear almost real to the relaxed spectator when projected on the screen. The motion picture directors use mechanical devices; we use the power of manipulation of the elements of light and sound. You were unimpressed by the experience, not because you knew the true nature of it — which you did not — but because you lived fully in the spirit of absolute truth.

"How often a Liberated Master reveals himself to a worthy disciple for a teaching of universal import. And notwithstanding all the evidence substantiating his tangibility, the student's mind fluctuates between doubt and rejection, and not infrequently defines the whole episode as a visionary creation of his imagination. After awhile, however, he retraces himself on the Path of the Real, and through a more intense application in rhythmic breathing and meditation, he perceives the uncontradictable Reality of the Self to Whom all things are possible; and as the Light from the heart reaches the head, the staggering vision of the First Cosmic Soul destroys the illusion of the limited consciousness.

"To be the recipient of inner experiences in an intermittent manner, should not cause undue elation or a feeling of spiritual success, but rather an attitude of more profound humility, a more intense desire for self-analysis, in order to avoid pitfalls and keep the path clear. An unkind word or thought, or an obstacle placed on someone's path of self-expression, cause an obstruction in the heart-to-head conduit and a severance of communication with God. This proves that the Spirit of God can only descend into man's heart by virtue of its power of cosmic gravitation. It cannot be forced, it cannot be called. Through intense yearning and fiery desire to seek spiritual elevation for its own sake, a vacuum is produced in the heart which is promptly filled with the Spirit of the First Cosmic Soul.

"This proves how inane was and is the militant attitude of the Christian missionaries who believed that by the babbling of words and a display of rituals and relics, they could spiritualize the so-called backward races. Actually they could not bring salvation to anyone because, in the first place, they did not have it themselves. With their minds crammed with diseased thoughts, and their sleeves filled with ungodly schemes, they marched side by side with the military conquerors, and with the crucifix in their hands proclaimed as pagan the religion of the inferior race and declared it to be a menace to civilization and an obstacle to the Gospel of Jesus Christ. Those who refused to accept the teaching were abandoned to the cold steel of their confreres in soldier's attire. This meant massacre, enslavement and exploitation of the natural resources of the land for the glory of the king and their own benefit.

"Because of this basic misinterpretation and misapplication of Master Jesus' Message, the white man developed a haughty and damnable attitude of superiority towards the nonwhite races. He elected himself master of the world and supreme arbiter of the destinies of the inferior races. In such a spirit he felt justified in taking over — unasked and uninvited — both the physical and spiritual domain of these people, bringing ruin and degeneration, trampling on the law of moral conduct and throwing them into a state of fear and turmoil, teaching them how to lie, hate and cheat, thus delaying for many centuries the realization of the commonwealth of all nations of earth. This is the story of colonialism: territorial aggrandizement and white supremacy based on persecution, exploitation and religion strangely mixed together.

"We do not deny the benefit derived by delving into other people's spiritual lore. It invigorates the soul and sets the mind to thinking and to perceive the subtle cosmic currents underlying all life. The Christian ethics could have reached the pinnacle of perfection, if the followers of the Gospel had approached the non-Christians in a spirit of active desirelessness, exactly as Master Jesus had commanded. In one respect, some of the "pagan" ethics are higher and nobler than that of the average individual Christian. If there is anything in which the white race, predominantly Christian, actually excels, it is applied science. There is more spirituality, selfless love, international collaboration, divine brotherhood and active desirelessness in a convention of scientists demonstrating how to grow food cheaply and keep the house clean almost effortlessly, than in the most elaborate display of religious *intentions* to bring man closer to God.

"When our brother Gautama Siddhartha established his teaching, which came to him exactly as Master Jesus', he did not force it upon anybody, nor did he organize religious companies with that militant spirit that marks the policy of many a monastic order of Europe, or the fanatic Mohammedans prior to the Crusades. It is registered in the Akashic Records that one day, long ago, on one of the streets of Benares in India, a passer-by met Gautama the Bodhisattwa, and noticing the extraordinary charm and self-possession of the Master, approached him with reverence and asked who he was that looked like the conqueror of life and the ruler of the universe. Gautama responded humbly:

" 'I AM I the Happy One, the Living Buddha.'

" 'And who is your teacher, tell me, that I might find him also and learn.'

" 'I have no teacher in the flesh, the I AM OM is my Teacher, my Ruler and my Lord; and IT dwells in my heart . . . I shall go my way dear brother, for you do not need me.' 'Please' — the inquirer insisted — 'Let me follow Thee, O Master, that I might be fed from the crumbs of thy heavenly banquet!'

"Thus Buddhism had its inception. Spiritual radiance based on Direct Perception, silently projected, has a tremendous power of penetration. This is the secret of success on earth for the true disciple of Light who is entrusted with the task of conquer-

451

ing both man and heaven. Forcefulness is the child of fear and inadequacy. The more one conquers oneself, the easier it is to conquer and hold others. The deeper your awareness of God, My disciples, the greater your power of influencing others on the path of spiritual ascendancy. You are on earth to recharge an ancient teaching with newer impulses generated from within, so that whoever is contacted by them is affected by his own reaction and according to his own inner urge. Such a task is placed on your shoulders because it fits you perfectly, due to repeated preparation in previous embodiments. See that you do not fall into the mire of transitory success, for it clogs and destroys the ideal conduit between your hearts and heads, and in turn it will destroy you. Be there where we send you, humble and proud, still and inwardly alert, trustful and desireless; we shall do the rest.

* * *

"Blessed disciples, you are about to enter the Circle of Absolute Contemplation where knowledge is absorbed through Self-diffusion and Self-retracing. There are subtle harmonies which you do not hear as yet, but which you must feel and raise onto the plane of Cosmic Silence, the Matrix of Universal Truth. Condense the wholeness of you to a pinpoint of light, and sink your mind deep into the most hidden recess of your heart . . . Well done! You are now in the Seventh Heaven illumined by the shadowless Light of the Mind of God. Here you shall learn the cause of the downfall of the two great continents of Lemuria and Atlantis, the former many thousands of years earlier than the latter, yet the cause was practically the same, showing how slow is humanity en masse to learn a lesson. Then you shall meet some of their inhabitants who now enjoy life everlasting.

"As both the Lemurian and Atlantean people reached an enviable level of civilization and prosperity, while the rest of the world remained steeped in intellectual and spiritual darkness, they became proud and selfish. No longer did they need God; to them the power of the mind was the all in all. The Source of Life was first discarded, then forgotten; materialism and physical possessions were sanctified; rhetoric and the letter of the law were exalted and given preference to the spirit of love and equity; diplomacy sunk into espionage and counterespionage; the forces of destruction, supported by an army of cruel and irresponsible henchmen, ruled despotically.

"In the midst of such debauchery lived small groups of light bearers, whom the Liberated Masters assisted in order for them to bear witness of the happenings to other races of the remaining continents. Alive and active in them were the noble attributes; the Logos OM was their Guide and Comforter. Their mode of living, however, changed to one of absolute simplicity and moderation, yet lacking nothing, including inner freedom and the realization of all constructive aspirations. Against such an impregnable fortress of ethical behavior, the ruling class devised newer and more diabolical ways of physical destruction and moral ruin. Accusations, slander and insinuation were duly legalized and applied without the right of self-defense.

"The people of Light, the Sun worshippers, faced the ordeal in a spirit of inner poise and love, and in dynamic expectation of loftier teachings from the Immortal Ones. As a result, neither their bodies nor their belongings or prestige suffered damage. Houses were set afire or subjected to demolition through the execution of arbitrary orders from the courts of law, or through acts of revenge from envious and inimical hoodlums, yet their homes and property resisted pillaging and devastation. People were ambushed, maimed or killed in violation of all human rights, yet the wounded and maimed were immediately restored to their physical wholeness, and those who had been murdered were resurrected by the power of collective prayers uttered by friends and relatives whose lives had been enriched by an accumulation of constructive karma.

"At this point the Law of Rebound commenced to take a prompt and greater toll. Often the evil doer found that his day's work of destroying someone else's life and property, had been transferred, by an invisible hand, to his own property and to the members of his own household. Returning home to his family at the end of the day, he found his house in a heap of ruins, with desolation, suffering and heartbreaking lamentation all about him.

"Thus on one side there was an expansion of light for those who were adhering to the unwritten law of ethics and love; while on the other side, all the signs of physical, economic, mental and spiritual decay, became more apparent and more menacing with each passing day. Many of the followers of the lunar path, because of their restricted attitude towards life, their lack of mental broadness, and daily violation of the rights of others, found themselves retreating into an ever smaller territory, living in overcrowded and neglected houses, and hating each other.

"Due to the destructive pressure imposed upon nature by the lunar-worshipping people, the land which they owned lost much of its value. Everybody wanted to sell and nobody had the desire to buy. All business enterprises were either at a standstill or being forced into foreclosure and bankruptcy. Real estate passed through many hands in a single transaction with considerable loss for the individual who had been forced to sell. Civic administrations, unable to secure needed revenue, dismissed civil service employees by the millions. Public buildings, parks and recreation centers were closed and heavily fenced for lack of maintenance. The police force disbanded their officers, some of whom turned their training to evil and lawlessness. Banking and financial institutes threw their securities and real estate holdings on the market in a vain attempt to secure liquid cash to satisfy the ever mounting claims of the frantic depositors. Mistrust and revenge grew parabolically in the rank and file of the evil doers, their leaders, acolytes and sycophants. Economic depression, famine, crime, physical disease, mental derangement and emotional collapse, collective despair and the heavily pressing hand of the law of rebound caused a physical and chemical rebellion in the action of the four elements.

"As fuel refused to ignite, fire could not be produced, consequently, light, energy and heat needed for home and industry, could not be manufactured. Yet when there was a conflagration, due to the people's negligence, it became uncontrollable. The atmosphere remained still, and the air stale and often unbreathable; but when the wind blew, its cyclonic impact caused damage of indescribable magnitude to human beings, houses, and whatever was left of cattle and vegetation. Rainstorms flooded the cities and countryside, and almost instantly the waters became polluted and utterly unfit for human consumption. The quarries refused to yield the needed masonry for building

454

construction, yet when an earthquake occurred, it reduced mountain ranges and whole cities to desert sand. Due to lack of solar magnetism, beautiful gardens changed into mephitic ponds, luxuriant valleys into seas of mud. The soil began to sag, lovely islands were seen listing like maimed giant ships. At this time cancer began to appear as the worst and most baffling of human scourges.

"The Liberated Masters observed all, saw the working of the law and witnessed the heartbreaking suffering, yet they were not permitted to lift a finger. Only during the last stage of destruction, They, in one voice, called to God for the application of the Law of Mercy. In response, the beings of the waters raised mountainous waves from the ocean and directed them inland, submerging the two mighty continents and their disobedient inhabitants.

"The families of Light, and those who were allowed to repent, climbed to the mountain peaks followed by the rising tides. They sang as they ascended, and as they reached where they could go no higher, legions of the Angelic Host welcomed them; their bodies were transmuted into light and they became starry dwellers for eternal years.

"In both instances, one thousand of the youth — the strongest and most daring in the field of inward search — were held by the Masters and given the power of transmutation of matter and energy, the gift of levitating their bodies, and the highest knowledge of the land in mathematics, applied science, the arts and political organization. With this knowledge sealed in their minds by the release of the gift of eternal remembrance, they were dispatched to other lands and peoples to relate what had happened to the sunken continents of Lemuria and Atlantis, and transmit all they knew for the benefit of posterity.

"The cruel suffering of those who had been the tools of pride and ignorance, was not devoid of reward of cosmic nature. The savage onslaught had purified and humbled their hearts, and revealed to their minds how insane they had been. They understood clearly that there is a Will higher than man's, a Spirit-ruler whose power and majesty do not tolerate infractions to Its Eternal laws.

"The nations and peoples of the rest of the world accepted the message of the One Thousand and changed, in various degrees, their mode of living. Various ethnical groups became the embodiment of divine justice, love expanded, and men experienced for the first time true happiness and peace, for these are, in the last analysis what humanity is seeking. Scientific research, the arts and philosophy, took a new and deeper stride for greater comfort, beauty, joy of living and understanding of the All-encompassing Spirit-Fire of the universe. The One Thousand Citizens of each of the lost continents became teachers and founders of universities, and counselors of kings and rulers, others wandered everywhere teaching the law to the common man who was eager to learn. *This is a story never told before.*

* * *

"Disciples" — the Master continued — "direct your attention to the First Cosmic Soul in your hearts, for a citizen of Light who once dwelt in the Land of Lemuria is approaching us. Listen to her message:"

"Worship, O children of earth, worship and contemplate the Immanent Spirit of Creation, and you shall become the recipient of Light that knows no darkness. I am Princess Yosana, the daughter of a deposed king and wise ruler of the Land of Lemuria. I was seven years old when ascending the mountain, the waters that were submerging the land caught my feet. I prayed to God with childlike transport, and, lo, I was transmuted into a body of light. With the power at my disposal derived from the new grace I drew both my Twin Flame and my parents into the Realm of Life Eternal. Here we are engaged in projects of interstellar magnitude, in obedience to those Who are greater than we. I welcome thee and thee, and congratulate you both for the ability to travel in the Realms of the Beyond, where human radiation and limited minds cannot penetrate. Once more you see and know that the highest earthly aspirations and the most cherished human desires are as flimsy toys compared with our state of being."

As Yosana ceased speaking, her Twin Flame, Tamos, appeared. What a matchless couple they were in their bodies of light and eternal youth. Presently other starry dwellers approached and surrounded Marco and Leonora in a festive welcome; then they all translated themselves to a beautiful, white mansion on the crest of a hill covered with flowering fruit trees. Seated on the spacious verandah Yosana spoke through radiated thoughts:

"It is not difficult for a sensitive person to feel and see the fellowship between Heaven and Earth, the latter being the footstool of the former, and Heaven the Ultimate Goal of every man. It is up to him to learn how to knit the two together.

"Let us consider a couple — man and wife — who through the reciprocal attitude of give and take live in happy oneness. Though occasionally beset by problems and disappointments, subdued and loving words are spoken to one another, sweet and tender is their relationship, a veritable heaven is their home life. Cleanliness, elegance and culture fill their house. Their business and social behavior move on a line of the highest ethics. They radiate kindness wherever they are, justify others' shortcomings, and never see evil in anyone. They have a son, whom they guide and counsel, love and reward, and yet discipline with a firm hand.

"Visualize this child, moving in such a highly rarefied atmosphere of dynamic holiness. On the table in the study he sees a book, perhaps 'The Light of Asia', or 'The Song Celestial', or 'The Upanishads'. He opens it and therein reads a moral maxim which impresses him deeply. Now he wants to know more about the great one who, in the meantime, has become his hero, his invisible guide and archetype. He reads and studies, and all that he learns changes into flesh of his flesh. With his heart and mind filled with awe, he lives in close adherence to both the letter and the spirit of the teaching. He feels proud and humble, and at moments wise also; the inner strength and power which permeate his being, compel his coevals to bow and reflect on that strange and unusual radiance. The new path, however, is not an easy one; our little student falls, now and then, into the grip of fear and loneliness, fear of being feared by his companions, of being misunderstood or unjustly criticized; yet, he cannot abandon his communion with his idealized master and teacher. In such a state of constant striving, pressed on every side by contradicting and opposing forces, now elated and now discouraged, our youth has grown to manhood with a well-developed analytical power. Forced to withdraw from the outer world by the superficiality of the masses, he returns therein as a fully majored Master of Life.

"Thus Heaven and Earth meet. Through a series of strokes in the sea of being — now advancing, now retreating and now standing still — yet with the mind well-fixed on the Supreme Goal, man cuts himself free from the shackles of limitation and sorrow and ascends towards the limitless expanse of Knowledge, Bliss and Immortality.

"The Earth today is filled with legions of unseen Liberated Masters, helping those who strive inwardly, exactly as they did during the last stage of the universal cataclysm in Lemuria. A cataclysm might either precede or follow an age of social enlightenment. Thus far in this century, humanity has experienced bloody clashes of unexpected magnitude, floods, hurricanes, earthquakes, famine, revolutions, persecutions, dictatorships and massacres whose destructive results could be equaled to the tragedies that have befallen mankind since the crucifixion of Master Jesus. Are they over? I am not permitted to say. But I do declare that more fearful uprisings are gaining momentum in the hearts, minds and worlds of millions of people throughout the Earth. Violators of the Law of love and ethics will fall victims to strange diseases whose cause will not be found by the standard method of laboratory research; financial fortunes unethically accumulated, shall blow up and vanish, and their owners torn asunder through physical, mental and emotional torment. Sons and daughters, abandoned by their parents, shall mercilessly pursue their fathers and mothers, in punishment of their crime for not having given them the needed discipline and love, and for having indulged instead in bickering, lewdness and craving for outer success. Hospitals will be stormed with a violence worse than that applied against the French Bastille, because of their inability to give shelter and alleviate the pain of the innumerable human beings. Communism will be submerged through a bloodless —though most severe — uprising of enlightened citizens. Cosmocracy will replace the corrupt and anachronistic democratic philosophy, as practiced even in this seeming highly civilized continent of North America. Then enlightenment shall descend, but true peace will not be a fact until the standard of living of the entire world is raised to that of your land and higher. And this shall be the beginning of the Golden Age."

As the radiation of Yosana's thoughts ceased, all the guests took their leave with the exception of two who slowly revealed themselves to be Elos and Beata. Only six spirit-forms remained on the verandah. Yosana and Tamos, Elos and Beata, and Marco and Leonora. For a few moments they stood in silent contemplation of God, then slowly began to rise and transmute their forms into enormous lotus flowers, each in a different color, and disposed themselves in the contour of a C, the symbol of Contemplation. Another lotus of larger dimensions and greater brilliancy appeared and surmounted the C.

Although they were in the form of flowers, they had, nevertheless, eyes to see, intelligence to perceive and the consciousness of God. From the lower end of the C, the first lotus, which was Elos, came forth and rose vertically many thousands of feet. He remained there for a moment, then changed into an immense flag of light with white and gold stripes; emblazoned in the center was a purple lotus with one-thousand-five-hundred-forty-seven stars in brilliant blue, corresponding to the star-planets of the first ninety-one solar systems. The voice from the lotus crowning the C spoke:

"This flag symbolizes the universal brotherhood of men and gods. A starry peace is herewith declared amongst all races and nations. It is the commencement of international collaboration!"

The second lotus, which was Beata, left the C and stood close to the flag. Assuming the form of a blazing torch, it projected radially beams of colorless fire, three of which were directed to the earth. Again the Master Lotus was heard:

"These symbolize the Triune Light of the Christine Era as a memento for all men to emulate the Master of Nazareth and attain Christhood."

The third lotus was Leonora. Standing next to the torch, it changed into a rain of golden-olive leaves descending to earth, bearing to mankind the message of faith, peace and love. The voice commented:

"These are the first gifts from the First Cosmic Soul, bestowed upon the meditative man."

"The fourth lotus was Marco. As it rose towards its twin lotus, it let petals of gold glide earthward. Three letters — PHK — were embossed on each petal, which stood for Perseverance, Humility, Knowledge. The voice explained:

"This is the winged loaf of freedom. Through Perseverance and Humility man shall likewise glide towards the knowledge of God. That Knowledge will make him free."

The lotus Tamos — which had changed into a blazing wheel with flaming spokes enclosed in a jeweled rim — rose and stood by the side of the lotus-Marco. It then made a complete turn forming a sphere of dazzling brilliancy. The voice continued:

"In the shape of a sphere is the pinpoint of Light in the heart of man, and this Light is the Hub of Life, the Source of Divine Intelligence and the Center of the Universe. When the mind identifies itself with this Light, all outer manifestations are equidistant from the Hub of Life, and therefore, perfect. Man can rule himself so as to make this perfection possible."

The lotus Yosana ascended and placing itself next to the sphere, projected a trumpet from its center and blew seven tremendous blasts. The sound changed into a spiral of light which enveloped the earth. The voice admonished:

"Hearken, hearken, ye teachers and disciples. The Gospel of Salvation must be conveyed to man in a clarion voice. Each statement of truth must be fully lived by him who utters it, or it will not bear conviction. The true teacher shall give and give, as the sun gives, in equal measure to both saint and sinner, rich and poor and anyone who approaches him.

"O teacher, remember: Never teach out of sheer vanity, or for the sake of rhetoric. Meditate, seek direct perception; then you shall truly teach like unto a Christ!"

The speaking lotus then ascended and as it reached the six lotus-symbols, it let a rain of jewels fall to earth: diamonds, rubies, emeralds, sapphires and other precious gems. The people were seen extending their hands to be filled. There was no rushing, trampling or vociferousness. Profound silence pervaded the earth, then all dropped the jewels in disappointment and gazed upward, their faces ablaze with light. The voice concluded:

"O teachers, O spiritual leaders, behold! Mankind yearns for light; it cannot be bribed with a dole of material wealth; and

460

it is in earnest. What a rich harvest for a true teacher. I say unto you, blessed disciples: Have courage, be wise harvesters, for the fruit is ripe and the hour has arrived. Do not let it fall to the ground, for there is a pack of famelic beasts ready to devour it. I say, have courage for the time has arrived for all religions to fold up and go!"

* * *

A few days later Marco and Leonora were summoned to appear before their Liberated Master-Teacher at the River Orio. As they arrived he welcomed them by touching their foreheads with the thumb of his right hand. "Your Inner Eye is now awake" — he said — "and you are ready to enter the Realm of the Fourth Dimension. Let a decisive stroke of your free will obliterate mind, senses and personality, and make you dynamically quiescent and void. Know that all is and is not because God pre-exists to both the manifest and the unmanifest. In the subjugation of the self man does not destroy his individuality; instead he allows the Real Essence of his Being to work unhindered in the world of form, producing all things in the image and likeness of that Essence, that is, perfect; and causing all men to acknowledge him as a superior being through whom that Essence has been given free play. Those who are unaware of the role of this Living Essence play the policy of absenteeism from the cosmic gathering of life; hence the suffering and bewilderment."

While their Master-Teacher was thus radiating to them his words of light, they passed through the Inner Circle of Contemplation on their way to the Spheric Garden of the Elohim. They were in a world of light, all was immersed in light, all was light; the soil, rocks and vegetation. Pulsating light emanated from their Spirit-forms. They had at last issued where pure light was the all in all.

"Yes" — the Master continued. "When the mind bows to the Buddhi, man's intellect penetrates the Essence of the things that surround him, and that Essence is Light, the Cause of Knowledge, the Source of Power and the basic Principle of Wisdom. When man listens to and obeys the Light in his heart, he gives a tremendous impetus to his power of intuition.

461

Why? Because by seeing light as the underlying essence of all things, he becomes aware of the rate of vibration of an object, its inherent possibilities and their infinite combinations and application in the world of form; he knows exactly the yet unknown power and hidden service that a certain substance can give.

"There are two paths leading to the acquisition of the power of intuition. The first is methodic introspection, as you already know; the second is scientific discipline and laboratory research whose outcome is compared with both the life within and the life of the world. In both instances man treads the path of Self-Knowledge.

"The opacity of certain types of substance and the incomprehensibility of certain phenomena are the result of man's non-attunement with the light in his heart, and the lack of scientific research. Should we allow the people of earth to come here en masse, their darkened consciousness, due to the lack of introspection, would reduce this starry heaven to the undesirable earthly state; all things would be seen with a confused, limited mental perception and, therefore, misunderstood. When the introspective power is active and the mind illumined, the intellect moves on the borderline of geniusship, and whatever it wants to investigate – the heart of a mountain, the depths of the ocean, events, animals, trees and the thoughts of man– it draws forth enduring truths.

"Come now and be attentive!" They approached a rose bush in full bloom. "Observe" – he said – "roots, stems, thorns, leaves and flowers. What are they? Intensify your power of introspection, and what do you see? Light, condensed and shaped in various forms, each vibrating at a certain rate, obeying a precise mathematical law, and yielding an incontrovertible and pre-established result, such as roots, or petals, or color, or fragrance, and so forth. Now again, while I hold you in this cosmic vibration, direct your attention to the planet earth."

It was midnight; their gaze embraced the continent of North America. They saw hundreds of millions of points of light swarming in the atmosphere; some were encased in human forms.

"I am holding your power of awareness within the boundaries of men and beasts only, for every point of light is either one

462

or the other. You do not see insects, fish or terrestrial and marine vegetation, though they are there, each entity another point of light. As you see they are all alike, equally pure and mighty, and devoid of diversification. The personality is asleep. This tiny spark of microcosmos, unhampered by the limitation of the mortal mind, is able to recharge every cell of the body with its own qualities and attributes which are of the same class of the First Cosmic Soul's. This explains, though tentatively, why an ailing body recuperates faster during sleep or while lost in dreamless slumber. It also explains why people pass away during sleep; the Point of Light, which is an emanation of the Immortal Soul, being unwilling to submit longer to the despotic pull of the mind — during the awakened state of the personality — simply withdraws from the human form which, unsustained by Its vivifying action, turns into a heap of decaying matter.

"The physical and mental buoyancy as well as all depressing moods, displayed by an individual during the day, are due in part to the increased or decreased radiance absorbed from the Point of Light while asleep. The acknowledgement of its existence, and the intense visualization of its vital dominance over mind and body could spell the difference between a meager existence and a life of unending rewards: physically, mentally, morally.

"Innumerable are the paths of perfection, varied the channels of visualization; however, one is the method that leads to victory: Meditation. One may meditate on this Point of Light, or on the root of the nose, or on the heart center, or on a moral maxim uttered by an accredited teacher. By concentrating the visualization on the fulcrum of your own choice at the exclusion of all else, you compel the Godhead to come to the rescue, and together draw the blueprint for a life of unending achievements, and every detail thereon marked shall come to pass."

❊ ❊ ❊

With their thoughts confined in the depths of their hearts, and their gaze fixed on the forehead of the Master, Marco and Leonora moved swiftly with him towards the half-hidden,

463

foliated rock basin, the source of the River Orio. There the divine guide stood for a few moments in deep mental concentration, in an attitude of blissful expectancy; then extended his arms and, lo, his immortal Twin Companion appeared. They took the students' hands in theirs and together rose towards the summit of a snow-capped mountain, from where they saw an immense semispherical valley covered with enormous scintillating flowering trees. Both the near and distant points of this panorama of breath-taking beauty were seen with the same clarity.

"Be alert" — the Master said — "for you are about to behold a cosmic spectacle which takes place only at the commencement of every new Cycle of Life."

From the symmetrical and picturesque valley they saw a pinpoint of light rising, rising, rising, and moving horizontally, transversally and spirally, now staying to describe a square, a circle or a sphere, in diverse colors and degrees of brilliancy. As it resumed the ascent, it expanded in size and radiance until it burst into an iridescent lotus of faultless perfection; it continued to grow until it displayed one-thousand petals of light, each petal of such immensity that it held comfortably one-thousand Twin Flame-couples. Soon two-million of these mighty Masters of Contemplation stood on the petals of the gigantic nelumbo, each equally close to the gaze of the onlooker. They wore robes of indestructible resplendence of every nation, continent and race, and of every historical epoch, including the lost continents of Atlantis and Lemuria. Their handsome and youthful faces were filled with joy, peace and passionless adoration of God. As every detail of the sublime spectacle registered in the consciousness of Marco and Leonora, they heard the voice of the First Cosmic Soul:

"You are in the highest plane of spiritual life brought to the conscious awareness of man who lives in harmony with the highest law of ethics. This is the Empyrean. Here dwells happiness as an expression of omnipotence and omniscience. It is the happiness that permeates him who has overpassed birth and death, health and disease, wisdom and ignorance, and knowledge and non-knowledge. This state, conceived by the purest and loftiest intellect still linked to earthly life, constitutes

464

the threshold of immortality unshaded by the faintest memory of human consciousness.

"These mighty Beings, true sons of the Spirit-Fire, have convened here as members of this Interstellar Congress of Light for final instructions, before taking over the rulership of Starry Empires of Light whose vastness is beyond man's highest visualization and measurement. They shall succeed still greater rulers whose inner growth has made them eligible for still higher duties. Man's march towards Infinitude never ceases.

"These great Lords of Light, in the absolute stillness of their Spirit-forms, have the ability to scan, in a timeless flash, their vast domains and enhance the intelligence of the billions of life-units therein for higher levels of thought without interfering with their power of free will. Their power to manipulate Matter, Force, Light and Intelligence, is so staggering that they take formless substance from the cosmic reservoir of life, and build, unbuild and rebuild stars, constellations and new orbits through visualization and wordless commands, for they know that there is none to compel, none to limit, none to encourage. They know that every speck of substance, being endowed with unqualified energy and unbound possibilities, is willing to obey the Voice of God, even in an unspoken state. And since a Master knows exactly what to ask from a being or a thing, the obedience is always prompt and complete. From a disciple the Master asks only what he can give; hence he should never hesitate to obey instructions and plunge into action, well-assured of His unfailing protection. *On the path of the Inner, neither forceful methods, nor pressure are ever applied.*

"When a disciple is ready, or when a Master thinks he is ready and receptive for instructions to carry out a certain mission, the Master directs his gaze towards the disciple and says: 'BE I AM OM'. If the command is freely and joyously accepted the four words sink first into the disciple's heart to don the Robe of the Logos which is the Power of the Christ. Then they proceed outwardly as light, sound, energy, intelligence, substance, life and love. They echo everywhere but mostly in the field of action specifically designated, rectifying all accounts — spiritual, ethical and material — correcting misdeeds, leveling karma, transferring wealth, causing wrong opinions and ill feelings to disappear, and establishing good will and love for the benefit of all concerned. And when the assigned task has been brought to completion a segment of humanity has been raised one step higher on the path of perfection. The obedient disciple has been promoted to a junior Christ.

"Blessed son and daughter from the planet Earth, play with Me the Ode of Peace and Brotherhood on earth on the strings of purity of heart and passionless love, wherefrom the Knowledge of God and Wisdom Divine emanate:

"I AM OM, the Spirit-Fire of Creation, the Voice of your hearts resounding in the Infinitude, reverberating in every mind that is attuned with ME.

"I AM OM, the Everliving Light, the Essence of Eternal Becoming.

"I AM OM, the First Mind-Buddhi, Self-thinking and Self-generating; all other minds issue from ME.

"I AM OM, the Bestower of Intelligence, the Seed of Genius, the Moving Force of all that lives.

"I AM OM, the Impersonal Power that sustains the three worlds with only an infinitesimal fraction of My all-resistless Strength.

"I AM OM, the undisputed dweller in the hearts of all.

"I AM OM, the One without beginning, the First without a second, the Last without end.

"I AM OM, There is nothing else! And now behold!"

＊　＊　＊

The two-million Twin-splendors, Masters and Lords of Creation, slowly and rhythmically were leaving the frosted violet petals of the cosmic lotus and commencing, high in the Empyreal Realms, the triumphal procession of the White-robed rulers of starry empires. Hovering above each couple was a celestial escort of ten flame-robed angelic beings. As the last of the Twin-contemplators left the nelumbo, the interminable procession halted, and all remained motionless, as if awaiting further orders from the Unseen Spirit. Then heightening the intensity of their radiance to blinding brilliancy they proceeded on wings of light towards the inter-solar horizon, accompanied by the mighty rhythm of the Symphony of Joy. The exalted Splendors, in all their majesty and glory, encircled our solar system three times, leaving in their wake a trackless path of purple fire.

The staggering magnificence of this cosmic spectacle cannot be described in words. The cogent image it depicted of the indestructibility of life, of the immortality of the Soul, of the unending progress of man, of his infinite avenues of self-expression, and undreamed of potentialities towards perfection, beauty and spiritual satisfaction will never be forgotten. While thus reflecting Marco and Leonora translated their spirit-forms to the banks of the River Orio, and found themselves in the loving embrace of their Liberated Master-Teacher.

"I welcome you" — the Master said — "as our Brother Jesus was welcomed by his Divine Master at the end of his earthly mission; not because you have reached his then spiritual level, but because I love you. Let this be a supporting vibration to the Self-elevating vibration that you already possess which expresses itself in such a stupendous manner. And as He became the I AM OM or the absolute identification of his human nature with the everliving Nature of God, so shall you and all those who practice meditation with the object of knowing the Supreme Self, the Light of the World, THAT which dwells in the heart of every man.

❊   ❊   ❊

"This is the Destination or the Ultimate Goal for all sentient beings — the humble, the proud, the tycoon, the political leader, the inventor, the playboy and the socially sophisticated, of every nationality and race. Both organically and spiritually, one is the common heritage of all men of Earth. Brotherhood, therefore, is a cosmic law, a compelling must in the social structure of the world. It is Christhood made manifest. The path of the inner leads to its realization. Meditate, O man, meditate! Wherever you are, in a silent desert or a throbbing city, in a dark cave or a palatial mansion, it is a fitting place to summon the Master-Soul for protection and guidance. This Master-Soul, being the very essence of you, is with you always. The Law of Life compels IT to keep man in an upright position, to answer his many quests and to provide the proper tools for the coalescence of every desire that harmonizes with the Law of Love and Order. Hence, O man, cultivate awareness of Its existence and presence. Awareness is vigilance, the virtue whereby man keeps himself in continual touch with the Cause of Truth and the Law of the Real, whose correct understanding enriches his mind

467

while on earth, and carries him away into the Octaves of immortality at the end of his worldly task.

"To facilitate, at the outset, the achievement of such a lofty status there are certain requirements that are essential: a home with a minimum of comfort and a maximum of cleanliness, with a quiet spot always available for immediate use, an economic freedom that gives no room for financial worries, a healthy body untouched by smoking, stimulants, depressants and drug addiction; an attitude of tolerance (at least) towards all races, the minority groups, the self-appointed foes, and all those who profess diverse religious creeds; a subdued feeling of rebelliousness against gambling, gossip, espionage, envy and sycophancy; a daily routine of work, rest and play — while still a neophite — and, finally a holy ambition to succeed. The more formidable one depicts the obstacles on the path, the easier it is to surmount them, the closer the ultimate victory. Rely on the Self of you with an all-absorbing faith; be humbly independent; then, O man, I shall be by thy side.

*   *   *

"I, the Master-coordinator of the Spirit-man for the Western World, shall cause my form to coalesce and make myself visible to you. Think of the thrill of having Me by your side, guiding you through the labyrinth of confusion and frustration onto a path of shadowless clarity where wisdom abides; the proper tools I will fashion for you alone to be used in coping with the seeming insolvable and perplexing problems encountered in your daily life.

"And if perchance your outer conditions seem determined to hold you in abjection, or if mediocrity or inharmony surrounds you, be not dismayed; be still and know that the I AM of you, the Master-Soul, was created for absolute victory and triumph. You are THAT! Wise retreat is not defeat. Think intensely, be inwardly perseverant, take refuge with unswerving trust in the Gift of Cosmic Dispensation that is flooding heaven and earth, at this very hour, with a positive and dynamic hope. Like all true candidates to Christhood of the past — like me when I had a human form — you shall come to grips with yourself, and weep and groan and shiver all over; it is the most redeeming blessing of your life, for you shall be cleansed and strengthened beyond all imagining; you have simply summoned Me by a different path. Now Master and disciple shall be together forever. I will not take you up into the clouds, nor offer you milk and honey; no, indeed! I will teach you instead how to live, think and work on earth with the same efficiency of a Liberated Master's. Your power of initiative, Self-will, Self-expression and success I will expand for you illimitably. You will receive the fundamentals on how to manipulate light, energy and substance which will initiate you into the Science of the Soul. And having thus become a Christ, all your achievements will bear the mark of the gods.

*　*　*

"This is the Path whereby man recaptures his own empire of Light to be ruled for eternal years and without written laws. It is a re-emergence into a state of being against which the limitation of earthly consciousness cannot prevail. How astounding and truly boundless is the joy of self-discipline, the rocky foundation upon which stands the pursuance of inner and outer liberty that defies and immobilizes persecution, intolerance and death itself. Now the disciple can truly declare: I AM the Christ, the Light of the World; I and the Father are One. For him this is, in truth, the Second Coming of the Christ; the direct, personal and redeeming touch forever, yes, FOREVER! The awareness of Its Presence, the incontestable certainty of Its ownership, the surrendering of the self at Its Lotus Feet, and the determination to listen to IT and abide to Its Law and Counsel, will usher the returning prodigal son into the Dawning of the Golden Age, bringing about the sublimation of matter and the triumph of the Spirit.

"Be still, My son, and receive this Truth, for this is thy Destination."